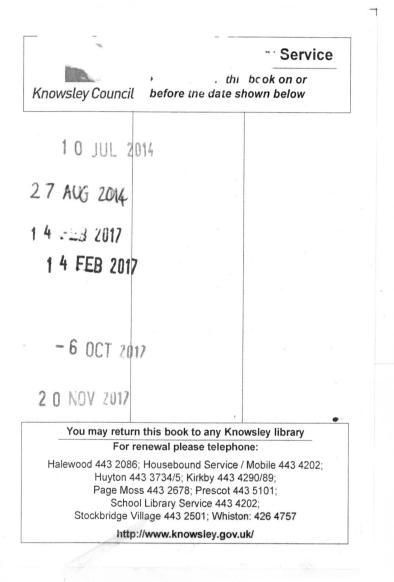

THE BLACK GUARD

A. J. Smith has been devising the worlds, histories and characters of the Long War chronicles for more than a decade. He was born in Birmingham and works in secondary education.

THE BLACK GUARD

A.J. SMITH

HEAD *of* ZEUS

First published in the UK in 2013 by Head of Zeus Ltd

9 7 5 3 1 2 4 6 8

A CIP catalogue record for this book is available from the British Library.

ISBN (eBook) 9781781853825
ISBN (HB) 9781781855621
ISBN (XTPB) 9781781855638

Typeset by Ben Cracknell Studios
Printed in Germany

Head of Zeus Ltd
Clerkenwell House
45–47 Clerkenwell Green
London EC1R 0HT

www.headofzeus.com

For Dad

FIRST CHRONICLE
OF THE LONG WAR

MAPS
BOOK ONE:
THE BLACK GUARD

FIRST CHRONICLE
OF THE LONG WAR

BOOK TWO:
DAUGHTER OF THE WOLF

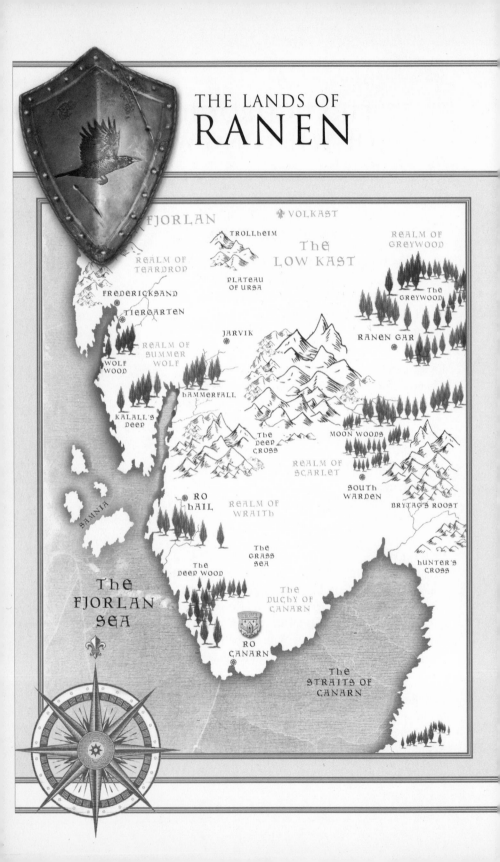

THE LANDS OF
RANEN

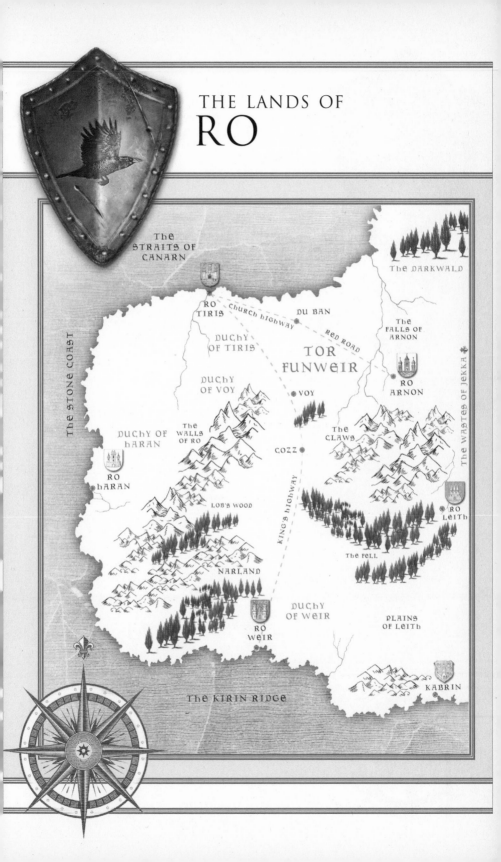

THE LANDS OF
RO

THE
STRAITS OF
CANARN

THE DARKWALD

RO
TIRIS

CHURCH HIGHWAY

DU BAN

RED ROAD

THE
FALLS OF
ARNON

DUCHY
OF TIRIS

TOR
FUNWEIR

THE STONE COAST

DUCHY
OF VOY

VOY

RO
ARNON

THE WASTES OF JEKKA

DUCHY OF
HARAN

THE
WALLS
OF RO

THE
CLAWS

RO
HARAN

COZZ

LOB'S WOOD

KING'S HIGHWAY

RO
LEITH

THE FELL

NARLAND

DUCHY
OF WEIR

PLAINS
OF LEITH

RO
WEIR

THE KIRIN RIDGE

KABRIN

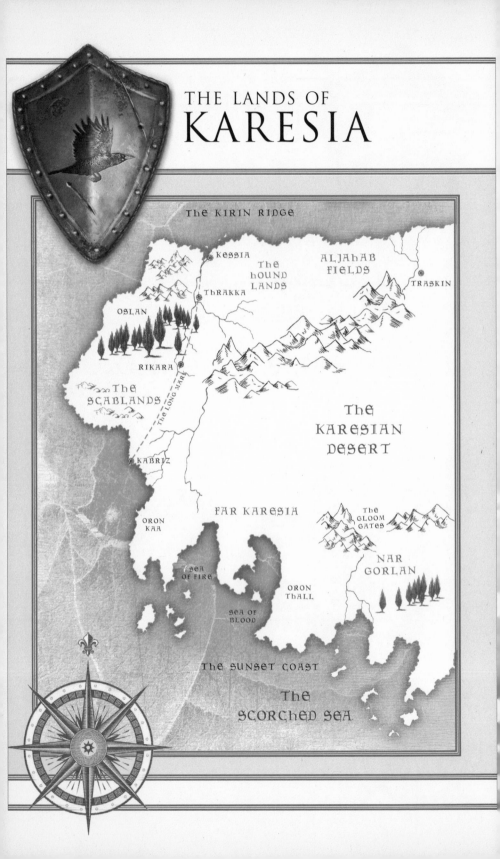

THE LANDS OF
KARESIA

THE KIRIN RIDGE

KESSIA

The
hOUND
LANDS

ALJAHAB
FIELDS

TRASKIN

ThRAKKA

OSLAN

RIKARA

The
SCABLANDS

The Long Mars

The
KARESIAN
DESERT

KABRIZ

FAR KARESIA

The
GLOOM
GATES

ORON
KAA

NAR
GORLAN

SEA
OF FIRE

ORON
ThALL

SEA OF
BLOOD

THE SUNSET COAST

The
SCORCHED SEA

BOOK ONE

THE BLACK GUARD

THE TALE OF THE GIANTS

I N THE LONG ages of deep time, uncountable millennia before
the rise of men, there lived a race of Giants.

Continents shifted and mountains rose and fell as the Giants
fought the Long War for the right to possess the lands of their
birth. The greatest Giants, mortal beings of huge size and power,
lived long enough, fought hard enough and gained enough wisdom
to become gods.

Rowanoco, the Ice Giant, claimed the cold northern lands and
was worshipped by the men of Ranen.

Jaa, the Fire Giant, ruled the burning desert sands to the south
and chose the men of Karesia as his followers.

The Stone Giant, known only as the One, held dominion over
the lush plains and towering mountains of Tor Funweir, and his
followers, the men of Ro, believed they had the right to rule all
the lands of men.

Other Giants there were also, though their names and their
followers are thought lost, and their empires buried, as victims
of the Long War.

The Giants have long since left these lands to the humans, but
their followers still worship them, invoke their names daily and
aggressively maintain their laws. The Giants themselves sit beyond
the perception of humans in their halls beyond the world while
their most trusted followers fight the Long War in their stead.

PROLOGUE

L ORD BROMVY OF Canarn stood by the docks of Ro Tiris
and wrapped his heavy travelling cloak tightly around his
shoulders. The city had two main docks, one used primarily
for trade ships and private galleons, while the other, the one near
which he currently stood, was exclusively for the king and his knights.
Brom had arrived via the smaller of the two harbours a few days
ago, leaving most of his lordly trappings back in his father's keep at
Ro Canarn. Only his longsword gave any indication of his heritage,
a finely crafted blade with the cast of a raven on the hilt. He wore
simple leather armour and looked more like a brigand than a noble,
with unkempt curly black hair and a thin beard which made him
look rather fierce. The young lord had travelled widely throughout
the lands of men and preferred to be an anonymous presence rather
than a visiting noble. The duchy of Canarn was over the sea from
the rest of Tor Funweir and a world away from the snobbery of
the other duchies. Bromvy and his sister Bronwyn had been raised
by their father, Duke Hector, to be as worldly as possible, and in
Brom's case this meant spending as much time away from home as
he could. He had just passed his twenty-fourth birthday and as he
gazed at the now empty docks Brom found himself wishing for the
simple life of an itinerant traveller.

The majority of the ships had been launched several hours
ago. Brom had watched as they sailed north towards his home,
the walled city of Ro Canarn. He hadn't counted the knights of
the Red on board, but it had looked to be a battle fleet capable
of sacking the city. The crossed swords mounted over a clenched

fist had been visible on their tabards and Brom knew this meant battle was intended. More worrying were the mercenary ships of Sir Hallam Pevain which accompanied the knights. They were swords for hire with a brutal reputation and Brom had fought the urge to roar out a challenge to the bastards as they'd left.

King Sebastian Tiris still stood on a high balcony overlooking the harbour, where he had watched his departing troops with an imperious sneer. He hadn't seen Brom skulking far below him, and the young lord stayed as far away as possible. He'd met the king once before and didn't want to take the chance that the lordly shit-stain would recognize him and have him arrested. If the king had made the move to assault Canarn, it meant that Duke Hector's children would already have been named to the Black Guard, as enemies of the crown.

Brom's mind was racing as he mentally chastised his father for being foolish and offering the king his chance to overthrow the house of Canarn and bring it securely within the lands of Ro. His home had always been seen as a forgotten province, over the sea and too close to the Freelands of Ranen for comfort. But the king had frequently stated his desire to *take back his land* from the liberal men of Canarn, and it seemed Duke Hector had finally given him his excuse.

Brom was angry but also largely helpless, and he began trying to contrive a way to get help. Most pressing on his mind was the woman who stood next to the king, her elegant hand holding back her lustrous black hair against the wind. She was a Karesian from the south and Brom knew her kind: an enchantress of the Seven Sisters, capable of swaying the will of men. What she was doing with the king of Tor Funweir he did not know, but Brom had seen her cackle as the ships were launched and King Tiris announced his intention to capture Ro Canarn. The euphoric look in the monarch's eyes as he looked at her had made Brom think that the enchantress was more than a simple consort. This was doubly concerning because, before he'd left, Brom had seen another of the Seven Sisters in Ro Canarn: an enchantress with a spider's web tattoo on her face, Ameira the Lady of Spiders. Why the Karesian enchantresses were interested in his homeland was not clear, but Brom left the docks with the intention of finding out.

As he turned towards the city with the vague goal of first finding a tavern and a drink, he began to think of all the people he could go to for aid. The list was not a long one and was comprised primarily of killers, criminals and scoundrels, men who had travelled with Brom as he learned how not to be a noble. None of them commanded an army, however, and he became increasingly despondent as he walked up the steep road that led away from the sea.

Brom loved his father and his sister and tried not to think of them in combat, or worse. His father's guardsmen were well trained and loyal, but no match for a battle fleet of knights of the Red, churchmen who represented the One God's red aspect of war, and who formed the armies of Tor Funweir. They were trained to a level of skill unmatched throughout the lands of men and dutiful in a way that bordered on fanatical. Brom knew of none of his people, the men of Canarn who unknowingly waited for the fleet to arrive, who could stand against the knights. His friend, Magnus Forkbeard, a Ranen priest from the far north, was in the city with Duke Hector and was possibly the only man able to match the knights for skill and ferocity – but Magnus was just one man and would not be able to sway the battle alone.

Brom was torn. Part of him wanted to find a boat and rush to the aid of his father. The more rational part knew that his sword would not sway the outcome and that he'd merely end up dead and unregarded on the cobbled streets of his home. If he could provide help, it would not be by standing beside his father and roaring challenges at the red men. The simple fact that one of Duke Hector's children would still be free was as much of a victory as he could hope for. As he passed through the northern gate of Ro Tiris, Bromvy of Canarn steeled himself to enter the underbelly of Tor Funweir and to stay free a while longer.

He needed no pass or official documentation to enter the city via the docks, though the gates leading inland were more closely guarded with squads of watchmen to suppress crime and patrols of king's guardsmen to make sure no undesirables could enter or exit the city. Brom smiled as he realized that he was the kind of undesirable that they were looking for, meaning he'd have to be on guard and at the least would have to locate a forger prepared to accept his coin.

Ro Tiris was an impressive sight to men who had not seen the towering White Spire of the King and the expansive Red cathedral. It was frequently cited, by the proud men of Ro, as the largest city in the world. Brom knew this to be, if not a deception, then at least misleading, because it was not even the largest city in Tor Funweir. It could make some claim to being the most densely populated, the best looked after, the richest and possibly the most crime-free, but Ro Weir to the south was a larger sprawl in terms of actual size. Though the southern city was dirty, hot and packed to the noxious walls with all manner of criminals and foreign influences, it had, in Brom's estimation, more life to it than Ro Tiris. The capital's stiff formality, and the large population of clerics and knights, got on his nerves.

The capital of Tor Funweir still offered certain opportunities for men who lived on the wrong side of the law, however, and Brom knew of several illicit traders and merchants who would be able to help him get out of the city and head south. He had a vaguely formed idea of finding an annoying Kirin acquaintance of his called Rham Jas Rami, a man who had certain skills Brom lacked and who owed the young lord several favours. If he could get a forged church seal and pass through the gates of Tiris unobserved, he knew that his chances of remaining free would be increased tenfold, as looking for a man in the wilds of Tor Funweir was no simple matter and the Purple clerics who would be despatched to find him were not suited to travelling rough.

PART ONE

CHAPTER ONE

RANDALL OF DARKWALD IN THE CITY OF RO TIRIS

'R ANDALL, IF I have to empty my own piss-pot again I'm going to bite your ear off. Get in here, boy.'

The knight was a sweaty old man, his best days behind him, with only alcohol and women to quicken his heart now that valour in battle was beyond him. He spent his days drinking, whoring and trading on his once great reputation. There were still plenty of tavern owners in Ro Tiris prepared to front a man a drink in exchange for tales of glory and battles won. The name of Sir Leon Great Claw was still sufficiently well known to guarantee a receptive audience. Only his young squire, Randall, knew the realities: Sir Leon was little more than a drunk, unable to buckle his armour or to last an hour asleep without a visit to the piss-pot.

As Randall entered the dirty tavern room, he was hit by the noxious smell, and the two whores who'd been keeping the old knight company left with a trail of insults regarding Sir Leon's personal cleanliness.

'You know we should charge extra for having to put up with the smell . . . he soiled himself while we were working.'

Randall felt sorry for them, but knew well enough that they were lucky not to have been beaten during their encounter. Sir Leon was not gentle to the women he paid, complaining – as he did about most things – *'No one knows how to treat a knight these days.'*

'Where have you been, boy? Do you want me lying in my own filth all day?' Sir Leon growled.

'Not at all, my lord, but the tavern owner is less than happy at the damage you caused last night and I needed to do a bit of work to appease him.'

Randall was used to his master being drunk, but the previous evening he had broken several more chairs and tables than was normal.

'Damage . . . what horse shit is this? I was telling a story, and when I tell a story I like to be expressive.' As if to emphasize the point, Sir Leon waved his arms around extravagantly.

'I appreciate that, my lord, but you headbutted a serving woman and attacked a lot of furniture with your sword.' Randall averted his eyes and tried not to offend his master.

'I was lost in the moment, my boy. Those were not tables last night, they were the armies of Karesia and I was wading through their blood as I did at the battle of Kabrin.'

The battle of Kabrin was twenty years ago when Sir Leon rode with the Red church knights against the Hounds of Karesia. In Randall's estimation, the old knight had told the story several hundred times and never the same way twice. He'd long been abandoned by the knights of the Red and forced to admit that the One God no longer needed his sword.

'Get rid of this shit and fetch me some wine.' Sir Leon kicked the piss-pot towards his squire and fell back heavily on to the stained bed.

'At once, my lord,' the squire said swiftly, catching his reflection in the side of the brass pot. Randall was tall for his age, but had not yet grown fully into his height and carried himself with a lope that made him appear gangly. At seventeen, he was considered a man, but everyone still called him boy and he hadn't yet summoned the courage to correct them. He kept his brown hair cut short at Sir Leon's request and the patchy stubble on his chin was shaved frequently. Randall thought that longer hair and a beard might make him appear older, but he knew that Sir Leon found something pleasing in his squire's youthful appearance.

Randall hefted the brass container up to his chest and did his best not to breathe in as he walked gingerly to the rear window of the inn. Several doors on the second floor were open and various unsavoury characters could be seen taking their morning wine or paying those with whom they'd spent the night.

It was a far cry from the lavish taverns Sir Leon used to frequent. Randall had been with him for three years and had observed the slow but sure decline in his sleeping arrangements. The last time they visited the capital, they had stayed at the Royal Arms, an inn reserved for the best knights and richest noblemen of Tor Funweir. This time, though, their experience of Ro Tiris was less capital city and more rat-infested back street. Not that Sir Leon seemed to mind. He took his decline with a pragmatic belligerence which Randall almost admired, though he thought it mostly a product of the knight's alcohol intake.

The rear window was positioned above a partially open sewer that ran from the old town of Tiris to the king's compound over-looking the harbour. Randall rested the filthy pot on the window ledge and tipped it out, tapping the bottom firmly to expel all of Sir Leon's nightly waste. It was a job that had become progressively more revolting over the years and Randall now wondered whether his sense of smell had been permanently damaged.

The splash below ended with an angry shout and Randall peered over the frame, looking down into the narrow alleyway into which he'd poured the pot.

'What in the name of the One do you think you're doing, boy?'

The words came from a steel-armoured man who had wandered into the alley to urinate. Randall gasped as he saw the cloak and scabbard that identified the man as a cleric of the Purple church, one who followed the One God's purple aspect of nobility. He wore a tabard displaying the sceptre of his order and had the bearing of a true fighting man.

'Apologies, my lord, I didn't look,' Randall said with sincerity.

'I should beat you till you bleed, you insolent serving rat!' The cleric pointed a huge, gauntleted fist at the young squire while Sir Leon's waste dripped from his formerly pristine purple cloak.

'I said I was sorry, and I'm not a servant, I'm squire to a knight of Tor Funweir,' Randall said more assertively than he had intended.

'You . . . a squire? Didn't your knight teach you the way of things? We of the Purple are the nobles of God. We own you and your pathetic life until the day you join the One, which won't be long if you disrespect me again,' the cleric said angrily.

'Sir, I will gladly wash your cloak if you'll permit me.' Randall had spent years listening to Sir Leon rant and rave about the Purple clerics. They supposedly represented the best and highest ideals of the One God, though Randall had seen very little noble about them the few times he'd crossed their path. They appeared arrogant, violent and unforgiving. He was, however, sensible enough to keep his opinions to himself.

'You'll do more than wash my cloak, boy, you'll take me to your master immediately.' He stormed out of the alley and made his way towards the front of the tavern.

Randall took a deep breath and turned back towards Sir Leon's room. Life was just beginning to creep into the inhabitants of Ro Tiris and the morning sounds of shops being opened and ships made ready filled the air. Tiris was the king's city and even in the poor quarter the buildings were well made of stone, but the streets were narrower, dirtier and more dangerous further away from the royal compound. A Purple cleric was out of place in such a disreputable area.

Randall did not know what to say to his master as he entered the room, but he hoped he hadn't done anything that would cause too much trouble. Sir Leon was lying spreadeagled across the bed, nothing but a filthy white smock covering his overweight frame. Randall coughed.

'Shut up, boy, I'm trying to sleep,' barked the old knight.

'I think there's a cleric downstairs who wants to speak to you, master,' Randall said quietly.

Sir Leon rolled over to face his squire, his eyes narrow and questioning. 'A cleric?' he asked suspiciously.

'Yes, my lord, I spoke to him just now, out of the window.' Randall felt nervous.

'And what colour robe was the cleric wearing?'

Randall paused, his eyes firmly on his boots, before he spoke. 'I think it was purple, master,' he muttered, making the word *purple* deliberately indistinct.

Sir Leon cleared his throat with a guttural growl. 'Now, young Randall, should I be concerned as to why this Purple bastard wants to speak to me?' The old knight looked long and hard at his squire, who shrank under his gaze.

'I think I offended him, without meaning to.' Randall doubted the details of the encounter would defuse the situation.

Sir Leon inhaled deeply, causing him to cough again, and this time he placed his hand over his mouth to catch the globule of blood and phlegm. He sat up on his bed, rubbing his considerable stomach as he did so.

'Well, I believe I should be properly attired so as not to offend her ladyship. Did he give a name?'

'No, we didn't really get to introduce ourselves.'

He shot Randall a hard glance. 'Enough of that cheek, boy. Fetch a basin so I can wash those women off my skin. The Purple arse-face would probably faint if he knew some people actually fucked.'

Randall had grown up in the Darkwald and knew little of the various coloured clerics and how they lived their lives in service to the One God. 'Are they not allowed to take a woman, master?'

Sir Leon stood and stretched as he answered, 'Some clerics do: the Black ones, and maybe the Brown. The knights of the Red and those Purple bastards are forbidden from the time they gain their cloak. It's one of the main reasons they get such pleasure from riding those armoured horses.' He laughed wickedly at his own commentary and narrowly averted another coughing fit. 'The Gold Church is another matter; those fat bastards can barely stand without a few paid women to carry their jewel-encrusted cocks.'

A bowl of relatively clean water was placed on a bench in front of the knight and he proceeded loudly to wash his corpulent frame. Randall had lost much of the revulsion he once felt at the sight of the overweight old man, but was still given to turn away when Sir Leon washed himself.

'Armour!' he said without looking up.

The knight's armour was burnished steel, fastened at the midriff and over each shoulder. Randall had adjusted it several times over the years and it now covered less than half of Sir Leon's upper body. If he had to fight while wearing it, he'd need to stand directly facing his opponent or else risk a fatal wound to his exposed sides. Not that he had fought in recent memory. In fact, Randall distinctly recalled the last time his master had been driven to violence. It was not a pleasant evening and had involved five dead town guardsmen and a very angry tavern owner. Sir Leon remained a dangerous man despite his years and poor health, and the guardsmen's jibes at his storytelling had angered the old knight. But that was two years ago and much alcohol had been consumed over the intervening time.

'Randall, get your fucking head together and dress me. Purple clerics are not known for their patience,' he said, flicking his dirty wash water on to the floor.

The armour went on quickly, giving the fat old drunkard a semblance of nobility. He was a tall man, though he rarely stood fully upright, and his beard and matted hair, even when swept back, gave him a wild appearance which he evidently found quite pleasing.

'Master, I think your armour may need adjusting again; the undercoat is showing through at the bottom . . . and I don't like the way your sides are exposed.'

'I like a bit of wear on it; shows it's not just an ornament. A real man's armour is stained, battered and ill-fitting.' Sir Leon posed, flexing his arms, before sitting back on the bed and pulling on his boots and greaves. 'Sword!' he said loudly.

Randall held out the ornate longsword, hilt-first, with the scabbard belt unfastened. Sir Leon grasped it firmly and, as he always did, gazed with genuine affection at the crest of Great Claw on the cross-piece, before buckling it around his waist.

'Right, lad, let's go and kiss his lordship's clerical arse,' said a defiant Sir Leon. He marched out of the room, the noise of his armour announcing his presence to everyone on that floor of the inn. Those who were sufficiently awake to open their doors were met with the sight of an imperious knight, hand rested on his sword hilt, ready for action. Randall followed close behind as the knight strode down the stairs to the common room below. He seemed clear-headed, the fog of alcohol masked to some degree, his hatred of the Purple church employed as a shield. A few men turned and showed their silent approval at the sight of the fully armoured knight. The tavern keeper looked daggers, remembering the destruction of the previous evening. The inn was a low-class establishment in the old town of Ro Tiris, with little finery and catering to those citizens who simply wanted somewhere to sleep, drink or find willing women. All three services were cheap and of the lowest possible quality. The broken wood caused by Sir Leon's extravagant storytelling had been piled by the fireplace, a testament to how much damage a drunken man in armour can cause. Sir Leon stood fully upright, glaring across the bar until his eyes fell upon the Purple cleric standing by the door.

The churchman was tall and broad-shouldered, with brown hair and a fierce look in his eyes. His features suggested a man in his middle thirties and his purple cloak, though stained, was still an evident symbol of his order. Those around him averted their gaze, knowing that a cleric of nobility held absolute power in Tor Funweir. The Purple clerics were feared throughout the kingdom and their arrogance and prowess in battle were legendary. Most men simply avoided them for the sake of an easy life. They were answerable only to the king and few men equalled them in power and influence.

The cleric straightened as Sir Leon entered the common room, an imperious look flowing across his face. He sneered at Randall, pulling his cloak around him as if to emphasize the stain. It was a considerable testament to Sir Leon's nightly visits to the piss-pot. Randall wondered if the old knight knew how many times he relieved himself each night, and how his alcohol intake had indirectly contributed to his squire covering a Purple cleric with his piss.

'You, knight.' The cleric spoke loudly, jutting his bearded jaw at Sir Leon. He then nodded towards Randall, who was standing behind the knight's left shoulder. 'That lad your squire?'

Sir Leon raised an eyebrow and slowly closed the distance to stand nose to nose with the cleric. He looked him up and down critically. The knight was several inches taller and, though in bad physical condition, still appeared the more imposing man. 'My name isn't knight; it's Sir Leon Great Claw,' he said clearly, making some effort to appear a well-spoken nobleman.

'I asked you a question, old man. Don't make me ask it again.' The cleric was clearly not intimidated by Sir Leon and did not flinch as they looked at each other. Randall stayed by the stairs at the far end of the common room. He hoped Sir Leon would handle this delicately and enable them to leave without angering the Purple church. However, this was unlikely as Sir Leon had, on several occasions, spoken of his desire to fight a Purple cleric.

'Did my squire do something to offend you, my lord?' The words were spoken with scorn, his hand resting suggestively on his sword hilt. 'He's young and has much to learn, your Purpleness. I seem to have neglected to teach him the proper etiquette for covering a cleric in piss.'

The churchman did not look impressed. 'If your intention is to exert some kind of dominance over me, old man, I should warn you that one more insult and I may have to skewer that fat belly of yours.'

The others in the tavern gasped and Randall held his breath. A few patrons quietly left, not wanting to be around if the cleric was driven to violence. Others sat open-mouthed, eagerly enjoying the spectacle of two men on the verge of a fight.

After a pause Sir Leon threw his head back in a throaty laugh. There was little humour in the sound and neither man backed away. He then asked quietly, 'What is your name, young cleric?'

'I am Brother Torian of Arnon, cleric of the quest and nobleman of the One God,' he said proudly and with deeply held conviction.

'That's a long name for a little man.' This comment left Sir Leon feeling rather pleased with himself and he flashed a wicked grin at Brother Torian, challenging him to react.

There was no anger as the cleric spoke. 'Your squire insulted me, Sir Leon. I stand before you wanting recompense and all I am given is further insult.' He narrowed his eyes and continued, 'You realize that you give me little choice but to kill you, old man?'

Sir Leon replied quickly and with venom. 'The two women I fucked last night might be a fairer fight for you . . . they stink of piss too.'

A man sitting nearby let out a sudden, involuntary laugh, causing all eyes to turn towards him. He began sweating and hurriedly turned his body away from the confrontation, focusing on his drink and curling up into the smallest ball his table and chair would allow. The laugh did little to defuse the situation and when the others' eyes returned to them, Sir Leon and Brother Torian were nose to nose.

Torian spoke first. 'You're a fat, old, stinking drunk,' he looked the knight up and down, 'with ill-fitting armour, an antique sword and no respect for your betters.' He moved quickly, his right hand striking Sir Leon sharply across the jaw. His fist was gauntleted and the blow caused blood and a sharp intake of breath from the old man.

Before Sir Leon straightened, the cleric had dropped his armoured shoulder and shoved the knight backwards. He fell heavily on to the wooden floorboards, his breastplate making a resounding clang as dust rose from the tavern floor. Sir Torian took a step forwards and quickly drew his longsword. 'You have one hour, Sir Leon.' He levelled his sword at the knight's neck. 'I will await you behind the tavern. If you are late, I will enter the tavern and kill you like a dog.'

Randall moved quickly to his master and helped him into a seated position. There was blood around his mouth and in his beard. He was winded and panting heavily. The Purple cleric held his sword an inch from Randall's face. 'And you, young man, maybe watching your master die will teach you humility.'

He deftly sheathed his sword and turned, looking taller and stronger now, as he strode from the tavern. The remaining patrons breathed a sigh of relief as it became clear they would not have to watch a man die while they were drinking. Duelling was forbidden to common men, but a frequent practice amongst nobles and churchmen.

Sir Leon let out a pained laugh. 'I wonder what I could have done to offend the little piss-stain.' Leaning on Randall, he breathed heavily and pulled himself to his feet. 'Right, I think I need a drink.' Still leaning on his squire, he shuffled towards the bar. 'I can manage from here, lad. Just needed to catch my breath.' He sat heavily on a bar stool, causing it to creak under his weight, and banged a metal fist on the wood. Pointing at the tavern keeper, he bellowed, 'Drink . . . here . . . now!'

Despite what he had just seen, the tavern keeper was not confident enough to deny the request and placed a large goblet of wine in front of Sir Leon. He then asked hesitantly, 'Er, should I expect your squire to pay for this, sir knight?'

Sir Leon shot the tavern keeper a glare and grabbed him by the throat. 'I expect to be dead in a little over an hour, you little shit. Sorry if I think this drink should be on the fucking house.' He paused, breathed in several times, and released his grip on the man, shoving him away.

Randall waited several moments, allowing the old knight to drink deeply from his goblet. He knew his master well and didn't want to interrupt what he imagined was a moment of deep thought. When he judged the time right, Randall approached slowly. 'Master . . .'

Sir Leon half smiled at the young man. 'Randall, you're, what, seventeen years?'

'Yes, master, I've been with you for three years.'

The smile became broader. 'You've been a good squire, lad. Never complained, always done what you were told.'

'Master . . . if you knew he was going to react like that, why did you provoke him?' Randall knew it was an impertinent question, but in the circumstances he cared little for propriety.

The laugh that preceded Sir Leon's answer was good-natured. 'I'm an old man, Randall. I know I can sometimes hide it, but I always feel it.' He took another long drink. 'I have wanted to be that rude to a Purple cleric since I first met one. It takes the pragmatism of advancing years to make a man truly free. It's just a shame I didn't have the balls to do it when I was younger and could have killed him.'

'But he's going to kill *you*, my lord!' Randall stated.

Sir Leon did not stop smiling. 'That is very likely. Yes, that is very likely indeed. I'd certainly recommend betting on him if the opportunity presents itself.' He laughed at his own joke and drained his goblet of wine.

He shouted to the tavern keeper. 'Just bring the whole bottle, that way I won't need to talk to you every time I want a drink.'

The man complied and a bottle of red wine was placed in front of the knight. He pulled out the cork with his teeth and poured himself a large measure. Randall knew that warning his master about drinking before a fight would be pointless and, in any case, it would not change the outcome. Sir Leon looked like a tired old man. He shifted his weight uncomfortably, the ill-fitting steel armour chafing his bulky frame.

'Don't panic, young Randall, even a burnt-out old drunk has a trick or two.'

He unbuckled his sword belt and panted, clearly more comfortable without it constricting his stomach. He held it out to his squire, who grasped the sword carefully and wrapped the leather belt around the scabbard. Randall still had a great affection for his master and began thinking about oiling the blade and adjusting his armour before Sir Leon had to fight the Purple cleric. 'Master, maybe you should remove your armour and let me add some side plates before your duel . . .'

Sir Leon laughed. 'In your estimation, how good am I with that thing?' He pointed to his sword.

'The last time I saw you use it, you were dangerous, master.'

'Well, as good as I may one day have been, that clerical bastard is a trained killer with youth and speed on his side.' He took another drink. 'I may get a lucky blow and win, or I may be able to rely on strength; either way, the state of my armour will make little difference. All it'll do is slow me down . . .' he chuckled to himself, 'and I'm slow enough already.'

* * *

The next twenty minutes or so passed in silence, with Sir Leon drinking and Randall not finding any words to say. The tavern began to empty as those who had spent the night removed themselves. Street cleaners and the city watch were abroad and Randall wondered about the legalities of fighting a duel in a back street. He guessed that, since both men were nobles of a sort, it was unlikely that the watch would intervene.

Unpleasant thoughts ran through Randall's mind. He wondered what he would do if faced with his master's dead body; would he have to take him to be buried, or would the city have arrangements for such things? He wondered, too, about his master's sword and armour; whether the Purple cleric would take them as a prize or whether they'd be left in the street to be stolen.

He also worried for himself. His home was a village in the Darkwald, many leagues from the capital, and Randall would not even know how to begin finding his way back there. He had travelled with Sir Leon to several of the great cities of Tor Funweir and disliked the idea of returning to the simple life of a commoner.

Time passed slowly, Sir Leon muttering to himself as he drank. He looked up rarely, moving only to scratch under his armour or shift his weight to a more comfortable position.

The sun began to shine through the tavern windows and Randall thought it would be a hot day. Ro Tiris was on the northern coast of Tor Funweir and the wind that blew across the straits of Canarn generally kept the capital cool. Across the straits lived the men of Canarn. Randall had never been to Ro Canarn, but the rumours he'd heard since arriving in Tiris made him think the city might not be currently very safe.

Randall was startled when Sir Leon banged his fist on the bar and proclaimed, 'Right, time to kill a cleric.' He stood up and puffed out his chest. 'Sword!' he demanded of his squire.

Randall gathered himself and passed the sword, still in its scabbard, with the belt wrapped carefully round it. Sir Leon took his time, looking fondly at the crest before buckling it around his waist.

He turned to his squire, the smell of wine heavy on his breath. 'Don't worry, lad. A poor old man like me shouldn't make you frown.' Smiling, he put his hand on Randall's shoulder. 'You're getting tall. Maybe it's time for you to get a sword of your own and find someone to show you how to use it.' Sir Leon had mentioned this before. It was the duty of a knight properly to school his squire in the way of handling a sword, but Sir Leon had simply never got round to it. He had shown Randall a couple of stances and the correct way to swing a longsword, but his squire was not a swordsman yet and had never possessed his own blade.

'Well,' said the knight with a grin, 'consider this your first real lesson.' He suddenly threw the empty wine bottle at the line of glasses next to the tavern keeper. The sound echoed around the empty common room and glass shards flew, causing the man to dive to the floor. Sir Leon didn't wait to see the reaction to his outburst, but simply strode towards the door.

Randall followed, several steps behind his master, and smiled awkwardly at the tavern keeper as he left.

The tavern doors were propped open and the street outside was relatively empty. The narrow cobbled back street was being swept clean by bound men of the crown – men paid in food, clothing and a place to sleep. They were doing a poor job and the street remained unpleasant. Sir Leon ignored the workers as he turned a sharp left into the street. He breathed in the air of the city and turned up his nose at the mix of alcohol, vomit and dirt. Randall followed behind him and had to run to keep up with the striding knight.

Sir Leon stopped at the corner of the tavern building and took a long look down the street. The buildings in the poor quarter were close together and little direct sunlight reached the ground. Debris from a hundred nights of revelry filled the narrow side street and Randall had to dodge bottles, crates and items of broken furniture as he struggled to keep up with his master. At the rear of the tavern was the alley into which Randall had thrown Sir Leon's waste, insulting Brother Torian in the process. Beyond were stables, serving several taverns and a number of brothels.

Sir Leon stepped over the open sewer and came to a halt. As Randall pulled up next to him, he saw Sir Leon's sturdy brown horse and his own black and grey pony mixed in with several mangy old horses munching on bales of straw. Standing in the middle of the stable was the Purple cleric, fully armoured and with sword in hand. His breastplate, greaves and gauntlets were of burnished steel. Although he had removed his cloak in preparation for the duel, other items of purple adorned his dress. His scabbard and belt both had an ornate purple design and the colour was repeated on most of the fabric that showed under his armour.

Now Brother Torian was wearing a steel helmet, and he raised his chin as he spoke. 'Good morning, Sir Leon. I believe we have business to settle.'

The old knight stepped forward and appeared to consider his words carefully. He puffed out his chest. 'I'm sorry, I've forgotten your name.' His mouth curled slowly into a defiant grin.

Brother Torian returned Sir Leon's smile with one of his own, though his was colder. His sword was already in his fist and he took a step backwards and flexed his arm, causing the blade to swing skilfully from side to side. Randall began imagining all the ways in which luck could play a part in the encounter. He thought that Sir Leon was the larger man and that his strength might prevail. The cleric looked like a true fighting man, but maybe he was green and would lack experience against a clever swordsman like Sir Leon. Either way, Randall estimated that skill, youth and fortitude would have to play a minimal part if his master were to emerge victorious.

Brother Torian kept his eyes on his opponent as he walked nimbly from side to side, stepping one foot over the other in practised fashion, his sword point held low. Sir Leon just stood there, not posturing or displaying any particular skill as he drew his treasured longsword.

'I was wrong, Sir Leon, I called that sword an antique. It seems I judged the blade by the state of the man who wore it.' Brother Torian looked at their swords. 'I would judge that our weapons have both seen much combat, though yours is of nobler lineage.'

Sir Leon did not respond with his customary humour. He raised his sword to look at the cleric over the cross-piece. 'This is the sword of Great Claw, an old noble house of the east. My father wore it before me and it has killed Kirin, Ranen, Jekkan, Karesian . . . even Ro.' Sir Leon was proud of his sword and the weight of nobility it bestowed upon him. An old drunk he might be, but he was still a knight of Tor Funweir, and whether he was to die in a stable or not, a knight he would remain. 'I don't apologize or ask for quarter, cleric.'

Torian came on guard. 'The time for apologies is gone and no quarter will be given. I mean to kill you, old man.'

Sir Leon attacked first, a clumsy overhead blow accompanied with a grunt of exertion. The sound of steel on steel was loud as Torian easily brought up his blade to parry the attack. He responded by kicking out forcefully at the off-balance knight and sending him back several feet, causing him to breathe heavily.

Neither man spoke as they began circling each other, Torian swinging his sword, while Sir Leon held his ready and low to the ground. Randall stepped back as far as he could to stand by Sir Leon's horse, well away from the fight. Both men looked dangerous. The sweat already flowing down Sir Leon's face made him look fierce, and Brother Torian was moving like a predator.

Again, it was the old knight who attacked – a thrust this time – aimed at the cleric's chest. Torian stepped to the side and deflected it, giving Sir Leon the chance to fall over if he was too off balance. He kept his footing, though, and pulled back his sword in time to parry an answering blow to his head. Brother Torian did not back off this time but pressed the attack, launching a series of high swings at the old knight. Each block that Sir Leon managed weakened him a little more and Randall thought the cleric needed only to wear him down in order to win. The attacks became relentless, the difference in fitness beginning to show.

The squire watched helplessly as the fight became one-sided, with Brother Torian slowing his attacks and forcibly pushing the old knight back until he was practically standing against one of the mangy horses. Sir Leon was panting and his face was bright red and moist with sweat. He'd parried every blow levelled at him and shown glimmers of skill, but he had not been able to find any small opening through which to test the cleric's defence.

Tentative faces appeared around the stable as locals, alerted by the sound, came to watch the fight. Several young children with dirty faces had clambered on the roof and now peered down from above. At the entrance to the alley a small group of four city watchmen had come to investigate the duel. Randall's hope that they would intervene and stop the fight was crushed when they saw the purple adornments of Brother Torian, and they made a display of ushering away the onlookers and standing guard over the stable entrance. Just as nobles and churchmen were allowed to bear arms, they were also allowed to use them.

Sir Leon roared with frustration and did not register the presence of the watch as Torian continued his methodical assault. Several blows began to buckle the knight's weak defensive parries and dents were appearing in his breastplate. Brother Torian was still fresh and was clearly conserving his strength, as his patterns of attack slowed again. He took several large strides backwards and disengaged, leaving Sir Leon to rave in anger. 'Come on, you purple pig-fucker,' he shouted between unintelligible grunts.

Brother Torian said nothing, but waved the knight back towards the centre of the stable.

Sir Leon was bent over and trying to catch his breath, panting heavily and dripping sweat on to the dusty stable floor. He looked at his sword again, the thinnest smile visible to Randall, and then, with a growl, lunged forward at the cleric.

Randall gasped and he desperately wanted to call out and urge his master to say something to placate the cleric, but he couldn't. The knight knew that this duel would mean his death, though Randall had hoped that something lucky or bizarre would happen to surprise everyone.

Brother Torian was expecting the desperate strike and, with grace and power, stepped forward. Sir Leon's thrust was weak and easily deflected, causing the old knight to fall to his knees as the cleric stepped past the thrust and kicked hard at the outstretched blade. The sword of Great Claw left Sir Leon's hand and fell to the stable floor several feet away.

Everything paused; the city watchmen were silent, the children looked wide-eyed and Randall held his breath. Sir Leon was on his knees, the last thrust having taken all his energy, and Brother Torian stood over him victorious. The Purple cleric held his sword against the back of the knight's neck and spoke clearly. 'Sir Leon Great Claw, knight of Tor Funweir, I take your head and repay your insult.'

With his last action before meeting the One God, Sir Leon directed a broad smile at his squire. Brother Torian swung swiftly and with great power, severing his opponent's neck with one blow.

Randall did not cry out, though tears began to form in his eyes as he looked at his master's headless body. Sir Leon had been all he had known for three years and now he was dead, beheaded in a dirty stable, answering an insult that Randall had given to a Purple cleric.

Torian did not address Randall straightaway, but dropped to one knee over his fallen opponent and offered a prayer to the One God. 'My sword and my life are yours. I fight for you, I kill for you, I die for you.' He then straightened and retrieved a stained cloth from his gauntlet and carefully cleaned his sword. The city watch still stood at the stable entrance and whispered to one another as they nervously approached the armoured cleric. They wore chain mail, belted at the waist and covered by a tabard displaying the symbol of the king – a white eagle in flight. As common men they were not permitted to carry longswords and so they all had crossbows and large knives.

'My lord, I am Sergeant Lux,' the eldest of the four watchmen said with a bow.

Brother Torian was silent. Randall saw that, despite the one-sided nature of the duel, the cleric at least took Sir Leon's death seriously and needed a moment to compose himself. 'Sergeant,' he nodded in greeting.

A few more onlookers emerged from around the stables, common men of Ro Tiris intrigued by the spectacle of true fighting men. Sergeant Lux waved at one of his men. 'Get rid of these street rats.'

The onlookers were dispersed quickly with a few directed shouts of authority from the watchmen, and the stable was again relatively quiet.

'Is he with you, your grace?' Lux pointed across the stable to where Randall stood, half leaning against Sir Leon's horse to steady his legs.

'Yes, I suppose he is, sergeant, though not in the way you mean.' The watchmen looked confused at this response, but Torian continued, 'He can remain. This duel was for his benefit on some level.'

Brother Torian sheathed his sword, removed his helmet and retrieved his purple cloak from its resting place across the back of a nearby horse. 'This is my first visit to the capital, sergeant; I assume you have arrangements for dealing with that . . .' He gestured towards the headless body of Sir Leon.

The watchmen looked at each other before Lux replied, 'We do, my lord, but if we're to return the body to his estate, we need to know to what house he belongs.'

Torian raised his chin and glanced at Randall before he spoke. 'He was of the house of Great Claw . . . somewhere to the east apparently.' He clapped his gauntleted hands together and the noise pulled Randall away from his grief. 'Squire . . . where are this man's lands to be found?'

Randall stepped away from the horse and, on weak legs, moved to the middle of the stable. He tried not to look down at the body and came to a halt off to the side of the watchmen. 'He has no lands.' Randall's voice quivered and his hands shook.

Torian narrowed his eyes and responded, 'He must have family or friends who would receive his body?'

The watchmen had begun to turn over Sir Leon's body, retrieving his head and attempting to keep the pool of blood from spreading across the stable floor. Randall spoke without thinking. 'Leave him.' He dropped to his knees next to the body and began to arrange his master in a dignified fashion.

Sergeant Lux paused for a second, surprised at Randall's impertinence, before slapping the squire's face. 'You will not speak unless directed to do so, boy.'

Randall fell, the slap causing his face to sting. 'My master had no family and no lands. His wife has been dead four years and he is without children . . .' More tears formed in Randall's eyes. 'He would want his body to be burned.'

Brother Torian nodded in approval. This was the honourable way for a nobleman to meet the One God. However, Sergeant Lux laughed. 'A pyre is expensive, lad . . . and who would arrange it?' He glanced back at his men as if Randall's words had showed extreme naivety. 'If he has no lands or family to receive his body, we'll have to throw him in the lime pits with the other scum that die in this part of Tiris.'

Randall's grief turned slowly to rage and only Brother Torian's restraining hand stopped him from clumsily attacking the sergeant.

'Enough, boy, see to your master.' Torian gently shoved Randall away from the watchmen. 'Show some respect, man, he was a knight of Tor Funweir,' he said to Lux. 'A fat, disrespectful old drunkard he may have been, but still a knight.' Torian reached into a pouch within his cloak and pulled out a small brown purse, throwing it at Lux's feet. He said, 'Burn him properly and have a Black cleric say the words.'

Sergeant Lux picked up the purse and seemed satisfied. 'Very well, my lord, it shall be done as you say.' The watchmen moved to Sir Leon's body and stopped in a circle behind Randall.

'Step away now, boy, his path is set,' said the cleric.

Randall didn't move. He straightened the body lying before him, pushing the legs together and resting the old man's arms across his battered steel breastplate. He still hadn't looked at the severed head and found himself wanting to keep hold of the old man's smile rather than the staring eyes of a dead man.

'Boy!' shouted Brother Torian, as he dragged Randall across the stable and shoved him against a wooden wall. Randall tried to look past him to ensure that the watchmen were treating Sir Leon with respect, but the cleric's armoured frame blocked the view.

'Your name, young squire?' Torian asked gently, as Randall stopped struggling and focused on the face before him.

'Randall . . . I'm from the Darkwald.' The words were hesitant.

'Very well, Randall of Darkwald, I think the One God has another path for you.' He stepped away from Randall, his bulk still obscuring Sir Leon's body.

One of the watchmen coughed to attract Torian's attention. 'Milord . . . what of the knight's blade?' The man picked up the sword of Great Claw, hefting it and feeling its weight in his hand.

'Watchman,' snapped Torian, 'that is the sword of a noble and not for the likes of you to wield.' The cleric closed the distance quickly and held out his hand. 'Give it here,' he said with quiet authority.

The longsword was placed, hilt-first, into his hand. Brother Torian inspected the blade and nodded his approval at its condition before turning back to Randall. 'I assume that, as a squire, the care of your master's blade was your primary responsibility, yes?'

Randall breathed in deeply. 'Sir Leon had other needs that took up a lot of time but, yes . . . I suppose I do look after the sword.' He felt no anger towards Brother Torian, but his grief at Sir Leon's death was enough to make him feel small and helpless. 'I was going to oil the blade before the fight, but he didn't let me . . . I thought . . .'

Torian interrupted him. 'This blade is well cared for. I don't think another coat of oil would have done much to help him.'

'That's what Sir Leon thought . . .' Another tear appeared as Randall continued. 'He knew he was going to die.'

Torian looked first at the sword and then at Randall, ignoring the squire's attempts to see past him. After a moment of thought he spoke with conviction. 'I've never had a squire. It's often seen as unseemly for a cleric of the Purple to need one . . .' He looked Randall up and down, shaking his head at the squire's common appearance. 'However, I am a cleric of the quest and outside of the usual traditions of my order.'

Randall didn't register the words and his mind filled instead with images of Sir Leon, laughing and joking as he drunkenly told unlikely stories of heroism.

'Are you listening, boy?' Torian asked sharply.

'No, I must confess that I'm not, Brother Torian . . . my mind is elsewhere, as I predict it will be for a while yet.' Randall had just seen his master killed and was not in the mood to be polite.

'You've a sharp tongue, boy . . . true to form, though, so I must at least commend you for consistency,' he said with an imperious smile. 'Now, this is my command . . .' He grasped Randall's face so that the squire could not help but look at him. 'You will become my squire and I will school you in the correct way of things,' he stated.

'My lord . . .?' Randall had a questioning look on his face.

'Did you not hear me, boy?'

'Er, I heard you, my lord, but I don't think I understand.' Randall was tired, confused and felt sick. The words of the cleric barely penetrated his mind.

'Randall, a cleric I may be, but I am not blind to the fact that I just killed your master. Nor am I a cruel man, despite what you may think.' His words were kinder now.

Randall shook his head and tried to focus. 'I doubt you care, but I don't hate you, my lord. My master wanted to die . . . he was old and tired and you could have been anybody.' Tears came again to his eyes. 'I think he just wanted to die fighting.'

Torian nodded with approval. 'That is a proper way for a knight to die . . . he taught you a valuable lesson today, boy.'

The watchmen had begun to remove Sir Leon's body. 'Lux . . . I will hear of it if that man is treated poorly,' said Torian.

The man bowed. 'Absolutely, milord, I'll see to the pyre myself.'

The watchmen left the stables, holding the body of Sir Leon respectfully. The man holding the head did so at arm's length and was making an effort to not look at Sir Leon's blank face.

Brother Torian turned back to Randall. 'Well then, squire, this is what you need to know of your new master. I am a cleric of the quest from Ro Arnon and I am here looking for a Black Guard named Bromvy of Canarn.'

Randall tried to stand upright. 'Yes, my lord . . . I understand. What has the man done?'

Torian looked quizzically at his new squire. 'Do you not know the meaning of the words *Black Guard*, boy?'

'I do not, sir.' Randall shook his head.

'Well, it seems that your education should begin immediately.' He passed Randall the sword of Great Claw. 'Here, take your new sword and let's be off. We have much to do.'

Randall paused and simply looked at the offered blade. 'My lord, I'm a commoner, not permitted to carry a longsword.'

Brother Torian raised his chin and puffed out his chest. 'You are now the squire of a Purple cleric and, if I say you can wear a sword, then you can wear a sword. Come now, belt it on and don't dawdle.' The cleric began to walk towards the stable entrance. 'Oh, and you'd probably better take Sir Leon's horse in addition to his sword,' he said before disappearing into the street.

* * *

Randall's first few days as squire to Brother Torian were strange. The cleric was an undemanding master, compared to Sir Leon. He talked a great deal, often unconcerned whether Randall was listening or not, and the young squire's head was a blur of clerical procedures and service to the One God.

Torian was from the Falls of Arnon and had never been to the capital before. He wore his armour throughout the day and largely ignored the fear he inspired in the general populace, most of whom he dismissed as simply common folk.

Randall learned quickly how to unbuckle the armour and greaves with Torian in a seated position. They were of high quality and needed little maintenance beyond a daily polish of the burnished steel. Torian appeared ill at ease with being waited on, but tried to smile as Randall ran around after him, automatically fetching his food and cleaning his clothes.

They stayed in a quiet tavern near the chapter house of the knights of the Red. It was an unremarkable area of the town, with little crime. The tavern was a low stone building with few comforts, though the rooms were clean and the staff respectful. Randall was permitted to sleep in a bed rather than on the rough bedroll he had been used to, and was even allowed time to himself each day. Torian disliked having Randall with him when he went into the poor quarter to make enquiries, saying that a squire would be a burden when the cleric needed to be focused.

Randall used this time to practise with his new sword and to read the books that Torian carried with him. The squire began to learn about the One God and even learned something of the other lands of men. He'd met Ranen and Karesians before, but had always thought them strange and difficult to understand. The books Brother Torian carried spoke of them as children of other gods, inferior to the One, but worthy of respect as enemies.

They rose early each day and Torian exercised for several hours, running on the spot and swinging his longsword with practised skill. Without his armour, the cleric was a muscular man, covered in scars and puncture wounds from crossbow bolts and longbow arrows. He deflected any talk of his wounds and Randall guessed that true fighting men didn't generally discuss their past battles. Sir Leon's tall tales began to make more sense and it occurred to Randall that the old knight had deliberately told different versions of the same story because the reality was neither glamorous nor exciting.

'Randall . . . daydreaming again, boy?' Torian was sitting on his bunk waiting to be attired in his clerical armour.

'Sorry, master, I was thinking of Sir Leon.' Randall quickly moved to the wooden chair that acted as an armour rack.

Torian flexed his arms, clearing the soreness from his morning exercise. 'The old man was a good first master for you, lad. He was demanding and taught you some humility.'

Randall hefted the bulky armour and swayed across the simple tavern room. 'I was just thinking that you and he may have got on well . . . If . . .'

'If his squire hadn't covered me in piss the first time we met?' he interrupted.

'Yes, master.' Randall blushed.

Torian laughed in response and held out his arms for Randall to place the breastplate across his chest. The purple undercoat was designed to show at the corners of the armour. The back plate was fastened by heavy leather straps at the waist and connected to the segmented metal of the arm pieces.

'How's your reading coming along?' Torian asked, as the armour went on.

'It's coming along well, master. I was learning about the other races of men.'

The cleric raised his eyebrows. 'So, tell me, what have you learned?'

Randall considered as he buckled up Torian's armour. 'The

men of Ranen worship an Ice Giant called Rowanoco and they live to the north.'

His master nodded. 'That's right, lad, they wear chain mail and normally carry axes. They're brutal, but cunning men.'

'Didn't the Ro once rule those lands, master?'

Torian nodded again. 'Indeed we did, though that was long ago. The Ranen were organized into work gangs by the Red knights.' His expression showed his distaste for this practice.

'You don't approve?' Randall queried.

'No, I do not, lad. The Ranen are primitive, but they were still vanquished enemies and should have been treated with respect.' He looked up at his squire. 'And if the knights hadn't organized them, the Ranen would never have formed the Free Companies and fought back.'

'Master?' Randall had not heard the term before.

'The work gangs were naturally made up of the strongest Ranen and they rebelled, took their wood-cutting axes and turned them on their masters. They called themselves the Free Companies and were surprisingly effective fighting men.' He stood up and flexed, feeling the weight of his armour. 'Ro Ranen became the Freelands of Ranen and the knights retreated south to the lands of Canarn . . . that was some two hundred years ago, but the Free Companies are still as stubborn and dangerous as they were then.'

Randall buckled on his master's longsword. The cleric raised a leg and rested his foot on a small wooden stool as Randall buckled on the steel greave.

'And what of the Karesians, master?'

'Well, we've never been truly at war with them, lad. They follow Jaa, the Fire Giant. They keep to themselves for the most part. Any you meet in Tor Funweir will likely be merchants or tavern keepers.' Torian seemed to have little time for the desert men.

'Sir Leon used to talk about the Hounds of Karesia.'

'Yes, the Hounds . . . the dreaded Hounds.' He chuckled to himself. 'The Karesians have little true military craft and so they rely on numbers. The Hounds are criminals, sentenced to serve time in the kennels as soldiers.' He placed his second leg on the stool. 'Jaa apparently taught that nobles should not fight . . . the dying should be left to the lowest classes of criminals and dishonourable men.' He turned to his squire. 'There are several hundred thousand of them, though.'

Randall finished dressing his master and took a step back to admire his work. The cleric was an imposing and noble figure when fully clad in his armour. The squire knew that he was a skilled swordsman but thought that, for most people, the flashes of purple would be enough to deflect trouble.

Brother Torian inspected himself carefully, noting any slight imperfections in his armour and pointing them out to his squire for later attention.

'And who are the Kirin, master?' Randall asked.

He'd known men claim to be Kirin and heard men referred to as such, but he'd always been confused by what the term meant. They were often swarthy-skinned men, though clearly not either Karesian or Ro and, by implication at least, they were mostly criminals.

Torian raised his eyebrows at this. 'You have no Kirin in the Darkwald?'

'Not that I remember, no. A few Ranen, but mostly men of Ro.'

'Well, the Kirin are the godless race that is produced when a Karesian and a Ro decide, for whatever reason, to mate.' He clearly took offence at the notion. 'They are mostly to be found in the forests along the southern shore of the Kirin Ridge, though some come to the Tor Funweir to ply their trade as slavers or rainbow merchants – that's drug dealers to you and me.' He picked up his purple tabard from the side of the bed and swung it over his head, letting the purple sceptre of nobility rest across his breastplate. 'They're not innately evil, but their mixed lineage makes it difficult for them to pursue an honest trade.'

Sir Leon had been quite hateful towards the Kirin, calling them all manner of names. Randall now thought this a little unfair, as it wasn't really their fault that their parents had decided to have sex.

Randall walked over to the windowsill and took a drink of water from the jug that was placed there. He had known that the Darkwald was an isolated area of Tor Funweir, but the sudden realization that Sir Leon had taught him virtually nothing in the time they'd been together was annoying. He'd learned more about the lands of men in the last few days than in the previous three years combined.

'Today, young Randall, I'm afraid your reading will have to wait. I need you to accompany me into the city.' Torian pointed to the sword of Great Claw hanging from a hook on the back of the door. 'You should wear your sword, boy . . .'

Randall let thoughts of Sir Leon and how poor a master he had been leave his mind. He screwed up his face, having barely been listening to his new master's words. 'Sorry, I was somewhere else for a moment. What did you say?' he asked.

Torian smiled as he spoke. 'Sometimes I envy the ability of youth to daydream. However, as a cleric I must chide you for your insolence,' he said warmly. 'I told you that you would be accompanying me into the city and that you should wear your longsword.'

Randall blushed, still uncomfortable owning such a weapon.

Torian sensed his misgiving and, with a condescending smile, moved to the door and picked up the scabbard. 'Come here, lad. Let's see how it looks.'

Randall stood in front of him and was taken aback as the cleric reached down and wrapped the belt around his squire's waist.

'Master . . .' Randall stuttered as he spoke. 'I should do that.'

Torian's smile became friendly as he positioned the scabbard on Randall's left hip. 'I gave you permission to wear it, so it seems fitting that I adorn you with it.' He stepped back and inspected the armed squire. 'There. Now all you need is armour and you'll look splendid.'

Randall breathed in and looked at the sword hilt. It was surprisingly light and didn't restrict his movement in the way he'd imagined it would. Despite his reservations, he felt older and stronger simply carrying such a noble weapon. The sword of Great Claw had been Sir Leon's pride and joy, and Randall wanted more than anything to do honour to the blade.

'Did Sir Leon at least teach you the correct way to hold such a weapon, Randall?'

'Well . . . not really, master. He showed me some basic positions, but he was drunk at the time and they didn't make much sense.'

'Hopefully, you won't need to use it then,' he said plainly, as he moved to his purple cloak hanging by the window. Randall was not permitted to touch the purple, aside from when he cleaned it, and Brother Torian treated it much as Sir Leon had treated his longsword.

'Where are we going, master?' Randall asked as Torian swung his cloak around his shoulders and fastened it at the neck.

'You'll be accompanying me to the Kasbah of Haq, outside the city walls. You've been reading about foreigners and so it seems only appropriate that you join me in going to a place where they gather. Be on your guard, though, these men are not friendly to Ro, especially clerics, and they will not want to volunteer the information that I seek.'

Before Randall could ask any more questions the sound of armoured feet began to be heard along the corridor outside. Torian was not concerned as he registered the sound and simply waved Randall away from the door.

The squire backed away and stood by the open window. The sound of metal feet rose in volume, but there seemed to be only one man approaching. Randall began to speak, but a raised hand from his master caused him to stay silent.

The armoured footsteps stopped just outside the door and a solid bang on the wood made Randall jump.

'Worry not, boy, this man is expected. The door is open, brother,' Torian called loudly.

The circular door handle turned and a gauntleted hand appeared. As the door was pushed open, Randall saw a burly, pale-skinned man of Ro. He was clad in steel armour of a similar fashion to Torian's, but more tarnished. He bore a large two-headed axe strapped across his back, but of most interest to Randall was the black tabard he wore, identifying him as a cleric of death. The black fabric showed a skeletal hand holding a goblet.

He was a man of middle years, perhaps in his late thirties. His skin was pallid and his hair white, and he looked like a ghost as he stepped into the room. Randall had never seen an albino and found his pink eyes more unnerving than his tabard. He directed a thin smile at Brother Torian and offered his hand. Randall saw a deep scar across the back of his neck, partially covered by his axe and a braided knot of hair that fell halfway down his back. The scar was old, but it looked to Randall that it must have been from a near-fatal wound.

Torian grasped the other cleric's hand, but didn't smile; instead, he bowed his head in a show of deep respect.

'Brother Utha . . . it has been too long,' Torian said, averting his eyes from the albino.

'Look up, Torian, we're not in Ro Arnon now and it's been many years since you needed to bow to anyone,' the Black cleric said, with what seemed like genuine affection. 'Besides, averting your eyes from a short-arse shit like me will strain your neck.'

Torian laughed and the tension released from his eyes. 'Come in, brother. I've no wine, but at least we have seats and fresh air . . .'

Randall knew that most clerics were forbidden from drinking alcohol, but the clerics of the Black were unknown to him – aside from the aura of fear that accompanied their station as brothers of death. They followed the darkest aspect of the One God and were present at funerals and large battles, wherever death was certain.

Utha surveyed the room. 'Last time we sat together, as I recall, my arse was perched on the only thing soft enough to cradle the arrow wound.'

Torian laughed again. 'As *I* recall, you were sitting on a dead mercenary outside a village near Ro Leith.'

Utha turned to Randall, though he still directed his words to Torian. 'Well, the rabid little shit had buried an arrow in a place that I like to keep free of wounds. It only seemed proper that I cleaved his head in. He was just a Kirin; I doubt the world has missed his stench since I threw him on the pyre.'

Randall withered a little under the cleric's gaze and looked down at the floor.

'This lad looks nervous, Torian. Perhaps he should go and fetch me some wine so that I don't die of fucking thirst while he looks at the floor.'

Torian nodded at Randall. 'Yes, of course. Go and fetch a couple of bottles, Randall,' he said.

Utha did not avert his pale eyes from the young squire as Randall quickly crossed the room and exited into the hall. He closed the door behind him and breathed out, more comfortable now that Utha was not standing on top of him. Randall had heard common folk speak of the Black clerics as if their very presence was a bad omen. It was said they could detect death's presence on the air, as a normal man would smell food or sense a beautiful woman.

Randall didn't linger outside the door and moved quickly along the corridor. The tavern was well maintained and a far cry from the establishments he had become used to during his service with Sir Leon. The floor was clean and free of dust, the doors all had locks and even the windows were of clear glass rather than shuttered with wood.

Randall spared a moment's thought on whatever it might be that brought a Black cleric to meet with Brother Torian, but he considered their business beyond him and focused on fetching the wine.

He walked to the end of the corridor and proceeded downwards, only vaguely registering that he was still wearing his sword. At the foot of the stairs, the tavern opened out. The common room had a high ceiling and was vaulted in wood, with church heraldry hanging from metal hooks. The crossed swords and clenched fist of the knights of the Red was most prominent, displayed next to the purple sceptre of nobility and the dove of the White. Randall found the tavern intimidating, as it was frequented mostly by Red knights and the city watch. Even in the morning several squads of armoured watchmen were sitting down to breakfast – small loaves of grainy bread with thick-cut slices of pork and steaming mugs of dark coffee. The kitchen beyond the polished wooden bar was active and Randall could hear orders being shouted amongst the tavern staff.

Randall walked along the bar and stopped in front of the young barmaid. 'Er, wine, please . . . red, I think,' he said.

She looked puzzled and leant on the bar, inspecting the young squire. 'Are you the one who brought that man of death into my father's tavern, boy?'

Randall thought her a little younger than himself and objected to being called *boy*, but he kept quiet. A number of the tavern staff, overhearing the girl, were now looking at him with interest. It was likely that Brother Utha had caused quite a stir when he walked through this room several minutes ago.

'Not me, exactly . . . he came to speak to my master,' Randall replied.

A watchman sitting at a table near the bar said, 'That was Utha the Ghost, lad . . . men should not talk to such creatures. Black clerics are barely men at all.'

Assorted nods of agreement flowed over his companions and Randall felt very small. The watchman walked to the bar. Placing several coins on the wood, he turned to Randall. 'They say the Ghost can see your time of death and smiles when it's close at hand. He carries an axe because the One will not permit him to carry the weapon of a noble.' The watchman looked down at the sword of Great Claw, sheathed at Randall's side. 'Nor does he permit a lowly squire who consorts with the men of death. I know you serve a man of the Purple, boy, but I object to you carrying that.'

The man was tall and looked down his nose at the squire. Another man joined him, younger than the first and only a few years older than Randall; he carried two short swords sheathed across his back. 'Leave him be, Robin, the lad's got enough problems. That's two clerics he's got to look after now.'

The first man laughed and returned to his table. The one who'd stood up remained leaning against the bar. 'More coffee, Lydia,' he said to the tavern keeper's daughter, before turning back to Randall. 'Don't mind him, boy, Black clerics make everyone nervous . . . especially that particular Black cleric.'

Randall smiled nervously back at the watchman. 'I hadn't heard of him before today. His name suits him, though,' he said, the image of the albino still in his head.

'More than you know, I'll bet. The Ghost is a crusader . . . he hunts risen men.'

Randall directed a questioning look at the man. He'd heard of the risen before, but considered them merely the stuff of tales. They were supposedly non-human beings who'd betrayed their loved ones and died a painful death, rising as monsters that detested and feared men. The deep forests of the Darkwald supposedly contained a village of the creatures, but the story was always told second-hand and Randall had never given the risen much thought.

'They actually exist?' he asked.

'There're a lot of dark places in the lands of men, boy; the Wastes of Jekka to the east contain more than just cannibal hill tribes,' the man said.

'Stop your lips from flapping, Elyot, you'll scare the boy,' said another man, older and wearing the insignia of a watch commander.

'Just warning him is all, sir. If he's going to be consorting with a cleric of death, he should know all he can,' Elyot said defensively.

'And you are clearly an expert, yes?' the commander chided.

Elyot turned a little red and smiled at Randall. 'Don't listen to me, squire . . . just stories is all . . . just stories.'

Randall felt a little awkward and turned back to Lydia, the barmaid. 'Wine . . .' he said again.

She looked as if she were going to raise an objection, but couldn't quite decide which objection to raise. After a momentary pause she produced a corked bottle of red wine. 'I'll add it to your master's bill,' she said scornfully.

'Thanks, you are very kind,' Randall replied, with deep irony.

He grabbed the bottle and stepped away from the bar. Turning, he began to walk towards the stairs. Elyot, the young watchman, put a hand on Randall's shoulder and caused him to turn back to face him. 'Listen to me, squire. I don't know what business the Ghost has with your master, but you mark me well, it's a bad omen.' The words were solemn and Randall nodded politely.

He backed away slowly, trying to smile at Elyot. A few steps back and he turned and walked quickly across the common room. He was not sure if the watchman's words were mere superstition or if the Black cleric truly heralded bad luck. Either way, he was glad to be leaving the common room and returning to Brother Torian. He breathed out heavily as he realized that meant he would have to face the Ghost again.

As he walked out of the common room, Randall thought of his home and the simple life that his people lived. He would most probably be a farmer or a blacksmith now if he'd not left the Darkwald and he would probably never have met a cleric either of the Purple or of the Black. Randall was not stupid or naive; he knew that he was a common boy and could not hope to raise himself much beyond the station of a squire. The cleric he served was a good master, a man of honour, despite his arrogance, and Randall was thankful for his position as his squire, despite the difficult days and constant need to be on guard. At least now he needed to worry about more than piss-pots and damaged furniture.

CHAPTER TWO

BROTHER UTHA THE GHOST
IN THE CITY OF RO TIRIS

U THA THE GHOST disliked his nickname. He'd heard it a lot since he left Ro Arnon and travelled west. It appeared that the men in the capital were more superstitious than those from the duchy of Arnon and he'd heard a hundred strange, or blatantly untrue, rumours about the Black church since he arrived. Utha was used to common folk being afraid of him – being a cleric of death – but to say that he was a *master* of death was overstating things a little.

He often thought that, if he hadn't been born an albino, he would have become a White churchman or maybe joined the Red knights. As it was, the cardinal of the Black had requested him on sight.

Utha had never known his parents and had never considered any other career than becoming a cleric of the One. He'd been given to the church in Ro Arnon when he was a baby; his pale skin and pink eyes were seen by the senior Purple clerics as a blessing from the Giants, and he'd joined the Black on his sixteenth birthday.

The Black church considered death a holy state, which they respected and feared in all its various manifestations. They were present at funeral pyres, and an army of Red knights was never permitted to go into battle without at least one Black chaplain. Their presence was held as a bad omen amongst the common people, with some justification, as they were also the One God's assassins, men skilled in dealing death as well as honouring it.

In contrast to clerics of the other orders, Utha was permitted to drink and fuck as the mood took him and he was thankful that he had joined the least *clerical* of the clerics.

'I'm not trying to make you jealous, Torian, but I've got a terrible thirst,' Utha said as the young squire left the room to fetch his wine, 'and it means we can talk without a serving boy listening in.'

'He's my squire. I killed his master in a duel and took over his tutelage.'

Utha raised his eyebrows and paused. After a few seconds he burst out laughing. 'Okay, so you've got a boy to hold your cock while you go for piss . . . that's not funny at all.'

'He's a good lad and, I admit, I felt bad about killing his master . . . He was an old fool, though. He backed me into a corner and I couldn't let him go unpunished,' Torian said seriously.

Utha had great affection for the Purple cleric but found his piety tiring. The clerics of nobility were generally a stiff-necked bunch and Torian was worse than most. He was honourable and trustworthy, but not a great companion if a man sought fun.

'What did he do?' Utha asked.

'I had a grievance with him and all he needed to do was show me a little respect. Instead, he insulted me, so I killed him in a fair fight.'

'For it to have been a fair fight he'd have needed to be as dangerous with a blade as you . . . and I consider that unlikely. You said he was an old man, so instantly I'm thinking you should have let it go.' Utha's voice had taken on a disapproving tone.

'He was an old man, yes, but an old man with a longsword, armour and a claim to nobility. If he was man enough to insult me, he should have been man enough to back it up with action.'

Utha smiled and sensed that Torian would take any further comments rather personally. 'Fair enough. Does the squire not have an issue with you having killed his former master?'

Torian shook his head. 'Randall thinks that he wanted to die and I was just a means to that end. As I said, he's a good lad.'

Utha let the matter drop and sat down on a small wooden stool, removing his axe from its sling and stretching his neck. 'I will never get used to riding horses. The bastards seem intent on causing me pain every time I get on one.'

Torian sat opposite him and looked down at the axe with appreciation. 'How's *Death's Embrace* serving you?'

Utha patted his axe fondly at the mention of its name. 'I haven't used her for a while . . . but I'm not regretting my choice, if that's what you're insinuating. A longsword just feels wrong somehow. Less satisfying when swung.'

Black clerics were permitted to wield any weapon they desired and, although most still wore a longsword, occasionally a cleric of death would select a more exotic weapon.

'Get your mind away from duels and weapons, Torian, we can tell each other stories later. For now, I have orders for you and I'd rather get them out of the way before your boy comes back.'

Torian frowned. 'Are we not going to talk about why *you* specifically were sent to accompany me?'

Utha had hoped that Torian wouldn't pry into the reasons why he was not still out hunting risen men. 'I requested that I be given a last mission before . . .'

Torian's frown broadened as he prompted Utha to continue. 'Before what?'

'I have to report to the Black cathedral in Tiris when you and I part ways. It seems that I must have my honour brought into question for some of my recent actions.' Utha was not going to tell Torian everything, partly because he didn't want to keep thinking about it, but mostly because he knew his friend would think less of him. 'I knew you'd been sent after the Black Guard, so I thought I could help. You are, after all, one of the few Purple clerics I can stand the sight of.'

Torian laughed, and Utha thought that he'd deflected any further queries for now.

'Okay,' Torian said with a smile, 'but before we *part ways*, you will have to tell me what you've done, and if it's just a tale involving a bottle of wine and a whore, I will be very disappointed.'

'How about . . . two bottles of wine and a room full of whores?' Utha joked.

'Just agree that you'll tell me.' Torian's smile faded and he looked serious again.

'I promise. Just not here and not now,' Utha said with honesty.

Torian relaxed a little and Utha's mind turned to the primary reason he was in Ro Tiris, to give Brother Torian news of the campaign in Ro Canarn and to inform him of his orders from Arnon.

'May I continue with official church business now?' he asked.

Torian nodded and leant in. 'What word from Canarn?'

'The city fell four days ago, just after you arrived in Tiris. Duke Hector has been captured and I'm sure the knights of the Red are being gracious in victory,' he said with irony.

Torian shook his head. 'Who commanded the fleet?'

'Sir Mortimer Rillion,' Utha replied in a tone that showed his distaste for the knight.

Torian evidently shared Utha's opinion and angrily banged his fist on his armoured thigh. 'So, the men of Canarn . . .?'

'Rillion took a company of knights and a bunch of mercenaries. I think Sir Pevain was with him and they didn't give the defenders much chance to surrender. I know that they took the keep within a few hours and, based on past form, I imagine they killed everyone that didn't kiss their arses when they entered the city. There was a Ranen Free Company there, but they left before the fight and the men that remained were no match for the knights.'

Torian could be sensitive when he perceived a lack of honour in his brother churchmen and he was flushed with anger as he spoke. 'The duke was a heretic, but the common men surely deserved better than to be hacked to pieces by mercenaries. There is no honour in attacking men who are defending their families and their lands,' he said through gritted teeth.

'What did you think was going to happen when you heard the fleet had launched? Stop being so fucking naive,' Utha said, with little tact.

'Brother . . .' Torian's face was shocked.

'Be serious. The Red knights were sent to kill everyone who got in their way. Rillion will be installed as knight protector and the duke will likely be beheaded.' Utha had little time for softening the realities of life.

It was the way of things. The knights of the Red were unleashed when the king commanded. They were the embodiment of the One God's aspect of war and conquest, and were little more than a blunt instrument. A week and a half ago they had been unleashed against the city of Ro Canarn and the house of Duke Hector. The men of that land had, for many generations, been friendly with the neighbouring Ranen and it appeared that the duke had asked the Ranen lords for sanctuary within the Freelands.

Utha had been told that King Sebastian had a spy in the court of Duke Hector, a Karesian enchantress called Ameira, which meant that they attacked with no warning and surprised the defenders of Canarn. The king's intolerance towards Hector and his Ranen allies had driven him to swift and brutal action.

However, it was not the place of humble clerics to question the will of the king, and Utha was nothing if not a dutiful cleric.

'Torian, we still have orders and those orders are not going to change just because you have a moment of petulance,' Utha said with friendly tolerance.

'Brother, we have known each other a long time, but I still find your manner a little difficult. Our ways are different.' He leant back a little and composed himself. 'Very well, brother, what are the orders from Arnon?'

'That's my boy,' Utha said with a smile. 'The duke's son is still at large somewhere and, as none of you have found him yet, I'm to accompany you and assist.'

'Utha, when I left Arnon, I was hunting a man whose father had been named a traitor, now I'm hunting a man whose homeland has been destroyed and his people massacred . . . the situation has changed somewhat, I'm sure you'll agree.'

Word had been sent to the church city at the same time as the

Red fleet had launched; Bromvy of Canarn was to be found and captured with all speed. He'd been named a Black Guard and stripped of his honour. Clerics of the quest had been despatched throughout Tor Funweir to search for the young lord, but so far he'd remained hidden, with only Torian reporting a possible lead.

'Actually, no, I don't agree. He still needs to be found and you still need to find him. What has changed?' Utha said sternly.

'He now has nothing to live for . . . that makes a man very dangerous,' Torian replied.

'Bromvy is still only twenty-four years old, worldly and clever for his age, but a young man nonetheless.' Utha put his hand on Torian's shoulder and smiled.

A knock on the door and the young squire tentatively poked his head into the room. 'May I enter, master?'

Torian kept his eyes on Utha for a moment. 'Yes, Randall, come in.'

The squire stepped in and closed the door behind him. He placed a bottle of red wine on the low wooden table and backed away quickly.

Utha grabbed the bottle and wrenched the cork out. 'To your good health, young Torian.'

He took a deep drink from the bottle. It was rich and fruity – not high in quality – but sufficient to slake his thirst. 'Now all we need are a couple of paid women and we have a party.' Utha grinned and decided to be more formal. 'What leads, brother, to where the young lord has fled?'

A thin smile intruded on Torian's stern features. 'This very day I was planning to go and meet with a man in the Kasbah who, I'm reliably informed, helped Bromvy escape Tiris – a man of Ro Leith called Glenwood, a forger by all accounts.'

Utha nodded and was glad that Torian was efficient. Despite what he may have said, he agreed that the knights of the Red had acted rashly. However, Utha was pragmatic towards the other clerics and considered it pointless to be angered by their actions.

'What led you to Glenwood?' asked the Black cleric.

'I paid a beggar in the poor quarter who saw the young lord riding south. This led me to a watchman who remembered his sword, an ornate blade and a noble pommel with a cast of Brytag, the World Raven. Everyone who leaves via the south gate is searched, but no one searched this man. There are only so many ways of leaving the city via the south without being questioned. Our young lord seems to have found one.'

Brytag was an old Ranen god and the patron of the house of Canarn. He was said to sit on Rowanoco's shoulder and to embody both luck and wisdom, which many Ranen saw as being the same thing.

'The watchman remembers him having an official seal from the Red church. He can't have got a genuine one, so I found the only forger in town who is stupid enough to deal with a Black Guard.'

Torian had not been idle in the week since he left Ro Arnon, and Utha was impressed with the work he'd done.

'So, I'll finish my wine and we'll go and see Mr Glenwood, yes?' Utha asked.

'That was my intention,' replied Torian.

Utha took another swig of wine, letting the liquid fall over his face and run down his chin. Then he stood up and turned to the young squire. Randall was a tall lad and Utha thought that he'd grow to a fair size in his next year or so of life.

As was his way, Utha decided to test the young squire's strength of mind. He crossed the room and motioned for Randall to stand, which he did quickly, with wide eyes.

'Torian has told me of your former master's dishonour, boy. I hope you realize that this does not reflect well on you. I'll be watching you, even if Torian is too blind to see the potential danger you pose.'

Utha didn't need to turn round to know that Torian would be shaking his head at this comment.

'So, boy, do you think yourself a suitable squire for a Purple churchman?' he asked.

The boy was nervous, but Utha noticed a certain intelligence in his eyes as he answered. 'I didn't even know that clerics took squires, my lord. So, in terms of suitability, I've nothing to compare myself to. Have you ever had a squire, Brother Utha?'

'You have a fast tongue, lad,' Utha said with a slight smile.

Randall looked a little embarrassed. 'You're not the first to remark on that, sir. I don't mean to be rude.'

'In answer to your question, no, I've never had a squire. Common men are ill suited to following around a man of my . . .' he chose his words carefully, '. . . responsibilities. Tell me, boy, where are you from? Some pox-ridden back street of whores and serfs, no doubt.'

Randall's eyes narrowed as he looked at the cleric. 'Er . . . I don't remember there being any whores, sir, but then cattle and farmers would make poor customers. I'm from a small village in the Darkwald, a hundred leagues to the north of Arnon. I think there were some serfs, my lord, but the lord of Darkwald was a kindly man, from what I remember. My people lived off the land, with little need to be bound to the nobility as serfs.'

Utha was often given to making quick decisions about people, especially those who took offence at his manner; however, he thought the squire had handled himself well. The Black cleric had made people cry on more than one occasion with a well-placed insult or a quick retort, but Randall had not withered under Utha's gaze.

'Well then, Randall, are you accompanying your master this day?' Utha asked.

Randall shot a glance at Torian, who nodded. The Purple cleric tolerated Utha's bullying, knowing it was the way he conducted himself with those outside the church.

'Yes, I think I am, milord.' He looked down at the ornate longsword belted at his waist. 'Though I think this might cause more problems than it solves.' He patted the hilt.

Torian stood and stepped past Utha. He rested his hand on Randall's shoulder and spoke with kindness. 'I told you that you were permitted to wear it. Any man who says otherwise is questioning my judgement and I would take great offence at that.'

Utha laughed. 'Ah, the offence of nobility . . . Is there a worse kind?'

Torian ignored him. 'Randall, when you learn how to use it properly, it'll feel more comfortable, trust me.' He then turned to face Utha. 'If you're quite finished, brother, we should get to work,' he said, with no hint of amusement.

'Indeed we should, before young Randall here shits himself and needs changing.' Utha had to confess to himself that he was being mean, but he delighted in causing Torian discomfort.

The Purple cleric pursed his lips, annoyed at the behaviour of his friend, but, as was his way, he let it slide with silent grace.

Utha smiled broadly at Randall. 'Don't worry, lad, none of the Purple have a sense of humour,' he said with a wink.

He thoroughly enjoyed the look of confusion on the young squire's face as the three men left the room.

'I saw a squad of watchmen in the bar on my way in; I think we should enlist their help,' Utha said as they reached the top of the stairs.

'For what purpose, brother?' Torian queried.

'Just for the sake of appearances, really. It never hurts to have lesser men who can be ordered around.'

'So, we're no longer making subtle enquiries?' Torian asked.

Utha stopped on the stairs and directed an ironic expression at the Purple cleric. 'Do you really think the enquiries you've made so far have been subtle? You carry a sword and wear purple, brother, nothing you do is subtle in the eyes of the common people. We are two clerics of the One; a squad of watchmen will do very little to increase our visibility.'

Torian considered it, but Utha detected no disagreement. 'The Kasbah will be unfriendly no matter how many men we take. Perhaps a little backup would be wise,' he conceded.

'Sensible, brother, very sensible indeed,' Utha replied.

They resumed walking down the wooden steps and entered the vaulted common room below. The squad of watchmen Utha had passed as he walked through earlier were still seated at the same table. Their breakfast had been cleared away and they were preparing to leave. Five men were seated round the circular wooden table, laughing at a joke the youngest of them had told. It took a moment for them to register the presence of the clerics, their laughter masking the sound of metal armour on wood. When they noticed, they leant in and began whispering quietly to each other.

'Allow me, brother,' Utha said confidently.

'There is no need to scare them. Could we perhaps proceed without your customary brand of coercion?' Torian asked.

Utha considered responding, but decided to smile wickedly instead. He crossed the tavern floor quickly, saying a silent prayer as he walked under the banner of the Black church hanging from the ceiling. The banner, with its skeletal hand holding a goblet, was smaller than the others, and it hung in its customary place away from the other banners. It was considered bad luck to hang the heraldry of all six clerical orders together, and the Black banner was traditionally the one that was separate.

As he approached the watchmen they locked their eyes on the wooden table in front of them, not daring to look up. Utha enjoyed their irrational fear and decided to stand over them for a moment before speaking. He knew that the moment's pause would cause them to remember a thousand stories they had heard about the Black clerics, and to imagine a thousand more.

Utha waited just long enough to make all of them feel uncomfortable before he spoke. 'You men will be coming with me,' he said softly.

The oldest of the watchmen, a man of perhaps forty years, glanced round the faces of his squad. 'My lord, we are due on street duty this morning,' he said nervously.

'What is your name, sergeant?'

'Clement, my lord,' he replied.

'Well, Sergeant Clement, your street duty will have to wait. You are required to assist me. Now, get your men up, we're travelling to the Kasbah of Haq outside the walls.' Utha spoke plainly and turned back to Torian without giving Clement any further chance to argue.

Torian was smiling with tolerance, though Utha knew that he would disapprove of the theatrical display. 'Not trying to instil a sense of loyalty in your troops then, brother?' Torian asked.

'Loyalty is overrated; I prefer fear,' Utha replied.

The five watchmen stood up slowly, sharing glances and whispered words as they straightened their chain mail and made sure their weapons were in place. Clement carried a heavy mace at his hip and a small crossbow, and the youngest of them had two short swords, one protruding at each shoulder. The other three all carried crossbows and large knives. They wore the white eagle of Tiris on their chests over dull steel chain mail. Utha was impressed enough to walk past them in review and nod approvingly.

'Gentlemen, if you would follow our lead,' he said with authority, before turning to smile at Torian and walk towards the tavern door.

Utha disliked the capital. The streets were packed together tightly and, although most buildings were made of stone, they were cheaply built and poorly maintained. The bound men who kept the cobbled streets clean did a half-arsed job and mostly shovelled the waste into the side streets to make it less obvious.

The chapter house of the knights of the Red towered over the buildings in this area and the crossed swords could be seen from virtually every street. Torian had wisely chosen to stay in a tavern that catered for men of discipline and respect, rather than in one of the numerous low-rent establishments that littered the city. Despite Tiris being the capital of Tor Funweir, it was still a dangerous place, where men needed to be on their guard.

Utha had been here before when he was a boy and the place had not noticeably changed. The conflicting smells were the same now as they had been then. He could detect meat, fish, tobacco, wine – both fresh and rancid – and the ever-present scent of vomit and faeces.

The streets of Ro Arnon, in contrast, were cleaned by the Brown church and were generally spotless.

The two clerics, the squire and the five watchmen walked along a bustling street adjacent to the farmer's guild assembly and emerged into a wide square. The paving stones here were octagonal and some effort had been made to keep them clean. The square was dominated by a statue of a Red knight on a horse, waving a banner of the One, and Utha was glad to be out of the claustrophobic side streets.

The guild assemblies framed the square and hundreds of people, both newcomers to the city and natives, jockeyed for position to enter the buildings and find work. The merchant's guild was the largest, followed by the watchmen's recruitment barracks. Both buildings had paid guards on their doors and were turning away most of the people who tried to enter.

To the east of the guild square Utha could see the White Spire of the King, an ancient watchtower that signified the vigilance of the house of Tiris. It rose high above the royal palace, dominating the skyline and dwarfing the Red cathedral, the banners of which could be seen clearly over the west of the square.

Squads of watchmen saluted as the clerics passed and common men averted their eyes. Utha saw a number of people point out the Black cleric to their fellows, and several gestures warding against evil. Utha had grown to enjoy this reaction and glared at those who had noticed him, increasing their nervousness.

He heard men whisper that *the Ghost was passing*, and that *the risen men should beware*, but nothing out of the ordinary or insulting was directed at him.

The King's Highway led from the northern corner of the guild square to the outer city walls and the ramshackle hamlets beyond. It was a wide, paved boulevard, patrolled by watchmen and used by men who could afford to pay the toll at the gate. Colourful banners hung from torch emplacements along the road, displaying the heraldry of the noble houses of Tor Funweir. The Black Raven of Ro Weir was placed next to the White Eagle of Tiris and the Grey Roc of Arnon. Utha thought the highway one of the nicer parts of the capital and breathed in deeply as he left the guild square.

Behind, Torian and the others followed him closely. Utha could see the young squire, Randall, deep in conversation with the youngest watchman. They were of a similar age and Utha thought the squire could learn much from a watchman who actually knew how to use a blade. However, he suspected that the watchman was simply telling Randall horror stories about the Black clerics, and he hoped that Randall was clever enough to disregard most of the tall tales he was hearing.

They walked along the well-tended cobblestones of the highway, passing mounted knights of the Red, chain-mail-clad watchmen and all manner of common citizenry. The fashion in Tiris currently favoured light-coloured robes, and both men and women were wearing full-length fabrics belted at the waist. Some men wore armour chosen for its fashionable appearance rather than its usefulness. Some breastplates were etched with family crests or coats of arms and a few longswords were on display – family heirlooms and designer steel.

Utha let his gaze wander to the women in the street. Some were nobles, wearing thin veils to hide their features from onlookers; others were paid women or servants. Scantily clad servants also appeared to be in fashion, as many merchants and noblemen were accompanied by several such. Utha winked at one as he passed and caused her to show an expression somewhere between fear and arousal as her master ushered her quickly away. She was wearing a revealing leather waistcoat and the cleric heartily approved of her more feminine qualities.

'Brother, now is not the time to be indulging your libido,' Torian said as he came to walk next to Utha.

'You're just jealous because you had yours removed when you took the Purple,' he replied, turning to watch the woman leave.

'You're strange, brother; with one breath you cause fear, with the other you're ruled by your cock.'

'Hopefully they didn't take that when you became a cleric,' Utha said with a wicked smile, 'though it would certainly explain your sour disposition.' He looked deliberately down at Torian's crotch. 'Did they put it in a jar and let you keep it?'

Torian replied calmly, 'I will rise above your taunts, brother . . . my love for the One is enough sustenance for me.' His words were sincere.

'Maybe I just have too much love and women allow me not to burst,' Utha replied. 'In that case, it would be reasonable to thank them for keeping me alive to do the One's good work.'

Torian shook his head and walked silently towards the end of the King's Highway. Utha thought it his duty to puncture the smug piety of the Purple clerics, and Torian was an enjoyable target. He took everything so very seriously and had been taught to abstain from pleasure from a young age. The Black clerics were supposed to take all they could from life, and this traditionally included alcohol and sex. If death was to be feared and respected, then life was to be enjoyed and celebrated. Utha had never been shy about his beliefs, and he knew they challenged Torian's faith – how could two clerics who followed the same god have such drastically different views of the world? What Torian didn't yet understand was that the One required all of his aspects in order to be whole.

They approached the outer wall of the city and Utha stopped at the side of the street. Ro Tiris was on the northern coast of Tor Funweir, with only a wide sea channel and the duchy of Canarn between the men of Ro and the Freelands of Ranen. Above the high stone walls Utha could see tall ships at anchor in the bay, and the smell of salt water was pronounced. Two turrets flanked the huge raised portcullis where the King's Highway passed out of Ro Tiris.

Utha and Torian stood off to the side of the open gate and the watchmen, with Randall in tow, stood in a rough semicircle around them. Sergeant Clement still looked uneasy at being ordered around by a cleric, but Utha sensed no hint of rebellion from the old watchman.

'Where are we going?' Utha asked Torian.

'The Kasbah of Haq. It's a Karesian marketplace down there.' He gestured to a road that snaked round the outside of the city wall. 'It's a strange-smelling place from what I hear, all manner of Karesian drugs and poisons filling the air.'

'Hm, I would have thought the watch would have dealt with the drugs by now.' Utha directed a questioning expression at Sergeant Clement, who looked surprised before stuttering out a reply. 'My lord . . . the watch have no real power outside the walls . . . we, er, tend to keep our distance from the Karesian mobsters . . . those bastards will cut your nose off if you give them reason to.'

'Relax, sergeant, Brother Utha is merely expressing his displeasure at the presence of foreign influence,' Torian said calmly, before turning back to Utha. 'Your need for theatrics aside, the Kasbah has a few establishments that provide feminine company for those who are inclined—'

'Do you mean brothels?' Utha interrupted.

'I believe that is the common term, yes. Either way, the forger Glenwood spends most evenings in one of these establishments. It is likely that he will just be waking up.'

'Let's go and be a nice morning surprise for him, then,' Utha replied, with his customary wicked smile.

They walked in loose formation out of the gates, sparing a respectful salute for the king's guard who patrolled the outer walls. The guardsmen carried longswords, wore ornate golden armour and were answerable only to the king. They remained within the walls of Ro Tiris, or at the king's side, and were charged with defending the city and the crown. Utha respected them far more than the watchmen, because they were true fighting men pledged to the crown from birth.

The guardsmen stopped anyone they did not recognize, taking a modest toll from those who wished to pass through the gates. Most common men were simply turned back along the highway and not permitted to leave the city. Utha knew that this was merely a ceremonial consideration and that if men truly wished to leave there were many secret ways and less secure gates they could use.

Beyond the walls, the outer city stretched along the coast in narrow streets framing the King's Highway. This was where Karesian rainbow merchants sold their illicit wares and low-born men of Ro came to forget about their lives. The smell of spices and other less savoury concoctions was thick in the air as soon as Utha stepped off the highway. He turned up his nose at the sickly sweet smell and held a hand over his face.

The buildings here were much lower and more closely packed than in the city and the colours were brighter. Utha thought it more vulgar and garish. Karesian and Ro men shouted the prices of their wares to all who passed; spices, foods, weapons and clothing were all on display. Utha could also see exotic animals from the far south, caged and poorly treated, waiting for a buyer rich enough to want a strange pet or hunting animal. Desert spiders the size of dogs sat next to strange many-headed birds and muzzled firedrakes.

Utha puffed out his chest and let all nearby see that a Black cleric was passing. Torian, the taller of the two men, swept his purple cloak back and proudly displayed his full plate armour. The watchmen, who stood behind them, looked nervous and their lack of authority outside the city walls was evident in their faces.

The populace here were less fearful of the clerics and most simply glanced at them and turned away, carrying on with their business. The stallholders and merchants continued shouting their prices and drumming up sales, paying little attention to Utha and Torian.

The Kasbah of Haq was like a dozen other marketplaces in the outer city, a roughly circular section of street dominated by colourful awnings and closely packed market stalls.

Torian pointed to a nondescript building set back from the market. 'That's the place. I believe it's called the Blue Feather.'

'The nicer the name, the shittier the brothel, as a general rule,' Utha replied, with a smile.

'Well, I've not actually been to many, so I'll defer to your expert opinion, brother,' Torian said snobbishly.

'You can look, you just can't touch . . . the women or yourself,' the Black cleric retorted crudely. 'Anyway, enough of what you can't do. I believe the man's name is Glenwood, yes?'

Torian nodded. 'He's a forger, known in certain circles, though he's seen as unreliable and reckless by many in the same trade.'

Utha shot him a questioning look. 'Have you been mixing in dark circles, brother?'

'Not by choice, but I had to immerse myself to a degree in order to get information. Criminals by their nature are very concerned with staying alive and an angry Purple cleric conjures images of death to such men. They can be very cooperative when threatened.'

Utha laughed. 'And you question my theatrics . . .'

'I use the gifts the One has given me, much as you do,' said Torian, with even more snobbery.

'Okay, so I'll let you talk to Glenwood. Just nod at me if you need help,' Utha said.

Torian took a deep breath and marched towards the Blue Feather, his hand firmly on his sword hilt. Utha motioned for the watchmen to follow and stepped slowly after the Purple cleric.

'My lord, is there likely to be trouble here?' Randall asked, as he came to walk next to Utha.

'Oh, I should think so, yes. Probably no death, but I would expect some people to get slapped around.' He grinned wickedly.

Randall smiled back politely, but Utha sensed that he didn't find the situation funny.

'Relax, lad, there aren't enough real men around here to cause your master any sweat,' he said in a vague attempt to be reassuring.

Torian stepped under a dark blue awning and approached a small group of Karesians seated on low wooden stools. The five men were armed with short scimitars and wore the flowing black robes of Karesian warriors. All had visible tattoos on their arms and their heads were shaved.

Utha stood behind him, staying outside the entrance awning but making his presence known. Sergeant Clement was still nervous and held his crossbow at the ready. Randall stood at the back, looking as if he was not prepared to take part in any violence, should it occur.

'The fear of Jaa upon thee,' one of the Karesians said with a florid bow. He spoke with a heavy Karesian accent. 'What does a man of the One require of us?' he asked respectfully of Torian, who answered with a shallow bow of his own.

'We're looking for a man of Ro called Glenwood. I hear that he frequents this . . . establishment.' The last word was said with scorn and Utha shook his head.

The Karesian stood and smiled at Torian, revealing several gold teeth. He was a tall man, looking down on the Purple cleric. 'Our clients are obviously men who desire discretion, my lord, and I regret that I cannot comment on who does or does not frequent this . . . establishment.' His words were still polite, but Utha sensed an edge of defiance.

Torian confidently sized up the man, looking at his scimitar and warrior's bearing. 'Discretion does not matter to me, neither does your primitive weapon. You will tell me whether the man I seek is present.' The words were spoken with authority and caused all five of the Karesians to become more alert as they looked at the two clerics and squad of watchmen.

The man who'd spoken narrowed his eyes, before letting his face flow into a broad smile. 'My lord, we are simple men, not used to the presence of clerics.' He bowed again. 'I mean no offence.'

'Then you will take us to Glenwood?' Torian asked.

The Karesian considered it and glanced at his four companions, all of whom looked worried. Utha detected a hint of fear and was optimistic that Torian was sufficiently intimidating to speed their passage.

'My lord cleric, I will take you to the man you seek for a small . . . price.' He rubbed his hands together suggestively. 'Think of it as a donation to the faithful of Jaa.' His face was contorted into an unpleasant grin and his gold teeth glinted as the morning sun passed through a gap in the awning.

Utha stood next to Torian, lending his best expression of right-eous annoyance to the one Torian already wore. The Karesian continued smiling, hoping that the two clerics would agree to bribe him. He slowly let the realization that this was unlikely intrude upon his grin and backed away, directing his eyes at the dusty street.

'I have asked you twice. If I have to ask you again, I may become rather more insistent,' Torian said plainly.

Utha smiled at the other four Karesians, showing a brazen confidence as he looked them up and down. Though they were obviously fighting men, they were poorly armed and would be no match for the two clerics.

The Karesian held his arms wide in a gesture of submission and bowed deeply. 'I apologize for any offence caused, the ways of the Ro are still new to me, my lord,' he said while still looking at the floor.

'I'm about to ask again . . . I suspect you don't want that,' Torian snarled aggressively.

The Karesian looked up, letting a frown of contempt show before he smiled again and motioned for Torian to follow him. 'You'll have to speak to the mistress,' he said as he led the way inside.

Utha continued smiling at the other men as Torian ducked under the low doorway that led into the brothel. Without turning, Utha motioned for the watchmen to go in, and then followed himself.

Inside, the building was dirty and badly maintained, with an unpleasant smell of incense which Utha suspected was used to mask the odour of sweaty men. A counter sat in the middle of a small entrance area, behind which sat a woman of Ro in her late forties. She was attractive but had hard eyes, and her tan suggested she had lived some of her life further south. Either side of the counter were yellow silk curtains hanging across doorways, and four mean-looking Karesian men stood idly around the counter.

Torian entered and all present looked up. Several of the Karesians appeared ready for action as the squad of watchmen followed, until the man who led Torian held his hands up to let them know that starting trouble was unwise. To emphasize this point, Utha walked in and did his best to look dangerous. His pale features, pink eyes and white hair made him distinctive, even amongst Karesians, and he thought that at least one of the men could connect the name *Utha the Ghost* to his face.

'And what can we do for such fine gentlemen?' the woman asked.

'Your man here was about to take us to see a client of yours. There is no need to worry yourself,' Torian said dismissively.

'They want to see Glenwood and are . . . rather insistent,' said the man who had led them inside.

The Karesian guards assessed the clerics and, much as those outside had done, deemed them too dangerous to be worth fighting. The woman looked flustered when she saw that none of her men was going to stop Utha and Torian from intruding.

'We have rules here, sir,' she said. 'Our customers pay for cunt or cock, not to be interrupted by clerics. A face like yours would put them right off their stride.' She screwed her face up in mock disgust and looked at Torian.

One of the Karesians laughed at this and the confidence shown by their mistress made all the guards feel more comfortable.

Utha made a low grunt of amusement and stepped past the Purple cleric. Leaning casually on the side of the counter and deliberately turning his back on the Karesian guards, he looked the woman square in the eyes. 'I'm the one with the sense of humour. My pious friend here thinks of you as little more than a river-dwelling rodent, given your profession. So I recommend you direct any further jokes to me,' he said with calculated aggression. 'Now, is there a joke you'd like to make about my face?' He stared her down with his piercing pink eyes.

The mistress maintained eye contact for a moment before looking over Utha's shoulder and nodding to one of her guards. He felt a hand on his shoulder as three of the guards moved in closer.

'There is no need for trouble. We can all be friendly, no?' The man who'd recognized Utha held his hands up. He had not advanced towards the cleric and was staring at Torian and the watchmen.

Utha didn't wait to see if the other guards had listened to him, as he judged the value of a quick show of violence would be considerable under the circumstances. He flexed his shoulder and elbowed the man who had grabbed him in the face, the steel plate making a satisfying clank against the man's jaw before he crumpled to the ground.

The other two guards seemed to consider attacking, but seeing Torian extravagantly draw his longsword persuaded them otherwise.

'I said that if I had to ask again, I would be more insistent.' He levelled his sword at the nearest man.

The woman backed away and didn't raise any more objections. She waved an arm towards the right-hand curtain and spoke quietly. 'He's in the fourth room along.'

Utha winked at the mistress and turned back to Torian. 'Handle this for a minute.'

He pulled back the curtain and entered the corridor beyond. A few scared faces, mostly male, poked out from behind coloured curtains, their time having been interrupted by the commotion outside. Utha spared a few glares to make the customers disappear back behind their curtains and moved to the fourth room, where he could hear hurried movement.

He pulled back the bright red curtain and saw a wiry man of Ro attempting to climb out of a narrow window. He was only half dressed and carried his boots and a sheathed longsword in his arms. The naked woman who lay on the wooden cot in the centre of the floor appeared unconcerned at the intrusion and looked bored as Utha quickly crossed the room and grabbed Glenwood's leg.

'I'm fairly sure I've not done anything to annoy the One recently,' he said as Utha roughly pulled him back. He was flushed from his recent sexual activity and barely struggled.

'Just make sure your cock's away. We need a little chat,' Utha said, with a gauntleted fist around Glenwood's neck. He picked the smaller man up with ease and held him off the ground for a moment.

Glenwood glanced over at the woman lying next to them. 'I don't suppose this makes me more desirable, does it?' he asked with a weak smile. The woman snorted in derision and rolled over to face the opposite wall.

'You're in the same room as me, Glenwood, you could never compete.' Utha smiled as he spoke and shoved the forger out of the room.

He stumbled to the ground, dropping his sword and boots on the wooden floor. A few faces again appeared from behind curtains, but most disappeared quickly for fear of involving themselves in whatever the Black cleric was doing.

'That looks very much like a longsword, Glenwood,' Utha said as he stepped casually out behind the forger. 'I assume that, as a common man, you were merely looking after it for a nobleman.' Criminals often thought they could get away with carrying a noble's weapon if they stayed away from clerics.

'Actually, no, brother cleric, it's mine . . . my father was . . . sort of noble.'

Utha laughed and solidly kicked the man down the corridor. Glenwood made a strange yelping sound and did an ungainly forward roll through the curtain into the entrance room. All those on the other side turned to look at the figure that had emerged so loudly amongst them.

The watchmen held their crossbows drawn and Sergeant Clement swung his heavy mace threateningly. Torian still held his longsword and Utha thought his brother cleric looked quite impressive as he glared at the men, the purple sceptre on his tabard shining brightly.

Glenwood had emerged with little elegance and was now draped in the yellow curtain through which he'd been thrown. Utha walked past him, absently grabbing the forger by the scruff of the neck, as he stepped into the entrance room.

The mistress of the Blue Feather was looking daggers at both clerics. 'Okay, you have your man, now get your pious arses out of my fuck shop.'

Torian directed his sword point at the woman. 'We will leave you to your immorality, woman. I believe I may return at a later time to instruct your men on the correct way to address a cleric of the One.'

The mistress looked as if she were about to burst with anger, but kept her words to herself and directed her men to stand down.

Utha dragged Glenwood roughly past the watchmen, holding the collar of his shirt and giving him several kicks to speed him along.

'Brother, I believe we have what we came for,' Utha said with a smile. 'Shall we depart?'

Torian allowed himself a slight show of amusement but quickly recovered his grim demeanour and backed away slowly, letting his hard glare move across the Karesians' faces.

The men outside had left as Utha emerged on to the street, and the sun had disappeared behind a cloud. The weather in Ro Tiris was changeable and a storm was imminent.

Torian and the watchmen backed out of the brothel and Utha noticed Randall for the first time since they'd entered. The young squire had hidden behind Sergeant Clement and done his best to remain invisible as the confrontation played out.

'You, Elyot,' Utha said to the youngest watchman, 'take hold of this *minor noble* and don't let him move too much.' He flung Glenwood at the watchman, who had his two short swords drawn.

Pulling Glenwood to his feet, Elyot placed one blade around the forger's neck and the other against his back. 'Move,' he said with practised authority.

'Is fucking suddenly against the One?' Glenwood asked.

He received a solid kick to the back of his legs from Elyot in response and fell to the floor again.

'Apparently so.' The forger grimaced in pain.

'We should take Glenwood somewhere more . . . appropriate,' Torian said with menace.

'Appropriate for what?' the prisoner asked, pulling himself to his feet.

Utha came to face him. 'I'll bet that you've done a multitude of foolish things in your life, but we are only interested in one of the more recent ones. Now cooperate and I won't bite your nose off. Clear?' he asked coldly.

Glenwood looked terrified and nodded, not trusting himself to speak. He smiled as Elyot, the young watchman, carefully placed the two short swords back where they had been a moment ago. 'Okay, I'm ready, let's go somewhere more . . . appropriate,' he said with nervous humour.

They were still concealed by the awning of the Blue Feather, but Utha noticed several men glance across and see the forger in the custody of the clerics. A man of Ro, with the glare of a fighting man, took particular interest and even locked eyes with the prisoner for a second, before disappearing into a side street.

Utha decided that walking back through the Kasbah would be unwise, as Glenwood would no doubt have friends who might consider a foolish rescue attempt. Instead, he led Torian and the watchmen into an alley that ran between the Blue Feather and an adjoining spice merchant's hut. It was wide enough for single file only, making Glenwood even more nervous, as he realized he was surrounded and unlikely to survive if he tried to get away.

Utha led the group down a second alleyway which passed behind the brothel and into a small yard. They were against the outer wall and in an isolated space used for alcohol storage. The back doors to several buildings opened out into the yard and crates of wine and beer were strewn around. Utha turned from his companions and perused the closest crate. Finding a bottle of Karesian red wine, he sat down on a low box. Torian stood next to him, his sword now sheathed, and the watchmen took seats on other crates. Elyot positioned Glenwood in front of the two clerics and then went to sit next to Randall.

'Now, let's get comfy shall we,' Utha said, uncorking the bottle of wine and taking a deep swig. Wincing at the taste, he placed the open bottle on the floor. 'Perhaps it needs to breathe a little.' He spat out the residue of vinegary liquid.

'Theatrics, brother?' questioned Torian, with a raise of his eyebrows.

'You have your sword, I have my theatrics; surely the value of both has been evident in the last hour?'

Torian shook his head and stepped forward to tower over Glenwood. The forger was around six feet in height, but thin and pasty-looking. The Purple cleric, in comparison, was fully armoured and looked like a mountain standing over the lesser man.

'How is the business in Red church seals these days, Glenwood?' Torian asked.

The forger looked surprised, but got the reaction quickly under control with the practised candour of a professional criminal.

'How many do you want?' he said, in a foolish attempt at humour, before quickly retracting the comment. 'Just joking, just a joke, my lords . . . there's no business in such things; no way of making enough money to justify the risk, anyway.'

'So, you admit that you're a forger?' Torian asked.

Glenwood frowned and said to Utha, 'So, I'm guessing you're the brains?' He turned back to Torian. 'Of course I'm a forger . . . there are a thousand people in Tiris who can tell you I'm a forger and a thousand more who can tell you where to find me.' He paused, shaking his head. 'But I'm not an idiot and I have enough friends in enough places to know that forgery is a relatively minor crime in the grand scheme of things and that two clerics are unlikely to be interested in minor criminal misdemeanours.' He spoke with the swagger of a man used to talking to the authorities. 'You want to arrest me? Be my guest, I guarantee I'll be free within the hour . . . probably on some technicality or other.'

Utha narrowed his eyes. 'You're evading the question . . . you're doing it very skilfully, but you're still evading the question.'

'Maybe, but I'm still not going to tell you anything, so put your arm round your lady friend here and go fuck yourself,' he said arrogantly. Torian quickly drew his sword and growled at Glenwood.

'Watch your tongue, piss-stain.' The words came from Sergeant Clement.

The watchman stepped forward and held his mace in front of Glenwood's head. Utha smiled at the forger, a vicious expression that made him shrink.

'I think I can handle the insult, sergeant,' the Black cleric said, before smashing his forehead into the bridge of Glenwood's nose.

The forger instantly dropped to the floor and yelped loudly, an incoherent sound of pain, anger and surprise.

Torian looked equally shocked and Clement backed sharply away from Glenwood's writhing form. Utha grabbed the forger by the throat and picked him up off the floor. He held the man away from him and punched him solidly in the chest, making him cough and spray blood on to the dusty floor. Utha then roughly spun him round and rested an armoured forearm across his throat.

'I'm not a watchman, I'm not a judge and I'm not a man who gives a Ranen's balls about what you think,' Utha said through gritted teeth. 'You sold a forged Red church seal to a man with an ornate longsword, yes?'

Glenwood was clearly dazed, his face covered in blood and his eyes unfocused, but the presence of a hulking Black cleric, ready to tear him apart, made him clear his mind quickly. 'Yes . . . yes, I did,' he said through a quivering mouth.

'Good. Now, I want you to tell us everything you know about the man with the longsword. Do you understand?' he asked.

Glenwood's eyes were wide and he no longer held his broken nose, as if Utha's words had made him forget the pain he was in. He nodded again in reply and started to retch. Utha released his arm and allowed Glenwood to double over and vomit on the floor.

The sound of Torian's squire also retching made everyone turn quickly. Randall didn't actually vomit, but he was clearly uneasy at the sight of blood and of Glenwood emptying his stomach.

'Easy, lad,' Torian said reassuringly, 'this streak of shit isn't worth feeling bad over.'

'That's a wise thing you just said, brother,' said Utha, as he pushed Glenwood into a sitting position.

The forger looked terrible, his nose was mangled across his face and his lips had gone a strange blue colour. Clement stood behind him and kicked Glenwood's leg to encourage him to straighten himself up. The other watchmen stayed back, thinking themselves largely unneeded.

Utha resumed his seat on the box and picked up the bottle of wine. Taking another drink, he said, 'Yes, it's much nicer after a little air. Now, Glenwood, if you will . . .' He waved his hand at the broken man sitting in front of him.

Glenwood straightened and pulled his legs back into a cross-legged position. 'I don't deal in church seals, but I owed him a favour, so . . .'

'Tell us about him,' Torian said as he sheathed his longsword and relaxed.

Glenwood spat out a mouthful of blood. 'He paid three hundred gold crowns for a clay seal that would get him out of the south gate without being stopped. I knew him years ago and felt like helping him.'

Utha shouted, 'Who was he?'

Glenwood looked across at the faces of, first the two clerics, then the five watchmen. He breathed in sharply, assessing his options. With a resigned sigh, he said, 'His name's Bromvy, people call him Brom. I think he's a noble of some sort . . . maybe Canarn or somewhere around there.'

Utha leant back in his seated position and looked up at Torian. 'There you go, theatrics work . . . I've proven it.' He turned back to Glenwood. 'And where was Lord Bromvy of Canarn intending to go?'

'I think he was looking for a friend. He asked me if I knew where he was. I think he wanted to know which gate he'd need to leave from,' he said quietly, as if ashamed at himself for giving this information.

'And . . . the friend . . . and his location?' Torian asked.

'The friend is a Kirin assassin – nasty bastard, kills anyone you pay him to – and, last I knew, he was in Ro Weir. He's called Rham Jas Rami and he and Brom go way back. They travelled together with another couple of wayward killers.'

Utha frowned at this. He knew a little about Bromvy and knew that he'd mixed with some unsavoury characters in his time. There were even rumours that Duke Hector's son had been a mercenary, but to hear that he associated with an assassin was a surprise, even to Utha.

'Weir is a three-week journey south at least,' Torian said to Utha.

Glenwood chuckled through the pain. 'I doubt it'd take Brom any more than two, maybe less. He's not like you pampered city folk, he's from Canarn, those men are tough. If you don't care for your horse or the need for sleep, you can get there shy of two weeks.'

Randall nervously raised his hand and spoke. 'Sir Leon used to talk about it, master. I think it's called the Kirin run. A way of criminals getting from one side of Tor Funweir to the other.'

Utha and Torian looked at each other and nodded. They had both heard of Kirin having ways of moving quickly through the land but had not expected them to be utilized by a lord of Tor Funweir.

Glenwood looked at Randall. 'Your boy has it right; the Kirin run cuts the journey in half. If you avoid Cozz and stay off the King's Highway . . .' He went to retch again but got it under control. 'And if you don't mind the big bastard spiders in Narland and Lob's Wood,' he smiled pathetically, 'and obviously if you know the way – which I don't, before you ask.'

Utha turned away from Glenwood. He motioned for Torian to join him and spoke quietly so as not to be overheard by the forger. 'We'll never find the way through Narland. We're better off taking the long route and hoping he's still there when we arrive.'

'I was told nothing of his criminal endeavours when I left Arnon,' Torian said with a shake of his head. 'As far as I know all the questing clerics who were sent for him are looking at the estates of his family, lesser nobles and the like.'

Utha took a moment to think, absently drumming his fingers on his black tabard. 'I know a few mercenaries were sent to the south . . . doubtful as far as Ro Weir, though.'

Torian straightened suddenly and let a rare smile flow across his face. 'Well, brother, it seems we have a direction in which to travel. Let us go to Ro Weir.'

Utha returned the smile and looked over Torian's shoulder at the watchmen standing round Glenwood. 'Sergeant Clement,' he said loudly, 'go and tell the lord marshal that you're accompanying Brothers Utha and Torian on a journey to the merchant enclave of Cozz and then on to Ro Weir.'

Clement didn't know how to react to this, but Utha enjoyed the helpless expression on his face.

CHAPTER THREE

MAGNUS FORKBEARD RAGNARSSON IN THE CITY OF RO CANARN

T HE CELL WAS cold and damp, with a simple straw bed on a
rickety wooden frame. Magnus wondered if the knights of
the Red who had thrown him in here knew how profound
an insult it was for a priest of the Order of the Hammer to be
summarily caged in this way. The knights were true fighting men,
for the most part, and Magnus found that he had to respect them
for that, but there were few other reasons to feel anything other
than anger at the way they'd assaulted Ro Canarn.

He looked out of the narrow cell window and clenched his fist,
imagining the feel of Skeld, his war-hammer. It was a childish
comfort to want the feel of his weapon's leather and brass grip in
his fist, but one that he allowed himself. To accept imprisonment
was almost as bad as being imprisoned in the first place.

The men of Ro who took the inner keep would have taken the
hammer and discarded it as a strange trophy of war, or kept it
to show that they'd bested a Ranen warrior. In reality, Magnus
knew that he'd not yet been bested. The knights had relied on
numbers rather than skill, and Magnus could take solace from
the fifteen he had killed before a cowardly crossbow bolt had
pierced his shoulder and allowed them to capture him. He flexed
his shoulders and rubbed the bandaged wound. It was not bad
and the Ranen priest's healing abilities had ensured the wound
would not fester.

Magnus was around seven feet in height, tall even for a Ranen, and although he had only recently passed his thirtieth year of life, his long blonde hair, dense beard and scarred body made him appear older. He'd been robbed of his chain mail and stood in simple woollen leggings and a black shirt. It was scant protection against the cold, but Magnus was a man of Fjorlan and the temperature was more reassuring than uncomfortable. His home, far to the north, was the oldest realm of the Freelands and the only province of Ranen that the south-men of Ro had never conquered.

Magnus had travelled throughout the northern lands. Like all priests of the Order of the Hammer, he was compelled to a perpetual wanderlust and had made friends in many distant parts. He found that a love of alcohol, women and song was an ideal way to taste a culture, and even the stiff-necked Ro could be likeable when drunk. Not that these knights of the Red seemed to drink, or even to laugh. They were dour men who lived only to follow orders and to maintain the laws of the One.

Somewhere above the cell, Magnus heard a scream of pain and he craned his neck to see out of the tiny window. The mercenaries who had come with the Red knights were not being kind to the defeated populace, and the last few hours had been punctured by a cacophony of screams and cries for help. The few Ranen who remained in the city with Magnus had already been executed by order of Sir Mortimer Rillion, under the questionable title of *traitors to the crown of Tor Funweir*. Several times he had heard a dying Ranen offer a defiant last prayer to Rowanoco before joining the Ice Giant in his halls beyond the world.

Magnus felt regret for the death of his countrymen, but he did not forget that they had had the choice to go or to stay, as was the way of the Free Companies. The few men of Wraith Company who'd stayed had at least got to dirty their axes with the blood of knights before they fell.

The small dungeon complex housed fewer than a hundred prisoners, mostly Duke Hector's guardsmen, men who had held the inner keep with Magnus after the city had fallen, and he wondered if they regretted their decision to fight when the battle fleet appeared on the horizon.

It was different for the Ranen. They hadn't fought for their home, their families or for a cause they believed in. Magnus suspected that the men of Wraith who'd stayed had merely wanted a good fight. The soldiers of Canarn had had much more to lose, and now they were prisoners of a victorious army.

The Ranen priest of Rowanoco, the Ice Giant, shook his head as he thought of Duke Hector. The lord of Canarn was, in Magnus's estimation, a good man, deserving of honour and respect, and to think of what the knights would do to him bothered Magnus greatly. The common people of Canarn and their duke had wanted nothing more than freedom from the church of Tor Funweir – a goal that Magnus thought achievable and, to a Ranen priest, wholly sensible – however, something had alerted the Red knights in Ro Tiris and they'd attacked without warning.

If Hector were still alive, he was probably to be made an example at a later date, paraded through the streets to be whipped and jeered at. Magnus had been fond of Duke Hector and he hoped that the killing of a noble was forbidden amongst the Ro. He knew little of their ways aside from what the duke's son had taught him during the time they had travelled together. Though much of his time with Bromvy had been spent drinking rather than learning. Magnus imagined a duke would be too important to be summarily executed like the other captives.

Hector's chaplain, a Brown cleric called Lanry, had been spared execution and Magnus hoped this rare vein of honour amongst the knights would stretch to the duke.

'You . . . Ranen,' shouted Castus, the bound Red knight currently supervising the many prisoners.

Magnus ignored him. He found the man's voice grating.

'I'm talking to you, priest,' barked the knight, as he approached the small cell where Magnus stood. 'Commander Rillion says I have to feed you. Personally, I think you should rot, like the barbarian scum you are.' He placed a small bowl of steaming liquid on the cold stone floor and kicked it through the hatch at the bottom of the door. Half the liquid spilled across the flagstones. 'Enjoy it, boy. You'll most likely lose your head this afternoon.'

Magnus took a step towards the door and looked through the bars and down at the man. The size difference was huge, Magnus towering a foot or more above the man of Ro.

As Castus turned to leave, Magnus spoke. 'Knight . . . I decided I was going to kill you just after we met. Now, I think I'll find your father and kill him too.' His accent was broad and his voice was deep, elongating and growling each word.

The bound man drew his sword and levelled the tip at the Ranen. 'I'll spit on your headless body and piss on your god,' he said.

Magnus grinned as he spoke. 'The only bit of him you could reach would be his foot, little man.'

Castus grunted and stomped loudly back to his guard post, leaving the Ranen with a thin smile on his face.

* * *

Several hours passed and Magnus still stood in his cell. He knew he would be summoned to appear before Rillion before the day was out, and refusing to sit was as much rebellion as his situation would allow. The minimal light that crept through the narrow window gave him a rough idea of the time, and Castus returned shortly before the sun had disappeared.

'Time's up. Sir Rillion requests the pleasure of your company.' The Red knight smirked broadly and Magnus imagined cutting off his ears to stop him smiling.

'No last meal, no last words. Hopefully, they'll just take off that head and put you down.'

He stood close to the cell bars and continued. 'Do you know what happened to the other Ranen? They were stripped naked, had their cocks cut off and we just let them bleed. They bled and they screamed and we just . . . we just laughed. Just when they started crying, Sir Rillion ordered their heads taken off and we threw them over the wall into the sea.'

Magnus considered it. The man of Ro was a vile worm, foolish and arrogant with none of the honour Magnus hoped he'd find in an enemy combatant. 'I am of the Order of the Hammer. I don't expect you to understand what that means because your god cares only for law and knows nothing of honour or courage.' Magnus stood just inches from Castus and continued, 'If I am to be killed, I will be killed with a roar on my lips. A small man like you can hope only for a whimper.' He paused. 'I want to kill you and I pray to Rowanoco that I live long enough to do so.'

Castus turned towards the corridor and bellowed, 'This pig-fucker thinks his god is gonna help him.'

The laugh that echoed from the guard station offended Magnus and he breathed in deeply. These men did not know how lucky they were. If he were armed, he knew they would run rather than fight him, but with manacles and crossbows they were brave indeed. They were not true fighting men and Magnus surmised that their station as gaolers was due to their lack of fighting skill.

Two more Red churchmen appeared from the corridor. Each carried a smug grin of victory and a loaded crossbow. They wore steel breastplates and bore the same red tabards as Castus, two swords across a clenched fist. With their weapons levelled at Magnus, they stood either side of the cell door.

Castus drew his sword and said, 'Take a step back, priest.'

Magnus contained his anger and stepped away from the churchmen. He was not accustomed to enemies who used bows; they were unheard of in Ranen as anything other than a hunting weapon. As a means of fighting, they were considered cowardly and dishonourable.

Castus produced a large metal key and began to unlock the cell door. His movements were slow and deliberate and his eyes remained on Magnus at all times. The door clicked open and Castus motioned for his men to cover him as he took a step into the cell.

His eyes betrayed a touch of fear as he realized he no longer had the safety of a large metal door between himself and the huge Ranen warrior.

Magnus stayed back, glaring down at the two crossbowmen standing either side of Castus. He thought it likely he'd survive the two crossbow bolts long enough to tear all three of them apart, but there was little to be gained by doing so. He would still be in a dungeon, ignorant of what had happened during his incarceration. He thought it best to let himself be taken before Sir Rillion.

'Turn round slowly, Ranen. Keep an eye on him, you two.'

Magnus turned, exposing the heavy steel manacles that bound his hands. Castus unlocked the chain that secured him to the wall and attached another set of manacles to his feet. The two restraints were then fastened securely together with a second steel chain.

Castus pulled hard on the chain and led Magnus backwards out of the cell. One of the crossbowmen stood in front and the other behind. All three of the men of Ro were on edge, as if they expected Magnus to erupt into violence at any moment.

He was moved under close escort along the dungeon corridor. The other prisoners flashed dark glances at Castus and several nodded silently in respect towards Magnus. A heavy wooden door was opened and they began to ascend the stairs to the keep above.

Magnus thought hard thoughts. He knew that these men of Ro cared little for honour or truth and he doubted anything he had to say to Sir Rillion would change the situation. The reality was that Magnus knew he'd have to kill a lot of men to escape from the city. He would feel no qualms at killing them, but he knew it would not help Duke Hector or the men of Canarn. They would have to endure the pain and indignity of being a subjugated people. The Red church would not be gentle to those so recently defeated in battle.

Magnus disliked it that the situation called for patience and thought rather than action. He was not used to such things and he hoped that Rowanoco watched him closely; he trusted the wisdom of his god would guide his words when it was needed.

The stone steps ended at another large wooden door and beyond he saw the darkening sky. The keep of Ro Canarn was drenched in rain, and the smell of blood and salt water filled Magnus's nostrils.

Young men of Canarn were cleaning the courtyard of debris and repairing various wooden structures that had been destroyed during the battle. Knights of the Red, still fully adorned in plate armour, patrolled the battlements and, high overhead, the banner of the One God had been raised above the keep.

Magnus was glad to see the open sky again and the rain was welcome on the priest's face. He had not been allowed to wash while imprisoned and he instantly felt better as the water cleaned off a layer of dirt.

In the days since his imprisonment, the knights of the Red had been busy. Though they had not repaired the broken sections of the city wall, they had cleared the bodies that littered the keep and, in the city beyond, funeral pyres could be seen.

A knight of the Red, older and more scarred than many of the others, stood up from his position round a fire and walked toward Castus. His head was shaved and his eyes were fierce, making him appear a little like a bird of prey. He regarded Magnus with interest before he spoke. 'Castus, would this be the fabled Magnus Forkbeard?'

Castus saluted with respect. 'Yes, my lord. He's been summoned before Knight Commander Rillion.'

'I have a report stating that this oversized Fjorlander killed close to thirty knights.' He stepped past Castus to stand before Magnus. 'You're bigger than I expected, Ranen . . . tell me, is this sadistic little shit treating you well?' He nodded towards Castus, who frowned at the unexpected insult.

Magnus smiled and threw a smirk at his tormentor before he spoke. 'I plan to kill him, so any insult will be repaid. He is a worm, not worthy to live, let alone fight.'

The senior knight chuckled and nodded agreement. Magnus found it gratifying that his opinion of Castus was shared by another, particularly a man of Ro.

'My lord . . .' Castus stuttered as he spoke.

'Quiet, soldier,' the knight interrupted him, 'this man is an enemy, but he is at least worthy of the respect due to his prowess in battle. I would kill him on a battlefield and be glad I had done so, but as a foe in chains he is a man to be treated well.'

Castus averted his eyes, not daring to contradict his superior. 'Yes, my lord Verellian.' He glanced at the two crossbow-men guarding Magnus and motioned them to lower their weapons.

'That's better.' Verellian spoke quietly and with a hard note of authority. Magnus guessed he was a true fighting man, which the dents in his armour confirmed. He carried a single-handed longsword, like all the knights of the Red, but his was older and obviously better maintained.

'Castus, take your men and return to the dungeon. I'll lead the prisoner to the great hall. A man in chains should be spared the additional torment of your company.' Verellian held his hand out to the bound man, who passed the chain to him after a momentary pause. 'Off you go, now, I'm sure there are other prisoners for you to abuse.'

Magnus smiled again and, sensing an opportunity, turned sharply, his huge shoulder connecting heavily with Castus. The gaoler stumbled and fell face-first on to the wet, muddy courtyard. Both crossbowmen raised their weapons and Verellian took a step back, grasping his sword hilt.

Magnus stood looking down at the man who'd repeatedly seen fit to insult him. When it became clear that he didn't intend to escape, the other knights relaxed.

'I'm sure you deserved that, soldier.' Verellian extended his hand and helped Castus to his feet. The man was covered in mud and growling with rage. A shake of the head from Verellian robbed him of any opportunity for retribution and he stomped back across the courtyard, swearing quietly to himself and motioning his men to follow.

'That was probably ill-advised, priest. I suspect you may be under his care again this evening.'

'Every insult will be repaid, sir knight.' Magnus spoke with conviction.

'I appreciate the man's . . . more detestable qualities, but pushing him into the mud was a little unnecessary.'

Magnus turned to face the knight and said, 'A man who defines himself as a gaoler has no honour. To cage a man of Ranen is the gravest insult to Rowanoco. Better your knights killed me than captured me . . . Though I pushed him over because you Ro have no sense of humour,' he added, with a smile.

Verellian chuckled. 'That at least may be true. Come, let us not keep the commander waiting.' He began to lead Magnus away, before pausing. 'You're from Fjorlan, aren't you; a man of the Low Kast?'

Magnus nodded. 'My brother and I were born in Fredericksand. It's the capital, on the coast of the Fjorlan Sea. The Low Kast is further inland.'

'I apologize, my knowledge of the lands of Ranen is minimal.' He was genuinely interested. 'Do all your people speak so well?'

'I speak better than most. Duke Hector's son taught me.' Magnus still had a heavy Fjorlan accent, but had learned to be understood in his time here; it was a matter of speaking slowly and with menace. Most Fjorlanders spoke enough of the language of Ro to converse, but they refused to call it *the common tongue*, the Ro name for it.

The knight resumed walking. 'And what's the correct form of address for a man of your station – Lord, Priest, Brother?'

'I am Father Magnus Forkbeard Ragnarsson, of the Order of the Hammer and priest of Rowanoco.' He knew his titles meant little to these men of the south. Verellian was impressed, however.

'Well, Father Magnus, I am Sir William of Verellian, knight captain of the Red and king's man.' He bowed as he introduced himself.

'You are the most polite man of Ro I have met since I came to your strange land. I was beginning to think only your women had manners.'

Verellian smiled again, showing himself more worldly that many of his comrades. 'Men like Castus are bound to the church from birth. They have no need of honour when they are required only to clean up the mess made by true fighting men.'

They crossed the courtyard and entered the great hall by a wooden staircase which wrapped itself around the southernmost tower. The last time Magnus had entered the hall of Canarn it had been at the side of Brother Lanry and as an ally and adviser to Duke Hector. He was now a prisoner and found the change an unwelcome one. From what he knew of Lord Mortimer Rillion he doubted he'd be treated well and he prepared himself to weather more insults.

As they reached the second landing, Magnus took a glance over his shoulder into the town, where he could see the central square lit up by funeral pyres. He was too far away to see who was being burned, but it was certain that Hallam Pevain's mercenaries were tending the pyres, and Magnus suspected the bodies of men and women of Canarn were providing the fuel.

On the edge of the square the small Brown chapel had not been touched, and Magnus hoped that Brother Lanry had been allowed to return to his flock.

The ornate double doors that separated the courtyard from the inner keep were flanked by two members of the king's guard, the elite group of soldiers charged with protecting the crown. They stood imperiously, looking down their noses at both Magnus and Verellian.

A gauntleted salute from one of them caused Verellian to stop. 'This is Father Magnus, he's to be taken to the great hall.'

The guards stepped aside with military precision and, in unison, reached out to grasp the two huge door handles. The tall wooden doors creaked open, allowing the warmth from within to wash over Magnus. He could smell meat cooking and beer. The fact that he'd been eating rancid gruel while the Ro feasted on meat angered him greatly.

Verellian stepped forward, lightly tugging on the chain to lead Magnus behind him. 'With me, Father; the knight commander awaits.'

'Will they let me taste meat and drink beer?' Magnus was hungry and thirsty and thought hospitality a knightly virtue.

Verellian raised an eyebrow at this and replied, 'I think you have more to worry about than a full belly, Father.'

Magnus walked into the dark hall. Either side of him wooden pillars displaying the banners of Canarn rose from floor to ceiling. The heraldry was in muted colours of green and brown, in sharp contrast to the blood-red tabards on display. Knights of the Red lined the walkway, their swords raised in ordered fashion. Each looked directly to the front, refusing to give in to their curiosity and observe the Ranen giant walking between them. Several of the knights wielded crossbows and Magnus again wondered about the honour of such a weapon.

As they neared the end of the walkway, he looked ahead to the feast hall before him. The huge vaulted ceiling made Duke Hector's great hall intimidating to lesser men. Magnus, however, had spent many hours here counselling the duke on the best way to keep his people alive while gaining their independence, and many more spent drinking and laughing. Now it seemed colder and less welcoming.

A small army of knights of the Red stood in ranks on either side of the raised platform at the far end of the hall. Cages, hung from the ceiling, held bruised and bloodied figures. Tables holding the remnants of a lavish feast stood behind the knights, and Magnus let his mind wander to thoughts of meat and beer.

'Enter and be judged,' a voice bellowed from the raised platform. 'In the name of King Sebastian Tiris, and within sight of the One, I claim the power to judge you.'

The assembled knights came to attention in unison, a loud clank of steel armour echoing throughout the hall. William of Verellian pushed his shoulders back and led the chained Ranen down the central red-carpeted aisle towards the platform.

He recognized a few faces as those in charge came into view. Sitting in Duke Hector's chair was a man of middle years, haughty and imperious-looking and wearing ornate red armour. This was

Lord Mortimer Rillion, a famous knight of Tor Funweir. His various exploits were told in stories to young Ro, and Magnus was impressed by his bearing. Whatever he might think of the knight of the Red, he had to concede that he was a true fighting man. He wore his beard short and well groomed and the flecks of grey added a note of nobility. He had a weathered face and the hard eyes of a man who was sure of his authority.

To the commander's left sat a Gold cleric, a follower of the One God's aspect of wealth and greed. Magnus did not recognize him, but disliked the way he was adorned in gold and jewels clearly plundered from the vaults of Canarn. The cleric was a fat man, wearing only white and gold robes, and he wore no sword or armour. He had a face resembling a pig and Magnus thought him a lesser man amongst the warriors.

Next to the Gold cleric stood a knight of the Red, a man still powerfully built despite his advancing years. He carried an axe slung across his back and Magnus recognized him as Sir Rashabald, the commander's executioner. This was the man responsible for beheading captive Ranen. He was grey-haired and nearing his fiftieth year, but was still ready for combat and his red armour was well used.

Skulking just off the raised platform was a huge man of Ro wearing black, full-plate armour. This was Sir Hallam Pevain and Magnus knew him well, though he had not expected to see him here. He was not a Red churchman but a mercenary knight with no lands or family, lending his huge two-handed sword to anyone who would pay. He was a bedraggled man with wild black hair, a straggly beard and a harsh face. Magnus had not seen him in three years, since he'd lent his sword to a vicious Ranen warlord many miles to the north. Pevain was a sadistic man, given to explosions of temper, and Magnus had fought him before. The sword he carried was responsible for a scar the Ranen wore on his right thigh and Magnus knew, too, that the knight carried several marks from Skeld.

Of most concern to Magnus, however, were the two women in view. One was Bronwyn, daughter to Duke Hector and someone for whom Magnus had great affection. She was not chained or bound, but was held in close guard by four Red knights. The leather armour she normally wore had been taken off and she was adorned in a simple woollen dress. She was tall and slender, with long brown hair tied in a braid. Her skin was pale and Magnus thought her beautiful.

The second woman was a Karesian from the lands of Jaa. She stood close to the commander and looked out of place. Her robes were black and the spider's web tattoo on her face worried Magnus. He had heard stories of the Seven Sisters and hoped she was not one of them. He knew that the enchantresses of Karesia had the power to entrance men and he had encountered their kind before. Rowanoco gave him certain powers against sorcery, but he still considered the Seven Sisters to be dangerous foes.

Verellian brought Magnus to a halt in front of the platform, a rank of kneeling Red knights between him and the commander.

'My Lord Verellian, you may depart.' Rillion waved his hand dismissively.

'I'd rather stay, my lord. Father Magnus has not been treated well thus far,' Verellian said loudly.

A laugh erupted from the Gold cleric and was echoed around the hall as various churchmen showed their disdain for the Ranen priest. Rillion did not join in the laughter but clearly thought nothing of Verellian's concern. 'Sir knight, please rejoin your unit in the courtyard.'

Verellian took a step closer to Magnus and whispered, 'My apologies, father, my word has no weight here.' He saluted towards the raised platform, took a few steps backwards, turned and marched back down the aisle.

Magnus stood alone, chained and disarmed, surrounded by enemies. Even if he could break the chains, he was forced to admit that fighting his way out would be difficult. He took a closer look around the hall, hoping to see his war-hammer, Skeld, in some disregarded corner. He clenched his fists several times, longing for the comforting feel of its leather grip. It was nowhere within sight and these men of the One God would not know of its significance. He turned back to the platform and puffed out his chest, letting all those assembled know that, although he was a prisoner, Father Magnus Forkbeard was still a proud man of Ranen.

Knight Commander Rillion spoke first. 'We have cleaned up the many dead, washed away the gallons of blood and sown the seeds of order . . . my heart is still troubled, however.' He stood and took several steps towards Magnus, still remaining behind the line of Red knights. 'You are a foreign man from a distant land and yet here you are, plotting with a traitorous duke to rob the crown of its lands.' He drew his sword. 'What would this north-man do if our positions were reversed?' Turning, he directed the query to his fellow Ro. 'He would not think to capture us alive and imprison us. No, we would be brutally slain, as is the Ranen way. We of the One God must strive to be better than these lesser men.'

Several of the kneeling Red knights banged their gauntleted fists on their armour, loudly proclaiming their support for their commander's words.

Rashabald the executioner spoke. 'My lord, this Ranen killed many knights of the Red. He is too dangerous to be released. My axe and the fist that wields it both hunger for the blood of this barbarian.'

This sentiment was echoed by the Gold cleric, who chuckled to himself before speaking in a high-pitched, effeminate voice. 'You men of the Red value combat and strength, let us amuse ourselves with this heathen. Have him fight wild animals and let his screams be music to our ears.'

Magnus glared at the fat cleric, hoping there were enough men of honour here to ensure that his own death, if it were to come, would be a swift one.

Rillion turned to the Karesian woman and spoke directly to her. 'And you, noble sister, your counsel has been wise thus far. Tell us what you would have done with this prisoner.'

She spoke with a thick Karesian accent, her words lyrical and seductive. 'This man is brave and strong.' She cast her eyes from Magnus's feet up to the hard expression on his face. 'He hates you, my lord, and he would gladly kill all present.' She closed her eyes for a moment and breathed in, smiling as she did so. 'He is not afraid, nor does he care for his own survival.'

As Magnus had feared, the woman had revealed herself to be one of the Seven Sisters, enchantresses of power and ruthless reputation. He did not know why a woman of her kind would be accompanying a Red church army, but he considered it a bad omen.

She sensed his thoughts and smiled again. 'You have heard of my order, I see. I am Ameira the Lady of Spiders,' she paused, with wicked intent on her face, '. . . and I know your brother.'

None of the churchmen recognized the significance of this comment, and Magnus was glad they knew nothing of his family. His brother was Algenon Teardrop Ragnarsson, the high thain of Ranen and commander of the dragon fleet.

'If he cares nothing for himself, to whom has he pledged his support?' Rillion asked of the enchantress.

'He cares for the Duke Hector's children, particularly his daughter, though the son is an old and trusted friend.' She looked deeply into Magnus's eyes and continued. 'He is also concerned for Brother Lanry, the Brown cleric . . . but paramount in his mind is the fate of the duke himself. He worries that his friend may be dead and this thought displeases him.'

The Gold cleric laughed. 'Ha, he looks every bit the warrior, but he's as soft as my arse when a woman and his friends are threatened. I will never understand how this backward people have halted our knights for so long.'

Magnus remained silent and looked around the hall, counting the knights arrayed against him. At least a hundred armoured men stood in the great hall of Canarn, and he was chained, without armour, and Skeld was nowhere to be seen. This was as bad a situation as he had ever found himself in and he tried to calm his mind with thoughts of past adventures and of those who had fallen under his hammer. He had friends who would laugh if they were to see him now, friends who would teach these men of Ro that a few men can be mighty when the need arises.

Lord Rillion raised his hand. 'Enough, I have made my decision.'

The hall fell silent and Rillion slowly moved to resume his seat. Rashabald and the Gold cleric both looked intently at the commander, their desire to see the Ranen killed clear on their faces. Magnus scanned the faces of the other Red knights and was glad to see they appeared dispassionate towards him. Sir Pevain, the mercenary knight, was staring at the Ranen, bloodlust in his eyes. Magnus considered him one of the more dangerous men in the room and doubted he'd stay neutral if the Red church had paid him.

Rillion then spoke, loudly and clearly. 'This man is a foreigner and his ignorance is the only thing that makes me not take his head.' The others on the raised platform showed their disagreement, but they kept quiet and allowed the commander to continue. 'However, his friend, the duke, is worthy of no such mercy. I think to witness the justice of the One God will be punishment enough for his foolish actions.' He waved a hand behind him. 'Sir Pevain, fetch the duke and bring him before us.'

Magnus kept his eyes on the large mercenary knight as he walked past the platform and through a side door, exiting the great hall.

Rillion then stood and addressed Magnus directly. 'The children, Bronwyn and Bromvy, will bear the dishonour of being named to the Black Guard until their deaths.'

Bronwyn looked through the ranks of Red knights, towards Magnus, and the huge Ranen saw real fear in her eyes. She was a young woman, the twin sister of Brom, Duke Hector's heir, and Magnus had grown to care greatly for her in the short time he had been in Ro Canarn. To brand her face with a mark of dishonour was unthinkable, and anger began steadily to build up within him.

The women of Ro were rarely allowed to wear armour or wield a blade, but Bronwyn was becoming a skilled swordswoman, a testament to her father's insistence that all his children should be able to fight for their lands if the need arose.

Sir Pevain returned, carrying a heavy steel chain and leading a broken and bloodied figure into the great hall. Duke Hector had been stripped naked and was bleeding from several wounds to his chest and face, making Magnus think he had been whipped.

The duke stumbled as Pevain pulled hard on the chain and he had to be dragged before the raised platform. Behind him, with a fearful look in his eyes, came Brother Lanry, the chaplain of Ro Canarn. The Brown cleric was a portly man wearing only the heavy brown robes of his order. He was a cleric who represented the One God's aspect of poverty and charity and Magnus thought him honourable. The chaplain had wielded his quarterstaff against the Red knights and had only been spared because he was a churchman.

Magnus took an involuntary step forwards, wanting with all his being to throw the line of Red knights out of his path and to help his friend. In response to the movement, the executioner stood and hefted his large axe. 'My Lord Rillion, if this peasant priest moves again may I have permission to cut off his hand and let him bleed?'

With rising anger, and with little thought, Magnus broke his silence and shouted out a response to the executioner's threat. 'You are a coward . . .' The hall fell silent. 'Remove these chains, give me my hammer, and no man here would stand before me.' He took another step forward, now standing inches from the kneeling line of knights.

Brother Lanry saw Magnus through the press of knights and a shallow nod of greeting passed between the two men. The cleric looked exhausted, but uninjured. Rillion maintained his calm, Rashabald and the Gold cleric looked as if they were about to burst with rage, and Sir Pevain smiled an ugly smile. Out of the corner of his eye Magnus could see the guards standing round Bronwyn move closer; they were physically holding her now and she was clearly distressed at not being able to see her father through the crowd of knights.

'I was told knights of the Red had honour . . . this is not honour.' He roared out the last few words and tensed his huge arms, feeling the heavy steel chains that bound him.

'My knights, stand to,' ordered Rillion, and the line of Red knights stood and drew their swords in practised military fashion. 'One more aggressive movement from this man and you are to subdue him. Wound, but do not kill.'

Bronwyn cried out from the side of the hall, 'Father . . .' The word was choked with tears and elicited a sharp slap from one of her guards.

'Knight,' Magnus shouted at the man who'd struck her, 'touch the woman again and I'll eat through these chains to reach you.'

Magnus maintained his glare and felt his arms strain against the manacles. He offered a quiet prayer to his god. 'Rowanoco, let not these dishonourable men take the lives of my friends; and if that is not within your power, grant me the strength to avenge them or face an honourable death. Let me not feel the cold stone of a prison cell again.'

The line of knights in front of him formed a circle, surrounding Magnus and cutting off any chance of action. Rillion and Rashabald stepped off the platform and stood over the broken duke of Canarn.

Pevain pulled on the chain, making the steel collar strain around Hector's neck. His head was pulled to face the commander and the extent of his injuries became evident. He had lost an eye to a sword point, a fresh cut indicating that the wound had been inflicted after the battle. His teeth had been smashed out and he shook violently. Magnus doubted he even knew where he was.

'Look well upon this traitor, you Ranen dog,' Rillion said loudly.

'My lord, can I be the one to take his head?' It was Pevain who spoke, and he did so with glee.

Sir Rashabald was clearly unhappy with this and looked questioningly at the commander. Rillion appeared to consider it, but then shook his head and wordlessly gestured to his executioner. Rashabald smiled and hefted his axe several times while Pevain removed the prisoner's metal collar.

Magnus scowled as he looked on and took sharp breaths, glaring at the men of Ro standing before him, the men about to kill his friend. He could hear Bronwyn crying, but did not look round to see. He was thankful she would not be able to see her father killed.

Duke Hector was a small figure, naked and broken; he barely looked up as Rashabald placed the axe against his neck. Rillion raised his hand above his head and everyone present paused, waiting for him to lower it, giving the executioner his order to strike. When it happened, it seemed to Magnus to happen in slow motion. Rashabald raised his axe high above his head, Rillion lowered his hand, and the axe fell.

The sound was of steel cutting flesh and bone, punctuated by a grunt of exertion from the executioner, and Duke Hector Canarn was dead. His head struck the stone floor and his body went limp, falling at Pevain's feet.

There was a moment of silence, the only sound being a low sob from the duke's daughter, as Sir Rillion leant down and lifted up the head to show the company of knights. The duke's face was a mask of anger and torment. Brother Lanry began to weep as his master's head was paraded in front of him.

Ameira, the Karesian enchantress, cackled. Her eyes were wide with euphoria at the sight of the dead duke.

The strength of Rowanoco now within him, Magnus roared to the ceiling at the sight of his friend's head. His hands gripped the steel manacles that held him and, with power unlike anything these men of Ro had seen, the steel links began to bend and buckle. His rage had taken over and he could no longer be contained by metal. The guards surrounding him looked on with wide-eyed amazement as, with a swift jerk of his shoulders, the huge Ranen warrior broke his restraints. Rowanoco hated nothing more than to see his people caged and he lent his rage to the priest.

91

All eyes turned and Magnus was faced with over a hundred armoured men, drawing their swords. He looked at the faces of the senior knights and the old executioner, then back at the men standing directly in front of him. His eyes had turned black and foam flecked the corners of his mouth.

'Men, restrain the Ranen.' Rillion stumbled over his words; even he was intimidated by the battle rage of Rowanoco.

The Karesian enchantress moved quickly to the commander's side and whispered in his ear before lightly touching his hand.

The first knight to thrust at Magnus died quickly with a sheared metal link jammed into his throat. His body was then hefted and thrown at the next man. Magnus easily deflected a hesitant downward swing, grabbing the blade in his hand and reversing it to stab through the wielder's face, killing him instantly.

Commotion engulfed the hall, with men jockeying to get close to the fight. Rillion issued commands to several knights and the Gold cleric was quickly removed from the hall. Pevain was stepping towards the melee and unsheathing his huge two-handed sword, while Sir Rashabald adopted a protective stance in front of the commander.

Magnus kept hold of the longsword and quickly killed two more knights with powerful downward blows. The other Red knights, now encircling him, stayed several steps away and held a guarded pose.

Magnus stood with four dead knights around him in a spreading pool of blood. 'Face me now, cowards,' he roared. 'I will be your death . . .'

With one hand he swung the broken chain around his head, keeping the knights at bay, while with the other he brandished his newly acquired sword with skill and menace. Rillion stood beyond the circle of knights; calmer now that Magnus was contained, he gestured to Pevain to enter the melee and shouted across the hall to his crossbowmen.

Magnus advanced on the encircling knights and swung the chain at those close by. The knights retreated a few steps and refused to engage. They held their swords low to the ground and closed ranks round him.

He crouched, his sword and chain both loose in his hands. The battle rage of Rowanoco had changed into a predatory desire for freedom. He was feeling the survival instinct of a caged animal and barely registered the huge figure of Sir Pevain entering the circle of knights.

'Pevain, I want him alive,' Rillion commanded from his position of safety. The enchantress stood close to him and continued to whisper.

The crossbowmen pushed their way to stand within the circle of knights, their cowardly weapons drawn and aimed at Magnus. The sound of Bronwyn crying was the only thing that entered Magnus's perception, but it was enough to keep his mind sufficiently clear to parry when Pevain launched a huge overhead strike at him. Magnus buckled under the strain, but his strength held and stopped the blow from landing.

'I said I want him alive. Don't disappoint me, Pevain,' Rillion repeated.

Magnus swung out his legs and aimed a kick at Pevain's armoured thighs. The mercenary rocked back, but didn't fall, and Magnus rolled out of range of the answering sword thrust.

The mercenary knight let out a grunt as he grasped his sword in both hands and launched an overhead swing at Magnus's unprotected shoulder. It was powerful, but clumsy, and Pevain relied on the plate armour he wore and the disproportionate size of his sword rather than any great skill.

Magnus was fast and knew how to deal with a man encumbered with steel armour. He didn't try to parry the blow, instead darting to the left and letting the swing strike the stone floor. Dust flew up and the flagstone cracked, causing Rillion to push his way to the front and bark at Pevain a third time. 'Sir knight, if you kill that man, you follow him.'

Ameira the Lady of Spiders stayed beyond the circle, but appeared distressed at the suggestion that Pevain might kill Magnus.

'My lord, we should rid ourselves of this fucking animal,' Pevain replied through gritted teeth. 'Let me kill him . . . let me kill him now.' He didn't take his eyes from Magnus, who was again crouched, sword at the ready.

Rillion drew his own sword and entered the circle, causing Rashabald to hurry in behind him. 'Pevain, I won't tell you again,' the commander said quietly, his eyes watchful and his sword held low.

Magnus was clear now of the battle rage and was looking for an opportunity to escape. He was surrounded by a wide circle of closely packed knights of the Red which left little opening for an attack. He could no longer hear Bronwyn crying.

Pevain breathed heavily, angry at being robbed of the opportunity to fight Magnus. He lowered his sword and, still looking directly at the Ranen, backed away to the edge of the circle. The crossbowmen emerged between the Red knights and took aim, waiting for the order to fire. Rillion stayed back, but carried himself with the practised motion of a skilled swordsman.

'I have made my decision, this brute is to be kept alive,' he said, looking down at the four dead knights of the Red. 'But a few arrows in the leg won't kill him.'

He nodded at the nearest bowman and a bolt was fired. It pierced Magnus above the knee, causing him to cry out in pain and fall to the floor. Before he could gather himself, Sir Pevain kicked him solidly in the face with his armoured foot and Magnus lost consciousness.

CHAPTER FOUR

LADY BRONWYN IN THE CITY OF RO CANARN

L ADY BRONWYN OF Canarn stood off to the side in the great hall of her father's keep. She had lost sight of Father Magnus amidst the melee of knights and she could no longer hear his primal roars of defiance. Her four guards were distracted, being the only knights not involved in the confrontation, and she steeled herself to act.

Her tears at the death of her father had been genuine, but those around her thought the duke's daughter weak and she had played on this, appearing anguished beyond the capacity to act. Currently, she knelt on the floor of the hall with her head in her hands. With one eye she regarded those around her. They stood peering towards the platform, wishing they were involved in what was going on. One of them, still standing behind her, had drawn his sword as a reflex when Magnus broke his chains, but the others remained unarmed.

She could still see the Karesian woman, Ameira, whose attention was fixed on the fight. She had a twisted euphoria on her face, as if drugged or intoxicated.

Bronwyn breathed in and tensed her body. Just as she was about to act, a vicious-looking Karesian kris blade skidded across the floor and came to rest next to her left hand. The four knights around her scarcely looked down, the nearby combat masking the sound. She smiled to herself, recognizing the ruby-encrusted knife as she reached for it. As the knight behind her began to call

95

out, an arm wrapped round his neck and a scimitar was drawn across his throat.

The dark-skinned man who appeared over the dying knight's shoulder took the time to wink at Bronwyn before kicking the dead knight to the floor and killing a second with a fast upward cut to the man's head. Bronwyn reacted quickly and thrust the kris blade into the exposed inner thigh of the man to her left. He fell, crying loudly, blood gushing from the wound. The last man involuntarily turned towards Bronwyn, opening himself to a swift cut across the back of his exposed neck from the dark-skinned man.

All four guards had fallen in a few seconds and Bronwyn leapt quickly to her feet, her simple brown dress now covered in blood. The intruder smiled and grabbed her arm.

'Time to go, sweetness,' he said, with a slight Karesian accent.

She let herself be grabbed and, sparing a quick look over her shoulder, ran with the man towards a side door. Ameira had seen her, as had half a dozen knights by the main door, but Rillion and the others were too preoccupied to act. The knight Bronwyn had stabbed was still alive and his cries rose in volume as she darted from the great hall with the intruder.

He was Al-Hasim, called the Prince of the Wastes by his friends. Bronwyn knew he'd been in Ro Canarn before the battle but had thought him dead along with so many others. He was a Karesian and occasional sword for hire, though he'd been in Canarn as a favour to Algenon Teardrop, the Ranen warlord, Magnus's elder brother.

Her father had disliked him but Bronwyn found his constant flirting funny. Now she was glad of his stealth and skill with a scimitar. He was of medium height, but wiry and lightning-fast with sword and knife. His jet-black hair was tied roughly at the nape of his neck and he had the exotic bearing of a prince from a distant land. Bronwyn knew he had no actual claim to nobility, but he often spoke as if he did.

The two of them ran from the hall. The corridors of Duke Hector's keep were narrow and labyrinthine, designed to confuse an invader, but his daughter knew them well. She wriggled out of Hasim's grasp and darted left into an antechamber.

'Er, your ladyship . . . the way out is this way.' Hasim pointed along the vaulted corridor.

'Yes, but the way to stay hidden is this way,' Bronwyn answered, entering the antechamber and moving quickly to the weapon rack against the far wall. The chamber was part of the armoury, connected on three levels of the keep by wooden stairs.

Hasim looked concerned, but followed after a momentary pause.

Sounds from the great hall indicated that Magnus had been subdued and Bronwyn's escape had been noticed. She removed a light short sword and pressed a wooden panel on the wall, causing a secret passage to open.

'Why did no one tell me this place had secret doors? It would have made the rescue so much easier,' Hasim said as he followed her into the narrow passageway, adding, '. . . but not as stylish.'

Bronwyn breathed heavily, pushing thoughts of her father to the back of her mind. She wished she had her armour. The brown dress she'd been given was ill suited to running along the small, dusty tunnel.

Her armour, a present from her father, had been roughly torn off by disrespectful knights of the Red and discarded somewhere in the keep. The knights had not touched her, save to disarm and restrain her, and she wished for another opportunity to prove she could hold her own against metal-armoured men.

Bronwyn led Hasim down the passage for several minutes. It curved left and right and, at intervals, rough-hewn stairs led further down, taking them out of the inner keep. Her grandfather had built these tunnels into the city walls long before she was born, and her father used to tell her and her brother stories about how he got lost in them as a child.

'Bronwyn, where exactly does this tunnel go?' Hasim pushed past her and peered into the gloomy darkness. 'Oh, and I need my knife back.' He held out his hand and Bronwyn placed the bloodstained kris blade, hilt-first, in his palm. It was the mark of the Karesian warrior class, a wavy-bladed knife with a vicious edge designed to cause wounds that wouldn't close.

'Are we going to come out of here in the middle of an army? Am I going to have to rescue you again?' he asked.

'I think it leads to the cliff overlooking the inner harbour.' Bronwyn wasn't sure, but she recalled playing in here with her brother when they were young. 'It should end in a wooden door that's hidden behind a boulder.'

Hasim did not look convinced. 'Okay, but let me go first.' He stood protectively over her.

'I'm not weak, Karesian,' she snapped.

Hasim frowned. 'I know. A weak woman would have flinched before sticking a man in the thigh . . . you barely thought about it.' He looked her up and down. 'You may look like a serving wench at the moment, but you've your father's strength . . . and your brother's edge.'

Bromvy, her twin, was not in the city during the attack. He'd been in Ro Tiris when the fleet had appeared on the horizon. Bronwyn hoped her father had got word to him not to return, but she knew he'd still probably be found and branded a Black Guard.

Ahead, a dim light could be seen. Bronwyn knew it would be getting dark soon and she wanted to be out of the city before then. Hasim motioned for her to stay back and stepped cautiously towards the light. A few feet down the tunnel, he paused to look at something.

'What is it?' Bronwyn asked.

He slowly turned back to her. 'I think the fleet of Red knights breached the city wall with catapults . . . I can see down into the town beyond the keep.'

Bronwyn moved to join him but was stopped by a swiftly raised hand. 'Are you sure you want to see this, your ladyship?' Hasim had a serious expression on his dark features.

'My father is dead and my brother is running for his life. I think that makes me duchess of Canarn.' She firmly pushed aside

Hasim's hand. 'You can step aside and do as you're told, or leave me alone.'

The Karesian did not move. 'Look, woman, I am not here to make this difficult for you, but I am not your subject . . . so you can dispense with this duchess shit.' He stared directly into her eyes as he spoke. 'You can look out into the town if you want, but if you do you will see blood and death.' He stepped aside. 'It's your choice, your ladyship.' His bow was shallow and mocking.

Bronwyn stepped towards the light. The secret passage ran along the inside of one of the outer city walls, and a huge rock had been catapulted through the stone. A gap had appeared at head height where the boulder had hit the battlements above, and Bronwyn could see down across the buildings to the town square of Canarn.

The sight was indeed one of blood and death, and Bronwyn looked with cold eyes at the spectacle of Red knights and mercenaries piling up dead bodies. Several houses had been torn down to provide wood, and funeral pyres burned the fallen people of Canarn. The knights had discarded their swords and were pushing wooden carts of the dead from all corners of the city. They piled them up in the town square to await a fiery meeting with the One God, an old Black cleric intoning words over them.

The knights of the Red numbered nearly a thousand and they had been more than a match for the untrained defenders, men defending their livelihoods as much as their home. Bronwyn thought she recognized a farmer called Hobb, a man who had grown cabbages to the north of the city, and had wanted only to protect his land and family.

She didn't cry, though she thought maybe that was wrong. More than anything, she wanted to turn back time and tell her father to retreat, not to stay and fight the knights.

'Bronwyn, we need to leave.' Hasim put a gentle hand on her arm. 'They're looking for us.' He moved to stand in front of her, blocking her view. 'At least, they're looking for you.'

She looked him in the eye and pushed him aside. She didn't

know what she expected to achieve by continuing to look at the scene of death below, but Bronwyn was the lady of Canarn and felt deep kinship with her people.

Hasim breathed in and firmly grabbed her by the shoulders, pulling her away and holding her against the opposite wall.

'Listen to me, woman . . .' he said through gritted teeth, 'that Karesian witch, the marked woman . . .'

Bronwyn struggled in his grip. 'How dare you . . .'

'Listen . . . she's of the Seven Sisters and if you stay in the city, she *will* find you.' He released his grip and stepped back. 'We need to get to the Grass Sea to the north. The witch won't follow into the lands of Ranen.'

Bronwyn stopped struggling and looked at the ground, tears appearing in her eyes. 'Why is this happening? What did my father do . . .?' She didn't look up, or expect an answer, but felt her legs give way as the enormity of what she'd seen flowed over her. Hasim held her, more tenderly this time, and pulled her upright to face him.

'Rillion is weak. For all the strength in his sword arm, he has let himself become thrall to a Karesian witch.' He unsheathed his kris blade and held it with the point facing downwards. 'That's why I'm here. Algenon Teardrop knew she was in Canarn . . . somehow . . . and he sent me to find out what she was doing here. I sent a report back just after the battle.'

Bronwyn processed this slowly, shaking her head and wiping away the tears. 'I thought . . .' she began, only to be interrupted by Hasim.

'You thought that I was here to look after Magnus.' He smiled. 'Trust me, he can look after himself. The enchantress has Rillion's heart and head in her elegant hand. Algenon doesn't confide in me, but he knew something was going on,' he said quietly. 'I try not to worry about things I'm not told, but there's something at work here beyond your father's actions and the king's pride.'

A sound from above caused them both to look up and dust fell from the wooden ceiling. Several men were walking through a parallel passageway. 'Fuck . . . they've found the secret passages.'

Hasim turned to look further along the tunnel and asked, 'How far to the exit?'

Bronwyn looked the same way and considered a moment before speaking. 'I think the passage turns right up ahead and then down into a cave. The doorway is through the cave.'

Hasim stepped back, sheathed his knife and drew his scimitar. 'Then we move quickly, your ladyship.'

The two of them ran along the dark tunnel. Hasim stayed ahead and held his scimitar loosely. Before the tunnel turned right another sound alerted them, this time from further along the passageway. Hasim stopped suddenly and backed against the wall, placing a restraining arm across Bronwyn and pushing her back to stand next to him. He placed a finger across his mouth as the flickering light of a torch appeared round the corner.

Hasim nodded towards the short sword tucked in Bronwyn's belt. 'How good are you with that?' he whispered.

She tried to smile but rising fear overtook the expression before it reached her mouth. 'Brom taught me how to use it, but I've never fought in a dress before.'

As the distinctive sound of armoured men approached, Hasim said, 'Well, you may soon get a chance to test your brother's tutelage.' He stood close to the wall, letting the vertical wooden supports act as cover. The tunnel was dark and both Bronwyn and Hasim wore dark clothing. Maybe they could stay hidden.

As the globe of torchlight grew larger and the sound louder, Hasim drew his kris blade and held the two weapons across his chest. 'Let them get close. Armoured men fight poorly in confined spaces.'

She breathed heavily and felt sweat appear on her forehead.

'Strike for the face and neck, they won't be wearing helmets and you'd never get that blade through their armour. If you need to, drop to your knees and go for the thighs and groin.'

She was barely listening and her vision was cloudy.

'Bronwyn . . .' he said quietly. 'You need to focus. These men will kill you.'

She wished she was somewhere else, far from this narrow passageway and the Karesian who stood next to her.

Hasim slapped her sharply across the face. 'Your ladyship, I cannot kill them all if you are going to pieces.'

She stared at him, not with indignity, but with newfound steel. Several deep breaths and she nodded at her rescuer.

Sword in hand, she waited. Hasim did not look along the passageway but focused on the opposite wall and she heard him whisper a quiet prayer to Jaa, the Fire Giant.

Words could now be heard from those approaching; the accent was Ro and the voices were unmistakably those of knights of the Red. Bronwyn heard five distinct voices and bit her lower lip at the odds.

The voices were relaxed and she was certain they were one of many patrols sent into the secret tunnels. They would not be expecting a fight and she was glad of the element of surprise. Hasim finished his prayer and kissed his kris blade, before leaning back close to the wall, his eyes watchful and alert.

The torchlight rounded the corner and an armoured knight emerged, peering into the darkness, followed by four more knights. All five wore full plate armour and their tabards showed the red aspect of the One God.

Bronwyn tried to stay as far behind the concealing beam as possible. Hasim turned to her and smiled in an effort to ease the tension. She found herself wanting to slap him as he had slapped her, but all she did was smile thinly back at him.

The knights approached. 'Soldier, do you see anything?' asked one at the rear.

The man holding the torch peered along the dark corridor. 'No, my lord, the tunnel looks like it goes a way along the wall.'

The knights were now only a blade's distance from Hasim. The torchbearer extended his hand and the fire passed close to Hasim's concealed face.

'Let's see where it goes,' said the knight at the rear, and all five began to move noisily along the tunnel.

The torchbearer had stepped past Hasim before he turned and showed wide-eyed surprise at Bronwyn, skulking in the darkness. 'My lord—' his words were cut off as she thrust at his neck, skewering his windpipe.

Blood splattered across her face and the knight fell. She withdrew her blade and stumbled forwards, the weight of the armoured man putting her off balance. The other four knights were off guard and paused for a second as Bronwyn fell awkwardly.

Hasim remained hidden for another moment and let a second knight advance before he emerged. The man was focused on Bronwyn and turned too late to parry Hasim's kris blade as it plunged into his eye. The remaining three knights began shouting, 'They're here . . .' The sound of armoured men clattering against wooden walls echoed along the passage.

Hasim, keeping hold of his kris blade, shoved the dead knight backwards. The body fell heavily against the next man, sending both to the floor. Blood sprayed out from the man's eye as Hasim withdrew his knife and dived forward. He jumped over the fallen man and tackled the next knight to the ground, a sword swipe catching him in the leg as he did so.

Bronwyn saw Hasim with his knee to the throat of one knight as he raised his scimitar to parry the downward swing of another. The knight who had been pushed to the floor by the body of his fellow was getting to his feet, Hasim's back exposed before him. The man advanced without seeming to notice Bronwyn, now standing upright in the narrow tunnel.

She didn't hesitate and stepped quickly behind him, aiming her blade at the back of his neck. He crumpled to the floor at her feet.

'Stay there,' Hasim shouted without turning.

It was taking all his strength to keep one knight subdued while parrying the swings of the other. Only the close quarters of the passageway prevented the man getting a full swing at the Karesian in front of him. The knight on the floor had lost his sword and was trying to lift Hasim's knee from his throat.

The last knight pulled back his sword and aimed a thrust at

Hasim's chest. The blow was strong and showed skill, but Hasim was fast and unencumbered by steel armour. He removed his knee from the fallen knight and rolled out of the way, hitting the wooden wall. He slashed out at the knight, his scimitar cutting deeply across the back of the man's leg.

Crying out in pain, the knight swung again, but this time he was off balance and his sword hit the wooden beam above. The blade bit deeply into the wood and he could not react as Hasim darted past him. From behind, the Karesian wrapped an arm round his neck and, with near-surgical precision, slid his knife under the man's armour and up into his side.

The knight spewed up blood as Hasim wrenched the blade inside him and roughly jerked it free.

The man Hasim had restrained with his knee was coughing and trying to catch his breath, as he felt on the floor for his sword. As his gauntleted fist found the weapon, Bronwyn advanced and the man looked up.

'Knight!' Hasim roared at the man, who turned from Bronwyn to stare at the Karesian. Hasim held up a hand to tell Bronwyn to stay back and took a step towards the Red knight.

'Time to die for your heresy, godless Karesian.'

'I'm not a hundred years old and I see no harem of beautiful women, so it's definitely not my time to die,' Hasim shot back in reply.

The knight thrust forward with strength. Hasim deflected the blow with his scimitar and attacked with his knife. The knight grabbed his wrist and kicked Hasim solidly in the chest, sending him back down the tunnel.

Bronwyn gasped as Hasim fell to the floor, losing his footing as he tripped over one of the fallen knights.

She didn't react; her short sword felt small in her hand now that the knight was armed and aware. Hasim tried to roll backwards and regain his feet, but the knight was quickly upon him, levelling another solid kick at the Karesian's side. He gasped for breath, the wind knocked out of him, as he lost his grip on his scimitar.

Bronwyn thought she saw panic in his eyes for a second, before he lunged forwards and wrapped himself around the knight's legs. The two men fell back against the wall with Hasim entangled around the knight's lower body. The armoured man growled in anger and swiped downwards, causing a vicious-looking cut across Hasim's back. The Karesian didn't make more than a slight grunting sound at the wound, but wriggled himself round the knight, who growled with frustration as he struggled to free his arm for another strike.

Hasim found an exposed area of leg and savagely buried his teeth in the man's flesh, causing him to raise his head and cry out in pain. Bronwyn darted forward, anxious that Hasim could not best this man now that surprise was no longer on his side. He didn't see her at first, but her thrust was delivered with a shaking hand and caused only the smallest dent in his breastplate.

'I said, stay there . . .' Hasim growled as he jammed his kris blade up into the knight's groin. His cry was louder this time but ended sharply in a gurgle, as the life left his eyes.

Hasim shoved the knight away and fell to the floor, blood covering much of his body. Bronwyn moved to his side and helped him sit upright against the tunnel wall. Most of the blood was not his, but the wounds in his back and leg were deep and jagged.

Hasim breathed deeply. 'It's not easy, is it, killing men?' He smiled and, wrapping an arm round Bronwyn's shoulder, pulled himself to his feet, wincing in pain as he did so.

'We're alive, they're not . . . simple if not easy,' Bronwyn replied.

He chuckled and winced again. 'Don't make me laugh, your ladyship. It hurts.'

He surveyed the five dead knights and took a moment to listen. No sounds could be heard, but his expression made Bronwyn think they should be moving quickly away from the scene.

'You did well, my sweet . . . that first knight shit himself when he saw a woman sticking him with a short sword.'

'Don't call me that,' she said.

'Apologies, my lady, blood loss softens a man's head and causes him to speak out of turn.' Hasim was still trying to smile as he spoke. 'We need to move.'

He was strong and, though his wounds looked bad, he moved as quickly as he could down the passage. Bronwyn helped, letting him lean on her and carrying his weapons.

As the tunnel turned where the knights had emerged, they saw stairs leading down and an open door on the landing below.

'Where does that lead?' Hasim asked.

'I'm not sure, maybe the base of one of the wall turrets,' Bronwyn answered.

'Well, the only way is down,' he said with another smile.

Bronwyn led Hasim down the stairs, where they stopped several feet before the door. She helped him rest against the wall and quietly crept up to investigate.

The door opened out on to a back street under the far wall of the city, and beyond she could see cobbled streets leading to the keep. Smoke rose from the town square several streets away as the funeral pyres burned and Bronwyn identified several landmarks she recognized. The tower of Brytag the World Raven, patron god of Canarn, was nearby, as was the crossed-swords emblem of the Street of Steel. No one was in the little street and she guessed they must be close to where the secret passage entered the cave. Taking a quick look along the street in both directions she retreated into the tunnel and closed the door behind her.

Hasim was leaning against the wall and his breathing was slow. He was holding the wound on his back with one hand and wincing in pain as he tried to move. 'Bronwyn, I do believe that knight of the Red cut me good and proper.' He tried to stand. 'I don't think I can move that fast without losing blood.' He smiled a weak smile. 'And that dress of yours is already blood-stained enough.'

Bronwyn leant down to help him as best she could. He was heavy and she could barely stand as she tried to take his weight on her shoulders. 'If I can't cry, then you can't whinge . . . and that is that, my lord Karesian,' she said through gritted teeth.

'In the name of Jaa, Bronwyn, I'm cut and I'm bleeding and I will slow you down,' Hasim said through the pain.

She pulled his arm over her shoulder and tensed her back against the wall as she began to heft his weight upwards. Hasim tried not to cry out, but the wound on his back was bleeding heavily and his strength was ebbing away.

'Look, your ladyship, I am not dead yet, but I can't help you like this. There's a chance you can get out of here if you move quickly, but with me on your shoulder . . .' He fell back against the wall. Bronwyn not finding the strength to hold him, they both slid down into a seated position.

'I can stay alive . . . trust me, I can . . . but you have other things to worry about, my lady. To the north is a blasted tree, split down the middle by a lightning strike. Find the tree and take the track to the west.'

'Shut up, Hasim. I just need to put you on a horse and you'll be able to ride as well as me.' The thought of having to escape the city on her own was terrifying, as was the thought of this man dying. He had saved her life in the great hall and again in the secret tunnel. The allies of her house were dead, imprisoned or scattered, and she could not afford to lose another here.

'Listen to me, woman, I've had bad wounds before and I'm not dead yet, but I will be if I trudge along this tunnel any more. You need to run, I need to find a healer; it seems our paths are no longer entwined.' His words were cold, as if he'd already decided what needed to be done.

Bronwyn looked at him with hard eyes, trying to think of an objection that would make him change his mind and leave the city with her. She could think of nothing. Hasim was a clever man with a well-defined survival instinct and she knew that he was right. She had seen few such wounds in her life, but enough to know that those the Karesian bore would be fatal without proper attention.

'And then . . .?' she asked.

'And then what? Make sense, woman.' His eyes were closed and he was sweating profusely.

'I go west at the blasted tree, and then?' she clarified.

He coughed as he laughed, a small droplet of blood appearing at the corner of his mouth. 'As I said, Bronwyn, you've your brother's coldness. But currently I'm glad of it. As the track turns west, ride hard towards the mountains. The river marks the border of the Freelands and the ruins of Ro Hail are a few leagues beyond. It's a two-week ride and I can't guarantee what reception you'll receive, but Wraith Company holds the ruins. Find Captain Horrock Green Blade and tell him what you saw in the great hall . . . especially about the Karesian enchantress, don't miss that bit out.'

Bronwyn nodded and began mentally preparing for her escape. Alone, she could move quickly, but without Hasim's scimitar and his hand to wield it she would be vulnerable. She knew the way out of the tunnels and hoped that the Red knights had not yet found the cave or the exit by the outer harbour. If they were still looking in the tunnels of the keep, she had a chance of escape. Finding a horse would be her biggest challenge, and she thought of the stables by the docks and wondered if they'd been burned during the assault. If she had to go further afield, there was a possibility one of the outer farms would still have their horses. They would be pack animals, not used to being ridden, but would have to do.

'You need to move quickly, Bronwyn. The knights have no reason to watch the north yet, but the longer you're missing, the more likely they are to think you've left the city. If they post crossbowmen on the northern ramparts you'll be lucky to travel half an hour without being shot or ridden down.' Hasim spluttered as he spoke and coughed up more blood. 'Go, woman, get your noble arse out of this death trap,' he snapped.

'I hope you stay alive, Karesian,' Bronwyn said, placing his scimitar and kris blade on the floor next to him. She didn't look back, and heard no response as she moved quickly along the tunnel.

* * *

Al-Hasim, Prince of the Wastes, was hurt. He'd been hurt before, but rarely in a situation where getting healed would be such an endeavour. He'd watched Bronwyn disappear into the darkness and, no matter what he'd led her to believe, he thought it unlikely that she'd escape the city. The Karesian witch, Ameira the Lady of Spiders, was probably using her dark magic to track the young woman even now and would find her within the hour.

He'd done his best to help her, nearly dying as a result, but he owed her twin brother much and considered him a friend. Hasim wasn't sure if he had any sisters himself, but trusted that Brom would have done the same if their situations were reversed. As he lay bleeding against the wooden wall, it occurred to him that dying in a secret passage in a backwater city of Tor Funweir was a deeply undignified way to meet Jaa, though he smiled at the thought of having bested five Red knights with only a couple of cuts to show for it. Their fabled skill was all very well on the battlefield, but they lacked the cunning of those who have lived by their wits since childhood.

Desperation was a great motivator and Hasim had been a desperate man for much of his life. His greatest regret, as he sat in a pool of his own blood, was that he hadn't had the presence of mind to say something witty to the Red knight before he'd punctured his groin. Hasim prided himself on doing things with a certain elegance, but he had needed to shelve this trait temporarily in order to stay alive.

'Right, you son of a whore, get your arse up and let's see how long we can stay alive,' he said to himself, tensing his arms against the wall and edging slowly up into a standing position.

The pain was tremendous and every slight movement was accompanied with a flood of grimaces, winces and grunts of exertion. Hasim had long ago come to terms with pain and had trained himself not to cry out, but he was still bleeding and felt weak. Looking down at where he'd been sitting, he saw a disconcerting amount of blood.

Removing his sword belt, he buckled it tightly round his leg to stop the bleeding. The pain was masked by light-headedness and his deep-rooted survival instinct. He stumbled for several steps and fell against the wall as he struggled to take any weight on his leg. Edging along, he came to rest next to the door that Bronwyn had closed. He held his kris blade in his teeth, but silently lamented the fact that his scimitar would have to stay where it was, as it was too cumbersome to carry in his current state.

He steadied himself and gripped the edge of the door, pulling it slowly inwards. The tunnel was dark now and the moonlight outside provided only minimal illumination. He could hear the crackle of fire as he ducked under the low door frame to peer out into the street, but could not see the flames. He would be lucky not to run into any of the companies of knights currently in the city.

As Bronwyn had discovered, the street was empty. The knights were busy and the remaining people of Canarn, those who had not fought, would be barricaded in their homes or huddled in Brother Lanry's church.

Hasim found his bearings quickly, identifying the Street of Steel, the tower of the World Raven and a tavern owned by a man of the name of Fulton. He had two allies in the city, men who would probably still be hidden, but looking for them now would be nearly impossible. He knew the Brown chapel would have been left alone and would be a safe place to heal his wounds, but it lay close to the inner keep and would certainly be guarded. As he inched along the wall, he left a smear of blood along the stone.

The street was unlit and as he reached its end he crouched into the shadows as best he could and looked out at the crossroads. A fenced oak tree sat in the middle, the only sign of greenery in view. Resting next to the tree was an untended wooden cart containing half a dozen dead men of Canarn. Hasim scanned a line of low stone buildings, dark-fronted, with all their windows and doors locked tightly shut. If people were alive within, they were sitting in the dark.

Ro Canarn had been a lively coastal city, full of activity and rarely quiet. Hasim had spent many happy nights here, drinking and laughing with Magnus before Duke Hector had made his fatal mistake and tried to break away from the king of Tor Funweir. He had been in the city in secret when the warning horn had sounded from the southern battlements and the Red battle fleet had appeared. And now, four days later, the city was like a tomb, deathly quiet and safe only for the knights of the Red and their allies.

Hasim had not known about the fleet, but he had known about the Karesian enchantress. She'd entered the city quietly a few weeks before the battle and had sent word to Ro Tiris of the duke's plans. Hasim had not known this when he heard the warning horn, but only when he'd seen her and Rillion in a passionate embrace after the battle. She had enchanted Rillion in the same way her sister had enchanted the king, and now it seemed they had got what they wanted – the attention of Algenon Teardrop.

Magnus's elder brother had paid Hasim a substantial amount of gold to find the witch, but his plans had been interrupted by the arrival of the Red battle fleet. Exactly why the Ranen warlord and the Karesian witch hated each other was not so clear, but Hasim had overheard several conversations since the battle that made him certain that Rillion was keeping Magnus alive because the enchantress wanted to send a message to Algenon.

Hasim had briefly considered trying to kill her, but thought better of it. The Seven Sisters were supposedly impossible to strike with weapons. He'd seen men from his homeland try to cut them with swords, shoot them with bows, even throw rocks at them, and all attempts had missed. Jaa gave his power sparingly, but had gifted the Sisters the ability to avoid death, even if they didn't know it was coming. Al-Hasim had heard stories of men hiding on rooftops and behind buildings, remaining silent as they struck. The blows still missed and, without exception, the men had died shortly afterwards.

The only time one had successfully been killed was when an old friend of Hasim's, a Kirin scoundrel called Rham Jas Rami, had shot one in the forehead with his longbow. To this day neither Hasim nor Rham Jas knew how he'd managed it.

There was much Hasim didn't know, though he had to confess that knowledge was currently of secondary importance. Whatever games were afoot, Hasim had been thrust into them unwillingly, and he allowed himself a pained laugh at his predicament.

He reached the corner of the line of buildings and took several deep breaths. The untended cart was his best option, though the Red knight it belonged to would not be far away. He had to cross the street to reach it and there was nothing to lean on.

He steeled himself, feeling nauseous and weak, and tried his best to stand unaided. He baulked at the pain and fell back against the corner of the last building. He briefly considered hopping across the open ground to keep the weight off his leg, but thought that a foolish idea and tried to stand again. This time he swayed, but did not fall, and began to hobble forwards.

Hearing the sound of clanking metal to his left, Hasim stopped and fell forwards, staying as low to the ground as he could. The Karesian was in the middle of the street but there were few lights in the city and he thought a quick glance would not reveal his presence.

The sound came from a knight of the Red, bearing a flaming torch and inspecting a fallen wooden building on the far side of the fenced oak tree. Hasim crawled forward, keeping his leg straight and trying not to aggravate his wounds any further. The knight had his back to him as he placed the torch on the floor and leant forward into the wooden rubble.

Hasim pulled himself forwards, arm over arm, using his remaining strength to reach the cart. The smell was bad and he guessed the dead men had been lying untended for several days. Most were missing body parts, and from the size and severity of their wounds Hasim guessed they had been caused by catapult stones and splintered wood rather than longswords.

Placing his kris blade inside his tunic, Hasim hauled himself up on to the flat wooden base of the cart. He lay across the back of a headless corpse, letting his arms go limp as he played the part of a dead man. He tried to slow his laboured breathing as he wriggled into the pile of dead men of Canarn.

Within moments he was fighting to retain consciousness, his vision blurring now he had ceased to move and his head swimming from loss of blood.

He woke sharply as the armoured knight of the Red hefted the wooden cart into motion. He had been unconscious only a few seconds, but was as near death as he had ever been. His only hope was that the knight would unwittingly take him somewhere he could get help. The cart moved slowly, rocking from side to side as the wheels ran roughly over uneven cobblestones. Hasim allowed his head to move, giving him a view of the city past the distended and bloodied arm lying in front of him.

He could see plumes of smoke from the town square, closer now, and he could sense the heat from the fires. There was an area of rubble around the square where the wooden shops and stalls had been torn down. The only structures left between him and the keep were made of stone.

He could see squads of Red knights and mercenaries tending the fires and chained corrals of the few people they'd taken alive. Men, women and children – from the look of them, none of them had been combatants and all had been stripped to their undergarments. The mercenaries jeered at them, brandishing the arms, legs and heads of the dead as trophies.

A call of 'was this your brother?' from one of them caused a woman to break into tears.

The knights tending the fires were unconcerned at this behaviour and several of them joined in as the prisoners were tormented. A few of the mercenaries were eyeing up the younger women captives, arguing loudly about who would get to rape whom. These were the bastards who followed Sir Hallam Pevain, and Hasim thought them the lowest form of scum.

Several knights, whom Hasim took to be commanders, were standing on the lowered drawbridge that led up to the keep. They had disapproving looks on their faces as they surveyed the scene below. Many of the Red knights in the square were men bound to the church from birth, rather than true fighting men, and their behaviour did not impress their leaders.

Hasim saw a man in leather armour, caught in the act of raping a young woman, have his throat slit by a knight lieutenant of the

Red. Another, who had smashed out the teeth of an older captive, had his face slammed against the cobbles and his hand crushed by an armoured foot.

'Let no man take his payment in blood and flesh,' shouted a senior knight from the drawbridge.

Hasim had seen much pain and death in his life; he'd been a mercenary, a brigand and even a thief, but the treatment shown to the people of Canarn appeared vile even to him. The senior knights were displaying a little honour by trying to stop it, but to Hasim's mind it was enough to condemn all of them.

The cart was pulled across the edge of the square and Hasim saw crossbowmen moving along the battlements of the inner keep. They were spreading out and emerging on to the city walls and he worried that they would patrol the northern battlements and see Bronwyn as she made for the plains. She was a good rider, but a crossbow bolt flew faster than a horse could run and they'd surely capture her.

Hasim breathed heavily and spat out rancid blood. He couldn't help Bronwyn, but thinking about her safety had quickened his heart and driven away the pain of his wounds. For a brief moment, he thought clearly. The cart was moving past the huge walls of the inner keep and he could see down to the cell windows a few feet above the cobbles. The walls were hollow and wide, and the keep held three levels of dungeons below ground level. Each barred window was at the bottom of a shallow trough, down which food could be thrown from the city. It was the way prisoners had been fed by the Ranen lords who held the keep long ago.

Hasim blinked; the light from nearby fires and the stench of death made the air shimmer, but he saw a line of cell windows through the haze. In some the occupants were standing defiantly, still wearing the remnants of their armour. Others appeared to be empty or to contain the dead or dying. Hasim had a chance; if he could locate the cell that contained Father Magnus, he knew that the Ranen would be able to summon the voice of Rowanoco to heal his wounds.

The cart was pulled away from the main square; the Red knight was going to the southern corner of the city to collect more of the dead. Hasim wriggled backwards and positioned himself at the edge of the cart. No one was paying any attention and he tensed his body to roll on to the cobbles. He estimated that he'd hit the ground on the opposite side to the town square and, if he moved quickly and stayed low to the ground, he had a chance of staying hidden.

He held his breath and rolled off the cart, biting his lip as he fell to stop himself screaming in pain. The cart continued to move, the Red knight pulling it unaware that one of his dead bodies had shown itself to be alive. Hasim began to crawl weakly towards the dungeons. He could not feel his wounded leg, and most of his body had gone numb. He was cold and knew he'd soon be dead.

At the base of the wall, he crawled into the shadows and pulled himself into one of the feeding troughs. He rolled several feet and came to rest next to a small barred window. Within the cell was a man of the duke's guard, battered and stripped of his armour. Hasim recognized him as Haake, a sergeant of the keep.

'Sergeant Haake . . .' he whispered through his pain.

The duke's man started with surprise and turned to look at the bloody face at his cell window. 'Who're you?' he asked softly.

'I'm a friend of Father Magnus, called Hasim . . . I bought you a mug of Ranen wheat beer on the duke's birthday.'

'I remember . . . You're wounded, sir,' Haake said with concern.

'Indeed, I do appear to be. Sergeant, I'm leaking blood all over the place and need to find the priest. Is Magnus on this level?' he asked.

Haake came to stand next to the window and inspected the wounded Karesian. 'Aye, lad, he's down the end of the corridor. They brought him back maybe ten minutes ago. He was unconscious and didn't look in a good way himself.'

Hasim winced in pain and narrowly avoided losing consciousness again. 'Which way to his cell?' he asked.

Sergeant Haake placed a hand on his chest and pointed to the left with his index finger. 'Be careful, Hasim, the gaoler is a fucking pig,' he warned.

'Songs will be sung, Haake, they will be sung loud and they will be sung often,' he said in thanks.

The duke's man nodded. 'Brytag go with you, brother,' he said, turning from the window.

Hasim looked along the line of windows to the left and began to move. He could only edge along the bottom of the stone troughs using the window bars as a ladder to pull him along. There were six or seven windows and Hasim felt light-headed as he passed the third one along. The cell contained a mortally wounded man, bleeding his last on the dusty stone floor. The next window gave on to an empty cell. Hasim felt himself beginning to lose consciousness and lunged forwards as far as possible. He doubted he'd be able to move again and hoped Magnus was within reach.

Hasim's head had just landed in front of the last cell window and, although he was fading, he could still make out the enormous lump lying in the middle of the small cell below.

Father Magnus was face down and clearly wounded. A crossbow bolt was protruding from his right leg. Hasim had not seen exactly what had happened in the great hall earlier in the evening, but he hoped his friend was okay.

'Get up, you Ranen fathead . . . I'm more wounded than you.' He choked the words out.

Magnus turned with a terrifying scowl on his face accompanying a deep red bruise where he'd been struck across the temple. He blinked a few times and moved into a crouched position.

'Hasim?' he asked in his heavy Ranen accent.

'Yup, think so . . . just about . . . I'm . . . dead,' his friend replied.

Magnus looked out of the cell door and, seeing no sign of the gaoler, stood and moved to the window. Hasim smiled at the sight of his old friend, but that was all he could do before he slouched against the bars and lost consciousness.

* * *

Magnus tried to remain as quiet as he could while he reached through the bars to investigate Hasim's wounds. The Karesian was cut badly across his left thigh and, although he'd stopped much of the bleeding with his belt, the wound was ugly-looking. The cut on his lower back was of more concern and it was still bleeding. Magnus knew Hasim was strong and wouldn't give his life away easily, but the Ranen was nonetheless impressed that his friend was still alive.

The Ranen priest closed his eyes and attempted to calm his mind. He had never called on the battle rage and the voice of Rowanoco in the same day, and he knew he needed to be at peace for the healing to work.

Hasim was an old friend, from the days when Magnus had journeyed with Brom and, although he'd not known that the Karesian was in the city, his presence made sense. The last he had heard, Hasim was in Fjorlan, sampling the local wheat beer and telling Ranen women outrageous lies about his heritage.

Hasim had got on well with Algenon, Magnus's elder brother and thain of Fredericksand, and Magnus knew Hasim would be the ideal person for his brother to send south. Magnus did not concern himself with Hasim's mission. He was a simple man, not given to worrying about things beyond his control, and currently he needed to focus on summoning the voice of his god.

With a hand placed through the bars, he lifted the remains of Hasim's tunic and touched the wound on his back. 'Rowanoco, the earth shakes at your passing, let it be healed by your voice.'

His hand remained on the wound, but the voice did not come. 'Rowanoco, hear me now. I am your child, your servant, your hand and your will. This man is my friend and I would see him live. Talk to him now, let him receive your voice and be a man again.' The words he spoke caused tears to appear in his eyes as he let himself feel pain, anguish and regret at the recent treatment meted out to those he held dear. Rowanoco would lend him his

117

power only if his priest was truly in need, and Magnus knew this meant he needed to soften his iron will and let his emotions flow through him.

'Rowanoco, father of all, blessed of the Low Kast, of the plateaus of Ursa, of the frozen wastes, visit us now and heal this man . . . please.'

The last word stretched on the Ranen priest's lips and he felt his hand become warm. In the deep recesses of his mind he heard a distant rumble as if an earthquake were echoing through his head. The voice of Rowanoco the Earth Shaker, god of the Ranen, began to fill him.

More tears came into his eyes as his god leant down and spoke to him. He felt peace, calm and tranquillity at the sound of the Giant's words and, although he could not hope to understand what was being said to him, he sensed a strength of purpose that he had rarely felt. His hand began to glow as he became a conduit for the god's power.

Rowanoco, the Ice Giant, reached across uncounted layers of the world and lent his power to the priest. Magnus's hand smoothly ran across Hasim's back and the wound began to close. Slowly at first, he felt the blood stop flowing and the flesh knit itself back together. He heard Hasim's heartbeat quicken a pace as the deep cut became no more than a scar and the blood around it disappeared.

Without thinking, Magnus moved his glowing hand to rest on Hasim's leg and, with merely a touch, the second wound was healed, leaving only a mark that looked as if it had been there for years.

Hasim coughed as Magnus fell back on to the floor of his cell. The Ranen glanced around and was glad to see that he'd been quiet and had not alerted Castus, the gaoler.

He breathed heavily, shaking his head to clear a slight residual dizziness. Above, he saw Hasim slowly open his eyes and blink rapidly, his face pressed against the barred window. The Karesian groaned and moved only tentatively, slowly letting his senses reorder themselves. He looked down at the belt still tied tightly round his leg.

With a smile he turned to look through the bars at Magnus. The priest smiled back and the two old friends looked at each other for a few moments before Hasim spoke. 'I think Bronwyn is safe, I got her as far as I could,' he said weakly. 'I just hope Brom is still alive somewhere.'

CHAPTER FIVE

RHAM JAS RAMI IN THE CITY OF RO WEIR

EIR WAS THE only city in the lands of Ro where a
Kirin man could live without being constantly hounded
by clerics. The Kirin were the mongrel offspring of
Karesian and Ro, and they were generally dismissed as criminals
and slavers by both their parent races. Rham Jas was no slaver
and thought that, on some level, he was a good man; however,
he had to concede that he was currently working as an assassin.

Weir rested on the Kirin Ridge, a narrow sea channel between
Tor Funweir and the arid expanse of Karesia to the south. It
was a hot, dirty and dangerous city, and Kirin criminals and
Karesian mobsters controlled at least a third of it. Rham Jas
despised the majority of them, but he was clever enough to trade
on the misplaced sense of brotherhood they showed towards him.
He knew he was safe as long as the Kirin hated the Ro more than
they hated each other.

Like all Kirin, Rham Jas was dark-skinned, lighter than the men
of Karesia but swarthy in comparison to the Ro. He was tall, but
slender, and had eyes that were never still and a near-permanent
grin. His hair was wavy and thin, hanging in lank curls to his
shoulders. He was approaching his thirty-sixth year of life, but
felt much older and enjoyed moments of immaturity to remind
him that age was not a good thing.

Currently, he was sitting in the shadows on the roof of a particularly nasty inn called The Dirty Beggar. He'd been up here for

about an hour and was beginning to think that he'd been given bad information. Rham Jas had been paid a decent amount of gold to kill a drunkard named Lyle. Apparently, Lyle had got into debt to the wrong people and was having his account closed. In Weir, that tended to mean death or something approximating permanent incapacity. Rham Jas had certainly been hired to cut off legs in the past.

He had been making a living from the mobsters of Ro Weir and other undesirables for nearly ten years. In that time, he'd discovered that he had a knack for assassination. Previously he'd been a hunter and a family man, living in a small village in a particularly isolated spot along the Kirin Ridge. Now he was discovering that a longbow was also an excellent way to kill people.

Rham Jas also carried a katana at his side. It was a gift from his wife and, though he rarely used it, he thought it wise to carry a sword when on a job – and it held certain sentimental value.

He pulled his cloak tightly around his shoulders and peered over the edge of the building to the street below. The Dirty Beggar was full and sounds of drunken revelry filled the night air. Outside stood a group of leather-armoured thugs, a local gang paid to keep order in the street. Several patrons of the tavern were being told to leave, and several more were vomiting on the flagstones. It was getting late and Rham Jas hoped he'd be able to finish the job tonight. Having to return to kill the man tomorrow would be annoying.

A gentle breeze passed overheard, carrying with it the scent of a nearby man. Rham Jas had an excellent sense of smell and guessed that someone was trying to sneak up on him from across the roof. He spun round quickly, levelling his bow with lightning speed at the dark figure several metres away.

'You speak or you die . . . it's that simple.'

The figure held his hands wide in a gesture of submission and stepped closer, pushing back the hood of his cloak and revealing a young face, no more than twenty-four years old. He had curly black hair and carried an ornate longsword. Rham Jas recognized him and slowly lowered his bow.

'And what do you want me to say, you Kirin horse-fucker?' The young man smiled, revealing youthful good looks despite his full beard.

'Perhaps tell me what you're doing here, you Ro bastard.' Rham Jas sat on the ground, leaning against the side of the roof, and loosened his hold on the longbow. He regarded the man closely. He had not seen him for at least a year and was impressed with how he carried himself. He had always been dangerous, despite his years, and now he had an air of menace that Rham Jas thought suited him.

'I'm glad you're still alive, Brom. I heard what happened at Canarn,' the Kirin said.

The young man looked down, showing signs of anguish. 'May I sit?'

Rham Jas reached for the bottle of wine he kept for jobs that involved lots of waiting and motioned to the ground next to him. 'Please. But keep your head down, I'm on a job.'

Lord Bromvy of Canarn, son to Duke Hector, ducked into the shadows and sat on the dirty tavern roof next to his old friend, leaning against a stone ledge which concealed them from the street below.

They sat silently for a minute, the bottle of wine passed between them, until Rham Jas judged it was time to speak. 'What of your father?' he asked gently.

Brom shook his head. 'I don't know. The last I heard, the knights of the Red had taken the keep and arrested him. I was in Ro Tiris when I got the news. Little I could do but run here.' He took a deep swig of wine. 'There's a price for my capture, the fucking Purple have enlisted every disease-ridden mercenary this side of Karesia to hunt me down.'

'You're worth something at last. I'd be flattered, Brom,' Rham Jas said with a grin.

'That's because you're a worthless Kirin mongrel,' his friend replied with little humour.

Rham Jas's smiled broadened. 'True enough, but I'm not yet a Black Guard.' The term was used for those whose family had betrayed the crown. It was a brand placed on the cheek to identify a man as belonging to a dishonourable house. Brom had been named to the Black Guard, but not yet captured and branded. Rham Jas assumed that the young lord was unlikely to turn himself in.

Movement from the street below caught the Kirin's eye and he placed a finger across his mouth. With slow, deliberate movements, Rham Jas stood and positioned himself above the ledge. Drawing back on his longbow, he scanned the street. He saw a fat man, dressed in a bright green robe, accompanied by two paid women. Lyle did not look worried and Rham Jas guessed he was not aware of the grievous insult he'd given to the local mobster – nor of the fact that he was about to die.

'What's this man done exactly?' Brom whispered.

Without taking his eyes from his target, Rham Jas said, 'Not sure,' before releasing an arrow from his hunter's bow. It hit the mark, just above Lyle's right ear; a good shot, thought the Kirin, as blood erupted from the wound. Lyle was clearly dead and the two women screamed and looked in horror at the pieces of skull and flesh that now covered their clothes.

'Right, off we go then,' Rham Jas said cheerfully.

He winked at Brom and darted back across the roof, grabbing his backpack and ducking to remain in the shadows. At the far side of the roof was a wooden staircase which snaked its way round the corner of the building. Rham Jas didn't look back to see if his friend had followed as he darted off the roof and deftly descended the stairs. He could hear distant sounds of commotion from the street and knew he needed to remove himself as quickly as possible.

He heard Brom running behind him, making more noise than Rham Jas thought was wise, as they leapt off the staircase to land on a lower building opposite.

Rham Jas loved the feeling of having got away with a crime. He also loved the feeling of shooting an arrow through the head of a Ro. He rarely took jobs that required him to kill Karesians or Ranen, and his inherent hatred of the Ro had earned him a certain reputation amongst the mobsters of Ro Weir. Prejudice was greatly prized where assassins were concerned.

The two men moved quickly across the second roof and came to a stop at a window leading to an adjoining tower. Rham Jas had propped the window open earlier, and now he swiftly jumped to grab the robe he'd fastened to a beam within.

Brom looked impressed as the Kirin climbed nimbly through the open window. He disappeared inside for a moment before reappearing at the window ledge. 'Do you want a fucking invitation, your lordship?' he said to Brom.

The man below smiled and began climbing the rope. Once Brom had joined him inside, Rham Jas pulled up the rope and closed the window.

The room they had entered was a storage room of sorts, with several racks of clothing and several more of dried food rations. Brom looked around with curiosity while Rham Jas removed his armour and dressed in a set of commoner's clothes he had prepared beforehand.

'Rham Jas, where exactly have you brought us?' he asked.

'It's the lower level of a drunk tank, where people with nowhere else to go end up when Brown clerics find them being sick in back alleys. This is where they keep the crap they give homeless folk. The food costs money, but occasionally a drunk has a few coins on him.'

'And why are we here exactly?' Brom asked.

Rham Jas sat on the floor and removed his sword belt, placing his katana on a rack behind a stack of clothes. 'Well, I thought being drunk in the tank was a good alibi when the watchmen come and ask me if I shot a man in the head. I stashed my armour and bow here earlier and then vomited in an alley outside. The Brown clerics ushered me in.' His constant smile beamed brighter than usual as he looked at his friend. 'I stayed up there a good hour or so and then came down here, got my stuff and killed that man.' He reached under one of the racks and produced a bottle of strong Ranen whisky.

'Drink?' he asked with good humour.

Brom shook his head. 'I don't think I'll be joining you in the tank and I don't want to see any watchmen, whether they're looking for you or me.'

A quizzical look crossed Rham Jas's face as he spoke. 'Yes, you're the wanted one. What exactly happened in Canarn?'

Brom looked as though he didn't want to revisit what had happened to his homeland, but he gathered himself and faced Rham Jas. 'Magnus came south again and my father asked for sanctuary. The old fool actually tried to join the Freelands of Ranen.' He tried to smile, but the expression never reached his eyes, and Rham Jas thought he was close to tears.

He looked out of the window, into the loud night of Ro Weir, and continued, 'Someone betrayed them and a battle fleet of Red knights attacked. Rillion and that bastard Pevain massacred anyone who tried to defend the town and the knights took the keep.'

Rham Jas knew how much the fall of Ro Canarn would affect the young lord and he felt a momentary pang of concern for Magnus. The dopey Ranen was far too proud to leave the city and actually stay alive. 'I bet Magnus did some fucking damage before they took him down. I've seen that man take a dozen swords and stick them up their owners' arses.'

Brom looked up. 'I don't know what happened to him. I still don't really know what happened after the battle ended. I just know that they took my father alive.'

'Your sister?' asked Rham Jas.

'She'd have drawn a sword and fought if Father let her . . .' He shook his head. 'But I don't know whether they'd kill her or not.'

'Knights of the Red aren't squeamish about killing women,' offered Rham Jas, with little tact, causing Brom to direct a hard look at him. 'What? If you expect me to hold you and make everything better, you're talking to the wrong Kirin.' Rham Jas felt for his friend's loss, but he had concerns of his own. 'Look, Brom, I wish I could help, but I've really got to go upstairs and pretend to be drunk.' He finished getting dressed and stood up. 'Now, how do I look?'

'Like a filthy Kirin scumbag.' Brom spoke with no humour and Rham Jas felt guilty for being so dismissive of his friend's pain.

He took a moment to consider his words and spoke again. 'Brom, I owe you a lot . . . you know I do, but we're a long way from Ro Canarn and I don't see how I can help. If Magnus and your father are both captured or killed, then you and I should be grateful we weren't there at the time.' He put a comforting hand on Brom's shoulder. 'You're a dangerous little bastard, I reckon you could make a decent living with that overly shiny sword of yours.'

'Go and pretend to be a drunk, Rham Jas. Maybe it was a mistake to look for you.' Brom stood up and grasped his old friend's hand. 'Now, can I get out through that door or should I climb back out of the window?'

Rham Jas was not used to feeling guilt, but he was pragmatic enough to know that whatever the young lord was planning would be very unwise indeed. Rham Jas was a clever man and was not given to foolish displays of courage. He had stayed alive for most of his thirty or so years through his wits, skill and good humour, and he didn't want to make a foolish move now.

'Go through the door and take the stairs to the street. The door's in a back street behind a brothel. No one will see you.'

Brom maintained eye contact for a moment, but turned to leave the storeroom with no more words. 'Brom,' Rham Jas spoke as his friend opened the door. 'What did you want from me?'

The young lord of Canarn looked down, then back at his friend, but he said nothing and left the room, closing the wooden door softly behind him.

Rham Jas let his smile disappear and kicked a pile of clothes out of frustration. He paced back and forth in front of the window for several minutes, trying to convince himself that he had done the right thing and that nothing Brom could have had to say would be for his benefit. But Rham Jas owed him his life.

The young lord had saved him from being hanged three years ago. Rham Jas and a Karesian bastard called Al-Hasim had foolishly broken into a Purple church in the city of Ro Tiris. They were drunk and were following a tip-off that the church had little security and easily accessible caches of gold.

Hasim was no thief and Rham Jas was not stupid, but they'd plied each other with just enough drink to make them think it was an amazing idea. The two of them, more out of boredom than need for gold, had climbed up a neighbouring building and jumped through a glass window to enter the church.

Rham Jas hadn't thought about the incident for a while and found his memories difficult to put in order. He remembered Hasim laughing while sitting on the altar and pretending to defecate, and he remembered the shouts of anger from the Purple clerics who emerged from below the knave.

There was definitely a fight and, as Rham Jas looked down at a faint scar on his chest, he thought how lucky he'd been not to die right there, in the sight of a god he didn't follow. The Purple clerics had probably been so taken aback by the sight of two laughing foreigners pissing on an effigy of the One God that they didn't fight at their best.

Rham Jas took a swig from his bottle of Ranen whisky and sat on the floor, temporarily forgetting that he'd just killed a man and would be being hunted by the city watch. His thoughts were elsewhere, as he remembered being dragged from the church, blood covering his clothes and vomit barely contained behind his lips.

The clerics had beaten the two of them insensible and the memory of exactly how Rham Jas had ended up with a noose round his neck was rather fuzzy. He was sure that Hasim was unconscious and vaguely recalled a list of charges being read out. He'd been told since that the clerics hadn't waited for any kind of official justice and were simply going to hang the two foreigners from a wooden beam in the church stables.

What happened next had been told to him by Brom and Magnus on a number of occasions and he still didn't know which version to believe. What was certain was that the young lord had taken his Ranen friend on a visit to the capital in order to help him understand the Ro. They'd been drinking too, though not to the extremes of Rham Jas and Hasim, and they had found themselves in the streets of Ro Tiris, alerted to the sounds of swearing and commotion from the Purple church.

Brom had always claimed that he tried to reason with the clerics, considering it his duty as a noble to stop what he saw as a miscarriage of justice. Whereas Magnus remembered the fight starting almost instantly. Either way, Magnus and Brom fought and bested four Purple clerics and rescued the drunken thieves from a pathetic death.

The first clear memory Rham Jas had was of Brom throwing a bucket of freezing water over him and Magnus barking out something about Rowanoco. The four men left Ro Tiris the next day and hid in the town of Cozz for several weeks until Brom was sure the encounter had not been seen by anyone and no one was looking for them.

Rham Jas had ingratiated himself with Brom straightaway, the young lord appreciating the Kirin's sense of humour. Magnus and Al-Hasim shared a love of alcohol and women that made them near-instant friends and the four men spent their time in Cozz laughing, drinking and mocking the clerics.

A Karesian, a Ranen, a Ro and a Kirin were an odd mix in any of the lands of men, but they developed a swift and strong bond over their shared hatred of the laws of Tor Funweir.

The four men travelled together for over a year, Magnus learning about the culture of Tor Funweir, Rham Jas getting Brom into trouble, and Al-Hasim exploring the country through the medium of whores and wine. They teased Brom for being a Ro and antagonized Magnus into more than one pointless tavern fight, but they remained friends.

Rham Jas had few genuine friends and counted Brom as one of the best. A Kirin assassin and a Ro lord were unlikely companions, but the various times they had met since their initial encounter had simply confirmed that Brom was an honourable man and one of the few that Rham Jas could trust.

A noise pulled him from his thoughts and caused him to stand up quickly. He could hear the sound of chain mail and metal-shod feet from the street-level door three storeys below.

He swore to himself as he realized that he'd lingered in the store-room too long. Quickly checking that all of his gear was hidden, Rham Jas opened the door and stole a peek down the wooden staircase. He swore again as he glimpsed a squad of watchmen ascending the stairs.

Taking a quick swig of whisky, he left the room. Silently closing the door, he took the steps leading up to the drunk tank three at a time. He was now barefoot and made little sound as he splashed whisky on his clothes so as to smell like a drunkard.

Two floors up and Rham Jas emerged into the tank. Within were five long wooden benches, each seating a dozen or so drunken men, secured in an upright position by a length of thick rope stretched across their chests. Rham Jas was glad to see an array of blank faces as all the men were either asleep or in various states of insensibility.

The spot left by the Kirin two hours ago was still empty and Rham Jas hoped his absence had not been noticed. The Brown clerics who maintained the tank would not return until daybreak to check on the occupants.

Rham Jas splashed more whisky on his face and downed as much as he could without vomiting. He dropped the bottle in a large piss-pot and tiptoed across the room to his seat. With great dexterity he wriggled under the restraining rope and took his place amongst the faceless drunks of Ro Weir. Leaning forward against the rope, he looked down, letting his hair fall over his face.

He didn't spare a look up as the door opened and five watchmen in chain mail entered the room. They spread out loudly across the tank, shaking a few men into vague consciousness as they began checking faces.

Rham Jas kept cool and shook his head, playing the part of a drunk who'd been roused from his sleep. He felt a hand grab his hair and his head was pulled back. Through feigned bleariness he looked into the face of the watchman, a man wearing a belted chain-mail shirt and the tabard of Ro Weir, a black crow in flight.

'Sergeant . . . over here,' the watchman said, still holding Rham Jas's head back.

Two of the watchmen remained by the door while the other two moved over to stand in front of Rham Jas. Several of the drunks were now awake. A few mumbled swear words and requests for quiet, and were answered with an array of kicks and slaps.

'Well, well, if it isn't our Kirin friend,' the sergeant said with a sneer, as he levelled his crossbow at Rham Jas.

In response, the Kirin groaned and shook his head, making some show of trying to raise his arms and rub his eyes. The rope restricted movement and Rham Jas pretended he had just woken up and wasn't sure what was happening.

'Straighten yourself up, you Kirin piss-stain.' The sergeant slapped Rham Jas hard across the face. 'Where's your bow?'

Rham Jas blinked rapidly several times and tasted the blood on his lower lip. 'I don't know what . . .' The Kirin accentuated his accent and made a show of appearing the ignorant foreigner.

The sergeant turned to one of his men. 'Get him up, soldier.'

The watchman grabbed Rham Jas by the throat and pulled him upright, the rope restricting his stomach and making it difficult to stand. The smell of whisky was strong and the watchman held Rham Jas at arm's length. 'He stinks of cheap Ranen shit, sir.'

The sergeant leant in and immediately baulked at the smell. 'Rham Jas, you smell like you've been swimming in the stuff.'

The Kirin smiled and made a show of retching. All three watchmen stepped back, leaving Rham Jas to fall theatrically to the floor.

'A thousand apologies, my noble lords . . . I seem to be in a state unsuited for the company of dignified men such as yourselves.' He spat on the floor and retched again, holding his hand up to the watchmen and asking for a moment.

'Kirin, look at me,' the sergeant said. 'A man got a longbow arrow in the head less than half an hour ago.' He held out the bloodied shaft of one of Rham Jas's arrows. 'Know anything about that, boy?'

Rham Jas looked up, letting a helpless and pathetic expression flow across his face. 'Sorry, milord, I sold my bow to buy the cheap shit I've been swimming in . . . whisky is a much better master than death.' His smile was broad, but unfocused, and Rham Jas retched again, this time summoning a small amount of vomit and aiming it at the sergeant's feet.

'Get the fuck away from me, you filthy Kirin.' The sergeant roughly pushed Rham Jas back and turned to his men. 'This piece of work can barely stand, let alone string a bow. He could maybe vomit a man to death, but he's not our killer.'

Rham Jas saluted in a mocking gesture and fell face-first on to the floor, drooling and making low groaning sounds .

The watchmen laughed and mocked him loudly as they walked back to the door. The room filled with swearing from the assembled drunks for a few moments, but silence quickly returned to the tank and the sound of the metal-clad watchmen disappeared below.

Rham Jas allowed himself a smile, but remained on the ground, thinking a few moments of rest wouldn't hurt.

* * *

Several hours later and Rham Jas found himself sitting outside a tavern on the far side of town. He'd retrieved his weapons and armour when the Brown cleric had come to wake everyone up, and the Kirin had swiftly removed himself and his belongings to a place of relative safety.

The sun had been up for less than an hour and Rham Jas had enjoyed watching the night turn to day from a wooden bench overlooking the port. The tavern was not yet open, but he liked the view of stone houses, tall ships and life slowly creeping into the streets.

Ro Weir was built on a hill with all the city streets sloping down towards the large harbour and the Kirin Ridge beyond.

His homeland was over the sea and deep in the primeval forests that lined the Ridge. There was a waterfall and a narrow wooded valley through which ran a sparkling river. His farm was one of several at the southern end of the valley. It was a land called Oslan by those that lived there, Lislan by the Karesians, and simply the Kirin woods by the Ro.

He'd not been back there for many years and he doubted there would be much left of his home. His wife was dead, as were all his friends and neighbours, killed by the Purple clerics who had assaulted his village looking for risen men. His children had survived, but were taken after the battle by Karesian slavers as they tried to find their father in the woods. Purple clerics were often followed by such men, who thought a cleric attack a good opportunity to secure new slaves.

Rham Jas had been deep in the forests of Oslan hunting Gorlan when he'd seen the plumes of smoke. He'd known what it meant as he'd personally helped repulse several such attacks in the past, but he arrived only in time to see the tracks of a slaver wagon and the ruins of his home.

The clerics of nobility disliked people following dead gods, and the strange darkwood tree that lay in the middle of the valley had long been a focus of worship for the Kirin who lived there. The name of the god it symbolized was not known, but the simple people of Oslan did not need the One, Rowanoco or Jaa to help them sow crops and pray for a mild winter. The risen men who shared the valley, called the Dokkalfar in their own language, had long been allies of the Kirin and let them worship at the foot of their sacred tree.

The first time the Purple had attacked, years before Rham Jas was a father, the Kirin had ended up pinned to the tree itself by a crossbow bolt. He'd hung there for several hours, as the other farmers held the village, getting weaker with each minute. However, the experience had changed Rham Jas. His blood had mixed with the sap of the strange tree and something in that union had given him sharper reflexes, a keener mind and a certain knowledge that other gods had once existed. Even now, thirteen years later, he still felt the strength that the tree had given him. He healed quickly and had, more than once, survived wounds that would kill a normal man.

As he thought of his past, Rham Jas shook his head as if to clear his mind. He disliked the thoughts, which were inevitably of the heat of burning wood and the bloodied body of his wife. Her name was Alice, and he missed her more than he could adequately express. His life since her death had been full, but he had never lost the feeling that, without her, no one truly understood him.

Rham Jas smiled as the breeze hit his face and he pictured Alice's beautiful features. The grief he felt for his children was different, somehow more hollow, because he had never avenged them. He'd tracked the slavers to the city of Kessia, the capital of Karesia, but he had let his anger at the clerics take over and had left. His children had been lost to the slave markets and, when Rham Jas returned to pursue them, he and Al-Hasim had run into trouble that made returning to Karesia almost impossible.

Al-Hasim used to try and get Rham Jas to talk about his grief, as if it would help him overcome it. What his friend didn't understand was that Rham Jas had already overcome his grief. He'd spent six years hunting down every single Purple cleric who had come to his village and had killed them all. Rham Jas had lost count of how many churchmen had died at the tip of an arrow or the point of his katana, but it was at least twenty. He'd hunted one through the wilds of the Fell on foot for three days, killing the man with his bare hands when he backed him into a wolf snare and strangled him. Another was asleep in a tavern in Ro Arnon when Rham Jas covered his mouth and slit his throat. He'd paid a group of mercenaries to assault a squad of watchmen in order to get to the cleric they were escorting and eventually he'd found the commander cowering in an old church beyond the plains of Leith. The leader of the squad that had burned Rham Jas's village knew that death was looking for him; he wore his purple robes only to weekly prayers and had let his armour rust. He had even pleaded with the Kirin, saying that he had renounced violence and asked the One for forgiveness daily. Rham Jas remembered with exact detail what he'd said to the cleric before he'd cut off his arms and legs and watched him bleed to death.

The cleric had looked him in the eye and said that the One God was watching and would forgive him his heathen worship of a dead god. Rham Jas had replied simply, 'Your god already has a taste for blood, so he should enjoy this.'

Once the last cleric was dead, Rham Jas was no longer the man who had lost a wife and two children. He became the Kirin assassin Rham Jas Rami and had no further use for soft talk of grief or kind words of comfort. He'd given up on goodness and had come to believe that no amount of good deeds could make a difference to the world.

The happiest he remembered being in the years since his wife had died was the time he'd spent travelling with Al-Hasim and later Brom and Magnus. He met the Karesian first, some months after he'd killed the commander, and they bonded quickly. Both men had a hatred of the church of Ro and both had reasons for not being able to return to their own lands.

They'd spent many months moving throughout Tor Funweir, sharing stories, alcohol and women. They'd been thieves, brigands, mercenaries and con men, never staying in the same place for long and constantly seeing the spectre of the clerics round each corner.

Rham Jas had never been charged with the numerous murders he'd committed and, after seven years, he thought his facility for stealth and assassination precluded any chance of the Purple clerics arresting him. He guessed that the varied ways in which he'd killed his wife's murderers, and the time he'd waited in between, had been sufficient to confuse any clerics who had sought to investigate the killings.

No men knew of what he'd done; even Al-Hasim knew only that he'd wandered through the lands of men after his village had been burned, but not the true purpose of his wandering. When they returned to Karesia together to look for his children, Rham Jas had lied about what he'd been doing to delay the search.

'Brom, are you going to hide in that alleyway and spy on me all morning?' Rham Jas had already seen the young lord of Canarn several times as he'd walked away from the drunk tank.

Brom was a dangerous man, but stealth was not one of his gifts. Now he stepped out from his place of concealment and came to sit on the bench next to Rham Jas, sharing the impressive view of Ro Weir.

'Your boots have steel buckles on them, much better quality than most around here can afford. They make a cleaner sound and don't grate as much as cheaper ones,' Rham Jas said as he turned to look at his friend. 'You look tired. Maybe you should get a few hours' rest before you try to persuade me again. I don't want your mind to be addled by fatigue.'

Brom didn't smile or turn to face his friend. He shielded his eyes from the sun and continued to gaze down over the roofs of stone houses to the tall ships at anchor in the harbour. The Kirin thought he saw a tear in his friend's eye, but it may have been a trick of the light. Brom was a guarded man, not given to displays of emotion, and Rham Jas guessed that he was composing himself. With patience and a rare acknowledgement that he had nothing immediately pressing to attend to, Rham Jas waited, giving Brom as much time as he needed.

'This is as far south as the knights of the Red have ever been. Did you know that, Rham Jas?' Brom asked.

The Kirin knew little of the history of Tor Funweir, but he'd certainly never heard of the knights crossing the Ridge. 'Men in steel armour don't fight well in the desert, I suppose,' he replied.

'Too cold or too hot and they go home. It's strange that their supposed honour takes a back seat to temperature. They never got as far north as Fjorlan either . . . too cold,' Brom said.

Rham Jas had endured many nights of Magnus going on and on about his land being unconquered. The men of Ranen thought it a great thing that the north of the Freelands had never been invaded by the Ro.

'I don't like the cold either,' Rham Jas said, 'but then I'm not a conquering army of warriors . . . I suppose I'm probably a poor example.'

Brom didn't smile. 'Even the Kirin woods and scablands are

too hot for them. I'm amazed they've held on to Ro Weir for this long . . . though, I suppose, the sea breeze does cool the place down,' he said.

Rham Jas had first-hand experience of the Purple clerics' various low-key expeditions into Oslan on the far side of the Ridge, but they had never gone there in force. Brom was probably right – bringing the word of the One was apparently conditional on the temperature being just right.

'Is this as far south as you were planning to run?' Rham Jas asked.

Brom leant back and let the bright morning sunshine play across his face. 'I wasn't running. I was looking for you,' he replied.

Rham Jas was uncomfortable with responsibility and thought his friend was far too distraught to be thinking clearly. He decided to try and lighten the mood. 'How about we go and get properly drunk and let a few women tell us how amazing we are?' he suggested cheerfully. 'There's a whore around here somewhere called Jacinta . . . seriously, the way she purred my name made me melt. I reckon she could roll Lord Bromvy of Canarn around her mouth a few times, yes?'

Again, Brom gave no reaction to his friend's attempt at humour. He breathed in deeply and shifted his weight, pulling his longsword across his lap. 'How much gold did you make for killing that man last night?' he asked.

'Enough for us to get a woman each, just like old times . . . well, without Magnus entertaining half a dozen of them in the next room.'

Brom finally decided to smile and turned to face his friend. 'Rham Jas, I appreciate your attempts at making light of absolutely everything, but I don't want a woman and I don't want to be cheered up. You're welcome to go and visit Jacinta if you wish, but I'll be waiting for you outside when you're finished.'

Rham Jas stood up sharply. 'Then what the fuck do you want, Brom? You didn't come all the way here to drink, fuck and be merry, and you certainly didn't come for my company,' he rattled off angrily, missing a few syllables and letting his Kirin accent become broad.

For a second, Brom looked confused as he tried to make sense of his friend. 'Rham Jas, sit down, anger doesn't suit you,' he said calmly, 'and you never could curse convincingly.'

Rham Jas felt a moment of childish petulance at being told off, but he slowly sat down nonetheless. He crossed his arms and adopted a rather comical display of annoyance. He had never been good at showing concern or being serious and he wished that Brom had sought out someone else. His friend's pain was difficult for Rham Jas to understand; he had long since reconciled his own grief, and did not like seeing it in others.

'Brom . . . I don't know what to say to you,' he said with as much sincerity as he could muster. 'Your father, your sister, your people . . . I wouldn't know what to say to them either . . . that's why I'm here and not taking part in glorious battles and hopeless defences. I'm just a lone man with a bow and a bad attitude. I kill for money . . . I'd kill you if I was paid enough.'

Brom raised an eyebrow. 'You'd try,' he said, patting the hilt of his sword. 'Rham Jas, I'm not leaving until you agree to help me. Now, I'm prepared to follow you around Weir for a few days if that's what it takes, but I'd rather you just gave in now.'

Rham Jas considered it. His friend had not told him what he wanted and the Kirin really didn't want to know. Brom was brave, clever and impulsive, a mixture of traits that Rham Jas knew well and heartily disliked. He let the moment stretch and thought about the faces of his few living friends. Magnus might be dead, Al-Hasim was probably on his back in Fredericksand, and Brom was sitting next to him. One couldn't be helped, the other didn't need help, and the third was asking for help. Much as Rham Jas would have liked to believe that he was a cold, heartless killer, it simply wasn't the truth.

'Tell me what you want,' he said quietly.

Brom nodded and his eyes softened slightly before he spoke. 'I need to know how you managed to kill one of the Seven Sisters.'

Rham Jas raised his eyebrows. 'Er . . . I put an arrow in her forehead . . . that was . . . maybe four years ago, not long before I met you,' he replied.

'I know you shot her in the head, but how did you manage to do it? As far as I know, no one has ever succeeded in killing one before or after you. Anyone who swings a blade or pulls back on a bow string misses. Jaa gives them some way of avoiding death,' Brom said angrily.

Rham Jas was a little confused by this. He'd thought that Brom would want his help in exacting revenge, or something similar. To hear that he was trying to kill a Karesian enchantress was a little concerning.

'Look, I've been asked about this before, you know I have. All I can tell you is that I stood . . . maybe . . . ten feet from her. She smiled at me for some reason, perhaps thinking I would be bewitched and be unable to let the arrow go . . . then I just shot her in the forehead and she died,' he said. 'Brom, what do the Seven Sisters have to do with you?'

'That's why I wasn't in Canarn during the battle. I saw the Lady of Spiders in the town and went to Tiris looking for you or Al-Hasim.' He looked down at his feet and shielded his face from the heat of the sun. 'When I saw the Red fleet launch I saw another Karesian witch at the king's left shoulder,' he said. 'That makes two of the Seven Sisters somehow involved in the attack on my homeland.'

Rham Jas considered it. Not much solid information was known about the enchantresses or their designs, but Rham Jas and Hasim had got on the wrong side of one in Kessia. She had been a beautiful woman, despite her facial tattoos, and Al-Hasim had made an inappropriate suggestion to her. Neither of them had known who she was, and they were surprised when she spoke some words and made blood appear from Hasim's mouth and eyes. Rham Jas had warned her and, when she'd refused to release his friend, he'd shot her. It was only afterwards that they had learned of who she was and the enormity of her death. It meant little to

Rham Jas, except that he could never safely return to Karesia. Al-Hasim, however, had never accepted the fact that he could not return to his homeland for fear of reprisals from the Sisters. The Karesian's father had been tasked with executing Al-Hasim and, in an uncharacteristic show of paternal affection, had let him flee to Tor Funweir instead.

'Which one did you see in Tiris?' he asked Brom.

The Seven Sisters recycled the same few names, using them as an honorific. The one Rham Jas had killed was called Lillian the Lady of Death and he'd heard of another since with the same name.

'I didn't get close enough to introduce myself, I just recognized the tattoo on her face and the dumb grin she put on the king's face,' he replied.

'I don't understand why the Seven Sisters would give a peasant's piss for Ro Canarn. It's a very long way from Kessia,' Rham Jas said, shaking his head.

'True, but they are less bothered by the cold than the knights of the Red. I didn't know why Ameira was in Canarn. It never occurred to me that the city would be destroyed while I was away. Magnus was there, I thought . . . I don't know what I thought.' He rubbed his eyes and panted heavily, showing the exhaustion he'd been hiding. 'I should have told someone . . .'

'Brom, don't have an emotional breakdown now. You were doing so well at being all cold and uncaring. I like the crying Brom so much less,' Rham Jas said with a broad grin. 'If you'd told someone, and they'd approached her, she'd have bewitched them. If you'd approached her yourself, she'd have bewitched you. As far as I know, they've never been involved in this kind of thing before. You had no way of knowing what was going to happen.' He thought for a second. 'If anything, you were sensible to remain free. That way you can maybe get help.'

Brom turned to his friend and nodded, making Rham Jas realize that he had backed himself into a corner and was now obliged to help. 'It's me, isn't it, I'm the help you sought?' he asked with resignation.

Brom continued to nod. 'We're an army of two, Rham Jas.'

'This is so much horseshit I can barely talk because of the smell,' Rham Jas replied, 'but okay, an army of two we are.' He held out his hand and they shared a firm handshake. 'So, what do we do now, my lord?'

'My land has been taken, my house has fallen and my family are imprisoned . . . we do what my father wanted, we gain freedom for the people of Canarn,' he said grandly.

'And after that?' Rham Jas asked with a smile. 'Can we at least spend a few days in the bottom of a bottle or between a woman's legs in celebration?'

'Get me back into Canarn and help me kill the witch and we can do whatever you like,' he answered.

'We'll have to go back via Cozz,' Rham Jas said, deep in thought, 'there's a blacksmith there who does a nice sideline in fraudulent travel documents. Unless you want to use Glenwood, but I don't trust that little snake.'

Brom chuckled. 'He got me out of Tiris,' he said, reaching into his tunic and producing the forged Red church seal he'd used to leave the capital. On closer inspection, the clay tablet was of poor quality and Glenwood had left out two of the six church banners that official seals usually contained.

'That streak of Ro shit couldn't forge my arse if I shoved it in his face and gave him a really close look,' Rham Jas said, shaking his head at the forged seal. 'You were lucky, the gate guards in Tiris were probably drunk. No, if we're planning a sea voyage, I'd rather get clay that doesn't turn to mud within twenty minutes.' As if to emphasize the point, he pulled off a corner of Glenwood's forgery and crumbled it into reddish mud between his fingers.

'Okay, so we take the Kirin run to Cozz,' Brom replied.

'And, just so I'm clear, we're killing anyone that tries to stop us, right?' Rham Jas knew his friend was a cold bastard but Brom could also be kind-hearted and, if they were being hunted by Purple clerics, it was unlikely they would be able to talk their way out of trouble. The churchmen of the One God were determined, and

Rham Jas shook his head as he thought of killing another Purple cleric or two.

'Hopefully, they won't find us and we won't have to decide whether to kill them or not,' replied Brom.

Rham Jas nodded and reconciled himself to the fact that he would always have helped his friend; he just needed a little time to realize he wasn't a cold, heartless assassin.

Something occurred to him and he leant forward and said conspiratorially, 'Do you think they know who Magnus's brother is?'

'I've no idea,' replied Brom, 'but, from what I remember of Algenon, he's not someone to trifle with.'

Rham Jas had only met the high thain of Ranen once before and was certain that Algenon Teardrop did not like him, but he was a fearsome man to be on the wrong side of and a devoted elder brother to Magnus.

PART TWO

CHAPTER SIX

ALGENON TEARDROP RAGNARSSON IN THE CITY OF FREDERICKSAND

T HE RANEN ASSEMBLY sat on the coast of the Fjorlan Sea. It was one of only two stone buildings in Fredericksand, the other being a chapel to Rowanoco, the Ice Giant. Algenon stood in the heavy wooden doorway and wrapped his bearskin cloak around him. The ice had come early this year and the wooden houses of his city were covered with a layer of snow, broken only by chimneys and plumes of smoke. The city rose from the low fjords and spread out as it crept up the rocky coast of Fjorlan.

Algenon held the title of thain. He was the chieftain of the realm of Teardrop, high thain of Ranen, and bearer of his father's name. A man of over seven feet tall, he hunched often and, due to an old shoulder wound, found it difficult to stand fully upright. His hair was black, as had been his father's, and well groomed, long and tied back in a braid. The men of Ranen wore beards to guard against the cold and Algenon's was thick and plaited and flecked with grey.

His younger brother, Magnus Forkbeard, had inherited the golden hair of his mother, Ragnar Teardrop's third wife and a woman only a little older than Algenon. The brothers looked little alike aside from their height and size, but nonetheless the thain loved his younger brother dearly.

Their paths in life had been radically different, too, with Magnus accepting the voice of Rowanoco from a young age and joining the Order of the Hammer. Algenon had stayed at his father's side and had known that he would rule when the time came. Magnus had been a precocious child, fighting and arguing at every turn. Algenon had tried to look after the boy, but after their father died he'd been more concerned with his duties as thain and had largely ignored the boy. As a result, Magnus had become strong and independent. He was widely travelled for a Ranen and had spent little time in the Freelands after he had first visited Canarn some eight years ago.

In contrast, Algenon had always been a quiet man, considering his words carefully and not being given to the violence for which his people were known. When he fought he did so to kill, and he had never felt the need to brag or impress with deeds or skill. With an axe in his hand he was still the most dangerous man in Fredericksand, but the older he had become the less combat had filled his mind and the more likely he was to try to talk his way past obstacles.

'My lord thain.' The words came from behind him and Algenon recognized the speaker as Wulfrick, one of his battle-brothers and a trusted friend.

The thain did not turn, but kept his steely gaze on the icy seas of Fjorlan, deep in thought and letting images of his brother's stern face play on his mind. He had not seen Magnus for nearly a year, but had received frequent messages regarding his foolish endeavours in the south, and Algenon wished that he'd forbidden him from leaving Fredericksand all those years ago.

'Algenon,' Wulfrick spoke again, more insistent this time.

'What do you want?' he asked without turning.

'The assembly awaits you, my thain.' Wulfrick bowed his head as he spoke.

Algenon took one last long look out to sea and turned, marching forcefully through the huge wooden doors of the Ranen assembly. His chain shirt was covered with moulded leather armour, containing steel plates, and the sound of metal on metal was loud as he entered the hall.

The Ranen assembly was a high-ceilinged building of white stone that rose in a circle to a skylight fifty feet above the floor. The lords of Ranen sat on stone benches rising from an open floor and on a raised platform was the single chair reserved for the thain of Fredericksand.

They sat in fur and hide clothing, bearded and battle-hardened; the thains and battle lords of Fjorlan were an intimidating presence for most men. Algenon had called them here for two reasons, one of which was unlikely to win much support. As he approached his chair he hoped that the news of Magnus's imprisonment would be enough to convince the lords to launch the dragon fleet.

In unison the two hundred Ranen lords stood and held their fists high in a gesture of respect. The only man who remained seated was Thorfan, the lore-master, a man in his eightieth year of life who was bound to hold the books of the Earth Shaker, the few texts that chronicled the will of Rowanoco.

Wulfrick moved past Algenon to sit at the front of the raised auditorium. As axe-master he was the only man permitted to face the lords rather than the thain. His position rendered his honour unquestionable.

The lords remained standing as Algenon reached into his cloak and removed two small throwing-axes, one from each hip, and placed them on the floor in front of his chair. In response, each of the assembled lords held aloft a single axe and placed it on the white stone floor of the assembly. The sound was clear and drove all other noise from the hall, with only the whistling cold wind echoing around the building.

This opening ritual complete, Algenon took his seat at the front of the auditorium and looked up at the semicircle of Ranen lords seated before him. Wulfrick unslung his huge two-handed axe and banged the haft twice on the stone floor. He was the biggest man in the assembly and his job was to maintain the rituals and laws of Rowanoco.

'My lords,' Wulfrick began, 'our thain has called for this assembly.' He spoke clearly in the archaic Ranen language reserved only for official business. 'We will hear his words in reach of our axes and in sight of our god.' A third bang of his axe accompanied his closing words. 'Rowanoco, look on your people with pride and let us not disappoint you.'

Algenon rested one leg across the arm of his wooden chair and, with cold eyes, looked over the faces before him. He let the silence linger and the cold wind swirl around the hall before he spoke.

'Brothers, far to the south lies the city of Ro Canarn.' Recognition on many faces showed that these men knew of the city. 'The ruler of that city, an honourable man of Ro called Hector, has asked my brother for sanctuary.'

Algenon paused as the lords gasped and whispered comments of incredulity at the news. Another strike on the floor from Wulfrick's axe and silence returned to the hall.

Algenon glanced around the room, his eyes falling on the figure of Lord Aleph Summer Wolf, an old and respected thain from the ancient city of Tiergarten. Aleph was not gasping or whispering, but looked with interest at his lord. Algenon knew the man well and smiled at the expression on his face. If he could interest all present in the same way, he knew his words would carry enough weight to persuade the assembly.

Aleph maintained eye contact with the thain and, after a second of thought, returned his thin smile. Then he stood and reached for his hand-axe. With his head held high, he banged the haft of his axe on the white stone in front of him. Wulfrick looked up and nodded.

'My lords, you know me . . .' Aleph spoke loudly and with a gravelly voice. 'Lord Algenon is wise, but given to theatre when the mood takes him. I ask that he tell the entire story and not pause for dramatic effect more than twice more.' He smiled and a thin laugh echoed around the assembly.

Algenon chuckled as Wulfrick once again called for silence. The assembled lords of Ranen turned back to the high thain and awaited his words.

'Well,' Algenon smiled and straightened in his chair as he spoke, 'Aleph makes his point with the elegance of an axe to the face, but he is wiser than I.' He stood and began to pace in front of the assembly, stepping over his two throwing-axes. 'Magnus is a young man with the exuberance of a mountain wolf, but he is not stupid, nor is he given to lending his hammer to dishonourable men.' Algenon paused for a second to judge the reaction of those before him. He saw a sea of nodding heads as all present signified their acceptance that Magnus was a man of honour.

'That makes what has happened all the more disturbing.' This caused the lords to look intently at the thain. 'Magnus offered the blessing of Rowanoco to Duke Hector and he called him brother.' Algenon returned to his chair and almost growled the next sentence. 'The Knights of the One God then descended on the city and massacred the men of Canarn.'

The reaction was instantaneous. The assembled lords stood and began to shout curses and challenges at the god of the southmen. The Freelands of Ranen had once been under the control of the One God and his clerics. All the assembled lords knew the stories – how the Purple had torn down the shrines to Rowanoco, how the Black had desecrated their funeral mounds, and how the Red had enslaved any able-bodied Ranen man. It had been two hundred years since the Free Companies had formed and bought back their lands with blood and death, but the men of Ranen still felt as much hate for the clerics and knights now as they had done then.

Aleph held out his hands. 'Brothers, I call for silence,' he bellowed. 'Do not let anger displace wisdom. These halls do not curse without reason and we should follow their example. Lord Teardrop has more to tell us, I am sure. We should take our seats and listen; maybe we will hear why this tragedy has taken place.' He spoke with wisdom, but Algenon knew that he was a potential rival in the assembly.

He picked up one of his axes and looked intently at the floor. 'My brother stands in a cell. This makes me angry. This makes Rowanoco angry. Magnus is of the Order of the Hammer and is worthy of more than a stone room and a locked door.'

The lords again showed their displeasure. A cage was the most insulting thing to a Ranen and a priest in a cage was the gravest insult imaginable. Death was a thing to be celebrated and sung about, whereas to be defeated and imprisoned was to be without honour in the sight of Rowanoco. The men of Ro knew little of true honour and had unknowingly committed one of the most heinous crimes.

'My lords, there is more . . .' Algenon had thought a great deal about how to approach the issue of the Seven Sisters and he was still unsure as to the best way to explain it. Al-Hasim, his spy and his brother's dear friend, had told him little in his last message save that the witch had enchanted at least one of the senior knights. 'The Red knights have amongst them a Karesian witch, one of the Sisters of Jaa, and her hand touches the weak minds of the men of Ro. Her designs are at work here,' he said, just loud enough to be heard.

One of the lords to his left stood and banged his axe on the stone, asking to be heard. Wulfrick acknowledged him and all turned to hear his words.

The man was Lord Rulag Ursa, chieftain of Jarvik. He was not a thain, but was known and feared for his prowess in battle. Rulag commanded a fleet of dragon ships and fifteen thousand warriors. He scanned the room, looking at the faces of his fellow lords.

'I am as aggrieved at the treatment of the priest as any man here,' he began, 'but I much question Lord Teardrop's motivation. If his intention is to go to war over an insult paid to him by a witch—' a few lords considered his words and several nodded in agreement—'maybe he should go there himself and call this woman out. Does the assembly need to meet in order to pander to our thain's ego?' His voice rose in volume as he finished speaking.

Shouting erupted from the men as several came to Algenon's defence, and those seated around Rulag stood and shouted challenges across the hall.

Axes were brandished and insults exchanged as Algenon sat quietly and waited. He had feared this reaction and knew that not all the lords of Ranen cared for talk of sorcery. Many were simple warriors, believing only in what they could see, hear and kill. The Order of the Hammer possessed certain divine gifts, but the rage and the voice of Rowanoco were things the Ranen had grown up with and most did not consider them sorcery.

Wulfrick let the challenges go, because axes were being brandished and Rowanoco had decreed that casting one's axe to settle an argument was an honourable way of deciding matters. None had been thrown yet, but Algenon could see that the hall had become split down the middle, with half wanting Rulag to retract his insult and the other half coming to his defence.

Wulfrick spared a glance over his shoulder to look at Algenon. Both men knew that the only way to silence the lords would be for an axe to be cast or for Algenon to speak. No axes were thrown and the thain waited for several moments, assessing the strength of the opposition.

Breathing in deeply, he rose from his chair and picked up both of his throwing-axes. Wulfrick, with a slight smile at his thain, banged his axe on the white stone floor and all the lords were silent. Most remained standing and Rulag thrust out his chin towards Algenon, displaying his reluctance to retract the insult.

'My lords,' Algenon said loudly, 'the point is a fair one, though the manner of its delivery could have been better considered.' This caused a low rumble of laughter from certain quarters. 'Whether my Lord Ursa wants to accept the fact or not is irrelevant, the witches of Jaa have taken a hand in this . . . they have broken a law laid down by Rowanoco himself.' Algenon deliberately invoked the name of the Ice Giant, knowing that the lords who supported him would now do so even more, and those who supported Rulag would be having doubts.

Wulfrick banged the haft of his axe on the floor three times before he spoke. 'The word of Rowanoco has been spoken. The law will be stated.'

Thorfan, the lore-master, who had virtually fallen asleep in his chair, jolted himself upright and reached for a heavy leather-bound book on a stand to his left.

He cleared his throat and placed the book in his lap. Opening it, he proclaimed, 'The word of Rowanoco, as passed down to us by Kalall of the Legion, the first lore-master of Fredericksand, will be heard.' He leafed through the pages, taking his time as he looked for the relevant passage. His eyes were narrow and he squinted to read the archaic script of the book. Making low muttering sounds to himself, he cleared his throat again before continuing, 'The Ice Giant decreed that the men of Ranen, the free men of the north, those of the Low Kast, the clans of the Plateau of Ursa, the men of the Deep Cross, the priests and lords of Hammerfall . . .' he breathed in sharply and let a cough escape his lips before continuing, 'shall never allow a man, a woman or an instrument of another god to imprison one of their own or, through design or action, make war or force subjugation on their brothers.'

This passage was well known to most of the men present. It had been paraphrased a hundred times over the years and used as a rallying cry for all manner of inadvisable endeavours and at least one truly just cause. This decree of Rowanoco had been the spur for the formation of the Free Companies and had ultimately led to the Ro being thrown back across the sea to Tor Funweir.

The laws of the Ice Giant were chaotic and open to interpretation, serving noble thain and violent warlord alike. Algenon knew that it was a risky ploy to use the decree of Rowanoco in this way, but he also knew that the alternative was to kill Rulag.

Aleph Summer Wolf stood and broke the silence by striking his axe against stone. Rulag Ursa also still stood, as did half a dozen other warlords from around Jarvik. Algenon saw Rulag's son, Kalag, clenching his fist angrily around his throwing-axe, seemingly waiting for an opportunity to throw it. The lords of Jarvik were feared enough to make several of the neighbouring realms ally themselves with him for fear of later retribution, and Algenon counted fifteen lords who were supporting Rulag. Aleph looked over at the other standing men and then flashed Algenon a knowing look; he, too, had assessed the strength of the high thain's opposition.

'We know this law, brothers,' Aleph began, 'and we know how it has been used and misused in the past.' He shot another glance at Algenon, as if to say sorry for what he was about to do. 'Lord Algenon seems to think we are all as simple as Lord Ganek of Tiergarten, an old lordling of mine who used this decree to kill a neighbouring lord for imprisoning his winter pigs,' he said with a smile, as at least half the assembled Ranen began to laugh. 'Apparently, as the pigs provided food for his wife and two fair daughters, he considered them part of the family and therefore brothers.' The laughter rose and Algenon thought that even Rulag looked amused at the story.

'My lord thain,' Aleph addressed Algenon directly, 'I have great affection for your brother. I would doubt that there is a man here that does not feel personally insulted by his treatment at the hands of the One.' He addressed the other lords, 'But if the thain wishes to launch the dragon fleet against the city of Ro Canarn and the knights of the One—' all were silent as he spoke—'then I must voice my considered objection. A single priest of the Hammer does not warrant the deaths of hundreds of men.' He sat down, as shouting erupted from the other Ranen.

Algenon sat back down as two hundred Ranen lords shouted at each other. Following the words of Aleph, the opposition to Algenon had become stronger than his support, and Rulag Ursa felt he had right and wisdom on his side.

Wulfrick was silent, but the glance he directed at his thain showed his concern that Algenon could not out-think Aleph.

The thain of Fredericksand considered his next move carefully. He saw little option and stood up with purpose, picking up his axes and keeping his eyes on the floor.

Wulfrick banged his axe loudly on the floor twice and, when silence only slowly returned to the hall, shouted in a booming voice, 'The high thain wishes to speak.'

Algenon was glad of the axe-master's support, even if it was more ceremonial than tangibly useful. He held both his throwing-axes loosely in his hands as he stepped forwards and came to stand before the raised seats. 'Lord Aleph once again shows his cunning, his wit and his considerable wisdom. I salute you, my lord, but I mean to launch the dragon fleet and rescue my brother.'

The assembled lords were now deathly silent, knowing that Algenon was not a man to trifle with when he had made up his mind. They began to take their seats as the thain raised his eyes and looked over the faces of the men who had spoken against him. Rulag met his gaze for a second before turning away and sitting down, resting his axe on the floor. Kalag Ursa appeared surprised that his father had yielded, but followed his lead and sat down.

Aleph, who had already taken his seat, looked suspiciously at Algenon, his eyes narrowing as he glanced at his own throwing-axe on the stone before him.

Algenon looked at the old lord and felt a moment's regret before he took a step forwards and launched one of his axes at Aleph. The axe spun through the air as Aleph widened his eyes and followed its trajectory into his chest. It was a good throw and Aleph was allowed only a moment to gasp for breath before he slumped forwards, dead.

His robes were dark brown, covered in bearskin, and the blood that flowed freely over his body left little evident stain before it spilled on to the white stone. The lords around him moved along in their seats, but they did so only to avoid his blood and everyone else bowed their heads in silent respect.

Algenon held his other axe tightly in his fist and swung it slowly back and forth, allowing anyone who wanted to cast his axe in return to do so. None did, and, after a minute, Wulfrick struck the floor again.

Thorfan, the lore-master, said with practised formality, 'An axe has been cast in favour of the motion and none have been cast against. The motion is as Lord Teardrop says.'

Algenon did not let any doubt show on his face, but he felt foolish for having resorted to killing Aleph. In the eight years he'd been thain of Fredericksand this was only the third time he had cast an axe, and he thought the lords now feared him more than they had done before. He'd been careful to cultivate an image of inscrutability and ruthlessness, but had rarely had to resort to his weapons.

What the others didn't understand, and what he could never make them understand, was that Algenon spoke for Rowanoco, and the Ice Giant had asked him to sail for Ro Canarn and stand against the Karesian enchantress.

He was not of the Order of the Hammer, but he had, since he had come to the office of high thain, a more direct way of communicating with his god.

Silently, he resumed his seat. 'I expect all warlords, battle-brothers and fleet captains to attend me in my hall before morning.' He turned to the man seated to the right of Aleph. 'Lord Borrin Iron Beard,' he said to the axe-master of Tiergarten, 'you will speak for your land in your master's place.'

Borrin was younger than Aleph, barely in his thirtieth year, but his eyes were those of a seasoned warrior, and he glared at Algenon. 'Your word is my law,' he said quietly, 'and the axe of Tiergarten is yours, my lord.'

No more words were spoken. Algenon stood and turned back to the huge wooden doors of the assembly. The sound of Wulfrick signalling the end of the session with his axe echoed around the hall as Algenon strode from the Ranen assembly.

Outside the harsh wind once again struck his face, and he allowed himself a moment of quiet reflection while looking out to sea, before making his way back to Fredericksand and the duties that lay before him.

* * *

The hall of Teardrop was a long wooden building with high-vaulted ceilings coming to a point, and a dozen chimneys to let the smoke from the fire-pits escape. Ancient weapons – axes, spears, falchions and hammers – hung from the walls, and the skulls of trolls, Gorlan spiders and lesser-known beasts adorned the hall. None of the weapons or kills belonged to Algenon, but he kept them there as a testament to the old lords of Fjorlan, men who, it was said, had fought from one side of the Low Kast to the other to clear a land for the men of Rowanoco.

Tapestries hung from the high ceiling depicting Giants in battle and the Krakens of the Fjorlan Sea devouring ships. The hall was used for meetings, feasts and ritual combat, and it was where Algenon Teardrop held court. His home was in a small adjoining building and, as he sat on his father's chair at the far end of the hall, he wished that he had leisure to go and spend a few uncomplicated hours with his children. Unfortunately, he had cast his axe and the way forward was now written in the rock of Fjorlan.

Wulfrick stood at his right side and allowed the Ranen lords to enter one by one to pledge their support to the high thain. Each man walked with a small retinue from the open doors to where Algenon sat. The hall was otherwise empty, and the lords had to pass seven long feast tables as they walked towards him. Wulfrick had often commented that Algenon's ancestors, who had built the hall, had a way of making their battle-brothers uncomfortable, as the walk was long and they remained in the thain's sight the entire way.

Rulag Ursa and the lords of Jarvik appeared to have been reconciled to the plan, and they now hungered for combat. Borrin Iron Beard, Aleph's axe-master, was curt but respectful and had pledged three dragon ships and five hundred warriors.

The lords of the Low Kast and Hammerfell had been less keen to pledge their full support, but threats and reminders of their duty had gained a further thirty ships with battle-hardened crews.

'How many is that?' Algenon asked his axe-master.

'That's fifteen lords and their battle-brothers, my thain.' He was looking over a piece of parchment that sat on a table in front of him. 'We have a hundred and twelve ships and no small amount of bloodlust.'

Algenon shot a dark glance at Wulfrick. 'You think I'm wrong to do this?'

'Yes, my lord, you are wrong to do this,' he said with no humour, 'but you knew that when you did it.' Wulfrick had known the thain all of his life and felt free to speak his mind. 'I don't know what Samson the Liar told you that pushed you into this, but we're going to war against the knights of the One. You can rationalize it as a decree of Rowanoco, or even say you're going to try and kill an immortal Karesian witch, but the reality is that we're going to war with those Red bastards.'

Algenon looked down at the floor. 'Samson is closer to Rowanoco than any priest of the Hammer and his counsel . . . on certain matters . . . is without equal.'

He may have pushed the lords into war, but he had not done so on a whim. He was following the will of his god and he had never felt he could question such a command. He wished he could tell Wulfrick about his duty, but he was forbidden from doing so.

The only Ranen who knew of the legacy of the thains of Fredericksand was the old-blooded Samson. He had the blood of Giants and, through thousands of generations, could claim a familial bond with the ancient Ice Giants that once walked the land. He was largely insane and was seen as a dishonourable old liar by most, but he had come to Algenon on the day of Ragnar Teardrop's death and told him of his hereditary duty – that the high thain of Ranen is the exemplar of Rowanoco and is pledged to the Long War, the endless battle between the Giants.

'Tell the other lords to return tomorrow.' Algenon rubbed his eyes. 'I'm tired and night is well into the sky.' He got up slowly. 'You're my friend, but I need trust now and not friendship,' he said to his axe-master.

'You will always have both, my lord,' Wulfrick said plainly, 'but a friend tells a friend when he's being foolish, and so I think we'll stay friends for a while.' He offered his hand to Algenon who took it warmly.

The battle-brothers stood face to face for a moment before Wulfrick spoke with a smile. 'I assume you had considered talking to Aleph's daughter?'

'I had considered it, yes. That, too, can be dealt with tomorrow,' Algenon said with no smile.

Wulfrick took the long walk to the entrance and left the hall, leaving Algenon standing by his chair, deep in thought. He had much to do before he could sail for the lands of Ro and most of it needed to be done in private.

Speaking to Halla Summer Wolf, Aleph's daughter, was necessary, but not likely to end in bloodshed. The axe-maiden was a hard woman and knew the way of things, having fought in many conflicts between rival lords. Algenon hoped she would accompany the fleet and do her father honour.

He tried to rub the fatigue from his eyes, but with his mind able to fix on nothing but the night, Algenon Teardrop Ragnarsson, high thain of Ranen and exemplar of Rowanoco, decided to go to bed.

He walked from the centre of the long hall to the tall wooden door behind his chair. The door was closed, but not locked, and Algenon paused a second to listen against the wood before knocking quietly. He stepped back as the circular handle was turned and the door swung slowly outwards. Towards the bottom of the door the face of a child peered out.

'I hope your brother knows that you're still awake and that you've been listening at doors?' he asked his daughter.

Ingrid Teardrop was nine years old and was becoming more mischievous with each passing winter. She had her father's black hair and her mother's deep blue eyes, but the grin was all her own.

She looked at her father with wide-eyed fear for a second. 'Erm, Alahan's asleep and I thought I should listen to what was going on. To find out about things,' she said.

'Things?' queried Algenon.

'For when I'm thainess,' she said proudly.

'I've told you before, Ingrid, there is no such position as thainess. The position is thain and, as I've told you a thousand times, a woman cannot become one,' he answered with a smile.

'But that's stupid. I'm cleverer than Alahan and I'm faster and, when I'm older, I bet I'll be better with an axe.' She had an expression of mock hurt on her face and Algenon pulled the door further open and put his arm round her.

She was wearing clothes handed down from her twenty-four-year-old brother and was trying to look more like a man. She was barefoot, clearly in an attempt to remain silent, and her knees bore scrape marks from where she'd been clambering around the great hall. She was very quick and agile for her age, and Algenon had given up trying to chase her when she misbehaved.

'Little wolf,' he said affectionately, 'you'll grow strong and tall and give birth to mighty Ranen children.'

She shot him a disgusted expression. 'I will not. I'll be the first thainess of Fredericksand.'

'Ingrid,' he said seriously, 'do you think combat and death holds more honour than bringing lives into this world and treating them with love?'

Ingrid looked as if she were about to break into a grin at her father's seriousness, but instead wriggled under his arm and darted back into the house.

'If you get out of bed again, you will have no story before bed tomorrow,' he chided gently.

She looked slightly hurt at her father's displeasure and said in a timid whisper, 'But you were telling me about the Krakens.'

'And if you want to hear any more about the Krakens, little wolf, you'll do as I say.'

Algenon's home was a simple place, a far cry from his cavernous feast hall. It had three rooms around a central area used for all things from cooking to bathing. The two smallest rooms slept Ingrid and Alahan, and were large enough for his daughter to keep untidy and his son to use only rarely. The room he had shared with his wife was now just a bare chamber with a bed in it. He'd removed all of the decorations when she died and had never spent more than a night in there since.

Ingrid disappeared into her room and then slowly poked her head back round the door. 'Father, that monster man came to see you again,' she said, referring to Samson the Liar. 'He gibbered a bit at Alahan and then left. I think he was annoyed you weren't here. I miss Hasim, is he coming back soon?'

'Go to bed, little wolf.'

Al-Hasim had been an infrequent guest over the last few years and had grown to become an uncle of sorts to Ingrid. He told her outrageous lies about his adventures and was punched by Alahan on a number of occasions.

She grinned and closed the door, though Algenon doubted she'd go to sleep. He briefly considered waking his son to discuss his responsibilities while his father was away, but thought better of it as he yawned again.

The small fireplace in the central room burned all day and night to keep out the cold and Algenon warmed himself for a moment before clumsily removing his armour. The outer leather was heavy and the metal plates within made it awkward as he placed it over a chair. Once his chain mail was unbelted at the waist, it could simply be shrugged off and left to fall to the ground, making a loud clank as it hit the bearskin rug under his feet. Now, wearing a simple black shirt, Algenon looked into a small mirror for a moment. The scarred and bearded face he saw looking back at him seemed nothing but a tired old man and eventually he trudged across the room to his bed.

* * *

It was a cold and clear morning as Halla Summer Wolf, axe-maiden of Rowanoco and bearer of her father's name, came to the great hall of Fredericksand to meet with Lord Algenon.

She stood at the huge oak doors with her bearskin cloak wrapped tight around her and her red hair flowing down to the small of her back. Halla was a woman of six feet in height and thirty years of age. Her chain mail and battleaxe were constant adornments and she took her role as axe-maiden very seriously. She'd lost her left eye to a thrown axe some years ago and wore a black eyepatch across the empty socket. She was still occasionally called *one-eye the axe-woman*, but had perfected her glare sufficiently to render the insult infrequent.

Her father had produced no sons and Halla felt the weight

of her name more acutely as a result. She was quick to fight and cultivated a reputation for being bad-tempered and violent.

The great hall sat on a hill overlooking the town and was set back from the low wooden buildings that stretched down to the Fjorlan Sea. Halla had received the news of her father's death late the previous night, when Borrin had come to speak to her. She'd come to Fredericksand with her father from their home in Tiergarten three days before in answer to the high thain's summons. They'd travelled up the coast with a small contingent of battle-brothers, unaware of what awaited them. Aleph Summer Wolf had told his daughter to remain away from the assembly, knowing that many of the lords would be angry at the presence of a woman. The Tiergarten assembly, though half as big as the Fredericksand hall, sat several women – Halla's axe-maidens and some of the bravest fighters in Fjorlan. However, she was still seen as a curiosity by most, rather than a true warrior.

She'd met Algenon Teardrop before and found his inscrutable face disconcerting. It was as if he always knew what someone was thinking, and her father had often said he was the most dangerous man in Fjorlan.

The door to the hall opened and Wulfrick, the axe-master of Fredericksand, took a step out into the cold morning air. He raised his eyebrows at seeing Halla so early in the morning. He moved slowly from the doorway to stand before her, pushing the door closed behind him.

'Cold this morning, isn't it?' He pulled his own heavy cloak around his shoulders. 'The ice came early this year. I think we're in for a bad winter.' He didn't look at Halla but kept his gaze directed over the roofs of the town to the Fjorlan Sea beyond.

Wulfrick was sometimes jokingly called the half-giant, due to his size. He wasn't exceedingly tall for a Ranen, but his shoulders were enormous and his arms were the size of tree trunks. He wasn't a true old-blood, but he was the most imposing man Halla had ever seen. His unkempt brown hair was never tied back and he wore troll-hide armour that gave out a constant background odour.

'I need to speak to Lord Algenon,' she said.

He smiled before he spoke. 'And I thought we were having a pleasant chat about the weather,' he replied without looking at Halla. 'I assume that Borrin has spoken to you?'

Halla nodded and looked down, refusing to let grief show on her face. 'I wanted to speak to the thain . . .'

'For what reason?' Wulfrick interrupted. 'You know what happened, so you'll only torture yourself by prying into the details.' He turned to face her. 'You've sat in the assembly before and you've seen men die to secure lesser objectives than this.' He was speaking abruptly, but Halla detected concern in his eyes. 'He was planning to speak to you today, but it's not appropriate for you to be here.'

'I'm not going to ask him why he killed my father. I know why he killed my father. I was going to . . . I don't know . . . look into his eyes or something.' Halla had not thought about what she'd say when she faced her father's killer. All she knew was that sleep had left her as the sun had risen and she had felt compelled to address the high thain.

'My father had no sons and Tiergarten needs a thain. Maybe you can tell me what that means?' she asked curtly.

Wulfrick looked down at her. 'It means that the lords of the realm of Summer Wolf will fight until one emerges strongest and that man will be thain. Borrin Iron Beard is a good man and a good axe-master, he'll make sure things are done properly,' Wulfrick said with a degree of formality.

Halla maintained eye contact with the huge axe-master. 'And what of me, do I get to become battle-sister to the new thain and forever lament that I was born a woman?'

He smiled warmly. 'You sound like Algenon's daughter – Ingrid thinks that thainess sounds much better than thain.' He relaxed his gaze. 'There's wisdom in youth and often foolishness in tradition, but we are bound by the latter. I know he would want you to join the dragon fleet.'

Halla considered the axe-master's words for a moment and

then turned and marched past him. 'Then let him tell me that,' she said defiantly.

Wulfrick didn't stop her, but simply followed behind as she pulled the huge wooden door open. 'This won't end well, Halla. You should return to your own hall and wait for him.'

She didn't reply and marched into the great hall, her leather boots echoing off the stone floor. She had been here once before, when she was a girl, and remembered it being impossibly large. Now it looked only slightly bigger than her father's hall in Tiergarten.

An old grey-robed man was busy lighting the three fire-pits that ran along the length of the hall. The warmth from the fires had not yet fully filled the room and the hall was almost as cold as the street outside. The old man quickly became flustered as Halla marched past him, but a calming hand from Wulfrick silenced any objection before it came. She strode past the empty feast tables, sparing only the slightest glance at the huge troll skulls that hung from the ceiling, and slowed as she reached the high thain's chair at the end of the hall.

Three Ranen warriors sat at a small table off to the side and all looked up as Halla approached. She recognized two of them as Rulag Ursa of Jarvik and his son Kalag. The third man carried a huge axe across his back and Halla guessed he was their axe-master. Rulag and Kalag both had deep green eyes, a remnant of the old thain of Jarvik, Golag Emerald Eyes, a man who'd been hanged by Rulag from his own dragon ship's mast when he'd stolen control of the town. The Order of the Hammer had condemned the family of Ursa to bear forever the same deep green eyes, to mark them out as the killers of their thain.

The axe-master strode towards Halla. 'This is a place for men, one-eye. You may wait outside until we need a serving wench for our meat.'

Wulfrick stood next to Halla. 'You see, you're not the first to arrive this morning, nor are you the first to be told to wait.' He ignored the axe-master of Jarvik.

Halla looked past the axe-master and let her gaze flow over Rulag and his son. 'When some men get here, I'll gladly serve them,' she said. The insult was deliberate.

Kalag, a man of no more than twenty years, stood with anger and roared, 'I will cut out your other eye, red woman, and see how quick your tongue is then.'

Halla smiled. 'The young lord seems to have forgotten his manners. With his father's permission, I'll gladly teach him the proper way to address an axe-maiden of Rowanoco,' she said, casually removing her battleaxe.

Wulfrick laughed at this, but put a restraining hand on Halla's shoulder. 'Enough, it's too early and too cold to be killing lordlings,' he said, with a relaxed wave of his hand, which was sufficient to give Kalag pause.

Rulag, the lord of Jarvik, was smiling and had not taken any great offence at Halla's words. He stood and ushered his son back to his chair. 'Apologies, Master Wulfrick, my son is exuberant when talk of battle fills the air. We were discussing the deployment of our ships along the Fjorlan coast and your woman interrupted at a tense moment. Kalag is a little anxious that he won't be at the vanguard of the fleet, at least until we pass Samnia.'

Kalag had a petulant expression on his face as he sat down and turned his fiery glare away from Halla.

His father slapped him on the back. 'Cheer up, son, one-eye here would have cut your cock off before you had a chance to draw your axe,' he said with good humour.

The Jarvik axe-master still stood close to Halla and his stare remained hostile. As Rulag resumed his seat, Halla took a step forward and stood nose to nose with the axe-master.

'Your lord may call me what he wishes, little man,' she said, staring him down. 'You, however, will address me as Lady Halla or axe-mistress.' She paused, deliberately sizing him up. 'If you call me one-eye again, I'll kill you . . . and I won't break sweat doing it.'

Rulag and Wulfrick both laughed at this, though the axe-master of Jarvik looked as if he were about to burst with rage. Halla didn't soften her gaze as she spoke. 'Go on, call me one-eye again . . .'

Halla was not the equal of these men for strength, but she knew that she was faster and more skilful.

Rulag also knew this and he barked at his axe-master, 'Jalek, sit down.' The lord of Jarvik then turned to Wulfrick. 'Fun as all this cock waving is, do we know when Lord Algenon will be returning?'

Halla shot a dark glare at Wulfrick. 'He's not here?'

'I did tell you to wait, but you're an impatient sort, Halla,' he replied with a smile.

'Father's gone to see the monster man,' said a child's voice from the back of the feast hall and Ingrid Teardrop, little wolf of Fredericksand, walked towards the seated men.

Halla was slightly uncomfortable in her presence, as Ingrid idolized the axe-maiden. They had met only a few times, but she constantly asked questions about combat and about the traditions of Rowanoco.

The child came to stand next to Wulfrick and smiled warmly at Halla. She wore simple clothes of spun wool and a tight-fitting cloak crested with wolf fur. She was barefoot, as was often the case, and Halla thought how cold her toes must be.

'I might attach a troll bell to your ankle, little wolf; that way you won't be able to sneak up on people,' Wulfrick said with the stern look of a favoured uncle.

Ingrid was abashed and looked down at the floor. 'But it's harder to listen to what you're saying when you know I'm there.'

Rulag Ursa laughed loudly. 'Algenon has a budding spy,' he said, chewing on a piece of crusty bread. 'She can join that Karesian troll cunt and go spy on the Ro.'

Both Wulfrick and Ingrid glared at the lord of Jarvik, and Halla sensed that both of them liked *that Karesian*, whoever he was.

Ingrid turned back to look up at the huge figure of Wulfrick. 'He's nice, isn't he? Don't we like Hasim?'

'Whether we do or not we should mind our manners around

children,' the axe-master said, without averting his glare from Rulag.

Halla smiled at him and placed a hand on his shoulder, causing Wulfrick to turn away. 'As I said, men seem to be in short supply in this hall at present,' she said quietly enough for the lords of Jarvik not to hear her properly.

Ingrid interposed herself between Halla and Wulfrick and looked up defiantly at Rulag. 'Well, we like Hasim and my father likes him too.'

Rulag scowled at the three of them and his son looked deeply offended. He threw his half-eaten bread down on a map of the Fjorlan coast and rose from his seat.

'Master Wulfrick, I can say what I please to whomever I please and there is nothing you or your . . .' he glanced first at Halla then at Ingrid, 'your women can do about it. Now where is Lord Algenon? I tire of being made to wait.'

Wulfrick smiled, but made a slight nod of deference to Rulag, and Halla thought he appreciated his position as axe-master was insufficient to challenge a battle-lord. He turned and looked down at Ingrid.

'Would the *monster man* be Samson?' he asked the girl.

Ingrid simply nodded.

The lords of Jarvik exchanged glances at the mention of the old-blood and Kalag stood from his chair. 'He takes counsel from the liar? Are not the Order of the Hammer sufficient wisdom for him?'

'He'll be back soon, my lords. In the meantime, he has left instructions about the deployment,' Wulfrick said while untangling his legs from Ingrid. 'Little wolf, please go back to bed, and no more spying.' He gently shoved her towards the back of the hall and, after looking hurt for a moment, she rushed to the door that led to her home.

Wulfrick turned to Halla. 'I'm afraid you'll have to wait outside,' he said plainly. 'You haven't even agreed to join us yet.'

Halla considered saying something cutting, and even thought about making a fuss or accusing Wulfrick of having insulted her, but she bit her lip and decided to save her anger. With a shallow nod to Rulag and his son she strode from the feast hall.

Her father was dead and she knew she would get no answers as to why, whether she was insistent or not. As she opened the huge wooden doors and felt the freezing air hit her face, she hoped only that her father had died to secure an honourable cause and that Lord Algenon was worthy of her axe. The way south to Ro Canarn was long and treacherous, passing dangerous semi-submerged rocks, sheet ice and dense fog. If she was to take her people and their ships through such dangers, she needed to know it was worth the risk. Her father's sea charts were familiar to her, but she was no expert and would need Borrin's help if she was going to join the fleet.

Somewhere, deep in the back of her mind, Halla found the idea of such a voyage exciting. She'd never sailed past Kalall's Deep or seen the icy straits of Samnia where, according to half-whispered stories, the blind, mindless Krakens still dwelt, a remnant of the Giant age that Ranen sailors sought to avoid.

* * *

Algenon Teardrop, high thain of Ranen, had a master. To the people of the Freelands, the thain of Fredericksand was the all-high of the dragon fleet and lord of all free Ranen. The reality was that Algenon himself was not a free man. He was bound to the service of Rowanoco in a way that no priest of the Order of the Hammer could hope to understand. He could not summon the battle rage or heal wounds by channelling the voice, but he was compelled to follow a more literal avatar.

He'd risen early, before first light, and walked into his town. With his black hood obscuring his face, Algenon was an anony-mous presence in the quiet, snow-covered streets. He'd walked past the steel shops where the furnaces were already lit and working. He'd taken time to stop at Alguin's Mount, where the Ice Giant supposedly first appeared to the Ranen, and now he waited outside Rowanoco's chapel.

The sun was just peeking over the high plateau and the snowy forests beyond were glinting in the light. Fredericksand was a beautiful place in the autumn months, before the ice took hold completely. Algenon knew that within a few months no ship would be able to launch from the Fjorlan coast, and only Volk ice-breakers would be able to traverse the sea. The ice that came each winter was the greatest defence his realm had and, once the passes of the Deep Cross were iced over, no army could march north.

Algenon judged that he had waited long enough and banged his fist against the small wooden door that led down into the chapel. The building was built largely into the rock, with only a small white dome protruding above the ground. All chapels to Rowanoco were like this, unadorned buildings dug into the stone of Ranen. The only sign of its importance was the shallow stone relief of a hammer etched on to the surface of the dome. The wooden doors required all who entered to duck, and the stairs down were steep with worn, rounded edges.

Algenon banged a second time and added a solid kick. Samson the Liar did not sleep and Algenon could only assume that the old-blood was making him wait on purpose. He may have been summoned, but he was still high thain of Ranen and wasn't prepared to let Samson treat him like an errand boy.

The doors began to open and Algenon wondered how Samson had managed to ascend the stairs so silently. The double doors were shoved roughly outwards, pushing snow across the street, and a huge head poked out of the darkness.

Samson the Liar had the blood of Giants, something the people of Ranen considered both a great gift and a tremendous curse. Through a thousand thousand generations, Samson could claim to be related to the Ice Giants that lived in the lands of Fjorlan before the men of Ranen. He was huge in size, approaching nine feet tall, but ungainly, and his limbs were swollen and oversized rather than in proportion. He was flabby, with little muscle, though still immensely strong. His hair was grey and his beard covered much of his face and neck, making him look like a wild man as he grunted at Algenon.

'The exemplar is here,' he said in a voice deeper than any man, and waved an enormous hand at the thain. 'He comes in, out of the cold.'

Samson loped back down the stairs. He was bent over and needed to use all four of his limbs to crawl up and down the narrow space, though his shoulders still rubbed against the wall and gave the impression that he was squeezing himself down a tunnel too narrow for his passing. Algenon ducked under the door frame and steadied himself before gingerly descending the stairs after the old-blood.

'Samson, is there any way you could walk backwards down these stairs so I'm not faced with your enormous arse the entire way?'

Samson craned his neck round to peer back up at the thain. 'He is in bad spirits,' he said, before hurrying down the stairs with unusual dexterity for a man of his size.

Algenon was more tolerant of Samson than were many others, but he still disliked his peculiar manner. Across the north of the Freelands maybe five men in recent memory could claim to be true old-bloods, and all of them had displayed the same swollen appearance and strange speech patterns. Samson was the oldest known – several hundred years by his own reckoning – and was the only one ever to be permitted to live in a town. Algenon knew of another that had once haunted the woods of Hammerfall, a feral creature known as Louhi the Beast – more of a wild animal than a man. Al-Hasim used to talk about a Karesian old-blood he'd known near the town of Rikara in the south. Those with Fire Giant blood in their veins were even more unstable, and the man had been known for waylaying and eating travellers before he was executed by the Hounds of Karesia. As far as the thain knew, the men of Ro had hunted down and killed any men with Giant blood long ago, and Samson and his Ranen kin remained the only real legacy of the Long War.

At the bottom of the narrow staircase the chapel was warm, heated by the ever-burning brazier that Samson maintained. The rocky cave had smooth walls and low passageways leading in a web out from the central chamber. Few men were permitted to enter, and most preferred simply to stand around the dome if they felt the need to pray. Rowanoco was not a demanding god to worship and just required that his followers take time to drink, feast and sing, as had always been the Ranen way. The priests of the Order of the Hammer were the only men to show any formality in their worship, and even they tended to merely drink, eat and sing in greater quantities.

Samson had been allowed to live in the chapel by Ragnar Teardrop some fifty years ago and, though the men of Fredericksand knew he was down there, he was a largely invisible presence to all but Algenon.

The thain stood in front of the fire and warmed his hands, giving Samson time to haul his enormous bulk around the cave and get comfortable. The old-blood had a simple bedroll and a wooden table, upon which were a meagre amount of personal possessions: a small hourglass, a book of poems and a ruby pendant, each with their own significance to Samson. On the floor sat a huge warhammer, an ornate weapon with well-worn silver engravings of Giants in battle, and to the old-blood's left sat a simple cooking pot. It was a humble place for a mighty being to live, but Algenon knew that Samson had little need of comforts and was happiest when at rest.

'The exemplar has done well,' Samson grunted as he sat on the stone floor.

'Will you now tell me more, or should I take men to their deaths ignorant?' Algenon was not bitter, but neither was he naive and he knew how important such information could be.

'The Ice Father wished it . . . it is done,' the old-blood answered cryptically.

'It's not done yet, Samson, there's a lot of blood between now and this being *done*,' the thain quickly replied. 'The dragon fleet will launch. A hundred ships and over five thousand battle-brothers will descend on Ro Canarn.'

Samson smiled broadly and clapped his hands like an excited child. 'It is well, it is well. The Ice Father desires it. The witch is not outside the word of law. You will show her.'

Algenon sighed. The old-blood was given to hysteria and often appeared quite mad. However, his connection to the Giants could not be ignored and, on the few occasions when he'd shared his vision with Algenon, he'd seemed the wisest man in the Freelands. He stopped clapping and let a frown intrude upon his oversized face.

'The exemplar needs more?' he asked with a cunning glint in his eye.

Algenon considered it and said, 'Yes, I need more,' with a low nod of his head.

Samson pulled himself across the floor, using only his huge arms, and looked through the flickering brazier at the thain. He leant on a single arm and reached a hand round the fire, inviting Algenon to take it. He hesitated a second before placing his hand in the old-blood's.

Samson did not hear the voice of Rowanoco either. Instead, he knew the will of Rowanoco. It was a gift that only old-bloods could possess, and most of them went insane the first time they used it. The Giant blood they possessed made it possible for them to reach across countless layers of the world and contact the gods themselves.

Algenon closed his eyes and felt his body relax as he was pulled by Samson into the ice halls beyond the world where sat Rowanoco the Earth Shaker.

He felt detached as he dropped through layers of rock and earth, following Samson into realms that men could not know. His mind was protected from the will of his god by Samson's power, and Algenon had felt increasingly humble and insignificant each time he'd experienced it. He'd taken Samson's hand four times before, on each occasion learning more about the nature of his god and the position of exemplar. Each of the three highest gods of men possessed one, and they had been the gods' generals in the Long War.

The thain didn't question Rowanoco's motives when, through Samson, the Ice Giant let his will be known, but Algenon had over the years begun to think of the races of men as mere puppets in the war fought over their land by the Giants. Algenon had even stopped thinking of the world as *the lands of men* and was now of the opinion that the lesser species simply looked after it for their masters.

Deep in his mind, Algenon felt cold, as if his thoughts themselves now lacked a body in which to stay warm. He couldn't perceive shapes or colours, but simply the sensation of being tiny in the presence of enormity, as if shapes beyond a size he could comprehend stood over him. He was aware that Samson was still with him, the old-blood's power the only thing that kept him whole and sane, but he still felt vulnerable and helpless.

When it came, the voice was felt rather than heard, and it was that of Samson. 'You have questions?' He was clearer and more lucid, as if the edge of insanity that he wore in the lands of men had been shrugged off.

'I would know why I take my battle-brothers to war,' Algenon said in his mind. He felt his lips move but was unsure whether or not he was actually speaking.

'The rule of law has been broken, you will redress the balance,' Samson said, channelling the will of Rowanoco. 'It was not thought possible, but it has happened.'

He sensed fear and something akin to annoyance. These were not his emotions and he doubted they belonged to Samson.

'Then I would know what has happened in the lands of men to cause such a reaction in the land of Giants. I know only that a servant of Jaa has swayed the servants of the One, though I do not know why . . . why they have done it and why it concerns my god.' Algenon now sensed pride mixed with curiosity. Unwittingly, he had said something clever and impressed Rowanoco.

Samson's voice had an edge of humour to it. 'Your words have the sharp edge of an axe, exemplar, and cut to the heart.'

The voice in Algenon's head had another voice cutting through it, as if not every sound came from Samson's mouth. 'The exemplar of the One is charged with stopping such interference, much as you are charged with stopping the servants of other gods influencing my people. It is the first rule of law, that the Long War will be fought directly. If Jaa's witches are coercing the One's priests, it bodes ill for the exemplar . . . and it means that the word of Jaa is being ignored by his followers.'

Algenon considered this for a moment. Not in his lifetime had the Seven Sisters influenced the clerics, nor vice versa, and he recalled no tales of it having happened. The Ranen, the Karesians and the Ro had been at war with each other numerous times; the Ro had subjugated the Ranen and, long ago, the Karesians had nearly subjugated the Ro, but it had always been done directly.

His thoughts were not private within the ice halls and he again sensed pride. Algenon felt even smaller as the crushing sense of his god's approval washed over him. It was a feeling that every priest of the Order of the Hammer spent his life seeking, but Algenon found it uncomfortable and difficult to comprehend.

He projected his next words gently. 'It is not possible and yet it is happening . . . so he who is charged with stopping it must not be able to . . .' he paused, 'or is being stopped from doing so.'

Samson's voice flowed into a laugh and Algenon almost cried out as his mind bent into impossible shapes trying to understand the concept of the god's humour.

Algenon felt Samson standing over him in an effort to shield his mind. He tried to ask two final questions. His mind was weak and the words were quiet and mumbled, but he asked, 'What has happened to the exemplar of the One? And how can the Sisters act against Jaa?'

As he fell into a deep sleep, largely oblivious to his surroundings, Algenon thought of his brother and hoped that the world had not shifted sufficiently for honour to no longer mean anything. Magnus would give his life for Rowanoco, as would any true Ranen, but their fate was being manipulated by others and Algenon feared that the men of Ro were deep within the designs of the Seven Sisters and that Ro Canarn was merely the beginning.

CHAPTER SEVEN

SIR WILLIAM OF VERELLIAN IN THE CITY OF RO CANARN

WILLIAM HAD BEEN in Canarn five days. He had been at the vanguard of the assaulting army of knights and he was one of the first to enter the inner keep. He'd seen much death since he arrived in the city and had caused his fair share. He was a veteran of many campaigns and had seen both the best and the worst that the knights of the Red could do. As he stood on the heavy wooden drawbridge of the inner keep, William of Verellian thought that the sacking of Ro Canarn was one of the darker days he had witnessed.

The knights of the Red were pledged to the One God as warriors and conquerors. They served the aspect of war and were called upon by the king whenever battle was required. William had been from a noble house of Tiris and had joined the knights at the age of twelve. His family had served the One for as many generations as could be counted, though William was the first of his line to wear the red tabard.

He was a man of nearly forty years in age and had the scarred face of a seasoned soldier. His head was shaved and he wore no beard, making him distinctive among the Red knights.

As he looked down from the keep into the town square beyond, he was struck with a sense of shame, something he rarely felt. He could see funeral pyres of men – hundreds of burnt, distended bodies littering the cobbled streets. The mercenaries commanded by Sir Pevain were taking their payment from the populace, raping and stealing as they pleased. The city was dark and outside the central square no life could be seen.

William thought himself a true fighting man, a man who had joined the Red knights from choice, unlike the bound men below. He thought their behaviour deplorable and that the red tabards they wore should count for more than this.

Lieutenant Fallon, who stood nearby, had his hand on the hilt of his longsword and was glaring at the mercenaries below.

'Fallon,' William said sharply.

The knight saluted his captain. 'My lord?'

'Keep that hand steady,' William said, pointing to his longsword.

'Sergeant Callis, get those scum away from the women. Let no man take his payment in blood or flesh,' he said quietly to the man at his left.

Callis nodded and turned to issue orders to other knights. 'Right, lads, the captain wants those mercenaries taught about proper manners. Get your boots in and let's cause a few wounds,' he said plainly, with the practised bluster of the seasoned soldier.

Five knights drew their swords and marched down the drawbridge to the square beyond. Sergeant Callis began shouting orders at the mercenaries as he entered the square. They were silhouetted against the fire as William looked down, a grim expression on his face.

Fallon nodded approval at his captain and released his grip on his sword hilt. He was a good soldier and had been William's adjutant for six years. The captain thought that if Fallon were in the square he'd probably kill any man that looked at him, whereas Callis would simply follow orders and stop the worst atrocities.

The mercenaries argued as the knights approached, saying that the women were spoils of war and theirs by right. Callis ignored them and simply kicked the nearest one in the groin.

'Listen, you filthy bastards, you will stop this heathen shit right now or I will personally remove your fucking eyeballs.' He directed his knights to various mercenaries who had ignored him and stood with his chin thrust out.

William watched as several mercenaries were beaten and one was killed, though he felt no better now that an element of calm had returned to the square. He was still a knight captain of the Red and felt that a vanquished foe should be treated with respect. He was considered old-fashioned by many of the other knights, but he cared little for their approval and preferred simply to challenge and kill any who questioned his ethics too hard.

Knight Captain Nathan of Du Ban appeared over William's right shoulder and surveyed the square below. 'You can't stop this, you know?'

'I can,' William replied plainly.

'Those men have been promised plunder. That means they get to rape, torture and steal to their hearts' content.'

'They're vultures, picking on the bones of a defeated enemy.' William was angry and let it show in his words.

'Verellian, you would gladly kill the prisoners if they raised a sword to you. Why are you so squeamish about the afters?' he asked.

'If you were in command, you could watch. I am in command and I can't. It's simple.' William was not naive, but he did not like needless suffering.

Nathan smiled and realized he wasn't going to win the argument. 'How many dead?' he asked.

'Two hundred and fifty during the battle, a hundred in the keep and around two thousand in the last four days,' William answered. 'We took the city easily. These men were farmers and tradesmen, not warriors. The men in the keep fought well, but they were outmatched. Father Magnus was the only man to give our knights pause.'

Nathan sneered at the mention of the Ranen priest. 'He's a big boy, but I don't believe he killed ten knights.'

'He killed twenty-three knights and fourteen mercenaries. He had a huge war-hammer and apparently his eyes turned black. It's a gift of the Ranen priests, their god gives them strength when they call on it.'

William had seen the huge Ranen kill a number of knights but had been occupied with the duke's guard for the majority of the battle. Having spoken to the Ranen briefly before he entered the hall, William did not doubt the reports he'd heard. 'It doesn't matter now, Rillion will likely torture him to death for what happened in the great hall.'

'I doubt it,' Nathan replied.

William looked at him, his eyes betraying an element of suspicion. 'What do you know, captain?'

'Just that the Karesian witch seems intent on preserving the big man's life . . . Tobias was on guard duty outside the commander's room after the battle and swears he heard Rillion grunting like a novice whore within five minutes of the bitch going to see him.'

William shook his head. Knights of the Red were forbidden from taking women, and although past commanders he'd known had ignored the rule, he was disappointed that Rillion would be so brazen. It was an insult to the One, who had decreed the knights were to pledge all their energy to worship and to fulfilling the wishes of their god. The Gold church priests were infamous for their whoring and the Black tried to take as much out of life as they could, but the knights of the Red were to remain celibate.

Added to that was the unpleasant reality of who the woman was. William was not schooled in the ways of the Karesian witches, but had heard a hundred tales to make him fear and dislike the Seven Sisters of Karesia. Ameira had had too much influence over Rillion's actions and William thought his honour had now come into question. If the company had been still in Ro Arnon, William would have gone to see the abbot about his commander's behaviour; but as it was, they were far from home, in a city that had just been sacked, and William had no option but to accept Rillion's actions.

'Are you going to have Callis clean up the whole city, or is watching him beat a few heads in sufficient?' Nathan queried in a mocking tone. 'I suppose we could fight the mercenaries now there aren't any men of Canarn left . . . they might put up a better fight.'

'Has the abbot found out about your bastard son yet, Nathan?' William asked with venom.

The other knight scowled and moved to block William's view of the square. 'The piety is getting old, Verellian. Half the men under your command have bastards, and the other half haven't fathered any simply because they're too scared of you. It might make you better company if you got your cock wet occasionally.' Nathan cast a vicious grin at William.

He was of the same rank as Verellian but commanded a separate unit. His men were in the great hall, standing guard over the commander and they had been stationed inside the city during the attack on the keep. Nathan's home, the town of Du Ban, was several leagues north and west of Arnon and famed for producing arrogant and violent knights of the Red.

Knight Lieutenant Fallon, who had heard the conversation, approached the two captains and shot a dark look at Nathan.

William maintained eye contact with the other captain, but he tried not to let the insult make him angry. The man was a fool, but William thought that being foolish should not be enough to get your legs broken.

He took a step forwards. 'If you mistake honour for piety again, brother knight, I'll call you out and kill you in front of all your men. You might even die with honour.'

Fallon drew his sword and stood next to his captain. Staring intently at Nathan, he said, 'I would gladly fight the duel in your stead, my lord. I think I could teach my brother knight about respect and devotion to the One.' He swung his sword suggestively as he spoke and William smiled. Nathan was not the first man to insult him and Verellian thought him a streak of piss next to any true fighting man.

Nathan sneered and tried to look down his nose at William and his lieutenant. He briefly considered saying something clever, but the confident smile on William's face persuaded him otherwise and he left quickly, his steel armour loudly sounding his retreat on the wooden drawbridge.

Fallon sheathed his sword and chuckled to himself as he watched Nathan go. He then turned to his captain and banged his fist on his red tabard in salute. 'Shall I go and slit his throat, my lord?'

'Maybe later,' replied William.

* * *

Several hours passed and William maintained a vigil over the town square, ordering Callis to intervene whenever the mercenaries became too rowdy.

He had been ordered to enter the great hall at midnight, but decided to be slightly late. William considered his commander a man of little honour and felt he would be allowed ten minutes of tardiness.

'Fallon, you're with me, Callis can handle this,' he said, turning sharply and walking back up the drawbridge.

Most of William's men were sitting round small cooking fires in the courtyard of the keep, trying to ward off the cold. The wind blowing off the sea of Canarn penetrated the stone walls and made the temperature drop sharply during the night.

These men were not interested in pillaging the fallen city and most were simply waiting for their orders to return to Ro Arnon. William was proud of the way they had conducted themselves. They had fought hard and with ruthless skill, but they had also treated fallen enemies with respect.

'Captain Verellian, do we have orders yet, sir?' asked an old knight sergeant called Bracha.

'Not yet, Sergeant, there's no sign of the way home. Though the commander may yet have orders for me.'

He looked over the faces of his men. They wore hard expressions and William guessed that they, too, found the treatment of the people of Canarn distasteful.

'If any of those mercenaries or bound men find their way into the keep, be sure to remind them that we command here, not that horse-fucker Pevain. Understood, sergeant?'

Bracha smiled as he saluted. 'Perfectly clear, sir, we'll make sure they remember their manners.'

William commanded a company of one hundred men, though only twenty-five of them had come to Ro Canarn. The rest were still in Arnon, probably glad they had stayed in barracks. Four of his men had died in the attack on the keep and they had already been burned. Their funeral pyre was now just a small mound of blackened wood, and the knights' ashes had been gathered and scattered from the high battlements.

'How long do we have to stay here?' Fallon asked as they walked across the courtyard. 'I object to seeing men die to secure a pointless objective.'

'Pointless?' William questioned.

'What would you call it, my lord, a strategic campaign?'

William allowed his lieutenant to speak his mind and was happy with whatever he wanted to say in private, so long as he followed orders and didn't question his captain in public.

'I'd call it what it is . . . we sacked Ro Canarn because we were ordered to do so,' William answered. 'If we had the leisure to choose where we fight, we wouldn't be very good knights, would we?'

'Sir, I am a knight of the Red and I fight and die where I'm told to, but a child with a farming tool could have bested most of the defenders and the city has done nothing to warrant the treatment it's getting. I'm not a complete bastard who enjoys killing weaker men.' He paused. 'I'm a bastard, admittedly, but . . .'

'Fallon, could we leave this for now? I'm sure we'll be here a while and I'll no doubt have ample opportunity to hear about how unfair you think the world is.'

William was used to hearing the man's complaints and he had long since realized that most of them were simply a plea for a worthy opponent. Fallon was the best swordsman William had ever known and was rarely challenged when he had his blade in his hand. He took great offence at having to watch a mismatched fight, and this extended to seeing mercenaries rape and torture captives who could not fight back.

'Why can't we fight men worthy of our steel? Is it too much to ask, am I being arrogant to want to test myself?' he asked, seemingly addressing the query skyward, towards the One God.

'If you wait long enough, he might give you a sign.' William said ironically. 'Or you could just shut up.'

Fallon screwed up his face as if the choice were a genuine one. 'I believe, on reflection, I'll shut up, my lord.'

'Good news at last, perhaps Commander Rillion will promote you for showing such wisdom,' William said as the two of them reached the wooden staircase leading from the courtyard to the great hall.

William had been in his armour for four days, removing it only to sleep and wash, and his under-tunic and leggings were stuck to his skin with sweat and grime. He looked down at his tarnished breastplate and the red tabard that covered it – both were badly in need of repair. Fallon was in a similar state. On official occasions, and when required to stand before their commanders, it was normally the done thing for knights to appear at their best. Currently, their best was several hundred leagues away in the barracks of Ro Arnon.

William still wore his red cloak, though it was stained and torn. Fallon had lost his at some point since the battle and had not thought to find a replacement. As they walked up the stairs and reached the first of three landings, William stopped and looked critically at his lieutenant's appearance.

In response, Fallon held his arms out and asked, 'What, am I not suitably attired to meet men of quality?'

'You're never attired to meet men of quality, but right now neither of us looks any better that a city watchman.'

'I put on my best for men I respect, my lord. Even if I did have my ceremonial cloak, I'd probably find a reason to lose it,' Fallon said with a hard look in his eyes.

'That's enough of that . . . I think he's a shit-stain as well, but we will show him every courtesy to his face. Clear?' William spoke with practised authority.

'As the Ranen sea, my lord.'

William chuckled and resumed his march up the stairs. This was the second time he had walked up here since nightfall. The first time, he had been escorting Father Magnus, the Ranen priest who had killed two members of his company. Now he was to receive orders from Knight Commander Rillion and he doubted he'd be treated to the same display of knights in ceremonial garb as the Ranen. Rillion was inclined to show off for defeated enemies, confident that it would discourage further conflict. In fact, it served mostly to anger people who hated the Ro and their One God.

The same two guardsmen were on duty outside the door to the great hall and William once more thought it strange that the king's guard should be in Ro Canarn. It was probable that if the king were coming here, William would have been told. However, King Sebastian was a cunning man and his leaving Ro Tiris in secret would not be out of character.

'You know what Bracha thinks?' Fallon asked as they neared the door.

'No, lieutenant, what does Bracha think?' William said with a groan.

'He swears that the king's guard are here because the king is bringing a huge army to the Grass Sea. He says he heard one of Nathan's sergeants talking about an actual invasion,' Fallon replied in a conspiratorial whisper.

The guardsmen saluted as the two knights approached, their fists striking firmly on their gold breastplates. Both William and Fallon responded in kind and the door was swiftly opened.

As they entered the great hall, William leant towards Fallon and said quietly, 'Don't you think we'd know if we were going to be invading the Freelands?'

Fallon responded with a sceptical look, the expression of a soldier who expects the worst of his superiors.

Within, the hall was cold and dark, lit only by a few flickering torches held in dark metal braziers. The line of crossbowmen was gone and William walked slowly across the dark stone floor. The banners of Canarn now appeared more sombre: dark images of Brytag, horses and swords in colours of green, black and brown. Three ranks of wooden pillars spread away from the corridor and little could be seen in the darkness between them.

'Before we came here, I heard that Duke Hector's hall was one of the most welcoming places in Tor Funweir,' said Fallon with a sneer.

'It was brighter a few hours ago. Rillion put on a bit of a show for the Ranen,' William replied.

'Do we not warrant a bit of a show, then?'

'We barely warrant any lights, apparently,' William said, sharing Fallon's laugh.

'Captain Verellian,' a voice bellowed from the hall, 'this is not the proper time for laughter.' The voice came from an old man seated by the feast tables. 'Men are dead and the One is displeased.' He mumbled to himself before he continued. 'Though he seems displeased by much these days . . . perhaps laughter is the proper response.' He waved a frail hand towards the two knights and beckoned them over to him.

He was a man of at least seventy years and his plain white robe showed no sign of any of the clerical orders. If the man was a churchman, he was very much off duty.

William raised his eyebrows and glanced at Fallon before walking over to the old man. He sat alone in the great hall, surrounded by the remnants of a large feast. The central fire-pit was down to smouldering embers and all the assembled knights had left for other duties. The huge vaulted ceiling rendered the hall cavernous and dark; the only lights were at ground level.

'You wear no rank, sir, to whom do we speak?' William asked politely of the old man.

'You speak . . . you speak as a man of import, young sir,' he muttered, looking through narrow eyes at William. 'You are Marcus of Verellian's son?'

'I am, sir, though I've not see my father for many years,' William replied, although his manner was abrupt. The old man had not identified himself and William was suspicious of such men, no matter how old.

The man's breath carried the stench of wine and William guessed that he was a little drunk.

'I heard that you and your knights were here and I see now that the sword you carry looked better at your father's waist.' He squinted to get a better look at William. 'Though you look nothing like him,' he added venomously.

Fallon chuckled and William shot a glare at his lieutenant, before turning back to the old man. 'No, sir, I still have both of my legs and my father has not spoken, let alone held a sword, for some ten years.'

'Well, you are the lord of Verellian, whether you deserve it or not. Now, smarten yourselves up, the noble Lord Mortimer Rillion awaits you.' He looked at the tarnished and battered armour worn by the two knights. 'Hopefully, he'll remember that he is a gentleman as he assesses your worth.'

Neither William nor his lieutenant laughed at this, and the old man appeared oblivious of the fact that both of the knights were thinking about punching him. He chuckled to himself and reached for a goblet of wine.

Fallon took a step forward and looked down at the seated man. 'Tell us who you are, old man, or I may have to become unpleasant.'

The man did not stop chuckling. He noisily took a gulp of wine and squinted up at the lieutenant. 'Put your cock away, boy, I'm not a fight for you. I'm Roderick of the Black, a cleric with far too much time to drink and insult knights.'

Fallon took a step back, but didn't retreat entirely. 'You were in the square earlier, giving last rites to the funeral pyres.' His demeanour softened.

The Black cleric started laughing, took another swig of wine, and had begun crying by the time the goblet left his lips.

Both the Red knights had seen this before; clerics of the Black had an ability to feel the emptiness of death and could become quite volatile when faced with large amounts of it. Most became

185

crusaders or ministers so as to avoid such things and it was unusual to see a Black cleric of such an age accompanying a battle fleet.

'Brother Roderick, perhaps you should sleep. It is dark outside and I'm sure your bed is preferable to an empty hall,' William said gently.

He nodded to Fallon to help him and reached for the cleric's shoulders. The two knights helped the old man to his feet and led him away from the table.

'I can manage, I'm still fit enough to best any man you care to put before me. I certainly don't need any help getting to bed,' he said with irritation, pushing away William and Fallon. He stumbled forwards a few steps, aiming at a side door.

Before William could speak, Brother Roderick stopped and swung round. 'Knight Commander Rillion awaits you in the antechamber yonder.' He gestured extravagantly towards an open doorway behind the raised platform.

William raised his eyebrows at Fallon and started towards the open door. Brother Roderick made it to the side door and leant heavily on the door frame, before clumsily leaving the hall.

'I'm not sure the chance to fuck and drink is worth having to experience that,' Fallon said grimly.

'He should have retired to a nice, cosy church,' William replied. 'Though, if he's the Sir Roderick from the Falls of Arnon, I may have heard of him.'

'Oh really, what's he done?'

'I think he was a crusader, the abbot of the Gray Keep, and from what I hear a cleric who refused to continue killing risen men.'

It was unusual, but not unheard of, for a Black cleric to see some humanity in the faces of the risen and to fall from the crusade.

'He was the man who claimed he saw the light of a dead god in the eyes of the last one he killed,' William added.

'Yeah, yeah, I've heard that swill before. I leave weighty matters to my betters, sir. I prefer just to think of them as undead monstrosities and leave it at that.' Fallon was a simple man and had not given the other clerical orders much thought.

He screwed up his face as he spoke. 'Although, it explains why they've got him ministering to funeral pyres at his age . . . former abbot or not, he disobeyed orders.'

The two knights of the Red crossed the hall and approached the open doorway. The raised platform, where Duke Hector once sat, had been stripped of adornments. The bloodstains had been recently cleaned from the flagstone floor where the duke had been executed and Father Magnus had entered his battle rage.

'He killed four knights apparently,' William said to his lieutenant. 'He broke his chains when Rashabald beheaded the duke.'

Fallon shook his head. 'Any knight who wants to be an executioner is not fit to execute men.'

William knew his lieutenant had an extreme dislike for Sir Rashabald and had, on more than one occasion, tried to call him out and kill him. Rillion had always intervened and protected the old executioner: he liked a man with a sadistic streak similar to his own.

The doorway led through to the duke's personal chambers where Sir Rillion had positioned himself. The dark wooden desk had been cleared of Hector's belongings and now contained piles of paper, troop rosters, maps and injury reports. Two members of Nathan's company stood guard within the room, their armour untarnished by battle or from sleeping in the courtyard. Fallon glared at them and picked an imaginary bit of dust from the armour of one.

Within the room sat Rillion, Brother Animustus of the Gold church, and Ameira, the Karesian witch William had heard called the Lady of Spiders. Two more knights stood guard in ceremonial armour behind their commander, and the crossed swords and clenched fist of the Red church hung defiantly from the ceiling.

Commander Rillion still wore his armour and looked up across the light of several candles to William and Fallon. The room was primarily lit by flaming braziers in the four corners, but Rillion had clearly been studying papers and squinted to focus on the two knights before him.

'Verellian, please come in,' he said with a wave of his hand. 'I'll try to ignore the lateness and put it down to a head injury during the battle.' His tone was mocking and his scarred face twisted in an unpleasant sneer.

William and Fallon came to stand in front of the desk and both the knights banged their fists on their breastplates in salute. Animustus, the Gold cleric, was drinking wine from a large brass goblet and barely acknowledged the two knights.

'My lord, we've been busy supervising the mercenaries in the town. It takes more work than we thought,' William said.

'Yes, Captain Nathan stomped through here a minute ago complaining about your supervising tactics. He thinks you're too soft,' Rillion replied, leaning back in his chair.

'Captain Nathan should be careful what he says. I already have several reasons to call him out.' William could see the smile on Fallon's face.

Rillion chuckled and the Gold cleric gave an amused snort, showing that he was listening. 'Well, then, I'd say Captain Nathan should thank me for the orders I'm about to give you.' The commander shifted his weight, flexing his neck to remove the stiffness. 'The duke's daughter has eluded the squads of knights sent into the tunnels.' He turned to the Karesian enchantress. 'The noble lady Ameira believes that the Black Guard Bronwyn has already made it out of the city.'

William disliked the way the commander looked at Ameira and again sensed that she exerted more influence over him than his knights knew.

Ameira stepped forward and William thought for a moment that she had detected what he was thinking. The witch had lustrous black hair and deep green eyes. Her robes were black and flattering in a way that was clearly not accidental. William disliked her spider's web tattoo and did not want to be too close to her. He was not naive enough to believe every story he had heard about the Seven Sisters, but he did not doubt that Jaa had gifted them with strange hypnotic abilities.

The witch locked eyes with him for a second and William looked away sharply. 'My lord, I am not comfortable in the presence of an enchantress,' he said with conviction.

Ameira laughed, a lyrical sound that made Rillion smile with a slight euphoria. She stepped forward and stood in front of the commander's desk, making it difficult for William to not look at her. 'Sir Verellian, surely you do not think me a danger?'

'Enough of this,' Rillion interrupted sharply. 'Ameira, please don't tease the captain. William, you are to travel north and apprehend the girl. Clear?'

The witch smiled and backed away, returning to stand at the commander's shoulder.

'It is clear, my lord,' William said. 'Do we know where she went?'

'She had help escaping. A Karesian spy called Al-Hasim killed eight knights and then escaped somewhere into the town. When Pevain finds him, we'll know where she went.'

'Surely he left town with Bronwyn?' Fallon asked.

Sir Rillion looked at the lieutenant as if he disliked being spoken to by an adjutant. His eyes narrowed and his face fell back into its customary sneer.

'Well, Lieutenant Fallon of Leith, I imagine we must appear very stupid to you. Hasim was seen shortly after Father Magnus had healed him. Castus, the gaoler, saw the spy leaving via the food trough but he couldn't level his crossbow in time to kill the dog. It seems the heathen powers of the Ranen make a considerable glow when they are used, and Castus was alerted. Sir Pevain was despatched an hour ago and will capture the man and extract the necessary information.

'In the meantime, you will ride north to the Grass Sea.' He stroked his beard as he spoke. 'We will send a fast rider with news of her location when we know it. Pevain has men with him who are skilled at . . . extracting information.'

The euphemism for torture bothered William. He knew that it was often thought okay for those under the command of knights to engage in such activities, so long as the knights themselves did not, but the practice was very much a grey area within the church.

'Is that all, my Lord Rillion?' William asked. 'Travel north and try to find the girl?'

The commander glanced at Ameira before he answered. 'And you are to kill any members of Wraith Company you encounter.'

William narrowed his eyes and considered the order for a second before he spoke. 'My lord, I wasn't aware that we were at war with the Free Companies?'

'We are not, and if you keep them away from the city, hopefully we will remain not at war with them.'

'If those are your orders, my lord.' William was a seasoned knight and wasn't going to argue. 'We'll muster the men and leave within the hour.'

Rillion waved his hand as if to dismiss them. William and Fallon repeated the salute and turned to leave.

William gave in to curiosity as he went to exit the room and turned back to his commander. 'My lord, am I to understand that the king is coming here?'

Rillion scowled at the knight and, with another glance at Ameira, said, 'Yes, Verellian, he'll be here within the next two weeks. The death of Hector the betrayer was only the beginning of our work in Ro Canarn. King Sebastian has other duties for us to perform.' He narrowed his eyes and became guarded. 'Do not worry, Captain Verellian, by the time you return from the Grass Sea, our duty will be clear.'

'Yes, sir,' William said wearily as he turned away.

Once the knights were out of earshot, Fallon turned to his captain. 'What about him,' he said with anger, 'can I slit his throat?'

'I'm not sure we can justify killing the new knight protector of Ro Canarn.'

William was deep in thought and greatly troubled that the words of a follower of Jaa should hold so much influence over a knight of the Red. Even more worrying was that Fallon's gossip might be true, and that the king might be intending to attack the Freelands.

'So, what do we do, sir?' Fallon asked.

'We follow orders, my dear boy,' he replied. 'We follow orders and die where we're told to die.'

* * *

Al-Hasim had seen the two knights enter the antechamber and had waited in the secret passage for them to emerge. He had heard much of what they'd spoken about with their commander and was worried for a number of reasons. He hoped that the two hours' head start Bronwyn had was enough, and that Wraith Company would find her before the knights did. It was at least a two-week journey to Ro Hail and Bronwyn would not know that she was being pursued. Either way, Hasim could do little to help her and she would need to show her mettle in order to remain free.

The secret passages provided an excellent way to move covertly around the keep and he'd spent half an hour or so curled up in a ball looking out of a secret door high in the rafters of the great hall. Magnus had healed him just in time, as the Red pig, Castus, had appeared and fired his crossbow at the Karesian a moment later. Since then, he'd tried to find Kohli and Jenner, the Karesian brothers who'd smuggled him into the town in the first place.

Sir Hallam Pevain was a tenacious pursuer and Hasim had been close to capture twice. First, when he'd hauled himself out of the trough, a shout from Castus had alerted the mercenaries above. He'd not stayed to fight, but had thrown himself into a nearby sewer which ran along the walls of the keep, and the smell had been enough to dissuade the mercenaries from following him. Around an hour after that, as he'd emerged from the sewer into a stable near the blacksmith's guild, he'd been spotted by Pevain's bastards and had to run into the dark streets of Canarn.

He'd not known that Pevain was after him personally until later, when he was hiding in the tunnels of the keep and overheard Rillion shouting at the mercenary knight for taking too long in finding him.

He had not yet had time to worry about the Lady of Spiders. Algenon had told him little about the witch. Hasim believed that she was manipulating Rillion – that much was obvious – but to what end, he was not sure.

The thain of Fredericksand was inscrutable at the best of times and, where the Seven Sisters were concerned, he was downright mysterious. Hasim trusted Algenon, though, and was now of the opinion that his next move should be to free Magnus from his gaol cell.

Kohli and Jenner would have gone to ground during the battle, and Hasim was certain they'd have found a warm place to hide with plenty to drink. The brothers were from Thrakka, a city several leagues to the south of Al-Hasim's home of Kessia, and were the kind of Karesian scum that Hasim liked. They worked for money to buy alcohol and women, making them very predictable in Hasim's eyes. They also owned a boat, which would be a likely escape route once Magnus was freed.

Hasim backed away from the hatchway high above the great hall and crawled back down the narrow tunnel. He wondered who would have installed such a covert listening point, but he was glad they had done. He'd found several such places throughout the keep – narrow passageways, large enough to crawl down, which looked in on most of the rooms in the building. He'd even found several spy-holes that looked in on the other secret tunnels, and had more than once observed Pevain's mercenaries as they searched for him. He'd remained hidden thus far, not wanting to alert them to his presence by killing any of them. However, he was becoming frustrated with his inability to move freely. Hasim was not used to being hunted and found it an unpleasant sensation.

As he left the watch-hole, he was faced with a steep set of stairs that led back down to the main body of secret passages. Beyond was a small wooden door, no more than five feet high and largely invisible from the other side. Each of the doors to the watch-holes had a small peephole, through which Hasim could make sure the way was clear.

As he walked down the small staircase, he thought quickly. Magnus would not be easy to break out of his cell and, even if Hasim could free his old friend, their position would still be a difficult one. He had to leave the city and he couldn't leave without the Ranen priest. He was fond of Magnus and had grown to value him as a friend. He'd miss the drinking sessions and talk of women bedded and battles won. Other than Brom and Rham Jas Rami, Magnus was the only other man Hasim had ever called brother, and that still meant something to him.

He looked through the peephole and saw nothing but a dark passageway. Beyond, he knew the tunnel led along the side of the great hall and then down through the walls adjacent to the keep. Al-Hasim had been in the tunnels for several hours and had already identified the best exits and the places least likely to be guarded. He needed to find Kohli and Jenner first, which meant exiting near the port. The Karesians would have retreated to their boat, hoping the knights wouldn't check the harbour. Hasim thought it unlikely that they'd have been able to leave the port after the battle and imagined they'd be cowering below decks with several bottles of wine.

Hasim opened the door slowly and immediately stopped. He felt pressure against the wood and was then flung back as the door was shoved back into him. Someone had been hiding beneath the peephole, waiting for him to leave.

Hasim hit his head firmly against the wooden steps and lost vision for a second as he heard a voice shout, 'Sergeant, I've found the Karesian!' followed by the sound of armoured steps moving quickly along the wooden tunnel beyond.

He tried to get to his feet, but fell back as an armoured knight of the Red flung the door open and advanced upon him. The sound of other knights approaching grew louder as Hasim inched back up the steps towards the watch-hole, drawing his kris blade and trying to focus on the advancing knight.

'You're mine, boy,' said the knight as he drew his sword, ducked under the small wooden doorway, and crouched at the foot of the stairs.

Hasim shook his head and hefted himself backwards on hands and knees. He was still dazed and only vaguely aware of the knight attempting to grab his foot as he scuttled back up the stairs to the watch-hole. He kicked out with as much strength as he could manage and heard a solid steel clang and a sharp intake of breath.

The knight stumbled back, getting his armour and sword tangled up in the narrow tunnel. Hasim swore to himself and rubbed his eyes. He could feel blood on the back of his head and was in considerable pain. Hasim turned and rapidly darted up the stairs.

'I'll make you bleed for that, horse-fucker,' shouted the knight as he advanced again towards the watch-hole.

Hasim briefly considered throwing his knife in order to silence the knight, but thought better of it as he reached the top of the narrow staircase. There was nowhere to go. The tunnel ended in the watch-hole overlooking the great hall and there was no way down, just a small grating through which the hall could be seen. He had to think fast, as reinforcements had reached the hatchway at the bottom of the stairs.

'He crawled up there. The scum's trapped, sir,' said the knight who'd found him.

'There's nowhere to go, boy, surrender and you may survive this,' said an older voice from the tunnel.

More men were converging on his location and Hasim could hear shouts and orders passed loudly along the tunnels. He breathed in heavily and shook his head. His wound was not bad and he began to think quickly.

Crouching, he moved as rapidly as he could down the tunnel towards the watch-hole. The knights below began moving through the hatchway and he could hear more men approaching. Holding the kris blade between his teeth, he reached the grating that overlooked the great hall of Ro Canarn and stopped.

'We're coming for you, little boy,' called the first knight, as he began ascending the cramped staircase.

Hasim couldn't fight his way through the knights. He was a realist and knew that, even in close quarters, there were too many, and this time he didn't have the advantage of surprise. Multiple shadows flowed over the top of the stairs and he could make out the voices of perhaps as many as ten knights approaching him. He started to laugh, an outburst of hysterical desperation.

Hasim glanced down through the watch-hole, took his kris blade from between his teeth and smashed it against the wood of the grate. The wood was solid, but Hasim was strong and he quickly broke off a piece. He hit it again and, as the first knight's head emerged at the top of the narrow stairs, he feverishly smashed at the wooden grating. Not enough of a gap had opened and he lay down on his back and kicked his feet into the wood. His left boot broke through, sending splinters into the hall below.

'Sergeant, the Karesian's trying to break through into the great hall.'

The sound of wood breaking was loud and Hasim could not hear if any of the knights were leaving. He spared a quick glance behind him and saw two men of Ro, their upper bodies squeezed into the narrow passageway at the top of the stairs. They began clumsily crawling towards him as he changed to a crouched position, braced himself, and flung his shoulder at the broken wooden grate. His weight was sufficient to finish the job his knife had started and, with a loud shout, he plummeted into the great hall.

He landed face up, with a thud, on one of the duke's feast tables. The fall had winded him and his shoulder felt as if it might be dislocated. Above, he saw the face of a knight poking through the broken watch-hole.

Hasim rolled off the table, got to his feet and quickly glanced around the hall. The main doors were open and beyond he could see the night. Behind the duke's platform several figures were emerging from an anteroom.

'You . . . Karesian,' shouted a voice from the antechamber, 'stop there!'

Hasim turned and saw Rillion and three knights, swords drawn, advancing on his position. He turned quickly and darted across the great hall. As he approached the darkness beyond the main doors, for a second he thought he might actually escape. As he began to smile he looked up and saw a figure approaching through the doors.

Sir Hallam Pevain entered the great hall slowly, his two-handed sword held casually across his shoulder blades. 'You're mine, Hasim,' he said with a growl.

A bell had begun to sound and Hasim could hear armoured feet approaching through several side entrances and antechambers. There was no obvious way of escape.

Behind him stood Commander Rillion and three knights of the Red, with Ameira, the Karesian enchantress, positioned in the doorway. The knights stood on the raised platform, by the duke's chair, content just to cut off Hasim's escape. In front of him, blocking his path to the main door, was Pevain and a dozen of his mercenaries. On both sides of the great hall, other Red knights appeared and encircled him. Hasim judged that he was finally captured.

Rillion drew his sword and stepped within ten feet of the Karesian. 'Al-Hasim, you are to stand down and be subject to the king's law,' he said with smug authority.

'And if I don't?' Hasim replied defiantly.

'Then I'll cut your arms off and give the rest of you to my boys,' Pevain butted in, grinning viciously and nodding at his mercenaries, who smiled and looked at Hasim as if he were a piece of meat.

'Pevain, we need information from this spy,' Rillion countered, causing the mercenary knight to look at the floor and nod with frustration. 'Don't kill him outright. Get the location of the girl from him and you can let your dogs turn him into a woman. Clear?'

Pevain and his men evidently liked this order. The bastards were known for not being too choosy when it came to rape, and Hasim had heard stories of men broken to the point of suicide after an encounter with them. Each of the dirty, grim-faced mercenaries was smiling at him, and a few even winked and licked their lips in anticipation.

Pevain advanced towards Hasim, his sword held low and his face twisted in a grotesque grin. Hasim had only his kris blade with which to defend himself.

'Do you yield?' Pevain asked mockingly.

'Do you?' Hasim shot back with venom.

He saw a group of five more knights of the Red enter the hall behind Pevain's mercenaries and stand in front of the large wooden doors, peering over the men in front.

Pevain didn't hesitate for more than a second before he lunged forward and aimed a powerful thrust at the Karesian's chest. He was a huge man and a skilled swordsman, but Hasim was faster and simply rolled to his right and across the wooden table he'd landed on.

Two mercenaries moved to cut him off and Pevain shouted, 'We can dance around the hall all night, Hasim, but you're going nowhere.'

Hasim found his feet on the other side of the table and crouched, spun round, and directed a lightning-fast kick at one of the mercenaries. The man's leg buckled and he fell, letting his longsword clatter to the ground. A second pursuer swung downwards at Hasim but missed as he darted back under the table, grabbing the fallen sword as he did so.

Pevain laughed as he said, 'The longer you wait the angrier my men will get . . . and they aren't gentle when they're angry. If you give up now, you might make a fine little Karesian wife.'

Hasim moved quickly along the floor as the mercenaries began to circle the table. Swords were swung at him, but either struck wooden chairs or missed entirely. Hasim had no real delusions about escaping, but was not going to give up easily. He did a forward roll out from under the table and knocked another mercenary to the floor as the others moved quickly in pursuit.

Pevain let out a roar of exertion and swung his huge sword downwards at the table between him and Hasim, splintering the wood down the middle. Hasim didn't turn to engage the huge mercenary knight but instead dived back across the broken table and rolled past him. He was met with a group of knights who had entered the hall from a side door and were brandishing weapons.

Hasim stopped, he was surrounded and out of options. The mercenaries and knights had him encircled and his room for movement was getting smaller and smaller as they penned him in. He held a longsword in one hand and his kris blade in the other, but he was faced with twenty or so Red knights and several dozen mercenaries.

He turned and was met with a powerful punch to the face from Sir Pevain. He felt blood flow from his nose and mouth and lost the strength in his legs for a moment, crumpling to a heap on the floor.

He looked up and rubbed the blood from his face, and saw dark faces loom into view. A kick to the stomach and he lost his breath, a kick to the back and he lost his grip on his weapons, and a kick to the groin and he exhaled sharply and involuntarily curled up into a ball on the stone floor.

'Don't kill him, you dogs, we need information from him,' ordered Rillion. His voice sounded close and Hasim was vaguely aware of him shoving the mercenaries aside. 'Pevain, control your bastards.'

Hasim was pulled roughly to his feet and received another punch in the face from Pevain, though this time he was held and not allowed to fall. He was shoved between the mercenaries for a few minutes, punched, kicked, insulted and goaded with promises of rape and worse. Then he was thrown against another table and doubled over, wheezing heavily and spitting blood.

Pevain grabbed him by the neck and held him up to his face. 'Where is the duke's slut of a daughter? Where did you send her?'

Hasim laughed weakly and spat blood in Pevain's face. 'A few kicks and punches I can handle, you sorry excuse for a knight,' he said, with as much bravado as he could muster.

Another powerful punch to the face and Hasim spat out a tooth and felt his lips and jaw swell up.

Pevain turned back to Rillion and said, 'My lord, we need to apply a bit more pressure to this Karesian pig-fucker. He's a tough little bastard.'

Rillion nodded and Hasim was thrown back to the mercenaries. 'Break him,' commanded Pevain simply.

He tried to resist, but many hands held him and he was weak and unfocused from the repeated blows to his head and body. He lashed out and struck wildly at the faces around him, but his arms were quickly wrenched behind his back and a forearm was wrapped roughly round his neck. Vile calls came from the mercenaries as they argued who would get to violate him first, and Rillion and his knights simply watched.

Hasim didn't stop struggling, but he knew he had no chance of resisting as he was punched repeatedly in the stomach and bent over a feast table, his arms held firmly and a rough hand grasping his hair.

Just as he began to pray to Jaa for a swift death, he heard a man shout, 'Let him go!'

Hasim turned his head and identified the speaker as William of Verellian. The hawk-faced knight captain was standing just inside the great hall with five of his knights, who looked at Pevain's men with disgust.

'Not your business, Verellian,' said Pevain in response.

The captain stepped forward and glared at the huge mercenary. 'No man will take his payment in blood or flesh. That applies to you and your men. Cage him, imprison him, question him,' he said with menace, looking directly into Pevain's eyes, 'but cause him to bleed again or violate his flesh and I'll kill you.'

Verellian's men drew their swords and faced off against the mercenaries, most of whom were decidedly afraid at the sight of Fallon of Leith, a man renowned as one of the finest swordsmen amongst the knights of the Red.

'Captain,' barked Rillion, 'you overstep your bounds. We need information from this man. He's a criminal and your knightly code does not apply.'

Verellian looked offended, but maintained his composure. 'Apologies, my lord, but my knightly code applies in all situations and with all prisoners. I will not disobey a direct order from my commander, but neither will I stand down and let these animals cause any more pain to a captive, criminal or not.'

Fallon and Verellian both looked dangerous with their swords drawn, and the men with them would clearly think nothing of killing the mercenaries if they were ordered to do so. Pevain glared at the captain, but his men were unsure, as if they would rather not have to test themselves against true fighting men.

Hasim remained still, but chanced a quick look at Ameira. She was standing behind Rillion, evidently enjoying the confrontation. This was the closest he had been to her since he had arrived in Ro Canarn and he wondered if she knew that he worked for Algenon Teardrop.

Rillion stepped forward to stand next to Pevain, considering what to say to Verellian. He narrowed his eyes and slowly smiled.

'I'm honestly not sure who would win if I let the two of you fight.' He sized up the two armoured knights.

Pevain was larger by nearly a foot, but William of Verellian was a hard man and had a reputation as a swordsman who could kill quickly and efficiently. Pevain was younger, though not by much, and the match was even.

William took a step forward and stared up at the mercenary. Lieutenant Fallon let a hard glare play over the faces of the others.

Verellian didn't move his eyes from Pevain as he spoke to his commander. 'My Lord Rillion, I will gladly kill this man and all his bastards if it will convince you that the Karesian should be treated with honour.'

Pevain smirked, showing that he wasn't scared of the Red knight. 'Commander, let this boy-fucker try and I'll make him my little whore the same as that Karesian pig.'

Verellian didn't change his expression as he rammed his forehead into Pevain's nose. He had to rise on to tiptoes to reach the taller man, but the blow landed solidly and sent Pevain to his knees, clutching his smashed nose.

Two of the closest mercenaries automatically moved to attack Verellian, their swords brandished and eyes wild with anger. Fallon grabbed the first by the throat and casually kicked away his sword. The second turned to thrust at him, but was met with a parry and Fallon's riposte was a swift cut to his neck. The wound was clearly fatal and the assembled knights and mercenaries paused and stared as the dying man slowly fell.

Pevain gathered himself and, panting heavily, rose to his feet. Fallon took a step towards the remaining mercenaries, stepping over the dead man and twirling his longsword with skill. Verellian didn't move an inch as Pevain again stood nose to nose with the knight.

Commander Rillion began to laugh, breaking the ominous silence. 'Pevain, if you strike Captain Verellian, he'll kill you. Fallon and the others will then kill all of your men and no order from me will stop them,' he said with quiet authority. 'Put your sword down and take your dead man out of my hall. Enough blood has been cleaned off the floor today.'

'You should listen to him,' said Verellian in a near-whisper.

Fallon simply smiled at the mercenaries, and Verellian's other knights stood with swords drawn.

The man restraining Hasim had turned away and the Karesian had slumped to the floor, leaning against a wooden chair. He managed a slight smile at the idea of his honour being defended by knights of the Red.

The mercenaries all looked towards Sir Pevain and Hasim sensed they'd rather their leader did not continue the argument. They were tough men, but no match for a group of hardened knights of the Red, especially not this particular group of knights of the Red. William of Verellian had been known to Hasim even before he overheard him talking to the commander. His skill and honour were well known in Tor Funweir.

Pevain was grunting under his breath and no doubt imagining all manner of unpleasant torments he would visit upon Verellian, but he turned to his men and waved them out of the main hall. He then nodded to Commander Rillion and left, gingerly touching his broken nose.

* * *

Hasim had been tied to a horse and he found himself waiting, flanked by knights of the Red, at the gatehouse leading north out of Ro Canarn. It was just starting to rain and he was still sore from the beating he had taken.

Knight Commander Rillion had not been pleased with William of Verellian's interference and, as punishment, he'd given Hasim into the care of the knights to be taken north in pursuit of Bronwyn. Rillion evidently thought that threatening Hasim's life would make Bronwyn less inclined to run. What he did not realize was that Verellian was a knight to whom displays of terror did not come naturally.

Hasim was used to having his fate dictated to by others, but he disliked the thought of those people's strings being held by a Karesian enchantress. As he sat on the horse, Hasim wondered where the other Seven Sisters were, and what interest they had in Ro Canarn.

CHAPTER EIGHT

ZELDANTOR IN THE CITY OF KESSIA

S LAVERY WAS A reality to many Karesians. Zel had been a slave since he was a child and had never questioned his position. His mother was a Kirin, living in the woods of Lislan, and had apparently been killed by churchmen of Ro. Slavers, following the clerics, had taken Zel when he was too small to remember. Zel was not bitter about this, primarily because he had never known his mother, but also because he found the life of a slave to be a relatively pleasant one. The slavers had given him to a mobster in Kessia as a show of respect and he'd served the man faithfully.

He now served a woman called Saara, though she was often referred to as the Mistress of Pain. She was of the Seven Sisters and had purchased Zel from the mobster shortly before Zel's twelfth birthday. He was now fifteen and largely enjoyed his duties. Previously he'd been required to care for the fat old mobster, cleaning his tattered clothes and fetching his meals. On occasion he'd even had to wash the man, scrubbing his back and shoulders while singing soothing songs or reciting poetry. When he wasn't being a body slave, he'd been trained in the use of a scimitar and told that, when he grew stronger, he'd be one of the man's many bodyguards.

Zel was glad that Saara did not require him to bathe her, or even repair her clothing. She liked him to wake her with breakfast and the gentle ringing of a bell, but her daily demands were few. She required that Zel accompanied her virtually everywhere and trusted his discretion, even going so far as to ask his opinion on matters when they were alone. In the time they'd been together, Zel had stood next to her at all manner of interesting meetings and encounters.

The Seven Sisters were the enchantresses of Jaa and universally feared by common Karesians. They had the power of life and death over all those who claimed Jaa as their god and they were able to make demands of virtually everyone. Even in Kessia, where the merchant princes ruled, Saara was treated with nervous respect.

'Slave!' The voice came from one of two wind claws waiting outside Saara's chambers.

The Mistress of Pain had chosen to stay in an opulent residence in the south of the city, a quiet place built in the form of three towers around three gardens of meditation. Saara had asked for the top floor of one of the towers to be cleared and she now held court overlooking a beautiful fountain and a carefully tended garden of brightly coloured plants.

Zel's mistress had just finished talking to a merchant prince called Zamam and had requested a short break. She had spoken to a number of princes during the morning, and several mobsters the previous evening, and Zel had advised that she take an hour's rest. He'd seen her through to her marble bedroom and had then taken some time for himself. Currently, he was on the terrace that led from the top floor to the stairs and the ten floors below.

The inner walls of the tower were open, allowing guests to look down on the garden, and Zel found the low babbling of water from the fountain most relaxing.

'Slave, are you listening, boy?' one of the wind claws asked again.

Zel sighed at being pulled away from his quiet contemplation, turned and bowed deeply to the man before him. The wind claws were tall men, wearing the flowing black robes common to their order, and both carried two wavy kris blades at each hip. The man who had spoken had long black hair, tied in a braided topknot.

'Many apologies, master, I was deep in thought,' the slave said.

'A slave to an enchantress is still a slave, boy. Please remember your manners or I'll have you beaten.'

It was not as much of a threat to Zel as it would have been to a younger slave. A beating was a simple thing, easily endured and soon forgotten, and yet the nobles of Karesia evidently found the notion pleasing on some level.

'I meant no offence, noble master,' Zel said, bowing even deeper and holding his arms wide in a fawning gesture. 'Were you waiting for my mistress?'

'Well, I was considering waiting for her, but after the procession of merchant princes I've seen walking up those stairs, I'd imagine my presence would be positively boring by comparison,' the wind claw said, clearly deep in thought.

'If you give me your name, master, I'll be sure to tell my mistress that you are waiting. She's resting at the moment, but will be available again shortly.'

The wind claw looked at him, letting his eyes narrow and his speech become suspicious. 'I am Dalian, called the Thief Taker. She will know me.'

He spoke with little ceremony, but Zel had heard the name before. The Thief Taker was an infamous man in Kessia, a man who enforced the will of Jaa and was frequently brutal in doing so. He was not gifted by the Fire Giant, as were the Seven Sisters, but had chosen to serve faithfully, frequently questioning the enchantresses and their use of the powers granted to them. He was the greatest of the wind claws, the men who made sure that common Karesians adhered to the word of Jaa.

'This is Larix, called the Traveller. He has just returned from Tor Funweir with a message from Katja the Hand of Despair for your mistress.' The second wind claw was a younger man, with lighter skin. His black robes were in pristine condition, suggesting to Zel that they had not been worn recently.

'I'll be sure to tell her that you are waiting, masters,' Zel said with deference. He had met wind claws before, but never the Thief

Taker himself, and Zel was moderately impressed at his bearing.

The slave continued bowing as he backed away from Dalian and Larix and approached the ornate white doors that led to Saara's chambers. He turned slowly and opened the doors, not looking back to see if the wind claws had any other words for him. Zel enjoyed a degree of arrogance, being slave to one of the Seven Sisters, but, faced with a man of such reputation, he felt his self-confidence wither.

The Thief Taker had recently been responsible for the death of an old-blood, an insane Karesian with the blood of Giants who'd been hounding an outlying village. Another of the Seven Sisters had asked him to do so and, if rumour were to be believed, Dalian had burned the old-blood alive. This brutality was apparently typical of the man and Zel was glad to be out of his presence.

He walked through the white and gold sitting room to the bedroom door. The quarters were opulent and spotlessly clean, with four quilted chairs positioned round a central table. Zel was not permitted to sit on any of the chairs and had only been present in the sitting room while standing behind his mistress.

He straightened his light blue tunic and knocked gently at the wooden door. At fifteen, Zel was almost a man in Karesia, though his mixed lineage meant that little was expected of him. Even as a slave, being a Kirin meant he'd be looked down on for the rest of his life. He was short and slim from years of hard work and meagre diet, but his mind was sharp and his time with Saara had taught him much of the world.

Zel knocked again and heard his mistress stirring. She coughed and said, 'Zel, I need to rest. Whatever you want can wait.'

'Many apologies, my lady, but two wind claws are waiting outside and I believe one of them is called Dalian Thief Taker.'

There was a momentary pause. 'Very well, come in.'

Zel opened the door slowly and peered in. Seeing Saara lying across a white-sheeted bed of expensive fabrics, he moved to stand inside the room.

'The second man is called Larix and has a message from your sister in Tor Funweir, mistress.'

Saara smiled, a thin expression masked a little by sleep. 'Excellent,' she said, 'I think the Traveller may have good news for us.'

'Mistress . . .' Zel said, not moving from his position by the door, 'I'm confused.'

Saara rubbed the tiredness from her eyes and sat up, letting the covers fall from her body, exposing her naked breasts.

She smiled warmly at her slave. 'You are often confused, young Zeldantor. Come, rub my shoulders and tell me what you are confused about.'

The slave walked round the large bed and picked up a small vial of scented oil from Saara's bedside table. The enchantress removed the bedclothes entirely and shifted position to sit naked and cross-legged in the middle of the bed. Zel removed his sandals and climbed on to the mattress, kneeling behind his mistress. Her skin was smooth and light for a Karesian, and her lustrous black hair was delicately placed around her neck so as to allow Zel to reach her shoulders unhindered. The young Kirin had seen her naked numerous times and no longer felt embarrassed at the sight; in fact, he'd come to enjoy seeing his mistress unclothed, as she represented the ideal of womanhood to him. Though most men would never admit it, for fear of retribution, the Seven Sisters were all beautiful women. Even those who were plain when they were chosen gradually took on the same beauty within a few years. It was a part of their gift, and Zel assumed it was to make the act of seduction and enchantment easier, for that was the way of the Seven Sisters.

Zel uncorked the vial of oil, poured a small amount into the palm of his hand and began to rub it smoothly into her bare shoulders. Saara leant forward and closed her eyes as he began to massage her skin.

After a moment or two, his mistress straightened her neck. 'So, let us talk about this confusion of yours, Zel.'

'It can wait if you'd rather bathe and prepare to receive the wind claws, mistress.'

She turned her head and smiled warmly. 'Dalian can wait.

I would rather my body slave was fully informed of my actions before I see any more men.'

'Very well, mistress. Thank you.' He bowed his head.

'As long as you can talk and massage at the same time,' she said with a slight chuckle, a lyrical sound that reminded Zel of the way a songbird calls for a mate.

'Of course, mistress, your words to my actions,' he replied formally, as he continued to massage her shoulders and back. 'I'm confused about some of what has transpired since we arrived in Kessia, mistress,' he began. 'I understand that your sister had Dalian and the wind claws kill Jennek the old-blood, and I remember from a meeting you held with Lillian the Lady of Death, that the intention was to cause someone to leave the city ...' He paused as Saara half turned to look at him more directly.

'And?' she said.

'Well, I am confused about why the wind claws needed to be tricked and why you desired that the vizier of Jaa leave Kessia,' Zel continued politely.

Zel had been present when Saara had instructed her younger sister Lillian to enchant Dalian Thief Taker into hunting down Jennek of the mist, a strange old Karesian with Fire Giant blood. The goal had been to cause the spiritual leader of the city to leave in search of another old-blood, though Zel had been unable to discern why his mistress had done this.

The vizier was called Voon of Rikara. He was chief adviser to the emperor and a man whose word could sway all but the Seven Sisters. Voon had left Kessia shortly after the old-blood had been killed and the common belief was that he'd had a spiritual crisis of some kind, but Zel knew his departure had been a deliberate design of the enchantresses.

Saara smiled tolerantly and gently patted Zel on the cheek. 'It's really very simple, young Zel. With no old-blood to counsel him, Voon cannot hear the will of Jaa. Now, do you remember when we spoke about exemplars?'

Zel nodded. 'Yes, mistress, they were the Giants' commanders in the Long War. The knowledge of them and their purpose is hidden from most men becuase the gods dislike their intentions to be known.' Zel recited this verbatim from the time he'd been schooled by his mistress on the nature of the gods. 'But if we all serve Jaa, why would it be necessary to remove the only man in Karesia with a direct conduit to the Fire Giant?'

'You're still young, Zel, and though I trust you as only a mistress can trust her slave, I cannot tell you everything,' she said, peering into his eyes. 'If you had the chance to live free and whole without the influence of those who would seek to use you, would you take it?'

'I'm not sure I understand, mistress.' Zel shook his head and screwed up his face in confusion. 'I'm your slave and exist only to serve your needs,' he said with genuine sincerity.

'But I am a human of the lands of men. The beings that try to control us are neither of those things. They are Giants of their own realms and lack understanding of our lands.'

Saara had spoken of this before and Zel had come to accept that the Seven Sisters had a different perspective on the gods from that of the common people. Saara generally referred to them as Giants, and was less than happy to acknowledge their divinity. Zel had always imagined that this was a luxury afforded only to the highest followers of Jaa, but he was unsure where this belief had come from. The Seven Sisters were the priesthood of Jaa, much as the clerics of Ro or the priests of the Order of the Hammer were the servants of the other gods.

Saara sensed Zel's confusion and patted his cheek again, more tenderly this time. 'My dear Zel, the day may come when the world will not be as you imagine it. On that day, you will understand; until then, you must listen and learn all you can.'

Zel had left the bedroom door open and a loud bang on the outer doors of Saara's apartment caused both mistress and slave to jump.

'I think the Thief Taker may be getting impatient, mistress,' said Zel as he climbed off the bed.

'Well, perhaps making him wait will help him to learn his place,' Saara replied with an arrogant smile.

She slid gracefully to the floor and stretched her arms and back, leaning forward in a pose that would have caused many men of Karesia to feel uneasy. Her naked body was toned, with little fat, and she bore a tree-shaped scar on her lower back. Zel had asked her about it before and had been told that it was a darkwood tree, and that all the Seven Sisters had a similar mark.

Dalian banged loudly on the outer door a second time and Saara glared across her apartments angrily. 'Zel, please go and tell the wind claw that I will be with him presently and that his insistence is beginning to irritate me.'

Zel made his way to the apartment doors and gathered himself, adopting his customary expression of serenity, before he opened the door and smiled. The wind claws both looked irritated, though Larix stood further back and appeared less keen to knock on the door.

Dalian, however, had an imperious expression on his face and looked down his nose at Zel. 'Must we wait all day, Kirin?'

'Not all day, no. I shouldn't think you'll have to wait much longer, master,' Zel replied with a shallow bow.

Dalian stepped closer towards him, trying to exert his authority over the slave. Zel merely smiled, not letting the wind claw intimidate him.

'Dalian, there's no need for you to wait, I can see the enchantress on my own,' Larix said in an attempt to calm his companion.

The Thief Taker didn't move his eyes from Zel and he spoke slowly and deliberately. 'Your mistress should remember to treat Larix with the same respect with which she'd treat me. Is that clear?'

* * *

Larix the Traveller sat on a low reclining chair. He didn't lean back or relax, but merely perched on the edge of the chair, a controlled look on his face. Zel placed a jug of sweet desert nectar

and two glass goblets on the table and then went to stand behind
Saara. Larix averted his eyes from the enchantress and kept his
gaze directed at the floor. It was a common tactic with those who
sought an audience with the Seven Sisters, as general wisdom held
that the Sisters required eye contact in order to enchant people.
Zel knew that this wasn't the case, but he also knew that Saara
liked men to think that it was.

'My lady, I bring news from the north,' Larix began.

'Really? News from the north. I see,' Saara replied with just a
hint of mock naivety. 'Please tell me your news from the north.'

Larix looked briefly up, before pursing his lips and looking
back down at the floor. 'Your sister Ameira sends word that
her work is nearing completion in Ro Canarn, and Katja sends
word from Ro Tiris that they have begun capturing risen men
and have located the Ghost. It seems that whatever designs you
have in Tor Funweir are proceeding smoothly.' The words were
spoken plainly, as if Larix did not know the meaning behind
the Sisters' actions and was merely presenting facts as he had
been told them.

'I sense your confusion, sweet Larix,' Saara said in a low, husky
voice. 'I believe I also sense your disapproval.'

The Traveller shook his head and suddenly appeared to be in
some discomfort. Zel noticed Saara smile and saw her slender hand
make subtle patterns in the air between them. Larix held the sides
of his head firmly and involuntarily looked up, locking eyes with
Saara for the first time. The enchantress opened her mouth and
breathed out, a gentle distortion of the air, visible as it passed from
her lips across the low table to Larix. As she worked her subtle
magic, Zel wondered if Larix knew he was now in thrall to two
of the Seven Sisters.

'Larix the Traveller, warrior of the wind claws, you are a loyal
and dutiful servant of Jaa . . .' she closed her eyes and let out a
small whimper of pleasure, 'and you should be rewarded for your
faithful service. The view from my window is most enchanting,
please go and see for yourself.'

Larix now looked with blank eyes at Saara. His hands had fallen limply by his sides and he was entered into a trance. With little pause, he stood and walked directly to the open window which looked out over the meditation garden ten floors below. Placing both hands on the windowsill, he peered down. Saara did not stand or turn to look at him, but continued to moan in pleasure as the feeling of enchanting another filled her body.

She squirmed slightly in her chair and breathed the words, 'The garden is beautiful, dear, sweet Larix. You must take a closer look.'

Larix the Traveller didn't look back, he simply hefted himself up on to the window ledge and flung himself out, making no sound as he fell until his life ended with the sound of the impact below. Zel heard screaming from the garden and ran to the window. Ten floors below he saw the smashed body of the wind claw lying across the rim of an ornamental fountain. His blood was spreading into the water and the dark red formed an ugly contrast to the light-coloured blooms of the garden.

A sound from his mistress made him turn back and he saw her writhing with pleasure on her chair, eyes closed and in a state of bliss. Zel considered saying something, but thought better of it and turned back to the window. A small group of people had gathered round Larix's body and several guardsmen were trying to make sense of what had happened.

'Zel, come away from the window,' said Saara between deep, pleasurable breaths. She had exerted herself considerably and looked flushed. Her slave moved quickly to kneel on the floor in front of her.

'Are you well, mistress? Perhaps another short rest might be in order,' he said with concern.

She smiled thinly. 'I think I am, but thank you for your concern. Maybe just an hour or two would be wise.'

Zel's mind swam with questions, but he thought of his duties first. He must ensure that Saara was well and rested; questions about Larix's death would have to wait. His mistress would tell him in good time, he thought, as he poured her a glass of desert nectar and stood before her with his head bowed. Saara took the glass and drank deeply of the sweet liquor, panting between mouthfuls. She let Zel take her arm as she swayed towards the bedroom, gently pushing him away at the edge of the bed.

Zel closed the door quietly as Saara lay down on her bed. The slave knew that using her powers was an exhausting activity and that she'd be too fatigued to rise from her bed for several hours. He did worry, however, that Dalian Thief Taker would return to find out what had happened to Larix and that the enchantress would have to rise early to deal with the wind claw.

Saara had already told Zel that, depending on what news she received, they would probably be taking a trip to Tor Funweir in the near future; he'd even heard his mistress talking to a whip-master of the Hounds about the pack of soldiers that would be accompanying them. Exactly why Saara was planning to sail across the Kirin Ridge to Ro Weir with ten thousand Hounds was not clear. Zel did not think it an invasion, nor did he think they'd be occupying the city. From what he could gather, the king of Tor Funweir had given the Hounds permission to cross the sea and the whip-master had begun preparing his pack several weeks ago. Zel thought it inconceivable that such a build-up of soldiers would remain invisible to the Ro, so they must be compliant to some degree.

Of the Seven Sisters, two were currently in Tor Funweir and the other four were in Kessia awaiting instructions from Saara. The news Larix had delivered was clearly favourable and the final stages of a long game were being played out in the lands of men.

* * *

Several hours passed before Saara rose from her bed. Zel had been sitting on the balcony of their apartment watching the scene build up around the dead body of Larix. Guardsmen had arrived quickly and ushered away the various onlookers; the residents of the building – rich merchants for the most part – had begun to leave when they realized who had died. The death of a wind claw was not an insignificant thing and many had simply wanted to distance themselves from the scene.

The body had been removed within the hour and several guardsmen had tentatively enquired after Saara, though most had simply knocked and left when Zel didn't answer the door. Zel thought that his mistress was the only person in the building not to have been spoken to by the city officials. He had witnessed the questioning take place, with only a vague level of interest, as if the guardsmen knew that sooner or later they would have to speak to the enchantress.

Dalian Thief Taker had not reappeared and Zel hoped he wouldn't learn of his companion's death until later, allowing Saara time to be fully rested before the inevitable confrontation. Zel had to admit to himself that he was afraid of the wind claw and would rather not have to explain to him how Larix had fallen to his death.

'Zel, has the commotion played out yet?' Saara asked as she entered the sitting area and took her place on a luxurious couch. She was wearing a thin silk dressing gown and had a look of natural beauty about her.

'Not yet, mistress, I think the guardsmen are just wasting time interrogating the residents until they can speak to you. I've ignored their knocks at the door so far,' the Kirin slave replied, turning to smile broadly at Saara.

'Very well, maybe you could go and summon the head guardsman for me and we can sort this out quickly, before . . .' she paused, looking at the sundial positioned next to Zel on the balcony, 'my appointment at the Well of Spells.'

'At once, mistress,' Zel said with a nod of his head which flowed into a deep bow of respect.

He backed away from Saara and opened the apartment door. Stepping out on to the landing, he was greeted by four guardsmen waiting nervously outside. They had been quiet as they waited and Zel thought they must just be staying on the off-chance that the enchantress would be willing to speak to them. They looked up as the slave emerged and smiled serenely at them.

'My mistress would like to speak to whichever of you is in charge,' he said with a shallow bow.

The guardsmen looked at each other before one of them moved to the railing that overlooked the garden and shouted down to his commander. 'Master Lorkesh, the enchantress wants to see you,' he said loudly.

The other men were relieved that they would not be required to enter Saara's rooms and Zel thought he heard a quiet prayer to Jaa from one of them. Common men of Kessia were deeply superstitious, a predilection actively encouraged by the wind claws and the Seven Sisters, who both understood that Jaa valued fear above all things.

The man called Lorkesh walked slowly up the stairs to the tenth floor, where Zel waited. The slave continued to smile calmly and enjoyed the thought that he was making the guardsmen nervous by maintaining direct eye contact with each of them. Zel was proud of the sinister air he'd cultivated since he had begun working for Saara.

It took some time for Lorkesh to reach the tenth floor of the building. He was older than the men outside the apartment and was wheezing as he emerged at the top of the staircase.

'Why is it that people of station always feel the need to stay as high up as possible?' he asked rhetorically. 'Is the ground somehow offensive to important people?'

One of the other men saluted him and motioned towards Zel. 'The slave tells us that the enchantress will see you, sir,' he said, glad to be able to turn away from Zel's serene gaze.

Lorkesh stood, leaning against the open ledge and breathing heavily from the ascent. The way he averted his eyes from looking down made Zel think the man was uncomfortable with heights. He puffed out his chest and turned to Zel. Lorkesh was a rather fat man, not as vigorous as a guardsman should be, and his world-weary features suggested someone built for wit rather than action.

'You're slave to the enchantress?' he asked. 'But you're a Kirin.' He raised his eyebrows at Zel's mixed lineage.

'Indeed, sir,' Zel replied. 'I see the guard of Kessia are ruthless in their pursuit of truth.'

Lorkesh was uncertain whether the slave was trying to be funny, but made a slight grunt and dismissed the comment.

'Very well, show me through to your mistress.' He leant in close to one of the other men. 'What's this one called?'

'Saara the Mistress of Pain, sir,' the guardsman replied.

'Wonderful,' Lorkesh said ironically, as he followed Zel into the apartments, his breathing now more shallow and regular.

Saara still sat on the couch, her legs crossed and several inches of thigh showing under her dressing gown. She smiled as Zel and Lorkesh entered and beckoned for the guardsman to come closer and sit opposite her. Zel remained by the door, closing it with a thud that made Lorkesh jump.

'Please, have a seat,' Saara said in her sensual, lyrical voice.

Lorkesh was making some effort to not look at the enchantress as he nervously crossed the apartment and sat.

'Right, your . . . Sister-ness, ladyship . . . er, hello.' He smiled slightly. 'A man we believe to be Larix the Traveller of the wind claws was found dead beneath your balcony some time ago. I obviously need to ask you some questions,' he said with practised discretion.

The guardsmen of Kessia were professional men, neither nobles nor slaves, and maintained order in the dangerous city. Lorkesh clearly took no pleasure in talking to Saara, but his oath as a vizier's man made it impossible to overlook the death of a wind claw and the presence of an enchantress.

'You have need of answers and I will provide all the answers you need,' Saara said quietly.

Zel once again saw her moving her hands as she breathed out and began to work her enchantment on Lorkesh. The guardsman looked up involuntarily and a faraway look flowed across his face. He was not a wind claw and his resistance was minimal. There was no pain and no attempt to break away, and the effect, when it came, was subtle.

Saara leant forward and said, 'The man you seek is Dalian Thief Taker, he betrayed his brother and threw him from a window of this building before he fled into the city.'

Zel was a little surprised at this, but eagerly awaited his mistress's next words.

'You will assemble the necessary squad of men and arrest the Thief Taker; if he resists, you will kill him; if his brother wind claws attempt to intervene, you will kill them too,' she said through pursed lips and with her eyes closed. 'You have spoken to several residents in this building, all of whom confirm that the Thief Taker was here with Larix shortly before his unfortunate death.' Saara opened her eyes and smiled at the blank, compliant look that covered Lorkesh's face. 'Is this clear?' she asked with less seductiveness and more authority.

'It is clear,' he responded, speaking in a monotone.

'You may leave and go about your work now,' Saara concluded with a wave of her hand.

The guardsman stood up in one jerky movement and walked blankly away from the enchantress. His eyes blinked slowly, and Zel thought he was gradually regaining his senses as he opened the door and left the apartment.

Zel walked over to stand before his mistress. 'Shall I lay out some appropriate clothes for your appointment at the Well of Spells, mistress?'

She considered this for a moment before saying, 'Yes, I believe I'll wear something blue today.'

* * *

Kessia was built in a series of walled circles, stretching out from the imperial compound and the Tower of Viziers at its centre. The first two circles were home to the richest merchant princes and most influential mobsters, housing them in opulent luxury, surrounded by slaves and armies of paid guardsmen. The third and fourth circles were for the less well-off, and by the outer wall of the fourth circle the sprawling rainbow slum stretched across the arid plain.

Class was everything in Kessia, and these Karesians would spend as much time amassing a fortune as looking over their shoulders to make sure no one was planning to take it from them. It was a paranoid city which lacked the strict laws of Tor Funweir and the honour-bound traditions of the Freelands.

Zel tried not to have too many opinions, preferring to rely solely on what his mistress instructed him to think; however, he disliked the capital and the pervading aura of fear that hung over it. These Karesians had no time to relax and enjoy their lives. Nor could they raise their families in any kind of positive atmosphere. At all times, the people of Kessia were obsessed about their place in the larger order of things and how someone might be trying to do them out of it.

The Well of Spells was situated in the middle of this carousel of status and fear. It was one of three buildings that dominated the central piazza of Kessia, the others being the imperial palace and the Tower of Viziers. The Well was home to the Seven Sisters, and only they and their servants were permitted to enter. It exercised the highest authority in Karesia, though Saara had frequently instructed her slave to keep this knowledge secret, as the common citizenry preferred to believe that the wind claws and the high vizier held the power. In reality, nothing happened in the vast lands of Karesia without one of the Seven Sisters willing it to happen.

The Well was small compared with the huge white marble palace and the lofty tower, but no less significant for its subtlety. The architecture was strange, not employing the clean, rounded lines of traditional Karesian buildings, and no balconies, minarets or open terraces could be seen. It formed a heptagon with a featureless grey wall on each side, possessing no doorways or windows. Looking up, Zel had always found the castellated rooftop five storeys from the ground more reminiscent of a Ro fort than a Karesian building, and the Well was rugged and somehow more solid than the neighbouring buildings.

Saara was wearing her customary black robe, chosen to keep her identity a mystery as she walked amongst the people of the city. She enjoyed the anonymity and Zel often saw her smiling to herself as they passed guardsmen, wind claws and others who would have been shocked to see an enchantress in their midst.

She didn't stop as they approached the Well of Spells, causing passers-by to look with interest at the woman who stepped closer to the building than most would dare. The area immediately around the Well was always deserted, for people feared to step too close and risk the Sisters' wrath. With her slave close behind, Saara strode across the empty ground and stopped within a few feet of the featureless wall.

With a dozen or so of the people of Kessia watching, Saara held out her hand for Zel to take. The slave complied and she cradled it tenderly before closing her eyes and willing the two of them inside.

Zel had been transported inside the building several times in the past and was always disappointed that he never got to see the reactions of the common citizenry when they saw a woman and her slave vanish before their eyes.

Within, the Well of Spells was radically different from its outward appearance. Sparkling white columns emblazoned with arcane symbols circled an open central yard, and the darkwood tree in the centre was well maintained and tended by a stone golem. The golem was large, over seven feet tall, and possessed shining red eyes. It was constructed to be a facsimile of a man, but had no features save for a rudimentary mouth, and its limbs were huge with stone hinges replacing the joints. The building in which it lived had no interior walls and was spacious and airy, with a permanent and barely perceptible chime in the background.

The golem rose from its crouched position at the base of the tree and moved, in a jerky fashion, across to Saara. The creature had been constructed long ago by the first of the Seven Sisters to serve all those who came after. Zel found the construct fascinating and enjoyed talking to it when he had the chance.

'Mistress of Pain, welcome. Zeldantor of Lislan, welcome,' the construct said in a rumbling voice that echoed from all around the building. 'You are expected.' The stone golem slowly turned back to the tree and loudly returned to its work.

Saara and Zel walked round the outer line of pillars to a raised platform against one of the seven walls. The Mistress of Pain was the eldest sister and, as such, held the high chair and was responsible for all of the enchantresses' designs.

As they walked up the white steps to the high chair, Zel could hear the golem talking to itself. 'The Sisters meet. What will they discuss? The Sisters meet. We tend the tree while the Sisters meet. We will be quiet and the tree will be cared for.'

'Mistress,' Zel said, as Saara took her seat, 'how much does the golem know . . . about the world outside, I mean?'

Saara smiled warmly at her slave. 'The golem has been here for as long as there has been a Well of Spells and, in all of those hundreds of years, it has never ventured outside. I don't think it's even aware of the lands of men. It lives only to maintain the tree and to protect the Well from those who would seek improperly to gain entrance.'

Zel had often wondered about the darkwood tree that stood in the centre of the Well of Spells. He had even asked Saara about it, confused about her birthmark and the significance of the tree. In response she'd always spoken vaguely about a dead god; the tree was the last remnant of lost divine power – *the priest and the altar*, she had often said. In fact, she had once told Zel that the place of his birth, deep in the forests of Lislan, had been peopled by Kirin who revered a similar tree. Zel knew that this was part of the reason he had been selected to be a slave to the Mistress of Pain, but the exact details about the tree and the god it symbolized had never fully been explained to him.

The tree was black and gnarled, with a thick trunk and a strangely squat appearance. The only branches it had protruded directly from the top of the trunk and snaked out in an irregular fashion, creating the impression of black, writhing tentacles.

The golem rose to its feet again and several slight distortions appeared in the air around the outer edges of the Well. Two more of the Seven Sisters appeared and were approached by the golem.

'Isabel the Seductress, she is welcome to the Well of Spells,' the Golem said to the younger of the two enchantresses. It then moved jerkily to the second woman and said, 'Shilpa the Shadow of Lies, she is also welcome to the Well of Spells.'

Isabel and Shilpa both bowed with deep respect towards, first the Golem, then the seated form of Saara. Neither of these women had slaves and Zel was again reminded of the fact that he was unique, being the only man ever to have become slave to one of the Seven Sisters.

Saara rose from her chair and crossed the open space to greet her younger sisters. The greeting was formal at first, with each sister bowing respectfully, but the mask cracked quickly and the three women shared smiles and hugs of genuine warmth.

'It has been, what, three years since we met as a group?' Saara asked her sisters.

'I think four of us met last winter,' replied Isabel, 'though my memory may be faulty.'

Shilpa nodded and said, 'Yes, that sounds right. Last winter was when Ameira and Katja left for Ro Tiris.'

Saara laughed a silvery peal of amusement. 'Ah, yes, I remember Katja complaining about the need to go somewhere so cold.'

'It's Ameira I feel sorry for, she's been with the men of Canarn. That land is cold *and* uncivilized. At least Katja has been afforded the comfort of King Sebastian's hospitality in a civilized land,' responded Shilpa, as she joined in her elder sister's laugh.

Zel was struck with how similar the three women appeared. All were tall, with lustrous dark hair and curvaceous bodies. Isabel was a little younger and had a playful glint in her eye; Saara had deep green eyes that stood out next to the blue eyes of the other two, and Shilpa possessed a languid grace, as if she were always dancing as she moved. Saara had no facial tattoo, a privilege of being the eldest sister; the other two both had intricate patterns in black ink across their left cheeks. Shilpa's was a series of birds in flight, and Isabel's a coiled snake. Both shone brighter within the Well of Spells and Zel couldn't take his eyes from the beautiful designs. Despite the differences, Zel thought there were many more similarities and from a distance it would be difficult to tell them apart.

'And how is young Zeldantor today?' asked Isabel with a girlish smile.

'He's well,' replied Saara. 'Zel, come and pay your respects to Isabel and Shilpa.'

The Kirin slave bowed his head and glided across the floor to stand in front of the three enchantresses. 'It is an undreamt of honour to see you both again, most noble sisters of my mistress,' he said with formality.

All three laughed and Zel closed his eyes for a moment to enjoy the sound. Their voices harmonized and rose in volume beyond a simple laugh to become something magical to Zel's ears.

'And will your other sisters be joining us today, mistress?' he asked Saara.

'The two others who remain in Karesia have all been summoned. Katja and Ameira are otherwise occupied and, based on the news I received from Larix earlier today, I would surmise that they have met with success in their endeavours.'

Shilpa and Isabel had not heard this news and both had eager and excited looks on their faces. Zel knew that whatever had transpired in Ro Canarn had done so at the Sisters' urging and the plan, whatever it was, was proceeding well.

More subtle distortions in the air followed and two more beautiful women appeared at opposite sides of the central room. The golem rose and approached each in turn.

'Lillian the Lady of Death, she is welcome in the Well of Spells,' it said in its rumbling tones, before quickly crossing the room to stand before the last of the sisters to arrive.

'Sasha the Illusionist, she is also welcome in the Well of Spells.'

The golem returned to its tree-tending duties, removing moss and lichen growing around the base of the sacred tree, as Sasha and Lillian moved to occupy two of the seven faces of the central room.

Saara sat in her raised chair and looked out with fondness at her four sisters. Zel stood behind her left shoulder and glanced around the room, witnessing possibly the largest meeting of the Seven Sisters in several years and certainly the first to include a male slave. On all of the previous occasions that Zel had been to the Well, it had been to accompany his mistress during a time of contemplation, but he'd never felt as dwarfed by power as he did now.

The last two sisters looked much as the others did, although Lillian was the tallest and Sasha had slightly darker skin. Much like Shilpa and Isabel, their facial tattoos appeared less subtle within the Well of Spells and Zel found himself staring. Lillian was to his right and was the closest to him. Her design, featuring a hand drawn as if grasping her face, was the most sinister-looking amongst them and in sharp contrast to the beautiful flowering rose on Sasha's cheek.

'Sisters,' Saara began, 'we are five. Let us look at the empty spaces and include in our deliberations the shadows of our absent sisters.'

The five enchantresses turned to the vacant spaces and Zel thought he detected warm remembrance on their faces, as if they were all recalling some pleasant memory of Katja and Ameira.

Saara let the silence linger for several minutes while all present closed their eyes, and Zel imagined a collective working of magic was being undertaken, though he could not perceive its effects. When they opened their eyes it was clear they had been communicating with each other on a level the slave could not detect, and the smiles they wore lightened the room. Zel found it disconcerting that several of them glanced at him with interest, and Saara nodded as if to confirm something to her fellow enchantresses.

'It has been five years,' said Saara, 'five years since we found the true significance of this tree and all those like it; five years since we uncovered the grand deception of our former master.' Her words made the smiles on her sisters' faces turn to hard and resolute expressions of defiance. 'And now,' she continued, letting her voice rise in volume, 'our plan is nearing its end.'

223

'What news, sister?' Shilpa asked eagerly. 'What news from the north?'

Saara smiled as she replied. 'Good news, yes, good news indeed. Ameira has successfully enchanted the Red knights of Ro and their hearts are hers. Katja has successfully enchanted the king and his fool son; these weak men are hers to command. And Bartholomew Tiris, the exemplar of the One, is trapped by one of the Dark Young. He can be of no further use to his god. His son, King Sebastian, signed the order to cage Bartholomew personally. The house of Tiris is ours.'

'And the One's last remaining old-blood?' asked Shilpa, the eagerness on her face turning to near-euphoria.

'The Stone Giant old-blood that Bartholomew kept chained under the house of Tiris has been executed by order of the king. Even if the exemplar were free, his channel to the One has been severed.'

A chorus of chuckles, laughs and sounds of gleeful excitement filled the room. Zel began to piece things together. He found it strange that the sisters had orchestrated the imprisonment of one exemplar and the forced exile of another. In the slave's estimation, that only left the exemplar of Rowanoco the Ice Giant.

Voon of Rikara had been the exemplar of Jaa, supposedly the father of the Seven Sisters. However, through the death of his old-blood, the vizier had been forced to journey to the south and was, to all intents and purposes, inert. This meant that two of the three Giants had no way of communicating with their followers, whether the common people realized it or not.

Zel found this disturbing and the motivations of his mistress were obscure in the extreme. The Sisters had done this purposefully, but their designs were a mystery to the slave.

'The king of Tor Funweir will soon be in Ro Canarn himself with an army of Red knights sufficient to assault the Freelands,' Saara continued.

This caused concern on the faces of some of the enchantresses, and Zel thought he detected fear in Isabel's eyes.

'My dear sister,' said Isabel, 'what of Teardrop and his unwashed berserkers? Surely they will resist.'

She spoke of Algenon Teardrop, a name well known to Zel and one of the few men the Seven Sisters held in respect. He was the exemplar of Rowanoco and, by all accounts, a most dangerous man.

Saara smiled again and nodded towards Lillian the Lady of Death. 'Sister, if you would alleviate dear Isabel's fears.'

'Of course, beloved sister,' began Lillian. 'Last year I had occasion to visit a particularly unpleasant mercenary knight named Hallam Pevain. Sir Pevain has, in the past, lent his sword to various Ranen warlords and we are assured that one of Algenon's battle-brothers, a barbarian called Rulag Ursa, is, in fact, our man.' The last two words were spoken with delicious relish and Zel detected pride in Lillian's demeanour.

'I am assured that, should it be launched, the dragon fleet will never make landfall. I believe that Ursa plans to wake the Krakens of the Fjorlan Sea,' Lillian said, evidently relishing the prospect.

Zel had read about Ithqas and Aqas, the blind and mindless Krakens of the Fjorlan Sea, and he had in the past been assured by Saara that the monsters were very real and woke every few years to devour anything in their path. He shuddered as he recalled the strange pictures of tentacled monsters rising from the waters.

Lillian was smiling broadly as she continued speaking. 'Once Algenon and his fleet are gone, by axe or by the Krakens, the Red knights need only deal with a few ragtag Free Companies. Ursa requires only that we assist him to become the new high thain of Ranen. His vanity and ambition have made him an easy ally.'

All five of the Sisters were looking pleased with themselves and Saara nodded with pleasure at Lillian's words. She then looked towards Isabel the Seductress and motioned for her to talk.

'My sisters, I have made all the necessary preparations for the occupation of Ro Weir. The Hounds are supplied and their kennel-masters understand what is expected of them. Duke Lyam of Ro Weir is . . .' she smiled broadly, 'most pleased to accept our occupation.'

Zel knew what this meant, that Isabel had enchanted the duke and he had agreed to allow the army of Hounds to sail across the Kirin straits. The bloodless occupation of a major city of Tor Funweir was to Zel an ingenious scheme, well worthy of the Seven Sisters.

Saara closed her eyes, lost in concentration. The other enchant-resses joined her and together the Sisters threw back their heads and spoke in unison. 'We are not of Jaa. We possess the power of a Giant killed by other Giants.' They almost sang the words.

Now Zel was even more startled. The Seven Sisters were the priesthood of the Fire Giant, Jaa. At least, that was what Zel had always thought, and what the people of Karesia and the lands of men had always thought.

'We pledge ourselves to the Dead God, the Forest Giant of pain and pleasure with a thousand young. We are your servants in the Long War and we will claim these lands in your honour.'

As Saara finished her prayer to the Dead God, Zel gasped as he saw the black tree move. The golem stepped away and stood silently, as all of the enchantresses looked on in silent euphoria.

The bark of the tree cracked and splintered, flowing more like flesh than wood, and the branches began to coil up. A deep rumbling sound accompanied the movement, like the throaty growl of a beast, indistinct, but organic.

'As Jaa stole your power and gifted it to us,' proclaimed Saara, 'we now use it to awaken your Dark Young and worship at their feet . . . the priest and the altar . . . the priest and the altar.'

Zel froze in place as the Dark Young of the Dead God shrugged off its torpid state and reared up, its many thick, branch-like tentacles thrashing in the air, before firmly bracing on the marble floor and slowly lifting the trunk out of the earth.

The base of the tree shook off the earth and Zel saw a mass of smaller tentacles, like feelers, and in the centre of the trunk a gaping maw was revealed. The mouth and feelers had been buried in the ground, somehow providing the creature with nutrition and keeping it alive.

The trunk swivelled forward until it was horizontal and the tentacles could function as legs. The Dark Young now resembled a tree only vaguely, and Zel could no longer comprehend that it had ever been anything other than the tentacled monstrosity before him. Its mouth was toothless but each of its numerous feelers was tipped with a fine, needle-like appendage.

The realization that he was to be a sacrifice only slowly dawned on Zel, as Saara looked with genuine tenderness at her slave.

'You are the son of a man called Rham Jas Rami, my dear Zeldantor,' she said. 'You have served me well, but we no longer have any need to keep you close. Your father will now be powerless to harm us and the Dark Young is hungry.'

'The priest and the altar . . . the priest and the altar,' chanted the Seven Sisters.

Zel tried to maintain his serenity as the Dark Young moved towards him, its mouth growing wider and its feelers writhing in the air. There was no pain, only a sweet taste in his mouth, when the needles entered his body and he became limp and began slowly to dissolve.

CHAPTER NINE

RANDALL OF DARKWALD IN THE MERCHANT ENCLAVE OF COZZ

·············•••••••••••••••••••••••>{{<•••••••••••••••••••••••·············

J UST OUTSIDE COZZ there was a strange local curiosity, long ago purchased by an affluent Ro silk dealer. It was supposedly the only remaining darkwood tree in Tor Funweir and the silk dealer had fought for years to keep it safe from the Purple clerics who desired its destruction. Randall had never seen one before, though he'd known people who claimed to have seen them in the Darkwald. It looked like no tree he'd ever seen, with a short, squat trunk and strange branches that bore no leaves or fruit of any kind.

'People actually pay to climb it, you know,' said Elyot as he pulled his horse in next to Randall.

'Why?' Randall was unnerved by the tree and couldn't imagine why anyone would want to be close to it.

'Because it's forbidden, I suppose. The clerics claim it is blasphemy just to acknowledge it.' He gestured towards where Torian and Utha rode, just ahead of the others.

Neither of the clerics had slowed to look at the tree and they were focused on the town of Cozz, just over the next hill.

It had taken two weeks for them to reach Cozz and Randall was saddle-sore. The merchant enclave was at the halfway point between Ro Tiris and Ro Weir, and Utha had insisted they stop for the night. The watchmen had been good company on the journey, assisting Randall each night with erecting a tent for Brother Torian and lighting a campfire, but he missed the comfort of a proper bed.

Elyot, the youngest of the watchmen, had ridden next to Randall for most of the journey and they had developed a friendship of sorts. He was a good swordsman for his age and delighted in appearing the seasoned soldier next to Torian's inexperienced squire.

Sergeant Clement had spent much of the time complaining about his poor treatment at the hands of the clerics. The names he called them in private were always whispered and Randall knew he was terrified that he would be overheard. Clement was particularly afraid of Brother Utha and always referred to him as *the Ghost* when the cleric was out of earshot.

Randall had heard a hundred stories in the last two weeks, mostly about risen men and Utha's legendary exploits. Strangely, none of the watchmen could agree on precisely what those exploits were. Elyot claimed that Utha was a crusader for the One and hunted down the risen throughout Tor Funweir. Whereas another man, called Robin, was certain that Utha had spent two years living amongst the risen men, learning their ways in order the better to hunt them. The most consistent story was that Brother Utha had once made a friend of a risen man during the siege of Kabrin, when he'd been wounded by a Karesian horse archer.

Randall had heard the story told a few different ways, but the details were always roughly the same – that Utha had been shot from his position in a watchtower, near the town, and had fallen into dense forest below. As the Karesians passed him, he was dragged into the woods by a risen man and his wounds were treated and he was nursed back to health. Elyot believed that his white hair and pale skin were a legacy from this encounter. Strangely, this was the only thing that Utha himself denied when he overheard them talking one night. The Black cleric had apparently been born an albino and took offence when it was suggested otherwise.

Randall didn't like the Black cleric. He took pleasure in mocking other men and used the fact that most were afraid of him to display his wit. He also thought Randall should attend to him as much as he did to Brother Torian. He was clearly aware of what a squire was supposed to do, and for whom, but he took the opportunity to make Randall feel uncomfortable.

'I think there's a cosy little place near the river, can't remember the name, but the woman that runs it is definitely called Beatrix,' Utha said from horseback as they approached Cozz.

'Is it a clean and moral establishment,' asked Torian, 'or am I going to have to share lodgings with whores and drunkards?'

'This is Cozz, brother, not the back streets of Ro Tiris. When I say *cosy* I mean it has a nice drinking terrace and a roaring fire, not a hundred willing women.'

Utha and Torian always rode in the lead, with the watchmen fanned out behind. They let Randall position himself wherever he wanted, which normally meant at the back since he was an average rider at best.

The clerics had slowed as they reached the grassy verge beyond which sat the merchant enclave of Cozz. It was a moderate-sized town, with no duke and no church, having been founded by the traders' guild some fifty years before. It functioned as a way station for most of the trade that passed through the western duchies of Tor Funweir. The merchants of Cozz set the prices for goods all over the country, with traders from Ro Leith to Ro Tiris having to keep their charges at the same level. Randall had been here before with Sir Leon and he was not fond of the place. He was not a greedy person and found the avaricious nature of the traders annoying.

The town was walled, with four open gates at the points of the compass. Signs at the northern gate indicated that Cozz was no more than two weeks' travel from any of the great cities of Tor Funweir: Ro Arnon to the east, Ro Haran to the west, and Ro Weir to the south. Randall, the watchmen and the two clerics had travelled along the King's Highway from Ro Tiris and were still two weeks from their destination.

The group moved slowly along the highway towards the northern gate of Cozz and Randall found himself riding close to all manner of traders coming and going from the enclave. Torian and Utha wore their cloaks gathered around their armour and were not obviously churchmen, meaning that the common people no longer gave them a wide berth or made warding signs at the sight of a Black cleric. If anything, Utha's white hair and pink eyes made people look at him with interest, even pointing him out to their friends and sharing a laugh at the albino. Utha didn't appear to notice, although Randall had spent enough time with the Black cleric to think it likely that he saw and heard more than he let on.

Randall was surprised to see many different races of men on the highway leading to Cozz. Ranen steel merchants from the north mixed happily with Karesian spice traders and Ro craftsmen. He saw wagons containing racks of swords and blacksmithing equipment queuing to be registered to trade in Cozz. Most were owned by Ranen, and the Ro watchmen on the gate were being deliberately awkward in letting the northmen proceed. Merchants of Ro, many from Tiris, were allowed in with nothing but a cursory glance, and Randall guessed that being foreign was not an advantage in Cozz. The watchmen were accepting money from the Ro; the bribery was overt and Randall wondered if Brother Torian would take offence at the evident corruption.

'How old are you, Randall?' asked Elyot as they approached the north gate.

Randall thought for a second and realized that, with the upheaval of the last few weeks, he'd failed to notice that his eighteenth birthday was fast approaching.

'I'll be eighteen before winter,' he replied, pulling back on his reins and moving to ride next to the young watchman. 'Sometimes I feel older.'

Elyot spoke louder so the other watchmen could hear. 'Is this the first time you've grown a beard?' he asked with good humour, evoking a ripple of laughter from the other men.

Utha and Torian were further ahead and were engaged in their own conversation, though a backward glance from Utha showed that he had acknowledged the laughter.

Randall smiled politely, but didn't like being made fun of. He turned away from Elyot and looked at the road ahead before he spoke. 'My old master didn't let me grow a beard and before that I was too young.'

'Don't worry, lad,' said Sergeant Clement, 'we'll make a man out of you with all this travelling. You never know, a good fight might make that beard sprout full and bushy.'

Randall shivered at the thought of having to fight. He knew that Clement was trying to be kind, but he had still not drawn the sword of Great Claw and was afraid of doing so.

The chatter continued as Randall and the watchmen followed the clerics off the main King's Highway to ride past the approaching merchants and enter the town.

* * *

Randall breathed in deeply as he stepped out of the tavern and into the dusty streets of Cozz. He was tired and his head was more of a blur than usual, filled with all manner of things, from clerics to watchmen, the Black Guard and risen men. He knew he should go and sleep, but sharing a room with five other men did not give him the peace he currently craved. He wanted some time alone with his thoughts, to walk and think and relax into his current position, maybe even to spare a few moments to remember Sir Leon Great Claw.

Utha and Torian had sequestered themselves away in the loft room of the tavern, and the watchmen had claimed a large area of the common room in which to drink and relax. It was rapidly growing dark and Randall wanted to spend the twilight hour walking around Cozz before returning to his duties.

The registered market square was half empty, with most merchants having already closed their stalls and returned to warehouses, homes and taverns. A few remained, though Randall thought they must be the lesser stallholders, perhaps relying on the extra custom that would appear late in the day.

As the squire ambled along the outer road of stalls he thought that night-time business looked thin on the ground, and he saw several merchants nervously counting their day's take. A few looked up as he walked past, hoping he'd have business for them, but most sat behind their stalls bemoaning their bad luck.

The registered market was a tough place to do business as the prices were all set by the merchants' guild, making competition fierce. The closer to the centre of the spiral market your stall, the greater your business. Those that languished on the outer ring had to rely on leftover business and opportunistic shoppers. The alternative was the unregistered market, towards the southern gate. There, goods and prices were not regulated, and it was full of unscrupulous merchants.

Randall quickened his pace to leave the market square and find a nicer area for a walk. He was still a simple man at heart and, for the first time in weeks, admitted to himself that he really needed a rest.

Beyond the square the town was tinged with green, and several small hills, each surmounted with a manor house, rose around the walls. It lacked the opulence of Ro Tiris as the money was made here by common men rather than nobles, and they had a different idea of how to live well on their fortunes.

Randall stopped on a leafy road encircling a rugged-looking hill. The street lamps were being lit by bound men and the cobbled road was pleasantly free of rubbish. Randall was the only person out for a walk and he breathed in, enjoying the quiet street. He perched on a wall and looked around, watching a darkening sky and hearing the merchants' bell tolling the end of registered trading for the day. A few shops in the blacksmiths' quarter were still open, but the market stalls were obliged to close by this same time.

Once the bell had sounded, the merchant enclave of Cozz became quiet, the only sounds of activity coming from the taverns. A few bound men, performing the functions of watchmen, began to patrol the streets, wearing rough leather armour and carrying crossbows, but otherwise Randall was mostly alone.

He settled back on to the low stone wall, raising his feet off the ground and slouching over, a position Torian would have chided him for adopting. The Purple cleric insisted that his squire sit up straight at all times, and Randall smiled as he realized he'd missed being able to slouch.

The sword at his side made his position slightly awkward, but hefting the scabbard across his lap meant he could get comfortable fairly easily. He sat below a flickering street light – a large candle in a glass orb – one of the many that illuminated the area. His seated position was between the market square and the street of blacksmiths, on a winding road flanked by well-maintained shrubbery and tall trees.

Randall was too tired to think of anything in much detail, but he was enjoying being away for a while from the teasing of the watchmen, Utha's insults and the work required by Torian.

He rubbed his patchy beard and gazed blankly into the grey twilight. He could feel his eyelids begin to droop and he knew that shortly he'd need to be heading back to the tavern.

Just as Randall made a move to stand up, he heard a sound from behind the wall. Turning round, he could see over a large bramble bush into the yard of a smithy, apparently still open for business. Three men stood talking under a wooden lean-to in a secluded area of the yard, with their backs to him.

One of the men was a fat blacksmith, still wearing his stained apron and absently toying with a huge hammer resting on an anvil. The other two were obviously not tradesmen. One was a Kirin and had a longbow slung across his back and a curved katana belted at his side. The other was a tall man of Ro with curly black hair and a fierce-looking beard. He looked young, but his steel-reinforced leather armour and ornate longsword made Randall take note. The sword had a cast of a raven on its hilt and looked to be the weapon of a noble. The Kirin was glancing around the yard and something about the way his eyes darted from side to side made the squire think him a dangerous man. The young Ro was engaged in animated conversation with the blacksmith and Randall gasped when he heard the name *Brom*.

The squire leant in and listened as best he could across the small area of grass between the wall and the yard.

The blacksmith was upset about something. 'I'm not your dad, your brother or your friend, so tell me why I should help you . . . for so little money?'

The man of Ro considered for a moment and Randall saw a youthful smile appear on his face. 'Because you hate the knights of the Red as much as I do and you know we have few other options.'

The Kirin interjected in a thick accent, 'And if you don't help us, Tobin, I'm going to shove your head into your anvil until both you and it are very red indeed.'

Randall ducked down and thought for a moment. He was sure he hadn't been seen and the darkness would act as cover if he tried to get closer. However, he would look very foolish if he were to be found out and give the Black Guard a chance to escape. Weighing up his options, he decided to run back to the tavern and alert the clerics that he'd seen Lord Bromvy of Canarn.

* * *

'How the fuck did he get here so quickly?' Utha demanded in irritation as he hurriedly pulled on his black armour. 'It took us two weeks to get here from Tiris and that bastard has made it to Weir and back.'

'The criminal classes have their ways, brother,' Torian replied.

Randall had been allowed to enter the loft apartment and had found the clerics deep in conversation about something relating to Utha's past. The squire had interrupted and weathered a barrage of abuse from the Black cleric before he managed to explain that he'd identified their quarry.

The watchmen waited by the door, having only to pull on their chain mail to be ready. However, Randall was sure several of them were the worse for drink and not in prime fighting condition.

'A yard in the street of smiths, yes?' Torian asked his squire.

Randall nodded. 'A little way past the market. I saw them from the road.'

'And you're sure you remained unobserved?' Torian pressed.

'As sure as I can be. I didn't hang around because the Kirin man looked quite watchful.'

'That would be Rham Jas Rami, then,' exclaimed Utha. 'One less assassin in the world is no bad thing.' The Black cleric picked up his axe and placed it across his back. 'So, we give them the chance to stand down and then kill the Kirin and capture the young lord?'

The Purple cleric considered it. 'Let's just hope they are still there, brother.'

Randall spoke. 'They were arguing with the blacksmith, so I'd say they'll be there a while, at least until their business is concluded.'

The clerics finished getting ready, making sure they were identifiable as men of the One God, and left the room.

Clement, Elyot and the watchmen followed them down the three flights of stairs to the tavern's common room and the group exited into the now dark streets of Cozz. Randall tried to smile at the men in the rear, but sensed they were not happy at being dragged from a night of leisure. Clement was certainly a little drunk and only reluctantly accompanied the clerics, while shooting hard glances at the squire responsible for making him leave the warmth of the tavern.

'Randall, come here, lad,' ordered Torian from the front of the group.

The squire jogged past the watchmen and fell in next to the clerics as they walked quickly towards the market.

'This will likely turn nasty. Brom is known to be a dangerous man and a Kirin assassin wouldn't think twice about killing all of us, so don't do anything stupid,' Torian said plainly, causing Utha to chuckle to himself as they sped along the cobbled streets.

'And what stupid things are you expecting me to do, master?' asked Randall, with a little more cheek than he intended.

Torian raised his eyebrows at the comment, but let the tone slide. 'Well, you carry a sword and you travel with true fighting men. Don't, however, get the idea that you are one yourself.' It was said sharply, but Randall knew it was meant as a kindness. If fighting began, the squire would just get in the way.

'I'll try to keep my stupidity in check, master,' the squire replied as humbly as he could.

'Keep that brain of yours active, though, boy,' said Utha. 'You've got more of a mind than these men.' He gestured at the five grumbling watchmen. 'And you'll no doubt get a chance to prove it soon enough. Fights can be won with words as easily as with blades.'

The Black cleric was still a mystery to Randall. He sometimes appreciated Randall's quick wit and sharp tongue, but at other times was highly irritated by them.

The group of men hurried round the outer edges of the market and quickly reached the street where Randall had sat less than twenty minutes ago. Torian signalled that they should stop and gestured to several nearby bound men to disperse. The bound men looked surprised at the sight of two armoured clerics and obeyed instantly, quickly melting away into the side streets.

'Show me where you saw him, Randall,' Torian said in a low whisper.

Randall took a step forward and pointed a little way along the street. 'The fourth street light along, there's a bramble bush behind it and I could see through to a yard opposite.'

Torian nodded and turned to Sergeant Clement. 'Take your men round that way,' he said, pointing along the edge of the market. 'Come into the yard from the north. We'll head down this street and approach from the south. Do not engage anyone, do you understand, sergeant?'

'Of course, sir,' Clement replied. 'With me, lads.'

'Clement,' said Utha. 'I know you've been at the ale, but just stand there blocking his escape and try to look mean.'

Clement looked embarrassed, but nodded as he and his men moved quickly towards the northern edge of the market.

Torian, Utha and Randall began moving slowly down the cobbled street and Randall felt the adrenalin rising in him. He paused briefly by the bramble bush and pointed across the grass towards the yard. Utha and Torian crouched and peered into the darkness.

The blacksmith, Tobin, was still there, perched on the edge of his anvil, swigging from a bottle of wine, and Lord Bromvy was leaning against the upright support of the wooden lean-to.

'Well, paint my cock green, the bastard is actually here,' Utha said with obvious surprise. 'Where's the Kirin?'

'Not seen,' replied Torian. 'No matter, let's approach quietly and, Randall . . . keep your eyes peeled for the assassin.'

Randall simply nodded, not knowing how he would go about looking for the man called Rham Jas Rami.

Utha and Torian looked at each other and began slowly and quietly to move towards the yard. Randall listened. He couldn't hear Clement and the watchmen either, and he began to think that Lord Bromvy might just surrender at the sight of eight armed men – though he hesitated to number himself as one of the eight.

He crouched down to stay hidden by the wall and followed closely behind the two clerics as they reached the bottom of the street and turned sharp right. The entrance to the blacksmith's yard was lit by two wooden posts holding globed candles, and beyond was the glow of several forges still burning. Utha was in the lead and sneaked up to one of the posts, making sure to stay in the darkness as he poked his head round the corner to look into the yard.

'He's right where we left him,' Utha whispered to Torian.

The Purple cleric glanced towards the yard and asked, 'Should we give Clement time to get into position?'

Utha smiled. Before the Purple cleric could object, Utha had turned, striding into the yard with no further attempt to stay quiet. Torian shook his head, but quickly stood and followed his brother cleric.

Randall was a little way behind and tried to keep his eyes on the surrounding buildings, watching for signs of the Kirin assassin. The yard was comprised of several wooden lean-tos, each containing anvils, stored weaponry and blacksmithing equipment. All but one of the buildings was deserted and Randall could see no other people in the yard. The lean-tos had flat roofs and he identified a number of places where a longbow could be used to devastating effect.

'Bromvy of Canarn,' bellowed Torian as he strode forward.

Brom and the blacksmith both jumped at the sight of the clerics, but the young lord quickly regained his composure and stepped out from the smithy into the yard.

The blacksmith hurried away, saying, 'Sorry, Brom, I don't need this kind of trouble.'

His path was suddenly blocked by Clement, Elyot and the three other watchmen of Tiris who had quietly positioned themselves to cut off any escape. The blacksmith swore to himself and turned to look imploringly both at Brom and at the clerics.

'The blacksmith can leave,' said Torian quietly.

Clement stepped aside and motioned for the man to depart. He spared an apologetic glance back at Brom, but darted quickly out of the yard and Randall saw relief on his face.

Utha and Torian walked to the middle of the yard and Bromvy strolled slowly to meet them. He was tall and carried himself with the practised step of a skilled swordsman. His black curly hair was unkempt and a little wild, but his beard was trimmed close and gave him a fierce look in the glow of the street lights. The sword at his side was clearly the weapon of a noble and he casually rested his right hand on the hilt as he stopped a few feet in front of Torian.

'Where's your friend, Black Guard?' asked Utha with scorn.

'I have many friends, cleric, you'll have to narrow down the question,' Brom replied defiantly. He showed no fear of the Black cleric, though Randall thought that he had disliked being called a Black Guard.

Torian had not drawn his sword and was calm as he motioned around the yard, pointing out the watchmen and indicating that Brom was trapped.

'You can't escape, my lord, surrender your blade and you will not be harmed,' he said slowly and deliberately, emphasizing each word.

Brom glanced at the watchmen behind him and took note of the weapons on display. He wasn't concerned by the mace carried by Clement or by Elyot's twin short swords. However, he frowned at the three loaded crossbows.

He turned back to face the clerics, assessing his options. Randall was glad that the Black Guard had not noticed him – or, if he had, he clearly didn't see him as a threat.

To the young squire, the odds appeared overwhelming – a single man facing a group of well-trained watchmen and two dangerous clerics. Randall had seen Torian fight Sir Leon and he knew how formidable he was with his longsword in hand. Utha, too, was clearly not a man to be trifled with, and Brom had taken note of the Black cleric's axe, which, though not in hand, could be drawn swiftly with a shrug of the shoulders.

'I have no desire to fight two clerics, but I can't let you take me,' the Black Guard said regretfully. 'The knights of the Red destroyed my homeland and I cannot abandon my father and my people to dishonour and imprisonment.'

The clerics looked at each other and Randall thought Brom could not know about Duke Hector's execution. Torian shook his head to silence Utha and took a step forward to stand close to the Black Guard.

'Your father, Duke Hector of Canarn, has been executed for treason,' he said formally.

The young lord didn't react straightaway, but simply looked at the ground and took a deep breath. Randall thought he saw a tear appear in his eye, but no other sign of emotion could be seen. When the Black Guard raised his head, he had a thin smile on his lips and a hard look in his eyes.

'And there's no way I can persuade you to forget that you found me?' he asked, with obvious gallows humour, eliciting a low snort of amusement from Utha.

'Not a chance, my lord,' replied Torian. 'However, we have no intention of harming you unless you resist capture.'

Brom nodded and again scanned the yard. Randall followed

his eyes and thought he saw a shape moving across one of the rooftops, though it may have been a trick of the light, for he could hear no accompanying sound.

Brom turned back to Torian. 'What's your name, cleric?'

'I am Brother Torian of Arnon, cleric of the quest and nobleman of the One God,' he answered with pride.

'Well, Brother Torian, I'm sorry you have to die,' he said quietly, just as Randall saw a definite shape emerge on top of a wooden building opposite.

'Master . . .' he called out just as the sound of a bow string being released and the whistle of an arrow reached everyone's ears.

Torian had heard Randall's warning, but turned too late as the arrow hit him in the throat. Brom didn't turn away or look surprised as the Purple cleric gasped for breath and with wide, staring eyes slowly fell to the dusty ground.

'No . . .' Randall cried out.

Utha and the watchmen turned involuntarily, stunned for a second by what had happened.

Brom had clearly known Rham Jas was there as he reacted quickly, levelling an elbow at Utha's face, smashing his nose, and sending the Black cleric staggering to his knees.

Two of the crossbowmen fired wildly at the rooftop but both bolts hit the wood and Randall saw a dark shape roll backwards into the shadows. The third crossbowmen fired at Brom but missed, as he darted to the side and dived over the anvil, doing a forward roll under the blacksmith's lean-to.

Utha grabbed his broken nose and tried to focus through the blood. The Black cleric looked at the body of Brother Torian staring blankly from the ground and roared as he unsheathed his battleaxe.

Turning to the crossbowmen, he barked, 'Kill that fucking Kirin.'

The three watchmen quickly reloaded their weapons and advanced in a line towards the opposite building. The assassin, Rham Jas, had disappeared and the men appeared nervous, each with an eye on the body of the Purple cleric lying spreadeagled on the floor.

Clement and Elyot, weapons at the ready, advanced on Brom, who had stood up inside the lean-to and swiftly drawn his ornate longsword. Clement swung his heavy mace in a wide overhead arc directed at the young lord's head, but for all his strength the blow was poorly timed and gave Brom the opportunity to parry and drop his shoulder into the watchman's chest, shoving him backwards into a wooden supporting beam. Elyot quickly attacked the Black Guard, using his youth and speed momentarily to drive him back.

Randall held his breath and looked on terrified as Elyot realized he was outmatched by the young lord of Canarn. The two short swords he carried allowed him to keep Brom from making a riposte, until a swift kick to the groin winded the watchman and a powerful downward swing of the longsword severed Elyot's right arm just below the elbow. The young watchman cried out in pain and fell against the wall, thrashing around as blood sprayed from the stump of his arm.

The crossbowmen turned to see what had happened, and a second longbow arrow appeared from nowhere and pierced the stomach of the man called Robin, who shouted out before dropping his crossbow and doubling over on to the floor.

Randall didn't see where the second shot had come from, but it was at ground level, indicating that the Kirin had quickly changed position. The two remaining crossbowmen fired into the darkness between two wooden buildings and Randall thought he heard a grunt of pain.

Torian, Elyot and Robin had been killed or incapacitated in a matter of moments. Randall felt panic rising within him. He drew the sword of Great Claw almost as a reflex, but made no attempt to attack either Brom or the unseen Kirin assassin. He looked at the body of his master and then at Utha, as the Black cleric pulled himself upright and shook his head.

Clement had again engaged Brom and the older watchman was roaring with anger as he delivered a frenetic series of blows at the young lord. Brom parried a few of them, but he was fast enough to avoid all of them and let the heavy mace strike wood

242

instead of flesh. Each strike took considerable effort and Clement was tiring quickly.

The watchman glanced over Brom's shoulder and saw that Utha was approaching the fight on unsteady feet. Brom, too, realized this, and with a quick look to assess the remaining men arrayed against him, he attacked Clement furiously. The young lord was a fearsome swordsman and Randall could barely see all of the lightning-fast blows that rained down on Clement. The old watchman held his mace above his head in a desperate attempt to stay alive until Utha arrived, but Brom was now trying to kill and a pivot of his shoulder allowed his sword to slip under Clement's mace and dig deeply into his side. The watchman's chain mail made a grating sound as the longsword tore into it, and Randall saw blood appear at the corners of Clement's mouth and the life quickly drain from his eyes.

'Black Guard,' roared Utha, 'time to die.'

He hefted his axe and shoved the metal anvil out of the way. Stepping past the now unconscious form of Elyot, he stood in a guarded pose. The two remaining watchmen had entered the gap between buildings and Randall had lost sight of them as they looked for the Kirin. A few sharp sounds of steel on steel indicated that they'd found him.

All the squire could do was to stand there, sword in hand, and watch. He knew he couldn't help in any useful way and, with his eyes still fixed on Brother Torian's body, he doubted his legs had the strength to move.

The squire managed to force his head to turn and focus on Utha. The bodies of Clement and Elyot were sprawled across the smithy and Randall couldn't believe how much blood there was. It was proving an obstacle to Brom as he stood awaiting the Black cleric.

Utha was a spectacle of rage as he swung his axe with skill and growled at the Black Guard. 'Torian was my friend and your father was a son of a whore.'

Brom looked angry, but controlled, as Utha reached him and their weapons clashed. The battleaxe swung high and Brom buckled under the strength of Utha's attack, his longsword barely keeping the blow from landing. Randall looked on as they fought furiously. Brom was the faster, but Utha by far the stronger, though both men were skilled.

The duel continued with each man holding his ground, as Utha carried on roaring challenges and Brom did his best to stay on the move and avoid the vicious battleaxe.

Across the yard, Randall saw a man emerge tentatively from the gap between buildings. He was a Kirin and held a blood-covered katana loosely in his hand. Randall could see a crossbow bolt protruding from his side and he looked to be in great pain.

Without thinking, Randall stepped into the middle of the yard and brandished his longsword, trying to summon up his courage and to keep Rham Jas from attacking Utha. No one else was alive and he felt that he had no choice but to join the fight. The Kirin was wounded and the squire thought he might be able at least to delay him until Utha had dealt with Brom.

The Kirin was swarthy-skinned with thin, black hair falling loosely to his shoulders. He was sweating and wincing with pain as he walked. Randall turned his back on Brom and Utha and, in spite of the sound of shouting and steel, tried to clear his mind and focus on defeating the Kirin. He could see the bodies of two watchmen lying in the darkness between buildings, testament to the speed with which the assassin had killed them.

Rham Jas moved towards the young squire and shot him a confused look before directing his eyes to the frenzied duel between Brom and Utha. Randall looked at him wide-eyed and forced himself to take a step towards the Kirin, holding his longsword at the ready.

'Randall . . . step back, boy,' shouted Utha, as a grunt of pain from Brom indicated that the Black cleric was gaining the upper hand.

'You should listen to him, lad,' said the Kirin. 'I won't kill a boy whose hand shakes holding a longsword.'

Randall glanced down at his hand and saw that it did indeed shake violently, making his grip on the sword tentative at best.

Glancing behind him, he saw Utha had backed Brom into a corner and the Black Guard was trying to defend himself from repeated axe blows. The lord wore only light leather armour, insufficient to withstand a single blow from Utha's battleaxe. As Randall stepped aside and let the sword of Great Claw fall from his hand, Utha began a combination of overhead blows that made Brom shrink as he raised his sword in both hands to block the strikes.

Rham Jas ran past Randall, wincing with pain and grabbing the protruding crossbow bolt as he did so. Before he reached the lean-to, Utha delivered a feint with his axe and rammed the hilt up into Brom's chin, causing teeth to fly from his mouth, and a follow-up kick to his chest sent the Black Guard to the ground as Rham Jas advanced. Brom was unconscious and Utha turned, his face still a mask of rage.

'You killed my friend,' he said to Rham Jas through gritted teeth.

'I'm sure he'd done something to deserve it,' the Kirin replied with a maddening grin. 'Putting on that purple tabard . . . it was only a matter of time till someone put him down.'

Randall looked again at his master's body and felt shame at not being able to fight the Kirin. He still shook as he watched Utha and Rham Jas circle each other. The katana held by the Kirin was a vicious-looking weapon with a long handle and a narrow curved blade. His movements were graceful as he stepped one foot over the other and his eyes were fixed on the Black cleric before him.

'No one needed to die here, you Kirin pig,' said Utha. 'Death should not be so casually handed out.'

Randall could see real pain in Utha's eyes, not from any wound, but from the experience of being around swift death. For a moment, the young squire didn't see the caustic man who had bullied him, just an enraged cleric of death.

'Tell it to your One God, because I'm not fucking listening,' replied Rham Jas, as he pulled the crossbow bolt from his side.

Utha did not attack with the ferocity he'd levelled at Brom but was increasingly measured, as if he considered the

Kirin the more dangerous opponent. The katana, too, was a weapon that required a different approach, and Utha adopted a defensive stance.

As they circled each other, the Kirin's face came into view and Randall thought for a moment he looked confused.

'You're Utha the Ghost!' the Kirin said. 'I've heard of you, you're friend to the Dokkalfar.'

The word meant nothing to Randall, but Utha's reaction was instant. He levelled the head of his axe at the Kirin and demanded, 'Where did you hear that name?'

Rham Jas merely smiled and nimbly darted forward with the elegance of a dancer. Utha pulled back his axe just in time to deflect the katana as it whirled within inches of his face, and Rham Jas disengaged to begin circling him again.

'They wouldn't like it if I killed you, cleric . . . but I doubt you'd just let me leave with Brom, so I'm afraid I must put you down,' he said, his grin returning.

Randall could barely believe how fast Rham Jas moved – he almost blinked from one spot to another as he launched single attacks at Utha. No combinations, just a series of swift, darting runs from one side to the other. Each attack left Utha off balance and his axe was now cumbersome and ill suited to duelling with the Kirin.

'Stay fucking still, you coward,' the cleric shouted with frustration, as a glancing blow from Rham Jas opened up a shallow cut on Utha's left cheek.

'Yes, that sounds like a good idea. I'll definitely do that,' mocked the Kirin.

He pressed a hand to his side and checked his wound. No blood was visible and Randall thought the arrow hole had begun to close.

Rham Jas didn't stop smiling as he ran at Utha again, this time spinning at the last moment and delivering a solid blow to the cleric's back. His armour bore the brunt of it, but Utha was still pushed sharply forwards and lost his footing, stumbling awkwardly to the ground.

The Kirin was quickly on him and kicked out at his axe, sending the weapon skidding from Utha's hand. He then drove his katana downward, piercing the cleric's shoulder and pinning him to the ground.

Utha shook violently, but remained still, and slowly turned his head to look at the blade protruding from his shoulder. 'Do it clean, you Kirin horse-fucker.'

'As I said, the forest-dwellers wouldn't like it if I killed you. They seem to think you are worthy. Personally, I think you are a troll cunt, but what do I know? I'm just a man.' Rham Jas grasped the hilt of his katana and pulled it quickly from Utha's shoulder, making the cleric cry out in pain and move his hand to the bloodstain between the steel plates.

'Boy . . .' Rham Jas called out to Randall, 'you'd better help him get his armour off and clean that wound.'

Randall was stuck in place with fear, barely able to feel his legs, as the Kirin assassin calmly sheathed his katana and crossed the yard to retrieve his longbow and quiver.

'Get to it, lad, we wouldn't want the fabled Utha the Ghost to die such a pointless death, would we?'

Randall slowly walked towards the shaking form of Utha. He tried not to look at Torian's lifeless body as he wiped the sweat from his eyes and knelt to pick up the sword of Great Claw. He couldn't focus clearly but he saw Rham Jas stow his weaponry and move to help Lord Bromvy of Canarn, who was just regaining consciousness and spitting out blood.

'You killed a Purple cleric, Rham Jas,' said Utha weakly. 'The One doesn't forget.'

Rham Jas helped Brom to his feet. 'The One can go fuck himself. Pray to him and tell him that, Ro.'

Randall reached the bleeding body of Utha and knelt down, allowing the Black cleric to grasp his hand firmly. The squire focused on Utha, but he could hear Rham Jas and Brom leaving and Utha's hate-filled eyes didn't move from the departing pair. The wound looked bad and blood was flowing on to the dusty floor of the yard. Slowly, and with his eyes still focused over Randall's shoulder, Brother Utha the Ghost lost consciousness.

* * *

Bound men began to appear as soon as Rham Jas and Brom had left. Men holding crossbows in shaking hands and wearing ill-fitting chain coats and pot helmets appeared from both sides of the blacksmith's yard. Two of them were instantly sick at the sight of the mutilated bodies and copious blood. Another one left quickly when he saw a dead Purple cleric, and several more looked around nervously, trying to fathom what circumstances could have led to a cleric of nobility being shot in the neck with an arrow. Ten or more bound men spread around the yard, but this was clearly an uncommon sight in Cozz and it was a few minutes before they noticed that three men were still alive.

Randall was unhurt and sat cradling the unconscious Utha. Nearby, Robin was lying on his back with an arrow protruding from his stomach, calling weakly for help. Within the blacksmith's lean-to, Elyot lay against a wooden wall. He'd regained consciousness, but he was deathly pale from loss of blood and fighting to stay awake as he held the stump of his arm firmly under his armpit to stop the bleeding.

Randall was certain that Clement, Torian and the other two watchmen of Tiris were dead. Rham Jas had cut one of them in two and he lay in an undignified slump in the small space between two wooden buildings. The other man had died from a katana thrust to the head and his face was mostly unrecognizable.

'The One preserve us,' said one of the bound men as he moved to help Elyot. 'What happened here, lad?' he asked Randall across the yard.

The squire didn't answer straightaway. He took a minute to look around him before he said, 'What do you think happened? People are dead. Maybe you should help those that aren't.' He spoke with deliberate anger and the note of authority in his voice surprised the bound man.

If his head had been clearer, his words would have surprised himself as well, but with so much blood and death Randall had no time for propriety.

'Yes . . . of course, sir,' said the bound man, unaware that Randall was just a commoner.

'Get some more men here . . . and a healer,' Randall grunted. 'Now!' he shouted.

Several of the men saluted and moved quickly out of the yard, while others helped Elyot and Robin into more comfortable positions, lying flat on the floor. Torian was not moved at first as the bound men clearly didn't want to touch a Purple cleric, dead or not, so Randall walked slowly over to the body of his master.

Brother Torian of Arnon was lying in a pool of blood spreading from the wound in his neck. The longbow arrow had hit his jugular and travelled downwards, exiting close to the angle between shoulder and neck. Randall guessed he'd died quickly as the arrowhead was wide and designed to cause large entry and exit wounds. His sword was still in its scabbard and his armour was unmarked. By any definition, the cleric had not died well; he had not even seen the face of his killer. Randall thought a man like Torian deserved better.

Two bound men helped him move the body and place it in a dignified position next to the other dead men. Randall then turned his attention back to Utha. The Black cleric was hurt, but with proper care his wounds would not be fatal. He was still unconscious from the pain and the wound in his shoulder was wide and jagged.

'You there,' shouted a man from the yard entrance, 'explain this mess immediately.'

He was a fat man of Ro wearing a heavy felt overcoat and carrying a slender rapier. The tabard he wore across his chest showed that he was a town official of some kind. Cozz had no traditional heraldry like the major cities of Tor Funweir, although the merchants in charge had adopted the image of a purse as their symbol.

Without paying much attention to the man, Randall replied, 'What kind of explanation would you like? A short explanation, a long explanation, or maybe you could tell me why your bound men were so close at hand and yet did nothing to help.' Randall's voice rose in volume as he finished speaking.

The fat man spluttered as he replied. 'I . . . er, we . . . didn't think it our place to interfere,' he said, with less confidence than he'd initially displayed. 'We only arrived at the end of the encounter anyway. We could have been no real help.'

Randall looked up and glared at the man. 'And you didn't think to apprehend the men that did this? The men that killed a cleric of the fucking Purple.' The last words were shouted and Randall chided himself for letting his anger show.

His wrath had the desired effect and the official quickly barked out orders to the bound men to close the town gates and make an effort to stop Rham Jas and Brom from leaving Cozz. Randall thought it a little too late.

* * *

It was well past dawn before Utha regained consciousness. Randall had drifted off into a restless sleep several times since arriving in the guildhall of Cozz. Although he had not been given a bed, he had managed to position two wooden chairs to give him a degree of comfort. The town official, who had identified himself as Marshal Lynch, was awkward, disrespectful and, in Randall's estimation, an idiot.

The town had no White chapel and no dedicated healer. The townsfolk accepted the inevitability of having to ride to the duchy of Voy, some days' travel northwards, if they needed serious healing. All other wounds were patched up by the bound men, unless the injured party was lucky enough to employ a healer of his own. Randall had directed a string of coarse insults at Lynch, which rather took the man aback, in an attempt to get a healer, any healer, to come and tend to Utha. The man who had been sent was in the employ of a horse trader from Leith, more used to wounds from riding accidents or horseshoes to the face than fighting injuries, but his skill was sufficient to stop the bleeding and stabilize the Black cleric.

They had been given a chamber in which to recuperate in the guildhall, ordinarily used for private business dealings, and Randall had insisted that a bed be positioned in the small room. On reflection, the squire wished that he'd insisted on two beds as his neck was stiff from sleeping on the wooden chairs. Elyot and Robin were back at the inn and the healer assured Randall that both would recover fully in time, though Elyot would be without his left arm.

The bodies of Torian and the watchmen had been stored, with as much dignity as possible, in the only church building in town – a small chapel to the Gold aspect of the One God – and Randall had insisted that Torian's corpse be guarded until they were ready to claim him and leave Cozz.

'I assume I'm still alive . . . or that the One has not blessed me with a place in his hall beyond the world,' said Utha weakly, jolting Randall awake.

'You're awake,' the squire said excitedly.

'Where's my armour?'

Randall pointed to a crumpled pile of black plate steel in the corner of the room. 'I don't know how much use you can salvage from it, we had to cut a lot of it off you. The Kirin was stronger than he looked.'

Utha looked paler than usual, if such a thing were possible, and he lay on the bed in nothing but a simple blue cotton gown. Randall had been close at hand when the healer had seen to him and the squire repeatedly had to tell him to shut up when Utha's reputation and his albinism were mentioned.

'Where's Torian?' Utha's eyes betrayed the fondness he had developed for his brother cleric.

'I made sure they will keep his body safe until we're ready to leave. These people aren't used to clerics and, between you and me, most of them aren't overly encumbered with brains.'

251

Utha laughed, wincing as he did so. 'I told you to keep your mind sharp, lad, it looks like you took that advice to heart.' He narrowed his eyes. 'Well, with the exception of trying to fight that Kirin.'

'I didn't know what else to do. I wasn't thinking very clearly.' Randall was spluttering a bit and trying to think of a justification for his foolish attempt to take on Rham Jas.

'Randall,' Utha interrupted, 'you did well. I'm alive and Torian is being treated with respect in death . . .' he paused a moment, 'though the death of a Purple cleric is no small thing and, mark my words, I at least will have to account for what we did here.'

'You did nothing wrong,' Randall said without really thinking.

'Did I not?' Utha asked rhetorically with raised eyebrows. 'I got him killed. Whichever way you look at it, my reckless insistence on making a show gave the assassin his shot . . . and he took it well.'

Randall had not considered this and felt a sudden pang of anger at the idea of Utha being blamed for the encounter. He had many reasons to dislike the Black cleric – his constant teasing, his aggressive manner – but he knew that Utha and Torian had been friends, almost brothers, and to blame one for the death of the other was unfair.

'Don't worry, young Randall, any recriminations are far off. I need to rest and we need to conspire a way to return to Tiris,' he said, as his eyes closed again and weariness took hold.

'Brother Utha,' Randall began, with a questioning tone to his voice.

'Yes, Randall . . .' said Utha wearily, not opening his eyes.

'What does that word mean? The one Rham Jas said to you, Dokkal . . . something.'

Utha turned to the squire, opened his eyes, and grew more alert. Randall thought the cleric was about to unleash a string of his customary insults, but instead he paused and considered his reply.

'Dokkalfar . . . it's a very old word in a very old language. Not a word you'll hear on the streets of any of the cities of men.'

'The word seems to bother you,' Randall pointed out, 'but it also seemed to be the reason Rham Jas didn't kill you.'

Utha smiled thinly and shook his head, as if conceding defeat. 'You're too clever to be a squire, Randall of Darkwald, but you should be careful where you direct that mind of yours.' Utha was still smiling but seriousness showed in his pale eyes. 'Some knowledge is dangerous . . . and some knowledge can get you killed.'

'He said that you were their friend.' Randall was sure that Utha didn't want to talk about this, but his natural curiosity got the better of him. 'Who are they?'

The Black cleric flexed his neck and moved the white pillow beneath him into a more upright position, the better to direct his pale eyes at Randall. 'Did Torian tell you why I was sent to accompany him? It must have looked strange for a cleric of death to be helping to track down one of the Black Guard. Not our usual kind of work.'

Randall had not really thought about it. Utha was the first Black cleric he'd met and, for most of the weeks they'd spent together, Randall had tried to avoid the caustic churchman. 'I didn't . . .'

'No, I suppose a simple squire would have little knowledge of the clerical orders,' Utha replied gently, and Randall thought that he was less on guard than usual, probably as a result of his weakened condition. 'I was disgraced and relieved of my previous duties. Torian was an old friend and needed help so I requested I be allowed to accompany him while the Black cardinal of Tiris decided what to do with me.' He had a look of shame in his eyes and Randall again thought that the cleric didn't want to talk about it.

'I don't mean to pry. We can leave it for now, if you wish,' the squire said.

Utha smiled, more genuinely this time. 'I'm not your master, Randall, and given a few weeks to recuperate, I suspect I'll be ministering death rights to pigs in Ro Leith, so don't worry.'

Randall shared the cleric's smile and poured a glass of water from the jug he'd placed on a nearby table. He rested it next to

Utha's lips and helped him drink. 'The healer put some kind of soothing root mixture in the water. He said it'll help you relax.'

'I don't recall doing anything to warrant such kind treatment, lad. In fact, I'm fairly sure that I've given you every reason to hate me.'

Randall didn't reply to this, but sat back down in his wooden chair and waited for Utha to continue. The cleric blinked a few times to regain some focus and made an effort to sit more upright.

'I was a crusader, a hunter of risen men. It was my calling, my . . . duty. From as early as I can remember I was trained to find them and . . . kill them.' He said the last two words with a deep well of regret in his eyes, and for the first time Randall saw a simple man under the armour of caustic wit the churchman usually wore. 'I have scars from fighting them and burn marks from killing them,' he said, showing Randall an unpleasant mark on his leg.

'Why would you have burn marks?'

'Dokkalfar burst into flames when they die. It's not something that we tell people about. It makes them seem strange, and the One dislikes deviance.'

Randall was listening intently and again thought that the world was a more complicated place than he could have imagined.

'I was disgraced because I disobeyed orders and refused to continue killing them . . .' He paused, as if remembering. 'I betrayed the One, I betrayed my church . . . and . . .' he closed his eyes, 'I know I was right.' The last words were spoken with stubborn indignation.

'But why?' asked Randall. 'The risen are monsters that prey on the living, aren't they?'

Utha kept his eyes closed and rubbed the stiffness from his wounded shoulder. 'The list of people who have saved my life is a short one. You can make a claim to it – getting a healer, stopping my wound from festering, insisting I be cared for properly. But before today only one name was on that list, a risen man called Tyr Weera.'

Randall was shocked at this. Shocked that the creatures had names, and equally shocked that one would deign to help a cleric of the One. 'I don't understand.'

'The Purple clerics have long believed, much as you do, that the risen are undead monsters deserving of nothing but death. It's not a lie or a deception, because they genuinely believe it. The One decreed it, the clerics maintain it and no one questions it.

'Dokkalfar is their name for themselves . . . and I only know that because I lived for a short time in a village of the creatures in the Fell,' he said, as if divulging a dark secret. 'I was dying. The wound down my back . . . you may have seen it.' He pointed vaguely towards the vicious scar that Randall had seen when he first met the Black cleric. 'A Karesian Hound attacked me from behind and nearly split me in two with his scimitar. I was left for dead on the edges of the Fell until Weera dragged me into the woods.'

Randall considered it. The risen were the stuff of myths and stories, rarely encountered, but always feared as if they were the remnants of some ancient evil. Even when he was a boy, Randall had only half believed the stories he'd heard about them living in the Darkwald. Now, not only was he faced with the reality of their existence, but also with their status as more than simple monsters.

'I don't know what to ask,' he said bluntly to Utha. 'It seems that a lot of people have the wrong idea. But why would this mean your disgrace? Surely the Purple should be told so that they stop ordering them to be killed.'

Utha opened his eyes and laughed. 'That's a little naive, don't you think? Try convincing a Purple cleric of anything other than the word of the One and you'll go mad before they yield. I tried to tell them . . . really I did. I even found an old Black cleric who thought as I did, but he was quickly ushered out of Arnon and given some spurious task to keep him quiet.' He bowed his head. 'And now they'll do the same to me. Torian's death just gives them one more justification for hiding me in a shit-stained village somewhere.'

'And Rham Jas, what does he know of them?'

Utha shrugged. 'I don't know. I can guess, but I don't know. He's likely from the Kirin woods far to the south and I was told that many Kirin down there still live side by side with the risen and could even claim friendship with them. It's another reason why the Purple clerics occasionally cross the Kirin Ridge and clear the villages.

'Randall, I appreciate all you've done, but I need to rest. Soon enough I'll return to the Black cathedral in Tiris and I'll be given robes and told to leave my axe in the care of a more worthy man.' He slid down the bed to lie on his back.

'And what of me?' Randall asked, instantly feeling selfish as he did so.

'We'll see, young squire . . . we'll see,' Utha said, before drifting off to sleep.

CHAPTER TEN

RHAM JAS RAMI IN
THE WILDS OF TOR FUNWEIR

R HAM JAS RAMI was tired. He'd pulled a concussed
Brom across the saddle of a stolen horse and ridden
out of Cozz several hours before. His own horse was
a cantankerous old bastard, chosen primarily because it had
belonged to a city official and it pleased the Kirin to steal from
those in authority. The bound men who'd come looking for them
after the fight had done a rather poor job of securing the town
and Rham Jas had easily managed to lead Brom out of a horse
merchant's private yard. Cozz was not a secure walled city like
Tiris or Weir and there were dozens of ways to leave quietly if a
man was sufficiently motivated.

Brom rode behind him over uneven terrain to the north and
west of the merchant enclave. The young lord had said little and
Rham Jas decided to let him process the death of his father in
peace. Rham Jas knew that in any case Brom's pathetic attempts
at navigating in the wilds would be of no assistance. Brom had
many gifts – he was clever, tough and ruthless – but survival in
the wilderness was not one of his skills.

'I don't mind handling the navigation, but if you're going to
ride behind me you could at least say something now and then,'
Rham Jas said in a slight huff.

They were approaching a low, forested gully that led between
hills away from Cozz. Two days ahead of them were the Walls of
Ro, the mountains that led north and signalled part of the Kirin

run. Rham Jas knew the route well and estimated that they'd be approaching Ro Tiris within a week.

'I don't feel like talking.' Brom had taken a nasty blow to the jaw and his words were muffled. He'd recover quickly, but the Black cleric was a strong brute and had knocked out one of his teeth.

'Well, it'll be a long and lonely journey if you keep saying that.' The Kirin was grumpy and let it show as he spoke.

'Just ride, Rham Jas . . . just ride.' Brom sounded tired and his words were indistinct.

Rham Jas let it drop and looked ahead to the darkening sky above the Walls of Ro. He didn't think they were being followed and the way ahead was clear, with only a few big Gorlan spiders and the odd bandit to worry about.

As he replayed the fight in his head, Rham Jas regretted not killing the Black cleric. He felt no compunction whatsoever about taking down the Purple man, but he had broken his own rules by leaving a witness. Killing a Purple cleric was no small thing in Tor Funweir and he silently lamented the fact that his face would be adorning wanted posters within a few days.

As he rode quietly down the gully towards the thinly spaced trees, he rolled up his right sleeve and surveyed the twenty or so cuts along his forearm – each a Purple cleric's death mark – cut into his flesh so that he would never forget whom he had killed and why. Grasping his horse's reins in his teeth, he unsheathed a small hunting knife and drew it slowly across an empty piece of skin near his wrist. He was running out of space and wondered how many more of the bastards there were for him to kill. He mused that placing the death marks on his legs might be a solution, or maybe even his chest, though that idea was less appealing.

Rubbing the new wound to relieve the slight pain it caused, he retrieved the reins and rolled down his sleeve. The cut would heal within a few minutes and the slight scar would be the only testament to the death of Brother Torian of Arnon – which Rham Jas thought was a stupid name. The men of Ro were obsessed with lengthening their names by adding titles, locations, job descriptions and all manner of unnecessary appendages. Even Brom had a tendency towards extravagance where his name was concerned. Lord Bromvy of Canarn, protector of the northern mark and scion of the duchy of Canarn went, in the Kirin's estimation, far beyond the information necessary in a name. The only appendage to his own was the addition of the word *Rami*, meaning *archer* in old Karesian.

'Why didn't you kill the Black cleric?' asked Brom, echoing Rham Jas's own doubts.

'Decided to talk, have we?'

'He's likely to cause us trouble, not to mention that we didn't get the clay for passage to Canarn.'

The blacksmith had still been arguing over the details when Rham Jas had gone for some food, and then had come back to find Brom being questioned by the clerics. They were without the necessary documents and the Kirin knew that getting out of Tiris by sea would be difficult without them.

'I didn't kill him because we . . . share some of the same friends,' Rham Jas said, immediately realizing how foolish it must sound.

Brom laughed for the first time since leaving Cozz. 'Sorry, I didn't realize you were a regular at the Black churchmen's annual parties.'

'It's not like that,' Rham Jas muttered, again letting his petulance show. 'I've heard of him is all.'

'So have I, though I would still have killed him.'

'Then maybe you should practise a bit more so he doesn't beat the snot out of you next time you meet.' Rham Jas spoke with more venom than he had intended.

Brom reined in his horse and stopped a few feet behind his friend. 'I know I'm being quiet, but keep that shit to yourself.'

Brom was more than physically wounded by his encounter with Utha the Ghost. Rham Jas didn't stop, but spoke over his shoulder as he led the horse further into the secluded gully. 'I'm just pointing out that, if you want to decide who gets to live and who gets to die, maybe you should get better with that shiny sword. I beat him, so I get to decide whether he lives or not.'

Rham Jas heard Brom grunt, a sound that was equal parts anger and agreement. The sound that followed, as Brom kicked his heels into the horse's flanks, was pure anger and the Kirin turned just in time to see Brom jump from his horse to tackle him to the ground.

The friends landed in a heap on the grassy track, with Brom positioned on top of Rham Jas. 'I can still pummel a little shit like you, Kirin,' the young lord shouted as he smashed his fist into Rham Jas's face.

The blow was solid and unexpected, and Rham Jas had to roll to the side to avoid further punches. He raised his leg sharply and kicked Brom in the back before shoving him roughly off to the side.

'Is that the best you've got, Ro?' Rham Jas shouted back, as he got to his feet and kicked Brom in the stomach, knocking the breath out of him.

Brom growled in anger and dived at the Kirin's legs, again tackling him to the ground.

'It takes a brave man to shoot a longbow, you horse-fucker.'

Brom punched and kicked wildly at Rham Jas. Most of the blows landed, but they caused minimal damage. The Kirin held his hands up to protect his face, but got a nasty knee to the side which made him wince with pain. He grabbed out at the Ro's neck, causing Brom to pull his punches and try to wrestle free from the choke hold. A solid palm strike from Rham Jas sent Brom backwards and allowed the two men to get to their feet, panting.

They stood looking at each other. Both men were bleeding from various minor wounds.

'Are you finished?' he asked the young lord of Canarn. 'Because this isn't terribly helpful.'

Brom was scowling and touching his jaw. Rham Jas had deliberately struck him on his existing wound and made it worse. Blood was visible at the corners of his mouth and his beard was stained red. He stood, scowling for a further moment, before straightening up and spitting out a globule of blood.

'Do you have anything to drink?' he asked.

The Kirin turned to where their horses stood grazing next to a copse of trees, oblivious to the fight. 'There's a bottle of Darkwald red in my saddle pack,' Rham Jas replied, letting his customary grin return, 'but I stole it, so I get more than you.'

'I don't give a shit, I just want something that'll make me drunk.' Brom sat down heavily on the side of the track.

Rham Jas shook his head and walked away from Brom to fetch their horses. He led them off the track and a short way into the trees, making sure they were out of the sight of any other travellers who might be using the Kirin run. He then turned to Brom, who hadn't moved from his position on the ground and was still spitting out blood.

'Get off the track, Brom. If we're going to get drunk, we should maybe take some sort of cover.'

Rham Jas tied the horses' reins to a thick tree trunk and Brom stood up. He was rubbing his back where Rham Jas had kicked him and his jaw was possibly now broken. Rham Jas knew that the bumps and bruises Brom had given him would disappear quickly and he'd be able to tease his friend about his weak constitution.

They settled down quickly and Rham Jas sensed his friend would much rather drink than talk.

'One bottle of wine isn't enough to forget anything of note, Rham Jas,' Brom stated.

'True, but the kindly old gentleman I stole it from had other interests too.' The Kirin retrieved a small leather pouch from his saddlebag. 'Do you know what this is?'

Brom looked at the pouch and shook his head. 'Is it a very small bottle of Volk whisky?'

Rham Jas opened the pouch and produced a bronze pipe and a circular container. 'This, my dear boy, is rainbow smoke. It seems that drugs are rife in your country, whether the clerics want to admit it or not.'

Brom laughed, shifting his position to lean more easily against a tree. 'So, if we get caught, we'll be babbling like fools? I like it.'

'Don't worry, we're in no real danger of getting caught,' Rham Jas replied as he unscrewed the container. 'Cozz has no clerics and the bound men there would never chase us up here. The Black churchman will have to get back to Tiris before they can seriously start looking for us again.'

Brom considered this and didn't look especially reassured. 'That's where we're heading too. We're walking into the troll's mouth, wouldn't you agree?'

Rham Jas liked Brom a great deal, but the young lord could be terribly dim-witted sometimes. 'We'll get there days ahead of them and, as far as I remember, you didn't explain your plan to them. They'll just assume we'll go into the wilds and lie low. The idea of us going to Tiris is so stupid it won't occur to them.'

'So, our stupidity is what's going to keep us alive?' Brom raised an eyebrow.

'Precisely . . . I wouldn't have it any other way.'

Rham Jas realized Brom must be in turmoil now that he knew his father was dead, but if his friend could take away some of the burden with humour, drugs and alcohol, then he would.

Rham Jas carefully loaded the pipe with a pinch of brightly coloured powder and sat back next to Brom.

'We're going to die, you know,' the Kirin said, with no real build-up.

Brom looked at him. 'What?'

'Well, there are only two of us . . . your father is dead, which means the city has likely been sacked and, by the time we get there, there may not be anyone to save.'

Brom bowed his head. 'It means something else as well.' His words were quiet and solemn. 'It means that I'm now the duke of Canarn.'

Rham Jas offered his friend the bronze pipe. 'Dukes first, my lord,' he said with a grin.

Brom took the pipe and, using a flint and steel from the pouch, touched a small flame to the bowl. He drew in a deep breath and Rham Jas sensed the familiar smell of high-quality Karesian rainbow smoke. Brom held his breath in for a moment and nearly coughed. Then he slowly breathed out a plume of sweet-smelling smoke and let his head fall back against the tree trunk.

'Do you think Bronwyn . . .?' Rham Jas began, only to be cut off by Brom.

'Don't,' he said. 'As things stand, I can imagine she's still alive, hiding somewhere in the secret tunnels. Maybe she even got out of the city.'

Rham Jas took the pipe. 'Whereas my customary brand of optimism would paint a rather grimmer picture of things?' He tapped the pipe against his boot to remove the burnt crust of powder.

'Exactly . . . just let me think happy thoughts for a moment.'

Rham Jas took a deep pull on the pipe and let the effects wash over him.

* * *

Karesian rainbow smoke was considered a decadent pleasure in Tor Funweir, illegal and possible to obtain only from mobsters and other shady characters. Rham Jas liked it as an aid to relaxation and found the Ro objection to it bizarre – probably just another example of the clerics disliking something simply because it was foreign and they didn't understand it.

The effects were mild. A feeling of comfortable lethargy made thinking happen slowly and an elevated mood usually followed within a few minutes. The stronger stuff produced more of a mellow high that enabled long periods of sitting around with few cares and a tendency to babble.

Rham Jas and Brom had emptied the pouch within the hour and, with breaks to pass round the bottle of wine, had successfully achieved a degree of calm.

They'd tied the horses securely and retreated deeper into the trees to lie across a grassy hillock well off the track. They'd ridden away from Cozz through the night and now, as they lay looking up at the cloudy sky, Rham Jas estimated that it was nearly midday. Neither man had said much as they let the rainbow smoke flow through their bodies and, with the exception of the occasional contented exhalation, they lay in silence.

Rham Jas was still worried about his friend. When Brom had arrived in Ro Weir, several weeks ago, his intention had been to return home as a liberator. Now, with the knowledge that Duke Hector had been executed, the young lord would have to reassess his plan. Rham Jas thought that getting into Ro Canarn would not be too tricky – finding a ship from Tiris would be possible and it should be fairly easy to stay hidden while they did so. The uncomfortable truth that informed the Kirin's thinking, however, was that the two of them would need help to make any impact when they reached Canarn. Rham Jas was a killer with few equals and Brom was a dangerous swordsman, but an army they were not.

'What did you mean?' Brom broke the silence.

'What did I mean about what?' replied Rham Jas vaguely, rubbing his eyes to focus through the drug-induced haze.

'The Black cleric . . . Utha the Ghost. You said you knew him.'

'Actually, I said that we have some friends in common,' corrected Rham Jas, 'but I get what you're saying.'

Brom half turned and rested his head on his hand. 'So?'

'It's quite a long story . . . and I may not be in the best condition to do it justice,' Rham Jas answered with a dopey grin.

Brom lay back down and breathed out, letting a manic chuckle escape his lips. 'Hasim always said you were no good to anyone after rainbow smoke.'

'I wouldn't listen to Hasim about . . . well, anything, really.' Rham Jas didn't lose his grin, but sat up, immediately feeling light-headed.

'I didn't kill Utha because some people I respect think well of him.' The Kirin knew that the risen could be found in the Deep Wood of Canarn, but he doubted Brom would ever have had contact with them. 'Do you remember that tree I told you about?' he asked.

'The black heartwood tree,' replied Brom

'Well, it was . . . sort of sacred to my people . . . and to some other people that lived in Oslan.'

'Other people? Make sense, man.' Brom was becoming irritable.

Rham Jas had long thought the trees extinct in Tor Funweir, that the Purple clerics had cut down or burned every one they could find. They could still be found in some places in Ranen, but the main concentration was in the Kirin woods.

'The forest-dwellers revere the trees. They call them the Dark Young of the Dead God. I suppose they're afraid of them, as if they're not exactly what they seem to be. They just looked like ancient, strange-looking trees to me.'

Brom was confused and gazed up at the dark sky. 'What does this have to do with Utha?'

Rham Jas smiled. 'I did say I was a little too far gone to be a good storyteller,' he said, wishing they had some more wine and rainbow smoke. 'I lived side by side with the risen most of my young life. I hadn't even heard the term *risen men* until I came to Tor Funweir; they were always the Dokkalfar to me.'

Brom's expression showed that he, like most men of Ro, believed the church's propaganda that the risen were monstrous beings. 'I thought . . .' he began.

'Yes, yes, you thought they were undead monsters. Everyone in your stupid country does. Except maybe Utha the Ghost.'

Brom looked even more confused. 'He's a crusader, Rham Jas, which means he hunts and kills risen men.'

'All I know is that they like him. Their taste may be suspect, I grant you, but they see him as a man of honour and I won't kill a man who is counted amongst the Dokkalfar's few friends.'

Rham Jas had not asked exactly why they considered the Black cleric a friend, but, during a recent trip to the Fell, he'd heard the name Utha the Ghost spoken with fondness. The Dokkalfar were paranoid and did not give their trust or friendship easily – their treatment at the hands of men had taught them to be wary – but Utha had done something to make up for the dozens he'd killed.

Rham Jas had never had to earn their friendship as his first twenty years of life had been spent living alongside them, and their strange tree had gifted him with extraordinary abilities.

His wife used to enjoy walking in the Oslan woods and listening to the strange beings singing, a sound Rham Jas, too, missed when he was away from them for too long. Even now, he looked for any opportunity to return to the deepest woods and spend time with the Dokkalfar.

'Was it worth it?' Brom asked. 'Leaving him alive to continue chasing us?'

Rham Jas lay back down. 'I have a feeling about that cleric,' he said mysteriously. 'I suspect he won't be chasing us any more.'

'You still should have killed him . . . but I don't want another fight about it.' The laugh accompanying Brom's words showed that the rainbow smoke had relaxed him considerably.

'Maybe. But I didn't,' replied the Kirin.

Something occurred to Brom, and he again directed a puzzled look at his friend. 'How is it that I don't know you at all?'

'You've known me for years, you idiot,' Rham Jas answered.

'But I didn't know any of that. I doubt Hasim or Magnus knew any of that either. Does anyone actually know you, Rham Jas?' Brom was prying in a way that the Kirin didn't like, but he meant well, so Rham Jas let it slide.

'There was someone, but she was killed by Purple clerics . . .'

'Oh, I'm sorry,' said Brom quietly, resting his arms under his head.

His few friends knew that there were certain lines beyond which Rham Jas should not be pushed. He rarely talked about his wife and had long ago learned that the mere mention of her would cause people to stop talking to him.

Rham Jas shook his head and an idea began to form in his mind – the kind of idea that only occurred to him when his mind was totally relaxed with the drug.

'Brom . . .' he began in a quizzical fashion.

'Yes, Rham Jas.'

'I think I may know where we can get some help.' The Kirin knew that it was a poor idea, but marching into Canarn alone was worse.

'Do you have an army of assassin friends somewhere around here?' Brom asked with a gormless smile.

'No, but I know a . . . well . . . a man . . . not that the word *man* really applies,' he answered. 'His name is Nanon and he lives in the Deep Wood of Canarn.'

'He has a strange name.' Brom suddenly looked suspicious and sat up to look down at Rham Jas. 'Who is he?'

The Kirin sighed. 'He's Dokkalfar . . . in their language he's a Tyr, which sort of translates as warrior.'

Brom's drugged state softened his reaction to this information and he merely directed a doubting expression at his friend. 'And he lives in the woods of my homeland?'

'Not just him. He told me there was a big settlement there – maybe a few hundred of them – deep in the woods.'

'Surely we'd know if there was a village of risen men that close to Ro Canarn.' Brom's expression was sceptical, and Rham Jas knew the young lord was cynical and not given to what he thought of as fantasy.

'They're quite good at staying hidden. Your god is obsessed with hunting them down.'

Brom suddenly looked offended. 'Do I look like a cleric to you?'

'No, but you're still a Ro. I can sense the wanton arrogance coming off you from here.' Rham Jas grinned broadly and made his friend laugh in spite of himself.

'Okay, so how can a risen man help us?' Brom asked when he'd stopped laughing.

'Well, if I can persuade him, he may have a few friends.' Rham Jas closed his eyes to shield them from the sun as it poked out from behind a cloud. It was going to be a hot day. 'It's the best plan . . . if you can call it that . . . that I can think of.'

'Why would he want to help me reclaim my home?'

'Well, they have no love for the church of Ro, so the chance to kill a bunch of Red knights might appeal to them.' Rham Jas grinned. 'And it might help if you promised them sanctuary in the woods when you become duke.'

Brom shook his head and rubbed his eyes. 'I don't think I'll become duke any time soon. Canarn will either be independent or Ranen.'

'So, you'll be a thain.' Rham Jas was still grinning, which only made Brom more irritable.

'I think I know who we need to speak to when we get to Canarn. It's been rolling around my head since we left Weir and I'm fairly sure he'll still be alive,' the young lord said, trying not to look at his friend. 'The knights wouldn't kill other churchmen, so Brother Lanry should still be somewhere in the town.'

'Brown cleric?' asked Rham Jas, vaguely remembering the man from the last time he had been in Ro Canarn with Al-Hasim and Magnus.

'He was my father's chaplain and he probably hates the Red knights more than you.' Brom at least had a smile on his face and Rham Jas guessed that the rainbow smoke would stop him getting too annoyed now.

'Okay, so if they haven't killed, buggered or caged him . . .' Rham Jas directed his grin upward as he spoke. 'He might have . . . what, a secret way in?'

Brom shot him a dark look and came out of his drugged state for a moment. 'Rham Jas, Ro Canarn had a population of five thousand men, women and children. If it's all right with you I'd like to see if any of them are still alive.' His voice rose in pitch and his eyes conveyed anger.

Rham Jas wasn't comfortable with grief and he had tried not to broach the subject of Ro Canarn's citizens. They'd have fought when the Red knights appeared and Rham Jas doubted the survivors would have been treated kindly. The city had formerly been a vibrant place, with taverns, shops and a populace of good, honest people – very different from the paranoid social climbers of the rest of Tor Funweir – and Rham Jas hoped some of their spirit might remain.

Brom, as the nascent ruler of the city, had a different perspective – he saw a population in need of rescue from an occupying force. In many ways, Rham Jas thought, he already resembled a Ranen thain more than a Ro duke.

'Okay, I apologize for my . . . idiotic rambling, brought on by . . . you know, drugs and stuff.' Rham Jas winced at his terrible apology, but decided to soldier on. 'We'll go and see the Brown cleric when we get to Canarn. He'll at least be able to tell us how many Red fuckers we have to kill and if Magnus is still in one piece.'

Brom snorted and Rham Jas was glad that his friend's drugged haze was rapidly returning. 'If he's still alive, Magnus is the second person we should go and see. Spring him from prison and he's worth four or five knights of the Red.'

'If he's still alive . . . and if we get help . . . and if we don't get killed on our way there.' Rham Jas was pessimistic about all the *if*s, but he was beyond the point where he could just leave Brom and return to Ro Weir. He was committed to seeing this through.

Brom considered the last words spoken by the Kirin for a long moment, gazing off the hillock and down into the loosely spaced trees to the north. 'You are aware that our horses may well have been eaten by Gorlan while we've been lying here?' he said, trying to focus on something more immediate than their strategy for retaking Canarn.

'Doubtful. Horses make a hell of a sound when they see the nasty little fuckers . . . we'd have heard,' Rham Jas replied, without much certainty.

Brom raised his eyebrows and they shared a doubtful look, before the Kirin said, 'Okay, we'd better move, just in case. I don't fancy walking to Ro Tiris.' He retrieved his longbow and quiver of arrows from the ground.

The two friends pulled themselves heavily to their feet and trudged slowly back to the trees. The hillock was only slightly raised from the forest floor, but the gentle gradient was enough to cause both men to stumble. At the tree line below, Rham Jas peered into the forest before slowly walking towards the horses.

They were picketed to a low tree trunk, next to a dense bramble bush, and Brom stepped past Rham Jas and drew his sword awkwardly as they approached the small clearing.

'Oh, troll shit,' said the young lord, as they both saw the dense web that was being wrapped round the twitching body of Brom's horse.

The other animal was unharmed and was snorting quietly and kicking at the ground as three large Gorlan spiders crawled all over the fallen animal. Each was the size of a large dog and coloured deep black with a bright flash of red on its bloated abdomen. They were sleek, rather than hairy, and weren't quite large enough to attack men; but their oversized fangs, currently stuck in the flanks of the horse, could nonetheless cause a vicious wound and recovery from thier paralysing venom would require several days in bed.

The largest of the three reared up at the sight of Rham Jas and Brom, raising its front two legs off the ground and bearing its fangs in a threat display. It made a loud hissing sound and poised to strike if they came too close.

'Look, you little eight-legged bastard . . . fuck off,' said Rham Jas irritably. 'We have enough problems without you adding to it.'

'I don't think it speaks Ro,' Brom said, without taking his eyes from the Gorlan.

Rham Jas guessed that his friend was a little scared of spiders and secretly determined to tease him about it later.

Rham Jas waved his arms in the air to attract the attention of all three spiders, and clapped his hands together in an attempt to spook them.

'I don't want to kill you, spiders,' he said, almost regretfully, 'but I will shoot you up if you don't leave.' He slowly pulled an arrow from his quiver and notched it to his bow.

'Rham Jas, just shoot the spiders,' Brom said, brandishing his sword.

The Kirin didn't like killing animals, but Gorlan were aggressive predators and would not leave a feast the size of a fully grown horse without a fight.

270

He slowly drew back on his bow and pursed his lips before shooting the spider between its fangs. The creature instantly flew backwards and its legs curled up, became rigid. The other two quickly fled into the brambles and the sound of them scuttling away disappeared after a few seconds.

Brom lowered his sword and breathed easier now that the creatures were out of view. 'I really hate those things.'

'They're not too bad. It's the really big ones you need to worry about. There are Gorlan in Lob's Wood that take three or four arrows to put down . . . tasty, though,' Rham Jas added with a smile.

* * *

Rham Jas enjoyed fried Gorlan legs – they were crunchy and surprisingly meaty. The abdomen could be sliced and deep-fried, but without proper cooking implements they'd had to throw it away. Brom was noticeably less keen on eating the spider. He'd eaten sparingly, concentrating mainly on the dried beef in their saddle packs. Rham Jas had teased him about being scared of Gorlan, but he didn't seem to mind so long as the others didn't come back.

Rham Jas was used to them and had seen huge specimens in his time. He'd even heard rumours that some of the largest, far to the south, had a primitive ability to speak. Whether that was true or not, the Kirin of Oslan had long realized that the bigger they were, the less hostile they were, as if intelligence were a privilege of size amongst the Gorlan.

They rode, Brom sitting behind Rham Jas, on the only horse they had left. The low wooded gully became a dense forest a day or so beyond Cozz. Rham Jas was not overly concerned about entering the woods of Voy as there was unlikely to be anything there that would cause a genuine threat to the two of them. Any bandits would provide a quick fight and maybe even a second horse, but the kind of scum who preyed on the Kirin run were usually broken men, with few options but to risk death. Not men who would cause Rham Jas to sweat.

'Stop moving so much,' Brom said grumpily.

271

'I didn't eat your horse, don't blame me.' Rham Jas gently elbowed his friend in the ribs.

'Just ride and try to keep still.' Brom had still not fully regained his composure and had been silent for several hours as they rode away from the dead horse.

Rham Jas had to admit that he wanted to fill the air with point-less conversation in order to not have to think about contacting the Dokkalfar. It would be an awkward encounter, bringing a lord of the Ro into the Deep Wood, but Rham Jas knew a little about how they thought and had high hopes that they would help. Nanon, in particular, favoured the idea of fighting back over just sitting in the woods to be picked off by clerics. So far, his more violent impulses had been curtailed by their Vithar shamans – the eldest of their people, whose counsel was always that the Dokkalfar must simply *endure until the time is right*. They had a strange view of vengeance and were more patient that any people Rham Jas had met. As long as Brom was quiet and let Rham Jas do the talking, they should be okay, he thought. They might even stand a chance of assaulting Canarn and killing enough of the knights moderately to inconvenience the church before they were hacked to pieces by longswords.

* * *

The days passed slowly as Brom and Rham Jas made their way through the foothills of the Walls of Ro and on to the forested northern plains of Tor Funweir. The Kirin run was decidedly empty and Rham Jas was glad not to encounter any random bandits or larger Gorlan. It suited those travellers who used the route to foster the image of the Kirin run as a dangerous and hostile environment. In reality, if you were well enough connected to know about it, and tough enough to use it, you were probably safe. Rham Jas had travelled Tor Funweir widely and the wilds held no fear for him. He was a crack shot with his longbow and a nightmare with his katana, and he had well-placed confidence when it came to killing things.

Brom was still quiet and, aside from the odd comment about his father or sister, he'd remained morose and sullen since Cozz. They had meagre daily rations and the young lord of Canarn had steadfastly refused to supplement his diet with Gorlan. He'd even turned his nose up at Rham Jas's nutritious spider and nettle broth, a rich concoction that was quite a delicacy in Oslan. The smaller Gorlan they encountered in the woods were perfect for eating, but Brom was clearly bothered by the creatures and became twitchy whenever they approached a nest.

'Rham Jas, what's that?' Brom pointed through the trees off to their left.

It was just approaching twilight and they had been talking about finding a place to camp. The woodland they travelled through had thinly spaced trees and was dotted with rocky crevices and dry river beds.

Brom was pointing to a slight glow emanating from a low fire in the distance. 'Is that a campfire?'

'I should think so, unless the moss has started to glow,' Rham Jas replied flippantly.

The fire was flickering close to the ground and far enough away that they couldn't see any movement around the area. Rham Jas reined in the horse and leant forward to stroke the animal's muzzle to keep it quiet.

'Hold the reins,' he said over his shoulder to Brom, and began to dismount.

Once on the ground, Rham Jas crouched and tried to focus through the grey evening air to see the campfire. The sky was rapidly becoming dark and Rham Jas couldn't make out any definite shapes through the trees, though he could hear distant rustling and footsteps consistent with a small group of people.

'I need to get closer to see, but it's probably just a bandit gang or a group of travellers,' Rham Jas whispered to Brom. 'If we're going to be sleeping around here as well, I'd like to know who our neighbours are.'

Brom dismounted and pulled the horse over to a nearby rock, tying the reins securely, before drawing his sword and crouching down next to Rham Jas.

'I know stealth isn't a speciality of yours, Brom, but try not to make too much noise . . . let me go first,' Rham Jas said with his customary grin.

'Oh, just shut up and get on with it,' he replied, clearly not in a jovial mood.

Rham Jas quickly retrieved his longbow from the horse and notched an arrow loosely against the string before making his way into the trees. He walked slowly, one foot over the other, moving in the practised fashion of a man used to sneaking up on people in the dark. Brom stayed a little way back and Rham Jas was glad that his blundering through the undergrowth produced only a little sound.

As he edged closer to the fire, Rham Jas could hear words spoken in the accent of Ro. Several men were standing around the fire and two were sitting on bedrolls. At first it appeared as if his guess about a gang of bandits had been correct, but as he passed a bramble thicket and secreted himself behind a thick tree trunk, it became clear that only those men standing up were bandits and those sitting down were being robbed.

Five men, with crossbows and short swords, stood in a rough circle round the fire, aiming their weapons at the two seated men.

Rham Jas decided to get a little closer and held a hand up to Brom, indicating that he should hold his position. The Kirin assassin moved swiftly and silently to stand behind a rocky protrusion within earshot of the camp.

The bandits were in good humour at having found two men alone in the wilds and Rham Jas guessed that the victims were not fighting men. One of the bandits had his back to Rham Jas and the Kirin could just about make out a seated Karesian not far in front of him.

'You're a long way from home, desert men . . . maybe you should think twice about coming through our land again, hey?' said a gruff man of Ro, smirking and showing brown teeth and gums.

'Mott, these bastards ain't got much.' The other man was riffling through a series of large rucksacks next to the fire. 'Except wine, they've got a lot of that.'

'Where's your coin, Karesian?' said the man identified as Mott.

Rham Jas estimated that the two Karesians were a little drunk, as they were gazing off into the night rather than focusing on the men robbing them. He couldn't make out their faces, but thought they looked rather relaxed, reclining in front of their fire and making no particular effort to stop the robbery.

'I'm talking to you,' Mott said, slapping one of their faces.

'I know you're talking to me, you stupid Ro. I chose not to answer. Brains are clearly not required for banditry,' slurred one of the Karesians in a voice that Rham Jas vaguely recognized.

The Karesian received another slap and toppled over on his bedroll. 'Hitting me is not going to make finding my coin any easier, fuckpiece,' he said with venom, the insult indistinct with the combination of accent and alcohol.

The speaker was called Kohli and Rham Jas guessed that his companion would be Jenner. They were Karesian brothers and smugglers from the far city of Thrakka, though what they were doing here was a mystery. The last time Rham Jas had met them, they, and Al-Hasim, had swindled a boat out of someone and were running illegal Karesian desert nectar into Ro Tiris. Rham Jas remembered them well enough to know that fighting was not counted amongst their skills, and he decided to intervene.

He waved back for Brom to approach through the trees and then moved to position himself as close to one of the bandits as possible, crouched in darkness a few feet from the man's back.

'We don't like Karesian scum in these woods so you'd better come up with something or my boys will have to take payment in blood,' Mott growled at the seated Karesians.

Rham Jas placed his bow on the floor and silently drew his katana. The five bandits were all facing inwards and were clearly not prepared for an ambush. He took a further step closer to the nearest man's back and then darted forward, wrapping one arm around his neck and swinging his blade round to rest against the man's cheek.

'And how do you feel about Kirin?' he asked loudly, as all the men present turned to look at him.

'Where the fuck did you come from?' Mott loudly retorted.

Kohli clapped his hands drunkenly. 'Rham Jas, perfect timing. Will you join me and my bandit friends in a drink? They are most interested in coin, but I'm sure they're just misunderstood.'

The other four bandits pointed their crossbows at Rham Jas and moved to stand in a line opposite him. 'Let him go, Kirin, and you may live.'

'Fuck off and *you* may live,' replied Rham Jas quickly.

The bandits laughed with misplaced confidence as Brom suddenly appeared from the darkness, sword in hand. He had no cover from the crossbows, and to Rham Jas his eyes looked colder than usual.

'Listen to the Kirin, he's not as stupid as he looks and you're not as dangerous as you think you are,' said the lord of Canarn.

'That's a nice sword. I think I'll take it from you when you're lying bleeding at my feet, boy,' Mott said, levelling his crossbow.

'Come and take it, little man.' Brom had murder in his eyes.

The macho posturing was becoming tiresome to Rham Jas. 'Oh, this is getting silly,' he said, realizing that his friend was going to get himself shot full off bolts if he wasn't careful.

With a swift jerk of his sword arm he cut the throat of the man he was holding and shoved the dying bandit into the fire. The others were sufficiently distracted by the eruption of sparks and smoke for Rham Jas to dart to the side and kick a burning branch into the face of a second bandit.

Brom also used the distraction to move round the other side and roar an unnecessary challenge at the bandits. Rham Jas shook his head at Brom's display, as the Kirin delivered a fatal downward strike to one man's chest and spun dexterously to give a second man a solid kick in the stomach, winding him and sending him to the floor.

Two crossbow bolts were loosed, but these were not true fighting men and the distraction of two killers setting about them was sufficient to cause the shots to miss their mark.

Brom engaged a startled Mott and proceeded to teach him a lesson in swordsmanship, effortlessly disassembling the bandit's technique and knocking away his short sword within moments. Brom punched him viciously to the floor.

'Brom, that's enough, they're only bandits. Not worth more than a quick scrap.' Rham Jas could see real anger in his friend's eyes and guessed that this was the eruption of several days' worth of pent-up rage.

Mott held his face and winced in pain as Brom levelled his longsword at the bandit's neck. The two others who were still alive stayed on the floor, looking up in fear at Rham Jas.

'Oh, stop that,' he said to the cowering pair. 'If your idiot boss hadn't mentioned taking my friend's sword, you might all have got away alive.' Rham Jas didn't like unnecessary death and these men were simply common folk making a dirty living.

'You . . . Mott, whatever your name is,' ordered Rham Jas, 'pick up your men and leave . . . now. If I see you again, I'll wear your skin as a hat. Do you understand me?' Rham Jas was irritated at having to rescue two drunken friends and stop a sober one from giving in to bloodlust.

Mott nodded, not taking his eyes from Brom's sword as it swayed next to his throat. The two other bandits stood up and, in obvious distress, picked up their two dead companions and began to back out of the clearing. Mott moved away from Brom, not thinking to pick up his weapons, quickly darted past his men and disappeared into the darkening forest.

'You're Lord Bromvy?' asked Kohli from beside the fire.

Neither of the Karesian brothers was overly concerned about the fight they had witnessed, Rham Jas thought. Jenner was mostly preoccupied with keeping himself upright and not being sick.

Brom didn't answer the question and glared at the patch of darkness through which the bandits had retreated.

'Yes, he is,' said Rham Jas. 'And Kohli, what are you doing here? Isn't there a child in need of drugs somewhere?'

Kohli blinked a few times. He, too, was considerably the worse for drink. 'We lost our boat in Tiris when . . .' he shot a dark look at his brother, 'someone demanded we stop for some female company and the port authorities impounded it.'

'The same boat you and Hasim stole last year?' asked Rham Jas.

'Yup, I think someone at the lord marshal's office recognized it and we had to run from the city. Luckily, these Ro aren't too bothered by forged clay documents.'

'Glenwood?' The Kirin was amazed that such a poor forger was still in business.

'We didn't know anyone else and he told us you were probably in Weir, so we thought we'd come and find you,' he said with a drunken grin which, for some reason, made Rham Jas irrationally annoyed.

'You thought you'd come and find me? Using the Kirin run, a route the two of you are spectacularly unsuited to travel?' he asked with the tone of a disapproving parent.

Jenner retched a couple of times and held his hands against his head, rubbing his temples. 'What's going on?' he asked vaguely. 'Are we being robbed?'

Kohli looked across at his drunken brother and smiled. 'Go to sleep, Jenner, we haven't been robbed. Rham Jas is here.'

The two Karesians had the deeply bloodshot eyes of men who drink to excess and each was thin, with frail limbs and blotchy skin. The last time Rham Jas had seen them, they'd been celebrating their twenty-fifth birthdays in Ro Weir. The year that had passed since then had not been kind to the brothers. Their clothes were poor and travel-stained, and their belongings consisted mostly of wine. Rham Jas couldn't see any weapons and neither was in any condition to defend himself if attacked.

Jenner straightened and said, 'Rham Jas, excellent. We told Hasim that we'd find him. That's, that's really good.' The last few words were said with a dopey grin and Jenner toppled over when he'd finished speaking.

Brom directed a quizzical look at the now unconscious form of Jenner. Rham Jas raised his eyebrows and stepped in front of Kohli, who was swaying contentedly.

'What's he talking about?' Rham Jas asked, pointing at Jenner.

'We were in Ro Canarn with Hasim,' Kohli said, as if it were the most normal thing in the world.

Brom nearly dropped his sword as he clumsily moved across the small camp and knelt down in front of the swaying Karesian smuggler.

Holding the man by the shoulders, he demanded, 'When?'

'We left about two weeks ago, just after Hasim got captured by the Red knights.' Kohli's eyes became unfocused and Rham Jas guessed he'd soon pass out from the wine.

'Why were you there . . . why was Hasim there?' Brom tumbled over the words as he tried to find out what the drunken man knew.

'Easy, Brom, he won't be much use until he's sober.' Rham Jas was almost as interested as his friend, but knew Kohli well enough to realize he was unlikely to prove coherent.

His words appeared prophetic, as Kohli collapsed forwards into Brom's arms, his eyes glazing over and a foam of vomit appearing at his mouth.

'Wake up, you fucking shit-stain,' shouted Brom at the unconscious man.

Rham Jas let his friend shout racial insults at Kohli for a few minutes. He thought that, since he'd denied Brom the chance of killing the bandits, he should at least allow him to scream at a drunken smuggler. The Kirin assassin simply sheathed his katana, retrieved his longbow, and sat down by the fire.

Kohli and Jenner were human refuse – men who were useful if you needed something done quietly, but otherwise Rham Jas despised them. They had no cause beyond money – and wine – and their only loyalty lay with whoever gave them coin. Al-Hasim had often tried to defend them, telling Rham Jas that they were simply men outside the law who hated the Ro. This might be true, but they were still annoying drunkards with few discernible talents.

After a few minutes Brom slumped down on the uneven ground. He didn't look away from the two unconscious Karesians and was panting rapidly, clenching and unclenching his fists. Rham Jas took a bottle of Kohli's wine and pulled out the cork with his teeth. It was of decent quality and he took a deep swig before passing it to his friend.

'I hate this . . .' Brom said darkly.

Rham Jas knew what he meant, but asked anyway. 'What do you hate?'

'All this,' he said, pointing to Kohli and Jenner and then gesturing around to the thinly spaced trees of the Kirin run. 'The thieves, the running, the death . . . the clerics, all of it.'

Rham Jas nodded and realized that any residual excitement Brom might have felt about the itinerant lifestyle was rapidly wearing off. The young lord of Canarn had spent much of his life with Rham Jas, Magnus and Hasim, and had essentially lived the life of a criminal – travelling, causing trouble and having a good time. But this was different. Brom finally knew why some men *had* to live this life. Before, he'd been doing it from choice, for the adventure or just so as to spend time with his unlikely friends. Now he was named to the Black Guard, wanted by the clerics, and with a shattered homeland.

'You get used to it, my friend,' Rham Jas replied gently.

'I don't think I want to get used to it.' Brom shifted himself around and kicked Kohli off his bedroll. Taking a swig of wine, he lay on his back, looking up at the thin canopy of branches above.

'Just be patient, these idiots will wake up in a few hours and they can tell you everything.'

Rham Jas, too, was surprised to hear that Al-Hasim had been in Ro Canarn. The last he'd known, the Karesian scoundrel had been in Fredericksand, enjoying Algenon Teardrop's hospitality.

'Why would Hasim be there?' Brom asked, not expecting an answer.

'Not sure, but at least we may find out whether your sister is still alive.' Rham Jas was speaking quietly and not pushing Brom any more. Rham Jas knew the signs and could see his friend was close to the edge. All he needed was for something else bad or frustrating to happen and he'd have some kind of breakdown.

'Try and get some sleep, Brom, all these questions will wait until tomorrow.'

* * *

Rham Jas didn't sleep at all. He sat in the same position for several hours, while Brom slowly drifted off into a fitful slumber. Then the Kirin decided to go for a walk in the woods.

A little moonlight shone through the trees, but the thin forest was otherwise dark and Rham Jas ghosted through the woods, making no sound. He didn't really know how he had found himself in this situation, accompanying a Black Guard to a walled city occupied by Red knights. Despite his skill and bravado, Rham Jas was mostly concerned to be left alone to live his life and not to become involved in such foolish endeavours.

Brom knew virtually nothing about what had happened in Ro Canarn, other than the certain death of his father, and Rham Jas wondered if anything the drunken Karesians would have to say would lessen the young lord's anger.

EPILOGUE

BRONWYN HUDDLED AS close as possible to the soft, mossy tree trunk. The canopy above sheltered her from the worst of the rain, but frequent drips, enough to prevent her sleeping, kept finding their way through the branches.

She was far enough from the road and deep enough within the small wood to feel moderately safe from discovery, but the weather and the need to sleep rough had soured the young noblewoman's disposition to a point where she almost wished for capture. At least a gaol cell in Canarn would be out of the weather.

She'd seen no sign of pursuit, though she was sure knights would have been sent after her, and had focused on the advice given her by Al-Hasim. He'd told her to turn due west at the blasted tree and contact Wraith Company in the ruins of Ro Hail. Whether that was wisdom or desperation didn't really matter – either way, Bronwyn was getting further from home and growing more miserable with each step.

As the darkness grew and the moonlight was obscured by branches, Bronwyn of Canarn drifted into a restless sleep.

Her dreams when growing up had always been curiously vivid, and frequently shared by her twin brother. Their father used to say that Bromvy and Bronwyn were bound by more than simply their blood, and that Brytag the World Raven allowed them to experience each other's worries and fears. Whether that was just an old man's story or a true reflection of the twins' bond was not clear, but she had felt better every time she had shared a dream with her brother.

She found herself viewing Ro Canarn from above, a lump of stone and smoke perched on a low cliff side and battered by waves. It was dark and lifeless, with individual buildings impossible to discern, though the tower of the World Raven acted as a lighthouse of sorts for her dreaming consciousness.

As she plummeted further down, the sound of the sea growing to a roar and the dark stone gaining texture, she saw people in the streets of her home. The figures were armoured, though none wore the tabard of Canarn – a raven with talons bared – and most were evidently foreigners. They patrolled the empty streets, between ruined buildings of wood and stone, their eyes wary and their weapons ready.

Bronwyn found herself at street level, drifting between mercenaries and knights, trying to get her bearings. If it weren't for the World Raven shining overhead, she thought she would easily have become lost, for Canarn had changed. It was no longer vibrant and friendly – those things were for a peaceful and stable population – instead, it was dark and brooding, and she thought it owed its continued existence to stubbornness: the stubbornness of Brother Lanry determined to keep his chapel safe and the population alive; the stubbornness of Father Magnus, who refused to be cowed by Rillion; and, most of all, the stubbornness of Bronwyn and her brother, who were both still free.

The entrance to the keep was stained with blood and she remembered the desperate fight to hold the drawbridge. Dozens of men had died, standing their ground against the knights of the Red. Even now, a stack of crossbows, swords and shields was piled next to the drawbridge. Each item bore the raven of Canarn – the heraldry most prominent on the shields – but most had sword cuts and puncture marks which defaced the image of Brytag.

The central square was much as she remembered it from her flight with Al-Hasim, though the funeral pyres had now reduced to embers and the corralled population had been allowed sanctuary in the Brown chapel.

If she'd been awake, Bronwyn knew she would be reduced to

tears. As it was, she allowed her dream to remind her of why she must remain free.

'This isn't the end of the tale.' The voice was familiar.

She let herself turn and identified the speaker as her brother, Bromvy, standing next to the drawbridge.

'It seems like the end,' she replied.

Brom wore his armour of steel-reinforced leather and his sword was sheathed. He was dressed as he had been the morning he left for Ro Tiris, shortly before the assault, and Bronwyn was glad to see him.

'Are you dreaming as well, brother?' she asked.

He looked upwards and smiled at the tower of the World Raven. 'It would appear so.'

'Father is dead.' Bronwyn spoke plainly. 'That makes you the duke of Canarn.'

Brom bowed his head. 'I don't feel like a duke. I feel like a criminal . . . and my back's sore from sleeping rough.'

'But you are safe?' she pressed.

'After a fashion. I'm still alive . . . and I plan to remain so.'

She wished that she could fling her arms around his neck and cry long and hard into his shoulder. She wished that her dream would allow her to grieve, to weep, even to feel vulnerable for a moment, but all she could do was look at him.

'And you?' he asked. 'Please tell me you're not the trophy wife of some mercenary.'

A moment of silence, before laughter erupted suddenly from both of them.

'Thank you for making a joke,' Bronwyn said wearily.

Their eyes were both drawn to the World Raven, looking down on them. The tower was an unassuming structure, with a small statue of Brytag, wings spread and talons bared, perched on a flat plinth high above. In their dream, the tower was taller, its lines starker against the dark greys and browns of Ro Canarn, and Brytag himself was much larger, looming over his town to look down at the twins.

'Are we really dreaming?' asked Bronwyn, not sure whether to address the query to Brom or to the World Raven.

'He wants us both to see something,' replied Brom. 'Father always said that Brytag was fond of twins.'

They were drawn towards the keep, their feet barely touching the bloodstained cobbled streets. Bronwyn felt no sea breeze and no cold touched her limbs, making the city of her birth feel alien and far-off. Her brother glided next to her and the twins emerged into the central keep of Canarn, a square courtyard framed by high stone walls. The area was dominated by cooking fires and stowed weaponry, as knights of the Red camped on the cold stone.

'Bronwyn,' said Brom, pointing into the shadowy courtyard, 'do you see those shapes?'

She directed her eyes where he pointed and saw a number of strange, indistinct figures moving around the edges of the keep. They moved with inhuman grace and wielded leaf-shaped knives. She perceived that the knights had not seen them and something about their presence was comforting and strangely alien.

'I see them,' she replied, 'but I don't know what . . . who they are.'

The scene froze and the twins tried to get a clear look at the shadowy figures, only to be denied by a rapid movement that whisked them away from the keep and towards the Brown chapel. It was clear that this dream, if that were what it was, was being directed by a force they couldn't truly understand.

The chapel was unmolested, though the greenery that used to surround it was now mud, trampled by patrolling mercenaries. They joked and cursed, waiting for the order to clear the chapel – an order that would hopefully never come. Bronwyn knew, from the time she'd spent in Canarn after the battle, that Commander Rillion was reluctant to defile the humble Brown chapel.

Brom looked at the men, his hands twitching with anger and a deep-seated desire to draw his sword and kill these invaders. His anger was different from Bronwyn's, it came from a sense of duty imparted by their father. He was the duke and his honour would forever be linked to Ro Canarn. He could live as one of the Black Guard, or he could retake his city – there could be no in-between.

'Settle, brother. Brytag isn't showing us this to increase our anger.' She again wished she could reach out to touch Brom.

'I wish I could turn it off . . . just for a while, but I can't see beyond the rage.' A tear appeared at the corner of his eye. 'I hope Lanry is still alive.'

'Let us see,' replied Bronwyn.

They moved smoothly over the mud and past the mercenaries. The chapel was large enough to house many people – but it was not a tavern, and those inside could hope only for shelter, not for comfort.

The scene within made Bronwyn gasp. The seats had been shoved to the sides of the nave and in their place lay a hundred hastily laid bedrolls, occupied by quivering bodies. There were few lights and a figure, robed in brown, hunched his way to each person in turn, using a globed candle to minister healing. Some wounds were minor, bruises and cuts, but many of the commoners within had serious injuries and missing limbs.

'The knights haven't allowed them proper healing,' said Brom, letting his tear-filled eyes play over the gruesome scene.

Gathered around the humble Brown altar were uninjured citizens of Canarn, and the staircase leading down showed that many more were resident in the chapel's undercroft.

'This isn't war . . . I don't know what it is.' Brom no longer looked angry. Instead, his eyes were downcast and his hand shook.

Five thousand people had lived in Ro Canarn, with many more in the surrounding farmlands. The survivors, huddled in the Brown chapel, numbered fewer than five hundred. Bronwyn hoped that more had survived the battle and were hidden elsewhere in the town, but the knights had done their work well.

The brown-robed figure looked up. Brother Lanry was an old man, but he appeared even older in the minimal candlelight, the lines on his face deeper and the pain in his eyes more pronounced. For a moment, Bronwyn thought he saw them, but she knew that wasn't possible.

The sound of a raven calling jolted both the twins away from the chapel.

* * *

Brom woke suddenly, light rain caressing his neck. The face of his sister and the calling of Brytag faded only slowly, and the Black Guard sat in a moment of quiet remembrance.

Above him were trees, next to him the unconscious Karesian criminals and his friend, Rham Jas Rami. Somewhere to the north, over the sea, and occupied by knights and mercenaries, was his home. As he blinked his eyes to focus in the morning gloom of the Kirin run, Lord Bromvy Black Guard of Canarn decided that he would not yield, he would not surrender. He would not stop until his people were free and the One had paid for what his knights had done.

BOOK TWO

DAUGHTER
OF THE WOLF

THE TALE OF THE WATER GIANTS

A S GODS SLOWLY ascended and empires of might and terror were formed, the Giants did war upon each other. The battlegrounds of air, fire, earth and water were joined by shadow, forest, dust and void until all the land was broken. Alliances were formed, Giants fell, and the wars raged longer than the understanding of mortal men.

Each Giant saw himself a god and each god grew strong or died, falling to the inexorable passage of Deep Time.

The Water Giants, more alien than most, fought with malign cunning and chose the Ice Giants as their chief foe, doing war upon them as mountains rose and the land changed shape.

As ages passed and Rowanoco ascended to the ice halls beyond the world, the Water Giants sensed that their end was near. Their race, who had missed godhood by a hair's breadth, cried tears of pain and their tears became the rolling seas of the north. Their leaders, the twin Giants Ithqas and Aqas, were felled by Rowanoco himself and sent to the bottom of the deepest seas to gnaw on rock and fish.

Rowanoco gave no thought to his fallen foes, but the twins remained, mindless and primal, swirling endlessly amidst the watery tears of their long-dead kin.

PROLOGUE

T HE BROWN CHAPEL of Ro Canarn was never a warm or comforting place. It was cheap to build, cheap to maintain, and possessed few accoutrements of wealth or prosperity. It was the only building of worship in the city and, as such, was large and functional. It had also been the home of Brother Lanry for many years, though it was currently much more crowded than it had ever been.

The population of the city – those who had not been imprisoned or murdered by the knights of the Red and their mercenary allies – had sought refuge in the only building that even the invaders refused to violate. Lanry was glad that some things were still sacred and the knights had left his chapel and its several hundred new inhabitants alone. They'd stationed guards outside and taken careful note of the families that sheltered within, but had not sought entrance or questioned the cleric of poverty's motives in allowing the common folk sanctuary.

'Brother Lanry,' said a child's voice next to the old cleric.

'Yes, Rodgar,' he replied with an affectionate smile.

'When can we go home? The stone floor is hurting my mum's feet.' The lad was no more than six years old and had not fully grasped what was occurring in his home city.

Either side of the old cleric were around a dozen children, ranging from youngsters who could barely talk to young teenagers. Many of their parents were either dead or captive, and Lanry would tell the children stories to keep them amused. The other adults in the Brown chapel were doing their best as well, but Lanry had a peaceful and fatherly quality that helped relax the younger citizens of Ro Canarn.

'You'll be home in no time at all, my dear boy,' he replied, 'and your mother can put her feet up in front of a nice roaring fire.'

A slight sneer from one of the older girls made it clear that not all of the children were as trusting as young Rodgar. The girl, whose name was Lyssa, was the child of a blacksmith – a man missing, presumed dead – and she'd developed a hard and uncaring edge.

'I'm sorry, young Lyssa,' said Lanry tenderly. 'We all need different kinds of encouragement.'

'We'll never be able to go home,' she replied, folding her arms and glaring at the old cleric. 'We'll be slaves . . . or worse.'

'Now, that's enough,' said Lanry, by way of a gentle reprimand.

Rodgar sat up a little and looked at Lyssa with innocent eyes. 'But Lord Bromvy and Lady Bronwyn are still alive. They won't let us suffer . . . isn't that right, Brother Lanry?'

'That's right, my lad.' The cleric ruffled Rodgar's hair and smiled. 'The house of Canarn will not abandon its people.' He thought for a moment. 'Have I told you children the story of Lord Bullvy and Lady Brunhilde?'

A few shook their heads. The younger children looked up at Lanry, eagerly wanting a story, while the teenagers rolled their eyes. The Brown cleric had remained stubbornly optimistic and so far had chosen serenely to ignore the cynicism that surrounded him. This had become harder as the days of occupation had turned into weeks, but he was determined to act as Duke Hector would have wanted.

'Lord Bullvy was the first duke of Ro Canarn. A very long time ago, two hundred years at least, the king of Tor Funweir ruled the Freelands of Ranen. Does anyone know what the Freelands were called in those days?'

'Tor Ranen?' answered Rodgar.

'That's right, lad, Tor Ranen.' Lanry kept smiling. 'Things were never peaceful, though, and the men of Ranen didn't like being ruled . . . freedom is very important to the children of Rowanoco.

'The Ranen were organized into work gangs by the Purple and, once they rebelled, those gangs became the first Free Companies and fought back hard.'

A few of the teenagers had softer faces now and were listening to the old cleric's story.

'I bet the Purple didn't like that,' said Lyssa, thinking she was being clever.

'No, no, they did not,' replied Lanry. 'They massacred hundreds of Ranen and called on the knights of the Red to kill the rest. Many lords of Ro went to fight, seeking honour or glory, and the Ranen could never win.'

Rodgar and the younger children were enjoying the tale, especially the bits that involved blood and death. Lanry occasionally lamented that so many stories were stained in blood and that he knew so few tales of love and peace.

'Lord Bullvy and his twin sister were minor nobles from Hunter's Cross and went to war when they were called upon.'

Lyssa yawned theatrically, causing several of the other girls to giggle. Lanry joined in the laugh and was glad of the jollity, even if he was the butt of the joke.

'The story does get more exciting, I assure you,' said the cleric with a chuckle. 'Just when Ranen was a breath away from being reconquered, the clerics and knights began to feel a cold wind blow from the north and the battle-brothers of Fjorlan joined the fight. Their dragon ships landed all along the coast, their berserkers flooded out of the Deep Cross and their priests and warriors threw down the banners of the One.'

Lyssa snorted at the story. 'How could they beat the knights?' she asked, as if no force could stand against the One God's aspect of war.

'They were stronger, I suppose,' replied Lanry. 'It suits the arrogance of the Red to imagine they are unstoppable . . . the reality is open to question, it would seem.

'Anyway, where was I?' The old cleric found his memory faltering a little. 'Ah, yes, the Red knights were forced to retreat from the rampaging Fjorlanders. They abandoned Ro Hail, leaving only a minor noble and his sister to hold the town against thousands of Ranen.'

'And that was Lord Bullvy?' asked Rodgar eagerly.

Lanry nodded. 'He and his twin sister, a woman who could shoot the legs from a Gorlan at a hundred paces, refused to surrender. They held Ro Hail for thirty days with barely a hundred men. On the thirty-first day, a priest of Brytag the World Raven arrived at the siege and stopped the Ranen attacking. Brytag has a fondness for twins, you see, and the priest demanded they be given safe passage to Ro Canarn.'

'They were spared?' asked Rodgar, biting on his thumbnails.

'They were. The Ranen escorted them all the way south and treated them with high honours. The clerics and knights had pulled back to Ro Tiris and left the twins and their men to hold Canarn. The Ranen wouldn't attack the city while Bullvy and Brunhilde were there, so the king had no choice but to name him duke.'

It was an old tale and one that Lanry enjoyed remembering. Hector was descended from Bullvy, a man who had fought on long after he should have surrendered and who had earned the respect of the Ranen. The house of Canarn had been a bastion of peace between the Ro and the Ranen for two hundred years, with each successive duke strengthening the truce. Whether Brytag, the sly old Raven of Rowanoco, had known of Bullvy and Brunhilde's importance, or if he just liked twins, Lanry didn't know. Either way, the peace had been hard fought, and the old cleric hoped it had not yet ended.

Rodgar clapped his hands excitedly. 'Brytag will look after Lord Bromvy, won't he? And Lady Bronwyn . . . they'll both be okay, won't they?'

'I always try to put my faith in the One, but, as I said, the World Raven is fond of twins. Brytag believes that luck and wisdom are the same thing in the end, and Hector's children seem to have both.'

There was still much work to be done – many people to be healed and cared for, and many more stories he'd need to tell, but for now he felt better. If a few words from an old Brown cleric could help calm the children, maybe their situation wasn't hopeless after all.

PART ONE

CHAPTER ONE

LADY BRONWYN IN
THE RUINS OF RO HAIL

IT HAD STARTED raining within a few hours of Bronwyn's escape from Canarn and had not stopped for two weeks. Her horse, a large, sad-looking work animal taken from a discarded supply cart, had shown his displeasure at the rain and had decided not to move any further.

She had stopped on the edge of a cluster of trees, too small to be called a forest and too widely spaced to afford much shelter, but the horse was happier with a few branches to hide under. Bronwyn sat, leaning against a tree trunk with her cloak pulled tightly around her. She felt no guilt at having acquired the horse and supplies – after all, the beast would have died with no one to tend it – but she did feel sadness for the dead men from whom she had taken the clothing. She didn't know their names, or why they had fought, but they had all been hacked apart with longswords and left by the road. The knights of the Red had killed indiscriminately and it was possible that the dead men had just been common folk.

She'd taken trousers, boots, a cloak and a crossbow. There had been no armour to speak of, but a heavy leather waistcoat was sturdy enough to be a good substitute. The dress she'd escaped in had been torn around the waist and now served as a light vest, with the rest of the fabric fashioned into a hood of sorts. The bloodstains that remained would serve Bronwyn as a reminder of what had happened to get her out of the city. She thought that

Al-Hasim would probably have been killed or captured, and that Father Magnus would still be in a cell.

She would not admit, even to herself, that she had little hope. Bronwyn was stubborn and had learned from her father that surrender was a poor substitute for death. She hadn't actually seen him die, though the Red knights blocking her view had done little to mask what had happened.

He was dead. Her father, Duke Hector of Canarn, had been beheaded by Red knights. This fact had kept her going into the endless Grass Sea long after she had wanted to give up.

She had taken plenty of supplies, but dried bread, fruit and porridge would only get her so far. She had reached the blasted tree after a week and had travelled west for another week, but had not yet seen the ruins of Ro Hail and only had Al-Hasim's word that the directions were correct. She'd had ample opportunity to improve her skill with the crossbow she'd acquired, and she was now able to hit rabbits and other game. So far, however, she'd been loath to make a fire of sufficient size to cook them properly. Porridge needed only a small flame and a bit of rainwater, but cooking meat might well alert anyone who was pursuing her.

She'd seen small nests of Gorlan spiders throughout the two weeks she'd been travelling but had not quite summoned the courage to snare one. Al-Hasim had told her several times that in Karesia fried Gorlan legs were a delicacy. However, the size and ferocity of the bloated arachnids was enough to put her off approaching a nest. Even in the small wood she was sheltering in there were cobwebs, and she guessed that the Gorlan claimed much of the southlands of Ranen as their hunting grounds.

Bronwyn felt a drop of rain hit the back of her neck and she shivered uncomfortably as it made its way inside her cloak. She'd slept rough before; many times in her life she'd camped out with Bromvy, and they'd both enjoyed the feeling of freedom that the open expanse of the Grass Sea gave them. This was different, though. She didn't have a tent, or a change of clothes, or her brother to keep her spirits up, and the only thing she had to focus on was to stay at liberty and get to the ruins of Ro Hail. Even that was only the vaguest of goals and she had no idea what she would do if she did actually manage to make contact with Wraith Company.

The ability of men like Brom and Hasim to stay cheerful in the face of despair was a trick she'd never learned. Her mother had offered few words of wisdom on the subject. Marlena of Du Ban had not been a loving or attentive mother. She'd died when Bronwyn and her brother were barely ten years old, but she'd spoken of a woman's duty as if she believed it was the one thing she had to offer her daughter.

The place of the noblewomen of Ro is to support the noblemen and to remain silent, she'd said. *They must show their emotions and never forget that they are the gentle counterpoint to the warrior men of Tor Funweir.*

Bronwyn had disliked this advice and had never really accepted that her place was dictated by birth and gender. However, despite her sword and crossbow, she felt alone and vulnerable.

As the sky began to darken, Bronwyn let her eyelids droop and she suddenly felt exhausted. The adrenalin that had kept her going since she left her home had steadily dwindled away and now all she felt was tired. Her horse was whinnying quietly and directed a glare at Bronwyn, as if to remind her how much he disliked the wet weather. She'd fed him some of the bale of straw she'd recovered from the wagon and hoped he'd allow her a few hours' sleep.

As she settled back against the trunk of a tree and tried to achieve a degree of comfort, the horse reared his head and made a loud wheezing sound, spraying spittle from his mouth. His nostrils were twitching and the way his hooves pawed at the muddy earth made Bronwyn sit up. The horse had caught the whiff of something on the wind and, though Bronwyn was not an experienced tracker, she knew enough not to ignore the keener senses of her mount.

She pulled her hood up over her head and scanned the horizon to the south. The Grass Sea was a vast, open plain, dotted with small farmsteads, woods and hills. She'd been careful to stay off the main route north and had avoided settlements and the better-travelled areas. The southern plains seemed to stretch forever, with only the city of Ro Canarn and the sea to end the emptiness.

The horse became more agitated. Bronwyn picked up her crossbow with shivering hands, carefully placed a bolt, and pulled back on the drawstring. She glanced to the west and hoped that Ro Hail was nearby as Al-Hasim had led her to believe, though it offered no guarantee of safety.

Then she heard a sound. It was distant and indistinct, but it made Bronwyn stand and start to pack up her things, ready to move if need be. Somewhere along the southern horizon, beneath a rapidly darkening sky and relentless rain clouds, she was sure she could hear the movement of horses. There was a low accompaniment to the noise, reminiscent of the sound of armoured men. She knew that the farmers of the duchy would not be so attired and began to feel apprehension.

She wrapped up her bedroll and fastened it to her saddle. Her short sword was at her side as she placed the straw and dried rations back in the saddlebag and took a firm hold on the reins.

She waited, standing behind the animal, with her crossbow pointing south, resting across the saddle. A few tense moments passed with the sound of approaching horses growing in volume until a small company of men came into view. They rode slowly and looked to be finding the going difficult, weaving left and right to avoid the boggy ground underfoot.

Bronwyn began breathing heavily as she saw the dark red cloaks the riders wore, the sound of metal on metal now indicating that the men were heavily armoured. They were knights of the Red, some twenty of them, although she was too far away to make out their faces. She clenched her fists and tried to calm herself as she backed away from the tree line. They were still far off, moving slowly, and had probably not seen her. She placed a hand across the horse's nose, gently encouraging him to remain silent as she began to lead him back into the trees. The horse complied and they made their way into the small wood. Bronwyn thought the men were most probably looking for her, but, given that they were moving slowly and making no effort to remain hidden, she guessed that they did not think she was so close.

Leading the horse through the trees, she glanced back to the south and was gratified that she could no longer see the knights through the wood. The rain was now heavier and made the ground treacherous as she tried to lead the horse down a steep incline. He bucked at her sharply, nearly causing her to lose her footing and slide down the small hill, but she held the reins firmly and slowly coaxed the animal down the slope.

A shallow stream ran along the base and the sound of rain hitting the water covered the stubborn complaining sounds of her mount. She pulled him down into the stream and, stepping on rocks and the narrow muddy banks, turned to the west and moved through the wood as quickly as possible. She hoped the western tree line was out of sight of the direction from which the knights were approaching; she could no longer hear them, but knew they'd be moving directly towards her position. If they hadn't captured Hasim, she thought they might not know where she was heading and there might be a chance of escape.

Bronwyn nearly fell several times as she led the horse through the narrow stream and, after a few minutes, she could see the western edge of the small wood. The horse was still complaining, and now that there was no real tree cover to keep them out of the rain, both horse and rider were soaking wet.

She could distantly hear the sound of armoured men moving slowly across boggy ground, but was shielded from them by black, leafless tree trunks and the shallow incline she'd descended to reach the stream. Beyond the wood to the west, Bronwyn could see little save for a sheet of rain and the endless Grass Sea.

The stream continued past the trees and the steep bank turned into a low rocky hillside within a few feet. If she broke cover, the knights would probably not be able to see her provided she remained behind the hill, and she was hopeful that Ro Hail was nearby, perhaps obscured by the rain, the hills and the approaching darkness. Bronwyn breathed in deeply, took a firm grip of the reins and walked slowly towards the tree line. She was tentative as she exited the wood, resting one hand on the horse's nose to keep it from making a sound. She proceeded close to the rocky bank, walking to the west as the rain grew even harder.

Bronwyn squinted to see through the gloom, wiping rainwater from her face and keeping a comforting hand on the horse. The animal was grumpy and his dark brown eyes conveyed worlds of anger. She decided, almost absent-mindedly, to give him a name, calling him Moody under her breath as she gently stroked his nose.

The rain made a considerable noise and she could no longer hear the knights. She hoped she could simply slip away, leaving her pursuers behind, though her optimism was tempered with the fear of being caught and branded a Black Guard.

The rain made it difficult to see far ahead, but as she left the wood behind and moved across the Grass Sea she thought she saw a break in the cloud and beneath it, perhaps, shadows indicating a structure of some kind. If the ruins of Ro Hail were close by, Bronwyn could perhaps hide and maybe even find shelter from the rain. She paused briefly to look back and saw no signs of the knights. Placing a foot in the stirrup she decided it would be wise to ride away from the wood, figuring that she could move faster and that it might even improve Moody's disposition. He would at least have something else to think about as she pulled herself up into the saddle and dug in her heels. She moved forward, slowly at first, letting the horse find his feet on the uneven ground. At the height she sat, Bronwyn could see over the bank and was gratified that she could see no knights of the Red.

Suddenly a sound from above made her look up. A shape appeared through the gloom. The man's metal armour made a distinctive sound but the rain had masked his presence until he was virtually on top of Bronwyn. Moody reared up and snorted, causing the man to pull back on his own reins and peer down into the darkness.

Bronwyn froze, the rain flowing down over her face as she looked up at the knight. She couldn't be sure if he was looking back at her, but he gestured over his shoulder and shouted, 'Captain, I believe there is a rain-soaked girl hiding under the bank.'

The words were spoken with amusement and Bronwyn didn't know how to react for a moment as she heard other armoured men approaching.

A sound from behind caused her to turn and she saw two knights of the Red moving swiftly down the rocky bank behind her.

'Bronwyn of Canarn . . .' The voice came from behind. 'You'll be coming with us.' Bronwyn thought she recognized the speaker as Sir William of Verellian.

More knights appeared at the top of the bank and Moody reared up again, his snort loud enough to be heard over the rain. Bronwyn didn't wait for more than a second before she rammed her heels into the horse's flanks. Moody began to run forward with Bronwyn clinging on to his neck as hard as she could.

The knights shouted after her and she could clearly hear armoured men moving down the bank in pursuit.

'Run, you miserable old horse,' she shouted to Moody, as she pulled him away from the bank and let him stretch his legs across the muddy ground.

Sparing a glance behind, she saw shapes moving quickly to assemble at the bottom of the bank. She had stolen a march on them and Moody was a big horse, with a long stride, enabling him to move quickly away from her pursuers. The ground was boggy, but Moody was unconcerned and Bronwyn even thought he was cheering up at the opportunity to run. Holding on tight, she looked up through the rain and saw nothing but a dark, featureless plain. Behind, the sound of the knights suggested they had all made it down the incline and were now in full pursuit.

Ahead, a dark shape loomed through the sheet of rain and Bronwyn thought she could make out a stone structure a little way ahead of her. Pulling back on Moody's reins, she rode hard towards the building, hoping it was more than just a lone structure.

She almost smiled as she saw other buildings appearing through the gloom. The horse's hooves struck stone and Bronwyn looked down to see the remnants of a road, partially obscured by mud and grass. Moody put on a burst of speed across this more even ground and they plunged into the rain-soaked ruins of Ro Hail.

Bronwyn looked up and saw dark, moss-covered brickwork. She was riding towards a low gateway with a long-broken wooden gate hanging from rusted hinges. Crumbling buildings stretched out from the gatehouse and the remnants of battlements could be seen above.

Bronwyn had never been this far north and had only heard about Ro Hail in stories. As her horse ran through the gateway, she remembered her father telling her tales of the men of Ro who had held the town long after the Ranen had defeated the knights of the Red. Hail was the last town to fall when the Free Companies rose up against the knights and the defenders had fought with such ferocity that Wraith Company had allowed them to return to Canarn under truce.

To her perception, as she rode hard over the uneven cobbled streets, it was nothing but a mound of rocks shaped roughly like a town. The buildings had long ago fallen into ruin and few complete structures could be seen. Bronwyn scanned the rain-soaked court-yard for a place to hide amidst the ruins. Moody had his own ideas about their destination and didn't stop running, heading towards a half-destroyed building with an intact roof. The horse shook his head, spraying water over the moss-covered ground, and Bronwyn quickly dismounted. She pulled Moody further into the building and found a dark recess beyond a collapsed wall to hide in.

The sound of armoured men and horses was now loud on the cobbles as Verellian and his knights reached the gatehouse. They slowed as they entered the courtyard, and Bronwyn peered through a gap in the crumbled brickwork to see them fan out and stop. She counted twenty knights and a man who looked to be a prisoner, bound and gagged, his horse led by a knight. As they came closer, she gasped to see that the prisoner was Al-Hasim.

She noted a few wounds on his face and neck. They were mostly healed, though the Karesian looked as if he would have a couple of new scars. She was glad to see him alive, but thought it likely that he had been tortured to reveal her location.

'Lady Bronwyn, you will not be harmed,' shouted Sir Verellian, 'but you *will* be coming with us.' He nodded to the man at his left. 'Fallon, to the left. Callis, take the right. The sooner we find her, the sooner we can get out of the rain.'

'So it's come to this,' said the man called Fallon, 'searching for a woman in a fucking pile of rocks.'

'Enough,' shouted Verellian. 'Let's just get it done.'

'Captain, sir, she could be anywhere,' said another man, moving slowly to the right side of the courtyard.

'Maybe, but that horse she was riding would struggle to hide around here.' Verellian kicked the flanks of his own mount and advanced into the ruins at a walk.

Bronwyn stroked her hand over Moody's nose to quieten him. They hid within a building that might once have been a house, though now it was little more than a wall with two horizontal platforms to show that it had been a three-storey building. The inside wall was mostly debris and Bronwyn knew that if a knight were to look closely he would see Moody no matter how quiet he was.

As she hugged the wall, and tried to get herself and her horse as deep into the ruined building as she could, a sound from the battlements above alerted her. The knights clearly heard it too, and all of them were looking warily at the broken city walls. From several hidden locations among the ruins men appeared, carrying weapons and wearing chain mail.

These were Ranen men, of Wraith Company, protectors of the Grass Sea. All wore dark blue cloaks and they came on slowly, clearly not intending summarily to kill the knights of the Red. One man stepped forward and separated himself from the other Ranen, walking decisively towards Knight Captain William of Verellian. The man motioned to the twenty or so Ranen who had appeared around the knights to hold their positions, as if assessing the knights' strength. Verellian remained calm; though he, too, looked as if he was counting the Ranen men before him and taking note of their weapons.

The man approaching Verellian was on foot and appeared unconcerned that the knight was mounted. Several others were emerging from the broken buildings, guard towers and the battlements of Ro Hail. Bronwyn thought the Ranen must have seen the Red knights approaching and waited until they were within the courtyard. They hefted axes of various sizes and a few of the larger men carried massive war-hammers. Above where Lieutenant Fallon sat on his horse, a small group of Ranen appeared from the gatehouse and held small throwing-axes at the ready.

'Knights, to me,' ordered Verellian calmly, causing his men to re-form behind him.

None of the knights had drawn their swords, but the atmosphere was tense.

The Ranen who approached the knight captain was a large man, over six foot in height, and carried a two-headed axe loosely in both hands. Piercing blue eyes peered out from a matted brown beard and wavy hair fell over his shoulders. He was perhaps forty years old and wore the dark blue cloak of Wraith Company. Bronwyn thought that she had maybe seen him before, as a companion of Magnus when he'd first come to Ro Canarn to talk to her father.

The rain still fell heavily and the sky was black, though the men of Wraith appeared less concerned with the weather than the knights, who shifted uncomfortably in their saddles.

The Ranen didn't appear to be in any rush as his deep blue eyes slowly took in the twenty knights before him. He took an interest in Al-Hasim, narrowing his eyes at the sight of a Karesian prisoner accompanying knights of the Red.

Verellian and the Ranen before him looked at each other for several moments, before the man of Wraith spoke.

'That's a nice horse, Red man,' he said, with only a slight accent.

'It is a very fine animal, yes. But it's *my* animal,' replied Verellian.

The Ranen smiled and waved a hand over his shoulder, signal-ling to some more of his men who had emerged from a ruined building behind him. Bronwyn had lost count of the men of Wraith, but they now outnumbered the knights by at least three to one.

'You're not in Tor Fuck-weir any more, *sir* . . . or whatever I'm supposed to call you,' he responded with venom.

Another man of Wraith, carrying a large war-hammer and wearing heavy chain mail, stepped forward from the gatehouse to stand behind Fallon. He had four men with him, each holding a pair of throwing-axes. The lieutenant wheeled his horse round and saw that he was surrounded.

The man with the hammer was older than his fellows and had one white eye with a deep scar across the socket.

'No man in the Grass Sea is foolish enough to come here unannounced, Red man. Are you eager to die?' he asked with a broad grin, causing a dozen of the men of Wraith to laugh.

Fallon drew his sword. 'Watch your mouth, white-eye,' he barked.

'Fallon, sheathe that weapon now,' ordered Verellian.

Fallon did as he was told but kept a hard stare directed through the rain at the man with the hammer. The rest of the knights formed up in a rough circle, facing outwards towards the men of Wraith. A few un-slung shields from their saddles and held them defensively, taking heed of the numerous throwing-axes held by the Ranen.

'To whom am I speaking?' asked Verellian, still maintaining his calm.

'My name is Horrock. I'm called Green Blade. This is my land and these are my people,' he said loudly, evoking a muted cheer from the rest of Wraith Company. 'You are not welcome here, Red man. These are the Freelands of Ranen and your god has no power here.'

The men of Wraith were evidently ready for a fight. Bronwyn crouched down in her place of concealment, not wanting to become

311

involved if blood were to be spilt. She knew that the knights would not back down, as it was the way of the Red to answer a challenge and not to yield, even when faced with overwhelming odds.

Moody was happier now that he was out of the rain and was keeping quiet as Bronwyn watched the confrontation unfold.

Verellian was stony-faced as he surveyed the men of Wraith Company. 'I've been ordered to apprehend a fugitive from Ro Canarn and I plan to carry out my orders.' He shot a glance at Fallon – as if they had received other orders they were more reluctant to follow. 'I do not wish to fight you, but this is not your concern.'

Horrock laughed at this and hefted his axe threateningly. 'I don't give a troll's cock for your orders, Ro. This is the realm of Wraith Company and you will either turn round or die. It's simple, really.'

At Horrock's words, the other men of Wraith closed in round the knights. Fifty or more bearded men, clad in chain mail and fur cloaks and bearing well-used weapons, surrounded twenty knights of the Red. A further thirty Ranen stood on the battlements and on top of piles of rubble, ready to throw their hand-axes when the order was given.

The rain continued to beat down on the stone courtyard of Ro Hail. The Ranen displayed an array of vicious smiles, but the Ro looked grim.

Hasim was casting glances around the ruins, beyond the men of Wraith, and Bronwyn thought he was looking for her. There was no way she could signal to him without giving away her hiding place, but she hoped that, when swords were drawn, he'd be able to find cover. The steel manacles that bound his hands were linked to a chain held like a dog's lead in the hand of one of Verellian's sergeants.

Horrock relaxed his grip on his axe and walked closer to Verellian. He was now within striking distance, but he did not look concerned as he locked eyes with the mounted knight.

'Tell me something, knight. What happened to the men of Ranen who stayed in Canarn with Father Magnus?' He spoke in a quiet and ominous voice. 'I think fifteen of them stayed, maybe thinking you Red bastards would put up a good fight. If they died in battle, I may let you live. If not . . .' He left the sentence unfinished.

Bronwyn knew that the Ranen who had not died in battle had been tortured and executed by Pevain's mercenaries and bound Red knights. She'd seen some of them mutilated as a lesson to the people of Canarn that resistance would be unwise. Verellian knew this as well, and he paused and looked solemnly at the ground as he considered his reply.

The knight captain was about to speak, but something seemed to displease him and instead he turned to Lieutenant Fallon and directed a thin smile at him.

'Fallon, are these men worthy . . .' he began.

'. . . of my steel?' Fallon finished the question. 'We die where we're told to, Captain. That doesn't mean we have to die easy.'

A blur of motion followed as Knight Lieutenant Fallon drew his sword, wheeled his horse round, and struck downwards at the old, white-eyed Ranen. The sword connected with the top of the man's skull, making a sickening noise, and killing the man instantly.

'Knights, we fight,' shouted Verellian, drawing his sword and roaring a challenge at Horrock, who was backing away from the mounted knight.

The scene became chaotic as the Ranen threw their axes, clearly surprised by the knights' sudden ferocity. Two knights fell quickly as axes hit their exposed heads, but most of those that were thrown bounced harmlessly off raised shields and plate armour.

Two axes, thrown by the Ranen behind Horrock, caught Verellian's horse on the flanks and caused the animal to snort loudly and buckle to the ground, throwing its rider forward. Verellian fell clumsily on to the rain-soaked cobbles and was immediately attacked by two hammer-wielding Ranen.

The knight roared again, this time in frustration, narrowly avoiding the first hammer blow. The second strike caught him in the shoulder and sent him backwards into his dying horse.

Bronwyn saw Hasim deliberately roll from his saddle and pull the man holding his chain to the ground. The Karesian then kicked the knight squarely in the face and ran for cover, diving over a mound of rubble.

Fallon had advanced into the gatehouse and had already killed two of the Ranen behind him. Another was trying to pull him from his horse, but received a fatal cut to the back for his trouble.

The main body of knights were still in a rough circle, holding off the men of Wraith with desperate parrying and sword thrusts. They were severely outnumbered and, though Bronwyn thought them the more skilled fighters, it looked as if they'd be overwhelmed.

It appeared that Verellian knew this as well, and Bronwyn saw concern on his face as he got to his feet and saw his knights pulled from their saddles and killed by the men of Wraith. His expression turned to one of grim determination as he pointed his sword at Horrock.

'We are knights of the Red and we will make you pay for each of our deaths,' he cried.

Horrock hefted his axe and ran at the knight. Verellian parried the first blow and answered with a quick riposte to Horrock's side. The Ranen spun with the stroke and minimized its effect, slashing his axe at Verellian's legs. The knight jumped over the attack and kicked out, sending Horrock back a little. Verellian then launched a series of high attacks on the Ranen, who barely managed to resist the weight of the persistent blows. Verellian was a skilled swordsman and Horrock quickly realized he was outmatched.

As Fallon continued to clear the path behind them, and other knights began to gain the upper hand, a further volley of throwing-axes, better aimed than the first, was directed at the knights. Three fell quickly, their blood spraying across the ground and mingling with the rain. Another two were thrown when their horses received wounds, and Verellian was caught in the back by a glancing blow.

Bronwyn had seen combat before, but this was brutal and somehow dirtier and less noble. Men hacked at each other with axes and swords; blood flowed into the gaps between the flag-stones. She saw the remaining knights fighting desperately and the bodies of dead men, both Ro and Ranen, littering the courtyard.

Verellian was hurt but didn't stop attacking Horrock, the dent in his armour depriving his thrusts of some of their power. Horrock now parried his blows more easily and his own ripostes drove the knight backwards.

Another throwing-axe hit Verellian, catching his hand and causing him to drop his sword and cry out in pain as two of his fingers were severed. Horrock responded quickly and his axe hit the knight's chest, buckling his breastplate and sending him to the ground.

Bronwyn watched, wide-eyed, as Verellian looked up. His face was wet with the rain and his expression was one of pain and resignation as he looked across the courtyard towards Fallon. His knights were nearly all dead and the Ranen were closing in on his adjutant. Fallon met his captain's look and paused for a moment, realizing they had lost. The way behind him was clear of Ranen and Verellian nodded across the battleground, signalling that he should ride to safety.

The few remaining knights of the Red were surrounded and pulled from their horses to meet a violent death on the cobbles; only Fallon remained, astride his horse in the gatehouse of Ro Hail.

'Ride, you pig-fucker,' Verellian shouted across the courtyard.

Fallon took one last look at the dying knights and at the remaining men of Wraith before he wheeled his horse and rode under the gate, his longsword still in his hand as he retreated from the ruined city.

Men of Wraith began to pursue him, but on foot, and he quickly left them behind. Only Knight Captain Verellian remained alive in the soaking-wet courtyard. The knight of the Red was badly hurt, but Horrock's axe blow had not penetrated his breastplate more than a few inches and, although blood was visible, the wound was not fatal. Of more concern to the man of Ro was the wound to his hand, and he looked at the bloodied stumps where two of his fingers had been. Then he rolled on to his back and began to laugh loudly, the rain falling heavily on his face.

Al-Hasim was still crouched behind the mound of rubble in front and to the left of where Bronwyn and Moody were concealed. He peeked out to where the men of Wraith were delivering death blows to anyone who had not yet fully expired. Bronwyn thought he was talking to himself, maybe trying to think of the best approach to the Free Company men. After a minute of contemplation, the Karesian stepped out.

'Captain Horrock Green Blade,' he said loudly across the courtyard.

Several dozen blood-soaked Ranen turned towards him, brandishing axes and growling challenges. Horrock waved a silencing hand at his men and stepped over the still-laughing form of Verellian.

'Identify yourself, man of Jaa,' Horrock commanded suspiciously.

Hasim raised his eyebrows and pointed to William of Verellian. 'Don't you want to deal with him first? Kill him or make him shut up? He's not a bad man for a knight . . . honourable, clever . . . still a knight of the Red, though.'

Horrock pulled a small hand-axe from his belt and threw it with tremendous strength towards Hasim. The axe hit the ground between his feet with a resounding thump.

'I said, *Identify yourself*. Don't make me say it again,' he said in a manner that did not encourage dissent.

Hasim raised his hands and smiled nervously. 'I'm Al-Hasim, called the Prince of the Wastes. I am friend to Magnus Forkbeard and Lord Algenon Teardrop.'

The names were clearly known to the men of Wraith and all turned and looked through narrow eyes at Hasim.

'Those are strong names to be throwing around, Karesian,' said Horrock. 'Why are you riding with these men?'

'I helped Duke Hector's daughter escape. The knights in Canarn wanted her back, so they brought me with them to find her.' Hasim was talking quickly, as if he thought these men would kill him if they didn't like what he said.

Horrock nodded. 'Well, let's get out of the rain and discuss it, shall we?' He glanced up at the black sky. 'Stone Dog,' he called to one of the Ranen behind him, 'go fetch the girl and that stupid big horse from the old bakery.'

The Ranen he'd spoken to was young and lithe, in stark contrast to the burly men around him. He had two throwing-axes in his belt, neither of which he'd thrown, and a vicious-looking, hook-pointed Lochaber axe in his hands. Bronwyn didn't move as he walked towards her place of concealment.

Stone Dog approached the hole through which Bronwyn had observed the fight and leant forwards to peer into the darkness. 'Hello, sweetness,' he said with a grin. 'Are you going to come out like a good little girl or am I going to have to come in after you?'

Moody made an unimpressed sound and Bronwyn glared at him. 'You come in after me, little boy, and I'll make you bleed,' she shot back.

Several of the nearby Ranen burst out laughing. Al-Hasim looked across at Horrock and chuckled.

'She's not too ladylike, I'm afraid,' he said to the man of Wraith.

'Evidently,' replied Horrock. 'Stone Dog, stop flirting with the young noblewoman and get her out here.'

Hasim smiled and walked over to the young Ranen. 'Allow me,' he said to Stone Dog.

'Be my guest.' The young man of Wraith didn't appear offended by Bronwyn's words.

Hasim leant casually against the wall next to the broken section. 'Bronwyn, my dear, would you mind coming out, so I can get my sensitive arse out of this fucking rain?'

Bronwyn suddenly felt rather foolish, as a kick to Verellian's head rendered the knight unconscious and his laughter stopped.

*   *   *

It took over an hour for the courtyard to be cleared of bodies, and the rain didn't stop. Twenty knights of the Red and half as many again of the Ranen had been killed, and several more had received near-fatal

317

or crippling injuries. The injured Ro were despatched quickly and the injured Ranen taken indoors, down a steep set of stairs that led to intact basements where Wraith Company had made their home.

The only surviving knight was William of Verellian, and Horrock agonized about what to do with him. In the end, his unconscious body was taken with the injured Ranen. The knight looked less like a bird of prey when he wasn't standing upright, glaring at people, and his shaven head was covered in blood.

Bronwyn had stood off to the side with Hasim and the man called Stone Dog. Moody was not allowed into the Ranen head-quarters and the large horse had been tied to a wooden post, under a partial stone roof, near the staircase.

Bronwyn and Hasim sheltered near the gatehouse as the men of Wraith said prayers to Rowanoco over the fallen. Bronwyn was impressed that they showed equal respect for the dead Ro, and she heard several words suggesting they thought these particular knights were fearsome opponents and men of honour.

'See the man with one white eye,' Stone Dog said to Hasim as they quickly crossed the courtyard to follow Horrock and his men into shelter.

'What, the man Fallon split down the middle?' asked Hasim, with a gesture towards the old man who was being carried reverently under cover.

Stone Dog was annoyed at the Karesian's flippancy, but he smiled after a moment. The men of Ranen were famous for finding humour in death and Bronwyn was pleased that they were less pious than the men she was used to.

'His name was Dorron Moon Eye and he was our priest. Your man Fallon killed a man of the Hammer.'

Hasim frowned, clearly aware of the significance of such a death.

Bronwyn interjected as they reached the top of the staircase leading down. 'He was of the same order as Magnus?'

Stone Dog ushered the two of them down the stairs and glanced around the courtyard to make sure they were the last.

'Dorron wouldn't come with us when we went to Canarn. He said it was foolish to accept the hand of a duke of Tor Funweir.' He faced Bronwyn. 'And Magnus told him he was an old fool who should stop living in the past.' He smiled.

The stairs dived steeply into an old stone basement underneath the courtyard and opened up into a series of low rooms and passageways. The area looked extensive and Bronwyn saw more homely comforts than she might have expected. Rooms with solidly built doors and cosy sitting rooms made the basement appear like a well-maintained tavern or even a small settlement.

She also saw numerous people who had not been in the court-yard during the fight. Women and children, most wearing the blue cloaks of Wraith Company, rushed to the returning warriors and tears flowed from the wives, sons and daughters of fallen men. The injured were taken quickly to places of healing. Mugs of strong beer were passed round and most of the warriors drank deeply while their chain mail was removed and their wounds tended.

Only Stone Dog paid Bronwyn and Hasim any attention amidst the commotion, and this took the form of keeping them out of the way. No woman or child came to greet the young Ranen, and Bronwyn detected a hint of emotion in his eye, as if once he'd had someone to rush up to him when he returned from battle. He did acknowledge an older Ranen woman, who shot him a quick glance and received in return a nod to signal that he was uninjured.

William of Verellian was still alive but Bronwyn could see large amounts of blood seeping through the axe wound in his armour.

'Stone Dog, is someone going to see to him?' she asked, gestur-ing towards the knight, who'd been placed on the floor at the foot of the stairs.

The young Ranen looked across at the other injured men. 'They'll get to him. He's not a priority,' he said, showing little regard for the life of a man of Ro. 'Dorron's dead, which means healing these men is going to take time, rest, recuperation. All that stuff we don't often need to bother with.'

Bronwyn turned to Hasim and wordlessly conveyed her concern that the knight would die before he'd been tended. The Karesian frowned and shook his head, as if he were wrestling with something.

'He's a knight of the Red, Bronwyn, keeping him alive might be a mistake.' He paused, breathing in sharply. 'But . . .'

Hasim crossed from where they stood, negotiating the people of Wraith struggling out of their armour. A few glanced up at him, registering surprise that a Karesian should be in their midst, but most were lost in post-battle weariness and simply ignored him. Bronwyn followed, trying to stay behind him.

They reached Verellian and Hasim crouched down next to the broken knight before speaking quietly. 'You probably saved my life in Canarn,' he said to the unconscious man, 'so, as a man of at least some honour, I should now save yours.' He inspected the knight and turned to Bronwyn. 'Help me get his armour off. I need to see how bad that axe wound is.'

Together they wrested the battered armour from Verellian. It was badly dented and two cuts appeared, one in the chest where Horrock had struck him and one in the back from a thrown axe.

Bronwyn knew a little of armour and thought it likely that the breastplate was now useless. The knight was still unconscious and it was a struggle to remove the steel from the large man. Hasim held both his arms out and Bronwyn unfastened the shoulder straps, letting the front plate detach, and allowing Hasim to pull off the segmented arm guards. Then they laid the knight down on his back and inspected his chest wound. It was an ugly, jagged line across his chest and stomach – not deep, but it bled profusely and Bronwyn thought he would die from loss of blood if it were not treated properly.

'Looks like you'll be alive a while yet, Ro horse-fucker,' murmured Hasim, mostly to himself, as he inspected the wound.

Turning back to Bronwyn he said, 'Water and dressings. They must have something around here.'

Bronwyn stood up and, moving quickly, returned to Stone Dog, who was still by the stairs.

'I need something to treat the knight's wounds,' she said quickly. 'He'll die if we don't stop the bleeding.'

'And we should use our meagre supplies to save a knight of Red?' Stone Dog replied angrily. 'I don't think so. We need everything we've got for our own men.'

'Keep the knight alive.' The words came from Horrock who was standing nearby with a woman massaging his shoulders.

Stone Dog paused a moment, clearly not happy about having to use their supplies on a man of Ro, but he didn't argue with his captain. He snapped his fingers at a young lad who was running around the room with bandages and buckets of water.

'Boy, tend to the knight when you're finished over there,' he said reluctantly.

Horrock ushered away the woman behind him and stepped closer to Hasim and Bronwyn. The captain of Wraith Company was not wounded and his piercing blue eyes regarded the two outsiders with interest. Bronwyn found his face inscrutable and could not read his intentions.

'I suppose we need to have a conversation. Would you agree, your ladyship?' he asked her.

She glanced at Hasim and was surprised that Horrock had addressed her first. The Karesian smiled reassuringly and nodded.

'Of course, Captain Horrock,' she replied, 'though, I would like to see the knight tended to first. He will die if someone doesn't look after him.'

It had occurred to Bronwyn that she was still technically a noblewoman of Tor Funweir and she had a certain obligation to see that William of Verellian was cared for properly.

Horrock grunted a sound that might have been one of amusement or of annoyance. 'Soft hearts don't last long around here,' he said, with a shallow nod of his head, making his words even more ambiguous.

'Neither do men with axe wounds to their back and chest,' Bronwyn shot back, eliciting a good-natured laugh from Hasim, which made several of the nearby Ranen glare at him.

'Sorry,' the Karesian said with an awkward smile, 'I can't help myself.'

'No need to apologize, Karesian,' said Horrock, 'but you must understand that many of my people have lost brothers, husbands, sons and friends. Humour is not easily found at such times.'

Bronwyn looked over the faces of the people of Wraith and, for a moment, she thought her insistence on proper care for the knight was petty. She could see many tearful faces. These people were not nobles, knights or soldiers. They were common men and women who had chosen to fight to protect the Freelands.

'Stone Dog,' ordered Horrock, 'care for the knight. See that he doesn't die.'

The young Ranen grumbled but he didn't argue as he moved to grab a wet towel and several bandages from the boy.

'He'll need those wounds sewn, Horrock.' Stone Dog knelt down next to the unconscious knight.

'You can handle a needle, boy. Get to it,' replied the captain of Wraith Company.

'You two,' he pointed at Hasim and Bronwyn, 'come with me.'

'Dispossessed minor nobles first,' Hasim said to Bronwyn, as he motioned for her to follow Horrock.

Bronwyn shot him a narrow glare, letting him know that she didn't appreciate his attempt at humour, and then walked after the Ranen. The two of them followed Horrock through the large entrance room, past wounded men lying on makeshift bedrolls and hastily erected tables. Many of the wounds were minor – thin cuts and shallow thrusts from the Red knights' longswords. A few looked more serious – severed limbs and wounds deep enough to be life-threatening. The women of Wraith were responsible for the care of the wounded and Bronwyn was impressed with their manner. Orders were barked almost in military fashion, and the uninjured men who remained in the basement were quickly made to help tend their fellows. Concoctions and poultices, producing strange earthy smells, were being prepared by several of the older women. Bronwyn realized the absence of a priest to heal the wounded was a major problem for the people of Wraith.

The Ranen barely registered the presence of Bronwyn and Hasim, standing only to nod to Horrock before returning to their bloody work. The Ranen captain led them through the main area and down a narrow stone corridor lit by globed candles and adorned with all manner of trophies. The Free Companies were renowned for taking items from fallen foes to remind them of their need to be ever vigilant, and the corridor was a grim sight for a woman of Ro.

Multiple broken longswords, some incredibly old, hung from the walls. Several flattened suits of armour had been riveted to the stone and Bronwyn was a little taken aback by the colours on display. It was clear that in their time Wraith Company had killed churchmen of multiple orders. Though red was the most common colour, Bronwyn could also identify purple armour, the brown robes and even a single suit of black armour, indicating that a cleric of death had fallen beneath a Ranen axe at some point in the past.

Horrock stopped at a heavy stone door, clearly more recent than the rest of the basement complex, and reached inside his tunic for a large iron key. He opened the door and Bronwyn could instantly smell the rain again as she saw a stone staircase leading back up towards the ruined town of Ro Hail.

'Things always look different when observed from higher up,' Horrock said without turning, as he began to ascend the stairs.

Bronwyn and Hasim followed and found themselves standing on the shattered balcony of a large stone building looking out towards what had once been the northern wall of the town. It was still raining, though a cleverly built awning protected them from the weather. The balcony was large enough comfortably to seat a dozen or more people and it held several chairs, a large stone table and an open cupboard containing bottles of dark liquid.

'Do you south folk drink ale, wine or something stronger?' asked Horrock, sitting down in the largest chair and gently nudging the cupboard with his foot.

Hasim crouched down in front of the bottles and began looking through the various kinds of liquor. He picked up a large bottle, which looked to Bronwyn to be made of stone rather than glass, and held it up towards Horrock.

'This is Volk frost beer. It's worth a small fortune in Ro Tiris,' he said with a twinkle in his eye.

'I'd better finish it before you steal it, then,' said Horrock, grabbing the bottle from Hasim's hand and removing the stopper.

Bronwyn sat opposite him and suddenly felt exhausted. She rubbed her eyes and breathed in and out heavily. Hasim put a comforting hand on her shoulder before taking a seat himself.

'I think you're safer than you've been for a few weeks, your ladyship,' he said gently. 'A drink couldn't hurt. There's some good Darkwald red in here.'

'That's the only bottle I have that was legally obtained,' Horrock interjected, and Bronwyn again found it difficult to tell whether the Ranen chieftain was joking or not.

Each of them selected a drink and within minutes the rain changed from a persistent annoyance to a relaxing accompaniment to a well-deserved rest. Bronwyn sipped on a glass of full-bodied red wine, Hasim drank some Karesian desert nectar straight from the bottle and Horrock took small mouthfuls of the fiery Volk frost beer.

'Now, am I expected to ask you questions?' Horrock suddenly asked. 'Or can we just assume I've asked them all and the two of you just tell me the whole story?'

Bronwyn nodded at Hasim, signifying that he should begin.

'Well, it's quite simple really, Algenon Teardrop sent me to find out why a Karesian enchantress was in Canarn.' He looked down at the floor and continued. 'It seems she was there to orchestrate the sacking of the city and the murder and imprisonment of its people.' There was regret in his voice. 'I found this out a bit late, though . . . around the same time I found out that the bitch had a company of Red knights suckling on her tits.'

Horrock narrowed his eyes. In Bronwyn's estimation, the man of Wraith would have known about the assault on her home, but not about the Seven Sisters' involvement. The Ranen considered the enchantresses their enemies and their presence was not tolerated as it was in Tor Funweir. The One God, it seemed, was less quick to anger than Rowanoco. Long ago, the Order of the Hammer had forbidden the Sisters from entering the Freelands.

'And you've told Teardrop this?' Horrock asked.

Hasim nodded. 'He gave me a cloud stone. I used it after the battle, so he knows roughly what happened.'

Ranen cloud stones were made from the deep ice of Fjorlan and the northern lords often used them to communicate across great distances. Bronwyn had seen a few in her time, and Magnus had explained that they allowed words to travel through the void of the Giants to reach anyone the speaker desired. He had evidently thought that was an adequate explanation. Suffice to say, they were powerful and much-coveted items.

'I'm more concerned with the balls it takes for a company of Red knights to march into Ro Hail and start throwing their weight around. Whether they accept it or not, this is *not* Tor Funweir.' Horrock had clearly taken offence at the idea of men of Ro being in the realm of Wraith. 'How many of them took the city?' he asked.

'A knight called Rillion led the assault with a couple of hundred Red men. It was the mercenaries that cleaned up though – a bastard called Pevain and his sadistic hired swords.'

Horrock shot an interested look at the Karesian. 'I've heard of this *Pevain*. He lent his sword to Rulag Ursa when he seized Jarvik . . . the man's a troll cunt.' Horrock took a large gulp of frost beer and looked out over the ruined town of Ro Hail, deep in thought.

Bronwyn took the break in conversation as a cue to relax into her chair. The wine she drank was full and rich and made the tiredness she already felt flow over her more acutely. Hasim looked equally tired, but he was also alert in a way that Bronwyn was not. This was all new to her – the riding, the sleeping rough, the brutal battle – and all she really wanted to do was sleep.

She looked at the captain of Wraith Company sitting opposite her. He was a hard-looking man, tall and broad-shouldered, with many scars, but Bronwyn thought his eyes betrayed a thought-fulness that struck her as out of place. He'd ordered Verellian kept alive, something that many Ranen warriors would have found unthinkable, and she guessed that Captain Horrock Green Blade of Wraith Company had achieved his position through brains as well as brawn.

'So, all my men who stayed behind are dead . . . and Father Magnus?' he asked, without turning back to Hasim and Bronwyn.

'I suspect that's why Verellian attacked. He knew that all your Ranen in Canarn had been killed by Pevain's men. Magnus was being kept alive for some reason – I think at the urging of the enchantress – but he was well when I left,' Hasim replied.

'Hopefully, the pile of red meat downstairs can tell us what the bastards are up to when . . . if . . . he wakes up.' Horrock drank deeply again and looked as if he had finished speaking for now.

CHAPTER TWO

SIR WILLIAM OF VERELLIAN
IN THE RUINS OF RO HAIL

WILLIAM WOKE UP slowly, his head pounding, his legs weak and his vision black and cloudy. He could taste blood on his lips and his right hand felt numb and painful. He was cold and couldn't feel his armour or greaves against his skin. Above him there was a light and crouching next to him was a young Ranen man, looking intently at a large white dressing across William's chest.

Another figure stood nearby and, through his blurry vision, William thought that this was a woman and that she was carrying something. He tried to speak but the sound came out as a barely audible grunt and William was hit by a wave of extreme fatigue. The woman hefted the object she was carrying and a bucket of freezing-cold water flooded over the injured Red knight.

'Well, I do believe our Red man is still alive,' said the man crouching next to him.

William spluttered through the water and panted heavily as his vision began to clear. He was in a stone basement, surrounded by other injured men, and people wearing the blue cloak of Wraith were feverishly running around tending to the wounded. As far as he could tell, William was the only knight there and a sinking feeling filled him as he realized his men were all dead.

'Don't try to move,' said the woman, 'you've been leaking blood all over the floor.'

She was an older Ranen woman, perhaps fifty years old,

and her hands were gnarled and bloodstained. She bore a slight resemblance to the young man of Wraith crouching next to him and William thought they were probably related.

He'd been positioned away from the majority of the injured Ranen and could see no few pairs of eyes glaring at him.

'I need a drink,' he said weakly. 'In a cup rather than a bucket, if that's possible.'

The young Ranen chuckled at this. 'Get him some water, Freya. Maybe in a golden goblet or something else suited to a knight of Tor Funweir.'

The woman smiled and William lost sight of her amidst the press of Ranen in the stone basement.

'Don't get delusions, Red man. I only saved your life because the captain asked me to. I'd happily cleave your head in.' The young Ranen punctuated this statement with an aggressive growl.

William shifted his weight and tried to raise himself up on his hands. He noticed that his right hand was bandaged and vaguely remembered losing some fingers to a thrown axe. The pain was dull and easy enough to ignore for a true fighting man, but William was concerned that his sword hand was badly impaired.

He managed to pull himself into a seated position and shuffled against the wall. The Ranen lent him a helping hand, which William felt was strange given the attitude he'd shown so far, but he clearly had no intention of disobeying his captain's orders.

'What's your name, man of Wraith?' William asked, trying to show gratitude for having his wounds treated.

'I'm Micah, called Stone Dog. And you're . . . somebody of Verellian?' he asked, making a slight mess of the pronunciation.

'Sir William of Verellian, knight captain of the Red.' He spoke his title with little grandeur, knowing it meant little among the Free Companies. 'Will I live?'

'Unfortunately, yes. It seems I'm actually quite a good healer. It's a shame really. Your back wound is minor, but Horrock split your breastplate with his axe and you had steel shards in the wound.'

William began to play the fight through in his mind, from

Fallon's initial attack to the axe blow that ended the encounter. He remembered seeing Sergeant Bracha pulled from his horse and beheaded in the stone courtyard, and Callis take a throwing-axe to the back of the head. He had left Ro Arnon with twenty-five men, all of whom were probably now dead, although he still hoped that Fallon had somehow managed to escape. His lieutenant was a cunning bastard and William suspected he'd be okay.

'Why am I being kept alive when all my men are dead?' he asked in a low, tired voice.

Stone Dog considered, while he looked at William's bandaged right hand. 'You're in charge, right? That means you can tell the captain why you decided to break a truce that has lasted two hundred years.'

William tried to reply quickly, but coughed involuntarily instead, and again felt deeply fatigued.

After a minute of laboured coughing, he said, 'I didn't break any truce. We came here looking for a fugitive and your men were going to kill us. The only chance of survival we had was to strike first.'

Stone Dog chuckled again. 'Turned out well for you, striking first,' he said plainly, reminding William that his men were all dead.

The older woman returned with a small clay cup and passed it to William. He could grasp it, but his hand felt weak and the water only just reached his lips. He looked at his intact left hand and wished he'd paid more attention to using both hands when he was on the training grounds of Ro Arnon. Learning to fight left-handed would be difficult for a seasoned knight like William. He was set in his ways and he wondered whether he'd ever be the same fearsome swordsman he'd once been.

'You're lucky, Red man,' said the woman. 'My boy here is well schooled in the healing arts and, since your man killed our priest, it was touch and go whether we could stop the bleeding.' She glanced around the stone basement. 'Plenty of our men weren't so lucky. We used valuable supplies to keep you alive.'

William leant back and took another drink of water, feeling strength return to his limbs. 'Do you really feel the need to remind me that I'm an outsider here? And that I'm lucky to be cared for? And that you'd both rather see me dead?'

Stone Dog and Freya looked at each other before they shared a laugh at William's words. The Free Companies were known for their boisterous sense of humour and cavalier attitude to death. In fact, their ability to laugh in the face of blood and slaughter was infamous.

'Of course, it's possible Horrock will still kill you . . . if he doesn't like what you have to say,' said Stone Dog.

'I don't know what he expects me to say. He's surely not an idiot and he was there. He saw what happened as much as I did.'

William had a certain instinct for survival and, like all knights of the Red, he would never give his life away easily. The thought of being summarily executed bothered him and he began thinking of ways to escape. However, his various wounds made it unlikely he'd be able to walk unaided, let alone run, any time soon. He resigned himself to his predicament and tried to relax. For now at least, he wasn't going anywhere.

The basement was becoming progressively emptier as the dead were removed and those who had been healed were taken to beds and rooms elsewhere within the underground complex. William had no hatred for the people of Wraith and he disliked it that he'd been forced into a position where confronting them was the only option. Tough as the men of Wraith Company were, he knew they couldn't stand up to a focused assault and, given the situation in Ro Canarn, he was sure they'd have to run if faced with an army of Red knights. An invasion of Ranen, which had been vaguely suggested by Knight Commander Rillion, was clearly not suspected by these people. William considered whether or not he should tell them. In his estimation, that would not be a betrayal because ultimately it would result in fewer deaths and a swift resolution to the campaign. Wraith Company would not be able to hold the Grass Sea against the kind of army the king would bring with him. To stay and fight would result in a massacre.

As he thought, William began to feel his eyelids droop and his fatigue turn into a desperate need for sleep. The floor was cold and he was dressed only in woollen leggings with a Wraith cloak wrapped around his shoulders, but he was tired enough to sleep regardless.

Stone Dog and Freya took a last look at his dressings and then returned to their business elsewhere in the ruins of Ro Hail. William was left more or less alone, though the heavy wooden door that led up from the basement was securely locked, making escape impossible for the time being. All things considered, Sir William of Verellian decided he would be best served by sleeping and trying to recover his strength.

* * *

He was woken sharply with a light kick to his legs. Standing over him, a loaf of bread in his hand, was the Karesian prisoner, Al-Hasim. He was dressed in light leather armour, presumably acquired from the men of Wraith, and he had found a scimitar from somewhere.

'Eat,' Hasim said, throwing the bread into William's lap. 'It's fresh and you need to get something other than an axe in your belly.'

'Thank you,' William said, looking up at the Karesian.

He was unsure about the prisoner. He'd stopped him being raped in Ro Canarn and had found him little trouble on the way north, but he was still a criminal and had thrown his lot in with Wraith Company.

'Our positions seem to be somewhat reversed, Hasim, wouldn't you agree?' He tore off a chunk of warm bread with his teeth.

Hasim pointed to a length of chain that had been attached to William's leg while he slept. It was fastened to a steel bracket on the wall and was a clear message that the knight was a prisoner.

'I should probably thank you a second time, Verellian.' The Karesian sat down on the stone floor next to William. 'If I hadn't been brought north with you and your men, I'd probably be Pevain's wife by now.' He was smiling and William found the situation bizarre, maybe even a little funny.

'So, what happens now?' he asked the Karesian.

'I think that depends on you. Horrock doesn't appear to be in any rush to kill you, but he's angry at the incursion. This is Ranen, not Tor Funweir.'

Hasim was a Karesian and further from home than William, making the Red knight wonder what had caused him to travel this far north.

'Where do you fit into this, Hasim?' William asked plainly.

He smiled and offered William a bottle of dark liquid. 'It's Volk whisky. I stole it from Horrock. Drink it, it'll help.'

William had heard about the Volk and their habit of brewing harsh liquor using frosted barrels, but his oath to the One precluded him from tasting alcohol. He waved his hand weakly, refusing the offered drink.

'Ah, yes, that's right, your god prefers blood to booze,' Hasim said, taking a deep slug from the bottle.

'Don't moralize, Karesian. I've fought the Hounds and we both know that Jaa is perfectly capable of bloodletting when the mood takes him.' William was a realist, but wasn't inclined to put up with hypocrisy. 'Not drinking alcohol is a fairly minor restriction in the grand scheme of things.'

'Okay, okay. Maybe we should start with what we do have in common. Neither of us is Ranen and this is not our land. Agreed?' Hasim asked with a friendly tone to his voice.

'Agreed,' William conceded, but he was unsure of the point Hasim was trying to make.

'So, you and yours did ride into Hail and start a fight,' he said grimly. 'You have to accept that they had as little choice as you.'

'Twenty or more of my men were killed. Don't expect me to forget that today or tomorrow.' William was a prisoner and planned to survive, but he still considered the Ranen his enemies.

'And the forty or so men of Wraith you tore apart are, what, insignificant?' Hasim shot back quickly. 'You're one of the few Ro who doesn't make me sick, but stop thinking you're the only men in this world. Everyone bleeds, Verellian: Ro, Ranen, Karesian

. . . even Kirin. Our blood is the same as yours.' He was clearly angry and William realized he'd never really taken an outsider's view of his own people.

The Red knight looked around the basement and saw blood-stains being scrubbed from the floor and the residue of a dozen or so bodies that had lain there. Near the doorway leading up to the courtyard was a young woman with blood on her hands and forearms. She was just sitting, looking at her reddened palms with wide eyes and with tears rolling down her face. There were others in the basement, mostly sitting or lying against the walls with a variety of exhausted and despairing expressions on their faces.

William was not a stranger to battle, or the aftermath of blood, bandages, screaming and death, but he had never seen women crying over their lost loved ones or common folk trying to save the lives of part-time warriors. His experiences had always involved the healing powers of the White clerics and an orderly triage with well-tended recovery time. These people had good healing skills, but their one priest was dead and bandages would only go so far with serious wounds.

He turned back to Hasim and gave him a shallow nod, before quietly saying, 'Okay, I'm sorry for my flippancy. This is new to me.'

'You've never been captured before?' he asked.

'I've never been defeated, let alone captured. I had a few bad injuries a couple of years ago, but I've never been on the losing side of a confrontation.' William found the position of defeated prisoner an uncomfortable one.

'Well, I've been in gaols and dungeons in more than one country, so take my word for it, things will get worse before they get better.' Hasim offered the bottle again.

'I'm not giving up on my oath just yet, Karesian,' William replied, with another wave of his hand. 'I still have an obligation to try to escape and return to Ro Canarn.'

Hasim directed a questioning look at the Red knight. 'Opti-mism, I respect that, but don't do anything stupid. It'd be a shame if you got yourself killed after I'd stuck my neck out to keep you alive.'

William rocked back against the wall and closed his eyes, letting air fill his lungs and trying to regain some strength by tensing his arms and legs. He was still tired and thought Hasim had woken him prematurely.

'Where's Horrock?' he asked.

'Probably sleeping off the first half of this bottle,' Hasim replied, indicating that the bottle of Volk whisky was nearly empty. 'It's still early morning and we were up late discussing what's to be done with you. Bronwyn, you'll be pleased to know, agreed with me and thinks you should be spared.'

'She's been named to the Black Guard, like her brother.' William realized that the laws of Tor Funweir meant little here, but it was easier to cling to duty and the last orders he had been given than to accept defeat. 'Unless something changes, she's a criminal in the lands of Ro.'

'I'm sure she gives a massive shit about that, Red man,' Hasim replied, with a good-humoured laugh. 'I'll leave this here, just in case you change your mind.' He placed the bottle of whisky on the floor next to William. 'Get some rest. Horrock will come and get you when he's ready.'

He stood up and, with a mocking salute, left William alone in the basement.

With a deep breath, the Red knight closed his eyes and felt sleep rapidly come over him. Being forced to see the aftermath of the battle from another point of view had been an eye-opening experience, and William felt humbled as he tried to shift himself into a more comfortable position.

He was no closer to a decision about what he should tell Horrock Green Blade. If he told the man of Wraith about the impending invasion of the Grass Sea, he would be no more or less likely to be executed and he might indirectly save many lives, though he had a nagging suspicion that the Ranen would choose to stay and fight rather than run for safety from the knights.

Commander Rillion would probably assume William had been lost. Unless Fallon made it back to Ro Canarn and orchestrated a rescue, he would be a prisoner for the foreseeable future. That made the decision about what to tell Horrock a little easier, because he knew he wouldn't be donning his Red armour and marching into battle any time soon, and any information he did give would not help the Ranen hold their lands against a concerted assault by seasoned knights.

* * *

William was glad Horrock had given him time to rest. He had no illusions that the man of Wraith was being charitable, but he needed time to clear his head and alleviate the extreme fatigue bought on by his wounds and the loss of blood.

He'd woken every few hours and had shaken off a little more of his weakness each time he'd done so. Ranen folk had come and gone throughout the next morning and, aside from the occasional insult or questioning look, the knight captain had largely been left alone, still chained to the wall and with only the remains of Hasim's bread for sustenance. He'd seen Micah Stone Dog several times, going up into the ruined town, and Freya had come to check on his dressings twice during the morning.

William was cold and he had to remind himself that he was further north than he'd ever been – across the Grass Sea of Ranen – and that he was a foreigner in the Freelands. He thought of Ro Arnon and the security he'd always taken for granted as a knight of the Red. He thought of Fallon and of his dead men, their bodies probably stacked on a pyre by now. He didn't want to admit that he'd been defeated and captured, but reality was a hard mistress and not gentle when a man was finally forced to admit defeat after years of victory. The most disquieting thought, though, was the rapidly growing empathy William was feeling towards the simple men of Wraith Company. As a churchman of the One God, William had always been insulated from what happened to the enemies of the Red knights; and now to see them bleed and die, trying to save their loved ones, had deeply affected him.

'Can you stand?' asked Stone Dog from nearby.

William felt his legs and rubbed his wounded chest before answering. 'I think so.'

'Well, up you get, then. Horrock would like a chat,' he said, producing a large iron key to unlock William's chain from the wall.

'Are you going to unlock that as well?' William pointed to the manacle around his ankle.

'Don't think so, you may do something stupid with a full stride.' Stone Dog's smile was good-natured.

'Don't worry, I'm perfectly capable of doing stupid things whether I can walk or not. My father lost both his legs to a Karesian Hound and he did stupid things for many years afterwards.' William was not trying to be especially friendly, but, reluctantly or not, Stone Dog had saved his life and so was worthy of politeness at least.

'So, stupidity runs in the family, Red man . . . I may get a chance to kill you yet.' The idea clearly still appealed to the young man of Wraith.

William pulled himself heavily to his feet and instantly vomited on the floor as a wave of pain flooded through him. It was not too pleasant, but William instantly felt better, despite the laughter from Stone Dog.

'Is that how tough churchmen try to escape, puking on their enemies?' he asked, with a broad grin.

'It's the first stage, yeah,' replied William as he spat on the floor, trying to clear the unpleasant taste from his mouth.

Stone Dog picked up the end of the chain attached to William's ankle and ruffled it as he would a dog's chain. 'Come on, boy, let's go for a walk.' He was enjoying the power he exercised over the Red knight.

'Don't push me, Ranen, I'm not planning to do anything stupid just yet, but I may change my mind if you talk to me like a dog again,' William said with an intimidating grin.

For a second he actually saw a hint of fear in the young Ranen's eyes, before he turned and led William of Verellian from the basement where he'd been chained for almost twelve hours.

He led him out of the room and down a long corridor where numerous exotic and mundane weapons hung on the stone walls. There were tabards and suits of armour also, and William narrowed his eyes at the presence of clerical and knightly armour among the trophies, showing that this was not the first fight these men had had with churchmen of the One.

Stone Dog led him along the corridor and through a heavy stone door and up the stairs beyond. William could hear talking above and he began to see the brightness of daylight spreading down the stairs. He'd been in a dark basement with no windows and he found his eyes a little sensitive to the light.

William moved his injured hand up to his face to shield it from the sunshine when they emerged at the top of the stairs and on to a stone balcony. The view was a sombre one as he looked through the bright, cold morning at the broken town of Ro Hail.

It had, long ago, been a mighty fortress of the Red knights, from where the subjugation of the Ranen people had been orchestrated. Centuries after that, it had been held by Duke Hector's ancestors in an infamous siege when they had defended the town for thirty days against the Free Companies.

It was now little more than a stone relic, with less than a handful of buildings still standing in any kind of recognizable form. William understood why Wraith Company lived underground and he guessed that they knew the city well enough to be able to appear and disappear with ease among the ruins.

Sitting in a casual circle on the balcony were Captain Horrock, Al-Hasim and the Lady Bronwyn. There were two other men of Wraith whom William didn't recognize. All present were armed and armoured. Horrock's deep blue eyes struck him as somehow more piercing in the daylight, despite the residual food lodged in his huge beard. Bronwyn had dressed herself in leather armour and looked more like a Ranen warrior woman than a noble of

Tor Funweir. Al-Hasim was yawning extravagantly as he leant back in his chair.

'Have a seat, Red man,' said Horrock in a casual, almost familiar, tone of voice.

Stone Dog threw William's chain to one of the other men of Wraith and quickly left the balcony. Verellian surmised that the young Ranen was not a senior member of Wraith Company, although he had not heard mention of any rank or chain of command beyond Captain Horrock.

William's chain was held loosely by an axe-man who leant on the balcony's railing. He made no particular effort to keep the chain taut or to restrict the knight's movements, but merely motioned for him to sit in one of the empty wooden chairs.

'My name is William of Verellian,' he said, sitting down carefully to avoid aggravating his chest wound.

'So?' replied Horrock.

'So . . . I prefer it to constantly being called *Red man*.' William maintained eye contact with the man of Wraith and tried his best to convey that he wasn't going to be cowed merely because he was a prisoner.

'Fair enough,' said Horrock, with no hint of humour. 'So, William of Verellian, how are you feeling?'

The Red knight laughed a little and held his arms wide to survey his various wounds. He still wore only woollen leggings and a cloak draped around his shoulders, making the large dressing across his chest stand out.

'Your axe sheared my breastplate, but, so long as I have time to heal without making it worse, I'll survive.' He looked at his injured hand and continued, 'Though I doubt I'll be drawing my sword any time soon.'

One of the Ranen warriors whom William didn't recognize snorted with amusement and said, 'Your sword got shattered as we moved the bodies, Red man. How about an axe?'

This caused a ripple of laughter from the Ranen, though neither Hasim nor Bronwyn joined in. Horrock merely smiled and directed a tolerant glance at the other men of Wraith.

'This is Haffen Red Face, my axe-master. He's here to kill you if I decide he needs to.' Horrock showed no emotion in his piercing blue eyes.

'And what conditions need to be met for me to die?' asked William, stony-faced.

Hasim and Bronwyn both looked at Horrock and William guessed that neither of them had any particular desire to see the knight executed.

'I probably won't order you killed,' the captain of Wraith Company said quietly, 'but I try to keep my options open when dealing with Ro . . . and Haffen is itching to kill another knight.'

As if to emphasize this point, Haffen grinned wickedly at William and twirled the chain in his hands.

'Well, I plan to live beyond today,' said William, still looking directly at Horrock.

'Can we dispense with the posturing, please?' asked Lady Bronwyn with a slight shake of her head. 'Sir Verellian, I know you had orders to apprehend me and, from what Hasim says, you're not a dishonourable man; but you are a knight of Tor Funweir in the Freelands of Ranen, so please . . . tell me what Sir Rillion plans to do with my home.' Her voice had a slight catch to it and William felt a moment's pity for the young woman. Her father was dead, her brother outlawed, and her home all but destroyed.

'It's not Rillion and it's not about Ro Canarn,' William replied, his eyes directed at the floor. 'It's the king.'

This immediately caught the attention of all present, even Al-Hasim who must have suspected that King Sebastian Tiris was involved.

'Speak plain, Verellian,' said Hasim. 'The king wasn't there when we left.'

'No, but I know the signs. His guardsmen had arrived and, if rumour and implication are to be trusted, the king plans to march into the Grass Sea.' William did not doubt this was true, but he had no solid proof, so he stated it in as simple and unadorned a manner as possible.

Horrock sat forward. It was the most animated William had seen him since they had fought. The two other Ranen directed angry glares at the knight, and Bronwyn gasped in surprise.

'He wouldn't be so stupid,' said Horrock. 'That would just lead to blood and nothing else. He has nothing to gain.'

'Neither he nor Rillion confide in me, but I wouldn't be surprised to hear that the Karesian witch has something to do with it,' responded William.

Horrock and Bronwyn both looked at Hasim, and William guessed that the Karesian was as concerned about the enchantress as he was. Al-Hasim gave Horrock a shallow nod before he turned to address William.

'I knew she had Rillion's balls in her hand, but to invade Ranen . . . what's the objective?' asked the Karesian.

'There is none,' replied Horrock, unable to comprehend why the king would break the truce. 'Algenon at his back and the Free Companies at his front. Even if he won, he'd get thousands killed and would *still* get stopped at the Deep Cross when winter came.'

William chanced his luck and interrupted the man of Wraith. 'If you believe that I'm an honourable man,' he said, glancing at Hasim and Bronwyn, both of whom seemed to confirm that he was, 'then believe what I say. King Tiris intends to invade and, I would assume, he'll be at the head of a large force of knights, clerics and yeomanry – Darkwald, Hunter's Cross, he's got no shortage of pressed troops.'

William was silent for a moment as the others threw comments back and forth, arguing over how and why the king of Tor Funweir could be so reckless. William could tell from the way Hasim sat, mostly in silence, with a troubled look on his dark features, that, besides himself, he alone realized that Ameira the Lady of Spiders was behind this.

Horrock stayed in his chair as Haffen Red Face growled out oaths of violence and challenges directed at King Sebastian Tiris.

The captain of Wraith Company let his man swear for a few minutes before he silenced him with a sharp motion of his hand.

'Haffen, that's enough. We all have work to do and defences to prepare,' he said, his mind clearly racing.

As William had feared, it looked as if Wraith Company would not be retreating to the safety of the eastern Freelands, or north to Hammerfall and Fjorlan. Horrock evidently had no intention of leaving the ruins of Ro Hail or the realm of Wraith to be overrun by knights of the Red.

'You could fall back,' said William hesitantly, causing the three Ranen men to stop talking and turn to him.

'Silence, Red man,' roared Haffen. 'You've said all you need to say.' He turned back to Horrock. 'Shall I chain him up downstairs again, captain, or maybe cleave in his head?'

To William's surprise, Horrock stood and slapped Haffen sharply across the face, causing blood to appear at the corner of his mouth.

'Calm down,' said Horrock quietly, maintaining a serene demeanour as he reprimanded his axe-master.

The big Ranen shook his head and then looked apologetically at the floor. 'I'm sorry, Horrock. I'm angry and I let it show in my words. It won't happen again.' With his head bowed, Haffen looked like a scolded child.

'Don't worry, just keep your head together and do as I say. Do you understand?'

He nodded. The respect the men of Wraith had for their captain was evident in their faces whenever they spoke to him, but William was still a little taken aback at the way the Free Company operated. They had no ranks, save captain, and clearly functioned on the basis of mutual need and respect. It was a far cry from the enforced servitude of the Ro church and the austere life of salutes and bowed heads that the knights of the Red had to endure.

Horrock turned to William and said softly, 'Yes, Sir Verellian, we could fall back. But until I know more than I do at this moment, we're not going to.'

He clearly didn't feel the need to explain himself further to William, as he turned back to Haffen and said, 'Send a fast rider to Johan Long Shadow at South Warden. He needs to muster Scarlet Company and ride west. Tell him what has happened here. I'll wait for him to talk to me through his cloud stone.'

Haffen stood listening to his captain speak. When he had understood everything, he nodded and quickly left the balcony, deliberately not looking at William as he did so.

Horrock then spoke to the other man, just as calmly. 'It'll take over a month, but ride hard for Ranen Gar and Greywood Company. Stop in the Deep Cross and have them get word to Fjorlan. Go, now.'

The second Ranen left with his instructions and Horrock slowly resumed his seat. Hasim was still deep in thought and Lady Bronwyn just looked upset, as if her world was collapsing around her.

William did not interrupt the silence, but merely looked out over the balcony towards the broken town beyond. Ro Hail was a meagre and unattractive prize, but an important one. It was the only staging point north of Canarn from which an invasion of Ranen would stand a chance, and its capture would have huge symbolic value to either side.

Wraith Company could do huge damage if an army simply rode into the ruins, but the Ranen could not possibly win if a large force of knights were to encircle the town, intent on its capture. If the Ro took the ruined position and fortified it, they would be very hard to shift, even if the men of Fjorlan came south as they had done two hundred years before when Ro Hail last changed hands. It had been attacked and defended numerous times since then but, for nearly fifty years now, it had been safe in Ranen hands. Duke Hector of Canarn and his father had both been moderate rulers, fostering friendly relations with the Free Companies and strengthening the truce.

'And what to do with you,' Horrock said suddenly, looking up to focus his piercing eyes on William, who was absently rubbing his shaven head.

'I ask for nothing, unless you'd consider letting me go,' the knight said with a thin smile.

The inscrutable Ranen showed no sign that he was amused by this comment and, after a moment, turned to Lady Bronwyn. 'He was your pursuer. Perhaps you should have the final say on his fate.'

Bronwyn looked uncomfortable with the responsibility for a man's life and involuntarily turned to Al-Hasim, who merely held his hands wide, indicating that he wasn't going to be much help.

'I don't want to see anyone else dead,' she said quietly, 'but we can't let him go. He'd just resume his command and you'd have to capture or kill him again.'

'Wise words,' said Horrock.

'So, we keep him as a captive?' she asked, clearly unsure of herself.

Hasim leant in and said, in a slightly patronizing tone, 'He gave you the right to decide, my lady. You don't need to ask permission.'

'And I don't need your commentary, Karesian,' she shot back with authority.

Horrock let out a slight laugh at this. 'She does have a noble streak, after all,' he said casually, before turning back to William. 'Lady Bronwyn of Canarn has spoken and you are now a captive of Wraith Company.'

William shook his head at the exchange. 'I knew that already, but thank you for the clarification.'

'But now, Sir Verellian, you don't need to worry about me or any of my men killing you on a whim,' Horrock said, as if it made all the difference in the world.

'And if I give you my word that I won't try to escape, will you allow me to take off this chain and . . . maybe put on some proper clothing?' William asked.

'No, I will not,' Horrock replied, with no hint of humour.

'Good, I'm so glad.' William was, to some degree, resigned to his fate, but he would still have liked to be treated with the respect due to his rank. 'I'm not sure you realize how cold it is in the north and this cloak is little protection against the weather.'

Hasim interjected, 'I can find you a tunic or something down-stairs, but no armour . . . but you'd have guessed that already,' he added with a broad smile.

Horrock sized up the knight of the Red, noting his shaven head and lack of facial hair. 'You should grow a man's beard, it'll help with the cold.' Again, he spoke in such a way that William couldn't tell if he was joking.

'Well, assuming you don't have a razor or soap for me to use, that decision may well be taken out of my hands,' he responded with a wry grin.

'You'd look less like a hawk and my men would be less wary around you. Most of them were raised never to trust a Ro or a man with no beard, so you are doubly distrusted,' Horrock said, reaching for a glass of something resting on a low table next to him. 'Hasim, if you'd take an instruction from me, go and see the knight properly attired. I need a word in private with her ladyship.'

Hasim nodded and placed a reassuring hand on Bronwyn's shoulder before standing and picking up the length of chain still attached to William's ankle.

As he was led back down into the ruined building, the knight captain thought he should pray. He'd been taught always to retreat into the ordered embrace of the One at times of stress; but he couldn't. He'd seen things in the last few hours that a knight of the Red is not supposed to see, and it had weakened his faith.

CHAPTER THREE

MAGNUS FORKBEARD RAGNARSSON IN THE CITY OF RO CANARN

M AGNUS HAD LOST track of the days he'd spent in the filthy cell, but it was probably at least two weeks. William of Verellian had made sure that he had water to wash himself, before the knight of the Red had journeyed north in pursuit of Bronwyn, and the luxury of clean water each day made Magnus's incarceration more bearable.

Castus, the gaoler, was less bothered about Magnus's desire for cleanliness, but the black eye he'd worn for several days after Verellian's lieutenant had struck him was enough motivation for him at least to follow orders. The gaoler had even begun feeding the prisoner properly, rather than simply throwing the food on the floor.

Magnus was tired and weak from languishing in a cell too small for exercise and too bare to sleep in comfortably. His shoulders ached and his throat felt scratchy and raw from breathing in the dust and debris from the funeral pyres that burned constantly in the square beyond his cell window. Sir Rillion had secured the town with brutality and the promise of a painful death for anyone who resisted his occupation. Now, weeks after the assault, Ro Canarn was a shadow of the town it had once been.

The Brown chapel had remained untouched and Brother Lanry had been allowed to return to the town to assist the populace. Those who had hidden in their homes during the assault were beginning to emerge and food was in short supply, with all the shops and businesses shut down, destroyed or pillaged clean by the mercenaries. The cleric was a good man and had quickly begun organizing the people to make sure everyone was fed. He'd probably butted heads with the mercenaries, but even they wouldn't think to kill a cleric of the One God.

Magnus had seen much from his cell window and had pieced together a picture of Rillion's actions. He had left the worst atrocities to Sir Hallam Pevain's mercenaries and Magnus thought the blind eye the commander turned to Pevain's actions cowardly and vile. The knights wouldn't torture, kill and rape the defeated populace themselves, but they openly allowed such behaviour on the part of their allies.

The level of dungeons in which Magnus was imprisoned had become progressively emptier over the weeks. With no fight left in the town, the mercenaries had begun to question, torture and then kill the duke's guard, leaving Magnus almost alone with dozens of empty cells around him. The commanders had been taken first, dragged from their cells by Pevain's men and tied alive to wooden stakes in the square. The last one had been burned several days ago – for no reason other than to amuse the mercenaries, thought Magnus. The rank and file soldiers of Canarn had met a similar fate, though they had been burned in groups of three or four, and the noise of their deaths had pained Magnus greatly. He knew that without Verellian's men in the keep, Pevain and his mercenaries had little to fear. Even the other knights of the Red had slowly disappeared from the town. Magnus thought Rillion must be pulling them back to the great hall for some reason, leaving the town to the ravages of the mercenaries, with only the old Brown cleric to stand up for the populace.

Magnus's thoughts were interrupted by sounds from the end of the cell block and he could hear armoured men moving with purpose along the hall. There were more feet than just those of Castus and his men approaching Magnus's cell, and he was filled with foreboding. With no one else left to interrogate, he thought his time had finally come and he would welcome the opportunity to stand before Rowanoco in his ice halls beyond the world.

The first knight to appear was Nathan of Du Ban, a worm of a man about whom Verellian had warned him. Behind him was Rashabald the executioner and trailing along at the back were Castus and his men.

'Magnus Forkbeard of Fredericksand, brother to Algenon Teardrop and priestly pain in the One's holy arse,' Nathan began, his blonde hair ruffled by the wind that perpetually blew along the prison corridor. 'You have been summoned by Lord Commander Rillion.'

Magnus stepped forward and regarded the knight. He was undoubtedly a true fighting man, as was the executioner, but both had the smug expressions of men who had never truly known hardship or had their roles in life questioned. These were high-born men, of the noble warrior class of the knights, each with a number of personal insignia and individual heraldic devices displayed on their armour. They were not clerics of the Purple, but among lesser men they wielded almost as much power, and Magnus knew that they had come to collect him personally for more reason than just the Ranen's fearsome martial prowess.

'So, I am to die today?' Magnus asked grimly.

Nathan smiled and Rashabald laughed. Castus began to join in the laughter, but a hard glare from the two knights shut him up. Magnus was again gratified that the bound man was not held in high regard by his superiors.

'I don't believe so, Ranen. Though Lord Rillion does not divulge his mind to me, so it is possible,' Nathan responded. 'You are to be a trophy of conquest, a symbol of our great victory over the traitorous men of Canarn.'

Magnus snarled and lunged forward, clamping his huge hands on to the cell bars and casting baleful eyes over Nathan's face. The knight did not react with anything more than an amused smile, but Rashabald and Castus both jumped at the sudden movement.

'Why am I tormented by petty men? Have I not done enough to warrant a clean and honourable death?' Magnus addressed the query skywards and almost shouted each word in anger and frustration.

Nathan turned to Rashabald. 'You see, brother, the instincts of a caged animal are common among the barbarian north men. I'm frequently amazed that they have proven such a thorn in our side for so long.'

The executioner responded with a nervous smile. To Magnus he appeared nothing more than an old man doing a coward's job. He was living on borrowed time, in Magnus's estimation, for his beheading of Duke Hector and numerous other honourable men. Magnus was ignorant of what had happened over the last two weeks, aside from the fact that Bronwyn had not yet been found and Hasim had been taken north with Verellian, but he could barely tolerate another moment in his cell and his mind was filled with thoughts of blood and vengeance.

'Step back, Ranen,' said Nathan, with scorn, as he drew his longsword.

Magnus didn't move; instead, he gripped the cell bars even harder, turning his knuckles red and growling down at the men of Ro. Nathan smiled viciously and stepped forward, coming to a stop within a few inches of the huge Ranen.

Nathan was a large man, though still small compared with Magnus, but his bearing and evident confidence rendered him a man to be taken seriously.

'I am not afraid of you, Father Magnus. If you try anything I don't like – and I do mean *anything* – I will gladly kill you, and Lord Rillion can parade lesser men before the king,' he said menacingly.

Magnus had suspected that King Sebastian Tiris would be arriving in Canarn at some point, so this was not a surprise. Rillion's order that the knights should pull back from the town and leave it in the care of Pevain's men was most likely in preparation for their monarch's arrival.

'Your king is here?' asked the Ranen priest, letting his growl die down and his hands relax slightly on the bars.

'He'll be arriving within the hour, at the head of a Red fleet, and you are to be brought before him as a sign of our victory,' Rashabald said, with a note of pride in his old, croaky voice.

'If your king has as little honour as you, I would rather spit in his face,' Magnus said in defiance.

Nathan didn't react to the insult and told Rashabald to be silent when the executioner began to splutter. Castus took a step forwards and half drew his longsword.

'My lord, shall I cut his filthy tongue out?' the gaoler asked, braver now that he had the backup of the knights.

'I don't think that would be wise,' Nathan replied, maintaining his calm. 'Rillion wants him unspoiled when he's presented to the king.'

Magnus was led from his cell, along the empty corridor and up into the keep. It was early morning and the air, though crisp and clear, still held the odour of death that hung across the courtyard. The knights were now in full dress uniform and arrayed in shallow columns lining the path from the drawbridge up to the great hall, though the city itself had been left in the charge of Hallam Pevain and his mercenaries.

All the knights sported freshly cleaned red cloaks and their armour had been mended and polished to a burnished shine, with the tabard of crossed longswords over a clenched fist visible on every chest. Magnus estimated that the knights were preparing for further action.

Dark thoughts again entered his mind, much as they had when he had been led to witness Duke Hector's execution several weeks ago, though what he now suspected was a potential invasion of the Grass Sea. Magnus couldn't think of any other reason for the knights' continued presence in the broken remains of Ro Canarn and for the arrival of King Sebastian Tiris.

The courtyard had been left much as it was the last time Magnus had seen it, and its lack of order and cleanliness spoke volumes about the knights' intentions. They had not made any particular effort to occupy the city, beyond subjugating its populace, and the ruined wooden buildings visible beyond the keep had been left where they had fallen. If Rillion and the king had truly cared about Canarn, they would not have allowed its rape and pillage at the hands of Pevain.

'Why have your knights not tried to repair the city?' Magnus asked of Captain Nathan as the small group moved down the line of knights and across the courtyard to the drawbridge leading into the town.

'Why should we? We're knights of the Red, not carpenters and masons,' Nathan replied with arrogance.

'It'll teach 'em a lesson to see their homes burning,' supplied Castus, with a vile grin.

Nathan again shot the gaoler a questioning look, but it turned to a smile of agreement.

'I still plan to kill you, gaoler,' said Magnus, without turning to look at the unpleasant little man.

'Stop!' ordered Nathan as he stepped in front of the chained Ranen and glared up into his eyes.

Rashabald tugged on the chain, causing Magnus to halt in front of the knight captain. 'Look around you, priest.' He gestured at the hundred or more armoured knights lining the courtyard. 'You are a man to be feared, no doubt, but this is not a fight for you. Castus is a man bound to the Red church and is accorded privilege as such. One more word of that kind and I *will* have to punish you.'

Magnus glared at the smaller man. Nathan was not making idle threats or exercising his authority for the sake of it and Magnus detected a sincerity in the knight's words. The Ranen had to conclude that Nathan was a professional soldier and meant every word he said.

'I'll say these things to myself in future, then,' Magnus replied in his Ranen drawl.

Nathan smiled in spite of himself. 'Very well, just don't think that I'll let another word of disobedience pass. I can't and I won't.'

I'm not William of Verellian and you'll find me less impressed with you.' He turned sharply and motioned for Rashabald to lead Magnus behind him.

At the top of the drawbridge stood a small group of knights and others, waiting for the king to arrive. Standing in the centre and wearing an ornately decorated red breastplate was Knight Commander Mortimer Rillion. He looked impressive, even to Magnus, and his high, crested helmet displayed old heraldry, indicating that the knight was of a nobler lineage than his fellows. His tabard had the same crossed swords as the other men, but it also had a laurel wreath placed above the clenched fist, the mark of a high noble of Tor Funweir and a distant relative of the house of Tiris.

To the commander's left stood Ameira the Lady of Spiders. She was standing a little way from the others, eagerly awaiting the arrival of the king's party. Magnus thought he detected a note of jealousy in Rillion's eyes as he looked at the Karesian witch. This again caused Magnus to question the motivation of the knights, as Ameira held a position on equal footing with Father Animustus, the Gold cleric who stood on the other side of Rillion. Two other senior knights of the Red stood with the commander in guarding positions and both turned with hard looks as Magnus approached.

Nathan saluted the commander as he arrived and Rashabald handed the chain to one of Rillion's guards.

'My Lord Rillion,' Nathan said, 'the prisoner has been fairly well behaved thus far, though I echo Verellian's words when I say that Castus has not endeared himself to the Ranen.' The last was spoken with a smile and caused both Rillion and the Gold cleric to laugh quietly.

'Very well, captain, please remain here in close guard. I don't want a repeat of his performance in the great hall,' Rillion said, referring to the knights who had died trying to restrain Magnus the last time he had been brought out of his cell. 'Make sure he is well secured.' The commander pointed at the leg and wrist manacles the Ranen priest wore, causing Rashabald to double-check the steel restraints.

Magnus did not resist. He was glad to be out of his cell and trusted that Rowanoco had plans for him that didn't involve his immediate death. The knights looked at him warily and he heard a few sergeants order their men to keep their eyes to the front and ignore the huge Ranen. He found this amusing, but didn't let it show; nor did he let the enchantress see that he thought her the most dangerous player in this game of conquest and subjugation.

Beyond the town, past the tower of the World Raven, Magnus could just make out the high rigging of tall ships in the harbour of Canarn, ships that had not previously been there. The banner of Tiris, a white eagle in flight, was caught in the breeze and indicated that King Sebastian Tiris, ruler of Tor Funweir, had landed in Ro Canarn.

Rillion ushered Nathan, Rashabald and Magnus off to the side and stood with his chest thrust out at the top of the drawbridge. The columns of Red knights came to attention, their steel armour clanking loudly in unison, and Magnus began to see movement in the city. From the southern harbour people emerged, walking in ordered fashion with pennants held above the marching soldiers. Magnus narrowed his eyes the better to look across the town and was taken aback by the numbers of soldiers he could see approaching. He guessed that, alongside the tall ships, there would be troop transports nestled just out of view. The red breastplates he could see marching through the ruined city indicated an army of considerable size, perhaps five thousand men, with several distinct companies of knights of the Red accompanying the king. To the rear, supply carts and engineers could be seen, with sapping tools and smelting equipment – anvils, portable forges, blocks of steel and spare segments of armour – all the necessary paraphernalia of a sizeable army.

This was an invasion force, and Magnus fidgeted uncomfortably as the army marched towards the keep. He could now make out individuals among the advancing knights – captains, lieutenants and several commanders, besides the rank and file knights of the Red. At the head of the column, seated on a white horse, one of only two men riding and not walking, was a figure resplendent in gold armour. On each side of his breastplate white eagles flanked an ornate crown design, and at his side hung a jewelled scabbard. He was a man of perhaps forty years, though he had neither scars nor a beard to lend any seasoning to his face, and Magnus was unimpressed with his bearing.

Either side of the advancing column, Pevain's bastards were peering out from between buildings to take a look at the king, and many of them seemed particularly interested in the Purple cleric who rode next to the monarch. Those knights in the keep who were close enough to see the riders began to whisper amongst themselves and Magnus heard the name Cardinal Mobius attached to the cleric. The cardinal wore unadorned steel armour, though his purple tabard, displaying the sceptre of nobility, was enough to make him stand out.

'What's he doing here?' Rillion asked of Animustus.

The Gold cleric was evidently distressed at the presence of the Purple cardinal, a man who clearly outranked him, but he mumbled a reply. 'Not known, but it doesn't bode well for your continued command, Mortimer,' the fat man said.

'Your highness, welcome to Ro Canarn,' Rillion said with a deep bow, causing the knights in the courtyard to snap abruptly to attention.

Magnus stood defiantly to one side, his restraining chain held by Sir Nathan, with Rashabald and two other knights standing in close guard. The Ranen priest didn't turn away from the king or avert his eyes as did most of the Ro, but instead he glared down at the monarch, letting the hatred and anger show in his dark eyes.

'Commander Rillion, my most loyal servant, it is a pleasure to see you again,' King Sebastian stated grandly, letting his voice rise to be heard throughout the keep. 'Brother Animustus, I hope that the assault on Ro Canarn has proved profitable for your order?'

He spoke to the Gold cleric in a tone that suggested to Magnus that the king did not hold the Gold church in high regard.

'Absolutely, your highness, the traitor's gold and valuables have been appropriated to the glory of the One,' Animustus replied with evident relish, rubbing his chubby hands together and looking most pleased with himself.

Cardinal Mobius handed the reins of his horse to a lesser Purple cleric who stood behind him and moved to stand next to the king. Rillion and Animustus both looked at the cardinal with a mixture of distrust and reverence, as if assessing where they stood in relation to the senior Purple churchman. Mobius didn't pay much attention to the looks he received, but simply stood close to the king's right shoulder.

'My king, we should get the men settled before we deal with the pleasantries,' he said quietly, before turning to Commander Rillion. 'Mortimer, I assume that you have done as we asked.' His tone suggested past familiarity between the two men.

Rillion nodded, but didn't take his eyes from the cardinal. 'Of course, the muster field is clear for your men . . . though I wasn't expecting so many.'

The king laughed. It was a practised sound, which struck a slightly false note. 'One cannot invade a country without an army, my dear Mortimer,' he said, with just a hint of arrogance.

Ameira shared his laugh and all the men present turned to look at her. 'And you must be the Lady Ameira.' King Sebastian reached for her hand and kissed it warmly, a vaguely euphoric look in his eyes, which Magnus had come to expect from those who fell under the sway of the Seven Sisters.

'Indeed, your highness, it is a pleasure finally to meet you,' Ameira said, holding on to his hand and laughing in a girlish fashion.

Rillion looked decidedly jealous but remained silent. Only Animustus and Magnus noticed his reaction, and Magnus released a low snort of amusement. Sir Nathan tugged on the chain and stepped back to stand as close to the Ranen as he dared.

'Keep quiet, priest, you're in the presence of royalty,' he said through gritted teeth.

'And who is this brute?' the king asked, doing his best to look imperious as he surveyed the Ranen warrior.

Rillion motioned to Nathan for Magnus to be led forward and a tug on his chain brought the prisoner to within a few feet of King Sebastian. 'This is Magnus Forkbeard, a Ranen priest of their Ice Giant. We believe he was Duke Hector's co-conspirator,' Rillion said, clearly still jealous of the attention Ameira was paying to the king.

Mobius moved quickly to stand between Magnus and the king. 'We should be wary of this one, my king. The Lady Katja warned us about him.' He rested a gauntleted hand on the hilt of his longsword.

Ameira smiled at the mention of her sister. 'My beloved sister is most wise, highness, though Father Magnus can be of no real danger to us any more,' she said cryptically. 'Perhaps we should go and discuss what is to be done with him. In private would be best.' Ameira still held the king's hand and Magnus could see her fingers lightly caressing his skin as she spoke.

Rillion clearly wanted to object, but he had simply to watch as King Sebastian Tiris was led away by the enchantress. Cardinal Mobius issued an order to a squad of guardsmen to accompany the king and the group quickly disappeared through a door and into the inner keep of Ro Canarn.

Mobius then turned back to Rillion. 'So, now that his highness is otherwise occupied, we can dispense with the feigned politeness, Mortimer.'

'What are you doing here, Mobius? This is a Red matter. Don't you have Kirin to hunt down or something?' Rillion asked with venom.

The Purple cardinal chuckled to himself and turned back to the lesser clerics behind him. 'Brother Jakan, have the advance guard set up in the great hall in preparation for the king's address to the troops. Send the rest of the knights to the muster field with Knight Commander Tristram.'

The cleric to whom he had spoken was a young man wearing the purple sceptre of nobility and he saluted formally before turning to the other clerics and relaying orders to the assembled knights and guardsmen. Magnus thought it a strange hierarchy – Purple clerics in command of knights of the Red. All were churchmen, but he'd never seen cooperation on this level before. To his perception the Purple clerics were warriors but not soldiers, and he thought this work more suited to the Red knights already in the town.

Mobius let his clerics move among the waiting army and, after a moment, stepped forward into the courtyard to stand with Rillion and Animustus.

'You have had it all your way so far, killing and destroying to your heart's content,' he said out of earshot of most of the other knights, 'but I'm here now and things will change. Do you understand me?'

Rillion sneered at the cardinal and glanced at Animustus, making sure he was not alone. 'You have no claim on me or my knights, Mobius. Be careful about throwing orders around,' he said, with an intentional threat in his words.

'This campaign will be conducted with efficiency,' the Purple cardinal said with a glance towards the destroyed town below. 'And preferably without mercenaries being involved. We have more than enough knights for the job and, with accurate intelligence provided by our Karesian allies, we are optimistic of a favourable outcome before winter. If we need additional forces, Lord Corkoson of Darkwald will be sent for with his yeomanry.'

Magnus growled at the suggestion that this army was going to invade the Freelands of Ranen and he made sure the cardinal heard his displeasure.

Nathan again yanked on his chain and barked, 'Silence, priest, I won't tell you again.'

Mobius turned away from Rillion and stood facing Magnus, his expression one of haughty superiority. As a Purple cleric the man was of the highest level of Ro nobility, a churchman whose word was absolute law for anyone lacking royal blood.

'Katja told me about you, priest, and about your brother. Algenon Teardrop isn't it?' he asked.

'*Lord* Algenon Teardrop Ragnarsson, high thain of Fjorlan and commander of the dragon fleet,' Magnus corrected, stating his elder brother's title with pride.

'Well, if we're throwing around names, I feel I should introduce myself properly. I am Cardinal Mobius of Arnon, cleric of the sword and nobleman of the One God,' he answered with equal pride. 'You must be uncomfortable with defeat and even more uncomfortable with being paraded around as a trophy.'

Magnus scowled, thinking the cardinal was stating the obvious, but he was at least being polite. 'I have long since stopped expecting honour from these knights,' Magnus said. 'They are cowards and murderers, and their allies are vile rapists.'

Cardinal Mobius nodded his head, considering Magnus's words. 'Well, worry not, priest, the invasion of your lands will not be undertaken by mercenaries and you have my word that all defeated opponents will be treated with appropriate honour.'

Magnus growled again at the news of this invasion. He was unsure precisely what was happening here. The knights of the Red had, long ago, subjugated the southern lands of Ranen, but for centuries the Freelands had existed without interference from the Ro.

'Why cause so much blood and death?' he asked Mobius. 'There is no goal or objective in my lands worth any of this. So why invade?' Magnus was angry but, more than that, he genuinely couldn't comprehend why the Ro would do such a thing. A war between the Ranen and the Ro would be devastating to both.

Mobius flashed him a knowing look and directed a haughty smile at Rillion and Animustus. 'Perhaps you should wait for the king's address before you put too much faith in your countrymen,' he said, with confidence.

* * *

The great hall of Ro Canarn was deathly quiet, with no man of Ro daring to speak until the king had broken the silence. He sat in Duke Hector's chair, surveying the assembled knights before him. Most of those that had arrived with the king were on the muster field to the north of the town, but those within the hall still numbered close to five hundred, organized in columns stretching back to the pillared entranceway and filling the huge hall. Magnus was held at the front, his chain still in the hand of Sir Nathan of Du Ban. None of Pevain's mercenaries had been allowed to enter the king's presence and Magnus thought they must have been given the job of keeping order in the town – not that it would be a difficult job, since most of the populace, not already killed or imprisoned, would be cowering behind barricaded doors in their homes or else clustered in Lanry's chapel.

The display of ornate red, gold and purple armour was impressive, even to the worldly Ranen priest, and he imagined that some of these well-adorned men might have honour and brains, more akin to Verellian than to Rillion or Nathan. However, the power in the room definitely lay with King Sebastian Tiris and with Cardinal Mobius, who had adopted a subservient position on a lower chair to the monarch's left. The Purple churchman held a reputation among the knights and, as Magnus looked across their faces, he guessed that the majority of them were scared of Mobius. Knight Commander Rillion was more his equal in status and the looks they exchanged betrayed a deep-seated rivalry. Rillion stood off the raised platform at the head of the column of knights and did not look pleased at having had to give up his seat.

As with the last time Magnus stood in the hall, the presence that worried him the most was Ameira the Lady of Spiders, the Karesian enchantress, whose designs were being played out at the heart of this charade. She sat next to the king and the two exchanged strange glances and thin smiles while the knights waited.

When Tiris stood up, all knights saluted with their fists struck solidly against their breastplates, and Mobius bowed his head slowly in a well-practised gesture of respect.

'My knights, my clerics,' he glanced at Magnus, 'and my captive.

Tor Funweir thanks you for your unswerving loyalty and diligence in bringing to justice the traitor, Hector of Canarn.'

Magnus scowled but remained silent as the king continued.

'However, much still needs to be done. The Ranen warlords have conspired with the traitorous former duke to supplant me and steal our land,' he said in a voice that rose in volume to something approaching a shout. 'And we will not allow these northern barbarians to act without punishment.' He stepped from the platform and walked deliberately towards Magnus. 'Tell me, priest, did you expect to get away with stealing my land?'

Magnus looked around the hall and saw hundreds of eyes regarding him, waiting for an answer that would play to the king's well-practised oration. Instead of growling an oath of challenge or attempting to break free, as he guessed they feared, Magnus leant forward and said, as quietly as he could, 'You are in thrall to a Karesian enchantress, your highness. She will have you invade my lands and see thousands of your men killed to secure no objective and to advance no cause.'

For a brief moment the king looked confused, but quickly regained his composure and glanced back up towards the seated figure of Ameira. They exchanged smiles of childlike adoration before Tiris turned back to Magnus and spoke again, this time with his chin raised in a self-righteous posture of authority.

'Your poisonous words serve only to damn you further, priest,' he said, loud enough for all to hear, 'and your lands will come under the sway of the One God, as all lands eventually will.' He then spoke more quietly, so that only those immediately around him could hear. 'And the thousands dead will be your barbarian cousins who presume to defy the might of Tor Funweir.' A look of euphoria entered his eyes as he stepped back on to the raised platform and began a lengthy and arrogant tirade against the Freelands of Ranen.

Magnus straightened as he felt a presence enter his mind and a female voice spoke clearly. 'You are wrong, Father Magnus Forkbeard,' said Ameira, through a means of communication that no one else in the hall could hear. 'There is indeed an objective, a clear and achievable one.'

Magnus looked past the ranting king and locked eyes with the enchantress. Allowing his mind to relax, he formed a question for her. 'What is all this for? What do you hope to gain? Your people have no stake in Ranen and Jaa cares nothing for these lands,' he said, with genuine confusion, finally sick of all the half-whispered games played around the rape of Canarn.

She smiled, though there was no humour as her words formed. 'Jaa? Is that the limit of your vision? Jaa is an old, decrepit Fire Giant, lamenting the loss of his supremacy. Rowanoco is a dull-witted axe-hurler, and as for the One, he lost touch with this world long ago, his people just haven't realized it yet.'

Magnus narrowed his eyes as the enchantress decried his god and, more surprisingly, her own. 'You speak in riddles, witch. Make sense.'

Another smile, and Magnus sensed that Ameira considered him more worthy than many of the men of Ro listening to the ranting of their king. 'You are a man after my own heart. If things had been different, perhaps we would have been allies. We both dislike these short-sighted men of the One and there might have been a place for you in the Dead God's empire of pleasure and blood.'

'You no longer follow the Fire Giant?' Magnus asked, with cold eyes directed towards the enchantress.

'And the axe finally falls. I thought you cleverer than this, Father Magnus. The men of the One are ours to control, the men of Jaa are deeply within our design. All that leaves is your pitiful nation of farmers and mindless axe-men. Assist me and I will swear to you that no more Ranen will die than is necessary.'

Magnus turned away and looked at the floor. Around him, knights of the Red cheered and banged their breastplates in loud agreement with their king's words, words designed by the enchantress to facilitate the invasion and subjugation of Magnus's people. These men were loyal to their king and the priest couldn't fault them for that, but they sat unknowingly within the thrall of a witch whose goal was not their own. Close to five thousand knights, clerics and guardsmen were massed on the plains of Canarn, ready to advance into the Grass Sea and the realm of Wraith beyond. Horrock's men would be no match for this army, and Magnus's thoughts turned to his brother and the fearsome warriors of Fjorlan.

'Your plan has a flaw, witch,' Magnus stated plainly in the dark recesses of his mind. 'You may have the knights and their king, you may even have the Hounds of Karesia and the people of your homeland, but you will never advance past the Deep Cross and take Fjorlan, not while my brother draws breath and the dragon fleet sails . . . your empire of blood and pleasure will forever be confined to the south while Rowanoco holds sway in the north.' It was a small victory, but one that gave Magnus heart for the coming war.

'Apologies, Lord Magnus, we must appear very foolish to you, not to have considered the dangers posed by Algenon.' Her words were mocking and Magnus felt a chill travel up his spine as if something beyond his perception was at work. 'There are many ambitious men in your homeland, men prepared to do much to gain power. Your brother should choose his allies more carefully.'

Magnus felt rage rise within him, but he closed his eyes and suppressed it. He knew that he'd be killed if he were to channel the rage of Rowanoco in the presence of the king, and nothing would be gained by killing a handful of knights before he fell. His mind raced as he searched for the meaning of Ameira's words. The Seven Sisters had clearly planned this invasion long before Canarn had been assaulted – the witch's confidence in her status in Karesia and Tor Funweir was testament to that – but he did not know how she could have neutralized Algenon. If the dragon fleet had launched it would be only a matter of days before it reached Ro Canarn and the king and his knights were up to their necks in blood. If the men of Ro left to invade the Grass Sea, they'd leave their rear exposed to the battle-brothers of Fjorlan and the possibility that the fleet could turn round

and sack Ro Tiris would quickly halt their advance. Magnus
had seen the barracks of Tiris and knew that few knights would
remain there. If his brother found Ro Canarn empty and an army
advancing north, he would blockade the capital of Tor Funweir
and bombard the city until the king retreated south. It was the
stalemate that had existed for centuries: the Ro were better on
land and the Ranen were better at sea. If the dragon fleet were
removed from the equation, however, the Freelands would be
vulnerable in the extreme.

'I can keep you alive for as long as I will it, Father Magnus.
Your fate is tied to my whim. How does that make you feel?' The
question Ameira asked was accompanied by a look of pleasure
in her eyes which no one but Magnus saw, and it made him even
angrier.

'You have nothing over me, witch. All you can do is kill me and
I am not afraid of that,' Magnus replied with sincerity.

Ameira's eyes disturbed Magnus. She was attempting to reach
into his mind and, although he felt strong, he knew she was powerful enough to influence him – but it would take time that she
didn't have. His will was greater than that of these weak men of
Ro, and the voice of his god flowed through him, strengthening
his resolve against the enchantment.

He smiled wickedly at the enchantress and his thoughts were
violent. 'Try it. Rowanoco dares you, bitch. You can't hide behind
these knights forever and I *will* find a way to kill you.'

'No, Father Magnus, you will not. I am untouchable by your
hand and, if you will not assist me, you will rot in a cell.'

Magnus's thoughts turned to Rham Jas Rami, the Kirin assassin
he'd not seen for over a year, the one man, he was assured by
Al-Hasim, that could kill the enchantresses. Where the Kirin was
now, Magnus didn't know, but as long as he existed somewhere in
the lands of men, the Seven Sisters would be vulnerable.

He heard a laugh in the deep recesses of his mind and Ameira
spoke again. 'Your Kirin friend is now powerless to injure us,
his son saw to that when we bought him from a Karesian slaver.

The Dead God gives us fresh power to resist his feeble attempts to kill us.'

Magnus knew that Rham Jas had once had children, but they were thought lost following the assault on the Kirin's village, somewhere in Oslan. To hear that the Seven Sisters had found his son would no doubt make Rham Jas happy and ferocious in equal measure.

'Maybe you should be more worried about his bow than my hammer.' Magnus projected his thought with a thin smile. 'He's a cunning bastard, witch, more than a match for you.'

'That may once have been true, but no longer. Let him draw his bow and you will see him as powerless as any in our presence.'

Magnus retained his smile, which appeared to infuriate the enchantress. The Ranen priest knew Rham Jas well enough to know that he was not a man whose actions were easy to predict; Magnus had, more than once, heard someone say he wasn't worried about the Kirin, only to be found with an arrow in his head shortly afterwards.

'Maybe this will silence you,' she said, reaching behind her chair and slowly producing Skeld, Magnus's war-hammer. 'I planned to give it to Knight Commander Rillion but, after your ill-advised insults, I may give it to Sir Hallam Pevain.'

Magnus stopped smiling and the thought of such a dishonourable man wielding Skeld caused him to breathe deeply in order to stop himself channelling the battle rage of Rowanoco and getting himself killed.

He gritted his teeth and projected his answer as calmly as he could manage. 'Give it to whomever you wish, but I assure you they will die at my hand before I take it back.'

Ameira the Lady of Spiders did not look impressed at the threat and, turning to look at the still ranting king of Tor Funweir and the cheering crowd of churchmen, she said, 'I will be sure to make your countrymen bleed, just so you may watch.'

* * *

Ameira left soon after the king had stopped speaking, and Magnus was then forced to endure hours of Ro back-slapping, knighthoods given out, bound men promoted to sergeant and promises of positions in the new duchy of Canarn.

Knight Commander Mortimer Rillion was named marshal of the city, with Nathan of Du Ban as his second in command. The king declared that his cousin, Jeremiah Tiris, would be named duke and Mobius would appoint a suitable Purple cleric to oversee the city's spiritual well-being. Animustus of Voy, the fat Gold cleric, would be returning to Ro Arnon with all of his plundered coin, and Pevain would receive another meaningless title to add to his list of accolades. The mercenary knight was also presented with Skeld as a mark of his *valuable service* to Tor Funweir – a gift that Magnus knew would see him killed more surely than his existing dishonour.

The majority of the knights of the Red would be travelling north with King Sebastian Tiris, Knight Commander Tristram and Cardinal Mobius, leaving Rillion with fifty knights and a hundred bound men as an occupying force in Ro Canarn. Pevain and his bastards were to be paid for a further month's work, apparently to assist Rillion in keeping order in the city, but Magnus knew that they would stay because the city had not yet been bled completely dry. Rillion's command would be a paltry three hundred and fifty men, and Magnus was amazed that no one seemed to regard the danger that the dragon fleet would pose to so few defenders.

Magnus was not so arrogant as to think Rillion, Mobius or the king stupid, so he imagined they must be privy to some information thus far hidden from the priest of Rowanoco.

Strangely, Ameira, the enchantress, was also to remain in Ro Canarn, and not to accompany the king into the Grass Sea. Magnus thought that Rowanoco's old decree that no witch would ever set foot in the Freelands of Ranen might still hold some sway and perhaps the Seven Sisters were not as free and untouchable as they might think.

As he was led back to his cell, Magnus thought of his brother once again and said quietly to himself, 'Please be wary, brother, these men have no honour and something is at work here beyond what I can see.'

CHAPTER FOUR

HALLA SUMMER WOLF
ABOARD THE DRAGON FLEET

ALL RANEN CHILDREN grew up hearing tales of monsters. Halla remembered having badgered her mother for a story each night before she would agree to go to bed, and her mother had always been willing to sit at her bedside and tell her tales of fearsome creatures and the Ranen heroes who had vanquished them.

The priests of the Order of the Hammer maintained the tradition that the children of Ranen should never forget that they were not alone in the world and that men did not hold dominion over the land, nor had they even held their portion of it for long. Halla remembered tales of trolls, the Ice Men of Rowanoco, who wandered the Low Kast, feeding on rocks, trees and unwary travellers. She loved the stories of the great Gorlan spiders that appeared out of nowhere during the summer months and built trapdoors from which to hunt across the lands of Hammerfall and the Deep Cross. She remembered huddling under her blanket as her mother told her of the scarred cannibal tribes of Jekka far to the east, beings not entirely human which struck at settlements and ate the inhabitants. Her mother's favourite stories were of the risen men, timid beings who lived in the deepest forests, had claimed the land for longer than men, and were hunted almost to extinction by the clerics of Ro.

She loved hearing fabulous stories, but of all those she remembered it was the ones her father had told her that stayed the clearest in her mind. Aleph Summer Wolf, the now deceased thain of Tiergarten, would wait until his wife was asleep to tell his daughter about Ithqas and Aqas, the blind, mindless Krakens of the Fjorlan Sea. Halla's mother did not approve of such stories, for the Krakens were more than simple monsters. The young axe-maiden loved the tales, however, and she would often pretend to be asleep in the hope that her mother would leave and that Aleph would take over the storytelling.

The Krakens were supposedly old gods, Giants worshipped by creatures lost in the mists of Deep Time. They were cast down by Rowanoco and made to gnaw on fish and rock in the deepest trenches of the ocean, their minds broken by the Ice Giant's wrath. Often Ranen sailors would return from their voyages with terrifying stories of encounters at sea, broken masts, ruptured hulls and lost men. Sometimes these were attributed to the Krakens and sometimes not, but Halla was fond of playing on the docks in the hope of seeing a returning ship and hearing a story about the Krakens.

The most infamous tale had come from a winter voyage when Halla was only seven years old. Five ships had left Tiergarten, bound for the mountainous islands of Samnia, but only one had returned, a wooden shell with a crew huddled below decks, half mad from the sight of the Krakens. None of the survivors could put into words what they had seen and they all died shortly after they returned, their bodies having simply given up on life and wasted away, while their minds could summon only shouted warnings of tentacles and death. No one knew exactly what had happened, but their ravings had been recorded by a priest and entered into the written record of Tiergarten as a warning for sailors. The ancient horn of the deep, a twisted brass instrument hanging outside a tidal cave on the coast of Samnia, was said to summon the beasts, and from ancient days the horn had been guarded at all times as a hereditary task by the Order of the Hammer. Only once had it been blown, by a mad axe-master of Hammerfall during the Ro occupation, and he'd had to kill two priests to get to it. The Krakens, when awoken, had provided the Ranen with little in the way of help against the Ro, for they had simply eaten the axe-master and sunk his ship before returning to the deep.

Halla stood against the railings of her father's ship and looked out across the slowly rolling seas of Fjorlan. It was now her ship and, although she was proud to be on board, it still felt strange. She'd fought all her life to be regarded as equal to men, but now that she was part of the battle fleet she could only think of the old stories of monsters.

The fleet had assembled quickly in Fredericksand, Algenon Teardrop calling his lords to come swiftly and with as many men as could be spared. They'd set sail a little over a week before and were now approaching the straits of Samnia; beyond, the seas of Canarn and Tiris marked the northern border of Tor Funweir.

Her ship, called the *Sea Wolf*, was towards the rear of the dragon fleet. She knew that if Aleph were still alive, the warriors of Tiergarten would have been closer to the vanguard, but with no thain to represent them they'd been pushed into a less glorious position. She had three hundred and twenty-five warriors spread across three ships and they formed the rearguard of the fleet, not generally considered a position to be coveted. Borrin Iron Beard, axe-master of Tiergarten, was acting as captain and had given the sailors to understand that a single derogatory word directed towards Halla would result in summary death by drowning. He was a good man, pledged to serve the family of Summer Wolf, and he'd known the axe-maiden all her life.

Far to the front she could see the banner of Teardrop, a black flag displaying a weeping dragon. The fog had not yet fully encompassed the fleet and Algenon's ship, the *Hammer of Fjorlan*, was just about visible in the distance. She knew that Wulfrick, Algenon's axe-master, had tried to speak for her and secure a more prestigious position for the battle-brothers of Tiergarten, but Rulag Ursa and the men of Jarvik had bullied the high thain into assigning her to the rearguard. The warlord of Jarvik had taken great offence at an axe-maiden being treated as heir to a thain, but, with no brothers, Halla had no choice but to speak for her people. Tiergarten was the second city of Fjorlan and she was not going to allow her father's death to affect the honour of his lands. The realm of Summer Wolf was the bread-basket of Fjorlan, the only place north of the Deep Cross where crops could be grown. The soil was dark and rich and, when the snows thawed, the forests and fields provided food for much of the north lands of Ranen. There were also few trolls, which meant that settlements would rarely just disappear overnight as sometimes happened in the Low Kast.

The fog began to grow thicker and Halla could hear bells rung throughout the fleet to alert the helmsmen to each ship's location. Behind her, dark, hard faces looked up from their oars and slowed their rowing. When the fog grew thick around Samnia, the danger of hitting a semi-submerged rock was ever present.

Borrin Iron Beard stood at the aft of the ship, looking out to sea. He slowly began to make his way past the oarsmen to the forward platform where Halla stood.

'Easy, lads,' he said as he walked past the front row of oarsmen. 'I've seen fog thicker than this. This is barely a wisp of cloud.'

He was lying, but Halla appreciated his attempt to calm the crew. She was not yet comfortable with the shouting and bullying that was required of a ship's captain and was glad of her axe-master's assistance.

'You look almost as grim as those dirty bastards,' Borrin said as he came to a halt next to Halla, joining her in looking forward, beyond the ship's rampant wolf figurehead.

'I'll be less grim when we clear Samnia and can see where we're going,' Halla replied, rubbing under her eyepatch.

'Just hope we don't get eaten by Krakens,' he said with an ironic grin, causing Halla to look displeased.

'It's ill-advised to joke about Giants, Borrin.' The comment was meant kindly, but the axe-maiden could not shake off her nervousness about travelling through the Kraken waters. It was a childish fear, and she knew it, but she'd never fully reconciled the reality of Ithqas and Aqas with the stories she'd been told as a child.

The fog bells continued to sound up ahead and Halla thought the vanguard of the fleet must have reached the islands. Her three dragon ships were close together, kept within visual range by their helmsmen.

'I hope Ursa can sail as well as he shouts,' Borrin said of the lord of Jarvik far to the front of the fleet. 'Algenon's men can negotiate these waters, but with Rulag and his idiot son to take care of, it'll be a squeeze to get us all through the Kraken waters to Kalall's Deep.'

The fleet had slowed considerably and Halla thought it was more than a simple precaution against the fog. If Rulag Ursa was being awkward about the sailing order of the ships, then it could be a long wait to get the whole fleet through the narrow channels of Samnia. Algenon and the *Hammer of Fjorlan* were at the head of the fleet, but his battle-brothers were flanked by the ships of Jarvik and Rulag's men.

The ringing of bells became more frequent and erratic and Borrin flashed a concerned look at Halla. 'What are they playing at up there?' he asked quietly. 'Sounds like the ships are too thinly spread or they're losing sight of each other in the fog.'

Halla stepped to the side and tried to focus her single eye forward into the dense mist; seeing only vague shapes in front of the *Sea Wolf*, she turned back to Borrin.

'Those are warning bells,' she said.

The rhythmic sound of bells was being echoed through the front few ranks of ships, indicating that they were trying to warn those on the flanks to stay close.

'Only a fool would break off in this,' Borrin said, going to the large brass bell that hung from a post.

He hefted the rope and rung the bell twice, loudly, a sound rapidly echoed by the other ships of Tiergarten.

Halla was confused. The fleet should be staying close in preparation for the journey through the narrow channels of Samnia. It made no sense that any ships should be breaking off, and yet the warning bells continued to sound. She stepped to the port side of her ship and tried to make out some kind of marker or feature that would tell her how close they were to land, but all she could see was fog and the rough outline of another ship from Tiergarten, equally confused as to what was going on.

'My stomach's rumbling, Halla,' said Borrin. 'That either means I'm hungry or that something bad is about to happen.'

The axe-master of Tiergarten was a superstitious man, very much of the opinion that his stomach could detect danger. Halla had never been sure whether he was joking or not when he claimed to have a stomach-related premonition, but now she had a similar sense of foreboding.

Borrin turned to address the battle-brothers of the *Sea Wolf*. 'Steady, lads, we'll be past the Kraken sea before you know it.'

His words did little to calm the sailors, but Halla guessed he'd said it as much for his own benefit as theirs.

Bells were now being rung rapidly and with a persistence that indicated something was genuinely wrong, though the dense fog meant that Halla, in the rearguard, could only guess at what was causing Algenon Teardrop and Wulfrick to ring such an insistent warning.

Borrin was deep in thought as he stood next to the axe-maiden and peered into the fog.

Suddenly he pointed to the port side of the ship and said, 'Halla, look. What do you make of that?'

She had to blink several times to focus properly, but sure enough, far ahead of her ship, on the port side, roughly where she imagined the inlets of Kalall's Deep must be, Halla could see what looked like fire. It was little more than an orange glow, but certainly fire. Then another dot of orange appeared, and then another, until a dozen or more fiery points could be seen through the fog to the port side of the dragon fleet.

Borrin looked confused at first and then, as grim realization dawned on him, he turned to Halla and said, 'Rowanoco save us, those are catapults.'

As he spoke, the dots of fire moved, shot sharply upwards into the fog, illuminating the sky as they became balls of fire flying towards the ships of the dragon fleet. A dozen or more catapults, hidden somewhere in the fog, fired one after another and the sailors of the *Sea Wolf* stood and watched dumbfounded as a ship of Hammerfall was hit amidships by a huge cask of flaming pitch. Ranen sailors, now visible to Halla, ran in panic trying to put out the fire, but the ship was ablaze and many of the men simply jumped overboard.

'Launch boats and help those men,' ordered Halla.

'Too late . . . look,' answered Borrin as more ships were hit and the dragon fleet came under fire from several hidden inlets off the coast of Samnia.

The catapults shot volley after volley into the fleet and ship and man alike were hit. The screams of Ranen burning to death took over from the bells and Halla could now see where the shots had come from. The fire had cleared a portion of the fog and she could see a tightly packed group of small ships emerging from a narrow channel. They flew the banners of Ursa, and Halla roared angrily as she recognized the treachery among the Ranen lords.

'Those are Rulag's cutters,' exclaimed Borrin.

Catapults fired from the starboard side of the fleet now, and Halla saw new cutters appear. The smaller ships were faster and more manoeuvrable than the large ships of the dragon fleet and each carried a catapult with a tremendous range.

The ships of Tiergarten, being in the rearguard, had not been hit by the flaming casks, although ahead of their position numerous ships, now burning furiously, had not been so lucky. Halla looked on helplessly as she saw men on fire diving into the icy water, and the way the ships slowly burned down to the water line made her even angrier. This was destruction by degrees, a carefully laid ambush designed to catch the ships in the narrowest channel where they couldn't manoeuvre to avoid the flaming catapults.

Battle chants could now be heard as some of the captains tried to break away to engage the ships of Rulag the betrayer. A ship of Fredericksand, one of Algenon's, with flaming sails and rapidly taking on water, plunged through the fleet to get to the cutters, but it was too big to avoid the other boats and its charge ended abruptly as it hit another ship. The cries of sailors echoed through the fleet as both vessels quickly sank.

'Fight or flee, Halla?' Borrin asked plainly.

Halla ignored him for a moment and shielded her eyes from the blazing fires in front of her. She was trying to find the *Hammer of Fjorlan* and hoping that Algenon and Wulfrick had managed to get away.

'Halla!'

'I can't see the vanguard. We can't leave until I know what has happened to the high thain.' Halla was an axe-maiden of Rowanoco and was not afraid of death.

She steeled herself and, stepping past her axe-master, shouted to the crew, 'To your oars, now! We need to get to the front of the fleet. Lord Algenon needs our help and Tiergarten will not disappoint him or Rowanoco by running.'

Her men paused for a moment, most of them still standing and staring at the burning ships ahead of them.

'Move!' shouted Borrin, causing each man quickly to regain his seat. 'If this ship isn't moving forward in two seconds, you'll have to worry about me *and* fire – and I am much scarier.'

He didn't question Halla's decision and she was deeply grateful for her axe-master's support, even as she strengthened herself for battle.

The *Sea Wolf* sprang into motion and moved quickly towards the wreckage of several ships from Hammerfall. Her other two ships followed suit and the three dragon ships of Tiergarten entered the fray.

'Keep us in the channel,' she said quickly to Borrin, who relayed the message to the helmsman.

A flaming ball flew overhead, narrowly missing the mast and thudding into the sea over the starboard side. Either side, the flaming shells of other Ranen ships continued to burn as the cutters of Jarvik maintained their bombardment. The fog was dense, but broken by shooting lines of fire, and Halla could sense the fleet was trapped between rocks ahead that required careful navigation and, on either side, the small, fast catapult ships hidden in narrow inlets. She could make out the looming cliffs of Samnia and knew that the water here was deep and freezing; a man in chain mail could survive for no more than a few minutes if he were to go overboard. The cutters were not coming close enough to be boarded and the remaining dragon ships were moving in circles, attempting to find a way out of the killing zone between the cliffs.

Banners of the Deep Cross and the Hammerfall intermingled as captains, lords and battle-brothers roared futile challenges and tried to keep their men alive. Several ships had been holed by the semi-submerged rocks and were slowly sinking while their crews attempted to launch rowing boats to escape the freezing water. Many were still undamaged, but were sailing in circles as the *Sea Wolf* plunged past them.

Halla un-slung her axe and began to bang a rhythm on the wooden deck. She turned towards the crew and saw they were starting to row with more purpose, keeping pace with her axe rhythm and gathering speed. Over on the port side a cry of warning came too late to stop a cask of flaming pitch smashing into one of the other Tiergarten ships.

Borrin reacted quickly, roaring, 'Eyes front, lads, we will honour them by staying alive. Now, forward!'

Halla glanced through the fog to see the other ship's captain raise his axe in salute to her before his vessel began to sink, with all hands feverishly trying to launch boats. Another flaming cask hit them amidships and Halla winced as she saw the captain suddenly engulfed in flame. The men abandoned the flaming boats and simply jumped into the freezing water to await death or rescue.

The men of the *Sea Wolf* looked grim, yet determined, as they rowed on into the narrow channel where the majority of ships were still trapped, many ablaze or holed by the hidden rocks. Halla could see the larger dragon ships of Rulag Ursa. The traitorous lord had broken off from the vanguard and left Algenon's ships isolated and trapped between the cliffs, with fire raining down on all sides.

'Faster,' roared Borrin, as he straddled the side of the ship and began to strike his axe on the hull, mirroring the tempo set by Halla.

Ahead, she could see the banner of Teardrop peeking out from between burning ships and the encircling cutters. The *Hammer of Fjorlan* was not ablaze and Halla suspected it had deliberately not been targeted. Beyond, the Kraken sea was clear to the south, but Algenon's single ship was trapped by Rulag's half-dozen and no aid was anywhere near, the majority of ships in the channel being now ablaze or sailing in circles to try to avoid running aground. She could see the dark coastline of Kalall's Deep over her port side, but the towering cliffs meant that escape overland would be difficult. The *Hammer of Fjorlan* could not last long if all of Rulag's ships closed in on it.

'Pull for the high thain,' Halla shouted.

A sickening sound came from her second escort ship as its hull was torn by semi-submerged rocks and it began to list badly to one side. The sailors had time to launch boats and escape, but they could be of no further help to the *Sea Wolf*. Bells were being rung on the attacking ships of Jarvik to alert Rulag that another dragon ship was approaching.

The ambush had been well planned, with many cutters, too small to be seen and in any case hidden by the fog, assaulting from all sides while staying out of the reach of the cumbersome dragon fleet. Rulag's larger ships, all of which had been in the vanguard, had broken off before they had reached the narrow channel, causing the *Hammer of Fjorlan* to become isolated, along with the other ships of Fredericksand, when the bombardment began. The traitorous lord had then turned about and encircled Algenon, allowing no means of escape, while panic had gripped the fleet.

Halla could see axes thrown from Rulag's ships thinning the ranks of Algenon's battle-brothers and softening them up for the inevitable boarding. Around her, she could see no other ships afloat save two that had managed to find their way down a side channel and were now out of range of the catapults. She felt rage growing within her at the sight of burning wood and the smell of burning flesh. Many were dead and many more would not survive the water. Behind her, she hoped some of the ships of Hammerfall and the Deep Cross, which had been closer to the rear, might have been able to turn and flee to the north.

She breathed in deeply and, with axe held aloft, roared a challenge at the nearest dragon ship of Jarvik. Several of Rulag's battle-brothers had turned to meet the *Sea Wolf*'s charge and she could see faces, ready for battle, beckoning her onwards.

'Aim for the gap and punch through, we . . . will . . . not . . . die . . . today.' Her words were loud and were spoken with deep conviction, making her men row all the faster and chant out oaths of battle and pledges to Tiergarten and the house of Summer Wolf.

Borrin continued to bang his axe on the hull, whipping himself up into a frenzy as he joined in the chanting. 'I'll tear your fucking faces off, you turncoat bastards . . . no soft death for betrayers.'

The warriors of Jarvik began to shout back, unaware that the two ships that had broken away had seen Halla's charge and were now turning to rejoin the battle, quickly making their way out of the narrow inlet and into the channel behind the *Sea Wolf*. Six dragon ships of Jarvik encircled the *Hammer of Fjorlan* and two had begun throwing grappling hooks and preparing to board, the remainder poised to meet the oncoming attack of Halla's ship.

'Halla, more approach,' shouted Borrin, pointing behind.

Halla saw several ships flying the banners of the Deep Cross plunging forward, shouting their own battle chants. They had not turned to flee when they had the chance, but had taken their cue from the *Sea Wolf* and were coming to assist their high thain.

Seven dragon ships were now sailing in loose formation towards the vanguard and the stricken *Hammer of Fjorlan*.

'Throw your oars . . . draw axes,' Halla ordered, causing her men quickly to pull their oars into the ship and across their benches, before standing as one and hefting an array of vicious-looking weapons.

The last few feet passed in slow motion and Halla saw faces fixed in battle fervour waiting on the ships of Jarvik. The *Sea Wolf* hit the gap between two of the ships, and splintered wood flew from all three vessels as the flagship of Tiergarten broke through. Others followed behind and the battle began.

Halla could see fighting on the deck of the *Hammer of Fjorlan* and could even make out the figure of Algenon Teardrop, swinging his axe in wide arcs, severing men at the neck, trying desperately to repulse the boarders. The men of Fredericksand were outnumbered but with Teardrop and Wulfrick in the fray they would always stand a chance. The axe-master was an immense presence, standing next to his thain and killing anyone who came close with thundering blows from his great axe.

More grappling hooks were thrown and it looked to Halla as if Algenon would quickly be overwhelmed. Her own men had moved to the sides of the *Sea Wolf* and were waiting for their opportunity to strike – an opportunity that came quickly when their ship abruptly stopped, wedging itself between the stern of the *Hammer of Fjorlan* and the port side of one of the attackers. Her battle-brothers roared out challenges and flooded from their ship on to the rear of the high thain's vessel, joining the fight alongside the men of Fredericksand.

The other ships that had joined them were engaged against the encircling vessels and a confusing melee ensued. No more flaming casks were being fired and the treachery had come down to steel against steel.

'Halla, cover the rear.' The command came from Wulfrick as he barrelled two attackers over the side and into the water.

She responded by swinging herself into the midst of a group of attackers and shouting a battle cry. The men of Jarvik looked surprised for a second and she didn't give them a chance to recover as her axe moved quickly, beheading the nearest man and cleaving through into the chest of another. Borrin was with her and, shouting insults at the Rulag Ursa's men, he began to hack at limbs and bodies. Her men were whipped up into a battle rage by her actions and she felt pride as they threw themselves at the attackers, caring little for their own survival. Their ferocity had stolen a march on Rulag's battle-brothers and she thought they might just stand a chance.

Rulag Ursa could not be seen, though Jalek, his axe-master, was leading the main assault and Halla saw him killing men of Fredericksand deftly and with skill, showing that he was a formidable opponent. She parried an incoming blow and quickly kicked the attacker overboard as she moved through the fray to reach Algenon. Borrin remained behind her, covering any attempt to strike at her and helping clear the way for more of her warriors to join the fight.

It was impossible to tell how they were faring as, in every direction, all she could see was Ranen killing Ranen, in a series of brutal and often desperate encounters. The men of Fredericksand were surrounded now and only Algenon and Wulfrick prevented them from being overwhelmed.

Another volley of throwing-axes was launched from a ship of Jarvik and more of the high thain's men fell on to the wide wooden deck.

'My life will not be given easily, you sons of whores,' roared Algenon Teardrop as he engaged three men, killing two quickly and then slicing the third almost completely in two, splattering blood over his face.

Halla had never seen him fight before and his reputation had been that of a man who would generally avoid violence, but now he appeared as dangerous a man as the axe-maiden had ever seen.

'And mine won't be given at all,' shouted Wulfrick, now standing back to back with his thain.

Halla and Borrin were trying to cut their way through to join Algenon and Wulfrick, but the sheer numbers of men in their way slowed them considerably. More axes killed all but a handful of the *Hammer of Fjorlan*'s crew and Halla's men now outnumbered Algenon's.

The Ranen who had joined Halla's charge were busy fighting on the decks of their own ships, preventing the betrayers from reaching the high thain, and their efforts were causing genuine concern to Rulag Ursa's men – men who now realized they might not be able to win.

Jalek, the axe-master of Jarvik, barked out an order to a group of men to deal with Halla's approaching warriors, before moving to engage Wulfrick himself. Eyes turned to see the weapons of the two axe-masters clash and the sound was deafening. Both were huge men and both were fighting for their lives, though Wulfrick was the more fearsome opponent and Jalek was taken aback by his ferocity.

Halla, Borrin and their battle-brothers moved forward in a wedge shape, hacking at the swarm of Rulag's men. More axes were thrown and several of the men of Tiergarten fell, and Borrin took a solid blow to the back. The axe-master went to his knees, but motioned for Halla to continue as he winced with pain and pulled himself back to his feet.

Wulfrick had pushed Jalek back to the railing of the ship and, with a shout of defiance, he raised his axe high overhead and cleaved in the other man's skull. Men of Jarvik roared in anger at the bloodied mess that used to be their axe-master and the fight became even more brutal. Now it was deeply personal on both sides.

Then Algenon jumped atop a nearby crate and growled out over the melee, 'I am Algenon Teardrop Ragnarsson, high thain of the Ranen, and I name you traitors and cowards.' He was clearly injured, with blood seeping out from under his cloak and a cut visible across his chest.

An answering roar of agreement sounded from the loyal men aboard the *Hammer of Fjorlan*, and a shout of defiance came back from the attackers. Halla joined in as she killed another man, beginning to lose track of the dead around her. Borrin had disappeared into the scrum of bodies and she hoped he would find a way to stay alive.

Wulfrick was red-eyed and foam could be seen at the corners of his mouth, his axe moving in deadly circles, killing men by the three and four, not waiting to fight individuals. Slowly the attackers were pushed back until the majority of Ranen aboard the ship were defenders, mostly battle-brothers of Tiergarten.

Then a distant horn sounded. The noise was deep and rumbled up from rock and earth, cutting through the fight to be heard over steel biting flesh and men screaming challenges. Almost instantly, the traitorous men of Jarvik began to withdraw, turning back to their own ships and fleeing from the defenders. The dragon ships of the Deep Cross that had joined the fight had cleared one of the attacking ships, and another was lost to a flood of loyal warriors, but four of Rulag's ships quickly disengaged in a planned manoeuvre.

The sound of the horn stopped any celebratory cheering from Algenon's ship and the hundred or so warriors who remained on the *Hammer of Fjorlan* fell deathly silent. Even Wulfrick just stood, blood-covered and panting, with no insults or shouts to see off the attackers.

Algenon stepped down from the crate to stand with his men as Halla's battle-brothers mingled with the thain's. 'Good to see you, Summer Wolf,' he said quietly. 'Do you know what that sound is?' Sweat was pouring down his face and he had a look of intense pain in his eyes.

She glanced at Wulfrick who, for the first time since she'd met him, looked afraid. The huge axe-master of Fredericksand had frequently said he feared nothing that could be killed with his axe, and Halla began to feel her own dread rising.

'That's the horn of the deep,' Algenon almost whispered. 'Rulag is trying to wake the Krakens.'

Halla's breathing speeded up and she looked across the deck. Behind her lay the body of Borrin Iron Beard, face down. An axe was buried in his back and his brown eyes were strangely peaceful.

Wulfrick darted back across the deck and looked up at the broken sail. The ship could not move and the vessels around it were in no condition to make way, with hundreds of men dead and more than one of the ships slowing sinking.

'Halla, will the *Sea Wolf* sail?' Wulfrick asked.

Several of her men had sat down heavily when the fight had ended and she saw the light leaving their eyes as the adrenalin of battle left them. One of them nodded at Wulfrick's question.

'She's splintered, but whole, my lord.'

'Get as many as can be saved to your ship. Do it now.' He moved quickly to Algenon, who was leaning against the railing of his ship.

Halla was glad of the obscuring fog as she ordered her men, 'Get the wounded over, anyone that still breathes.'

Her helmsman took over from Borrin and all of Algenon's men joined in, moving men too wounded to walk and those standing in shock amidst their dead battle-brothers. Death had a strange effect on the warriors and the bloodied flesh and bone disquieted them even as they prepared their escape.

Men from the other ships began throwing ropes across to the *Sea Wolf* and leaving their own stricken vessels. Warriors of the Deep Cross, Hammerfall, Fredericksand and Tiergarten moved in groups to the benches of Halla's ship. The oars were still intact and they sat quickly and stowed their weapons.

The sound of the horn trailed off and silence once again came over the fog-shrouded sea channel. Halla moved to join Wulfrick in assisting Algenon and the three of them were the last to leave the *Hammer of Fjorlan*.

'I'm sorry I had to kill your father,' the high thain said weakly. 'He deserved better.'

'Later, my lord, later . . . we need to leave . . . now,' she replied, a slight panic sounding in her voice.

Her arm was round Algenon's waist and she could feel the wetness of blood flowing down his back. He was strong, but she could tell he was badly hurt, and Wulfrick's tight jaw and grim expression showed that he, too, thought the thain would not survive.

A little more than two hundred warriors had survived the battle and the *Sea Wolf* was full to bursting as Wulfrick placed Algenon down on the deck and stood facing the crew.

'We're still alive, boys, no drinking with the Ice Giant for us.' The words were boisterous and Halla envied him his commanding presence, but fear remained in his eyes. 'Now, row for all you're worth.'

Algenon's eyes were beginning to close as the loyal men of Fjorlan extended the oars and heaved away. Halla crouched down next to the dying thain and raised his chin the better to look at him.

'You did well, Halla,' he said, registering her presence. 'Maybe it is time for a thainess after all.' He was smiling and Halla thought he no longer felt the pain of his wounds. 'Stay close to Wulfrick. If there's a way to survive, he'll find it.'

'Are there no priests among your men?' she asked, with a note of desperation in her voice.

'There were, but they were the first killed. I am spent, Halla . . . no priests, no healing, no tomorrow.' The last words trailed off as his eyelids drooped again.

Wulfrick came to join Halla next to the dying thain. The *Sea Wolf* began to move away from the *Hammer of Fjorlan* as the axe-master firmly grasped the hand of his lord.

'We're still alive, Algenon,' he said gently.

'Speak for yourself,' the thain replied with a pained chuckle. 'I am leaking all over your ship, Halla. I deeply apologize.'

The pool of blood was spreading from Algenon's back and his skin was pale and his eyes dark. Wulfrick's jaw was tight and the huge axe-master's knuckles were turning white as he gripped Algenon's hand.

'I don't know what to do,' he said, with tears appearing in his eyes. 'I always know what to do . . .' Halla thought he was wavering on the edge of despair as he looked at the dying man. 'I've let a traitor kill you. My honour is tied to yours and I've let you die.'

Algenon's eyes widened and he turned towards his axe-master. Grabbing his shoulders he pulled himself up to look into Wulfrick's eyes. 'You are my battle-brother and my friend. You are strong and you remain so. Tell my son . . .' He spluttered as blood appeared at the corners of his mouth. 'Tell Alahan . . . to rule well . . . and . . . to keep his axe sharp. Keep him alive, Wulfrick . . . keep him alive.' His voice trailed off and his head rocked limply forwards. Halla waited for more words, but none came and Algenon Teardrop Ragnarsson, high thain of Fjorlan, was dead.

Wulfrick didn't move from Algenon's side and sat with his head bowed, mouthing a silent prayer over the fallen thain.

'My Lord Wulfrick.' The words came from Rexel Falling Cloud, an axe-master of Hammerfall who had approached the position where they sat. 'We are but two hundred men and no thain has survived. What do we do?' There was a note of desperation in his voice.

Wulfrick ignored him and continued his prayer, his eyes closed. Halla took a deep breath and stood to face Falling Cloud.

'We row for the coast as swiftly as our backs will allow,' she said in a commanding voice.

Falling Cloud looked as if he were going to object to Halla's impertinence, but, after a momentary pause, he saluted her by smacking his fist on his chain mail. 'You are a brave woman, one-eye . . . you fought when you should have run.' He nodded his head in approval.

Halla let the name slide and stepped past Falling Cloud to look at the frightened faces crammed into her ship.

'Rexel,' she said over her shoulder, 'check how many axe-masters we have and organize these men properly, strong men to the rear and axe-men to the fore.'

Rexel Falling Cloud stepped next to her and said, 'You've a stomach of iron, Summer Wolf, but your words are wise. It shall be as you say.'

He moved quickly between the lines of benches, barking out orders at the rabble of men trying to row. A few axe-masters from minor towns in the Deep Cross and Hammerfall identified themselves and were quickly sent to Halla for instructions. None of them argued at being ordered around by a woman, as the name of Summer Wolf made her the senior warrior aboard the ship. Even Wulfrick was merely an axe-master with no claim to leadership once out of Fredericksand, whereas Halla was the only child of a deceased thain and her lineage was sufficient to make these men listen to her. It was possible that thains had survived on other ships, or had found a way to escape north, but the survivors of the *Hammer of Fjorlan* numbered no lords among them.

'The *Sea Wolf* is overburdened and cannot move swiftly, therefore we must ready ourselves for further attack,' she said to the assembled axe-masters. No one mentioned the Krakens, but all knew they were what she was referring to.

'What of the betrayer?' asked Rexel angrily.

'Time to hunt down Rulag Ursa is a luxury we do not have, Falling Cloud. His day will come. For now we must focus on keeping ourselves and our men alive.'

Halla was trying not to think too deeply, but to let her instinct come to the fore. She knew what to do, but had always been afraid of doing it for fear of appearing inadequate. However, as she looked into the thick fog around her ship and saw no sign of land or of other ships, she knew that someone had to take charge, and Wulfrick was still silently praying over Algenon's body. Borrin was dead and could no longer lend his voice to her instructions, leaving her alone and in command.

'Those benches are overcrowded. No more than four men to an oar. See to it at once,' she said to a minor axe-master, who instantly moved to carry out her orders.

'You,' she pointed to a man of the Deep Cross, 'set a fast stroke at the fore, enough to get us moving quickly.'

'Rexel, make a check of weapons and armour . . . and move the injured aft.'

'At once, my lady,' Falling Cloud replied formally.

Halla was glad of his assistance as it encouraged the lesser axe-masters to comply with her orders with equal alacrity, and within a few minutes some semblance of order was restored. Halla didn't want to admit that orders and activity were ways to distract the men from thoughts of the horn of the deep and the blind, mindless Krakens of the Fjorlan Sea.

As the *Sea Wolf* began to pick up speed and to move in the direction of Kalall's Deep, Halla turned her attention back to Wulfrick. The axe-master of Fredericksand was sitting next to his lord's body with a look of despair on his face. Halla offered him her hand.

'Would you like assistance in standing up, Master Wulfrick?' she asked.

He slowly cast his eyes upwards to glare at her. 'I can stand,' he said softly, pulling himself up, leaning on his huge axe. 'You seem to have found your balls, young Halla.' There was little humour in his words, however.

'Should I be insulted at your comparing me to a man?' she asked, with a similar absence of humour.

'Don't take it personally. You've done well.' Wulfrick nodded with tacit approval, composing himself. 'How far from land would you say we are?'

'That's not the important question, Wulfrick. The important question is how far from a *landing* are we . . . we saw cliffs on either side as we came into the channel. There was no low ground or beach that I could see.'

Before Wulfrick could say anything more a sound was heard from behind the *Sea Wolf*. It started as a low rumble, accompanied by rushing water, and began to rise in pitch to something akin to a throaty whine, echoing through the fog. The sailors paused in their rowing, and the sound felt louder without the noise of oars breaking the water.

'Who told you to stop fucking rowing?' roared Wulfrick, instantly making every man resume his duty.

The sound of displaced water continued from behind the *Sea Wolf* and Halla peered into the fog looking for signs of pursuit. She gasped as a shape darted across her field of vision, appearing and disappearing within a second, the fog rendering the movement indistinct. Then came another sound, deeper and more resounding – it seemed to be coming from all around the ship and the huddled men of Ranen looked close to panic as Falling Cloud ran among them, slapping backs and urging them to continue rowing. Halla felt her breathing quicken as she stared into the fog behind the vessel. A roar sounded from somewhere, a terrifying sound that no human mouth could make, growing from a grumbling murmur to a primal sound of anger.

Wulfrick had a look of stern defiance on his face as he came to stand next to Halla. 'Rowanoco save us,' he said, as both of them saw a huge shape rear up into the fog behind them.

The shape was taller by half than the mast of the ship and wider than the banks of oars. Halla was thankful for the obscuring fog, but the sound penetrated deeply into the minds of all the Ranen – a sound that none could ignore and none would forget. It was a growl, as if a beast had been awoken from its slumber, and it continued to grow louder and louder until a single greenish tentacle, the size of a broad tree trunk, swung sharply downwards, smashing into the rear of the *Sea Wolf*, feet from where Halla and Wulfrick were standing.

Shouts erupted from the oarsmen. Wulfrick continued to mouth prayers to Rowanoco as he pulled Halla against the railing and away from the splintered deck where the Kraken had struck.

'Row for all you're worth, you troll-fuckers . . . row for Fjorlan . . . for Ranen and for Algenon . . .' Wulfrick was wide-eyed, but he was thinking clearly.

They both leant over the rear of the *Sea Wolf* to look at the immense black shape undulating and writhing within the dense fog.

Then a momentary break in the mist gave them a glimpse of the creature. All at once and whole they saw the Kraken that pursued them. It was larger than any ship and rose, as a column of flesh, up from the ocean to move quickly forwards by an unseen means of locomotion. It appeared, to Halla's eyes, to have only a vague physical form and to comprise a pulpy mass of greenish-black ooze, with gummy, toothless mouths and sickly green tentacles appearing and disappearing within its gelatinous body. The oarsmen, all of whom were looking back, screamed in abject horror as the Kraken roared. Several men lost their senses upon seeing the beast and dived overboard to their deaths in the freezing water. Several more clasped their hands to their heads and screamed as if the beast had entered their minds.

Halla turned away and pulled Wulfrick down after her. They sat, their backs to the railing, looking at two hundred Ranen sailors with madness in their eyes.

'Don't look at it,' shouted Wulfrick, but his words were largely useless as the men were unable to tear their eyes from the horror that pursued them.

Falling Cloud was standing in the middle of the deck, following the erratic movements of the Kraken until the fog once more began to engulf the creature. Whether it was Ithqas or Aqas, Halla didn't know, but whichever of the blind, mindless Krakens chased them, it was far removed from the stories she'd been told as a child. There was nothing exciting or awe-inspiring about the beast, only primal terror.

Then another sound arose from in front of the ship and two huge tentacles, dripping with black slime, slammed on to the deck and sent a dozen or more Ranen into the water. The second Kraken was in front of them and the *Sea Wolf* was swiftly moving towards its destruction between the two mindless beasts. The ship was holed and water began to shoot up in a plume from the middle of the deck.

Halla held tightly on to Wulfrick and they looked deep into each other's eyes as the ship began to list and the sound of splintered wood signalled that the *Sea Wolf* was stricken.

She was glad the fog hid the approach of the Krakens as Wulfrick roughly grabbed her and jumped overboard, holding her in his arms. She felt the icy water fill her mouth and pull the breath from her lungs before she blacked out.

* * *

Halla awoke slowly. Her single eye opened by degrees and she saw a bright, glaring sky. She was numb with cold and could feel nothing below her neck as she blinked quickly and turned her head. She lay on a rocky beach with snow and driftwood all around her, her legs resting within the slowly rolling wash of the sea. It must have been freezing cold but she could barely feel it, and her breathing was shallow and caused a grating sensation in her throat. Halla could hear moaning and the sounds of discomfort coming from nearby. On both sides of her were other survivors of the dragon fleet, washed up on a rugged coast somewhere in the south lands of Ranen.

There was no longer any fog and she could see across the low, featureless expanse of the ocean, where there was no landmark in view. She began to move slowly, first her fingers and then her hands, gradually flexing her arms to relieve the stiffness. She reached to her hip and was gratified to feel that her axe was still at her side. With enormous effort she placed both hands on the rocky ground and pushed herself up into a seated position.

A fresh breeze hit her face and she closed her eye and breathed in deeply before opening it and looking around. The rocky coast stretched as far as she could see in both directions, and along the length of the beach lay smashed wood and broken bodies. Axe-heads, ripped chain mail, planks of wood with splintered edges and, near to where Halla lay, she could see the huge figure of Wulfrick lying spreadeagled across the rocks, still adorned in his smelly troll-hide armour. Just past the motionless axe-master of Fredericksand, Halla could see several battle-brothers of Tiergarten, her men from the destroyed *Sea Wolf*. Some were moving, but most were mangled into grotesque shapes and clearly dead. More worrying were those who were alive but who sat staring blankly out to sea with deranged and bloodshot eyes. The sight of the blind, mindless Krakens had robbed many of her men of their sanity, and Halla was thankful that she at least felt clear-headed.

Falling Cloud was sitting upright several feet away, with his head in his hands. He was shivering violently and looked to have a large wooden splinter stuck through his shin. The man was unaware of the wound and Halla hoped his mind had been strong enough to weather the sight of the Krakens.

'Rexel Falling Cloud, axe-master of Hammerfall,' she called out, spitting out salt water as she did so.

He looked up hesitantly, and Halla saw tears frozen on his cheeks and his eyes reddened and half closed. He rubbed his face and turned to the axe-maiden.

'My . . . lady,' he responded with weariness. 'I am alive. I am alive.'

'Yes, you are alive, and I need your help,' she said loudly, before pointing weakly to his wound. 'That needs seeing to.'

Falling Cloud looked down and registered the wound for the first time. 'Yes, though it doesn't hurt,' he said. 'The water is cold, but it has stopped the bleeding.' His eyes had a faraway look, but Halla was glad to see he could still think clearly.

'We need to see who is alive and who is dead, and where in the name of Rowanoco we've ended up.' She craned her neck round to look inland.

The coastline was rocky for a way up the beach and ended in a series of low cliffs, topped with snow-covered trees.

'Is this Hammerfall?' she asked the axe-master.

'No, my lady, there'd be more snow. We're further south,' he replied, shaking his head and trying to get his bearings. 'And there are no cliffs like that on Samnia, so we're on the mainland somewhere.'

Men lying on the rocks around them now registered the conversation and a few of them sat up, wincing in pain as they became aware of their wounds through the cold.

'I'm freezing my fucking balls off . . . and where's my fucking axe?' shouted Wulfrick, without moving.

'Master Wulfrick. Still alive, I see,' responded Halla with a gratified smile.

The huge axe-master of Fredericksand turned his head and said clearly, 'Someone tell me where I am and where is the person I should be killing.'

Falling Cloud let a slight laugh escape his lips and for a moment his head felt clearer. 'I think we're south of Hammerfall, maybe on the coast of Wraith land.'

'And my axe?' Wulfrick asked, still not moving his enormous body from the rocks.

'Master Wulfrick, your axe is not currently of primary importance. Please pull yourself together,' Halla responded, making no particular effort to be gentle.

He looked hurt for a moment and swung round to sit up, facing Falling Cloud and the axe-maiden. 'I'm together. It takes more than a few tentacles to get the better of me.'

* * *

Barely two hundred of the Ranen had survived the initial attack, the Krakens and the subsequent shipwreck. More had perhaps washed up on other coasts, or had managed to flee before the horn was blown, but Halla tried not to think about them. The situation could not be changed by hoping for a thain or two to appear over the hills, and she knew that if none did, she was in charge. Most of those who had gathered on the beach had been washed ashore from other ships and had not had to witness the Krakens – though the main topic of conversation while the men of Fjorlan were carrying out the orders Halla gave them was of tentacles and terror. Of her own men fewer than twenty were still alive, and she found herself giving orders to men from Fredericksand, Hammerfall and the Deep Cross.

Falling Cloud's injury was not bad and he fashioned a rudimentary splint that enabled him to walk across the rocks with relative ease. Halla thought him quieter and more solemn than he had been, but at least he was being helpful as he moved among the bodies looking for survivors. Wulfrick didn't move more than a few feet from where he'd washed up and remained deep in thought for some time before he joined the rest.

Halla issued many orders to the battle-brothers around her and didn't give more than a cursory acknowledgement when they were carried out. Then she just found other things for the men to do, and they seemed happy enough to be moving with purpose. A rough shelter was fashioned to protect against the cold wind, the bodies were assembled in several pyres, and she sent men to scout further inland. The various injuries were being tended to, but every few minutes Halla heard another dying Ranen offer a final prayer to Rowanoco.

A dozen or more Ranen had lost their minds at the sight of the Krakens and they sat in a rough circle, just inside the wash. None of them had spoken and they had ignored numerous shouts from the others. Halla had decided to leave them be for now; if they couldn't be roused when the time came to move, she'd count them among the lost.

The hours passed quickly and now the sun was beginning to fall in the sky, causing the temperature to drop sharply. Close to a hundred shivering Ranen huddled in the shell of a hull, dragged further inland and propped up to form a rudimentary windbreak. Other small groups of survivors were similarly sheltered along the beach. The body of Algenon Teardrop had not been found and Wulfrick was wandering the surf looking for his lord, refusing calls to come out of the weather and warm himself by the large fire they had now managed to light within the shelter.

One of the few men of Fredericksand to have survived was Oleff Hard Head, an old chain-master from Algenon's dungeon, and he'd been given the task of scouting further inland. The old axe-man was gruff and surly when he returned to the shelter after several hours of exploring.

'Tell us some good news, Oleff,' said Falling Cloud while he adjusted his leg brace.

Hard Head nestled as close to the fire as he could and rubbed his red hands together vigorously. Then he looked up at Halla and smiled thinly.

'My Lady Summer Wolf, it seems we are south of the Deep Cross. I can just about see the mountains to the north and, if my geography is right, we're in the realm of Wraith.'

A few of the men smiled, a few more laughed with relief, and Halla nodded at Oleff.

'Good, we'll move inland tomorrow and set up camp over the cliffs. The wounded need time to recover or die, and,' she gestured across to the men who had lost their minds, 'they need time to . . . I don't know, but I'm not prepared to give up on them just yet.'

Halla didn't know if it was the predicament they found themselves in, but the men of Fjorlan had not once questioned her orders or shown any sign of doubt that she was in charge. Even Wulfrick had not made any move towards taking over, and so Halla Summer Wolf steeled herself for more days of keeping these men together and alive. She had no real plan beyond that but entertained a vague notion of reaching the ruins of Ro Hail, making contact with Wraith Company, and finding a way north to see what Rulag Ursa had done in Algenon's absence.

Maybe four days, or a week at the most, would be needed to heal their injuries and prepare the men to move as a unit. Halla looked silently over the faces of her new subordinates and began assessing who would make appropriate lieutenants in the weeks to come, as they made their way north.

Rexel Falling Cloud was a good man and already an axe-master, so he'd be an invaluable adviser. Wulfrick would take whatever position he deemed necessary and Halla was aware of the need to be careful when ordering him around. He had, after all, been the high thain's closest ally and was the mightiest warrior of them all. Oleff Hard Head was a senior man of Fredericksand and would be a good and knowledgeable presence at her side. The others would have to wait for the results of her silent assessment.

'Get some sleep, gentlemen,' she said through a yawn. 'Tomorrow we move inland.'

CHAPTER FIVE

SAARA THE MISTRESS OF PAIN
IN THE CITY OF RO WEIR

S AARA CRADLED THE Ranen cloud stone gently in her hands
and peered through it into the eyes of Rulag Ursa, battle lord
of Jarvik, the traitorous warrior communicating with her
from half a world away.

'I need your assurance that Algenon Teardrop is dead,' she
asked the indistinct image that appeared in the stone.

'We have woken the Krakens, witch,' he said angrily, 'and don't
make the mistake of talking to me like your servant.'

'I meant no offence. I just need to know that the service we
have paid for has been carried out,' replied Saara, filing away the
insult for future repayment.

'You've paid for? I am to be high thain of Fjorlan. This is not
some fucking business deal. Rowanoco only values strength, and
I am the strongest.'

The Ranen was a worm of a man, but he was a necessary tool
in dealing with the exemplar of Rowanoco and Saara knew that
he could be easily manipulated with promises of power.

'Please answer the question, my Lord Ursa. It's as much in
your interest as mine to see Teardrop dead.' Saara tried to sound
patient and relaxed, though in truth she felt nothing but disgust
for the Fjorlander.

'He's done for. Most of his men are in pieces and the last
anyone saw he took an axe to his back and was bleeding out
over the deck. Ithqas and Aqas did the rest . . . if a hundred men

made it to shore, I'd be fucking surprised.' Rulag was decidedly pleased that he had massacred hundreds of his own people, and Saara felt a moment of pity for those who would have to live under his tyrannical rule.

'Very well,' she replied meekly, 'you may proceed with your plan. Communicate with me again when Fredericksand is in your charge.' Saara waited for an insult, but none came and she guessed Rulag was busy thinking about his impending elevation to the position of high thain.

The cloud stone faded into misty black and Rulag was gone. Saara smiled to herself and took a moment to appreciate the flowering of her plan. Algenon was no longer a threat and the dragon fleet had been neutralized. The invasion of the Freelands could now take place with minimal resistance, and the Seven Sisters would soon be able to kill the few remaining old-bloods and bring the worship of the Dead God to all the lands of men.

She replaced the cloud stone within her robes and left the building where she had paid for a room – an unremarkable tavern, chosen simply so she could be alone while she spoke with Rulag. She'd slipped away from the ten thousand Hounds that had travelled with her and she had a number of things that required her attention. Most importantly, the deal struck between the Seven Sisters, Sir Hallam Pevain and Rulag Ursa had been successful. Now she had further business in the old town of Weir. From within her cloak Saara retrieved a small piece of paper with hastily drawn directions scrawled on it.

Outside, the streets of Ro Weir were quiet and dark. Buildings loomed inwards over the cobbles. Saara was used to the wide boulevards and airy courtyards of Kessia and found the claustrophobic back streets of Weir an unwelcome contrast. She had been here for several days now, implementing the city's occupation by her pack of Hounds. Duke Lyam, the old noble nominally in charge, had a weaker mind than she was used to and Saara found she had to be gentle with him so as not to turn him into a gibbering mess, incapable of signing the decrees she required.

Master Turve, the whip-master of the Hounds, had taken command of the city's muster field and was making use of the barracks previously occupied by the knights of the Red, who were now accompanying the king into the Freelands of Ranen. Turve was using the city watchman to implement a low-key martial law, designed to keep the citizens calm and under control while Saara made sure the transition went smoothly and with little disruption. Duke Lyam had pledged his and the king's support for the enchantress's designs and, with a few key people in a few key places, Saara was happy with the way Ro Weir was coming under her charge. The huge population of Kirin criminals and Karesian merchants in Weir had made Saara smile, for she realized that her task was half completed before she even arrived. This was not Ro Tiris, and these citizens of Tor Funweir were accustomed to sharing their streets with non-Ro.

Officially, King Sebastian Tiris had agreed a treaty of mutual cooperation with the Seven Sisters. In reality, he had come under the thrall of first Katja and now Ameira, and the few dissenting voices had fallen silent for fear of being accused of treason to the crown.

All things considered, the plan was proceeding at a pace. Saara doubted that anyone could now stop the Seven Sisters from succeeding. By the time the Freelands were subdued, the Dead God would virtually have won the Long War, supplanting the murderous Giants who had stolen his power so long ago. Saara had even begun to hope that fresh worship from the lands of men would return their benefactor to his rightful place as the only permissible god – would breathe fresh life into the lost god of pleasure and blood with a thousand young.

Saara was smiling contentedly to herself as she proceeded down another dark street and entered the slum area called the Kirin Tor, a place built specifically to house the numerous itinerant Kirin who made their home in Ro Weir. She was walking alone through the midnight alleyways with her black cloak pulled tightly around her shoulders to guard against anyone who might recognize her, and she silently lamented the loss of her body slave. Zeldantor had been pleasant company in the years they'd been together and, although his sacrifice had been necessary both to appease the Dark Young and to protect the Seven Sisters from the wrath of Zeldantor's father, she missed his constant presence at her side. Even now, as she passed the gloomy side streets and dirty alleyways, she longed for his upbeat commentary on events and his unwavering loyalty. His father had been responsible for his death, and Saara consoled herself with the knowledge that Rham Jas Rami would now be powerless to strike at the Seven Sisters.

She stopped at a crossroads and checked the directions she'd been given. To her left, several rainbow junkies looked at her through red eyes – Kirin men with dirty faces and few possessions standing around a poorly constructed hut. Further ahead were a number of stone buildings nestled among rudimentary homes made of wood and scavenged metal. Her directions had been given her by a Ro thief who'd been spying on an old bookseller for her, and she guessed he'd not been paying much attention when he wrote them down, since they did not appear to correspond with the actual streets – although the possibility also existed that these makeshift buildings would move around from time to time.

Saara pulled her hood up the better to obscure her face as she approached the Kirin junkies. 'I seek a bookseller,' she asked in heavily accented Ro.

One of the Kirin, fatter and more diseased than the others, grinned and showed several missing teeth and stained gums.

'You're in the wrong part of town for learning, sweetheart ... why don't you come and join us,' he responded, with a deeply unpleasant leer.

'Yeah, we don't get fine-looking bitches like you too often,' said a second Kirin, licking his lips. 'Don't worry, we'll be nice to you.'

There were four of them, men evidently of vile intent and little in the way of brainpower, but Saara was in a hurry and not in the mood to play games.

'I said *I seek a bookseller,* if you can assist me . . .' she held her hands wide, awaiting a response.

'Oh, we can assist you, you fine-looking cunt,' the fat Kirin said and stepped forward, reaching for the enchantress with his grubby hands.

Saara stepped back and slapped him hard across the face. 'I will say it once more and if I get a response that is not helpful, I will cause each of you pain,' she stated calmly. 'Now, can you assist me?'

The fat Kirin shot her a look of deep indignation from his bloodshot eyes. 'I'll cut your face up for that, you Karesian whore,' he said, removing a rusty knife from inside his coat.

The other three grunted agreement and one jumped up and down excitedly. 'Let's fuck the bitch . . . let's fuck her now,' he cried gleefully, spitting over himself at the prospect of violating the enchantress.

The Kirin she'd slapped stepped forward and moved to place the knife at Saara's neck. She didn't move, but smiled with a predatory curl to her lips as the fat man paused, stopped by some invisible force. He began to wince in pain as he tried to raise the knife to stab her.

'Grab her . . . what you waiting for?' asked another, as the first Kirin was overcome with fear at his inability to strike the woman.

Slowly and gently, Saara took the man's hand and placed the knife next to her breast. 'Kill me . . . if you can,' she challenged.

'I . . . can't . . . move,' he almost shouted with rising panic.

His fellows moved to flank the enchantress and one of them aimed some punches at her, but none of the blows landed, and the confidence drained from their eyes as they found themselves rooted to the spot and unable to strike.

Saara gestured slightly with her hand and said, 'You are venomous little men, you will die in an appropriate fashion.'

The first Kirin started to retch as Saara caused poisonous Gorlan spiders to appear in his throat. His eyes widened and he coughed out several spiders the size of a fist, looking down in horror as they crawled over his body. He tried to scream, but the sound was lost under the pressure of spiders erupting from his throat and rapidly covering the upper part of his body, biting and crawling over each other to get inside his clothing. His arms shot out and shook violently as the venom flowed through his body, and he fell to the ground in convulsions.

Saara let two of the others run away with looks of abject terror on their faces. Another had his eyes fixed on his friend's body, which was disappearing under the crawling mound of spiders.

'Look at me.' She spoke with menace.

This last Kirin was the youngest and his eyes were as wide as could be, watching his friend being consumed before his eyes. Hesitantly, he looked up at the enchantress.

'I seek a bookseller. Do you know where I would find such a man in these streets?' she asked with a vicious smile. 'His name is Kabrizzi.'

The young Kirin forced his left arm to rise and point towards one of the stone buildings.

Saara turned to look in that direction and smiled, more genuinely this time, as she said, 'Thank you, you have been most helpful.'

Another wave of her hand caused the mass of Gorlan spiders to leave the dead man and scurry towards the young Kirin.

'But . . . I helped you,' he protested, as spiders swarmed up his legs.

'I . . . don't . . . care,' Saara replied, without turning back, as the Kirin began to scream in pain.

His cries ended in a grotesque gurgle and Saara walked down the adjacent street towards which the man had pointed. She thought allowing two of them to leave had been a wise move, because they would tell others what they had seen. She enjoyed the mysterious, half-whispered rumours that followed her around Karesia and, if she were to command Tor Funweir in the same way, the peasantry would need to fear her just as her own people did.

Kabrizzi's shop was an unadorned stone building with few signs that it was anything more than a squat for junkies and whores. There were no lights in the street and the darkness filled every corner and crevice. A small, rotten plaque next to the door, when Saara had rubbed it clean, read: *Emaniz Kabrizzi, purveyor of rare books and occult items.* He was not a famous man, nor a remarkable one, but he had one valuable asset that meant Saara needed his assistance. Her thief contact had confirmed that Kabrizzi had come across an old book, hidden in the bowels of a Blue church in Ro Haran. The book, seemingly of little interest to Ro scholars, was called *Ar Kral Desh Jek* in the ancient Jekkan language, which translated roughly as *The Book of the Lost.* Saara had not informed her sisters about the book, and she was eager to posses it for the knowledge it contained.

A single knock on the door was enough for her to hear movement from within and a crotchety voice, with a slight Karesian accent, barked, 'Fuck off, we're closed . . . we're always closed . . . so fuck off.'

'Please open the door. I am not a thief and you will like what I have to say.' Saara spoke calmly.

The voice didn't respond for a moment and she heard heavy, throaty breathing from behind the wood. A bolt was moved and a key was turned and the door inched open, displaying several heavy chains designed to keep it from being flung open by an intruder. Through the narrow gap, an old Karesian face squinted at the enchantress.

'Fuck me, it's one of the Seven Sisters. Which one are you, Jezebel the Bitch or Harlot the Not Particularly Pleasant?' Kabrizzi displayed the carelessness about insults that only the very old possessed. He chuckled to himself.

'My name is Saara the Mistress of Pain, and if you insult my order again, old man, I'll make you eat your own cock before I eat your heart,' she answered, narrowing her eyes into a girlish smile.

'All right, don't take it personally, witch. What do you want?' he asked, not visibly concerned about her threat.

'I am told that you recently came into possession of a very rare book. I wish to buy it from you.' Saara stepped forward so the old man could see her better in the dark street.

'Show me your coin,' he said suspiciously.

Saara produced a heavy purse and weighed it suggestively in her slender hand. Its size made Kabrizzi's eyes light up and a grotesque smile appeared through the gap in the doorway. Saara was gratified that, despite living in Tor Funweir, the old Karesian had not lost his people's avaricious streak.

'Open the door,' Saara said plainly, not wanting to converse across the chains any longer.

Kabrizzi pursed his lips and sized up the enchantress, looking her over from head to toe, assessing the dangers of allowing one of the Seven Sisters into his shop.

'You have nothing to fear from me, old man, I merely wish to see the book. You are, in a sense, merely a glorified doorman in this encounter.'

Her confident manner did nothing to speed up Kabrizzi's musings. 'If I let you in, you could bewitch me, or whatever it is you do.'

Saara nodded. 'Indeed, I could,' she replied, 'but what's to stop me merely making you open the door? You'll notice that you still have free will and I am being polite.'

That placated the old man a little and he nodded and disappeared inside for a moment. Saara heard the heavy chains being unlocked and a moment later the door was opened fully. He beckoned her in with a frail old hand and she left the dark street to enter an equally dark shop.

'Do you not have any lanterns?' she asked.

'No, lanterns are expensive. I have candles and books. If you want candles or books, I'm your man. If you want anything else, you can fuck off,' he said, shuffling inside.

'Yes, I believe we've covered that, thank you.' Saara could tolerate the old man's abrasive manner so long as she got what she wanted.

The shop was a low-ceilinged room with several equally cramped rooms spread out around it. She could see a filthy-looking bed in the furthermost room, meagre wash facilities in another, but every other conceivable space was taken up with books, some on bookshelves or in chests, but most simply piled from floor to ceiling. Kabrizzi had three or four candles lit at various points around the central room, but the illumination they provided was scant.

'Close the door, witch,' Kabrizzi said as he moved slowly to a gnarled old wooden desk that may, at one time, have been a shop counter.

Saara stole a look out into the dark street to make sure she had not been followed and then closed the door and replaced the rusty bolts.

'Now, what was the book's name?' the old man asked, opening a large leather-bound tome on the desk.

'*Ar Kral Desh Jek*,' Saara answered, making sure to pronounce each word slowly and deliberately.

Kabrizzi looked up and narrowed his eyes. Saara thought she detected a hint of fear as the old man looked at her.

'Some books are dangerous, witch . . . some books shouldn't be read.' He closed the tome and sat back in a rickety chair behind the desk, reaching for a clay pipe to his left.

'I am aware of that, but my request stands.' Saara was eager to read the text and tried not to let her excitement show. 'You've read it?' she asked.

Kabrizzi filled his pipe with sweet-smelling rainbow smoke and touched a taper to the bowl while inhaling deeply. He leant back and peered at Saara through the cloud of smoke.

'Ancient Jekkan is difficult to translate, my dear. It requires a detailed code to make sense of the characters. Luckily, I have such a code,' he said.

He took several more deep puffs on his pipe and his pupils dilated as the rainbow smoke flowed through his body and caused him to relax a little.

'I decoded enough not to want to decode the rest,' he added, with a catch to his voice.

'Show me the book,' Saara demanded with a note of authority.

Now that Kabrizzi was easier to see, his face illuminated by a flickering candle, Saara guessed his rainbow smoke habit was more than just recreational. He had deeply bloodshot eyes and the smoke was of a very high grade, the kind of drug that only a lifelong user would need.

'Money first,' he said, his hands visibly shaking.

Saara smiled and dropped her bag of coin on the rickety desk. It made a satisfying thump on the wood and Kabrizzi quickly pulled it into his lap and undid the tie to look inside.

'A small price to pay for your sanity,' he said with a vicious grin.

'I wouldn't concern yourself with my sanity, old man. Now, the book, if you please . . .' She held out her hand.

Kabrizzi stood up slowly and Saara inferred that he was giving her ample opportunity to change her mind. When it became clear that she wasn't going to, he shook his head and moved to a closed oak chest next to a rotting wooden bookcase.

'I locked it in here when I started having strange dreams. It doesn't stop me having them, but it makes me feel better to know it's locked away.'

Kabrizzi's hand shook as he removed a large key from a bookshelf and slowly turned it in the lock. Within, Saara could see two books, one was well wrapped in white cloth and the other was tightly locked with an iron clasp. Kabrizzi gingerly picked up the cloth-wrapped book and held it at arm's length. Saara didn't trouble herself with the other book. She felt her excitement rising as Kabrizzi crossed back to his desk.

'It took me a long time to find this and, most days, I wish I'd never heard of it,' he said, with fear in his eyes. 'The Blue cleric I got it from was half mad, living in a basement under the library of Ro Haran. He claimed it was the only remaining copy.'

Saara didn't reply at first but merely gazed at the tome, sensing a strange aura in the room. She looked up at the old Karesian bookseller.

'Step aside, Kabrizzi.'

He didn't argue, but held his hands away from the book and took two wide steps to the side.

Saara moved round the desk and brushed dust from the chair before sitting down, elegantly, with her fingers on the white cloth.

She began to unwrap it, winding the fabric around her hands to reveal the front cover of the book. It was leather-bound, with dark embossed writing. Rusted from years of neglect, the metal print was grainy and indistinct, but it nonetheless read *Ar Kral Desh Jek*, words of the ancient Jekkan language, long unspoken in the lands of men. The book was said to contain the chronicles of the Lost, those Giants who never became gods or else were cast down or killed by Rowanoco, Jaa and the One. The book was dangerous because the Lost were strange, alien entities whose existence was unknown to all but the most learned scholars, and the few who studied such beings ran the risk of exposure to things that men were not meant to know.

Saara was not afraid, as the Dead God's name was contained within, and she was guided by his hand across countless layers of the world and countless more beyond death. He had led her far, directed the Seven Sisters to kill old-bloods, to cage exemplars, to hunt the Dokkalfar and to invade the Freelands of Ranen. Now he had directed her to an old bookseller in the Kirin Tor of Ro Weir and to the book that was in her hands.

Kabrizzi had backed off a few steps and was too far away to read over Saara's shoulder.

'I'll just be back here . . . close the door when you leave,' he said as he moved quickly out of the central room and disappeared into the bedroom.

Saara composed herself and opened the book. Within, she saw strange Jekkan symbols and magical glyphs designed to compel the reader and to damage fragile minds. Saara had learned to read the language over the past few years and she knew that her mind was strong enough to resist the book's magical protection.

The pages were of thick, pale white paper with rough-cut edges and numerous dark stains and finger marks. The first few pages contained a warning that men were not meant to read this book – that their minds were not sufficiently advanced to comprehend its meaning. The book was meant for other beings – for Dokkalfar, Jekkan, maybe even for Giants – but it had outlived its previous readers and was now in the hands of a woman.

She bent forward over the desk and moved a candle the better to see the strange writing. It spoke of the Water Giants, Ithqas and Aqas, the creatures now called the Krakens, who had ascended to godhood but had been struck down by Rowanoco in an honour-fuelled rage.

She turned through pages of grotesque monsters from the far reaches of the world, creatures that had once been gods in the ages of Deep Time but were now merely numbered among the Lost, the losers in the Long War. Storm Giants who flew in packs over the highest peaks, Scaled Giants who forged an empire in the forgotten east, and strange, nameless beings that had once walked, crawled, flown or swum.

She leafed through the pages, keeping her mind clear and her will strong, as she searched for the Forest Giants, the Giants of pleasure and blood who birthed the Dark Young and were, long ago, worshipped out of fear by the Dokkalfar.

The lore contained within the book did not provide a time frame or a scale of things that any human could comprehend. It spoke in terms of the ages of the world and of the Deep Time between them, when mountains rose and fell and the continents formed. If the lands of men had existed for only a blink of an eye, the book in Saara's hands detailed beings that had lived millions of blinks ago. To men, the Giants were simply an ancient race of beings. The book, *Ar Kral Desh Jek*, however, spoke of them as a collection of races, and the word "Giants" was no more than a collective term for the variety of monstrous species that had lived during Deep Time.

Saara turned away and took a moment to calm her mind, realizing that even she, the greatest of the Seven Sisters, was not altogether immune to the book. It tried to scratch away at her mind in a way she had not previously experienced. There was no deliberate intent or enchantment at work, but a constant background grasping that she had to concentrate to avoid. The magic in the book was old and was not designed for men. It was like a weight pressing down on her head, oppressing her rational mind and making her light-headed and chaotic.

Saara clung to the power of the Dead God that dwelt deep within her and clenched her fists, breathing slowly and keeping her will strong. She needed to find the name, the lost name of her god, the name that no mortal being had spoken in many millions of years. It was within the pages at her fingertips and she knew that the high priestess of a god could never be complete without the name of her master.

Leaning in again and with a steely strength, Saara the Mistress of Pain continued to read. She reached pages that spoke of the Dokkalfar, the ancient and immortal forest-dwellers, remnants of the Giant age still present in the world. To her surprise, they were linked to Jaa and to the death of the Dead God. The book chronicled an uprising when the Dokkalfar had realized they were needed to birth the Dark Young and that without them the Dead God could not spawn new Young. She leant in even further and read that the forest-dwellers had been created only to be slain, their death releasing the spores that would ultimately give rise to new Dark Young; and that when the Fire Giant had slain their god, Jaa had gifted them with immolation at their death, a gift that stopped the spores from being produced. This simple act had prevented new Young from being born and had enabled the Dokkalfar to sever contact with their former master.

Saara read all this and sat back in her chair. All at once, she knew why the Dead God had led her to the book and why she had been drawn into hunting the Dokkalfar. With the Seven Sisters' designs nearing completion, Jaa had been separated from the world of men, his old-bloods dead and his exemplar inert. Saara knew this also meant that the power he had gifted the forest-dwellers must also have been severed. Kill a Dokkalfar now, she thought, and unless he is burnt after his death he will produce the spores that will enable new Dark Young to flourish and grow.

She smiled to herself, almost forgetting about the dangers of the book in her hand. A scratching sensation in her mind, however, made her quickly strengthen her resolve once more, close her eyes and breathe deeply.

The knowledge contained within *Ar Kral Desh Jek* was an ancient artefact of great power, which had changed hands throughout the world for centuries, moving from one scholar to another until someone capable of understanding it should appear. Saara knew it was not meant for her, but she also knew that the lore it contained was necessary for the Dead God's work.

She forced herself to continue reading and turned the pages quickly, looking for the entry concerning the Forest Giants. Each page contained depictions, in vivid colour, of nameless monstrosities and strange shapes which the book called living beings.

Then she paused. At the bottom of a page was a reference to the Dark Young's father, a fleeting mention that conveyed little save a name. She read it slowly, repeating the syllables and letting her mouth become used to the strange words. The book spoke of a Forest Giant that ascended to godhood and was slain by Jaa, the Fire Giant, as a single move in the Long War. The Giant's name was Shub-Nillurath. Saara felt a euphoria as she repeatedly spoke the name.

'Your name . . . I know your name,' she shouted upwards, her vision clouding over as pleasure and pain in equal measure flowed over the enchantress. 'Shub-Nillurath, the Black God of the Forest with a Thousand Young,' she proclaimed to the sky.

* * *

Dalian Thief Taker disliked the smell in Ro Weir. He had stowed away aboard a Hound troop carrier, disguised as a whip-master, and was now searching for a way to slip out of the newly erected barracks on the muster field of Weir. He had narrowly evaded capture in Kessia when the Seven Sisters had seen fit to frame him for the murder of Larix the Traveller, and if it hadn't been for his willingness to kill many of his pursuers, Dalian had no doubt he'd have been burned to death by now. He'd found masquerading as a Hound very easy – all he needed to do was scowl a lot and appear slightly psychotic. Both things were part of his general make-up anyway, so his presence was not questioned.

Izra Sabal, the sadistic whip-mistress, acting as Master Turve's adjutant, was Dalian's biggest problem. She was a brutal killer whose eyes never remained still and she had taken an interest in the new whip-master with the scarred face whom she didn't recognize. If Dalian could find an opportunity, he'd kill the bitch in a heartbeat, but the whip-mistress was constantly surrounded by her Hounds and he thought it the wiser course to slip away.

Jaa was Dalian Thief Taker's master and had always been so. He had no doubt that the Seven Sisters had betrayed the Fire Giant, but he was unable to persuade the other wind claws of this. His order was now deeply drawn within the designs of the enchantresses, and it was he who was the traitor, to be found, tortured and killed. He did not doubt his duty. If, as he suspected, he was Jaa's only servant not to be so enthralled, it was up to him to preserve the divine fear of the Fire Giant and to eliminate these pretenders. Dalian Thief Taker, greatest of the wind claws, felt revitalized and strong of purpose, forcing his body and mind to behave as if he were younger than his fifty years as he prayed for a swift end for Jaa's enemies.

'I am yours to command,' Dalian said quietly by way of a prayer, 'but I would have answered this calling more . . . lustily, were I twenty years younger.'

As the Thief Taker looked out from the canvas tent where he was lying low, he remembered a conversation he'd had with his son, many years ago. Dalian had been given the task of executing his boy for treason against the Seven Sisters and it was the only time in the wind claw's life when he had disobeyed an order. He had never been a loving father, largely leaving his son to do whatever he pleased, as was often the way in Karesia. However, he had found himself unable to deliver the killing blow and had instead allowed his child to escape to Tor Funweir. Dalian had never been called to account for his disloyalty; his superiors had believed him without question when he had lied about killing

Hasim. His son's Kirin companion had killed an enchantress – so far as Dalian knew, the only man ever to have done so – and equal blame had fallen on Al-Hasim of Kessia.

Dalian had not spoken to his son in nearly ten years and had no idea now how to go about finding him, but he was convinced that finding the nameless Kirin who'd managed to kill one of the Seven Sisters should be his primary goal.

The Seven Sisters had been dispersed throughout Tor Funweir by Saara the Mistress of Pain and they were now speeding to the cities of the Ro. They would be able to sway dukes and clerics to their will with minimal effort now that the king of Ro had been enchanted. Lillian the Lady of Death had been sent to Ro Arnon, Shilpa the Shadow of Lies was on her way to Ro Haran, and Isabel the Seductress was travelling east to Ro Leith. Katja the Hand of Despair was already in Ro Tiris, and Ameira the Lady of Spiders resided over the sea in Ro Canarn. He knew it was only a matter of time before all the civilized lands of men would be under their sway, with only the barbarian north free from their influence.

Dalian steeled himself for a brash escape and marched out of the tent. The muster field of Ro Weir was a sea of tents accommodating ten thousand Hounds of Karesia, fully armoured and ready for action. This was not an invasion and the Hounds were unsure how to act as an occupying force. They were all convicted criminals or low-born peasants, kept in line by enchantments, drugs and the savage whip-masters. Most were brutal and semi-suicidal, glad to give their lives for Karesia the moment they were required. Each wore black armour and a full-face helmet, and carried a heavy bladed scimitar, so that they appeared almost identical.

Dalian walked confidently through the camp, keeping half an eye on Izra and Turve's command tent at the end of the row. He could see a great deal of activity in front of the large tent and it looked as if the whip-masters were sending squads of Hounds into the city to suppress the small outbreaks of disobedience that had arisen since the Karesians had arrived in Ro Weir.

He moved between tents, stacked scimitars and small cooking

fires, trying to identify the best way to leave the muster field. He knew that the horses were corralled to the north and near to the King's Highway, but they were guarded and the Hounds on duty were unlikely to let him take one. The Karesian Hounds rarely used horses, but Saara had insisted they were necessary. She had also sent messages, via fast riders, to Katja and Ameira. The Mistress of Pain was very concerned to locate a man they called the Ghost. Apparently, he was a Cleric of the One and Saara had instructed her sisters, already installed in Tor Funweir, to apprehend him at all costs. *Travelling towards Ro Tiris* was all Dalian had managed to learn concerning the Ghost from a returning messenger whom he'd tortured for information.

He smiled as he approached the horses, thinking the underworld of Tiris would be the perfect place to start looking for his son. Dalian even began to think what he'd say when he came face to face with Al-Hasim.

'I am your servant as always, my lord.' Dalian once again spoke skywards, addressing the Fire Giant. 'But a glass of wine and someone to massage my feet would be welcome before I set off.'

PART TWO

CHAPTER SIX

RANDALL OF DARKWALD
IN THE CITY OF RO TIRIS

RETURNING TO RO Tiris was not a happy homecoming for Randall. A hardness had come over him since leaving Cozz, but he didn't like his new view of the world. Each time he'd raised a mirror to his face during the journey, he'd seen a man he didn't recognize looking back at him – bearded and solemn, with a sadness previously unknown to him.

Brother Torian's body was wrapped in a white shroud and laid across a wooden cart which Randall was driving. The Purple cleric had been treated with various preserving ointments and an image of his serene face could be made out through the weave of the shroud.

Utha had refused to talk about his friend's death since leaving Cozz. The Black cleric had changed in manner and appearance over the last few weeks. With no replacement armour, he wore a simple grey robe and now looked less like a warrior and more like a monk or Brown cleric. He'd begun to teach Randall how to hold a sword, concerned at the way he'd thrown himself into the fray against Rham Jas, and the young squire finally felt comfortable holding the sword of Great Claw.

Utha had become less caustic and showed more respect towards Randall, as a result of the way the squire had handled himself during the fight in Cozz. He even grudgingly accepted that the squire had probably saved his life.

'Now, attack high,' Utha said, as they engaged in their daily practice.

Randall swung at Utha's shoulder, meeting his axe in mid-swing and holding the position.

'Good, now answer my riposte.' The cleric swung low towards Randall's body and their weapons clashed again. 'Move your feet more, don't stay too still.'

They were a little way off the King's Highway, a few hours from the southern gate of the capital, and had spent the night under canvas rather than enter the city after dark. It was a bright and clear morning and Randall could see plumes of smoke rising from Tiris.

Randall stepped to the side and delivered a thrust towards Utha's side, his axe swinging down to answer the attack.

'Excellent, we'll make a swordsman out of you yet,' Utha said with a smile. 'Just don't attack any Kirin assassins and you should be fine.'

'The sword is still heavy in one hand,' Randall said.

He had tried using the blade with both one and two hands and found the single-handed technique made his shoulder ache.

'Of course it is, it's a big chunk of metal. If it was too light, it'd break.'

Utha hadn't entirely got over his dismissive attitude towards the young squire, but Randall thought that now there was a note of good humour to his jibes.

Elyot and Robin had remained in Cozz to recover from their wounds, so Randall had had only the Black cleric for company during the two weeks it had taken them to return to Ro Tiris. It had been a difficult journey for the first few days, with Utha saying little and Randall deep in thought. After they passed the town of Voy, the Black cleric had loosened up a little and begun to chat with Randall. The change had taken some getting used to, but the squire had found Utha pleasant enough company when he wasn't delivering barbed insults.

He had talked briefly about what would happen when they reached the capital, and Randall thought Utha's insistence on staying outside the city for one more night was largely to do with him not wanting to hasten his own punishment. The death of a Purple cleric, added to the trouble he was already in for disobeying orders, did not bode well for the Black churchman. Utha feared he'd be blamed for Torian's death and, despite Randall's insistence that it hadn't been his fault, his mood remained grim when he spoke of it. Secretly, Randall was terrified at the thought of accompanying Utha to the Black cathedral in Tiris, but, as the only witness able to speak about what had happened, he knew he had no choice. If his testimony could save Utha's honour, then it would be worth a few hours of discomfort.

They continued their morning practice for another hour, until the sun was just visible through the thin cloud. Utha's tutelage was good and Randall felt comfortable with his sword in hand. His strength had grown over the last month, and Utha's patient style of fencing had suited Randall's initial hesitancy. The cleric's axe was called Death's Embrace, and Randall had come to realize that if Utha were further disgraced as a result of his actions in pursuit of Brom, his weapon would be taken from him. This evidently worried the cleric and Randall often caught him gazing lovingly at the axe, in a manner similar to the way Sir Leon had stared at his longsword before Randall inherited it.

'You're still over-extending your arm,' Utha said, after Randall had lost his footing attempting a high strike. 'Don't let the blade get too far away from your body. It's a *long* sword, remember; it has enough reach without you sticking your arm out.'

'That's what happened to Elyot, isn't it?' Randall remembered the way the young watchman had been opened up by Brom and had lost his arm.

Utha nodded. 'Yes, he relied on having two blades to Brom's one, but forgot about the reach he was conceding to the longer blade. Never assume you have the better of your opponent, just fight and let your skill decide the result.' He smiled. 'And don't be afraid to kick or punch. You're using a one-handed blade, so it's not like your other hand is doing anything. Remember how Bromvy knocked me down?'

415

Randall found revisiting the encounter strange, though he knew that many valuable lessons could be drawn from the combat.

'He took you out of the fight,' he replied plainly.

'Indeed. He recognized me as the greatest threat and put me down so he could deal with Elyot and Clement, neither of whom was his equal.'

Swordplay, Randall realized now, was about much more than just hacking at men with a blade.

'How's the porridge?' Utha asked, as he sat down on his bedroll and placed his axe carefully on the saddle of his horse.

'It's done.' Randall spooned a large portion into a small wooden bowl.

They had eaten porridge every morning since leaving Cozz. Tomorrow they would be in Ro Tiris and could eat heartily at an inn – an enticing thought after the thick, slimy substance they had been living on.

They ate slowly and with little talk, both of them in their own world of contemplation. Randall thought of his life and the unexpected turns he'd endured over the past month, and he guessed that Utha was worrying about the Black cathedral. The Black clerics had their headquarters in Ro Tiris, unlike the other clerical orders, which were based in Ro Arnon. Utha had frequently spoken about the tradition of keeping the clerics of death close to the king and away from the Purple cardinals. He had been evasive as to the reason for this tradition, but the implication was that they were the one order that was always under the eye of the king.

'Time to go, young Randall,' Utha said, finishing his porridge. 'Get the camp together and I'll deal with the fire.'

Utha was wearing his cleric's boots – tough leather, with tight steel buckles – the only remnant of his armour that remained. He was still a huge, broad-shouldered lump of a man, but without his black armour he looked less intimidating. His pale skin and pink eyes were less striking and the scar down his neck was hidden by the hood of his grey robe.

They pulled down the small camp quickly and largely in silence. Randall tried to speak, but his light attempts at conversation met with a glare from Utha. The cleric spoke no words as he packed up his few belongings and sheathed his axe, taking a moment to look at the double-headed weapon before he stowed it for what might be the last time.

'Right, just so we're clear, Randall, as we ride through Tiris, keep your mouth shut. I don't want to talk to you. Understood?' He didn't look at the squire.

'I understand, but remind me again why I should obey your orders?'

The Black cleric shot him a threatening look. 'Because I will knock your teeth through your head if you don't.'

'I need to be able to speak to defend you, remember?' Randall had lost much of the fear he used to feel towards Utha and had no compunction about speaking his mind. 'It's not like I'm a squire any more.'

The cleric stood up and flexed his back, making a show of considering Randall's words. Then he turned and crossed quickly to stand in front of the squire. He saw the punch coming but couldn't get out of the way in time to avoid being knocked to the floor. He tasted blood on his lips, but the blow had not been meant to injure him.

'We're going to ride to the Black cathedral and you're going to keep your fucking mouth shut until I tell you to speak.' Utha reached inside his robe and threw a gold piece on the floor in front of Randall. 'There, now you're my paid squire, so do as you're fucking told.'

* * *

Randall kept his mouth shut as the two of them rode into Ro Tiris. He kept feeling the swelling on his lip and testing his teeth to make sure the punch hadn't loosened any of them. Utha was not a man to argue with, but Randall was fairly sure the Black cleric had lashed out from fear of returning to the cathedral.

They entered via the southern gate, the watchmen on duty recognizing Utha the Ghost and not daring to approach him as they rode into the city. Randall heard the customary whispered comments about the Black cleric – otherworldly suspicions and stories of risen men – but the young squire had become immune to the aura of fear that surrounded his new master and he barely listened as they rode along the King's Highway into the capital of Tor Funweir.

The Black cathedral was a smaller building than Randall had expected. It was nestled west of the guild square, in the shadow of the huge barracks of the knights of the Red. The streets were largely empty and Randall surmised that only the knights used the road between the two churches, rendering it off limits to the common men of Tiris. The cathedral was a plain building of black stone, with no adornments other than a single irregular spire which rose at an angle from the castellated roof.

He thought, as they rode through the streets, that the training grounds on each side of them were strangely empty. The knights of the Red were based in Ro Arnon, but the barracks of Ro Tiris were huge and held the king's army.

Utha noticed the empty streets too, and took a good look at the training grounds. 'A lot seems to have happened while we've been hunting the Black Guard,' he said. 'The last time I was here, the barracks held eight or nine thousand knights.'

'Where would they have gone?' Randall asked the cleric, momentarily forgetting that Utha had ordered him not to talk.

'I'm not sure, but the cynic in me suspects northwards. Look at that.'

He pointed to the White Spire of Tiris, the mark of the king. The banners displaying the white eagle of Ro Tiris were flying at half mast, indicating that King Sebastian Tiris was not currently in the city.

'I think someone has made a huge mistake,' Utha said, shaking his head. 'I might have cared about that a month ago.' He nudged his horse onwards.

Ahead of them, a small group of guardsmen stood, formally attired in gold, outside the vault-like door to the Black cathedral. There were six of them, each carrying a longsword at his side and a tall lance in his hand.

The leader of the group, a grey-haired warrior without a helmet, noticed the approaching cleric and stepped into the road, motioning his men to follow.

'Utha the Ghost,' he stated with a formal nod.

'It's actually Brother Utha of Arnon,' said Randall without thinking.

The guardsmen all looked at the squire and the grey-haired leader shot him a hard glance. 'Silence, boy.'

'That's my squire, guardsmen. If anyone tells him to shut up, it'll be me,' Utha said, turning to look at Randall. 'Thank you, lad. I'm glad someone remembers my actual name.' He smiled thinly at the squire before turning back to the leading guardsman. 'What do you want, lieutenant?'

'By order of Prince Christophe Tiris, you are to be taken into custody.' The six guardsmen had moved to form up round Utha and Randall, their lances held in practised fashion, pointing inwards at the two riders.

Utha didn't move and kept his hands in view as the lieutenant moved next to him. 'I'll have to take your axe, brother.'

'Careful, guardsman, I don't answer to you. My authority is in that building and I could with all legality take you and your men apart for hindering me.' He spoke quietly and Randall detected fear in the guardsmen's faces.

'Now, why am I being arrested?' Utha asked calmly.

'His highness does not reveal his mind to me, brother, but you will be coming with me.'

The huge black door that led to the cathedral of death began to open and everyone present turned to look. A black-robed figure had appeared in the doorway. His features were masked and his hands remained inside the sleeves of his robe, but he spoke clearly.

'Brother Utha is not yet expelled from the church, which places his fate in my hands . . . not yours, guardsman. He is God's man, not king's man.' The speaker did not raise his head or identify himself.

'Brother abbot, we have instructions to arrest this cleric and if you interfere, we are prepared to use force to do so. The house of Tiris rules here, not the Black church.' The guardsman spoke confidently and, from what Randall knew, the king's men were unswervingly loyal to the crown and unlikely to be cowed by the clerics.

Utha reached behind his back and placed his hand on the hilt of Death's Embrace. 'You are close to actions that will get you killed, lieutenant,' he said with anger in his pale eyes. 'The prince is brave indeed if he thinks he can overrule the One.'

The grey-haired lieutenant banged his longsword loudly on his gold breastplate and within moments another two squads of guardsmen had appeared from either side. They'd been hidden and waiting in the side streets should their commander call for aid, and now they lowered their lances and joined the first squad encircling Randall and Utha.

'Please, Brother Utha. This can be cordial or it can be bloody.' The guardsman spoke with sincerity. 'No one needs to die.'

The Black abbot, standing in the doorway, raised his head and Randall saw dark eyes regarding the large group of king's men. Utha slowly moved his hand from Death's Embrace and held his arms wide.

'You had better be sure of your actions, lieutenant,' he said.

'I am as sure as I can be, brother . . . as sure as my orders came from the house of Tiris and must be followed to the letter.' He continued, 'And, now, Brother Utha, I must take your axe.'

With lightning speed, Utha drew Death's Embrace and held it at arm's length, making the guardsmen jump. When it became clear that the Black cleric did not intend to fight, the lieutenant moved in and grasped the hilt of Utha's axe.

'Take care of that weapon,' the albino cleric said. 'It is dear to me.'

* * *

Randall and Utha had dismounted, been disarmed and were led under close guard through the streets of Ro Tiris. Utha was silent during the journey, taking note of landmarks and the route they had taken, as if he was attempting to ascertain where they were being led.

As they turned from a wide boulevard north of the guild square, Randall was taken aback for a moment as the royal compound came into view. The house of Tiris was a large white building set back from the rest of the city and overlooking the harbour. The smell of the sea carried down the street and hit Randall's nostrils, masking the city's usual odour and making him smile. He turned to Utha but saw no sign of a smile or anything other than concern on the cleric's face. He didn't appear to be surprised by their destination, and Randall wished he hadn't agreed to accompany him into the city.

'Utha,' Randall whispered, 'why are we being taken to the palace?'

'I don't know, Randall, but Prince Christophe must have either lost his mind or else be privy to more information than us to treat the Black church with so little respect.' He spoke quietly so the guardsmen couldn't hear, and his eyes were narrow and suspicious. 'Keep your mouth shut when we get inside and let me do the talking. Understand?'

Randall nodded and their march continued towards the White Spire of Tiris, towering over the royal compound.

The gates were open and within the ornate fence, a large area of courtyard separated the street from the huge golden doors. Ranks of armoured king's men patrolled the area, walking in step and turning to salute the White Spire whenever they passed the front of the palace. The barracks lay off to the side, behind a second fence and, just as he had at the Red cathedral, Randall thought the place strangely empty.

Most strange of all, however, were the covered prison wagons standing within the courtyard. They were empty, but Randall noted that all of the windows had been boarded shut and on the outsides were odd-shaped knives that had been thrown at each of the wagons. As they were led through the gates and into the courtyard, he could see guardsmen on stepladders trying to pull the weapons from the wood. They were struggling, for the leaf-shaped knives had evidently been thrown with some considerable force.

Utha noticed the knives too, and turned to address the lieutenant. 'Since when do guardsmen hunt risen men?' he asked, having recognized the strangely shaped weapons.

'Since we were ordered to,' the man replied. 'The house of Tiris has a new adviser who has provided intelligence on the monsters, enough to make hunting and capturing them easier.'

'Does this adviser have a name?' asked Utha.

'She's a Karesian enchantress called Katja . . . the Hand of Despair, or something. I think she's of the Seven Sisters.' The lieutenant had spoken the name with little judgement and Randall couldn't be sure how he viewed this woman.

Utha had recognized something in the man's words, however. It may have been the woman's name or the name of her order, but he visibly clenched his jaw at the news.

Randall moved to walk next to the cleric and asked, under his breath, 'Who are the Seven Sisters?'

'Enchantresses that shouldn't be here . . . shouldn't be counselling the prince and shouldn't be helping them hunt Dokkalfar,' he answered. 'She'll enter your mind if you let her, so if we should have to address the witch, keep your will strong.'

'And how do I do that?' Randall asked, unsure how he would *keep his will strong.*

'Just stand near me and look at the floor,' Utha responded dismissively.

The huge golden door was opened with an audible creak as they approached. As the interior came into view, the squire gasped once more at the golden opulence on display. This was the house of King Sebastian Tiris, his wife, the Lady Alexandra, and their son, Prince Christophe. It was formal and decorative in equal parts and Randall could see little in the way of comfort.

There were servants moving through the wide, carpeted rooms, cleaning and polishing the wooden and gold surfaces, and there were no small number of ceremonially attired guardsmen on duty. The squire thought it odd that they'd been led here rather than to a prison cell and wondered again what business the prince could have with them.

The entrance hall was dominated by a huge staircase that led up from the floor and curved round, forming a circular balcony above. The guardsmen led them past it and towards a less ornate door at ground level.

'We're not going to the bedchambers, then?' Utha asked with irony.

One of the guards took offence at this attempt at levity and slapped Utha across the back of the head. Several others glared at him, challenging the Black cleric to react.

Utha chuckled to himself and reached up to feel where he'd been hit. His hand came away with no blood on it and he nodded before turning to the man who'd struck him and punching him square in the face. The guardsman fell loudly, dropping his lance on the ornate carpet.

Utha just stood there, hands held wide in a gesture of submission to the other men, and made no further attempt to attack the man who'd fallen.

'You hit me, I hit you, it's really that simple, boy.' The imposing cleric spoke confidently.

The lieutenant interrupted, 'That's enough. Soldier, keep your hands to yourself.' He pointed to the man on the floor. 'Any reprimands will come from me. Brother Utha, I apologize, this man will be whipped for striking a cleric of the One.' He spoke formally, showing respect. 'You, get up and report to the guard marshal.'

The guardsman stood quickly, saluted and left, nursing what was quite possibly a broken jaw. Utha didn't look particularly happy or content with the result, and Randall guessed he was still deep in thought.

The door they approached was made of wood and iron, and was in sharp contrast with the opulence surrounding it. It was reminiscent of a door to a dungeon and Randall didn't like what that implied. The lieutenant opened it and they were led quickly down some narrow stone steps. The detachment of guardsmen spread out, with a few remaining at ground level, closing the door behind them.

The stairs were dimly lit and the bright morning sunshine did not penetrate into the basement. They were led in single file into a long corridor. As the group made its way further into the dungeon, on each side of the passageway Randall saw doors with steel gratings, indicating prison cells, although they were all empty.

'We're being taken to the oubliette?' asked Utha as they neared a single door in the middle of the corridor.

The lieutenant nodded. 'The prince wants to meet you as far away from others as possible. He seems to think you're dangerous, Brother Utha.'

'What's an oubliette?' asked Randall, suddenly feeling afraid.

'A place of forgetting,' replied the Black cleric. 'It's the worst kind of dungeon. The king uses it only when someone has committed treason and he wants to forget about them.' He locked eyes with the lieutenant. 'Have we committed treason?'

'I was only instructed to bring you here.' The guardsman was just following orders and was unlikely to be able to answer more questions.

The Black cleric looked at Randall and raised an eyebrow.

The man in the lead reached the door at the end of the corridor and produced a key. The door was well used and built for security rather than elegance. The key turned readily and the large door opened outwards, revealing a sizeable square room beyond.

The lieutenant stepped inside and motioned for the other guardsmen to lead Utha and Randall into the oubliette. The Black cleric was hesitant for a moment, then he entered slowly, placing his hand on his squire's shoulder and ushering him in.

Randall was afraid, but he tried to not let it show as he took in his surroundings. The room was large and filthy, with straw pallets arrayed across the floor. Around the edges of the room were a dozen or so cells, each separated from the main room by a steel gate. Randall thought he could see figures in most of the cells, but they were all hunched over or wrapped in brown blankets and he couldn't see who they were. In the corner of the oubliette was a staircase leading up to a large hatchway in the ceiling, which appeared considerably more ornate than the rest of the dungeon complex.

'Okay, we're here. You have done your duty, now tell me what the fuck is going on?' Utha demanded.

'You are to wait here until the prince is ready to see you. Now, if you'll excuse me . . .' The lieutenant moved to the staircase and climbed up to the hatch. He knocked and the door was unbolted and opened from the other side, allowing him to disappear above. He had taken Death's Embrace with him.

The remaining guardsmen placed their lances against the wall and encircled Utha and Randall. Their eyes looked hostile and Utha spoke with a wry smile. 'I don't think your lieutenant would like it if you decided to give us a beating.'

'Maybe you tried to escape,' said one of the guards, a bearded man, removing his gauntlets as he spoke.

'And maybe I'll break your face if you take another step towards me, piss-stain,' Utha said venomously, clenching his fists. 'You've only got nine friends, are you sure you don't want to go and get a few more to make it fair?'

Randall was within the circle, standing next to Utha, and was trembling. He did not share his new master's bravado.

When the hatch reopened, Randall's breathing slowed as he realized they had probably been saved a beating at the hands of the king's men. Utha looked disappointed and continued to clench his fists as he stared down each of the guardsmen in turn.

They retrieved their lances and, still glaring at the cleric, resumed their guard duties.

'Remember who you are and remember who I am and we'll get along fine,' Utha said with a vicious grin, turning to see who was coming through the hatch.

Out of the corner of his eye Randall caught movements in several of the cells, and in the nearest one he saw dark eyes peer out from under a thin blanket. It looked to be a man, but in the minimal light his skin looked grey and Randall couldn't make out his features or guess where he came from.

The first figure to descend the stairs made a considerable noise. He was quickly identifiable as an armoured Purple cleric of middle years. His longsword was sheathed and its scabbard bore elegant pictures of rampant lions, embossed in silver. He was older than Utha and the possessor of a mangled nose.

Behind him came a beautiful Karesian woman, who made Randall gasp. She swayed her hips as she walked down the stairs and wore a figure-hugging dress of deep red. As she reached the bottom of the steps, Randall could see a tattoo on her face showing a howling wolf and stretching from her neck across her left cheek.

On seeing the woman, Utha stepped next to his squire and whispered, 'We are in the presence of an enchantress, young Randall, so keep your wits about you.'

Again, Randall wondered how he was going to do this, but he tried not to look at the woman once she had noticed him and smiled.

The grey-haired lieutenant had come back through the hatchway but stood at the top of the stairs, as if waiting for someone else to enter. He was no longer carrying Death's Embrace.

'I think we can dispense with the guards,' said the Purple cleric. 'Go about your duties, gentlemen. You'll be summoned if necessary.'

The armoured men appeared reluctant to leave, but they did so with only a moment's hesitation. The door was again closed, leaving only the Purple cleric, the enchantress and the lieutenant in the oubliette with the prisoners.

'Brother Utha,' said the Purple cleric, bowing his head in a gesture of respect. Recognition had appeared on both their faces and it was clear to Randall that the two clerics knew each other.

'Brother Severen,' replied Utha, though he did not bow his head and displayed little evident affection for the older cleric. 'This is my squire, Randall of Darkwald. Say hello to Severen of Tiris, the prince's confessor.'

Randall managed to stumble through the moment and say, 'Hello, my lord.'

'A squire, Utha? That is highly irregular.' Severen spoke with a decidedly upper-class accent.

'So was the means of his employment. He was Torian's squire,' Utha replied. 'That is, until Torian was killed by the Black Guard's friend, a Kirin called Rham Jas Rami.'

Severen showed displeasure at the news that Torian was dead, but the most interesting reaction was the expression that came over the enchantress's face when Rham Jas Rami was mentioned. She seemed momentarily afraid at the name, though she quickly recovered her poise and resumed smiling.

'And you were with Brother Torian when he died?' Severen asked.

'I was standing a few feet away when a longbow arrow pierced his neck.' Utha was solemn and kept a tight rein on his emotions as he spoke of his friend's death.

'And yet you still did not apprehend Bromvy,' interjected the Karesian woman in a sultry drawl.

'And who are you to ask anything of me?' Utha growled.

'Mind your manners, Utha,' barked Severen. 'This is Katja the Hand of Despair. She is advising the house of Tiris on certain matters and she's worthy of your respect.'

Randall thought the name sharply at odds with the woman's pleasing appearance and girlish smile. She was a Karesian and had an exotic beauty that few women of Ro could match, but there was nothing in her demeanour to indicate that she was a *hand of despair*.

'The Seven Sisters are advising the prince?' Utha asked suspiciously.

'And the king,' stated Katja, with another disarming smile. 'We have been welcomed for the knowledge we possess and the advice we can give.'

'And why is the oubliette filled with risen men?' Utha gestured to the cells around them.

The Black cleric had not previously paid attention to the small cages and Randall thought it strange he should know who was in them without looking.

'I'm surprised to hear a crusader concerned with the fate of the risen,' Severen responded with an imperious glare.

'I'm not a crusader any more, as you well know.' Utha was not cowed by the Purple cleric or the enchantress, but Randall also noted that his master was on edge, keeping his fists clenched and trying not to look at Katja.

'The risen men are a danger to the stability of Tor Funweir and, with our assistance, the church of Ro has been able to hunt them with more success than before,' Katja responded. 'We plan to have them all imprisoned or killed within the year.'

Utha glared at her before addressing Severen directly. 'Brother, you and I have never been friends, but answer me this, why is this witch afforded such respect?'

Katja laughed and the room brightened visibly as she did so. Severen directed a gleeful smile at her and the lieutenant raised his head the better to hear the sound of her laughter. Randall and Utha looked at each other and the squire sensed that something was very wrong here.

'Answer me, Severen,' repeated Utha, more insistent this time.

'All answers will come in time, my dear Ghost,' replied Katja, not allowing the Purple cleric to answer.

'I don't recall speaking to you, witch,' shouted Utha, becoming angrier with each passing moment.

Severen was still smiling euphorically as he stepped forward and slapped Utha hard across the face. 'Mind your manners, Ghost,' he said, with a maddening smile.

Utha looked as if he were about to attack Severen, but was interrupted by movement from above. The lieutenant held the hatchway open as a man emerged. He was young, barely older than Randall, and his ornate gold armour spoke of ceremony rather than action. He carried a sword at his side, but the hilt and scabbard looked unused and his face betrayed little experience of hardship. He was blonde-haired and clean-cut, with no beard or blemishes on his face, lending him an almost angelic appearance.

This was Prince Christophe Tiris, heir to the throne of Tor Funweir. Both Katja and Severen bowed as the prince entered the oubliette, but Utha merely gave him a shallow nod.

'My prince,' said Severen respectfully. 'This is Brother Utha the Ghost, betrayer and turncoat.'

Utha nearly exploded with anger at these words, but a raised hand from Prince Christophe cut off his response.

'Brother Utha . . . why do they call you the Ghost?' Christophe asked with a lisp. He had evidently not registered the fact that Utha was an albino. The prince wore the same look of gleeful euphoria on his face as Severen.

'He is called the Ghost because he was cursed at birth, my prince,' responded Katja, levelling her beautiful brown eyes at Utha.

'Ah, I see . . . yes, the One can be cruel to unworthy men,' the prince said, sneering down at the Black cleric. 'Does he know why he is here?'

'No, my prince, we were awaiting your arrival.' Severen made sure he was standing between Utha and the prince. Randall thought whatever they believed his master had done must be very serious indeed.

'Well, now that I am here, we can begin, yes?'

'Indeed, your highness.' Severen turned to Utha. 'Brother Utha the Ghost, you are hereby found guilty of treason against the crown and people of Tor Funweir.' He spoke the words formally and motioned for the lieutenant to enter the oubliette and stand in close guard behind Utha.

Randall had been ignored up until this point and he was conscious of the fact that his longsword had not been taken. Utha seemed to realize this as well, and Randall caught his master glancing towards the sword of Great Claw.

Then Utha laughed. 'Treason? And here was I thinking we were being serious. Your highness, I do not know the purpose of this charade, or why you and Severen bend your knee to this witch, but I do not answer to the Purple. I am a cleric of the Black and I demand to be taken back to my order.'

The prince appeared livid at the interruption and put a hand to his sword hilt in a well-practised display of indignation. 'Silence, traitor.'

'I . . . am . . . no . . . traitor,' Utha shouted back in defiance, careless of the fact that he was addressing royalty.

Severen stepped past the prince and struck Utha again. This time with a closed fist, and the Black cleric dropped awkwardly to the ground and spat out blood.

'It's come to this, then . . . beating an unarmed man in a filthy dungeon?' asked Utha. 'How noble of you . . . Torian would be proud, you pig-fucker.' Utha's eyes flashed once again to the sword of Great Claw at Randall's side.

Katja stood inches from the fallen Black cleric. 'Dear, sweet, gentle Utha,' she said with a glint in her eye. 'You are guilty of aiding and sheltering risen men. It is a most heinous crime to choose undead monsters over your own people, but with proper guidance I'm sure I can cure you of this evil ailment.'

Utha looked confused for a second, before standing to face the enchantress. 'So, you've enchanted the prince,' he stated. 'And Severen too . . . and, I'll warrant, many more weak-minded men of Ro.'

She continued to smile at him but didn't nod to confirm his suspicion. 'The risen are born evil. It's not their fault, any more than it's your fault that they used their magic on you.' She spoke lyrically, with affection.

'We have questioned and tortured many of the risen over the past few weeks, Utha,' said Severen, 'and your name kept coming up. It seems the monsters consider you an ally. A friend to the forest-dwellers, they say.'

Utha closed his eyes and breathed in, composing himself. 'Don't we just kill them any more? Questioning the risen is unheard of.'

'The Lady Katja has advised us of a better way to proceed,' Severen responded. 'We now cage them and use pain to extract information. They are not human, so our clerical code doesn't prohibit such things.'

Utha took a step back and stood next to Randall, judging the height of his scabbard and the ease with which he could acquire the sword of Great Claw.

'You are not the first formerly honourable man to be found guilty on these charges, Utha,' Severen stated, returning to a more formal mode of speech. 'Others have been imprisoned for assisting the risen men in their campaign of terror against the noble men of Ro.'

'They have no campaign of terror,' Utha growled in frustration.

'You are damned by your own words, Ghost,' shouted the prince, in a high-pitched whine. 'You know nothing of the ways of the undead – cunning and evil, they will sway the will of weak men such as you, and my grandfather.'

At the mention of the prince's grandfather, Utha turned a questioning look on Severen. Randall had heard of Bartholomew Tiris – he was King Sebastian's father and was considered a wise man.

'Bartholomew doesn't have a traitorous bone in his body,' said Utha. 'This is a joke . . . or it would be if it were funny.'

Katja remained close to Utha and her words were whispered. 'You cannot win . . . you would be well advised to accept your punishment.' She paused, before continuing in a whisper only Utha and Randall could hear. 'Your land is too valuable to be left in the hands of Ro . . . old-blood.'

Utha tried to strike the enchantress, but his hands wouldn't move and Randall sensed his exertion as he tried to lash out. He had heard tales of the Seven Sisters and their reputation as beings it was impossible to kill, a reputation he was beginning to believe as he watched his master struggle to gain control.

'My dear Katja, we should show him what happens to traitors,' said the prince excitedly, pointing to a locked gate that led away from the oubliette.

'I would be happier if he were shackled first, my prince,' said Severen. 'Utha is a dangerous man, not to be treated lightly . . . Lieutenant,' he addressed the grey-haired guardsman, 'be sure he is under close guard.'

The lieutenant crossed to the door. He opened it and summoned two of the men from outside. Again, no one had paid any particular attention to Randall, and he realized he'd dug his fingernails into his palms with the tension.

'Maybe you will be more humble when you see how the house of Tiris deals with traitors to the crown,' said Prince Christophe, like a petulant child. 'Lead the way, Brother Severen.'

The Purple cleric locked eyes with Utha for a moment before he crossed the oubliette and unlocked the iron gate. It was the same as the cell doors where the risen men were imprisoned but led into an unlit stone corridor.

Randall chanced a look into one of the cells and, for the first time, had a clear look at a risen man, one of the beings Utha had called Dokkalfar. He – for it appeared to be a male – was hunched over, but nonetheless looked to be tall and gangly, with clear grey skin and round black eyes which had neither pupils nor irises. The creature directed a questioning look at the squire and tilted his head as he watched them pass his cell. Randall thought he looked little different from a man, although his elongated, leaf-shaped ears and long fingers gave the Dokkalfar an otherworldly appearance.

As Utha approached the door, he paused and turned to lock eyes with the risen man. Severen moved to stop him but Utha quickly crouched in front of the small cell and reached through the bars.

'I am sorry . . . I tried to tell them. I swear to you I tried.'

Randall sensed a deep sadness both in Utha's words and in the creature's black eyes, as Severen roughly grabbed the Black cleric and marched him away.

'You see,' proclaimed the prince, 'he cares for the beasts . . .

touches them and treats them better than his own people.' Randall decided that he disliked Prince Christophe intensely.

'They are not beasts . . . highness.' Utha virtually spat out the last word.

Severen drove his fist into the Black cleric's stomach and Utha doubled over as he lost his breath.

'I don't want to keep hitting you, brother,' he said as he pulled Utha upright and held him firmly.

Utha coughed and nodded. 'So, stop hitting me . . . brother.' He pushed Severen away and leant on Randall instead. The squire looked angrily at the Purple cleric and tried to help Utha upright. He was winded, but recovered his composure quickly.

The guardsmen led them down the corridor, past rotting brickwork, moss and damp. At the end Randall could see a barred door, wooden and more solid-looking than the iron grates, which appeared to be securely locked. The grey-haired lieutenant began to open the door, before turning to the prince and asking, 'Are we required within, my prince?' There was a trace of fear in his eyes and Randall wondered what lay within.

'Yes, you are, guardsman,' Prince Christophe replied, as if the question had been a stupid one. 'You must keep the traitor under guard.'

The three king's men looked wary, but they were not going to disobey the prince's orders. They formed up round Utha and the door was opened, releasing a noxious odour that assaulted the squire's nostrils and made him feel sick. It was dark within and Randall could see nothing except a swaying distortion in the air and the glow from a single torch.

'Move,' ordered Severen from the rear, shoving Utha into the darkness.

They entered one at a time until all were within the room. Katja moved round the walls with the torch, lighting half a dozen iron braziers around the circular space.

As the light spread, the room became illuminated and Randall's eyes widened as he saw a huge darkwood tree sprouting up from a patch of earth at the centre, and a decrepit old man tangled up in its branches. The man was Ro and wore a simple purple robe, though it was split in places, and the tree appeared to be connected to the man's flesh by needle-like growths along its black surface.

The man wasn't moving, but his eyes were open and his chest rose and fell, showing Randall that he was still alive. He bore a slight resemblance to Prince Christophe and the squire guessed that it must be Bartholomew Tiris. His eyes were bloodshot and showed no sign that he was aware of their presence.

Katja stepped forward and raised her hands in an extravagant gesture of worship towards the strange tree. Severen drew his sword and placed it against Utha's back, forcing him forward with a grunt of exertion.

'What have you done, prince?' demanded Utha, as he looked with horror at the king's father, tangled in the black, tentacle-like branches.

'Silence,' the prince ordered, with a cackle, mimicking Katja's gesture of worship. 'Wake the Young, Katja, wake the Young.'

They looked with astonishment at the prince as an insane fire appeared in his eyes and his cackling grew louder.

Randall spared a glance at the three guardsmen and saw that all were averting their eyes and making an effort to look at the floor. Brother Severen had a look of insane glee on his face, and Randall guessed that both prince and cleric of nobility were under Katja's spell. He turned to Utha and tried to convey his fear, but his master was focused on the tree as the gnarled branches began to move.

'We have found the Ghost,' Katja screamed. 'We have found the old-blood of the Shadow Giants . . . he is yours to consume.'

Her words caused the tree to shift violently and rear up, its branches starting to writhe in the air and its trunk slowly undulating. The body of Bartholomew Tiris was dropped to the floor and the pulsating tentacles moved down to connect with the ground, acting like legs as they wrenched the wide trunk from the earth.

Severen shoved Utha forward with his sword and the Black cleric appeared transfixed by the horror before him. The trunk was now in the air, shaking off mud like a beast as it tilted forwards to reveal a needle-filled maw reaching for the cleric. Randall was rooted to the ground with terror and could only watch as Katja danced around the floor and the prince clapped his hands together like a deranged child. The two of them had moved away from the door and were now on either side of the tree.

Severen had a malevolent grin on his face as he pushed Utha forwards, towards the thing that used to be a darkwood tree.

'The priest and the altar,' screamed Katja, 'the priest and the altar.'

Randall was transfixed until a strange moment of remembrance conjured up an image of Brother Torian. The Purple cleric, who had been Randall's master for less than a month, had held a sense of right and wrong for which Utha had frequently teased him – but at that moment, in the oubliette of Tiris, the memory of his face shook Randall from his terror and enabled him to think clearly.

The needles protruding from the beast's circular maw were reaching for Utha, extending and producing a sickly green fluid.

Randall didn't pause to think for more than another moment before he roared, 'Utha . . .' at the top of his voice, and deftly drew the sword of Great Claw.

The guards were still looking at the floor and Severen reacted only slowly, turning his head as he apparently noticed Randall for the first time. His own sword was at Utha's back and he couldn't raise it to parry as the squire struck. Randall was young and strong and his sword flew downwards, striking the Purple cleric at the shoulder and making a grating sound as it cut through the plate of his armour and bit into his flesh.

Severen's blood sprayed across Utha's face and the Black cleric shook his head, quickly regaining his senses and backing away from the monster.

'Randall, sword,' he barked, holding out his hand.

The squire threw his longsword the short distance into his

master's hands. The guards looked up and Randall guessed that they were not immune to the transfixing power of the monstrous tree. The grey-haired lieutenant was in control of his senses but the others were rooted to the spot with fear.

Utha turned away from the tree and, with cold, angry eyes, attacked the lieutenant. Brother Severen was alive but thrashing in pain on the stone floor and Randall knelt quickly and seized the Purple cleric's longsword.

'No . . . the Young must feed,' screamed Katja. 'The Dead God demands blood.'

The prince had also drawn his sword but was reluctant to advance on the Black cleric, and his path was blocked by the writhing monstrosity in the centre of the room. The tree was still reaching for Utha, but he'd moved out of its reach and was no longer looking at it.

Randall moved quickly with his newly acquired sword and shoved one of the transfixed guardsmen out of the way to clear the doorway. The man didn't resist but just fell limply to the floor as Randall grabbed the iron handle.

'Get it open, boy,' shouted Utha, as he drove the lieutenant against the wall with brutally efficient skill.

The door creaked and Randall had to throw all of his strength into one huge heave. It began to open and he saw three more guardsmen standing beyond. Behind him, Utha had despatched the lieutenant with a cut across his neck and was turning to receive the prince, who'd worked his way past the monster and, with a wild look in his eyes, leapt at the Black cleric.

Randall held his breath as Utha parried Prince Christophe's clumsy attack and kicked him solidly in the chest. The prince looked deeply indignant for a moment before the pain hit him and he fell back into the path of the tree.

Katja screamed, 'No . . . this cannot be,' as the writhing beast grabbed the crown prince of Tor Funweir.

The needle-like feelers in its mouth attached to the prince's body and in a second he had slumped into unconsciousness as the creature began to consume him whole, pulling the body head-first into its grotesque maw.

Utha watched for a moment as the beast slowed to digest its meal, before he turned sharply and kicked the last guardsman out of the way.

'Move or die, it's that simple,' Utha roared at the king's men who stood in their way.

All three paused, but they were professional soldiers and the threat fell on deaf ears. They couldn't see into the room and the tree was no longer advancing as they drew their swords.

Utha thrust forward, piercing the lead man in the stomach before he withdrew the blade and answered a high attack from another of them. Randall didn't stop to think as he joined his master in the corridor and engaged the last guardsman, swinging from high and keep his arms as close to his body as possible.

They fought, side by side, and Randall felt exhilaration as his sword clashed with the guardsman's. His lack of skill was offset by the cramped conditions and, as Utha clubbed his own opponent to the ground, Randall lashed out with the hilt of his sword and connected with the man's jaw.

One guardsman was dying, but the other two were merely dazed as Utha and Randall jumped over them and ran down the narrow stone corridor, with the Karesian enchantress screaming behind them.

'You hurt?' Utha asked as they approached the main room of the oubliette.

'No, no, I don't think so,' replied Randall.

He quickly checked himself and found no blood or wounds, although his mind was swimming with fear and exhilaration.

They reached the gate that led to the imprisoned Dokkalfar and Utha kicked open the door, sending dust and debris flying from the filthy dungeon floor. The Black cleric ran to the nearest cell and crouched, extending his hand as he had done before.

'Randall, help me get this cell open.'

The squire was frantic to escape and thought the idea of

pausing to rescue the other prisoners foolish.

'Did you hear me?' Utha shouted. 'Jam that sword in the hinges and help me wrench the door open.'

He did as he was told, automatically following his master's orders, and thrust his newly acquired sword into the thick iron hinge at the base of the cell door. Utha stood and kicked at the blade with all his strength, jamming it between the iron rivets and bending the hinge. Then he grabbed the hilt of the sword and pulled it sharply away from the cell door, causing the hinge to break and the door to buckle.

'Help me,' he shouted to Randall, and the two of them pulled frantically until the door was bent sufficiently to allow the being inside to escape.

'Quickly, we have to leave,' Utha said to the creature.

Now at its full height, Randall couldn't believe how tall the risen man was – seven foot at least, with a slender build. It moved towards them, its head tilting as it studied their faces.

'Utha the Shadow . . . you are our friend.' The Dokkalfar's voice sang from its thin and sensual mouth, though its accent was strange, placing stresses in the wrong places, Randall thought.

The Dokkalfar languishing in the other cells had all stood and looked silently into the central room as Utha helped the newly freed creature out of the cell. The Black cleric turned to the others and looked flustered as he registered how long it would take to rescue them all. His breathing quickened as shouting sounded from the chamber behind them. The guardsmen had recovered enough to begin to pursue them.

'Utha, we have to go,' shouted Randall, grabbing his master's arm and trying to pull him to the door of the oubliette.

'We need to save them,' Utha said quickly.

'If we try, they'll catch us . . . come on,' Randall shouted again, pulling more forcefully at Utha's arm.

The muscular cleric moved away only reluctantly, with the single freed Dokkalfar following close behind.

'I'm sorry,' he said quietly to the creatures who remained.

A guardsman, groggily swaying on his feet, appeared in the doorway and shouted, 'You killed the prince . . .'

Utha turned and, with anger in his eyes, hurled the sword of Great Claw at the man. The longsword thudded into him and skewered him through the chest. The cleric then grabbed the sword in Randall's hand and pulled open the door that led out of the oubliette.

Randall fought his rising fear and ran back across the central room to retrieve his sword. He removed it easily, but had to turn away to avoid the blood spray that came with it. Down the corridor he saw two guardsmen rising to their feet and, at the end of the passage, just emerging from the doorway, was Katja the Hand of Despair. The Karesian enchantress glared at Randall with staring eyes and the squire quickly looked away in order to avoid falling under her spell.

'Randall, hurry the fuck up,' shouted Utha from the door.

'They're coming.' Randall was breathless as he joined his master.

Out of the central room, Randall shut the door, jamming his dagger into the lock to keep it from being opened again. They ran out of the oubliette, the freed Dokkalfar behind them. Randall didn't look at the risen man and tried to focus on getting out of the royal compound alive. When he reached the door that led up to the house of Tiris, Utha frantically flung it inwards.

'Stop.' Randall placed his hand on Utha's shoulder. 'There are guards and servants up there. How are we going to get out?'

Utha growled, 'I'm going to kill anyone that tries to stop me and then we're going to steal that wagon.' With no more words, he slapped away Randall's hand and ran up the stairs.

The squire wiped sweat from his forehead and went to follow him, but was stopped by a restraining hand from the risen man. The tall creature had been silent as he ran and Randall felt his presence intimidating. The creature's skin was grey, and as more light played across his features the young squire could see no pigment or colour of any kind in the Dokkalfar's face. He was simply a non-human, a living being not of the race of men, and Randall involuntarily shied away from the creature.

'Do not think to stop the Shadow, young man of Ro,' it said in a sonorous voice. 'His *now* is more important than yours or mine.'

Randall didn't try to understand as he wriggled out of the creature's grasp and ran up the steps after Utha.

The Black cleric was moving, sword in hand, across the carpets. He was covered in blood and looked terrifying as he ran towards the courtyard. Randall followed and saw servants cowering, unwilling to challenge the enraged cleric and too afraid to run for help. They crossed the entranceway quickly, reaching the door unchallenged.

Utha paused at the door until Randall and the Dokkalfar had joined him. 'There are at least a dozen guardsmen in this courtyard,' he said through gritted teeth. 'There's also a wagon. You go for the wagon, I'll go for the guards. Clear?'

'As it needs to be,' replied Randall, too frantic to be scared.

Utha nodded and put his hand on Randall's shoulder. 'You've saved my life twice, boy, now get in the wagon and let's stay alive a while longer.'

Randall looked down to see that his hand was no longer shaking and the longsword of Great Claw felt lighter in his fist.

Utha breathed in deeply and scowled, opening the large door with an aggressive growl and tightening his hand around his new longsword. The glare of sun that hit them as they entered the courtyard made Randall squint as he followed his master.

Beyond, the gate was closed, and more than a dozen gold-armoured king's men stood in groups or walked in lone patrol around the yard, evidently unaware of what had transpired in the oubliette. The wagon was close, with three horses attached to the front and two guardsmen removing Dokkalfar knives from the carriage.

Utha didn't pause before running at the first two guardsmen. They saw him too late, and Randall saw the other king's men slowly realize that a roaring Black cleric was in their midst.

Utha swung with power at the first man, half severing his head, before spinning round and driving his blade through the breastplate of the second man. In a moment he'd cleared the wagon of guards.

'Guardsmen, to arms,' roared one of the king's men, standing at the main gate.

'Randall, the wagon,' Utha shouted as he kicked the dead bodies out of the way and turned to face the other guards, who were beginning to gather their senses.

The squire didn't take in the overwhelming odds arrayed against the cleric as he climbed into the wagon's driving position and grabbed the reins. The Dokkalfar, his face still masked by his hood, wrenched two knives from the wood and jumped up to sit next to Randall.

Utha picked up a second longsword from a fallen man and swung his two blades with intimidating skill, roaring at the guardsmen while running at them. The Black cleric moved like an enraged monster and Randall saw fear come into the eyes of those who were preparing to fight him.

Utha did not wait for the men to overwhelm him as he plunged into the mass of them. He lashed out with both blades, aiming to maim rather than kill as he severed one man's sword arm at the elbow and cut another viciously across the face.

'The gate,' he shouted to Randall, without looking back, and the squire flicked the reins roughly to spur the three large horses into movement.

As the wagon moved across the courtyard, two crossbow bolts thudded into the wood inches from where Randall sat. Looking up, he saw more armoured men emerge from the building behind him, reloading their crossbows. The squire recognized one of them from the oubliette and guessed that the enchantress would also be in pursuit.

To his surprise, the Dokkalfar stood up gracefully on the wagon's forward seat and launched both his newly acquired knives at the men surrounding Utha. Two died instantly as they were struck in the neck, and Utha killed another who had turned to see where the knives had come from. The Black cleric was now surrounded and only the two longswords he wielded kept his adversaries from closing in.

'Hold tight,' Randall said to the Dokkalfar, as the horses barrelled into the ornate gates of the royal compound.

The wagon juddered violently as the metal bent and buckled under the weight of the horses and the heavy wagon.

'Utha, move,' roared the squire over his shoulder. The way ahead was tantalizingly clear.

He pulled up on the reins to slow the carriage and turned to see Utha surrounded. Without thinking, Randall leapt from his seat and drew his sword. A guardsman with his back to the squire became the first man Randall had wilfully killed when the sword of Great Claw struck him at the neck and sheared down into his body. A second turned to engage the new combatant, but a moment later caught a Dokkalfar knife in the neck.

Utha roared again as an opening appeared among the encircling guards and he plunged forward, deflecting thrusts from the other men. With a skill and ferocity Randall had never seen, Brother Utha the Ghost engaged five men at once and fought to reach the carriage.

A glancing blow to his leg made the cleric buckle and it looked as if he'd be driven back until Randall moved in to join his master. He tried not to think, letting his mind forget Utha's lessons and just relying on instinct. He was not a match for these men in terms of skill or training, but the distraction provided by the ferocious cleric of Death gave Randall the chance he needed. His second kill came in the form of a thrust that pierced a young guardsman in the side, through the exposed middle section of his breastplate.

Through the press of guards, Randall saw Utha take another blow, this time a deep cut across his chest. The cleric forced himself upright and whirled his two swords in wide, skilful arcs, pushing the guardsmen back.

Then another knife was thrown and, for a second, there was no one between Utha and Randall. They locked eyes and Utha ran forwards. He caught several blows, but determination and anger spurred him on and he dived past the encircling knights into an ungainly forward roll on the flagstone courtyard.

Randall could see men emerging from the compound with drawn crossbows, and standing behind them was the cackling figure of Katja the Hand of Despair. With a wildness in her voice, she was directing men to stop Utha.

'He killed the prince, stop him at all costs.' Her voice cracked as she spoke.

Randall grabbed Utha and hefted him up as the Dokkalfar threw his last two knives, killing two more men and buying them a moment to haul themselves up into the wagon.

'Move,' shouted Utha weakly, and the carriage sprang into life again as the risen man grabbed the reins and drove the prison wagon forward.

Bolts thudded into the wood, but the shouting quickly died down as they made their escape. Utha was bloodied and pale even for an albino, as Randall pulled the wagon door shut and pushed open the front window to address the Dokkalfar.

'Just get out of the city. Don't stop for anything.' He had to shout to be heard over the noise of hooves on stone.

'We will not stop and they will not stop us,' the creature replied, as Randall slumped back inside the wagon beside Utha.

'That's three times, young Randall.' The cleric wore a thin smile. 'Take my hand.' Utha raised a blood-covered hand to the squire, which Randall grasped firmly. 'I would call you *brother*, Randall of Darkwald,' he said quietly, as his eyes began to close.

CHAPTER SEVEN

RHAM JAS RAMI IN THE STRAITS OF CANARN

R HAM JAS WAS cold and disliked the weather of the north. The ship was cheap and the captain had asked no questions, but comfort was in short supply. It was late and the temperature had dropped sharply as darkness had fallen. Their journey through Tiris had been swift and, with a little coin thrown around, relatively easy. Kohli and Jenner had remained in the city, planning to find a way of returning to Karesia and leaving Rham Jas and Bromvy with the words *Don't get killed and say hello to Al-Hasim.*

This advice had been playing on the Kirin's mind and he had spent the past week, as they'd crawled slowly north across the straits of Canarn, thinking how best to keep Brom and himself alive.

They were close now, within a day of the coast and the beach where Rham Jas had instructed the captain to put them ashore. The forests of Canarn were small, but their dense, tall trees provided perfect cover for the Dokkalfar that lived there. Rham Jas remembered the direction of travel, but his head was full of ways in which his plan could go wrong. But he'd agreed to help his friend and, try though he might, Rham Jas could not bring himself to abandon Brom. It had ceased to be about repayment for the young lord having saved his life and had become a personal goal – to see this done, to take Brom to his home and to play whatever part fate had in store for him.

It was approaching midday and Rham Jas could feel no warmth. The sun was permanently behind the rolling grey clouds and the sky was dark. Brom was below deck, as he'd been most of the past few days. He'd eaten and slept, but had otherwise done very little save sit in his cabin and mope. Rham Jas was used to spending time on his own, but still he would have liked a more talkative travelling companion. The Kirin had hoped for a relaxing evening of whores and wine in Ro Tiris, but Brom had not been keen and insisted they leave straightaway. Rham Jas had been forced to watch Kohli and Jenner stroll into the red-light district with smiles on their smug Karesian faces.

'Rham Jas . . .' The words came from Captain Makad, the Karesian trader who owed him a favour and had agreed to do the job for little money. 'The sea will be getting choppy. If you want me to put you ashore on that beach, you're going to have to row. I'm not getting near the rocks.'

'Don't worry, captain, we'll row,' he responded. 'And you'd better stay clear of Canarn.'

'That was the plan,' the captain said with a smile, before returning to his duty.

They had not been able to reach the barracks or the king's harbour, so neither Rham Jas nor Brom knew how many knights were in Ro Canarn. If Captain Makad were to come too close, he would risk being spotted and boarded by knights of the Red, and Rham Jas had no doubt that the captain would sell them out for very little money. Not that the knights would be able to find them in the Deep Wood, but it was still better if he and Brom remained invisible for now.

The sea was starting to get rough and Rham Jas doubted he would be able to sleep. They'd reach the coast tomorrow, and the Deep Wood a few hours after that, and he hoped he'd hear the song of the Dokkalfar for a few moments before they kicked him and Brom out of their realm.

* * *

The forest was dark and Rham Jas disliked not being able to see the sun through the dense canopy. The trees in the Deep Wood were tall and imposing, having been there long before the duchy of Canarn had been founded, and they had a solidity like towers constructed of wood and bark. The forest floor was free of the usual detritus of fallen branches and uneven ground, with only a thick scattering of leaves covering a grassy floor.

Despite having spent most of his young life within a few hours' travel of the Deep Wood Brom had never ventured into it before, and the look of awe on his face as he perceived the huge, majestic trees was testament to their near-magical presence.

Each tree had a name in the Dokkalfar language and though Rham Jas had never tried to learn, or even pronounce, their names, he knew that the reverence in which the Dokkalfar held the trees was more than a simple respect for nature. Long ago, the Dokkalfar had been bound to a Forest Giant and, unlike men, they understood that nature was both beautiful and terrible, deserving of fear as well as love. Animals of the forest were locked in a daily struggle for survival, constantly hunting and being hunted in an endless game of life and death. This had made the Dokkalfar suspicious, on edge at all times, never at rest.

Rham Jas liked them. Despite the opinion the majority of other men held, he respected their synergy with the woods and their ancient acceptance of persecution as something that had to be endured. As he led Brom deeper into the woods, the Kirin assassin felt a sense of calm that he rarely experienced. A quick look behind showed that Brom did not share this feeling, and Rham Jas had to remind himself that other humans were uneasy around the forest-dwellers.

'How much further?' asked the young lord.

'I don't know . . . maybe another hour, maybe two. They'll approach us when and if they choose to.' Rham Jas knew that actually looking for them was rather pointless. The Dokkalfar could remain hidden indefinitely; they hadn't survived for so long by being easy to find.

'This forest reminds me of the Fell.' Brom was walking slowly behind his friend and craning his neck to look up at the towering tree trunks.

'That's because the same trees grow here. I think the Fell is their . . . homeland, I suppose. Though I'm not sure if the term really applies.' Rham Jas slowed his pace to allow Brom to take in their surroundings.

'This forest has never been hunted by the Black clerics, so far as I know, so they should be more relaxed . . . shouldn't they?'

Rham Jas raised an eyebrow. 'It doesn't really work like that, I'm afraid. They communicate somehow over long distances; each settlement shares the pain of every other settlement that's attacked and every Dokkalfar that's killed. They call it the Slow Pain.'

'Interesting people,' Brom replied simply.

'They're not people, my friend, they're Dokkalfar.' It was a basic distinction, but a very important one. 'They don't like being compared to men.'

'But they look like men, don't they? I mean, I've never seen one, but I always imagined . . . two arms, two legs, a head.' Brom was nervous and Rham Jas allowed him to ask his questions.

'They have the same limbs and roughly the features as us, just a bit . . . different,' the Kirin replied, realizing that this answer was not hugely helpful. 'They're taller than you or I and they . . . they're just not human. You'll see.'

They walked through the dense wood slowly, Rham Jas taking note of familiar landmarks, but making no particular effort to be stealthy. He knew that to try and remain hidden in the Dokkalfar woods was largely pointless as they'd probably already have been seen. He guessed that the decision about what to do with the two humans who had wandered into the Deep Wood was currently being made somewhere out of view. He knew that he wouldn't be killed, but worried about Brom. The young lord was an outsider here and, as a noble of Tor Funweir, he was directly related to the noble families that had hunted the forest-dwellers throughout their lands – and the Dokkalfar were able to sense such things.

Rham Jas stopped as they reached a small patch of open ground, a clearing between the huge trunks of half a dozen trees where a single ray of sunshine lanced down through the canopy. The forest floor was flat and featureless, save for the ever-present carpet of green and brown leaves upon which they walked. Rham Jas recognized the place and decided to stop for a rest.

'Let's stop here for an hour or two and give the watchers a chance to get a good look at us.' He removed his longbow and sat at the base of a tree.

'They're watching us?' asked Brom, a little alarmed by the news.

'They have been since we entered the woods. It's their way.' Rham Jas knew that his friend was impatient, but the Kirin was not going to rush this encounter. The more insistent the visitor to the Deep Wood, the less likely he was to survive.

'Sit down, Brom, we may as well take some rest.'

Hesitantly, he joined Rham Jas against the broad tree trunk. From ground level, the forest had a strange ethereal quality and the single ray of sunlight made the leaves glint and shine. Distantly, Rham Jas could hear a slight sound, the rhythmic chanting of the Dokkalfar. It sounded like no other noise the Kirin had ever heard – a chorus of high-pitched notes that rose and fell with beautiful and elongated timing, each note swelling before lowering, only to rise again.

Brom heard the sound too and raised his head the better to listen to the beautiful song of the forest-dwellers. His eyes closed involuntarily and his head began to sway slightly as the rhythm increased in tempo and volume.

'It's beautiful,' Brom said as he listened. 'Is that really them singing?'

Rham Jas nodded. 'They say that it's how they talk to the trees and pass messages to other Dokkalfar settlements,' he said quietly, so as not to interrupt the song. 'My wife used to spend hours just listening to it in Oslan.'

They sat and let the song flow over them, neither of them speaking. Rham Jas sat cross-legged and Brom lay back as if bathing in the ethereal glow, letting the ray of sunlight play over his face. The song had calmed the young lord considerably, and Rham Jas allowed himself to hope that they would indeed find help from the forest-dwellers of Canarn.

The minutes stretched and flowed together as the two friends listened, until another sound came from high above. This sound was not music and it caused Brom to sit up sharply and reach for his sword.

'Easy,' said Rham Jas quietly. 'Keep it sheathed.'

They both looked up and Rham Jas saw a shape sitting in a high branch. The figure was crouched and holding two leaf-shaped blades, one in each hand, held across his chest. No face or features were visible in the high shadows, but the figure cocked its head to one side, as if studying the two humans. Size was difficult to gauge across the distance, but the figure appeared large and was cloaked in shadow, looming over them.

'Rham Jas . . .' said Brom, not taking his eyes from the figure.

'Relax. They'd have killed you by now if they were going to,' the Kirin replied simply, causing his friend to dart a questioning look at him.

'Don't you mean they'd have killed *us* by now?'

'Oh, no, I wasn't in any danger,' Rham Jas answered with a broad grin. 'You're Ro, remember – everyone hates the Ro.'

Brom glared at Rham Jas before turning back to the figure above. 'Can I say hello, or is that bad etiquette?'

'You can say what you like, but don't expect him to answer until he's ready,' Rham Jas replied.

A moment later the figure had blurred into motion, flexing his legs and jumping down to land gracefully on the forest floor. He crouched with one blade in front of his face and the other behind his back, in a guarded pose. Brom gasped as he looked into the face of a Dokkalfar for the first time.

It was a male, maybe seven feet tall, with long, jet-black hair hanging loosely down his back. His eyes were also black, reminiscent of pools of inky water, which seemed to flow from side to side as he looked at the humans. His skin was grey and he was slender with long, dextrous-looking fingers and sharp, talon-like nails. As he stood, his hair moved slowly to reveal large, leaf-shaped ears and no facial hair of any kind. His clothing was dark green, with flashes of black and grey inlaid within the thin fabric.

Brom didn't take his eyes from the forest-dweller, and Rham Jas could tell that his friend was trying to reconcile the graceful being in front of him with the oft-told stories of risen men.

The Dokkalfar male tilted his head and looked first at Brom, and then directed a long, disquieting look at Rham Jas. The Kirin smiled awkwardly, hoping the creature knew who he was. Rham Jas had visited several different Dokkalfar settlements and their Tyr warriors always seemed to know him, having received the information from distant forests. The fact that the Tyr had not attacked thus far meant Rham Jas was fairly optimistic, but he wished the creature would speak and lessen the tension.

When he did speak, it was in a deep, sonorous voice. '*Paivaa*, Rham Jas Rami. *Hauska tutustua*.' The Dokkalfar spoke a language unknown to man and Brom shot his friend a confused look.

'Erm . . . hello,' replied Rham Jas. 'Sorry, I don't speak your language. Nanon tried to teach me once, but I have no ear for it.' Rham Jas cleared his throat and tried to say the one phrase he had memorized. '*Puhut ko Ro?*' he asked, in an attempt to find out whether the creature spoke the common tongue.

The Dokkalfar appeared to smile, though the expression was thin and conveyed little friendliness. 'I know your speech,' he said, the words of man sounding somehow wrong as he spoke them, with the stresses in the wrong places.

'This is Bromvy of Canarn, a lord of the Ro,' Rham Jas said, anticipating some kind of reaction from the creature. When none came, he continued. 'We ask an audience with your Vithar.'

'You are friend to us, Rham Jas Rami. This man is not known.' The Dokkalfar's head was tilting from side to side as he spoke and Rham Jas thought he must be assessing Brom.

'I have need of you,' said Brom, unsure of his words.

'Need is a strange concept amongst your people,' the forest-dweller replied. 'You are impatient and your needs must always be *now* . . . *now* you will do something, *now* you need help, *now* you act. I have no interest in the *now* of men.'

'Nevertheless, we still ask an audience,' Rham Jas repeated.

The Dokkalfar stepped gracefully within a few feet of Brom, his height, his grey colouring and his expressionless eyes making him appear huge and intimidating. He still held his two knives, but they were loose in his hands and Rham Jas did not think he was about to erupt into violence. Brom didn't take his eyes from the creature and he raised his head the better to look up into his face, refusing to be cowed by the Dokkalfar.

'And what is your *now*, Bromvy of Canarn?' the Dokkalfar asked.

Brom glanced across at Rham Jas and tried to convey that he didn't understand. The beauty and otherworldly qualities of the creature had clearly shaken the young lord, but Rham Jas felt it wasn't his place to interfere. He stood off to the side of the forest clearing, gazing into the woods, as Brom and the forest-dweller searched for something in each other's face.

When the lord of Canarn spoke it was with hard-fought confidence. 'My *now* is a need to help my homeland and free my people,' he said with conviction. 'And to make those dishonourable men who murdered my father pay.'

The Dokkalfar paused, his head no longer tilting, and Rham Jas guessed that he was thinking about Brom's words. 'I am called Tyr Sigurd, it is . . . interesting to meet you.' The forest-dweller gave a shallow bow of his head. 'You will follow me.' Sigurd turned sharply and strode across the clearing, placing his leaf-blades across his back as he did so.

'What do we do?' Brom asked Rham Jas.

'We follow him, I suppose,' the Kirin replied. 'Oh, and Brom . . . well done, he didn't kill you.' Rham Jas smiled broadly and received a playful punch to the shoulder in return.

Sigurd walked slowly and frequently looked behind him, making an effort to move at a pace the humans could match. His stride was huge and he effortlessly avoided obstacles on the forest floor without looking down. He moved across fallen branches and the carpet of leaves, making no more than a slight rustle of sound, and his footsteps did nothing to disturb the detritus of the Deep Wood.

They followed him through tightly packed trees and down a sharp incline into a narrow valley, protected from the sun by an even denser canopy than before. The tree trunks here were thin and rose up from the flat valley floor with few roots at their base. Rham Jas knew that this signified a Dokkalfar settlement under the carpet of leaves. The tall trees had their roots lower down and a constructed floor, built halfway up the trunks, made the settlement all but invisible.

Sigurd stopped by one of the trees and turned back to the two humans. 'You will not be able to find this location again, so do not try . . . if you try and succeed, you will be killed,' he said in a matter-of-fact way, before reaching down to reveal a wooden hatchway hidden amongst the leaves.

The hatch was circular and had been woven out of thin branches, making it even more difficult to detect with a cursory look. Beneath, all Rham Jas could see was a slight yellow glow, though he smelled the telltale scent of Dokkalfar food – a form of nutrition that involved boiled vegetables and herbs, with no meat or bread but with a hearty flavour.

Sigurd jumped down, making no sound as he landed below. Brom looked at Rham Jas, and the Kirin smiled before he too jumped down, making a considerable noise as he thudded on to the tightly packed earth below. Brom followed a moment later and the two humans paused to get their bearings as the hatchway closed.

The forest floor above had given no indication of the huge space beneath, and both Rham Jas and Brom gasped as the glow increased in brightness to illuminate the Dokkalfar village. Starting a little way in front of them, the roots of the trees served as pillars, stretching away in chaotic lines. Around the base of each tree were simple, organic-looking structures which appeared at once beautifully constructed and entirely natural. There were no straight lines and neither windows nor doors, but leaf motifs were in abundance throughout the settlement. The forest floor above was a high ceiling, perhaps twenty feet from the actual ground, and Rham Jas could see beams and struts of twisted wood and earth acting as supports for the bed of leaves above their heads. He found it difficult to tell whether or not the supporting beams were natural or had been built by the craft of the Dokkalfar. The expression of awe on Brom's face indicated that his friend was just as confused.

Sigurd stood a little way ahead of them and waved elegantly, indicating that they should follow him deeper underground. Neither followed straightaway, as other Dokkalfar were visible in the settlement and, without exception, they had all directed their black eyes towards the two outsiders. The structures of which Rham Jas had taken note were little more than canopies or large awnings, and all kinds of Dokkalfar were peering out from their homes. Rham Jas felt self-conscious as several dozen heads tilted to regard the humans.

'You will follow,' Sigurd stated. 'No one here will harm you.' The words didn't reassure Brom, but with a gentle shove from Rham Jas they walked further into the Dokkalfar village.

Cooking pots of amber and baked mud hung from carefully constructed apparatus above glowing rocks. It seemed they did not use fire, but their craft nonetheless enabled them to heat things to a sufficient temperature.

Rham Jas walked after Sigurd, smiling nervously at the nearest Dokkalfar, and Brom followed closely behind. The forest-dwellers followed their movements and Rham Jas saw both curiosity and anger in their eyes, though he sensed no immediate danger.

Sigurd led them through the thinly spaced tree trunks past a Dokkalfar presence as diverse as any human settlement. Rham Jas saw children playing with branches and twigs as if they were swords, running across the dark forest floor, and Tyr warriors at work beside heated rocks that served as forges.

Brom was right when he said that Black clerics had never hunted in the Deep Wood of Canarn. Duke Hector had always resisted attempts by the church to set up a Black keep in the area, and although the men of Canarn were not aware of the forest-dwellers' presence, their distrust of the clerics had inadvertently protected their Dokkalfar neighbours.

The looks directed at the two men were hostile, however, and the children in particular whispered quiet insults at the humans.

'They don't seem to like us,' said Brom, stating the obvious.

'Just be thankful it's our race they dislike rather than us,' replied Rham Jas. 'If it were the latter, our heads would likely be adorning a high tree top by now.'

'Who are the Vithar?' Brom asked, as they followed Sigurd down an incline which led away from the majority of the dwellings.

'Shamans,' answered Rham Jas simply. 'The Dokkalfar don't have leaders as such, they take counsel with the Vithar shamans if a course of action is not clear. The Vithar invariably counsel patience and endurance.'

Brom nodded, but Rham Jas thought he was only half listening and had been talking mainly to alleviate his nervousness in the alien environment.

As they followed the Dokkalfar male away from the habitations, the settlement opened out as the ground sloped sharply away from them. The forest floor above was still at the same height, but the tree trunks below ground were now vast wooden pillars, as tall as the towers of Canarn, and a deep depression in the ground provided an awe-inspiring vista of walkways, galleries and platforms built in and around the trunks.

'Well, fuck me,' Brom said, as he paused and looked into the heart of the Deep Wood. 'How did I not know this was here?'

'Because the forest floor above is natural and flat. Men have walked over this ground a thousand times, never knowing what was beneath.'

Rham Jas was trying to act as if all this was only to be expected – in reality, he'd never seen anything like it either. The Dokkalfar settlements he'd seen in the Fell and in Oslan were humble tree houses by comparison.

'Any cleric blood left on those dirty hands of yours, Rham Jas Rami, Kirin man?' The voice came from a Dokkalfar perched on a branch overlooking where they stood.

Sigurd didn't look up, but paused as Brom and Rham Jas both craned their necks to see who had spoken. The Dokkalfar jumped down from his perch and landed nose to nose with Rham Jas.

'You look older,' Nanon stated, letting his eyes move slowly from the Kirin's feet to his head.

'You look the same,' replied Rham Jas, 'but then you would.'

He'd not seen Nanon for several years, when the Dokkalfar had helped him ambush a Purple cleric near Ro Leith. He looked exactly the same as he had done then – short for a forest-dweller, just over six foot tall, and his grey skin was scarred in places. Rham Jas knew that Nanon had travelled widely from his home in the Deep Wood and that he had a fascination with humans that was curiously out of place amongst his people.

'I am as old as I choose to appear, Kirin man. The *now* of man is the *forever* of the Dokkalfar,' he said with a smile, the first genuine display of emotion that either of the men had seen since they encountered Sigurd.

Brom relaxed slightly, for Nanon spoke the language of Ro with less of an accent and had a friendlier demeanour. Rham Jas knew that the Tyr was more dangerous than any of them, but he was also more worldly and more tolerant of men.

'Why are you and lord Ro man here? This is a dangerous *now* for men.' His eyes were just as black as Sigurd's but somehow conveyed more feeling, and he lacked the strange head tilt common to most of the forest-dwellers.

'Bromvy of Canarn,' Brom said by way of an introduction.

'We know your name, Ro man, and we know your anger . . . perhaps you should relax a little.' He turned from Rham Jas and stood equally close to Brom, assessing him in much the same way as he'd done with the Kirin.

'Tyr, I must take them to the Vithar,' said Sigurd.

Nanon didn't acknowledge this at first and continued staring at the lord of Canarn. Rham Jas thought Brom was becoming a little nervous under the Tyr's gaze, but he maintained his cool and simply let himself be studied.

'Very well,' said Nanon with another smile. 'I will accompany you.'

The old Tyr moved quickly to stand next to Sigurd, and the two Dokkalfar resumed walking. They led Rham Jas and Brom down the slope towards the base of the larger trees. All around them new vistas came into view with each step as high platforms and strange organic structures snaked their way across the settlement. Dokkalfar, mostly wearing simple green robes, made their way across platforms and walkways between the thick tree trunks, going about unknowable business and scarcely acknowledging the outsiders below.

It was bewildering to Rham Jas that the huge roof of the settlement was also the forest floor above; he simply couldn't conceive of the bizarre craft it must have taken to keep the floor – or ceiling – stable and invisible while all manner of animals and men walked across it. It was a knotted lattice of wood and sprouting plants, with nothing to give away its presence. He'd seen similar underground settlements in the south, but never anything on this scale, and he wondered if the Deep Wood held some particular significance for the Dokkalfar.

Ahead of them, Rham Jas could see the forest floor levelling out and the huge roots of trees became visible. As he looked up, he estimated the height of the trees to be fifty feet at least and a slight feeling of vertigo came over him at the enormity of the place. Next to the Kirin, Brom was similarly impressed and was standing with his mouth open and his eyes wide as he stared up at the trees. Rham Jas didn't know whether the Vithar would agree to help them, but he was sure that Brom's new station as ruler of Ro Canarn would be the key. If they were to succeed in liberating the city, and if Brom were installed as duke, he would have the opportunity to take the unprecedented step of declaring the Deep Wood a sanctuary for the Dokkalfar. Though, as Rham

Jas looked around the immense settlement, he wondered whether the forest-dwellers would care about such things.

'Follow,' ordered Sigurd, and he and Nanon stepped on to a wooden platform secured to a tree trunk by thick vines.

Brom glanced at Rham Jas and the two outsiders likewise stepped on to the platform – and nearly fell over as it began to rise and move across the settlement. Brom grasped a vine to steady himself.

Looking up, Rham Jas could see a dense tangle of similar vines all across the village. They ran the length of the tree trunks and held numerous platforms and hanging bridges within their mass. Some were moving, but most simply looked as if they were part of the trees to which they were attached. Again, this was like nothing Rham Jas had ever seen.

'Impressive, isn't it?' Nanon asked, with a degree of pride as the platform sped through the trees.

'It's making me sick,' joked Rham Jas. 'Could you get them to slow it down?'

Sigurd looked confused at the Kirin's humour, but Nanon laughed loudly – a sound that carried a fair distance through the trees and sounded strange coming from a Dokkalfar.

'You're still funny, Kirin man. I miss the wit of your people.'

'I've been with him for a month and I'm getting sick of it,' muttered Brom, still clinging on to the vine and trying not to look down to the forest floor.

Rham Jas was more sure-footed than his friend, but even he was clumsy in comparison with the Dokkalfar. Sigurd and Nanon stood with no assistance and appeared to know intuitively when to make the slight adjustments needed not to fall from the platform. Their grace was a thing of alien beauty and Brom struggled to reconcile the reality of these creatures with the stories he'd heard about the risen men.

Just when Brom looked as if he were about to be sick, the platform came to a sudden halt on a high terrace. The two Dokkalfar stepped off as soon as it stopped and the two men almost flew off the edge.

Rham Jas was saved by his ability to balance and Brom by the firm grip he held on the vine – but both looked ungainly and foolish as they stumbled after the forest-dwellers.

Rham Jas took a quick look around and saw they were about halfway up a huge tree trunk and within sight of a green auditorium arranged between branches. The bridge that led to the auditorium was hung with vines and swayed ominously as the Dokkalfar made their way across it.

'Did you know all this was here?' Brom asked.

'Of course . . . doesn't everyone?' Rham Jas lied with a maddening grin. 'Well, not *this* precisely, no, but something like it.'

Rham Jas could see seated Dokkalfar within the auditorium and guessed that the Vithar shamans were arrayed before them.

'Let me do the talking until they address you, okay?'

'No problem,' replied Brom. 'But if it looks as if they're going to attack us, try and give me some warning.' Rham Jas thought he was joking, but he couldn't be sure.

They stepped on to the swaying bridge and followed the Tyr on to a more stable platform at the front of the auditorium. Galleries comprised of twisted wood rose above it and spread out in irregular fashion, providing seats for several dozen Dokkalfar, though only a handful were currently occupied. Nanon and Sigurd held their position at the base of the auditorium and motioned for Rham Jas and Brom to pass them.

The Kirin put a hand on his friend's shoulder and the two of them stepped in front of the raised seating. There was little light in the settlement, but something about this area made their features stand out as if they were held by a gaze that penetrated the obfuscating darkness. Before them sat green-robed Dokkalfar.

'Rham Jas Rami dark-blood and friend to the Dokkalfar,' said the figure seated in the middle. 'You are welcome in the Heart.'

'Thank you,' Rham Jas replied, immediately thinking it a foolish thing to say. 'I wish to ask something of you and your people.'

The Dokkalfar who had spoken raised his head and Rham Jas saw his dark grey skin; blacker than the others, he melded into the darkness around him, becoming distinct only when he spoke.

'I am called Joror,' he said in a faltering accent, and Rham Jas guessed he had not spoken the language of Ro for some time. 'We are the Vithar and we will hear of your *now*.'

'Wait,' roared another voice from behind.

Rham Jas and Brom turned to see a large Tyr stride past Nanon and Sigurd, coming to a stop next to the humans. He was the largest Dokkalfar that Rham Jas had ever seen – not just tall but muscular and broad-shouldered. He wore a large leaf-sword across his back – a weapon that the Kirin doubted could be lifted by a man, let alone wielded in combat – and his black eyes looked at the humans with disdain.

'You may speak, Rafn,' said Joror with a bow of his head.

'I didn't ask permission,' replied the huge Tyr. 'I am not here for counsel. I am here to stop the *now* of these ignorant creatures being heard. Their poisonous words will serve only to damage us and I will see them killed before they talk.'

Rham Jas raised his eyebrows and turned away from the seated Dokkalfar to look up into the face of the creature called Rafn.

'Those are big words for a little girl,' he said, without a smile.

From behind him Nanon laughed, but every other Dokkalfar remained silent while Rham Jas stared up at Rafn.

'You are Rham Jas Rami dark-blood, friend to the Dokkalfar,' said Rafn. 'But he is a Ro man of noble blood and I will kill him for his people's murderous ways.'

The Tyr was angry at the human intrusion into his home and Rham Jas sized him up, looking for the best and quickest way to kill him if the need presented itself. He was huge, but the Kirin assassin knew he would bleed and die like any other creature.

'I am your friend and he is mine.' Rham Jas spoke loudly and with defiance. 'If our presence bothers you that much, I invite you to stay and hear our words . . . along with your Vithar.'

'You invite me? *You* invite *me*?' Rafn shouted.

Rham Jas didn't back away, though he could sense that Brom

had taken a step to the side, trying to keep closer to the friendlier presence of Sigurd and Nanon.

'I'm not a little boy who is scared of you, grey skin. Don't forget that,' Rham Jas said as he stared down the hulking Dokkalfar in front of him. 'This man is my friend and I will take you apart before I see you harm him.'

The Vithar called Joror stood from his seat and approached the confrontation. Rham Jas knew the shamans had no authority over the other Dokkalfar, except when counsel was needed, but he hoped their wisdom would stop him having to fight Rafn.

'This is foolish,' said Joror. 'This man is known to you . . . to all of us. He is our friend and if he says that the *now* of the other is worth listening to, we will hear it.'

Rafn had not turned from the Kirin, but he was evidently reluctant to answer the challenge with violence and, after another moment's tilting his head, he lowered his eyes and stepped back.

'Rham Jas Rami dark-blood, I will not strike you.' He turned to Joror and said, 'I will remain and hear the *now* of the Ro man.'

Calm returned to the platform and Rham Jas was secretly thankful he hadn't needed to test his skill against so intimidating an opponent. Brom also relaxed a little as he stepped back next to his friend.

'Could you have beaten him?' he asked in a whisper.

'No idea,' replied Rham Jas, 'but I stood more of a chance than you.' His wide grin returned and Brom chuckled involuntarily.

'Why do they call you dark-blood?' he asked.

'I'm not totally sure. I think it's got something to do with a darkwood tree I was pinned against for a few hours.' He had been called *dark-blood* before and had never given it much thought. 'They fear and respect the tree, so my having some of its sap in my bloodstream is a big deal to them, I suppose.'

Rafn took a seat next to Joror and, with Nanon and Sigurd standing behind them, the two men stepped forward to be heard by the assembled Vithar shamans.

'My friend is called Bromvy of Canarn, he is a noble of Tor

460

Funweir, the lands of Ro, and he has need of your help.' Rham Jas tried to speak as loudly and as formally as he could. 'He is an outlaw in his own lands, a Black Guard in the language of the clerics, and his father has been murdered by Red knights of the One God.' This caused a slight ripple among the Dokkalfar and Rham Jas was glad the forest-dwellers still loathed the church of Ro.

'Why does this concern us?' asked Rafn dismissively. 'Ro killing Ro simply means they will leave the forests alone for a time.'

A few nods from the others showed Rham Jas that the Dokkalfar were still too concerned with their own survival to care about Brom's predicament.

'I have words,' said Nanon from behind them.

'Tyr Nanon may speak,' announced Joror with a wave of his hand.

'I know this Kirin man better than most and I see his heart in his words. He is concerned by a *maleficium* that abides in the city of men.'

Rham Jas had not heard the term before, but the reaction of the Dokkalfar was instant and startling. The Vithar clenched their fists and shivered uncomfortably, and the Tyr almost involuntarily adopted a protective posture. The reaction calmed down after a moment, but Rham Jas had never seen anything like this among the forest-dwellers.

Nanon was looking into Rham Jas's eyes, searching for something. The Kirin knew that the longer a man spent with a Dokkalfar, the more understanding would exist between the two. In this case, it meant Nanon understood his humour better than the other Dokkalfar and had a rudimentary ability to know his mind.

'She is called the Lady of Spiders and she has the hearts of the Red men in her evil hands,' he said, plucking the knowledge from Rham Jas's mind.

'You know of the Seven Sisters?' asked Brom, forgetting his friend's advice to stay quiet.

'Silence, lesser being,' commanded Rafn, still uncomfortable with Brom's presence. 'You could not hope to understand what this being is capable of.' He was obviously disturbed by talk of the *maleficium* – apparently a Dokkalfar term that referred to the enchantresses of Karesia.

Brom took a step forward. 'This woman has manipulated the knights of the Red into invading my homeland, slaughtering my people and executing my father. I know what she is capable of.' He spoke defiantly.

Rafn was silent for a moment as he studied Brom's face. Then he turned to Joror and said quietly, 'The *now* of man coincides with the *forever* of the Dokkalfar . . . I would never have thought it possible.' Then a laugh erupted from the huge Tyr and Rafn stood and strode purposefully towards Brom.

Rham Jas made a move to intercept him, but Nanon held his arm and stopped him. Rafn didn't attack and Brom was in any case too angry to be cowed by the huge warrior before him.

'Tell me your name again, Ro man?' asked Rafn in a low growling voice.

'I am Lord Bromvy of Canarn, son to Duke Hector, and Black Guard of Tor Funweir.'

It was the first time that Rham Jas had heard Brom admit to being of the Black Guard and he thought his friend's predicament must have finally sunk in.

'Bromvy,' repeated Rafn, sounding out the strange human name. 'Your *now* is more dangerous than you know, for the *maleficium* seek to bring your lands crashing down and your gods to ruin.'

'I ask for your aid against the Lady of Spiders and her Red knight thralls.' Brom spoke with conviction, fighting the urge to back away from the huge Tyr.

A female voice spoke from under a hood several seats down from Joror. 'Listen to our *forever*, Bromvy and Rham Jas Rami of the lands of men.' The words were more lyrical and softer than those of the male Dokkalfar. 'The better you will understand why we will help you.'

The speaker pushed back her hood to reveal lighter grey skin – almost white in comparison with the males – and her ears were more elongated, parting her black hair as they rose in an elegant leaf shape.

'I am called Jofn and I speak the *forever* of ages past,' the female Dokkalfar began, holding the attention of all those present.

'We were much as your kind are now – with birth, life, love and death. We had lands, society and homes to call by our own names and a god whom we cherished.'

She spoke of things unknown even to Rham Jas. He had always thought the forest-dwellers to be a lost remnant of the Dead God's followers.

'Our Shadow Giant deity was slain ages past by the being you know as the Dead God – a Forest Giant of pleasure and blood, a chaotic being of purest malevolence, whom we served out of fear. Our own god was lost, one of many causalities of the Long War.'

The other Dokkalfar bowed their heads in remembrance, though Rham Jas could not truly comprehend the timescale of which she spoke. He knew that the forest-dwellers were long-lived and that they had dwelt in the land long before the rise of men, but the span of millennia it would require for gods to rise and fall made his head spin.

'The Dark Young of the Dead God were ours to birth. He twisted our forms from beings of light and beauty into the black countenances you see before you and used our deaths to create more of his monstrous servants.'

Rham Jas had heard the term 'Dark Young' applied to the darkwood trees, but he was confused as to their significance.

'And then, in the gaps between Deep Time, other gods rose and, as a bold move in the game they named the Long War, those Giants you call Rowanoco, Jaa and the One conspired to slay the Forest Giant and his twisted servitors, just as he had done to our forgotten Shadow Giant god, the one we loved.' A black tear appeared in her eye as she recounted the oldest tales of the Dokkalfar.

'The One found him, Rowanoco fought him and Jaa stole his power, thinking him dead. The arrogant Fire Giant gifted the Dokkalfar with immolation upon death, so we would no longer spawn the Dark Young, and that was how the world remained for countless millennia.

'Then, with the rise of man, the three Giants chose followers from the young races and gave them power to enforce their laws and to fight the Long War. Rowanoco and the One gave of their own being to strengthen their priesthoods, but Jaa . . . Jaa sought to gain advantage by giving none of his own strength. He used the stolen power of the Dead God to empower his enchantresses, unknowingly freeing them from the Fire Giant's laws.'

Brom and Rham Jas looked at one another in surprise and confusion at the Vithar's words. She spoke as if legend and myth were history.

'We are but men and you speak of things beyond us,' said Rham Jas as respectfully as he could.

'The *maleficium* in your city, Bromvy of Canarn, seeks to sever the power of the three and to bring back the worship of the Black God of the woods with a thousand young. The not so Dead God.'

'But that Giant was slain, how can it come back?' Rham Jas asked, already suspecting the answer.

'The power Jaa stole resides within the *maleficium* witches – the Seven Sisters of Karesia – and so long as they live the Dead God can never truly be dead.' She paused and a deep sadness entered her black eyes. 'In strange aeons even death may die.'

Rham Jas felt the enormity of the Vithar's words and knew that he was as nobody in comparison – a Kirin assassin who had, for whatever reason, decided to help one of his few friends.

'Rham Jas has killed one before,' said Brom, making the Kirin smile awkwardly as all those present turned to look at him.

The female Vithar called Jofn returned his smile, though hers was somehow more knowing.

'You also possess the power of the Dead God, Rham Jas Rami dark-blood. The essence of a Dark Young flows within your body, gifting you strength, speed and resilience. Their stolen powers do not work on you and you will *never* be their thrall and you will *never* be helpless in their presence.' She snapped out these last words as if she were speaking to spite the enchantresses. 'Our goals coincide, for the *maleficium* witches have realized the realities of their power and have willingly turned aside from Jaa to lay themselves at the feet of the Dead God.'

Tyr Rafn, who had been silent throughout the tale, now raised his chin and spoke clearly. 'These . . . witches have designed the severing of the three Giants and their evil scheme nears its end. They have only to sever the power of the Ice Giant Rowanoco and they will be free to implement fresh worship throughout your lands of men.'

'You knew this before today,' stated Brom. 'Why have you not acted? I see strength in your people, strength I hadn't dreamt of.'

The others turned to Joror, who, Rham Jas guessed, was as close to being an elder shaman as any of them.

The Dokkalfar Vithar cleared his throat and said, 'The *now* of man is a blink of an eye to us. The *maleficium* witches are human and their movements are too fast and too erratic for us to keep up with them. Dokkalfar do not adapt well to change. We know it to be true, as each of us can feel that Jaa's gift of immolation upon death has left us. This would only be possible if the last Fire Giant old-blood had been killed.'

Rham Jas knew a little of the old-bloods, but he could see confusion in his friend's eyes. However, the lord of Canarn shook off the confusion and stepped forward to stand close to Joror.

Looking down at the seated Dokkalfar, Bromvy said, 'What will you ask of me in exchange for your aid?'

'Ask of *us*,' corrected Rham Jas.

Joror didn't turn from Bromvy. 'You must give us your word that you will join us in opposing the *maleficium*. The Heart will remain free from the interference of men and in return we will aid you. Rham Jas Rami dark-blood may be the only creature able to slay the witches and we would ally with him.'

Rham Jas again felt the unwelcome weight of responsibility on his shoulders. He could handle killing and had hurt all manner of people in all manner of ways, but to think that he was in any way special or significant made him feel nauseous.

'I think I need a drink,' he said suddenly, causing everyone to stare at him with various sorts of disapproving looks. 'Just to steady my nerves.' He grinned nervously. 'Some Darkwald red would be nice.'

* * *

The Dokkalfar were not particularly interested in alcohol. After a few hours of trying to convince them that drinking oneself insensible was sometimes a desirable thing, Rham Jas had given up and settled for some kind of strange plant tea.

Nanon had taken Brom and Rham Jas to a high balcony, well above the Vithar auditorium, and they sat looking out over the beautiful Dokkalfar settlement. Rham Jas wasn't sure whether or not the Heart was their name for the place or just a description of its importance, but either way he'd learned more about the forest-dwellers in the past few hours than in the entirety of his life.

He tried to focus on the fact that Joror had agreed to help them and not to dwell on the *Rham Jas Rami saves the world* element. He'd killed one of the Seven Sisters, almost by accident, but to conspire to kill them all struck him as a little out of his league.

Brom and Nanon had been talking about Canarn and they had similar ideas about how to approach a potential assault. Nanon had spent enough time with Rham Jas to have a good grasp of humour and irony, and Brom had responded well to the forest-dweller's blunt appraisal of their chances.

'If we kill enough of them quickly, we can win,' Nanon was saying. 'If not, we'll all get killed.'

'We don't know how many there are,' responded Brom as he took a sip of his own tea. 'And Joror has yet to tell me how many of you will be coming with us.'

Nanon tilted his head, indicating that, despite his peculiarities, he was still Dokkalfar.

'Does it matter?' he asked.

Rham Jas knew that the forest-dwellers had a strange grasp of numbers. They found the concept of armies difficult to understand, because they generally thought in terms of individuals. As a long-lived race, they did not think of anyone as expendable or less important than any other, whereas the race of men had a habit of fielding masses of faceless soldiers. Rank, wealth and law left humans constantly questioning their station in life, and the habit of placing one man above another inevitably created a structure of perceived importance. This was bewildering to the Dokkalfar, who had no concept of leadership or seniority, but rather a society built on shared need and respect.

Brom was unaware of this and said, 'Of course it matters. If they have two thousand knights, we need enough to stand against them.'

'We'll have whoever comes with us,' responded Nanon, in a way that infuriated Brom. 'And that will have to be enough.'

'Enough?' Brom asked with irritation. 'Enough is whatever takes back my home.'

'Then whoever we have will have to be enough,' Nanon repeated.

Rham Jas thought he should interject before Brom became too annoyed. 'Your Brown cleric friend will be able to give us an idea of numbers. If you and I go and see him first, we'll form a plan based on that.' This calmed his friend somewhat. 'Nanon, do you have any black wart?' Rham Jas asked, his ever-present grin becoming broad enough to cover his whole face.

Both of them looked up at the Kirin – Nanon smiling and Brom looking confused.

'I'm sure I could find some,' replied the Dokkalfar. 'What are you thinking, Kirin man?'

'I'm thinking about a way to thin the ranks of knights and give us a chance.' Rham Jas was used to coming up with creative ways of killing people and a few sacks of Dokkalfar black wart would make a lovely surprise for the knights of the Red.

'I know I'm only an ignorant Ro,' said Brom, exasperated, 'but what the fuck is black wart?'

'It's like Karesian fire or Ranen pitch, but . . .' Rham Jas looked at Nanon and grinned, 'it's a little more explosive than flammable.'

Something seemed to occur to Nanon. 'That reminds me, every Dokkalfar that falls must be burned to ash within a few hours of death.'

Brom looked back at him. 'That's the Ro way of doing things anyway. Is it a particular funeral rite of your people?'

'No, it's simply the best way of stopping a hundred new Dark Young sprouting up from our bodies,' he said with deep sorrow in his eyes. 'Our gift from Jaa caused us to burst into flame upon death. But now we are without the Fire Giant's gift, and we need to think of other solutions . . . in your terminology, it's quite shit.'

* * *

They had spent a restless few hours trying to sleep in the high trees and now, just after midnight, they found themselves at the edge of the Deep Wood.

Brom stood next to Rham Jas and the two of them looked out across the duchy of Canarn. The young lord was wistful as he had his first glimpse of his home since he had been named to the Black Guard.

On either side of them a line of Tyr emerged from the trees, each carrying several small woven sacks containing explosive Dokkalfar black wart as well as a number of knives for throwing and fighting. Their blades were heavy and leaf-shaped with ornately designed handles, far more beautiful than the functional weapons of men. Brom had acquired one of the blades and wore it in his belt as a secondary weapon, and Rham Jas had been given a fresh quiver of finely crafted arrows, several of which had black wart on their tips. Both their swords had been sharpened and their armour reinforced with hard wooden struts. The two men felt as ready for combat as they would ever be.

They had forty Dokkalfar Tyr with them, including Nanon, Sigurd and the huge figure of Rafn. They were an intimidating presence, even to Rham Jas, but he was sceptical whether their numbers were sufficient. As things stood, they didn't even know how many knights held Canarn and it would require a stealthy incursion to see Brother Lanry before they could even begin to formulate a plan.

'Bronwyn had better still be alive,' grunted Brom, focusing on his sister's safety to distract himself from the dangerous job at hand.

Rham Jas simply nodded.

CHAPTER EIGHT

LADY BRONWYN IN
THE RUINS OF RO HAIL

BRONWYN ROSE EARLY from her bed and walked up to the forward battlements of Ro Hail. She had been sharing a small room with Stone Dog's mother, an old wise-woman of Wraith called Freya Cold Eyes, while Al-Hasim slept in the communal room surrounded by the Free Company men.

They'd be in Ro Hail for nearly two weeks while Horrock Green Blade and Haffen Red Face supervised the fortifications of the ruined city. The gate had been rebuilt using solid planks of hard wood, the battlements reinforced with fallen stones and mortar, and the buildings surrounding the central courtyard turned into axe-throwing platforms. The two hundred and fifty men of Wraith Company had gone about their tasks with gusto and solidarity, daily prepared to undertake back-breaking work in order to defend their land. Now, as time was beginning to run out, the city looked like a fort rather than a ruin.

'You can't hold it, you know,' Hasim was saying to Haffen as Bronwyn walked up the stone staircase leading to the gatehouse battlements overlooking the Grass Sea to the south.

'Horrock thinks we can,' replied the man of Wraith.

Hasim looked doubtful. 'No, he doesn't, he's just hoping that you can hold them off long enough for Scarlet Company to arrive.'

'What's wrong with that?' Haffen asked with slight annoyance.

'How many men does Johan Long Shadow command at South Warden?'

Haffen shrugged. 'I don't know . . . maybe a thousand axe-men.'

'A thousand . . . added to your two hundred and fifty makes one thousand two hundred and fifty – against five thousand knights, clerics and guardsmen. You can't win,' Hasim said plainly.

'And the Fjorlanders?' Haffen showed a stubborn refusal to accept defeat, a trait Bronwyn had noticed frequently among the men of Wraith Company.

'If they come, they'll come by sea and attack Canarn, which means they won't be here for a month at least. You can't hold out that long. I hate to say it, but you should listen to Verellian.' Hasim had counselled a withdrawal in line with the Red knight's insistence that a massacre would help no one.

'Horrock says we stay, so we stay,' Haffen grunted.

Bronwyn reached the battlements and approached the two men. It was just starting to grow light and the wind was biting and cold as it whistled north off the Grass Sea. Both men wore armour, though Hasim's was light and made of leather, in sharp contrast to the heavy chain mail worn by Haffen. Bronwyn had not yet donned her armour and wore a simple cotton dress which Freya had provided.

'We could still fall back,' she said by way of a greeting.

'Don't you start . . .' snapped Haffen. 'You two don't represent the bravery of Ro and Karesians, do you?'

'Do you represent the stubborn pig-headedness of the Ranen?' Bronwyn shot back.

'You say stubbornness, we say honour . . . did you roll over and accept the Red knights when they marched into your home?' Haffen asked, not happy at being ganged up on.

Bronwyn smiled slightly and shook her head. 'I didn't get much chance to fight, but no . . . I didn't,' she conceded.

The Grass Sea was barren and quiet as the three of them gazed southwards. The rain had stayed away for the past few days and, though a mist clung stubbornly to the plains, the weather had been kind to the defenders of Ro Hail, allowing them fair conditions to fortify their base. Most of the entrances to the underground complex had been sealed and Freya had been given the task of protecting the young and infirm once the time came to fight. Behind them, men of Wraith began their daily duties of patrolling and construction, intended by Horrock to keep every man ready for when the army arrived.

Bronwyn liked these men – they were commoners who had chosen to join the Free Companies and to defend the lands of Ranen from invaders. Although they had not been required to repel an attacking army for decades, they were stubborn now that the time was rapidly approaching when they might be required to die for their land.

'Al-Hasim,' shouted Stone Dog from below, 'Horrock wants you downstairs.'

The young man of Wraith had been assigned by the captain to look after William of Verellian during the knight's incarceration and this meant both Bronwyn and Hasim had spent much time with him. He was a proud young man who spoke with conviction about his duty to Wraith Company and the Freelands of Ranen, and he never went anywhere without his large, hook-pointed axe.

'What does he want?' asked Hasim.

'I don't know, just get your arse down here.' Stone Dog was frequently aggressive and blunt in his language, but he was a consummate soldier and did whatever Horrock asked of him, whether he thought it worthwhile or not.

'All right, give me a minute,' replied Hasim wearily. 'Maybe I'll get some sleep one of these days.' He winked at Bronwyn before turning to walk down the stairs.

'Lady Bronwyn too,' shouted Stone Dog.

'What does he want with me?'

'How am I any more likely to know that than what he wants with the Karesian?' he asked ironically. 'Just get a move on, he's impatient.'

Haffen smiled broadly and pulled his bearskin cloak tightly around his shoulders as the wind picked up and Bronwyn and Hasim turned to leave.

They walked down the newly repaired stone steps which ran parallel to the forward defences and headed across the courtyard. Either side of them, where before there had been only crumbling stone ruins, there now stood wooden constructions built to defend inwards should the knights breach the city gates. Bronwyn could see men of Wraith moving bundles of throwing-axes around and stowing them in hidden places behind the fortifications. The men were all clad in chain mail and Bronwyn knew they'd been on high alert for several days now, expecting an attack at any moment. From the newly constructed wooden walls, stairs had been built leading up to the stone battlements that looked out over the Grass Sea, and men stood at the high points, keeping a watch on the realm of Wraith.

Although the city was now well defended, Bronwyn could still not conceive how so few men could turn back five thousand knights of the Red.

'You and I could leave, you know?' Hasim said, echoing her thoughts. 'None of them would blame us if we fled north.'

Bronwyn looked at him and considered chiding him for cowardice, but she had to admit to herself that the idea of escape had occurred to her over the past two weeks.

'I couldn't do it,' she said. 'Even if I wanted to, I couldn't bring myself to abandon them.'

Hasim stopped and held Bronwyn's arm, pulling her to face him. 'You're not thinking about drawing that toothpick and attacking the knights are you?'

'I'm not staying in the basement with Freya. I have as many reasons to want to fight the knights as any man of Wraith.' Bronwyn knew that Hasim would play the part of a protector sooner or later, because his friendship with her brother dictated that he should try to take care of her.

'They won't think twice about cutting you down, noble or not. These men are not coming here to make a point: the fuckers are marching to war; they want to invade and conquer Ranen.' Hasim had a deadly serious look in his eyes as he spoke.

473

Stone Dog was a little way ahead of them and had reached one of the few doors to the basement that was still visible. He noticed that Bronwyn and Hasim had stopped in the courtyard and the young man of Wraith turned back to face them.

'Am I interrupting something?' he asked, with a mocking tone in his voice. 'I know you two foreigners need your sexual tension in order to function, but hurry the fuck up.'

Al-Hasim laughed and playfully slapped Bronwyn's behind. She didn't wait for more than a second before turning and punching him hard in the face. Stone Dog erupted in laughter and Hasim staggered back, feeling his bloody lip.

'Brom would kill you if he saw you doing that,' she threatened with a smile. 'And I might if you touch my arse again.'

Stone Dog sauntered slowly over to stand next to Hasim. 'When you've quite finished your bizarre flirting ritual,' he said with a grin. 'Horrock is long-suffering, but he did say to hurry up.'

They entered the underground complex and walked quickly through the now mostly empty basement. Healing supplies had been prepared and bandages and thread lay in baskets around the central room, but the place was otherwise bare.

Hasim and Bronwyn entered Horrock's chamber behind Stone Dog and immediately heard the captain of Wraith Company talking in a quiet and gentle voice. He was cradling a Ranen cloud stone and there was a look of deep concern in his eyes.

'Wait,' he said, 'I have some friends here now . . . try to stop crying, okay?' Horrock rarely showed emotion and Bronwyn was taken aback by this display.

Stone Dog stood at the door as Horrock motioned for Bronwyn and Hasim to come and join him. As they sat down around the central wooden table, Bronwyn could hear the sound of a child crying. It sounded like a girl, and her sobs were quiet and indistinct when filtered through the cloud stone.

'Hasim, I have a friend of yours here . . . and she says she'll only talk to you,' Horrock said, with a confused expression on his face. 'My children are all grown up and I think I lack the gentle touch.'

He placed the stone on the table and said, 'Al-Hasim is here.'

'Al-Hasim,' a child's voice exclaimed excitedly through her tears.

'Who is that?' Hasim asked with narrowed eyes.

'Ingrid Teardrop,' was the reply, causing Hasim and Bronwyn to look at each other.

'Ingrid, what are you doing?' the Karesian asked gently. 'How did you get hold of your father's cloud stone?'

More tears could be heard from the stone and Bronwyn leant forward to see the hazy image of a young girl. She was black-haired and blue-eyed and had tears streaming down her face.

'I don't know what to do,' she whimpered. 'Tell me what to do. They're hitting people with axes and I hid and I can't find Alahan and I took the stone and I hid.' The words tumbled out one after the other.

'Ingrid,' snapped Hasim, 'calm down. I need you to tell me what's happened. Breathe deeply and start again. Can you do that for me?'

Bronwyn was impressed with the way Hasim dealt with the young Ranen girl.

Algenon Teardrop's daughter paused and sniffed loudly several times, rubbing the tears from her eyes with the sleeve of her blue tunic.

'Father left a few weeks ago in his ship. He had lots and lots of men with him and they were going to rescue Uncle Magnus. I overheard them talking, they didn't think I was listening, but I was and I heard them.'

Horrock leant back. Bronwyn guessed he was pleased to hear the news of Algenon's launch, but concerned about what was happening in Fredericksand.

'Okay, then what happened?' Hasim asked gently.

Ingrid starting crying again as she said, 'Then the men from Jarvik turned up yesterday and started hurting people and they broke into the hall and smashed father's chair and they were looking for me, but they couldn't find me so they burnt down our house and started chanting things about a new high thain.' Again, the words were jumbled and Hasim shook his head trying to make sense of the child's speech.

'Men from Jarvik, what are they playing at?' Horrock directed the question at no one in particular and was growing more and more concerned with each passing moment.

'Ingrid, you're okay, I won't let them hurt you,' said Hasim with sincerity, 'but you need to focus. Imagine you're a thainess and Fredericksand is your city. Okay?'

Ingrid nodded and stopped crying momentarily, her big blue eyes pleading for Hasim to help her.

The Karesian picked up the cloud stone and tried to smile. 'What happened to your father?'

Ingrid was fighting back tears and she looked away, biting her lip and sniffing again.

'The big man that kicked over his chair was shouting about father being at the bottom of the Kraken sea. It's not true, is it? It can't be true. Father is the strongest man in the world and nothing can kill him.' Her words were at the very edge of despair and she desperately wanted someone to tell her that her father was alive and well.

Hasim, Bronwyn and Horrock shared dark looks across the table, but none of them said anything. Bronwyn could tell that Horrock was fighting back his anger and Hasim was close to tears himself as he spoke to Ingrid again.

'Where are you right at this moment, little wolf?' Hasim asked.

'I'm hiding in the monster man's chapel. I don't think the men with axes will look for me here. I need to find Alahan, he'll know what to do.' She was a little calmer now she had Hasim to talk to, but she was still not the ideal conveyer of dark news from Fjorlan.

'Monster man?' queried Horrock.

'It's what she calls Samson the Liar,' Hasim replied, not taking his eyes from the cloud stone, 'the old-blood of Fredericksand; she was always fascinated by him.'

Bronwyn knew of old-bloods – those who had the blood of Giants – but she had never seen one. They were supposedly extinct

476

in Tor Funweir, though stories occasionally surfaced of strange, semi-human beings hiding in caves or high up in mountain passes.

'Do you know who the big man was?' Hasim asked Ingrid. 'The man who said your father was . . . dead.' He said the last would in a low whisper, trying to not make Ingrid cry any more.

'Yes, I saw him with father before the ships left. He's called Rulag Ursa. I think he's a battle-master or something but Wulfrick and Halla thought he was an idiot. He was mean about you too. He said you were just a spy but I stuck up for you.'

Hasim flashed a weary smile at her. 'I'm lucky to have friends like you, little wolf.' He was concentrating hard on the cloud stone and Bronwyn could see he was struggling hard to think what to say to the girl.

'If Algenon's dead . . .' began Horrock, 'I don't want to think about what happened to the dragon fleet in the Kraken sea. Ursa would have had to kill thousands of men to get to the high thain.' He was speaking quietly and mostly to himself, keeping the words from Ingrid's ears.

'Ingrid, do you know what happened to Wulfrick?' Horrock asked.

'He left with Father on board the *Hammer of Fjorlan*. He wouldn't let them hurt Father, would he?'

A noise startled the young Ranen girl and she turned away from Hasim. 'Someone's coming. I can hear them on the stairs.' She was clearly frightened.

'Ingrid, stay quiet and find somewhere to hide,' Hasim ordered with authority in his voice.

Then a loud noise and, in the flowing mists around the image of Ingrid Teardrop, Bronwyn could see a huge figure move past her, holding an oversized hammer. Ingrid moved to stand behind the huge being, who put a protective arm around her.

'Samson, keep her safe,' shouted Hasim, recognizing the figure of Samson the Liar.

The images became even more blurred as other men entered the chapel and started to attack Samson. They could hear Ingrid screaming and she dropped the cloud stone at her feet and huddled in the corner. The view they were afforded was of the old-blood roaring and smashing his hammer into the traitorous battle-brothers of Jarvik.

Then darkness, as a stray axe blow smashed the cloud stone and cut off their view.

Hasim roared and threw the table across the room, breaking it against the wall. 'I'll feed the bastards to a fucking troll,' he shouted. 'She's just a child.' He was addressing the now silent cloud stone, wishing his words to be heard by the axe-men who pursued Ingrid. 'This is not honour . . . what is Rowanoco for if not for honour, you treacherous cunts.'

Horrock stood and grabbed hold of Hasim. The captain of Wraith Company was several inches taller than the Karesian and he held him firmly by the shoulders.

'Get a hold of yourself, Hasim, or I'll throw *you* against the wall,' he said with customary calmness.

Hasim was breathing heavily and his eyes were filled with rage, but he slowly slumped and just stared at Horrock.

'We're in trouble, captain,' he said quietly.

Both men sat down and Bronwyn saw a variety of expressions flow across their faces. Hasim's was still a mask of anger, but he was also deep in thought. Horrock's piercing eyes shot from side to side as if considering his options. Bronwyn herself was trying not to give in to despair. If the dragon fleet had been lost, her homeland would remain in the hands of the knights, and Ro Hail could not be held. The last few weeks had been filled with half-whispered hope that the Fjorlanders would come south and expel the knights from the Freelands of Ranen. It had happened once before, long ago, when the Ro had last tried to subjugate the Ranen. The men of Fjorlan were brutal and fearsome in battle, more warrior-like than the common men of the Free Companies, and even Horrock looked to them as their last hope for victory.

'How long until Johan Long Shadow gets here with Scarlet Company?' asked Hasim, after several minutes of silence.

'He said they'd leave just after I spoke to him . . . that was four days ago. If they ride hard, it'll still take a week to get here.' Horrock shrugged. 'If we can't count on help from Fjorlan . . .'

'We're fucked,' supplied Hasim, unhelpfully.

'We are, as you so eloquently say, fucked,' Horrock agreed. 'Either Rulag Ursa has gone mad or he is more power hungry than I thought. Not content with stealing the rulership of Jarvik, the bastard's getting delusions of grandeur.'

'Ursa used to be a friend of Hallam Pevain, didn't he?' asked Hasim.

Horrock nodded. 'Still is, as far as I know. Pevain helped him secure Jarvik, and they share a similarly lax attitude to honour.'

Bronwyn sensed that Horrock and Hasim were of the impression that a plot was being played out behind the scenes – a plot that had led to Algenon Teardrop's death and would soon lead to the sacking of Ro Hail.

Horrock started nodding to himself, as if he'd decided on a course of action. 'Okay, we leave,' he said. 'We can pack up food and provisions and be out of this death trap by nightfall. We'll head east and join up with Johan and Scarlet Company.'

* * *

Time moved at an agonizingly slow pace as the people of Wraith Company feverishly gathered their belongings and loaded carts with food and supplies. Word of Algenon's death and the presumed loss of the dragon fleet spread quickly through the city and Bronwyn detected a definite change in the demeanour of the Ranen. Before, they had stubbornly held on to the belief that if they could hold Ro Hail for a day or two, help would come, first from Scarlet Company, then from the north, and the knights of the Red could be pushed back. As she looked over their faces now, she saw men and women fearful for their lives in the knowledge that they simply couldn't win.

Haffen still wanted to stay and he didn't join the others in packing for a swift retreat. Instead, he stayed at his position on the forward battlements, keeping a silent vigil out towards the

Grass Sea. Horrock assured them that Haffen would be at the front of the retreating company and simply needed time to come round to the idea of running away rather than fighting. These were tough people, and Bronwyn could see that none of them liked the situation, where fighting was simply not an option. The Free Companies could not hope to match the armies of Tor Funweir when it came to skill, equipment or tactics, but they had always had an indomitable spirit that made them fearsome in combat. As the people of Wraith Company said goodbye to their home, the hardest thing of all was the realization that they would probably never return. Aside from the two hundred and fifty warriors, Wraith Company numbered some four hundred men, women and children who were not fighters, who were undertaking most of the preparations for the evacuation of Ro Hail.

Hasim had been quiet most of the day, confining himself to assisting by loading carts and weaponry for the long journey east. Whenever Bronwyn had seen him he'd looked close to tears, and she guessed that the probable death of Ingrid Teardrop was affecting him. The roguish Karesian had often spoken of his fondness for Fredericksand and his respect for the house of Teardrop, whether it was his friend Magnus, the high thain Algenon, or the children. The young warrior Alahan and the spirited Ingrid were like family to him. He was unique among Karesians in that he didn't seem to mind the weather in the far north and preferred the food and drink of Fjorlan to that of his desert homeland.

As evening fast approached, Bronwyn found herself with Stone Dog and Freya helping an old man of Wraith to climb the steps out of the basement.

'I've lived here all my life,' the old man muttered as he saw the darkening sky. 'If I were a few years younger, I'd show those damnable knights a thing or two about Wraith Company.'

'And they'd run, shrieking in terror, I'm sure,' quipped Stone Dog, as he held the man's arms and ushered him towards an empty wooden cart in the central courtyard.

Next to it were several dozen other carts loaded with all manner of belongings and supplies. Ro Hail may have been a ruin, but it had also been home to several hundred people, and Bronwyn felt sad looking at the piles of items of personal significance. She saw a mud-stained toy bear sitting in a basket next to an old flute and a dirty rocking horse. Another cart contained tables and chairs taken from the underground rooms, and a third was full to bursting with clothing and linen.

Plenty of carts already had drivers and it looked as if the population would be ready to leave by nightfall. They clustered in small family groups around their carts, and while most were unhappy to be leaving their home, Bronwyn could sense a community spirit that enabled them to remain upbeat as they wrapped up warm and prepared to strike out towards the realm of Scarlet Company.

Nearer the central courtyard, waiting by the gate, were the warriors of Wraith. All were attired in chain mail and heavily armed with axes, hammers and short bows for hunting. There was little talk amongst them, save for occasional jokes about the knights of the Red and vaguely formed plans to defecate in the courtyard as a welcoming gift to the Ro.

Haffen still stood on the battlements above the gatehouse, though he was now little but a shadow in the twilight. His back was facing the courtyard and Horrock had told them he'd keep watch until the last possible moment. Bronwyn thought that time was rapidly approaching, and she saw Hasim mounting the steps towards Haffen.

They helped the old man into a seated position in the back of the cart and Bronwyn watched Haffen and Hasim, waiting for them to come down and sound the evacuation. Instead, however, they were discussing something, and Haffen was gesturing off to the south-east. Hasim was peering into the grey evening and the two men were becoming animated as they spoke.

All of a sudden, Haffen turned sharply and scanned the courtyard. His eyes fixed on Horrock Green Blade standing among the carts and he shouted, 'Horrock, get up here.' His voice was urgent.

The people of Wraith stopped their own conversations and craned to look up at Haffen. The captain of Wraith Company appeared concerned as he walked rapidly from the carts to the stone steps. Bronwyn quickly left Stone Dog and moved to join the captain, as she'd decided shortly after arriving that she wasn't going to let anything happen without her knowing about it. She was still a noble and she felt that the least she could do was to listen to the others and offer counsel if she were able.

Horrock glanced at her as she joined him, but said nothing as the two of them rapidly ascended the steps. Once they reached the battlements, Bronwyn glanced out across the darkening Grass Sea and breathed a little easier when she didn't see any immediate cause for alarm. No campfires or other indicators of an advancing army were visible and she hoped whatever Haffen had spotted was not a precursor to an imminent attack.

'We're ready to leave, Haffen. What's the alarm?' Horrock asked wearily.

Haffen was still pointing off towards the south-east, roughly the same direction from which Bronwyn had approached Ro Hail two weeks ago. Hasim was standing next to him and peering along the length of his arm.

'Look over there, by the first line of trees,' Haffen said to his captain.

Horrock leant forward over the battlements.

'Are you sure you're not just looking for a reason to stay,' Bronwyn asked Haffen, trying to maintain a light mood.

He glared at her and replied, 'Just look over there, Bronwyn, and tell me if you see something by the tree line.'

She stood next to Hasim and took a long look out into the twilight. The trees began at the furthest extent of her vision and she could barely make out the area as the sky rapidly darkened.

The small copse was arranged in several lines and blowing gently in the wind. As they blew back, Bronwyn thought she saw something shining in the darkness – a dull, silvery surface which was out of place among the trees. All three involuntarily leant forward and Bronwyn held her breath as she saw, in a gap between the branches, an armoured knight, on horseback. with a red tabard. It was a momentary glimpse, nothing more, but a quick glance at the others' faces told her they had seen it too.

'Rowanoco save us,' said Haffen, 'that's a knight of the Red.'

Their eyes remained locked on the tree line as the quickening wind revealed a second knight and then a third and then, with a heavy gust, a full column of knights was briefly visible in the distance.

They remained silent for a moment before Horrock turned swiftly, strode to the inner edge of the battlements, and roared down at the assembled people of Wraith.

'The time to flee has passed . . . the men of Ro have come and we must fight for our land.' He paused for a moment while those below looked up with astonishment on their faces and fear in their eyes. 'Strength, my friends,' shouted Horrock. 'Strength for our sons and our daughters . . . if we are to die on this ground, defending this land.' His voice rose. 'We will make those that take our lives remember the night they fought the free people of Wraith.' His words carried conviction and Bronwyn could see the people stirred with anticipation, fear and rising bloodlust.

Haffen moved to join Horrock. 'We defend this ground,' ordered the captain. 'Get the wagons out of sight, the women and children into the basement and you lot,' he pointed to the battle-brothers of Wraith, 'kill anything that tries to breach the wall.'

'To your stations,' Haffen said quietly.

Movement erupted from below as they hurriedly carried out their instructions. The wagons were hastily pulled out of the way and into covered buildings to the north of the ruined town. The women, children and others who couldn't fight were corralled by Freya Cold Eyes into the basement complex, and Bronwyn saw the axe-men in the courtyard move quickly to the wooden fortifications.

'Go with Freya,' Hasim said to Bronwyn as they stood on the forward battlements.

'You know I'm not going to, so why do you ask?' she replied petulantly.

He turned to direct a hard stare at her. 'Because you're the lady of Ro Canarn and nothing would be served by you dying under a knight's blade.' He was deadly serious and Bronwyn noted the real concern for her safety in his words.

'Get the throwing-axes stowed, bundles at every point of the courtyard,' Haffen was shouting nearby. 'Stone Dog, you're up here with me.'

Bronwyn stepped close to Al-Hasim to speak more privately. 'I know you care, Karesian. Though I'm sure not wanting to annoy my brother has a lot to do with it . . . but I know you care all the same.'

'Just go with Freya,' he repeated tenderly, slowly reaching down to hold her hand.

Bronwyn involuntarily pulled it away. 'Don't do that,' she said. 'You're worried about the knights and it's making your head go soft.' She smiled at the Karesian scoundrel – a man, far from home, who'd found himself fighting alongside Ranen for a patch of land that was not his own. 'If the last few weeks have taught us anything, it's that survival is always possible, no matter what the odds.'

'This isn't an adventure, Bronwyn,' he said with sadness in his eyes. 'This is a war. I've never fought in one before, either. I've always gone out of my way to avoid them.' He reached for her hand again. 'Look around . . . look at Haffen, at Horrock, at all those people down there . . . by morning they will all be dead. If you're in the basement with the others, they may just spare your life.'

They stood looking at each other for several moments, saying nothing, until Bronwyn saw something bright on the distant horizon and turned. Hasim was still holding her hand and she found that she liked the warmth of it. The two of them moved side by side to look southwards and saw a line of fire in the distance.

'Haffen,' Hasim called over his shoulder. 'The knights mean to bombard us.' His words were quiet and solemn, and as Bronwyn peered into the twilight she could make out a heavy catapult under each fiery glow.

Haffen looked and swore loudly to the sky before quickly turning and shouting to the courtyard, 'Catapults, take cover.'

The men below ran for the cover of stone just as the audible sound of wood flexing signalled the release of flaming rocks.

The sky erupted in light as several dozen catapults shot trails of fire from the horizon towards the city. Bronwyn watched with wide eyes as the fire moved slowly through the sky and then thundered over her head. Horrock appeared behind them and dragged her and Hasim behind the battlements.

'Incoming!' shouted the captain of Wraith Company.

The men below took cover as the first flaming rock crashed into the courtyard, scattering the remaining carts and lighting up the ruins of Ro Hail. More rocks followed and wood and flame erupted across the courtyard, crushing men and breaking the fortifications. Men aflame ran frantically to find water or dropped to roll on the ground. Most of the wooden constructions were still intact, but some were on fire and Bronwyn gasped as she saw Freya, still above ground, running to a water barrel. The men of Wraith had secreted barrels of flammable pitch around the courtyard in preparation for use against the knights, and they hurried to move them away from the fires.

Then a horn sounded from the Grass Sea and a roar followed, signalling the knights' advance.

'To your stations,' Horrock ordered quietly as he unsheathed his two-headed axe and moved along the battlements.

Haffen took a last deep breath and turned to Bronwyn and Hasim. 'Let's die well, shall we?' he said with a vicious grin.

Hasim and Bronwyn shared a meaningful look and she realized he was still holding her hand.

* * *

The men of Wraith were poised behind the battlements as more rocks thudded into the outer walls and the reconstructed gates. Bronwyn was crouched above the gatehouse next to Al-Hasim, with Haffen and a dozen more members of Wraith Company on guard next to them. The knights were arrayed across the plain to the south, maybe five hundred of them, identified by Hasim as the army's advance guard. The knights of the Red shouted challenges at the battlements and banged their longswords on their red tabards. The catapults had been wheeled closer but now threw no fire. Instead, they heaved huge rocks into the air, designed to smash the walls and open the gate.

There had been no offer of parley and Bronwyn surmised that the knights simply planned to clear Ro Hail and hold it as a staging area. They had not surrounded the ruined town, but the Ranen made no attempt to escape. The knights had large warhorses and could easily ride down anyone who tried to break free from the barricades. She considered counselling surrender, but the faces of the Ranen warriors around her told of their intention to stay hidden until they saw the chance to kill.

They had no catapults or artillery with which to answer the bombardment and Horrock had quickly ordered them to take cover and remain patient. The knights would not have seen the majority of the Ranen, and Horrock was hoping they would enter the city unaware of those lying in wait for them. His tactical mind was focused on how to cause the most damage to the advance guard of knights and to buy time for the carts to escape via the north, where Freya had led most of the non-combatants through the underground complex.

Bronwyn could barely see down into the courtyard, but she could make out a large space filled only with the burning remnants of smashed carts and a few dead bodies. Patience was clearly not a common trait among the Free Companies and the men were shaking with battle fervour as they waited for the knights to enter the killing ground.

The wall shook as more boulders thudded into the stone and Bronwyn hunkered down behind the battlements. Hasim was still with her and had adopted a protective, crouched position above her, his scimitar held threateningly in his hand.

Then the sound of splintered wood sounded from below and the main gates of Ro Hail flew inwards. The knights of the Red let out a raucous cheer and a horn sounded to signal the charge. In unison, the column of five hundred knights wheeled their horses and rode hard for the open gates.

'Steady,' shouted Horrock, as the advance guard formed into a line narrow enough to pass through the gatehouse. 'Mark your targets well and make your aim true . . . I want fifty dead in the first volley.'

The Ranen, hidden below raised wooden fortifications, were poised for action. Each man held two throwing-axes, one in each hand, and close to a hundred of the battle-brothers of Wraith had been designated as axe-hurlers. Their job was to thin the ranks in preparation for a second line of Ranen to emerge at ground level and roll barrels of flaming pitch towards the mounted knights. If that didn't force the knights to retreat, the third rank, which included Hasim, Horrock and Haffen – and Bronwyn – would emerge and engage the knights in close combat.

Horrock held his axe up in readiness and shouted, 'Hold . . .'

The knights reached the southern wall and turned sharply to aim their horses at the gateway.

'Hold,' roared Horrock a second time, as the knights reached the gate and began to enter the courtyard.

'Hold,' he shouted for the last time, his voice raised above the sound of the armoured knights.

The men of Ro flooded in. Bronwyn was taken aback my how many there were. Five hundred fully armoured knights of the Red rode into the courtyard and fanned out in practised fashion. They held longswords aloft and roared challenges and promises of death at the men of Ranen.

'Now,' bellowed Horrock, and he stood and turned to face the advance guard of knights.

There was barely a moment between his command and the first volley of axes. The Ranen rose as one from their places of concealment overlooking the courtyard and shouted words of defiance as one hundred axes were hurled at the knights.

The ruined city burst into life as the men of Wraith Company unleashed their pent-up anger against the men of Ro. The sound was deafening and Bronwyn couldn't hear any of the knights over the shouting of the axe-men, but her vantage point gave her a good view of the courtyard and she saw men and horses hit by razor-sharp throwing-axes.

Horrock's demand that there be fifty dead in the first volley was close to the mark, as heads were cleaved, armour split, limbs severed and horses lamed or killed.

'This is the land of Wraith,' roared Haffen, standing high on the forward battlements and raising his axe above his head. 'You will not take it while we live.'

The knights had been taken aback by the first volley, but recovered quickly and Bronwyn saw their captain, protected by a circular shield, give orders to storm the barricades and kill the Ranen.

Then the second volley. Their aim was truer now and no few heads were split by the whirling steel of Wraith Company.

'That's it, lads.' Haffen continued to shout from the gatehouse. 'Show the bastards how the Ranen do things.'

Bronwyn and Al-Hasim were still behind the forward battlements, though less concerned to hide now the trap had been sprung. Bronwyn could still see the catapults across the misty plains to the south, but the bombardment had stopped once the knights had breached the town.

The two volleys of throwing-axes had killed or incapacitated more than a hundred of the knights and riderless horses were loose in the courtyard. Knights who were unhurt but had been unhorsed now pulled themselves to their feet.

'Fire the bastards,' shouted Horrock from his position on the stairs.

All around the ground-level barricades, flaming torches sprang into life as the second wave of Wraith Company opened wooden hatchways and rolled heavy barrels at the knights of the Red. Each was lit by a long wick at the end and several had been breached with axes to hasten the spread of the fire, as twenty or so barrels of sticky, flaming pitch raced towards the attackers.

The knights couldn't react quickly enough and were engulfed in flames within seconds. Screaming filled the courtyard as frightened horses reared and threw their riders. One clumsily stamped on a flaming barrel and sprayed sticky flames across the cobbles, setting light to a group of knights who were getting back to their feet in the middle of the killing ground.

Order disappeared from the knights' advance as flaming men and horses flailed around in an attempt to douse the fire. Bronwyn winced and turned away from the grisly scene.

The wooden barricades were splashed with water to stop the fire spreading to the Ranen defences, and the few knights who attempted to climb the fortifications were swiftly cut down by the defenders. The knight captain was alive and whirling his longsword defiantly overhead, mimicking Haffen's gesture.

'Rally to me,' he shouted at his remaining knights.

Less than half of the five hundred knights were still ready for combat and many of those had been unhorsed or were corralled by lines of flame and dead horses. The fire barrels had robbed them of any immediate chance of storming the barricades, but now they regrouped.

'To arms,' commanded Horrock, drawing his double-headed axe and descending the stairs to the raised wooden fortifications.

'That's us,' said Al-Hasim quietly to Bronwyn. 'Take this.' He handed her a small wooden shield. 'You've a better chance of staying alive with this than if you just rely on that big knife.' He pointed to her short sword.

'After you,' said Bronwyn, after a deep breath.

Haffen was nearby but had already begun to sprint across the high walls to join his captain. Other men of Wraith, wielding a variety of heavy axes and hammers, moved quickly to defend the inner fortifications and Bronwyn could see long spears being used by the axe-hurlers.

As she turned from the gatehouse, something caught her eye and she paused. 'Hasim,' she shouted. 'Look!'

Across the misty plain, just beyond the position of the catapults, dust was rising from the Grass Sea. Bronwyn could see an enormous line of horses riding into view. They were too numerous for her to count. High overhead, two banners flew erratically in the evening wind. One was the white eagle of Ro Tiris and the other the ominous purple sceptre of the clerics of nobility. Bronwyn swore to herself as the bulk of the king's army appeared within sight of Ro Hail.

Hasim joined her and looked out at the army of Ro arrayed across the Grass Sea. 'Jaa preserve us,' he said. 'So many . . .'

Bronwyn thought she detected fear on the Karesian's face.

'Horrock,' he shouted, 'it seems the king has arrived.'

If his words were heard, there was no sign that the captain of Wraith Company was going to alter his plan. Instead, he joined the third wave of defenders and began hacking at the few knights who were trying to breach the fortifications.

'Come on, they need help.' Hasim grabbed Bronwyn's arm and led her down the stone steps to the inner barricades.

She steadied herself and felt her hand shaking as it gripped the hilt of her short sword. She'd killed before, in the tunnels of Ro Canarn as she and Hasim were making their escape, but this was different – this was a battle and, if she could not strike to kill, she knew she'd be useless.

They reached the battlements and joined the other defenders. The knights had regrouped and were attempting to fight their way on to the wooden ramparts. They had only limited success as the long spears held by the axe-hurlers were keeping them at a distance, but Bronwyn thought it could only be a matter of time.

The knight captain was still on his horse directing his troops and determination was on the faces of the men of Ro as their professionalism and skill returned. They hacked at the ground-level wooden hatches and several of the Ranen who had lit the barrels died as longswords smashed and cut at the gaps between the wooden planks.

'Get those hatches open,' ordered the knight captain, shouting at the top of his voice to be heard over the melee.

Bronwyn found herself at the edge, looking down on the knights trying to break open the defences. She locked eyes with a man of Ro, burnt from the fire and angrily hacking at the wood. A moment later he took a spear to the chest and fell to the cobbled floor. A second man took his place and then another joined him as they began to smash open the hatch.

Hasim appeared next to her with a spear in his hands and grunted with exertion as he skewered a man through the neck. The blood sprayed over his fellow knights, who yelled angry insults and challenges from below.

Then a barrel of pitch that hadn't split open was thrown from the courtyard up on to the wooden battlements. Bronwyn held her breath as she saw it smash near to her and erupt into flame, sending two Ranen diving forward from their positions of safety. The flames spread quickly and she held up her shield arm to block the heat of the fire.

'Put that fire out,' shouted Horrock from nearby.

Several men ran to grab buckets of water, but the sticky pitch had quickly attached itself to a large area of wood and the fire was spreading.

With a roar of defiance, Captain Horrock Green Blade jumped down from the battlements and became the first man of Wraith to engage the knights in close combat. He killed one quickly, cleaving in his chest with a mighty blow from his axe, but other knights moved to engage him.

'Time to get bloody, lads,' announced Haffen with a grim smile, as he joined his captain in the fray.

Others followed, chanting, 'For Wraith!' as they set about the knights of the Red, until the majority of the third wave had left the fortifications and entered the courtyard.

'Stay here,' ordered Hasim, dropping the spear and drawing

his scimitar and kris blade.

'Not on your life,' Bronwyn replied.

He shot her a look of frustration but didn't argue as the two of them jumped down together.

'Stay close to me, then,' he conceded. 'Strike at the neck and head and keep that shield up.'

The fight they joined was brutal and desperate, with many Ranen going berserk as they hacked at the armoured knights. Haffen was particularly vicious and foam began to appear at the corners of his mouth as he grasped his axe in both hands and whirled round, killing anyone close to him. The knights initially backed away from the ferocious axe-man, but Bronwyn could tell that the men of Wraith were outmatched in terms of skill.

She could see Micah Stone Dog fighting desperately, with his back to a wall, against a young knight. Nearby, Horrock was engaged against two Ro, his size and strength the only thing preserving him. As Bronwyn began to sense hope slipping away she was faced with a battered knight launching a high attack at her. Without thinking, she raised her shield and buckled under the strength of the blow. Another high swing followed, and another, until she was barely able to stand.

'No way to treat a lady, you horse-fucker,' shouted Hasim, as he appeared behind the knight and deftly opened the man's throat with a single cut.

'I said, stay near me,' he repeated as he pulled Bronwyn to her feet. 'I will *not* let you die here.'

They fought back to back, both relying on speed to keep the knights at bay. Bronwyn began to use her shield more and more, with only occasional swift sword cuts directed at the attackers' faces and necks. She blinded one man and severed another's ear, but received several small wounds herself. Hasim was faring better and was largely unhurt as he killed another man with a well-placed thrust of his kris knife. Kicking the man off his blade, he shoved Bronwyn back out of the way as a huge knight charged at them.

'Fight me, you Karesian whoreson,' the knight shouted as he smashed his sword down at Hasim's head.

He narrowly avoided the blow by darting backwards and sticking his scimitar into the knight's side. The huge man cried out in pain, but grabbed the protruding blade and wrenched it from Hasim's grasp. Kicking out, he sent the Karesian tumbling to the ground.

'Bronwyn . . .' he shouted, as the knight advanced on the young lady of Canarn.

The Ro was too caught up in battle fervour to notice the wound Hasim had given him and he likewise ignored a glancing blow from a thrown axe.

'Time to die, Black Guard,' the knight said with a grotesque grin.

As he raised his sword overhead to deliver a killing blow, he paused and his eyes grew wide as a knife pushed its way into his neck and Freya Cold Eyes appeared over his enormous shoulders. The old Ranen woman twisted the knife to make sure the knight was dead before she pulled it back and let him drop to the floor.

'Freya . . .' Bronwyn breathed with gratitude as she quickly stood up.

'Don't thank me, young lady, just be more careful.' The old axe-maiden was smiling but the blood spreading down her face told Bronwyn she had been fighting as hard as any of them.

Hasim retrieved his scimitar from the fallen knight and pulled Bronwyn back out of the melee.

'It's not just about Brom, okay? I will *not* let you die.' He repeated the same phrase and Bronwyn could sense deep sincerity in the Karesian scoundrel's words. 'Now, I know you won't take cover, but at least stay away from big bastards like him.' He gestured to the large dead knight.

Bronwyn nodded and tenderly touched Hasim's face. Without more words, they returned to the courtyard. It was difficult to see who had the upper hand, but Horrock and Haffen were still alive and causing their fair share of slaughter. She could no longer see Stone Dog; and the majority of the knights were now on foot, with their warhorses either running in wild circles or having left the ruins altogether.

The next few minutes passed agonizingly slowly as hacked body parts and sprayed blood turned the courtyard of Ro Hail into a butcher's yard. Bronwyn stayed clear of the central melee and remained with Hasim on the fringes. Somewhere in the middle, she could hear Horrock roar a challenge at the knight captain, and the scrum parted briefly to allow the two captains to meet in the centre.

The axe-hurlers had joined the fight and the knights were largely penned in. As Horrock and the knight captain clashed, the other fights slowed to keep half an eye on the two men, each side investing heavily in the survival of their commander. Even Haffen had pulled back to the edge of the melee to take a moment's rest and wipe the blood and sweat from his face.

Horrock did not fight as he had against Verellian two weeks before, but rather fought dirty, employing kicks and punches to keep the knight off balance. Bronwyn sensed the man of Wraith was a fast learner. The knight captain quickly became frustrated with Horrock's dishonourable fighting style, but was helpless to stop him as axe blows began to land on his plate armour. As his breastplate became dented, his parries grew more awkward until a feint opened him up and a thunderous downward strike split his head down the middle.

As the bloody mess that had been their commander fell in a heap to the ground, the remaining knights of the Red broke and began to fall back. It was a disorderly retreat, with most of the men on foot, and several more died as they turned to flee. The knights ran towards the open gateway and fled into the Grass Sea beyond, as Wraith Company held their weapons aloft and roared their victory to the sky.

'Stop fucking cheering,' shouted an exhausted Horrock. 'Put that fire out and barricade the gate.' His men paused for a moment, looking at their captain. 'Move!' he bellowed, causing every man to hurry back to his position.

Haffen led a group of warriors to the gateway and piled the broken wood up in some semblance of a gate, using spears to wedge the makeshift door in place. Several dozen men shuttled buckets of water to the burning barricades. The remainder fell to the ground from sheer exhaustion.

Hasim and Bronwyn made their way across the killing ground to where Horrock sat, panting heavily.

'That was just the advance guard,' said the Karesian.

Horrock looked up as if this information was not helpful, but, after a moment, he smiled a thin smile.

'I know, but at least we've made them pause.' He stood again and surveyed the defences.

Bronwyn thought that only around half of the inner wooden fortifications now provided some cover, and the fire had caused a large section to collapse entirely. The courtyard was littered with the dead and, though there were many more Ro bodies than Ranen, she was still shocked at how many men of Wraith had fallen.

'We can't hold if they storm again,' she said without thinking.

'True enough,' replied Horrock, standing next to her, 'but they don't know that.' He was still panting, but Bronwyn sensed steely resolve in his piercing blue eyes.

'If I know the knights of the Red,' began Hasim, 'and I think I do, I don't think they'll risk another frontal assault.' He pointed to the gates that Haffen was hastily rebuilding. 'If we get those looking solid again, I think they'll try something different. The knights don't like getting a bloody nose and they won't risk it again.'

'So they'll just throw more rocks at us?' Horrock asked with gallows humour.

Hasim nodded. 'Probably, yes. But they're more likely to encircle the city and starve us out. They have the numbers to do it and now they know we're prepared to fight . . .'

'Of course, there is someone whose counsel may be useful right now,' Bronwyn interjected, referring to Sir William of Verellian.

They both looked at her with doubt on their faces.

'He's still a knight of the Red, Bronwyn,' responded Hasim. 'He wouldn't want to be too helpful, I'd guess.'

'True, but he's honourable. I think he'd help in any way that meant fewer people were killed.' She considered and continued, 'At least he'd be able to tell us what they're likely to do next.'

Hasim smiled. 'So, you're saying you don't trust my knowledge of knightly tactics?'

A man offered Horrock a bowl of water and he immediately washed his bloodstained face and then shook his head rapidly from side to side. As he wiped his face with a rag he stood up. 'Your knowledge may be extensive, Hasim, but you're not actually a knight,' he said.

His men were busily moving around the fortifications, repairing whatever could be quickly mended, moving bodies from the court-yard and collecting throwing-axes.

'If you'll take an order from me, Karesian, go and fetch the red man,' said Horrock, without turning away from his men. 'Find Stone Dog and take him with you . . . and keep the knight chained.'

Al-Hasim was not a Ranen, let alone a man of Wraith Company, but he responded to Horrock's order with only a slight pause, moving quickly away and across to the north side of the courtyard. Bronwyn followed his movements, mostly to confirm that Stone Dog was still alive.

'You did well, my lady,' Horrock said suddenly. 'You're covered in blood, have dents in your shield and you're still alive . . . this bodes well.'

'Freya had to save my life and I tried to stay away from the main fight, but yes, I'm still alive. A lot of your men aren't,' she responded sadly, unable to turn away from the butchered men in the courtyard.

Freya and several young Ranen from the basement were taking note of the dead and moving the wounded to the safety of the underground complex. The dead knights were treated with respect, but with no space to take them inside, they were simply stacked off to the side in a rough pyre. Haffen was still doing his best to repair the main gate. The wooden fortifications would function as axe-throwing platforms, but would be useless as a defensive position.

'You need a longer reach,' Horrock said to her out of the blue.

'Er, sorry . . . what do you mean?' Bronwyn asked.

'The shield works fine, but you actually need to attack occasionally, and that short sword and your short arms don't help.' Bronwyn laughed at his familiar manner. 'Ever swung an axe?' he asked.

'My brother taught me how to use a sword, but I hadn't attacked to kill until a month ago when we escaped Canarn,' she said quietly. 'I hadn't really thought about killing men. I suppose there were too many other things to think about.'

Horrock narrowed his blue eyes. 'I met Brom once. A cold bastard from what I remember.' He smiled. 'You're the same. Most people agonize over their first kill. You didn't even think about it.'

'There's a lot at stake . . . my home, my people, my family's honour . . .' She bowed her head. 'While Canarn is occupied, I'm not allowed to be squeamish.'

CHAPTER NINE

BROTHER LANRY IN
THE CITY OF RO CANARN

IT WAS JUST beginning to get dark as Lanry began his nightly
walk to the marshal's office. Sir Pevain insisted he arrive before
the mercenaries' nightly drunken ritual began. They were
difficult enough to deal with when sober, but Lanry disliked the
viciousness that accompanied their more drunken moments. He
had a great need of extra food and water. The people of Ro Canarn
who had stayed indoors during the battle were beginning to suffer
starvation. The mercenary knight had turned off the water pumps
and was using his control over food and water to keep the population
in order. The common people were being denied basic necessities,
and those who had recently lost their homes and families faced an
uncertain future.

'Fulton, hurry up,' Lanry said to the former taverner who
pulled the cart behind him. 'It's getting dark.'

'Why don't *you* pull the cart?' Fulton shot back, with droplets
of sweat forming on his forehead.

Lanry put a hand on the man's shoulder and smiled. 'Because
I'm a fat old man with a bad back and, if I was pulling it, we'd not
get there till tomorrow,' the cleric said with humour.

Lanry tried to stay jolly despite the broken town around him,
and since the death of Duke Hector the people had looked to the
cleric for leadership. He was not a man to abandon his home to
the ravages of war, and being a churchman of the Brown meant he
was largely immune to the torture and death that his fellow men of

Canarn had to endure. He'd seen much of both over the last month and had come to realize that the knights of the Red had a very different way of doing the One's work. The Brown clerics represented the One's aspect of poverty and charity, and Lanry had devoted his life to the care of the people of Ro Canarn. He had been the only churchman in the town and Duke Hector had allowed him to stay on sufferance. It had taken Lanry several years to convince the duke of his good intentions and now, twenty years after he had built the small Brown church, he was needed more than ever.

He smiled to himself as he recalled drawing his heavy quarterstaff and joining the duke's guard in defence of the town. He felt a little embarrassed at having actually clubbed a Red knight over the head and he secretly hoped that the man was all right. Lanry was not a fighter, but he had felt it was his duty to fight for his home as much as any other man of Canarn.

They led the cart past the main square and towards the lord marshal's office overlooking the docks. Pevain had killed the marshal and taken over the stone building, holding court like a conquering hero and dispensing random justice upon those who displeased him. The mercenary knight had executed more people than Lanry wished to recall, and he found himself ministering now to less than half the population. They still looked to him for guidance, but he was secretly crying over the torment his people had to endure. He'd seen children die of starvation, and with the lack of clean water disease was beginning to appear. Pevain gave him a daily ration, but it was barely enough for a hundred people and Lanry found himself having to arrange a rota system for the survivors. If a man got water one day, he'd have to do without the next. It was a painful thing for the cleric to have to do, but so far it had kept most of them alive.

'What if we just wait until they pass out with the wine and then help ourselves?' suggested Fulton, as they neared the tower of the World Raven.

'Interesting idea . . . though please be good enough to tell me what happens the day after you pass out from drinking?' responded Lanry, trying to be as tolerant as possible.

'You wake up with a headache . . . I do, anyway.'

'And what do you think these men will do when they *wake up with a headache* and realize we've pilfered their food and water?'

The taverner considered this. 'I suppose they'd come looking for us,' he eventually conceded.

'Endurance is our greatest weapon now, my friend,' Lanry said gently, placing a reassuring hand on Fulton's shoulder. 'Mark my words, your tavern will be open for business again one of these days.'

Lanry tried to remain optimistic when he was around the other men of Canarn, even going so far as to suggest that young Lord Bromvy would return to set them free. In private, however, the Brown cleric was close to despair and held out precious little hope that their situation would improve.

They rounded a street corner and the marshal's office came into view. Previously, the area had been a thriving port, with several good-humoured taverns and a small auditorium for fish trading. Now, everywhere was boarded up or torn down and the only activity was in the office itself, which had been turned into an improvised drinking establishment and headquarters for Pevain's mercenaries. Lights were on throughout and, even half a street away, activity could be seen and heard. The mercenaries were too numerous for all of them to find quarters within the building and so a rough camp had formed in the open square outside. They lounged around small fires, passing bottles of stolen wine and telling unlikely tales of their sexual prowess. Lanry recognized the faces of rapists, murderers and thieves – men who had been living off the bones and flesh of Ro Canarn for more than a month. With the exception of the dozen or so men on patrol in the town, they could all be found here, and Lanry gritted his teeth as he prepared to walk among them.

'Just keep your head down and ignore them,' he said over his shoulder to Fulton, who was becoming increasingly agitated.

They were noticed quickly and Lanry heard a number of off-colour comments thrown at them – nasty challenges to their masculinity and some physical gestures that the Brown cleric didn't fully understand. Dirty, bearded faces looked up at them, displaying unpleasant sneers. Lanry smiled politely, aware that these men wouldn't harm him, but making sure that Fulton stayed close behind him.

'What do you want, boy-fucker?' barked a toothless mercenary who stood nearby, on guard outside the marshal's office.

He was often the man who greeted Brother Lanry as he arrived for supplies each evening. The mercenary was illiterate and had no doubt had a poor start in life, but Brother Lanry still smiled at the thought of smashing his quarterstaff into the scumbag's face.

'I'm sorry, are you talking to me?' Lanry replied absently.

'You know I'm fucking talking to you, cleric,' said the mercenary with well-practised aggression.

'And you know what I want, so we're both being stupid.' Lanry directed a laconic expression at the idiot and then shooed him away dismissively. 'I'm not here to speak to you . . . I don't even like looking at you, so get out of my way,' the Brown cleric added.

Fulton narrowly suppressed a laugh and the mercenary looked confused, confirming Lanry's suspicions about his lack of education, but he got out of the way and they proceeded towards the open doorway.

'How do you get away with that?' asked Fulton quietly, with a nervous smile on his face.

'Because these people are worthy of nothing but scorn and sharp metal implements, my dear Fulton, and they're stupid enough not to realize how hateful they are.' He paused and turned to direct a serene smile at the taverner. 'I like to think that subconsciously they know they deserve these insults.' Lanry resumed walking, leaving Fulton looking confused as he followed on behind.

The door to the marshal's office used to be permanently open and any citizen of Canarn was able to enter freely. Since Sir Pevain had taken over, he'd stationed guards outside and only admitted people he wanted to see. The daily inquiries about food, water and housing bothered the mercenary knight and he had killed several men who had complained that their wine storehouse had been pillaged and burned down. Subsequently, the door had remained closed. Brother Lanry was the only citizen of Ro Canarn who Pevain would tolerate, and that was only because the mercenary was under orders not to harm him.

As Lanry and Fulton entered, an overpowering stench of wine and vomit assaulted their nostrils and both men involuntarily moved their hands to their mouths.

'Do they ever clean the place?' Fulton asked quietly.

'About as often as they clean themselves,' replied Lanry, 'and that, by the state of them, is infrequent.'

The door opened into the old town hall of Ro Canarn – a large, airy space that had been used variously as fish market, meeting place and assembly hall. The fishermen had stopped fishing now and the hall was little more than a dosshouse for Pevain's more trusted lieutenants. They lounged around on pillaged furniture, drinking stolen wine and eating stolen meat. These men were all of Ro, but belonged to the lowest level of society. They were swords for hire, men who'd found a way to indulge their fondness for killing, stealing and raping while still somehow remaining within the law. Lanry knew that criminality was a sketchy concept where war was concerned, but he still hoped that these scum would some day be made to answer for their cruelty.

They walked through the entrance hall, past small groups of black-armoured mercenaries, most of them the worse for drink, and ascended the central stairs to the marshal's office on the first floor. No more comments were directed at them and Fulton appeared a little more relaxed once they were away from the main force of mercenaries.

The taverner stopped at the top of the stairs and Lanry saw an expression of surprise and anger come over his friend's face.

'Fulton, what is it?' the cleric asked.

'That man . . .' he replied, pointing with a shaking hand at a large, bearded mercenary slouching on a bench outside Pevain's rooms. 'He's the one who . . . took Bella.'

Lanry frowned and remembered Fulton's cheerful wife. She was a cook who worked with her husband in the tavern they had owned. A mercenary had smashed his way into their home on the night of the attack and Bella had tried to fight him off with a kitchen knife. As a result, she'd been taken to the prison pens in the town square. Fulton had been trapped in the Brown church at the time and had only seen his wife again several nights later, as she was raped and beheaded by the man she'd tried to fight off – the man now laughing at some off-colour joke while relaxing outside his master's new office.

Lanry placed a restraining hand on Fulton's shoulder. 'Nothing will be served by you dying today, my friend,' the cleric said in a whisper. 'Just keep your head down and don't look at him.'

Fulton began to sob quietly, but he nodded and took heed of Lanry's counsel. The Brown cleric was as close to a leader as the people of Ro Canarn had left. Fulton was no warrior and he knew full well that Lanry's instruction was wise.

They walked past the man, who barely looked up from the conversation he was having with another mercenary, and Brother Lanry knocked on the office door.

'I'm busy,' was the immediate response from within.

'He's busy, brother,' repeated the man outside. 'Piss off and come back later.'

'If I do that, I'll be told that he's still busy,' said Lanry with as much pateince as he could muster. 'We do this every day. Can't I just glide past the usual dance of cock-waving and get to the part where I return to my church with food and water?'

The man laughed heartily and slapped Lanry on the back.

'You're all right, cleric,' he said with a smile, and banged on Pevain's door himself. 'Hallam, it's that Brown cleric.'

There was a momentary pause and then a frustrated voice from within said, 'All right, Lanry, get your clerical arse in here.'

Lanry smiled politely at the mercenary, taking care to keep Fulton as close to him as possible, turned the door handle and entered the marshal's office.

Within, he immediately averted his eyes from the spectacle of Sir Hallam Pevain, lounging back on his chair, his rough hand on the back of a young girl's head. Pevain's leather trousers were pulled down and the girl was crouched between his legs. There was a look of twisted pleasure on his face as he roughly jerked the girl's head back and forth, and she gripped his chair with red, trembling hands.

'I hope we're not disturbing you?' asked Lanry through gritted teeth, looking down at the floor.

'I said I was busy, cleric...' He didn't look at them.

He grabbed a handful of the girl's hair and pulled her away, making a loathsome sound of contentment as he did so. Lanry glanced up and recognized the girl. She was a servant from the inner keep, one of Lady Bronwyn's attendants. The cleric couldn't remember her name, but recalled having heard her sing at Duke Hector's birthday celebrations.

As Pevain roughly shoved her towards the door, the look on her face was of fear and revulsion. Brother Lanry stopped her momentarily, whispering, 'Strength, sister, strength and we will overcome.'

He hoped the words might help, but he also knew how petty they must sound to a young girl, no more than sixteen, who was daily being abused.

'Same time tomorrow, darlin',' said Pevain with a chuckle, as the girl hurriedly left the room.

Fulton hadn't looked up and Lanry thought that he ought to come alone in future, or at least leave his companion outside with the cart.

Lanry tried not to show his anger as he crossed the small office to stand in front of the desk. Pevain styled himself as some kind of military governor – a lesser master of Canarn now that Sir Rillion had made it clear he cared nothing for the common people. The knights of the Red were more honourable and, in their own way, kinder than the mercenaries. However, Lanry had not seen any of them since the larger force had moved through some two weeks ago, and he'd been stuck with Pevain and his bastards. Lanry wasn't sure whether *the bastards* was actually their name or just a fitting description, but either way the term had entered common usage.

'Food and water is it, Lanry?' asked Pevain, making a show of standing to fasten his trousers and stretch his back and arms.

'It is indeed. A little more than yesterday would be appreciated,' replied the cleric.

'You'll get what you get.' Pevain remained standing and glowered at Lanry. 'I only have so many supplies and my men need to eat and drink too.'

'But your men take it when they want it, my people have to ration the little I am allowed. People are dying, Pevain.'

The matter was serious and Lanry was responsible for their well-being now there was no duke to speak for them.

The mercenary laughed as though Lanry had said something funny. 'So, some peasant cunts lose a bit of weight . . . what's the big deal?'

Lanry clenched his jaw and felt a sudden urge to have a wash when he got home. Having to be in the presence of so refined a scumbag each day was not an easy thing to put up with.

'Just because you've killed half the population, it doesn't mean the remainder need any less food and water,' Lanry said, with as much restraint as he could manage. 'Wine we can do without, huge feasts of meat and fish are barely a distant memory, but bread, grain and water are essential . . . sir knight.'

Pevain moved round the desk and stood close to Brother Lanry. The knight was a very tall man and carried an unpleasant odour with him. The cleric had wondered recently whether Pevain actually cultivated the smell in order to make himself more memorable.

'Don't take things so seriously, Lanry. Why don't we open a bottle together and get some peasant bitch to make us glad we're men for a couple of hours?' Pevain's smile was almost as bad as the smell, and dirty, rotten teeth poked through his straggly black beard as he spoke.

'I am a cleric of the Brown first and foremost. I'll be sure to remind myself that I'm a man at a later date. For now, can I please have some supplies?' Lanry asked, allowing some offence to show in his voice.

Fulton was still looking at the floor and, aside from the odd frown of discomfort, the taverner had remained silent and expressionless. Pevain had not paid any particular attention to him up to this point but now he directed a questioning look at Lanry.

'Your friend looks nervous. Maybe he should be the one to remember he's a man.' The mercenary stepped in front of Fulton. 'How about it, little man? You want a girl to fuck?'

Lanry moved Fulton gently to the side and took his place under Pevain's glare. 'If you could . . . we are in a hurry,' he said politely.

'Very well.' The mercenary knight was irritated. 'You're all business, you church types. Follow me.'

Lanry breathed a little easier as Pevain walked to the side door and down the stairs beyond. The marshal's office was a stone structure on the outside but inside a latticework of wooden staircases led to various grain silos and food warehouses. In times of peace the storage spaces were used for salting and smoking meat and fish, and for stockpiling goods for the harsh winters of Canarn. While under the knights' occupation, the warehouses were largely used as a means to control the starving population.

Lanry and Fulton walked after Pevain and descended two flights of wooden stairs to a tunnel below. This led under the cobbled streets of the port side of Ro Canarn and was one of several entrances to the grain silos. They had been built underground by Duke Hector's father in order to protect against theft and to help preserve the goods. Formerly, the lord marshal had been responsible for them, but over the years Lanry had been in the town they'd been used less and less, as business flourished and the people had enjoyed several good harvests.

At the end of the tunnel more wooden staircases led back up to the streets. A small group of mercenaries was hanging around, watching the warehouses while drinking themselves insensible.

'All right, boss,' said one of the mercenaries by way of greeting to Pevain.

The knight ignored him and motioned for Lanry to ascend the nearest set of stairs.

'Are we not going to the warehouse?' the cleric asked.

'No,' replied Pevain. 'I thought that I'd have a few of my lads prepare your supplies ahead of time. It'll stop you looking longingly at the stuff you can't have.' His grotesque smile returned and Lanry felt a little sick. 'You see, brother,' he said, placing a patronizing arm round the cleric's shoulders, 'you need to know your place. I'm in charge here and that's not going to change. Get it?'

Lanry didn't look away from Pevain and smiled through gritted teeth. 'And if the supplies your men have prepared are not enough?'

'Then people may go hungry. It's up to you to make sure it goes far enough, brother. Isn't that what you Brown fuckers are all about? Charity and that?'

Pevain was as ignorant of charity as he was of kindness or honour, and Lanry again had to force himself not to be rude to the mercenary.

Not trusting himself to engage in further dialogue with the bastard – a term Lanry was beginning to think increasingly appropriate – the Brown cleric pulled himself up the steep wooden staircase and back up to the street. Fulton followed and they returned to the evening air of Canarn. They were just off the docks and underneath the tower of the World Raven. Lanry looked upwards and said a quiet prayer to Brytag, the Ranen god of luck and wisdom, before he was shoved out of the way by Pevain as the knight came out of the tunnel behind them.

At the side of the street, flanked by three mercenaries, were a number of barrels and a few sacks. Lanry estimated the contents would be barely enough for five hundred, let alone the two thousand hungry people who were waiting for food.

'Pevain, is this all?' Lanry asked without turning round.

'It is,' he replied. 'And you can address me as *sir knight*, cleric.'

'Very well. This isn't enough to stop starvation and I humbly request more . . . sir knight.' Lanry knew his duty to the people of Canarn must come before his personal feelings.

'Come back tomorrow, same time, and I'll see about a loaf or two extra,' Pevain replied, and the three mercenaries nearby chuckled to themselves.

'Fulton, go fetch the cart. I'll wait here,' Lanry said to the taverner.

His friend left quickly, and Lanry thought he'd be happier out of the presence of the mercenary knight.

Pevain let Fulton walk away towards the front of the marshal's office to retrieve the cart before he moved to stand in front of Brother Lanry.

'Right, you little shit-stain, now we can talk without the common citizenry listening, I want to make you an offer,' he said conspiratorially.

'I don't think I'd be interested in your offer, sir knight,' Lanry responded, with a slight bow of the head.

'Wait till you hear it.' Pevain was grinning broadly and his breath made Lanry feel nauseous. 'It might be a way for you to make things easier for yourself. After all, there's no reason why you and I shouldn't be friends.'

'I can think of several, sir knight, but none that I care to repeat to your face.'

Lanry was skirting round the edges of being rude, but he didn't want to push his luck too far. Pevain was unstable and, given sufficient motivation, Lanry was sure he'd ignore Rillion's order and kill the Brown cleric as soon as he'd kill anyone else.

'You're not an idiot, cleric,' said the knight, ignoring Lanry's half-insult. 'And you must appreciate that I'm in charge here and am gonna be for a while yet. So why make things difficult between us? If you play this right, I can see Brother Lanry becoming a rich man if he makes the right friends.'

Lanry smiled again, this time with his eyes locked on Pevain's. The knight was a large man, easily a foot taller than the Brown cleric, but Lanry didn't fear death and the sword and armour mattered little to him.

'You are a . . . singular man, with singular skills, sir knight. A humble cleric such as myself does not think of riches or station. We prefer to gain our reward in the grateful faces of our flock.' Inwardly, Lanry liked to play the piety card, and he saw a look of confusion come over Pevain's face, as if the mercenary simply didn't understand a man to whom money meant nothing.

'There must be something you want, cleric. Can the Brown take women?' he asked, raising his eyebrows in a suggestively vulgar expression.

'We can marry, yes,' Lanry replied. 'But not until our work for the One is completed, and I have much work left to do.'

Fulton appeared again at the corner of the marshal's office, pulling the cart behind him. Before he came within earshot, Pevain stepped closer to Lanry and whispered, 'All right, cleric, I understand. Just know that Hector is dead, Bromvy is dead and I'm all you've got left. You'd better get used to it.'

'Bromvy . . .?' queried Lanry, who had not heard that Hector's son had been captured, let alone killed. 'You know this?'

'It's only a matter of time. Purple clerics have been despatched after the lordling. Even with the nasty friends he's got, he's done for.' Pevain showed no respect towards the house of Canarn. 'So, unless Lady Bronwyn wants to ride into the city, I'd say the house of Canarn is dead and gone,' he added with a snarl.

'We'll see, sir knight,' was all Lanry said before turning to load the meagre supplies on to their cart.

* * *

The walk back to the Brown church was a sombre one. The streets were deserted and, once they were out of sight of the marshal's office, eerily silent as well. Fulton said nothing and merely concentrated on pulling the heavy cart over the uneven cobbles. It was a lighter load than Lanry had secured on previous evenings and he genuinely doubted the people of Canarn would survive much longer. Pevain had given them no new healing supplies and Lanry's skill would only go so far in helping those who were malnourished or injured. It would be a difficult night and, the cleric thought, it would get much worse before it got any better.

The Brown church of Canarn was a small building on the edge of the town square, previously a joyous place of market stalls and colour. Now, it resembled a cross between a builder's yard and a battleground, with wooden debris and the remnants of funeral pyres spread haphazardly across the cobbles. The pens that had been used to confine dissenting citizens were now empty, and the majority of the populace had returned to their houses, steadfastly refusing to give the mercenaries any excuse for further brutality. Those who had lost their homes during the battle or in the weeks that followed were staying in the vaults of the Brown church, which had formerly been used for storage and were now heaving with displaced common folk.

'It's not enough,' said Fulton, breaking the silence as they approached the church doors. 'There're two pregnant women, dozens of children and old people, and I've lost count of how many injured or starving. We can't live on porridge, dried fruit and water forever.'

'I know,' was Lanry's simple reply.

The Brown cleric paused before the door to his church and turned to face Fulton. He put an arm round the taverner's shoulder.

'Do you remember when Lord Bromvy had that tournament for his eighteenth birthday?'

Fulton's eyes widened slightly, as if he were trying to recall, and nodded slowly in response.

'Great fun, from what I remember,' supplied Lanry. 'Duke Hector allowed anyone to take part.' The cleric smiled. 'I even had a go at duelling with Brom. I lost, but he was nice enough not to crow about it.'

Fulton smiled weakly as he brought to mind the event that had taken place five years before. 'I think I unhorsed Haake in the joust,' he said. 'Though I'm pretty sure the guardsman let me win.'

'Do you remember what Duke Hector said as he gave out the prizes?' Lanry asked.

Fulton shook his head and Lanry placed a comforting arm round his friend's shoulder. Looking out across the deserted city of Canarn, the Brown cleric said, 'My memory may be failing me, but I think he said, *"Brothers and sisters, friends and family, we stand together as people of Canarn, people with an unbreakable spirit and inexhaustible warmth."'* Lanry was paraphrasing, but the words had stuck with him and he had recalled them often, particularly over the past month.

'Spirit and warmth need to be fuelled by food and water,' Fulton replied with a friendly smile.

'That may be true, but let's keep the old duke's words in mind as we try to make this stuff stretch, shall we?' He kept his arm round Fulton's shoulders and led him towards the door.

Within, the Brown church was quiet, and both men breathed a sigh of relief as if they felt safe once they were within its walls. The faces of men and women of Canarn looked up as they entered and Lanry saw weak smiles across the floor of the church. The seats had been set aside or made into makeshift beds, and the weakest and most needy had called this place home for several weeks. In the vaults below were those who simply needed a place to stay – men, women and children whose houses and businesses had been pillaged and destroyed.

A blacksmith named Carahan and his heavily pregnant wife, Jasmine, were closest and Lanry saw concern on the man's face as he looked at the meagre supplies.

'Is there another cart outside, brother?' Carahan asked.

'I'm afraid not. It seems Sir Pevain is not feeling especially charitable this evening,' Lanry replied, directing a thin smile at Jasmine, who shifted uncomfortably on her rickety bed.

'Any more healing supplies?' asked the blacksmith. 'We're almost out of etter root and the cramps are getting worse.'

Lanry shook his head and saw real concern on Jasmine's face. Etter root was a painkiller which was neither expensive nor difficult to find, but now the only apothecary in town had been destroyed and Pevain controlled the supply, it had become as rare as gold.

'I may be able to find some upstairs, but it'll be the last until the mercenaries let us have more. Unfortunately, I still have wounded who need it as well.'

Lanry hated having to ration medicine. It was the way of the Brown clerics to want to care for all people, and to have to decide who was the more deserving of pain relief was one of Lanry's most unpleasant responsibilities.

'Fulton,' he said to the taverner, 'Carahan will help you distribute what we have. Give to the neediest first, then those who had nothing yesterday. If there's anything left, ration it as usual. The same with the water.'

Fulton nodded and motioned for the blacksmith to assist him. Brother Lanry walked past the men and approached the stairs leading up to his personal chamber. He greeted people who stood eagerly awaiting a ration of grain and something to drink. At the end of the nave, the tubs for collecting water had been bought down from the roof and he saw the supply of rainwater was pitifully low.

'I can pray for salvation or I can pray for rain,' he said to himself, as he began to walk up the wooden stairs. 'I wonder which is more likely to yield results.'

At the top of the stairs he opened the simple oak door that led to his chamber. It had few comforts – all of his linen and clothing had already been distributed amongst the needy – but the small room was still a much-needed refuge from the despair all around him.

Brother Lanry, Brown cleric of the One God, sat down heavily in his old rocking chair and loosened the neck-fastenings of his robe. On a small table by his right arm were an oil lantern and his clay pipe. Allowing himself a moment of calm, Lanry loaded the pipe with sweet-smelling tobacco and touched a match to the bowl. He rocked back on his chair and turned to look out of the shuttered window. Seeing the dark, ghostly town beyond, he inhaled deeply and tried to think how to keep the people's spirits up. The weeks since the battle had passed slowly. Lanry thought the people of Canarn had endured more than their fair share of hardships at the hands of, first, the knights of the Red, and now the hateful mercenaries of Sir Hallam Pevain.

As he mused on the situation and puffed on his pipe, Lanry sensed someone behind him and began to turn round. He was stopped by a hand on his shoulder and an arm round his neck. The grip was not tight or constricting and was mostly designed to stop the cleric from turning round.

'Whoever you are, you sneaked in here without making any sound. That is to be commended,' Lanry said. 'I have little of value to steal, I'm afraid, so if burglary is your intention, may I recommend the lord marshal's office. Anything of worth left in the town is probably there somewhere.' He ignored the restraining arm and moved his pipe back up to his mouth.

'You should lock your window, Lanry,' said a familiar voice, at which the cleric swiftly removed the arm and spun round in his chair.

'My Lord Bromvy!' Lanry exclaimed with emotion in his old face. 'It is . . . beyond words.' The cleric abandoned any sense of propriety and flung his arms extravagantly round the young lord.

'Easy, brother,' said Brom. 'You look thin and I wouldn't want you to hurt yourself.'

Lanry looked down at his shrinking waistline. 'Yes, I have been on an enforced diet for a month,' he said with a smile.

Lord Bromvy of Canarn looked different – taller and more grizzled than the last time Lanry had seen him, with a hard look in his eyes and a few new scars on his face. His armour was of leather, with hardened wooden struts of a strange design. Lanry grinned broadly as he saw the cast of Brytag the World Raven on the hilt of Brom's sword – an insignia of the house of Canarn that had been presented to him by Duke Hector on his sixteenth birthday. It was strange to see the young lord again, and stranger still that Brom had managed to keep hold of his longsword – a weapon noble in appearance and dangerous for a Black Guard to carry.

'Did you return with an army?' Lanry asked, only half joking.

'No, but I'm here,' said another voice from a shadow in the corner of the room.

'Who . . .?' began the cleric, before a swarthy Kirin man stepped into the light.

He was shorter and thinner than Brom, with lank black hair hanging to his shoulders. He carried a longbow across his back and a thin-bladed katana at his side. The strangest thing about the Kirin was the broad grin splashed across his face.

'Rham Jas Rami. Pleased to meet you, Brother Lanry,' said the Kirin, extending his hand. 'I'd introduce you to our other friends, but they are a little shy, so they're waiting in the city.'

Lanry was perplexed at the notorious Kirin assassin accompanying Lord Bromvy, but he shook his hand nonetheless. Any allies are good allies, thought the cleric.

'Do your friends number in the hundreds?' he asked.

'Forty . . . not including us two,' said Brom, 'but we have a plan.'

CHAPTER TEN

HALLA SUMMER WOLF IN THE REALM OF WRAITH

T HE SNOW HAD disappeared swiftly as they moved inland and headed south-east from the frozen coastline, progressing slowly and with increasing caution as the days went on. Halla had insisted that her group of beleaguered Fjorlanders hold a defensive position close to the sea for no less than a week in order to allow wounds, both mental and physical, to heal as best they could, and now, a further week into their unplanned expedition, they were approaching the Grass Sea of Wraith Company.

Two hundred and five men of Fjorlan were all that had been accounted for. A further twenty had not left the beach and six had needed assistance to come this far. Most of the Ranen had taken off their armour and stowed it in carts they had manufactured out of the wreckage of the ships. They had no oil or metalworking equipment to care for their chain mail and breastplates, and Halla had ordered it to be preserved in case of need. They carried their weapons, though over the last week most had been used as walking sticks or for hunting, and the few whetstones that remained had been passed around to keep their blades sharp.

Hunting game on the low grassy plains was a challenge, and with no hunting bows or nets the party had been relying on stationary targets like Gorlan nests and edible mushrooms. Wulfrick had managed to sneak up on a deer and fell it with a well-aimed throw of his axe, but the meat had been tough and had not lasted long when divided among so large a group. Halla's men, as she had begun to think of them, had not complained about their empty bellies, and each had done his bit during their forced march inland.

Rexel Falling Cloud was still limping but he acted as an invaluable lieutenant to Halla and she was grateful to have someone else do the shouting. Oleff Hard Head, the chain-master of Fredericksand, had displayed an unlikely talent for singing during their journey and had done his bit to keep their spirits up. His songs were usually vulgar, but amusing, and he had made the men laugh at the most inappropriate times. Even Wulfrick had been caught in the midst of a raucous belly laugh at one of Oleff's songs – one of the few moments when he'd not been brooding over the loss of his thain.

'We should sight Ro Hail tomorrow, my lady,' said Falling Cloud, as they settled down for the night among the rocky protrusions at the edge of the Grass Sea.

'Have the men don armour in the morning, I don't want any surprises,' replied Halla, in the commanding voice she'd adopted since taking charge two weeks before.

The rocks rose from the grass in irregular pinnacles and provided one of the better rest spots of their journey. They were out of the wind and, with swiftly arranged canvas, out of the rain that frequently swept this land. It was warmer than Tiergarten and there was no snow, but without cold-weather clothing the men were feeling the biting breeze.

Wulfrick came to join Halla and Falling Cloud, plonking his enormous frame down on the grass next to their small cooking fire.

'Do we actually have anything to cook on that?' he asked, pointing to the low flames.

Halla shook her head. 'No, we're out of Gorlan parts and there's been no sign of game for a couple of days. You'd know that if you hadn't been off sulking.' She wasn't being mean, but was becoming increasingly annoyed with Wulfrick's mood.

'Sulking? Cheeky bitch,' he said with a mock hurt expression.

'My Lord Wulfrick,' interjected Falling Cloud, 'I must caution against speaking to my battle-mistress in that manner again.'

He was smiling, but the sentiment was appreciated by Halla.

'Okay, so I may have been a little . . . out of sorts,' Wulfrick conceded. 'Still alive, though.' The axe-master had used this phrase several times since the shipwreck and seemed to take comfort in the simple fact of his continued existence. 'I'll be better when I get back to Fredericksand and have a little chat with Rulag Ursa.'

'That's a long way north, brother,' said Falling Cloud, who often provided the level head among the boisterous axe-men.

'Indeed, but that's where I need to be. Alahan needs me, as his father did, and I'm still pledged to Fredericksand and the family of Teardrop.'

He took comfort in his honour, and Halla found that easier to deal with than his earlier complaining about how he had got Algenon killed.

'I'm quite eager to see who else got away as well. A ship or two of mentally unbalanced berserkers would be rather handy when I call out the traitorous bastard.' He hung his head for a moment. 'And I need to tell Alahan and Ingrid that their father has fallen.'

'Later, Wulfrick,' said Halla. 'Can we not have a single day pass without musing on the unfairness of our situation? We have pressing issues of survival to consider. Food is getting thin on the ground and if we don't reach Ro Hail soon, men are going to be too weak to make it through the Deep Cross.'

The mountain passes that led from the south land of the Free Companies to the north land of Fjorlan were a natural defensive line and during the colder months they were impossible to traverse. Halla knew that if they didn't reach the lowlands of the Deep Cross within a month, with the strength required to weather the high passes, they'd be trapped by snow and would die unremarked deaths.

'Find a troll and follow him,' Falling Cloud said with a smile. 'If you can stand the smell . . .'

'Have you ever met a troll with a sense of direction, Rexel?' asked Wulfrick with a grin. 'I've seen one of the big idiots dive off a cliff in pursuit of a bird.'

This caused a ripple of laughter among the men within earshot and Halla was again impressed at their ability to laugh in the face of adversity.

'I've never actually met one,' interjected Halla. 'I've seen them from a distance, but never close up.'

'You're not missing much,' said Falling Cloud. 'In Hammerfall, we lose settlements to the things every so often.'

'Troll bells,' supplied Wulfrick unhelpfully. 'At least you'll be able to hear them coming.'

'You need to shoot the bell into them first and we're a bit short of ballistae that can pierce their hides. Hammerfall is not Fredericksand, remember.'

Halla had been told by her mother of the troll-wranglers, who would enter the high passes with heavy, winch-operated ballistae designed to attach large bronze bells to the trolls. The oversized arrows didn't kill the creatures, but they were too dim-witted to realize what the ringing sound was, and stories existed of trolls remaining alive for centuries with ballista arrows stuck in their dense bodies.

'That's an obscure strategy,' Wulfrick mused cryptically.

'What is?' asked Halla.

'Well, if you could shepherd a bunch of trolls south, we could unleash them at the Ro.' The laughter caused by this comment was loud and echoing, sending a good-humoured ripple across the camp. 'I bet they'd enjoy eating steel plate armour.'

'Wouldn't the scrawny southern bastards get stuck in their teeth?' Falling Cloud joked. 'A troll with indigestion . . . not a pretty sight, I'd bet.'

The laughter continued well into twilight and Halla found herself enjoying the company of these men. They'd all lost their family and friends to the traitorous lord of Jarvik or to the Krakens, but despite their circumstances the men of Fjorlan were upbeat and glad simply to be alive. Wulfrick was just about recognizable once again as the boisterous axe-master he'd been before, and Halla thought him more focused and driven than he had been a week ago. The loss of his thain was still a topic of conversation, but he'd ceased to be offended when Halla told him to shut up, and now she regarded him as a valuable ally rather than a brooding deadweight. If they were to return home and bring Rulag Ursa to justice, the group would need their most fearsome warrior – and no one denied that Wulfrick had a totemic quality with his axe in hand.

She had also learned from Oleff the reason why Wulfrick had no family name – an anomaly among the Fjorlanders, who were traditionally very concerned with their family heritage. Halla was proud to be a Summer Wolf, just as Rexel was proud to be a Falling Cloud. Wulfrick, however, was only ever called by his first name and Halla had been told not to ask the reason for this. The story, apparently, was that Wulfrick the Enraged, son of Lars the Enraged, had been destined for greatness until his father had led a failed coup against Ragnar Teardrop and had been executed. Wulfrick had been spared, but he had had to pledge his life to serve the family of Teardrop. He'd given up his father's name as a way of wiping away the dishonour. In Halla's estimation, this also explained his fanaticism about serving Algenon and his children, and the extent of his indignation at Rulag's treachery.

She looked across the fire at the dark, bearded face of the axe-master and found herself valuing his presence. At the back of her mind was a half-whispered comment she'd heard just after they had left the beach. A young man from Hammerfall had said to a companion, 'We'll be okay, Wulfrick is still with us.' Halla knew that this sentiment was shared by others and she knew that her group would be much less intimidating without the huge axe-man.

'It'll be warmer tomorrow,' Falling Cloud said absently after the laughter had died down and night had begun to fall. 'Hopefully, Wraith Company can lay on a hearty meal for us. I think my belly may stop talking to me if I don't give it some meat soon.'

Halla smiled and realized that she too was starving. 'What do we have left?'

'Not much,' he replied. 'A few sacks of nettles and mushrooms, nothing too nutritious. We're okay for rainwater, but men need food as well as drink . . . women too. You all right?'

She was a little surprised at the show of concern and realized her sex had not been an issue since the shipwreck. She'd just been one of the men – in fact, she'd been in charge of the men, and if any doubted her abilities, they'd kept it quiet.

'I'm as fine as you . . . but thank you for the concern,' she said, scratching behind her eyepatch. Halla had found her missing eye grow more and more itchy over the past few days and she wondered if it was a nervous tic bought on by the unexpected command.

Just as they were beginning to settle down against the rocks, a distant sound was heard across the camp. It was far away, but it was like the noise of an impact, perhaps a landslide or stone striking stone.

Faces looked up from low-burning campfires and Halla perceived questioning looks on the faces of her men. No one said anything at first and they all listened as another sound was heard in the distance. A whistle followed by a dull impact. It wasn't a loud noise, but it carried across the still night air of the Grass Sea.

'Where's Oleff?' Halla asked Falling Cloud.

'He took a handful of men to higher ground, scouting for tomorrow.' He pointed to a jutting rocky promontory, just visible in the distance. 'He left a few hours ago. High places are rare around here and I think he wanted to make sure there weren't any surprises.'

Halla considered and quickly decided to go and investigate. 'Falling Cloud, stay here. Wulfrick, come with me. Let's go and find out what we can see.'

Neither of the men argued and Wulfrick swiftly picked up his axe and accompanied her through the rocky pinnacles. They passed small campfires and groups of Ranen shaken from their dozing by the same distant sound.

'Easy, lads,' Wulfrick said quietly, as they passed a group preparing to put on their armour. 'No alarms just yet.'

Halla received respectful nods of acknowledgement as they made their way through the camp and out on to the plain beyond. The promontory was still a distance away and Halla broke into a gentle run to cover the ground quickly.

Darkness had now descended and the Grass Sea was mist-shrouded and sinister-looking, dewy and wet underfoot, with little in the way of landmarks save for the jutting rocks ahead of them.

'Falling Cloud thinks we'll sight Ro Hail tomorrow,' Halla said to Wulfrick as they jogged across the plain. 'I've never been there.'

'I went once long ago. It was little more than a ruin, from what I remember. The men of Wraith lived in tunnels beneath the city and didn't bother about repairing the place,' Wulfrick responded, as he hefted his axe across his shoulders to run with greater ease. 'They'll be surprised to see us, though.'

'As long as they're not too surprised to offer us food.' Halla knew the men were counting on Wraith Company to supply them with provisions and rest, and she prayed their hope was not misplaced.

As they neared the rocks, Halla could see a small figure climbing down and moving towards them. He was making little effort to be stealthy and was running with a degree of urgency. She turned to Wulfrick and saw his eyes narrow with interest as the figure approached.

'Lady Summer Wolf,' the Ranen man said, clearly a little agitated. 'Oleff sent me to get you.'

'Well, you've got me. What's the noise?' she asked.

'You'd better come and see. Follow me.' He quickly spun round and ran back to the rocks.

'Should we be concerned?' Wulfrick asked as they sped up.

'Just follow me,' the man repeated.

At the foot of the promontory, Halla looked up and saw jagged rocks running in a line across her field of vision. There were small, irregular trees sprouting along the top, providing cover for Oleff's scouts, and numerous little crannies that made climbing relatively simple.

She got a firm handhold and pulled herself up. It was a short climb and by the time they'd reached the top she could tell why Oleff had chosen this for a scouting point. It was the highest ground anywhere within sight, and she could see the vast plains of the realm of Wraith stretching out on all sides.

Crouching down, she moved slowly through the trees, aware of the huge figure of Wulfrick behind her. He was finding it more difficult to haul his massive body through the trees and she could hear whispered swear words as he caught himself on some thorns.

'Halla, is that you?' asked a voice from a little way through the trees.

'Oleff . . .' she replied by way of greeting, as she joined the chain-master behind a rocky protrusion facing south-east.

Wulfrick came to crouch next to her and they both looked with astonishment at the source of the noise that had aroused them.

Across the Grass Sea, a few hundred paces distant, was a mass of campfires. Tents and fortifications for several thousand men had been set up on the plains and Halla gasped as she saw the fluttering banner of the Red knights of Ro flying overhead. There were other banners she didn't recognize, and siege equipment was visible at the front of the camp. Holding her breath, Halla surveyed the scene before her. The low walled shape of a city was just visible in the distance and the encircling army had begun to hurl huge rocks against the walls, which made a whistling sound as they sped through the air and a dull thud as they struck stone.

'Rowanoco save us,' whispered Wulfrick. 'That's Ro Hail.'

The city of Wraith Company was under siege by an army of knights of the Red, its walls battered by huge boulders and its defenders nowhere to be seen.

The camp was vast but was now largely deserted as the majority of the troops had been committed to encircling the town. Halla had never seen so many knights in one place, and as she looked over the wide circle set back from Ro Hail, she turned to Oleff and asked in a whisper, 'How many are there?'

'Five thousand, by my reckoning. Mostly knights, but there are Purple clerics and a detachment of king's guard as well,' he answered, without taking his eyes from the siege.

'King's guard?' questioned Wulfrick. 'What are they doing here?'

Oleff pointed to the other banners flying over the camp. 'You see the white bird on that flag? That's the banner of King Sebastian Tiris.'

Halla directed her one eye back towards the camp and could see only a very few armoured men around several large pavilion tents. Wulfrick was directing his gaze at the king's heraldry and a look of anger had come over his face.

'The king of Tor Funweir has marched into the Grass Sea?' he asked through gritted teeth. 'Such a thing has not happened for two hundred years.'

All Fjorlanders shared a common knowledge of the ages their southern brethren had spent under the yoke of Ro occupation and all were deeply offended by the notion that it might happen again. Wulfrick was clenching his fists and Halla even saw him reach for the comforting grip of his axe. The huge axe-master of Fredericksand inched forward and craned his neck to see better.

'The Wraith men are trapped . . . these Ro bastards will starve them out, bombard them till they can't hold the walls and then slowly sweep it clear.' He was clearly itching to get involved. 'Ro battle tactics rely on numbers, and cowardice will see you through . . . Wraith Company will fall without having had a chance to fight.'

Oleff and Wulfrick embarked on a lengthy tirade against the dishonourable tactics of the Ro, making each other more and more angry at their own helplessness.

Halla tuned out their whispers as an idea began to form. She turned away from the town and tried to focus on the camp below them. Few fires were visible, except around the pavilions, and she guessed that the knights surrounding Ro Hail would camp in their current positions, maintaining the siege for as long as necessary. An occasional suit of golden armour was visible, glinting in the moonlight through the tents, as she tried to assess the numbers remaining in the camp. Judging by the few fires and the ceremonial look of the gold-armoured guardsmen, Halla thought that only the king's personal guard was left – no more than three hundred men, maybe fewer. Of most interest, however, were the additional ballistae and catapults that stood unused at the edges of the camp. They had no crews but at least one looked as if it were loaded and ready to fire. It looked as if the artillery being used against the town comprised mostly short-range engines designed to breach defences, while the larger contraptions left at the camp were taller and could hurl rocks much further.

'I have an idea,' she said quietly, causing the two men to stop talking and turn to her. 'Wulfrick, return to the pinnacles and muster the men. Arms and light armour only, we need to be stealthy.'

He looked confused. 'Halla, I'm all for facing overwhelming odds, but attacking those knights is suicide.'

'I don't think we should attack those knights,' she responded, pointing at the city. 'I think we should attack *those* knights.' She then pointed with a grin at the king's camp. 'The king won't actually be involved in the siege, no?'

Oleff shook his head. 'I imagine he'll be sipping wine in front of his tent and being told how clever he is by the Purple clerics.'

'And we could end this siege swiftly if we were to capture him, yes?' she asked with a tone of authority in her voice.

The two men realized what she planned and Wulfrick bit his lip to stop himself erupting into a vicious laugh.

'Aleph Summer Wolf is alive and well and talking to us through his daughter,' he said with a broad smile.

'No, he's dead and the voice you hear is Halla Summer Wolf, axe-maiden of Rowanoco and lady of Tiergarten,' she responded with pride.

Wulfrick smiled. 'Yes, my lady.'

Oleff peered across the dark plain towards the camp, assessing their strength. 'If we move around these rocks and come at them directly east, we'll be masked by darkness, mist and those boulders. If we keep quiet, they won't know what's hit them.' He turned to Halla. 'I'm impressed, my lady. The camp's just far enough from the siege that it's doubtful the body of knights will notice us killing their men.'

'Wait until you hear the plan for those catapults the knights have so carelessly left unmanned.' Halla had counted ten catapults and five ballistae, enough to cause real damage to the besieging knights. 'Oleff, you'll take twenty men to the artillery and, once we have the king, you'll announce our presence to the army. Thin their ranks as much as you can before falling back to our position.'

This elicited a menacing chuckle from all three of them, and Halla was gratified that they didn't question her orders or try to usurp the command now that battle was planned.

'And if the king isn't cooperative, I'll start cutting off fingers till he is,' said Wulfrick, clutching his axe menacingly.

Halla directed a hard look at Wulfrick. 'I gave you orders, axe-master . . . what are you still doing here?' The hard look turned into a smile as Wulfrick banged his fist on his chest in salute and backed away. 'Bring them to the base of the rocks . . . remember, no heavy armour, we need to be quiet until the last possible moment.'

Halla kept a watchful eye on the scene before her, trying not to think about all the things that could go wrong with her plan. If capturing the king allowed the people of Wraith Company to escape east to the other Free Companies, she'd still have the issue of where to take her own men. Halla had no doubt that the king of Tor Funweir would place his own survival before that of his knights, but she suspected they'd have to keep him hostage for long enough to secure the escape of all the Ranen. Ultimately, the Fjorlanders needed to head north to the Deep Cross and to be pursued by five thousand Ro would not make the journey a pleasant one. The alternative was to give the monarch to Wraith Company as they moved east, practically ensuring that the Ro would follow in that direction. The simple conclusion was that, wherever the hostage was taken, the army of Red knights would surely follow.

'Oleff, how far to the Deep Cross from here?' she asked, assessing her options.

'Maybe three weeks . . . if we really moved. South Warden is closer, but if we don't get north of the passes soon, winter will arrive and we'll be stuck,' he responded.

'And the safest place for Wraith Company is South Warden, yes?' Halla knew that the combined might of the Free Companies would be enough to engage the army of knights, but they were spread thinly all over the southern Freelands and rarely massed as a single force.

'I'd say so, yes. It's a fortress – high walls, catapults, everything a defending force could need. Not enough men to face that lot directly, but they'd have more men and a better chance than defending Ro Hail.' Oleff was originally from Ranen Gar, the great southern stronghold of Greywood Company, and he knew the Freelands better than most Fjorlanders.

'Okay, so we demand the king lifts the siege and allows the people of Wraith to get to South Warden as quickly as possible. Once they're out of sight, we go north with the hostage.'

It was a bold plan and relied heavily on the knights not being willing to risk the life of their king, but these men were Ro to whom propriety and status meant everything. Halla was prepared to gamble on the king's life being more important than the need to kill Ranen.

'They'll follow us, you know?' he cautioned.

'Good. It'll give the Free Companies time to muster.' She tried to sound as confident as possible.

'And what do we do with the king once we reach the Deep Cross?' he asked, echoing Halla's own thoughts.

She wasn't sure how to answer and had to admit to herself that this part of the plan was, as yet, unformed. She tried to look confident as she replied, 'Maybe we'll release him in troll country and let the knights bang their heads against the mountains for a few weeks.'

Oleff laughed quietly and, after a moment's thought, said, 'I'm glad you're in charge, Lady Summer Wolf. You're going to save a lot of Ranen lives.'

It was a compliment that made Halla glow with pride, though she suppressed the urge to grin broadly and merely nodded formally at the chain-master of Fredericksand.

* * *

It took less than half an hour to assemble the men of Fjorlan at the base of the rocky outcrop and Halla had watched every man arrive to ensure that none were wearing heavy metal armour. Wulfrick had made her orders clear and most of the axe-men wore only toughened leather breastplates or no armour at all – even the axe-master himself had discarded his heavy troll-hide armour. They all looked lean and hungry for combat – hefting axes, gritting their teeth, flexing their muscles. The people of Fjorlan were warriors from their first steps and Halla thought her company looked as intimidating as any army.

'Silence from this point on,' she said under her breath. 'We have a few hundred paces of open ground to cover before we get to the camp. Oleff, take your men to the rear and secure the artillery. Falling Cloud, you're on the north side to guard against the knights returning – signal if they get wind of what we're doing. Everyone else, you're with me. We kill everyone as quickly and quietly as possible and secure the king.'

A wave of excited anticipation flowed over the waiting warriors; several of them were fighting the urge to roar out a challenge. With a wave of her hand, she and Wulfrick moved to the front and began to move along the base of the rocks. Halla was impressed at how quietly the warriors proceeded and she had to turn back and call for silence only once before they reached open ground.

Crouching at the edge of the rocks, she could just make out the camp through the misty darkness. The siege of Ro Hail was proceeding to the north and could mostly be observed as a series of campfires and the occasional boulder launched through the air. At ground level, she was now even more certain that they'd remain unseen as they assaulted the camp and, waving to her men to follow, she broke into a dead run.

They fanned out across the dew-covered grass and, with a bright moon overhead and weapons at the ready, the Fjorlanders sped towards the unsuspecting camp. Wulfrick held his two-handed axe braced across his shoulders. Halla felt better for having him at her side; the shudder of anticipation was visible in his huge body as he ran.

Halla felt no blood lust as she approached the camp, but rather a solemn sense of responsibility towards her men and an impatience to see their bloody work begin. The king's guardsmen would be tough opponents, but if they were caught unawares she knew the men of Fjorlan would be more than a match for them.

The line of deserted tents appeared just in front of them and Halla scanned her field of vision, looking for sentries. She could see none and hoped the arrogance of royalty meant the king had left his perimeter unguarded. Slowing down, she signalled behind her to Falling Cloud, who broke off with twenty men to circle towards the north to cover them. Another signal and Oleff headed towards the unmanned catapults and ballistae. The men of Fjorlan moved with purpose and Halla could see conviction on their faces as they followed her commands, without question.

'There,' said Wulfrick, pointing to a guard just visible at the edge of the empty tents. 'Silence,' he signalled to the men behind him.

They stopped and Wulfrick passed his axe to Halla before drawing a heavy dagger from his belt. Moving as low to the ground as he could, Wulfrick broke off from the others and sneaked up behind the nearest tent.

Wulfrick moved stealthily between the dark tents and emerged behind the single sentry. With a huge hand placed over his mouth, he eased the dagger into the guardsman's neck and cut his windpipe, holding the body tightly as the life ebbed from the man of Ro's eyes. Wulfrick was immensely strong and the man looked like a child in comparison as the huge axe-master killed him.

Halla motioned the others to follow and quickly crossed the remaining ground to the tents. Throwing the axe back to Wulfrick, she moved between dark canvas and smoking campfires. The men behind fanned out again and swept through the camp, staying in shadows and keeping as quiet as they could. Halla could see the banner of the king, a white eagle, flying overhead as they made their way towards the large pavilions at the centre of the camp. Another flag, showing a purple sceptre, was flying below the royal banner, signifying that a senior Purple churchman was also present.

She could see light from between the tents as they approached the king's pavilion. As she hoped, the king's men were totally oblivious and had not been expecting an attack. Signalling to Wulfrick to move round the side with half the men, she took a deep breath and advanced on the pavilion.

Her estimate of three hundred guardsmen looked about right, but they were not prepared for action and most were not even armed or armoured. The men of Ro were sitting round their campfires or within their white fabric tents and something about the way they were casually relaxing while Ro Hail was under siege annoyed the axe-maiden greatly. She moved with her men to the last line of deserted tents and paused until she was sure that Wulfrick and the others were in position.

'First blood is mine,' she said to the men behind her and stood, hefted her axe, and ran towards the first group of guardsmen.

As soon as Halla emerged through the line of tents and into the light, close to two hundred men of Fjorlan followed her and quickly flooded the area from all directions. A man of Ro, reclining next to a campfire and holding a bottle of wine, looked up to stare at her. She grunted at him before severing his head with a powerful swing of her axe, signalling the start of their assault.

Shouts of alarm only slowly went up from the king's men. By the time they realized what was happening, the rampaging axe-men had killed anyone in their path. Only a few of the men of Ro had weapons at the ready and most of them met their deaths swiftly, without even standing up.

Halla didn't stop moving and drove her men forward towards the centre of the camp, despatching anyone who clumsily attempted to stand in their way. She killed a man as he tried to pull on his gold breastplate and another as he wrestled with a stubborn scabbard. She could see Wulfrick nearby, as the huge axe-master cleared a wide path from the north towards the king's pavilion.

Then, all of a sudden, Halla, Wulfrick and their men were standing on the central ground in front of two large white pavilions, directly beneath the banners of Tor Funweir. Confused Purple clerics, armed and armoured, stood in their path and a detachment of spearmen closed ranks round the main pavilion.

'Kill them all,' roared Wulfrick, not missing a step as he swung his axe skilfully and advanced on the nearest cleric.

The silence evaporated as oaths were shouted and battle was joined. They'd killed numerous guardsmen and Halla was gratified to see that now the clerics and spearmen were heavily outnumbered by rampaging Fjorlanders.

The Purple clerics were skilled swordsmen and the the sound of steel on steel sounded through the camp. As she engaged a cleric, Halla hoped they were too far away from Ro Hail to alert the main army.

She was shaken back to matters more pressing when the cleric she was fighting deflected her axe and opened up her shoulder with a skilful thrust. Crying in pain, the axe-maiden fell to the ground, but was relieved to see another man cleave the cleric to the ground before moving on. Halla quickly got to her feet and tried to block out the pain as she rejoined her men.

Their advance had slowed and it was now a grim push through the last line of defenders to get to the king's pavilion. Halla tried to favour her uninjured shoulder as she parried a spear thrust and then severed the wielder's arm before kicking the guardsman out of her way.

To her left, Wulfrick was difficult to miss – towering over the other men, the axe-master of Fredericksand was a nightmare of whirling steel and rage as he annihilated any man foolish enough to stand in his way. Halla could see several clerics who looked older and more skilled than the rest and one of them, a dark-haired man wearing ornate armour, was moving intentionally towards Wulfrick. The Purple cleric killed several of Halla's men with lightning speed as he focused on the huge axe-man.

'Barbarian,' he roared, by way of a challenge, 'I am Cardinal Mobius of the Purple and your Ice Giant holds sway here no longer.'

Wulfrick roared skywards and Halla saw the foam of frenzy appear at the corners of his mouth as he beheaded two clerics and moved to engage the Purple cardinal. There were still men between them, but their intention was to fight each other. She tried to focus on the men in front of her, but secretly she worried for her friend. It was strange that, in the midst of brutal combat, it had occurred to her that Wulfrick had indeed become her friend.

She wrested a spear from a guardsman in front of her and threw it at a cleric standing over a fallen axe-man. The Ranen was wounded but alive, and weakly nodded his thanks to Halla before dragging himself away from the main combat. She spun round and saw no other men to fight in her immediate vicinity. The entrance to the main pavilion was still guarded by clerics, though Wulfrick and his men had pushed them back before Cardinal Mobius had appeared and stopped their advance. All around her lay dead men, mostly Ro, and the king's pavilion was now dangerously isolated.

'Help them,' she ordered all the men nearby, pointing to the Ranen at the pavilion entrance.

An axe-man, noticing her wound, offered her an arm and Halla Summer Wolf leant heavily against him before turning to see Wulfrick approach Cardinal Mobius.

The other warriors parted as the two men clashed. The sound of axe striking sword rang out loudly and Halla realized the cardinal was every bit as dangerous as Wulfrick. The two men fought in wildly different styles. Wulfrick relied on superior strength and unnatural speed, whereas Mobius was a duellist, giving and taking ground in a complex dance of steel. Their weapons differed too

– a two-handed axe versus a longsword and shield – and Halla thought the clash more than a simple fight between men.

The remaining spearmen were boxed in and were killed without mercy, leaving only a handful of clerics in front of the pavilion, where they were swiftly overwhelmed by Halla's men. To the north, the axe-maiden saw the signal from Falling Cloud indicating that they had cleared the few sentries and guardsmen in that direction, and she knew Oleff would be loading the catapults and making ready to fire.

Mobius dodged to the side of a powerful axe blow and nimbly thrust his blade into Wulfrick's side. It was a glancing blow, but one that made the axe-master wince and gave the surrounding Fjorlanders cause for concern.

'You're quick, purple man,' spat Wulfrick, as the two men circled each other.

Both men could see the fight was over, with the Ranen defiantly victorious. The Fjorlanders surrounded the pavilion and stood back from where Wulfrick and Mobius were sizing each other up.

'Wulfrick, we're done,' Halla shouted across the camp. 'You,' she nodded towards Mobius, 'stand down, you've lost.'

'I am a cleric of the One God, bitch,' he roared. 'I will never surrender to a barbarian.'

The Ranen shot him angry looks and moved in to isolate the Ro. Halla held up a hand, indicating they shouldn't kill him.

'Take his sword and tie him up,' she ordered the closest group of men.

A few of the men smiled as they got their first sight of a Purple cleric – men of Ro closely associated with the age-old oppression of the Ranen people. Ropes were retrieved from nearby tents and the Ranen began to circle the cleric with quickly fashioned lassoes. Halla moved past them and motioned for Wulfrick to join her. The wounded axe-master tore himself away from the cornered man of Ro and stepped into the pavilion entrance with four other axe-men.

'My king, we are defeated,' Cardinal Mobius shouted into the tent.

A tangle of legs and rope made him buckle awkwardly to the ground and drop his longsword.

'You cannot win, barbarians,' he growled angrily as his face hit the muddy ground and the men of Fjorlan quickly swarmed over him.

Kicking and punching, they rendered him unconscious in a matter of moments and secured ropes round his arms and legs.

'I would have won,' said Wulfrick quietly. 'It was just a matter of time.'

'Time we don't have,' replied Halla. 'Let's get this done.'

Wulfrick nodded and flung open the tent flap across the pavilion entrance. Halla and five men flooded into the command tent and Wulfrick followed. Observing a garish habitation of furs and heraldry, they quickly searched for the king of Tor Funweir.

The pavilion contained a large map, on a low table, showing the south lands of Ranen. Around the edges of the tent were banners of Tiris and the other houses of Tor Funweir – birds for the most part, of many different colours and breeds. A large feather bed of white linen looked as if it had been slept in and on a table next to it was a half-eaten meal of what looked like venison. Halla moved to the far side of the tent and heard what sounded like crying coming from the floor beneath the bed. She raised her eyebrows and pointed in the direction of the sound, causing Wulfrick to stride next to her and tip over the wooden bed.

Cowering on the floor, his head buried in his arms, and wearing a simple white robe, was a man in his mid-fifties, clean-shaven and smelling lightly of perfume. The figure of King Sebastian Tiris was not a noble sight and a pool of liquid spreading out by his leg indicated that the monarch was very scared indeed.

'Have we pissed ourselves, your highness?' asked Wulfrick with a vicious smile.

'Please,' the king cried, 'don't kill me . . . I can give you gold . . . gold and jewels . . . just spare my life.' He looked up at them through bloodshot eyes and Halla felt anger that such a cowardly worm could be responsible for so much death.

'We're not going to kill you . . . my lord.' She practically spat out the honorific. 'You are now a prisoner. Get used to it. My name is Halla Summer Wolf and this is Wulfrick, axe-master of Fredericksand.' She turned back to Wulfrick and said with aggression, 'Grab this little boy and bring him.'

'Come on, your highness, me and you are going to be good friends.' The axe-master roughly pulled the king to his feet and turned up his nose at the pool of urine.

'Are kings not taught to use the trench in Tor Funweir? I thought *we* were the barbarians,' Wulfrick said with a sneer.

He wrapped a huge arm round the cowering monarch and led him out of the pavilion. Outside, a muted cheer rose from the assembled Fjorlanders as they saw the terrified, captive figure of the king of Tor Funweir. His eyes opened as wide as they would go when he saw the mass of Ranen, who would all have gladly killed him at the slightest opportunity. He looked across the dead guardsmen and clerics and saw the bound and unconscious form of Cardinal Mobius hefted over a man's shoulder.

'Now, your highness,' said Halla, 'we need you to call off your attack.' She tried to convey as much menace as possible, despite the increasing pain in her shoulder. 'If you don't do exactly as I say . . . this man,' she gestured to the hulking form of Wulfrick, 'is going to start cutting things off.'

Wulfrick smiled and tightened his grip around King Sebastian's neck. 'I'll start with your fingers . . . then your hands . . . and by the time they get to identify your body, there won't be much left.'

The king was shaking violently in the axe-master's grasp and he nodded at Halla. He was utterly broken, and the men of Fjorlan were looking at her with silent admiration. Her plan had worked thus far, with only a handful of Ranen dead.

The company of men sheathed their weapons and made their way quickly through the tents to the north. Falling Cloud joined them after a moment and looked with concern at Wulfrick's side and Halla's shoulder.

'You two need healing,' he said.

'That can wait,' replied Halla. 'Rexel Falling Cloud, may I present King Sebastian Tiris.'

Wulfrick shoved the monarch forward and Falling Cloud looked at him, raising his eyebrows before smiling. 'Not very noble-looking, is he?'

'Rexel, don't be mean,' said Wulfrick. 'The little lamb is covered in his own piss . . . that would ruin anyone's day.'

A laugh erupted from several of the nearby Fjorlanders.

'There are still a lot of things that can go wrong with this,' said Halla, more nervously than she intended, 'so let's keep alert until it's done.'

Once they emerged through the last line of deserted tents and past the bodies of those killed by Falling Cloud and his men, Halla saw the wide vista of knights and catapults arrayed across the plain before them. The encircling troops were still distant, but Halla nevertheless gasped at the enormous numbers of troops laying siege to Ro Hail.

Immediately in front of them were ten catapults – tall wooden engines designed to throw boulders a great distance – and Oleff Hard Head grinned viciously as Halla arrived.

'Lady Summer Wolf, artillery at the ready,' he said cheerfully. 'Who's your friend, Wulfrick?'

'This? Oh, don't you worry about him, he's just a king I found cowering in a tent and begging for his life,' replied the huge axe-master.

Oleff took a step towards the captive monarch and paused, nose to nose with the king. 'Good evening, you cowardly troll cunt,' he grunted, showering the king with spit.

'Please,' King Sebastian pleaded, 'my life is worth much . . . you will be rich if you leave me unharmed.'

Oleff erupted into anger and said loudly, 'Look around you, shit-stain, do we look like money means anything to us?'

'Enough, Oleff,' ordered Halla. 'Are the catapults ready?'

The chain-master brought his anger under control and turned back to Halla. 'Sorry, my lady, it's rare I get to look into the face of a man responsible for so much needless death . . . killing Ro makes me lose my manners.' He breathed in deeply and continued, 'Ten catapults sighted and ready. They're pointed at the nearest company of knights and should get their attention.'

'Very well. Falling Cloud, assemble the men in columns behind us. Look mean, but don't start anything.'

Rexel nodded and turned to issue orders to the men of Fjorlan, who quickly responded by forming into loosely packed lines behind the catapults.

'Wulfrick, I imagine they'll charge us as soon as they realize what's going on,' she said to the axe-master, who was now holding the king off the ground with an enormous arm round his waist. 'As soon as they get close enough, show them our captive.'

'Let's just hope they stop,' Oleff joked.

'They will . . . they will,' spluttered the king from his undignified position under Wulfrick's arm. 'I'll order them to stop and they wouldn't risk my safety.' King Sebastian was less a king and more of a sheltered noble – a far cry from the rulers Halla Summer Wolf had been used to. Algenon Teardrop would have given his life rather than be captured and the axe-maiden momentarily pitied the men of Ro for having to live under the rule of such a man.

She crouched down next to King Sebastian and let her single eye stare into his face. 'You'd better scream your orders at the top of your lungs, your highness,' she said quietly. 'We wouldn't want the knights not to hear you now, would we? If they don't, I promise you, you'll be the first to die.'

Her men showed pride on their faces and she heard whispered words of triumph behind her. The survivors of the Kraken sea had had little to be happy about for weeks, but as they looked at their commanders and at the broken king, each battle-brother wore an expression of elation at the overwhelming odds they had overcome.

'Oleff, send the knights my warmest regards,' Halla ordered.

'A pleasure, my lady,' he responded, giving her a respectful salute.

A simple downward wave of his arm and the Ranen at the base of each catapult levered the engine into life. Each artillery piece gave out a loud noise as the wood of the arm struck the padded bracer at the top, and the catapults jumped forwards as ten huge boulders were launched high into the air. Halla smiled to herself and followed their trajectory as they flew into the dark sky, before arcing sharply down.

The first impact was loud and could be heard clearly, even at their distant position. Halla saw armoured men fly in all directions as the boulders smashed into the knights of the Red. She couldn't see their faces, of course, and could only guess at the confusion caused by the unexpected bombardment, but those companies that had been hit lost their formations instantly and others, not yet hit, began to move away from the city walls to regroup. She heard trumpets sound – no doubt an alarm call – and within moments a good quarter of the encircling troops were making their way quickly back towards the camp.

The knights were mounted and drew long lances as they plunged across the muddy ground. It was unlikely that they could see who had fired on them, but the fact that the shots had come from the king's position had clearly caused well-founded alarm.

'Hold your ground, lads,' ordered Wulfrick, still firmly holding the king. 'It looks scary, but they'll pull up soon enough.'

'Show them the prisoner,' Halla ordered quietly.

'Get ready to shout, your highness.'

Wulfrick pulled the smaller man round and held him up effortlessly. King Sebastian was not especially diminutive, but in Wulfrick's grasp he looked little more than a child as he was held aloft.

The knights charged towards the line of catapults at an alarming speed, and the assembled Fjorlanders stood their ground nervously, fervently hoping the charge would stop once the men of Ro saw their captured monarch. Halla could identify a Purple cleric among the riders and a decorated older man who she guessed was a knight commander.

'Halt,' shouted the king through a filter of tears and fear.

'Louder,' prompted Wulfrick, punching him lightly in the ribs.

'My knights, halt,' the king repeated loudly, genuinely shouting as loud as he could.

The Purple cleric was at the head of the knights and squinted to see who was shouting. Halla saw the realization only gradually dawn on his determined face, as he raised his lance and forcefully pulled up on his horse's reins. The knight commander looked with a mix of anger and surprise as he saw the line of Fjorlanders standing in ranks behind the captured king, and the knights that followed began to pull back on their reins too. Several horses buckled and threw their riders, and several others rode at full tilt into the men in front as the order to halt only gradually reached the back ranks.

Around a thousand mounted men of Ro stopped on the dark plain in front of the line of catapults. At least a hundred of them had been thrown and some of those had been trampled to death by the heavy warhorses.

'I think we got their attention,' quipped Oleff nervously, as he looked at the large company of knights.

The Purple cleric, a young man with an elaborately crested helmet, rode past the bulk of the riders and was joined by the older knight commander. They broke off from the knights and rode at a trot towards Halla's position. The other men of Ro followed only slowly, many of them still confused at what was going on.

'Release the king, Ranen heretic,' ordered the cleric, drawing his longsword.

'Brother Jakan,' said King Sebastian in a trembling voice, 'sheathe your sword immediately.'

Wulfrick slowly lowered the king to the ground and held him roughly with an axe blade across his throat.

The knight commander, less impetuous than the cleric, kicked his horse a little further forwards and looked at the Ranen warriors before him. His eye was drawn to the dead guardsmen littering the ground behind them and the unconscious body of Cardinal Mobius, casually thrown over a man's shoulder.

The knight of the Red was older than the cleric and bore numerous scars, including one that ran the length of his left cheek.

'Knight Commander Tristram,' the king said, addressing him, 'you are to lift the siege and stand down.' His voice was panicked and his eyes had not moved from the bloodstained axe that rested against his neck.

'We're a long way from Fjorlan,' the knight stated calmly, addressing Wulfrick. 'And that's barely a company . . . you have no army and no hope of survival.'

'I would listen to your king, red man,' growled Halla from her position next to Wulfrick. 'Lift the siege and no one else need die.'

'Silence, one-eye,' barked the cleric, causing every Fjorlander present to heft his axe and stand at the ready.

The churchman was clearly taken aback by this show of solidarity and his horse reared as two hundred axe-men growled at him with anger in their eyes.

'Talk to her like that again,' shouted Oleff, 'and my friend here will cut something off your king.'

To emphasize the point, Wulfrick grabbed one of the king's hands and bent back the fingers, with a vicious grin on his face. The king howled in pain and the men of Ro baulked at the sight.

'Enough,' shouted Brother Jakan. 'Release the King . . . now!' He still held his sword, despite the command to sheathe it, and Halla thought him likely to do something foolish.

She stepped close to the knight commander's horse and spoke quietly. 'This is what is going to happen, Sir Tristram, you are going to call all of your men back to this camp. We are going to take your king and enter Ro Hail – and you are going to let us.'

Halla glared at the Ro as she spoke and saw a serious look, tinged with confusion, staring back at her. Tristram was assessing his options as he listened to the axe-maiden, and he appeared to her much more level-headed than the Purple cleric, who was still holding his sword nearby.

'Very well,' he said plainly and with obvious reluctance. 'If the king is hurt in any way, I will hunt you to the ends of the earth, axe-bitch.'

Halla smiled. 'I'd expect no less. We will release him when Wraith Company is a week's travel to the east and we are a similar distance north. Understood?'

Tristram gritted his teeth and nodded, trying to keep his anger in check.

'This is heresy against the One,' roared the Purple cleric. 'You will release him *now*.'

The front line of Fjorlanders took a step forward at Falling Cloud's instruction, and Wulfrick grabbed the king's head, pulling it back to expose his neck.

'This is Rowanoco's land, boy,' said the axe-master. 'Your god doesn't like the cold.'

Halla stepped away from the knight and turned to address Brother Jakan as he glared at Wulfrick.

'If I see anyone leaving this camp while we are in the city, the king loses a hand. If you try to follow, he loses an arm,' she said loudly enough for all present to hear. 'I expect you to send someone to collect him in a week – no more than five men.' She smiled. 'We'll tie him to a tree and you'd better get to him before the trolls do.'

Brother Jakan was about to say something, but his words were cut off by Sir Tristram grabbing his sword arm and pulling him back. The knights of the Red looked dejected and Halla breathed a little more easily.

'Do what she says,' cried King Sebastian in the manner of a frightened child.

CHAPTER ELEVEN

MAGNUS FORKBEARD RAGNARSSON IN THE CITY OF RO CANARN

MAGNUS LOOKED UP through the feeding trough and saw the back of the guard silhouetted against the moon. Sir Nathan had insisted that a bound man be stationed there at all times, following Al-Hasim's appearance, and for almost a month he had been the only regular figure, aside from Castus, in Magnus's life.

If escape or rescue were still a possibility, the Ranen priest had largely stopped thinking about it. Instead, his head had been filled with concern for the fate of his people since he had seen the king's army ride north into the Grass Sea. Captain Horrock was an excellent commander, but he was still a common man leading other common men. If the Fjorlanders were unable to help, as the witch insisted, Magnus knew that Wraith Company would either be wiped out or driven north into the mountains. Added to this was his concern for the fate of Al-Hasim and Bronwyn. He had heard nothing of them since Verellian left almost a month ago, and their fate would now be tied to that of Horrock and the men of Wraith.

The world was changing and he hated it that he was stuck in a cell while wheels turned and games were played. He wanted to feel the sun on his face and Skeld in his hand. There was much combat and glory to be had and the Order of the Hammer were not animals to be ignored, but rather men to be on the front line, displaying the might of Rowanoco to the enemies of the Ranen people.

He could see the dark sky of Canarn over the shoulder of his guard and the smell of salt water had returned after weeks of nothing but the scent of death. Things in the town were moderately stable with Pevain and his bastards based in the old lord marshal's office on the waterfront and the knights largely confined to the inner keep and the great hall. The people of Canarn who remained free were locked in the daily ritual of queuing for the meagre food and water that Pevain allowed them, and almost half the population were either corralled like cattle and starving to death – or already dead, their ashes adorning the town square.

Rillion and Nathan cared nothing for the common folk of Canarn. Magnus had not seen or heard anything from the senior knights for nearly two weeks. He guessed that Rillion was still annoyed at being confined to the city while the king and Cardinal Mobius marched north. The knight commander had been left with just a skeleton garrison and the actual work was being left to the mercenaries, while the knights sat around and lamented their miserable assignment.

The enchantress was still here and her assurance that no battle fleet of Fjorlanders was likely to show up any time soon had allowed the knights to relax. The plain truth, as Magnus saw it, was that no one would be coming to his aid or that of Canarn.

The moon was full and the lack of cloud made for a cold night, though nothing like the extreme temperatures of Magnus's home, far to the north. He missed the fields of ice and snow and realized he'd not seen his brother or his homeland for a long time. Being in a cell was deeply insulting, but being helpless while his brother and his people struggled for survival was almost too much for the priest to bear.

He still wore the same woollen leggings and black shirt as when he'd been incarcerated over a month before, and the smell bothered him almost as much as his imprisonment. His face and skin were clean enough and he still received fresh water each day, along with thin, watery gruel and bread, but no change of clothes had been provided – and he longed for the comforting feel of chain mail.

As he looked out of the small cell, over the shoulder of the bound man, Magnus momentarily thought he saw movement further along the feeding trough. As he tried to focus, a dark shape appeared. Mostly hidden in shadow, the figure was silently moving towards the guard. Magnus squinted and thought he could identify the silhouette of a longbow as the figure crouched next to the adjoining cell. He couldn't see the silent intruder's face, but he knew of no man of Ro who would use such a weapon and a thin smile crossed his face as he also made out a sheathed katana at the figure's side. There was no indication that the bound man was aware of the intruder's presence and he was leaning against the stone wall, fed up with another night's mundane guard duty.

What the man didn't yet realize was that his night was about to become rather less mundane, as Rham Jas Rami, the Kirin assassin, started to ascend the feeding trough towards the guard's back.

It had been several years since Magnus had seen the Kirin. Rham Jas's face was covered by the hood of a black cloak and he crept like a predator as he came close to the guard. He moved with stealth to within a foot of his target, before slowly and silently drawing his katana and gradually standing up. The guard was completely unaware of the figure at his back and the man of Ro even yawned and puffed out his cheeks in an unconscious gesture of tiredness and boredom.

Rham Jas held his katana with the blade pointing down and gradually moved his arm round the guard's neck until, at the last possible moment, his hand darted to cover the man's mouth and the blade entered his side, just under the armpit, and angled sharply downwards, killing him instantly. The dead man made no sound beyond a faint groan as Rham Jas carefully removed his sword and cradled the body to the ground. The Kirin then poked his head out to check that no one had seen his target fall, before moving back into the shadows and carrying the dead man down the feeding trough to Magnus's window.

'You stink,' he said, with the same infuriating grin that had made Magnus punch him in the past.

'And you're ugly,' the priest replied, offering his hand to his old friend through the bars. 'Good to see you, Kirin.'

'And you, Ranen,' Rham Jas replied, with an even broader grin as he grasped Magnus's hand and shook it warmly.

'I have no idea why you are here, but it's a nice surprise. Did you bring an army with you?' Magnus asked.

'Not exactly.' Rham Jas pointed to something behind the priest.

Magnus turned quickly and saw Castus, the gaoler, standing wide-eyed in the dungeon passageway. He wasn't moving and his mouth was open, with a slight drizzle of blood on his lips. Then he crumpled limply to the ground and behind him appeared the figure of Lord Bromvy of Canarn, holding a bloodied longsword.

'Brom!' exclaimed Magnus, louder than he had intended.

'Stealth was never one of your gifts.' Brom smiled. 'Don't worry too much, though, the bound men that were with this pig are both dead.' He kicked the lifeless body of Castus to emphasize that he'd taken care of the other guards. 'Rham Jas, get to it,' he said to the Kirin through the cell window.

Rham Jas took a quick scan behind him to make sure the way was clear, then darted back out of the feeding trough and into the city.

'How did you get in here?' Magnus asked Brom, unsure what his two friends intended.

'Let me get you out of there first,' he said, retrieving the cell key from the gaoler. 'Where's Skeld?'

Magnus scowled. 'Pevain was given him as a trophy.' The fact that the dishonourable mercenary knight had his war-hammer still bothered Magnus greatly.

'Well, I hope you've been practising with a longsword,' Brom said with a smile, kicking the gaoler's sword towards the cell.

The young lord of Canarn was wearing tough-looking leather armour and carried a heavy-looking leaf-shaped blade in his belt.

Brom unlocked the door and the grating sound was like a strange kind of music to Magnus's ears as, for the first time in a month, he set foot out of his cell without a guard of Red knights for company.

'You're a wanted man, Brom. Coming here was not wise.' Magnus was deeply grateful to be rescued, but the last thing he wanted was to see either of Duke Hector's children captured and branded a Black Guard.

Brom shot him a serious look as the Ranen priest picked up the Ro longsword. 'You doubted I'd come back? The Red bastards killed my father, Magnus . . . they beheaded him as a traitor.' Brom's face had always looked fierce, but Magnus thought he'd gained an extra edge of darkness since they'd last met.

'They made me watch as they killed him . . . I mourn him too.' He directed a grim look at his friend.

'I know you'd have stopped them if you could.' Brom began to wipe the gaoler's blood from his sword and turned to look down the narrow stone passageway. 'Why are there so few knights here?' he asked, changing the subject. 'Lanry saw a massive army pass through, but he didn't know what was going on.'

'Rillion was left with only a token force to hold the city while the king went north,' Magnus replied.

Brom looked genuinely surprised by this news. 'The king? As in the king of Tor Funweir? As in King Sebastian Tiris?'

'I think that's what your people call him, yes,' replied Magnus. 'There's much you don't know, my friend.'

'That goes for you as well,' Brom said, still processing the news that the king had passed through the city. 'We ran into Kohli and Jenner, so we know Hasim was here and took my sister north. Please tell me you know what happened to her?' They began to walk back along the dungeon passageway. 'Please tell me she's still alive.'

'I wish I could answer you, my friend, but I haven't seen her since Hasim smuggled her out of the city.'

'Will she be safe in Ro Hail?'

Magnus frowned. 'Hard to say. If they got out before the king arrived . . .' He paused. 'It takes time for the Free Companies to muster.'

Brom resumed walking towards the guard station at the end of the passageway and Magnus could see two more dead knights, propped up against the wall with their throats slit. The young lord of Canarn was just as cold and dangerous as Magnus remembered, and the priest was impressed at the way he'd entered the dungeon and killed the three bound men without making a sound.

'Let's keep things simple for now,' Brom said, as he stepped over the dead knights. 'How many fighting men are left in the keep?'

'Fifty Red knights and a hundred bound men. I think Pevain has a couple of hundred mercenaries in the city . . . more than we can handle.'

'I know about Pevain and his bastards – Lanry has a surprise for them,' Brom stated.

'A few common men don't add much to our fighting strength,' Magnus said, beginning to wonder if Brom intended some kind of glorious last stand.

Brom turned off the passageway, before the stairs that led up to the keep, and stepped into a dusty antechamber that contained a disused slit trench.

'We have a few friends here as well. They're waiting for the signal to join us in the keep. We've got a chance, that's all.'

He had a vicious look on his face and Magnus thought Brom was very much on edge, wanting to get bloody as soon as possible. In fact, his friend was shaking with anticipation.

Magnus noticed that the iron grating above the disused toilet trench had been opened from within and realized how Brom had sneaked in without having to pass the knights in the courtyard above.

The Ranen priest paused as he watched Brom quickly move to the open grating. 'Brom,' he said quietly, making his friend turn back to him. 'You need to settle down. Your hand is shaking.'

Brom looked at his sword hand and smiled. 'I feel like I'm going to war for the first time.'

'Rillion and his knights are true fighting men. They'll kill you if you're not focused. You and I are not burdened with Rham Jas's gifts, Brom . . . simple men like us need to rely on skill, steel and luck. Take a moment to focus, my friend.'

The young lord had to wrestle with his impatience before he sat down heavily on the grating. He was breathing deeply and Magnus realized he had been functioning largely on adrenalin up to this point.

'Rham Jas is waiting upstairs, we can't take too long,' he said, glancing up at the huge Ranen priest. 'Apparently he's got a plan.'

'He's patient. The longer we give him, the more time he'll have to rub his hands together and be impressed at his own cleverness.'

The disused slit trench led out from the inner keep and it looked as if Brom had bypassed the courtyard entirely when he came to rescue Magnus.

'Does his plan involve getting out alive?' Magnus asked.

The lord of Ro glanced up and smiled thinly. 'If the plan works, we should be alive *and* able to stay in the city.'

'Sounds like a good plan, then,' Magnus said. 'If it works.'

'Well, you don't just have me and the Kirin to rely on . . . don't worry.' Brom puffed out his cheeks and stood up slowly. 'We've found some unlikely allies . . . and we gave Lanry something that should deal with Pevain.'

Magnus was curious but also eager to experience freedom. If they had allies and a plan, that could only be a good thing.

'We need to move,' said Brom, as he slid the steel grating aside.

'Are you calm?' asked Magnus.

'No, not at all . . . but we still need to move.'

Magnus wasn't going to patronize the young lord. He had got himself to Ro Canarn and sneaked into the city with only a Kirin scumbag for company. If he could do that, thought Magnus, maybe he wasn't just a Ro lord playing at being a brigand.

'Okay, so let's move,' he said, as Brom began to climb into the slit trench. 'And your allies had better be something special.'

They climbed down into a narrow stone tunnel just large enough to accommodate Magnus's huge shoulders. It was almost pitch-black, with only infrequent shards of moonlight penetrating from above, and Magnus was glad his friend knew the passages around his father's keep. The trench had numerous side tunnels which snaked round the castle, but they were heading now down a shallow incline that, long ago, had been part of the sewer system of Canarn. Duke Hector had not used the dungeon for many years and the trenches were rotten and grown over with moss.

Brom stopped after a few minutes of uncomfortable crawling and poked his head up out of the trench. Then he ducked back down and waved Magnus forward to join him. As the Ranen priest moved a part of the steel grating out of the way, he straightened and joined Brom in looking out on to Ro Canarn. There was a rope secured to the grating where Brom had climbed up from below, and the town square could be seen between buildings. Magnus quickly gained his bearings and saw the drawbridge to his right and the keep beyond. They had come out on the same level as the courtyard, and low cooking fires were just visible through another stone tunnel.

Brom tugged on the rope and signalled to someone below. Magnus couldn't see the face of the man standing at the base of the wall, but he was tall and cloaked.

'Who's your friend?' he asked Brom in a whisper.

'His name's Tyr Nanon. I'll introduce you to him if we don't get killed,' the Ro lord replied, with gallows humour.

'What's the Kirin's plan?' Magnus was still whispering and he could see no army to come to their aid.

'It involves explosions and surprise.' Brom turned to look at Magnus. 'Who do we need to worry about?'

'Rillion and Nathan are the senior knights and Pevain's in the town somewhere,' Magnus responded, secretly longing for a chance to kill the mercenary knight.

'Okay, let's get into position.' Brom had a look of extreme concentration on his face and Magnus realized his friend had been waiting for this opportunity for a while.

They climbed out of the slit trench and entered the semicircular drainage tunnel that led to the inner keep and past the drawbridge.

On the other side, Magnus gasped as he saw dark shapes moving like shadows through the streets of Ro Canarn. All the figures were tall and they moved with an inhuman grace as they made their way towards the drawbridge. Magnus saw three mercenaries hanging around by the entrance to the keep and all three died silently, pulled into the darkness and despatched by the rapidly moving figures below. Some of Brom's mysterious allies were carrying sacks slung across their backs, and all wielded large, leaf-shaped blades.

'Brom, did you enlist a company of ghosts to help you?' he asked, as he crawled after the young lord towards the cooking fires in the courtyard.

'They're friends of Rham Jas . . . and me as well, I suppose. Risen men, Dokkalfar, forest-dwellers – I've heard a few names for them over the last couple of days.'

Magnus was struck by this strange news, but asked pragmatically, 'Are they trustworthy and honourable?'

'I believe so. They've been fairly straight with us so far,' answered Brom over his shoulder. 'And Rham Jas trusts them.'

'Ha, the trust of a filthy Kirin, I bet that is hard-won,' Magnus said with as much humour as he could in the circumstances.

Rham Jas was his friend, but their relationship had been based on mutual teasing and the occasional fist fight. Brom knew this and snorted quietly with amusement as he reached the end of the tunnel.

In silence, the two of them crawled out of the semicircular drainage tunnel and crouched in darkness in the courtyard. Opposite, Magnus could see the tower that led to the great hall and the wooden stairs that snaked their way upwards from the dusty inner keep. Around the edges of the courtyard sat groups of bound soldiers – not true fighting men, but knights of the Red nonetheless, each carrying a longsword and wearing a steel breastplate. Magnus counted some fifty men and wondered how many of the strange forest-dwellers had come to help. The drawbridge was close by, maybe ten paces from their position, and he could just about make out dark figures forming at the top on the wooden ramp.

Brom gave a signal that the nearest figure registered, before moving silently to the winch that controlled the drawbridge. The plan was clearly to cut off reinforcements to the keep while they dealt with the smaller group of knights within, without interference from Pevain's bastards.

The risen man didn't raise the wooden ramp right away, but appeared to be waiting for something. Magnus thought that something must be the small figure moving across the battlements high above – whom the longbow in his hands identified as Rham Jas.

'Stay against the wall and be ready to duck back into the tunnel,' Brom said in a whisper.

Some of the shadowy figures massing just inside the keep moved slowly forward, taking care to stay out of the light and remain hidden. They held small sacks and, once they had come as close as they dared, they threw them towards the campfires.

Before the sacks landed the risen men had darted swiftly back and Magnus saw confusion on the faces of the Red knights as the parcels flew sedately past them and exploded when they touched the flames. Magnus had seen pitch and Karesian fire used in a similar way before, but never with such explosive results.

Sound, fire and light erupted in the dark courtyard as one after another the campfires exploded and men were torn to pieces. The knights reacted with nothing but panic and half of them had died within moments. In less than a second, the dark, silent keep had exploded into flames. Brom drew his sword as the signal to raise the drawbridge. As it creaked into life, a second, louder explosion could be heard from the town. Magnus glanced back out of the keep and could just see the edges of the marshal's office burning violently by the docks. Lanry and the people of Canarn had evidently decided that they didn't want Pevain around any more.

Noise and fire had burst upon the quiet of the evening, and Brom was framed in light as he shouted a defiant challenge at the panicked knights in the courtyard. The risen men were a step behind him and Magnus grinned broadly as he joined them.

The sacks had exploded violently but the fires had quickly

burned down. Brom was shouting as he hacked two knights to death with swipes of his longsword. Magnus disliked using a sword, but he was still more than the bound men could handle as he cleaved his way through their ranks, barely taking time to parry as their wild attacks were blunted by a swift death.

It was a bizarre sensation to be free and fighting after so many days of captivity and the Ranen priest was enjoying the feeling of men falling under his immense strength. The bound knights were poor enough opponents and Magnus could allow himself a glance across the courtyard to see the risen men dealing out death from the shadows. There looked to be around twenty of them and they whirled their leaf-blades with grace as they killed the startled men of Ro. The Ranen priest was taken aback by the creatures' otherworldly might and momentarily wondered why such people would ally themselves with an idiot like Rham Jas.

Magnus deflected a clumsy blow from a badly burned knight and decapitated him with a powerful backward swing of his sword. Nearby, Brom was holding a leaf-blade in his hand as he furiously killed any bound men who came across his path.

'Is this the best they've got?' he shouted across the melee.

As if in answer to the question, Magnus heard a shout from the wooden stairs that led to the keep and, looking up, saw more knights of the Red emerging from the great hall of Canarn. The churchmen that appeared were not bound men but true knights of the Red and dangerous foes. Magnus recognized them as some of Sir Nathan's company and guessed that Rillion's adjutant would be close behind his men.

High above, Magnus saw Rham Jas draw a flaming arrow and shoot across the keep towards the stairs. The arrow had something attached to it which exploded on impact, blowing several of the knights backwards, their broken bodies in flames. Several more fled back inside and Magnus experienced a moment of respect for the Kirin and his planning abilities. Raising the drawbridge had cut off the mercenaries and a well-aimed explosive arrow or two would cut off the true fighting men, leaving Brom and Magnus to finish off those in the courtyard. The old Brown cleric in the town must have killed a huge number of the mercenaries when he detonated the marshal's office.

As men died around them, it occurred to Magnus that if they were to kill the senior knights and retake Canarn, someone would have to fight Rillion – and he was not keen to see Brom take a foolish step towards his own death by challenging the knight commander. Hacking apart bound men was one thing, defeating a company of true fighting men was something else. Rham Jas was a killer without equal, Brom was a skilled swordsman and, from what he'd seen, the forest-dwellers were formidable, but Magnus doubted they had the strength to win against overwhelming odds. Also, it would be only a matter of time before Pevain found a way of lowering the drawbridge, or a path through the secret tunnels, and joined them in the courtyard with his men – although judging by the explosions still sounding in the town below, Brother Lanry was proving more than a minor inconvenience to the mercenaries.

He looked up and wiped blood from his face. Around him were slaughtered bound men and, at a quick glance, he could see none dead on his own side. Brom was conserving his energy and expending minimum effort in despatching the frantic knights, while high above Rham Jas was fighting several men who had emerged from the guard towers. The Kirin was every bit as dangerous as Magnus remembered, and his katana dealt out death with chilling precision, quickly clearing the battlements of bound men.

Magnus paused. The number of knights remaining was negligible and they were cowering and dropping to their knees in surrender.

'Kill them all,' shouted Brom coldly, and Magnus turned sharply to face his friend.

'No,' he responded, more loudly than the young lord. 'They've surrendered.'

Brom was doubled over and sweat was streaming down his face. He kicked a pleading knight out of the way and quickly sheathed his sword, before straightening up and breathing deeply.

'Your priest is wise, Bromvy,' said one of the risen men, a being shorter than his fellows but still tall and dangerous-looking. The risen men assembled the remaining knights into a group and Magnus could see that no more than six had survived the initial assault.

'Yes,' was all Magnus said in response before he turned back to the young lord of Canarn. 'Brom, you need to calm down. The plan is working thus far. What's next?'

'Magnus, this is Tyr Nanon,' Brom said quietly by way of introduction. The risen man's skin was grey and his ears were pointed, but Magnus was a Fjorlander and less startled by non-humans than the Ro, having grown up around trolls.

'Well met, Ranen man,' Nanon said, with a strange, thin expression which somehow resembled a smile.

Around them, the courtyard ran with blood – less than had been spilt a month before, when the Red knights first took the keep – but still a grisly scene of slaughter. The risen men had taken cover by a line of barrels at the base of the wooden stairs and Rham Jas was making his way across the battlements towards the great hall.

'The other Dokkalfar are in the secret tunnels. I gave them directions to get to the great hall,' said Brom, as he moved towards the line of barrels.

They all ducked down at the base of the stairs and paused. Rham Jas had disappeared again and the fire from his explosive arrows was just dying down.

'How many more are there?' Magnus asked, cleaning blood from Castus's longsword.

'Another twenty. They'll have started clearing the tunnels of knights by now,' his friend replied. 'Let's go and see Rillion, shall we?' Brom had calmed himself down, but Magnus decided to remain at his side for as long as he could.

More explosions sounded beyond the keep and Magnus guessed that Brother Lanry and the common folk of Canarn were taking back their town with Dokkalfar explosives. The Ranen priest smiled at the thought of Pevain's bastards being killed, but he regretted being unable to fight Pevain himself, and he was resigned to the idea that he would have to sift through the rubble to find Skeld.

Brom took the lead, with Magnus and Nanon close behind, and ascended the wooden stairs towards his father's great hall. The bodies of dead knights were strewn across the first landing and they had to step over bloodied chunks of flesh to reach the main door. The king's men who had been stationed at the door had gone north with the army and Nathan had not posted another guard – not that another man or two would have made any difference.

Brom reached the door and crouched down at the side with his hand on the handle. He motioned for Magnus and Nanon to join him, and the other risen men gracefully adopted combat poses either side of the landing. Brom looked behind him and Magnus saw Rham Jas was in position behind a turret, with another flaming arrow drawn on his bowstring. He had taken up a position where he would be able to fire down through the doorway and, having confirmed that the Kirin was ready, Brom flung the door open.

Instantly a flaming arrow flew past them. Shot with skill, it flew through the door, just under the frame, and travelled a short way into the hall before it thudded into the carpeted floor and exploded violently.

Magnus momentarily shied away from the bright flames and he heard screams from within as knights of the Red were caught in the explosion. Two risen men stepped forward and threw their sacks into the hall, causing more loud explosions within, and more screams of pain. A quick look through the door showed Magnus that Nathan's men were arrayed within, waiting for them to enter. The explosions had caused panic and disorder, but Nathan and the other senior knights – Rashabald the executioner and Rillion – were visible through the flames at the back of the huge hall.

Two more arrows, fired at the same time, flew through the door from a lower angle and Magnus saw that Rham Jas had quickly changed position. The arrows travelled further into the hall and one thudded into the breastplate of a knight before it exploded.

Knights dropped to the floor to extinguish the flames and ran back to get away from the fires. Rillion was roaring at the top of his voice, shouting at the knights to form a defensive line. Several men were still struggling to put on their armour.

Magnus searched the scene for Ameira the Lady of Spiders, but she was nowhere to be seen and he would have to keep his wits about him until the enchantress appeared. She was the unknown quantity in the assault – the one person who genuinely worried the Ranen priest.

Rham Jas had disappeared again and Magnus thought he must have ducked into the secret tunnels that led along the great hall. The fires were quickly dying down within the hall and beyond he could see the remaining knights of the Red forming up in front of the raised platform.

No more explosive sacks were thrown and the risen men were waiting silently, fanned out on either side of the landing, behind Brom and Magnus.

Then a booming voice sounded from the hall. 'Bromvy Black Guard,' shouted Knight Commander Rillion. 'I assume that it's you out there.'

A look of grim conviction had replaced Brom's smile as he prepared to advance on the knights. He held his longsword loosely in one hand and the heavy leaf-blade in the other. Magnus knew Brom well enough to guess he'd be preparing himself for a fight, the outcome of which would be uncertain. Rillion was renowned as one of the finest swordsmen in Tor Funweir and Magnus doubted whether Brom could best him. Over and above this was the question of Ameira the Lady of Spiders. He had not seen her in the great hall but suspected that her foul craft would yet play a part in this encounter. If, as she had boasted, Rham Jas was helpless against her, the well-planned assault would have all been for nothing and the witch would be able to sway their minds and escape. The people of Canarn might be free of the knights, but the enchantress would be able to continue her designs elsewhere.

'Don't forget about the enchantress,' Magnus said to Brom across the open doorway.

'Rham Jas has a plan for her too,' he replied.

'She was confident that the Kirin would be helpless against her.' Magnus kept the matter of Rham Jas's son to himself for now, knowing it would add unnecessary tension to an already fraught encounter.

'Let the Kirin worry about the witch. You and I have to worry about the knights,' Brom responded, clenching and unclenching his fists as he began to prepare for the hardest fight of his life.

'Okay, but at least let me handle Rillion,' said Magnus with some insistence.

Brom turned to look at him, a dark glare across the open doorway into his father's hall.

'You know I can't do that,' he replied. 'The bastard has to be mine. There are plenty of knights for you, my friend.' He tried to smile, to suggest it was just a question of Magnus's vanity.

'Don't be a fool, Brom,' said the Ranen, 'you can't handle him.'

Brom's smile grew more genuine as he nodded to his friend before saying, 'Then I'll die.' The young lord of Canarn stepped boldly through the door and into the great hall.

'Rowanoco's cock,' muttered Magnus before joining his friend.

The risen men moved as one to follow them and as a group of twenty or so they strode into the hall.

The fires were burning low and were now mostly confined to the backs of dead men and a few items of wooden furniture. The pillars leading from the door to the main hall were largely untouched and Magnus saw Brom glance at the heraldry of his house as he made his way through the carpeted entrance.

The knights stood in a line before the raised platform and made no effort to intercept them, fearful of coming too close and experiencing more explosions. The men of Ro just waited for the strange group of warriors to enter the great hall. Magnus noted that the forest-dwellers held no more sacks and he suspected that only Rham Jas was still in possession of explosives.

'Welcome to Ro Canarn, Bromvy Black Guard,' Rillion shouted from behind the line of knights. 'My hall may have lost some of its hospitality, but I assure you that you are welcome.'

Brom stepped into the light of the main hall. He looked around, taking in the huge space that had been his home for twenty-four years, and briefly closed his eyes.

Magnus and the risen men stepped after him and formed a line some ten paces in front of the knights. The odds had evened out considerably after a few well-aimed arrows from Rham Jas, and the true fighting men arrayed against them now numbered only a handful more than twenty. Magnus knew that others would still be in the keep, but Brom's assurance that more forest-dwellers would be dealing with them rendered the fight pleasingly even.

'Sir Rillion,' said Brom formally, 'I mean to kill you.' The words were spoken calmly and momentarily took the knight commander by surprise.

'You and your . . . friends will meet only the justice of the One today, Black Guard,' shouted Rashabald from nearby.

Magnus noted that Sir Nathan was glaring across the ground and focusing on the Ranen priest.

'You consort with the risen . . . I thought a duke's son would know them for the undead monsters they are,' Rillion said from behind his knights.

Tyr Nanon was standing next to Magnus and was the only one of the forest-dwellers to react to this. 'I forgive you your ignorance, Ro man,' he said with a smile. 'Your mind is not your own.'

'Silence!' shouted the commander.

The largest of the risen, a huge creature – taller than Magnus by nearly a foot – stepped next to Nanon and held his huge leaf-blade in front of his face.

'I am called Tyr Rafn, greatest of the defenders of the Heart, and I say you are cowards who prey on the weak.' His words were deep and gruff, like the growl of a troll. 'I give you the chance to prove yourselves worthy with blood and steel,' he said calmly, by way of challenge to the knights, who looked ill at ease in the presence of the huge creature.

'Will you stay behind your knights all evening?' asked Brom with a sneer.

Slowly, and with the movements of a seasoned soldier, Knight Commander Mortimer Rillion stepped off the platform and added his sword to the line of knights. Nathan of Du Ban and Rashabald the executioner followed. For the first time since Magnus had been captured, he saw the senior knights join their troops.

The two forces sized each other up and Magnus took note of Nathan opposite him, clearly intending to single him out for combat. The knight captain smiled and held up his longsword in salute. Magnus didn't respond and planned to kill the knight quickly so he could get to Rillion and assist Brom.

The stand-off lasted only moments before Brom yelled, 'For Canarn!' and ran at Rillion.

The others followed and the two lines of warriors clashed in the middle of the great hall. Magnus met Nathan and parried a furious series of high attacks from the knight's sword. The Ranen was a little startled by Nathan's skill, but gathered himself quickly and held his ground. To his left, Brom and Rillion exchanged barbed insults as they fought, Brom's second blade the only thing preventing Rillion from quickly killing the young lord. The risen men were less dangerous when not attacking from shadows and employing the element of surprise, but the fight was still agonizingly even. Nanon killed a knight with his first attack, running him through with a manoeuvre resembling a dance move, and Magnus surmised that the forest-dwellers' style of duelling was completely alien to the men of Ro. The huge figure of Tyr Rafn was the most intimidating presence on their side and only Sir Rashabald was prepared to fight him, using his two-handed sword to keep the risen man at bay.

Men and forest-dwellers died as swords and knives whirled, cutting and stabbing flesh as the hall became a battleground. The two lines broke up quickly and Magnus found it difficult to keep track of who was alive and who was dead. Nathan was a dangerous swordsman and he needed to concentrate on besting the knight, reluctantly turning his back on Brom who was being methodically pushed back by Rillion.

'You can't win, priest,' growled Nathan, as he levelled a thrust at Magnus's side. 'I don't want to have to kill you.'

Magnus laughed as he fought. It was a boisterous sound that cut through the noise of steel on steel. 'If you don't want to kill me, you've already lost because I want to kill *you*,' he roared, redoubling his efforts and using his superior strength to unbalance the knight.

Nathan fell back against the edge of the raised platform and rolled to the side, narrowly avoiding a high swipe from Magnus. The knight got to his feet and they squared off again, though Nathan was now more on the defensive as he realized Magnus had been keeping half an eye on the rest of the fight and not giving his full attention to the knight captain.

Over Nathan's shoulder, Brom could be seen. The lord of Canarn was fighting with his back to a large wooden feast table and there was a nasty cut on his face. Rillion had disarmed him of his leaf-blade and Brom was furiously trying to resist the knight's superior skill.

'Time to die, knight,' spat Magnus, intending to finish off Nathan and go to his friend's assistance.

Nearby, a sickening sound of steel cleaving flesh sounded over the melee and Magnus saw Tyr Rafn had delivered a huge overhead strike at Rashabald. The forest-dweller had struck with such power that he'd shattered the executioner's sword and split his head in two, driving his blade down past the knight's neck to end up wedged in his breastplate.

The death of Rashabald made Rillion roar with anger and he began a combination of lightning-fast strikes at Brom. The lord grasped his longsword in both hands in an attempt to keep off the attack. As he held the blade above his head, Rillion rotated his arm and his sword slipped under Brom's defence to deliver a vicious wound to his shoulder. Blood spurted from the wound and Brom fell to the floor. Magnus held his breath for a moment as Rillion pulled back his sword and prepared to finish him off. Just as he began the fatal strike, Nanon appeared to his side and roughly tackled him to the ground, causing both knight and forest-dweller to roll in a heap towards the far wall. Brom was moving only slowly, grasping the bloody wound and trying to focus through the pain.

Magnus kicked out at Nathan and received an answering cut to the stomach to remind him that the knight captain required all of his attention. He tried to concentrate on defeating the knight, but the spectacle of Brom lying on the floor was a powerful distraction. Forcing himself to focus on Nathan, Magnus delivered a feint and saw an opening emerge in the knight's defence. It was a small opportunity, but the Ranen was able to bypass the knight's longsword and spear Nathan through the side. The knight captain cried out in pain and almost laughed as he looked down to see the fatal wound in his side.

'I am killed, priest,' he said through the pain, dropping his sword and grabbing Magnus's shoulders.

'You died well, knight,' Magnus responded, as he slowly drove his sword further into Nathan's body, causing blood to appear at the corners of his mouth, and the life slowly drained from his eyes.

As Magnus turned, he saw Tyr Rafn desperately trying to pull his blade free from Rashabald's breastplate. The huge weapon was stuck and, as the body fell away from him, the forest-dweller stood unarmed for a moment. Magnus moved to assist him, but he was not quite close enough and three knights seized the opportunity and leapt at Rafn. He was unable to defend himself properly and could only answer the sword thrusts with powerful kicks and punches. The three knights stabbed at him, and grey blood seeped out from numerous wounds as he frantically tried to fight them off. As Magnus quickly killed a knight who'd moved to intercept him, he saw Rafn drop to his knees with knights jumping on him and stabbing furiously at his chest and back, causing the huge forest-dweller to cry out in pain and anger, before slumping to the floor in a bloody mess.

Near the far wall, Nanon was astride Rillion and pummelling him with his fists. Both had lost their swords and Rillion was at least neutralized for the moment. Magnus made his way across the hall, despatching any knights who got in his way with brutal efficiency, but the priest could see that more risen men lay dead than knights.

As he neared Brom's unconscious body a loud explosion sounded from above and Magnus looked up to see three knights of the Red fly from a broken watch-hole and fall dead into the great hall. From the hole a face emerged, and Rham Jas Rami jumped down to land gracefully on the stone floor.

'Rham Jas, where's the witch?' Magnus shouted across to his friend.

'She ran away from me, cackling,' he responded, as he took in the scene of bloody combat before him. He saw the mauled body of Rafn and the limp form of Brom, before stowing his longbow and deftly drawing his katana.

'Is he dead?' he asked, pointing to Brom.

'He will be,' answered Knight Commander Rillion as he smashed his forehead into Nanon's face and roughly kicked the forest-dweller off him.

Standing quickly, he retrieved his sword and picked up Nanon's leaf-blade in his other hand. The forest-dweller didn't move.

'Come on, priest,' he shouted at Magnus, by way of challenge, as he moved to stand before the Ranen.

'Let me,' said Rham Jas angrily, with a glance at Brom's bloodied body.

'No,' replied Magnus. 'You need to find the witch.' He locked eyes with Rillion, though Rham Jas didn't move. 'Kirin,' he shouted. 'I can't kill her . . . you need to move . . . now!'

Rham Jas nodded reluctantly and darted past them to exit the hall through a side door, his katana held low.

Both Magnus and Rillion allowed themselves a quick glance around the hall and both saw that more than half of their forces were either dead or dying. Nathan, Rashabald and Rafn were gone, and Brom and Nanon were out of the fight.

'Knights,' roared Rillion. 'Stand to.' The order caused the remaining knights of the Red to disengage and form up in a line, facing the risen men.

The forest-dwellers were confused for a moment, but Magnus raised a reassuring hand and they understood and pulled back to re-form their own line. Both forces were down to less than ten warriors and the stone floor between them was covered with broken bodies and blood. The battle for Ro Canarn had claimed more dead than Magnus could count – from the initial assault to the prisoners he'd seen executed to the dead mercenaries in the town. Ro, Ranen, risen men, commoners, knights, mercenaries and nobles – he wondered if any goal could be worth all of this blood, and if the survivors even knew that a Karesian witch was responsible.

Rillion and Magnus moved to a more central position as they circled each other, and it was clear that the result of their duel would decide the outcome of the fight. Ameira was still nowhere to be seen and Magnus had to hope the Kirin would be able to deal with her.

Then, with no more posturing, Rillion attacked. The knight commander was older than Magnus by more than ten years, but those years had given him experience and a skill that the priest of the Order of the Hammer had rarely encountered. He also wielded two blades to Magnus's one and he deftly pushed him back with a dizzying array of swordsmanship. They clashed with swift, glancing strikes and it was clear that Rillion was not going to trade powerful blows with Magnus or be drawn into a contest of strength that he couldn't win.

Magnus focused on the knight before him and managed to hold his ground, using his strength to keep Rillion in a defensive stance, as they fought back and forth across the bloodstained floor. The priest knew that the longer their duel lasted, the weaker Rillion would become. He couldn't find an opening in the knight's defence, but he knew that a long encounter would be more to his advantage than Rillion's. He didn't channel the rage of Rowanoco, knowing that to keep his wits about him would be the key to defeating such a skilled opponent.

Then, more risen men began to appear from the side doors and Magnus saw the odds change. Those that had entered the keep through the secret tunnels had done their work in despatching the other knights and now they moved to join the main force in the great hall. None of them paid any particular attention to Rafn or the other dead forest-dwellers but simply stood with their kin opposite the line of knights – a line that now looked small and inadequate. The knights numbered fewer than half the forest-dwellers and Magnus surmised that if Rillion were to fall, his men would surrender.

The knight commander's face showed anger and something akin to surprise as, maybe for the first time, he contemplated defeat. Magnus knew that their battle was still in question, however, and when Rillion attacked again the knight's skill was tinged with more ferocity than before. He abandoned his defensive stance and launched an all-out attack, raining swift cuts at Magnus from high and low. The Ranen priest pulled back and parried as best he could, but without armour Magnus knew that he was in trouble. He didn't allow himself to look at the risen men standing nearby, or at the bloodied form of Brom, as to do so would have meant his death.

Then a heavy blow from the knight connected. Magnus had parried a downward swing but had not been able to move aside to avoid the follow-up thrust, which caught him in the stomach. He'd managed to move far enough to ensure that the leaf-blade connected nearer his side than his middle, but in turning away from the blade he'd caused the wound to rip open.

Magnus didn't fall or drop his blade, though the pain was excruciating. He slapped the leaf-blade away and disengaged as quickly as he could.

Sweating and gritting his teeth, he said, 'You've lost, Rillion. Canarn is no longer yours and one way or another, you're dead.' He felt light-headed as he spoke and was struggling to stay standing.

Then Brom moved – slowly at first, as if he'd been conscious for a few moments and was now ready to act. His sword had not fallen far from his hand and he silently grasped it before lunging from the floor towards Knight Commander Rillion. The knight heard him grunt with the exertion and turned to see the ornate

cast of Brytag the World Raven just before the blade connected
with his breastplate and pierced far enough through to bite into
flesh. Brom collided heavily with the commander and didn't stop
moving forwards, pushing his sword deeper into Rillion's chest.
The knight didn't cry out as the sword emerged at an upward
angle through his back.

'Killed by a Black Guard . . . how dishonourable,' he whimpered.

Rillion was dead by the time he and Brom hit the floor and
all those present stood silent for a moment, the smell of blood,
death and burned wood hanging in the air. Brom didn't stand up
but just looked at the commander's face, while the remaining Red
knights were too stunned to act.

Magnus smiled and had a distant thought of his brother and
how proud Algenon would be of what had happened here. He
lamented not having told Rham Jas about his son. Then his wound
caused the darkness to cloud over his vision and he fell to the floor.

* * *

Rham Jas Rami was as silent as he knew how to be as he entered the
antechamber. Beyond, he caught a quick glimpse of the enchantress
as she made her way towards the great hall. They'd been playing
cat and mouse games for the past few minutes and the witch hadn't
stopped cackling to herself as Rham Jas had dealt one by one
with the many knights who were still in the keep. She'd protected
herself well with men of Ro, who were clearly prepared to die for
her. Rham Jas noticed the noise from the hall had decreased and
guessed that Magnus must have dealt with Rillion, leaving only
Ameira and Rham Jas to finish their game. The enchantress had
appeared somehow too confident, as if she had a card yet to play.

'Rham Jas!' a voice sounded from the hall.

Brom was clearly still alive and his cry indicated that Ameira
was entering the great hall. Rham Jas moved after her. He couldn't
see Ameira, but he knew she was close.

Rham Jas stayed silent as he stepped on to the carpet and made
his way towards the main hall. He could see the Dokkalfar and

Brom standing in the light next to a kneeling group of surrendered knights. Magnus was lying on the floor with two forest-dwellers tending to him. Rham Jas couldn't tell whether he was alive or not.

Suddenly the pressure in the air increased violently, causing everyone in the great hall frantically to raise their hands to their ears and to cry out. Ameira had appeared through the forest of pillars, her hands held wide and with a look of deviant pleasure on her face. Rham Jas smiled as he realized that whatever sorcery she was employing was not working on him. Slowly he drew an explosive arrow and moved round a pillar. He could see the knights and the Dokkalfar bent over in pain. Rham Jas could feel the pressure, but it was like a simple hum in his ears and not uncomfortable in any way.

'The Dead God will accept your lives as a sacrifice . . . may you die in exquisite pain,' said Ameira, contorting with pleasure as she spoke. 'Rham Jas Rami, come here . . .' She gestured with her hand and Rham Jas felt a gentle pull in her direction. It was easy enough to resist and he surmised that this was something else to which he was immune.

Notching the black-wart arrow to his bow and striking the wick into a gentle flame, the Kirin assassin stepped into view.

'You are powerless to harm me . . . we have consumed your offspring and with his blood we were granted new power over you. Your son was eaten . . . he was eaten.' She laughed manically as she spoke.

Rham Jas paused a moment, stunned by the words. Nearby, Brom was doubled over on the floor, pale with blood loss and holding his ears. His eyes were clouded as he looked up at his friend, imploring him to shoot.

With effort, he forced his mouth to frame the words and spat out, 'Light the bitch up.'

Rham Jas looked through the small flame at the end of his arrow and saw Ameira the Lady of Spiders laughing. Her body was undulating in a grotesque, inhuman dance and she directed baleful eyes at him. With a deep breath, Rham Jas Rami loosed his arrow. It flew straight and true and struck the enchantress in the breast, exploding violently. She didn't have time to register surprise before her body blew apart and spread across the stone floor of the great hall.

* * *

Saara the Mistress of Pain threw her head back and cried out in anguish as she felt her sister die. Somewhere to the north the unthinkable had happened, and Saara sat up in bed, her fingers grasping the bedclothes, sweat running down her body. The warm night air of Ro Weir blew briskly through the window as she quickly stood up, shaking off the intense nausea that Ameira's death had brought on.

Breathing deeply, Saara moved to the window and closed her eyes as she faced the breeze. Yesterday she had been told that the last remaining old-blood, Utha the Ghost, had escaped and today she had lost a sister. As far as their plan had come, and as close as Shub-Nillurath was to being reborn, things could still go wrong.

Saara had been told in her prayer to the Dead God that the blood-sacrifice of Zeldantor would protect them against his father. It was a blow to find out that he was still able to harm them. Saara began to think of a replacement sister. Seventeen women had borne the title of Lady of Spiders. She would have to send a message to the abbey at Oron Kaa to begin preparing an eighteenth.

As for her prayer to the Dead God, she determined to meditate on it and to find a new way of interpreting her master's will. She cared little or nothing for the chunk of flesh that had been Ameira, and she was strangely excited at the prospect of a challenge to her own might.

She smiled and thought of her next move. The subjugation of Ranen was all but a certainty, with Rulag Ursa in the north already having taken control of Fredericksand and the foolish Ro bringing their law to the south lands.

In Tor Funweir, Saara was confident that her Hounds would be adequate to the task of hunting down the Dokkalfar and herding them together for the purpose of birthing new Dark Young. Many had already been taken, and now that she had *Ar Kral Desh Jek* Saara knew that in the end she would triumph. It was inevitable.

EPILOGUE

BROMVY OF CANARN had no title. He was not a lord, a duke or a thain, and the name of Black Guard was not one that he could display.

As he stood on the high battlements of his father's keep, with the straits of Canarn below, he thought of the Seven Sisters and of his promise to the Dokkalfar. The forest-dwellers who had fallen during the fight had already been arranged into a pyre and Brother Lanry was about to set them alight.

Magnus lay face up on his own pyre, a white shroud covering his body in the Ranen way. The priest of the Order of the Hammer was one of the bravest men Brom had ever known and to see him dead was a hard thing to bear. If it was to be his and Rham Jas's task to stand against the Seven Sisters and their Dead God, Brom lamented that Magnus would not be at their side.

Pevain had fled with a few men aboard one of the Red knights' vessels, although several dozen mercenaries were still hiding in the city. Otherwise, Canarn was free.

Tyr Nanon appeared behind the Black Guard and coughed politely – a human gesture that the forest-dweller didn't quite get right.

'How's your wound?' he asked.

Brom looked at the bandage he wore across his shoulder and chest. 'Lanry says it'll heal and I'll be left with a *bastard of a scar* . . . his actual words.'

'I never fully understood the human need to curse for emphasis,' the Dokkalfar said, screwing up his face. 'Rafn just used to hit people. It had the same effect.'

Brom smiled and realized the cold wasn't bothering him. The winds that blew off the straits had a tendency to make the people of Canarn stay indoors and to build large fireplaces.

'We swear when we're angry . . . I do anyway. Lanry swears because no one expects him to.' The Brown cleric played the part of a kindly old man, but he was as jaded as any of the One God's followers.

He stepped away from the battlements and faced Nanon. 'Did you want something?'

The old Tyr nodded. 'I wanted to warn you.'

'About what?' Brom was confused.

'You've entered the fray, Ro man . . . this war is more dangerous than you can know,' Nanon replied cryptically.

'I may have missed something, my friend, but I thought we'd won.'

The Dokkalfar smiled. 'That's not what I mean . . . you're a soldier in the Long War now, whether you like it or not.' He put his hand on Brom's shoulder. 'Enjoy the moments of peace . . . the Giants' war doesn't allow them very often.'

Brom wished that he understood – he wished that he was with his father and sister and that he'd never heard of the Seven Sisters or their Dead God. To be a soldier in the Long War was beyond his understanding. The more time he spent with Nanon, the more helpless and insignificant he felt.

* * *

Several hours and several funeral pyres later and Brom was sitting in his father's study, the room Sir Rillion had used for the past month. He'd removed anything that was red in colour and had thrown two Red knight banners on the funeral pyres. He had not yet returned to his old room and he was not keen to see who had been sleeping there, or what state they'd left it in. Currently he was content merely to remove his armour, unbuckle his sword and have a drink. Lanry and Rham Jas had joined him and the mood was far from jovial.

'What if Pevain reaches Tiris and they send another fleet of knights?' asked Brother Lanry, taking a pull on his pipe.

'Unlikely,' replied Brom. 'From what the prisoners say, the barracks in Tiris are mostly empty now and any reinforcements will be sent to join the king. I don't think they ever really gave a peasant's piss for Ro Canarn.'

Lanry shook his head. 'So much death for so little gain.'

'And we're not exactly helpless anyway,' supplied Rham Jas with a grin. 'Nanon and a few of the others want to stay. You never know, Canarn may become the first place where men and Dokkalfar live side by side.' He considered his own words. 'You'll need to plant more trees, though.'

Brom took a long swig of ale and wiped the foam from his chin. 'There's much that needs doing and planting trees isn't near the top of my list. People are sick, homeless and many have lost family and friends. Canarn is not going to be the same for a long time yet.'

'Well, with no rationing of food and healing supplies, the worst of the despair will pass quickly,' said Lanry. 'Pevain had ample food and water for everyone, but refused to give it out. I've sent Fulton and a few others to open the warehouses and give the people back what was pillaged. Full bellies will make everything seem better in short order.'

Brom had left the Brown cleric to minister to the populace and, other than an address planned for the following morning, he thought his time would be best spent thinking about the army of knights of the Red far to the north and about his sister's safety. If Canarn could be made strong again, it would provide a pivotal southern fortress for the Freelands and, Brom hoped, it might even prevent reinforcements being sent across the straits. There was no other usable landing on the coast of Canarn and the docks of his city were the first thing that needed to be reinforced and defended. If the king wanted more men to come north, they would have to go overland through the Darkwald and Hunter's Cross.

'How long do you want me to stay for?' Rham Jas asked. The Kirin had been a little quieter since the death of Ameira and the

news of his son was clearly playing on his mind. 'I've got a few
. . . appointments.'

'I hope you're not planning to go on an enchantress killing
spree without me,' Brom said with a friendly smile.

'That was the plan,' Rham Jas replied without humour. 'I'm
the only one who is immune to their . . .' he wiggled his fingers in
the air, 'sorcery, or whatever you call it.'

BESTIARY
COMPANION WRITINGS ON BEASTS
BOTH FABULOUS & FEARSOME

THE TROLLS OF FJORLAN,
THE ICE MEN OF ROWANOCO

History does not record a time when the Ice Men did not prowl the wastes of Fjorlan. A constant hazard to common folk and warrior alike, the trolls are relentless eating machines; never replete, they consume rocks, trees, flesh and bone. A saying amongst the Order of the Hammer suggests that the only things they don't eat are snow and ice, and that this is out of reverence for their father, the Ice Giant himself.

Stories from my youth speak of great ballistae, mounted on carts, used to fire thick wooden arrows in defence of settlements. The trolls were confused by bells attached to the arrows and would often wander off rather than attack. Worryingly, there are few records of men killing the Ice Men, and those that do exist speak of wily battle-brothers stampeding them off high cliffs.

In quiet moments, with only a man of the Hammer for company, I wonder if the Ice Men have more of a claim on this land than us.

FROM 'MEMORIES FROM A HALL' BY ALGUIN TEARDROP LARSSON,
FIRST THAIN OF FREDERICKSAND

THE GORLAN SPIDERS

Of the beasts that crawl, swim and fly, none are as varied and unpredictable as the great spiders of Nar Gorlan. The northern men of Tor Funweir speak of hunting spiders, the size of large dogs, which carry virulent poisons and view men as just another kind of prey. Even the icy wastes of Fjorlan have trapdoor Gorlan, called ice spiders, which assail travellers and drain the body fluids from them.

However, none of these northerners know of the true eight-legged terror that exists in the world. These are great spiders, known in Karesia

as Gorlan Mothers, which can – and indeed do – speak. Not actually evil, they nonetheless possess a keen intelligence and a loathing for all things with two legs.

Beyond the Gloom Gates is a land of web and poison, a land of fang and silence and a land where man should not venture.

FROM 'FAR KARESIA: A LAND OF TERROR'
BY MARAZON VEKERIAN, LESSER VIZIER OF RIKARA

ITHQAS AND AQAS, THE BLIND AND MINDLESS KRAKENS OF THE FJORLAN SEA

It troubles me to write of the Kraken straits, for we have not had an attack for some years now and to do so would be like tempting fate. But I am the lore-master of Kalall's Deep and it must fall to me.

There are remnants of the Giant age abroad in our world and, to the eyes of this old man, they should be left alone. Not only for the sake of safety, but to remind us all that old stories are more terrifying when drawn into reality.

But I digress. The Giants of the ocean were formless, if legend is to be believed, and travelled with the endless and chaotic waters wherever tide and wind took them.

As a cough in Deep Time, they rose up against the Ice Giants and were vanquished. The greatest of the number – near-gods themselves – had the honour of being felled by the great ice hammer of the Earth Shaker and were sent down to gnaw on rocks and fish at the bottom of the endless seas. The Blind Idiot Gods they were called when men still thought to name such things. But as ages passed and men forgot, they simply became the Krakens, very real and more than enough when seen to drive the bravest man to his knees in terror.

FROM 'THE CHRONICLES OF THE SEAS', VOL. IV,
BY FATHER WESSEL ICE FANG, LORE-MASTER OF KALALL'S DEEP

THE DARK YOUNG

And it shall be as a priest when awake and it shall be as an altar when torpid, and it shall consume and terrify, and it shall follow none save its father, the Black God of the Forest with a Thousand Young. The priest and the altar. The priest and the altar.

FROM 'AR KRAL DESH JEK' (AUTHOR UNKNOWN)

THE DOKKALFAR

The forest-dwellers of the lands of men are many things. To the Ro, arrogant in their superiority, they are risen men – painted as undead monsters and hunted by crusaders of the Black church. To the Ranen, fascinated by youthful tales of monsters, they are otherworldly and terrifying, a remnant of the Giant age. To the Karesians, proud and inflexible, they are an enemy to be vanquished – warriors with stealth and blade.

But to the Kirin, to those of us who live alongside them, they are beautiful and ancient, deserving of respect and loyalty.

The song of the Dokkalfar travels a great distance in the wild forests of Oslan and more than one Kirin youth has spent hours sitting against a tree merely listening to the mournful songs of their neighbours.

They were here before us and will remain long after we have destroyed ourselves.

FROM 'SIGHTS AND SOUNDS OF OSLAN' BY VHAM DUSANI, KIRIN SCHOLAR

THE GREAT RACE OF ANCIENT JEKKA

To the east, beyond the plains of Leith, is the ruined land. Men have come to call it the Wastes of Jekka or the Cannibal Lands, for those tribes that dwell there are fond of human flesh.

However, those of us who study such things have discovered disturbing knowledge that paints these beings as more than simple beasts.

In the chronicles of Deep Time – in whatever form they yet exist – this cleric has discovered several references to the Great Race, references that do not speak of cannibalism but of chaos and empires to rival man, built on the bones of vanquished enemies and maintained through sacrifice and bizarre sexual rituals. They were proud, arrogant and utterly amoral, believing completely in their most immediate whims and nothing more.

Whatever the Great Race of Jekka might once have been, they are now a shadow and a myth, bearing no resemblance to the fanged hunters infrequently encountered by man.

FROM 'A TREATISE ON THE UNKNOWN', BY YACOB OF LEITH, BLUE CLERIC OF THE ONE GOD

CHARACTER LISTING

THE PEOPLE OF RO

The house of Canarn – descended from Lord Bullvy of Canarn
Hector of Canarn – Duke of Ro Canarn – *deceased*
Bromvy Black Guard of Canarn (Brom) – errant lord and son
of Duke Hector
Bronwyn of Canarn – daughter of Duke Hector, twin sister to
Bromvy
Haake of Canarn – Duke Hector's household guard

The house of Tiris – descended from High King Dashell Tiris
Sebastian Tiris – scion of the house of Tiris and king of Tor
Funweir
Lady Alexandra – wife of King Sabastian
Bartholomew Tiris – the king's father – *deceased*
Christophe Tiris – son to King Sebastian, prince of Tor Funweir
– *deceased*

Clerics of the One God
Mobius of the Falls of Arnon – Cardinal of the Purple
Severen of Voy – Cardinal of the Purple
Brother Jakan of Tiris – Purple cleric of the sword, protector to
King Sebastian Tiris
Brother Torian of Arnon – Purple cleric of the quest – *deceased*
Animustus of Voy – Gold cleric
Brother Lanry – Brown cleric, confessor to Duke Hector
Brother Utha the Ghost – Black cleric and old-blood of the
Shadow Giants
Brother Roderick of the Falls of Arnon – Black cleric

Knights and nobles
Mortimer Rillion – Knight Commander of the Red army –
deceased

Nathan of Du Ban – Knight Captain of the Red, adjutant to
Knight Commander Rillion – *deceased*
Rashabald of Haran – executioner and knight of the Red –
deceased
William of Verellian – Knight Captain of the Red
Fallon of Leith – Knight Lieutenant of the Red and the army's
finest swordsman, adjutant to Knight Captain Verellian
Tristram of Hunter's Cross – Knight Commander of the Red
Hallam Pevain – mercenary knight
Castus of Weir – bound man and gaoler – *deceased*
Leon Great Claw – a knight, first master to Randall of
Darkwald – *deceased*
Lyam of Weir – Duke of Ro Weir

Common folk
Bracha – old knight sergeant
Callis – sergeant in the Red army
Clement of Chase – watch sergeant of Ro Tiris
Elyot of the Tor – watchman of Ro Tiris
Fulton of Canarn – tavern keeper
Kale Glenwood (formerly Glen Ward) – forger, resident in
Ro Tiris
Lorkesh – guardsman
Lux – watch sergeant of Ro Tiris
Lyssa – child in the Brown chapel
Mott – a bandit
Randall of Darkwald – squire to, in succession: Sir Leon Great
Claw, Brother Torian of Arnon, and Brother Utha the Ghost
Robin of Tiris – watchmen of Ro Tiris
Rodgar – child in the Brown chapel
Tobin of Cozz – blacksmith and fixer

THE PEOPLE OF ROWANOCO

The Ranen of Fjorlan
*The high lords of Fjorlan have, since the first, sought to keep
their names alive through their children. Those of minor houses*

are afforded no such honour and many deliberately strike their father's name due to dishonourable actions.

The house of Teardrop – named for Alguin Teardrop, the first high thain of Fjorlan.
Ragnar Teardrop Larsson – father to Magnus Forkbeard Ragnarsson and Algenon Teardrop Ragnarsson – *deceased*
Magnus Forkbeard Ragnarsson – younger brother to Algenon Teardrop Ragnarsson, priest of the Order of the Hammer, friend to Lord Bromvy – *deceased*
Algenon Teardrop Ragnarsson – high thain of Ranen, elder brother to Magnus Forkbeard Ragnarsson – *deceased*
Ingrid Teardrop Algedottir – daughter to Algenon Teardrop Ragnarsson
Alahan Teardrop Algesson – son to Algenon Teardrop Ragnarsson
Wulfrick the Enraged – axe-master of Fredericksand
Thorfin Axe Hailer – lore-master of Fredericksand
Samson the Liar – old-blood of the Ice Giants

The house of Summer Wolf – an ancient and respected house, named for Kalall Summer Wolf
Aleph Summer Wolf Kallsson – thain of Tiergarten – *deceased*
Halla Summer Wolf Alephsdottir – daughter to Aleph Summer Wolf, axe-maiden
Borrin Iron Beard – axe-master of Tiergarten – *deceased*

The house of Ursa – A new house with no honourable lineage, they name as they see fit
Rulag Ursa Bear Tamer – thain of Jarvik, father to Kalag Ursa
Rodgar – child in the Brown chapel
Kalag Ursa Rulagsson – lordling of Jarvik
Lyssa – child in the Brown chapel
Jalek Blood – axe-master of Jarvik

Survivors of the dragon fleet
Rexel Falling Cloud – axe-master of Hammerfall
Oleff Hard Head – chain-master of Fredericksand

The Ranen of the south lands
*The Free Companies are common folk who earn their honour
names and have never sought nobility or family names.*

Wraith Company – protectors of the Grass Sea
Horrock Green Blade – captain of Wraith Company,
    commander of Ro Hail
Haffen Red Face – axe-master of Ro Hail
Freya Cold Eyes – wise-woman of Ro Hail
Micah Stone Dog – young axe-man of Ro Hail
Darron Moon Eye – priest – *deceased*
Johan Long Shadow – commander at South Warden

THE PEOPLE OF KARESIA

*The Seven Sisters – enchantresses, formerly of Jaa, now of Shub-
Nillurath*
Saara the Mistress of Pain – leader of the order of the Seven
    Sisters, bears no mark
Ameira the Lady of Spiders – a Seven Sister, marked with the
    sign of a spider's web – *deceased*
Katja the Hand of Despair – a Seven Sister, marked with the
    sign of a howling wolf
Sasha the Illusionist – a Seven Sister, marked with the sign of a
    flowering rose
Lillian the Lady of Death – a Seven Sister, marked with the sign
    of a hand
Shilpa the Shadow of Lies – a Seven Sister, marked with the sign
    of birds in flight
Isabel the Seductress – a Seven Sister, marked with the sign of a
    coiled snake

The Wind Claws – men who give their life to Jaa
Dalian Thief Taker – greatest of the wind claws
Larix the Traveller – a wind claw – *deceased*

The Hounds – criminals serving as the Karesian army
Izra Sabal – whip-mistress of the Hounds
Turve Ramhe – whip-master of the Hounds

Common folk
Al-Hasim, prince of the wastes – exile and thief, friend to the
　house of Canarn
Emaniz Kabrizzi – book dealer of Ro Weir
Jenner of Rikara – Karesian smuggler, brother to Kohli
Kohli of Rikara – Karesian smuggler, brother to Jenner
Voon of Rikara – exemplar of Jaa, missing somewhere in
　Karesia

THE GODLESS

Kirin – a mongrel race, neither Ro nor Karesian
Rham Jas Rami – assassin, dark-blood and friend to Bromvy,
　Black Guard of Canarn
Zeldantor – son to Rham Jas Rami, slave to Saara the Mistress
　of Pain

The Dokkalfar – an ancient race of non-human forest-dwellers.
Tyr Nanon the Shape Taker – warrior of the Heart
Tyr Rafn – warrior of the Heart – *deceased*
Tyr Sigurd – warrior of the Heart
Tyr Vasir – a forest-dweller held captive by the men of Ro
Vithar Joror – shaman of the Heart
Vithar Jofn – shaman of the Heart

ACKNOWLEDGEMENTS

I would like to thank the following people for more help, support and love than can be adequately expressed. You all contributed to this and I really hope you enjoy it.

Simon Hall, Mark Allen, Tony Carew, Martin Cubberley, Carrie Hall, Benjamin Hesford, Marcus Holland, Paolo Trepiccione, Alex Wallis, Karl Wustrau and my mum (who thinks the swearing a little unnecessary, but read the first three chapters anyway).